THE FIRST TRUE PASSION

He was panting harshly, looking down at her with almost ferocious triumph. He knew she had been scared. He had sensed, too, that despite being married, she was almost virginally inexperienced. He smiled and then, with utmost tenderness, he kissed her gently on the mouth.

"You're very special, Lizzie," he said huskily, tracing the line of her cheekbone and jaw with the tip of his finger. "So special that I'm never going to let you go."

She gazed up into his dark, gold-flecked eyes, so langorous from his lovemaking that she could hardly move. Slowly she shook her head against the sand.

"No," she said, and there was the regret of a lifetime in her voice. "I'm not yours to keep or let go, Raefe. I'm Adam's, and what happened today . . ." Her voice thickened, as if it were full of smoke. "What happened today can never happen again."

A Multitude of Sins

Margaret Pemberton

BANTAM BOOKS
TORONTO • NEW YORK • LONDON • SYDNEY • AUCKLAND

A MULTITUDE OF SINS
A Bantam Book / July 1988

ISBN 0-553-27263-2

Bantam Books are published by Bantam Books, a division of
Bantam Doubleday Dell Publishing Group, Inc. Its trademark,
consisting of the words "Bantam Books" and the portrayal of a
rooster, is Registered in U.S. Patent and Trademark Office and
in other countries. Marca Registrada. Bantam Books, 666 Fifth
Avenue, New York, New York 10103.

PRINTED IN THE UNITED STATES OF AMERICA

O   0 9 8 7 6 5 4 3 2 1

For Mike.
Again, as always.

Defeat cries aloud for explanations, whereas success, like charity, covers a multitude of sins.

Admiral Alfred Thayer Mahon.

A
Multitude
of Sins

Prologue

THE doorman, immaculate in his uniform bearing the gold crested insignia of the Victoria Hotel, Hong Kong, swung open the large glass door leading onto the street and saluted respectfully. Elizabeth gave him a slight smile, and stepped out into the pale light of early morning. It was barely dawn. The noise and tumult, so inherently a part of Hong Kong's street scene, was temporarily subdued. The city of Victoria was taking a brief rest, pausing before it launched itself into another frenetic and fevered day.

The sleek, low-slung sports car she had hired the previous evening had been brought around to the front of the hotel and was waiting for her. A bellboy opened the door for her, made certain she had everything she required, and sincerely wished her a good day. As she turned the key in the ignition, firing the engine into life, he stepped back. He watched as she pulled away from the curb, the same expression of admiration in his eyes as was lingering in the eyes of the doorman.

Lee Yiu Piu was sixty-two years old and he had been a doorman for over twenty years. The Victoria Hotel was one of the most prestigious in the world, and Lee Yiu Piu knew class when he met it. And Elizabeth, tall and slender and graceful, her pale blond hair coiled into a thick knot at the nape of her neck, her white linen suit starkly simple, her only jewelry the ring she wore on her left hand and the small pearl studs in her ears, reeked of it.

"Where can she be going at this time of the morning?" the bellboy asked curiously as he stepped back into the hotel's flower-filled lobby.

Lee Yiu Piu shrugged. He didn't know. It was certainly strange, especially so if the rumors he had heard were true. An airport taxi throbbed to a halt beneath the porte cochere

1

and a party of flight-weary reporters and cameramen spilled out. Lee Yiu Piu stepped forward, opening the massive glass doors for them. Their conversation as they entered the hotel indicated that the rumors *were* true. In that case, the beautiful Englishwoman's lonely dawn departure was even more puzzling.

Elizabeth's hands shook slightly on the steering wheel as she turned onto Chater Road and passed huge billboards announcing the televised concert that was to take place that evening. She had known her return to Hong Kong would be traumatic, but she hadn't expected such a physical onslaught on her senses; such a searing sensation of having been whisked back in time; of having never left.

She had flown into Kai Tak Airport late the previous evening, the island a dark hump in the silk-black sea, glittering like a Christmas tree with myriad twinkling lights. She was glad she'd never flown into Hong Kong before. The landing brought back no memories, no visions of the island as it had been on the sun-filled afternoon twelve years ago when she had first sighted it from the rails of the *Orient Princess*, its mountains soaring silver-gray, silver-tawny, and silver-green where they were gashed by ravines and tortuous valleys, the lower slopes dense with vegetation and thick with flame trees and vines and deep-scented hibiscus. So long ago. Before the war. Before the Japanese. Before Raefe.

As she sped through the narrow, gaudy streets the unmistakable, indefinable smell of Hong Kong assailed her, ripping wide the intervening years and sending them scattering. She was twenty-five again. Twenty-five and so deeply in love that the mere memory of it made her gasp for breath.

With her knuckles white, she turned inland, skirting the Happy Valley Racecourse and zigzagging up the mountain road that led to the Wong Nei Chung Gap, the center of the island. Behind her were stupendous views of the city and the harbor and Kowloon. In front of her, as she neared the gap, were glimpses of the bays and rocky inlets of the island's southern shore, milk-white beaches merging into an indigo sea. There was no other traffic; no other traveler in view. She drew to a halt, then opened the car door and stepped out onto the roughly made road. Wong Nei Chung Gap. Peaceful, serene—and the scene of a bloody carnage that had left scores of men dead and countless others wounded.

A sparrowhawk wheeled high above her head, disturbing the silence. No familiar landmarks remained. There was no sign of the brigade headquarters that had once nestled in a fold of the hills. No sign of the shelter that had been erected lower down, closer to the road. For Hong Kong, the war was over, forgotten. And for her? She sighed. Despite the huge billboards that lined Chater Road, despite the newspaper reporters already gathering, how could it ever be forgotten? How could she ever even wish to forget?

The sparrowhawk, sighting prey, plummeted. She watched the large wings flutter against the scrub and rock, and then it soared high, wheeling into a ravine, a small, unidentifiable mammal imprisoned in its talons. There was silence. In the distance, the sea shimmered, outlying islands insubstantial as shadows in the early morning heat. There was no one to be seen. On the most crowded island on earth she was, as she had wanted to be, alone.

She sat down on the grass, hugging her knees, knowing that before she returned to the teeming streets of Victoria, the past would have to be faced and the most important decision of her life made.

Chapter One

❦

SNOW fell steadily over the bowed heads of the mourners as they gathered at Serena Kingsley's graveside. The autumn of 1924 had been chill and bleak and now, in January, an arctic frost showed no sign of giving London relief. As the familiar words of the Anglican burial service were read, more than one woman surreptitiously lifted the cuff of a mink or vicuña coat with an elegantly gloved hand to glance at a wristwatch and estimate how much longer it would be before the service was over. There would be heart-warming French cognac and a lavish buffet awaiting them at Jerome Kingsley's Belgravia home, and a chance to indulge in the social gossip that was even more their meat and drink.

The mourners were fewer in number than they would have been if Serena had died at a more suitable time of the year. Winter, for the Kingsleys' friends and acquaintances, was a time of migration. They either sought refuge in the milder climate of the Riviera, or sailed south to the more exotic retreat of Madeira. Apart from the Kingsleys' only child, their daughter Elizabeth, there was no family present. Serena's parents had died in a yachting tragedy many years previously and Jerome Kingsley's antecedents were a mystery. If he had a family, it was one he never acknowledged. He had appeared on the London scene in 1905, polished and assured, and the possessor of a talent for financial manipulation that amounted to near wizardry. By the time he was thirty-two and had proposed marriage to Serena Hughendon, one of the most eligible heiresses of the season, he was able to be accepted with society doing little more than raising a delicate eyebrow. Self-made millionaires cannot, with impunity, be accused of fortune-hunting.

The marriage was a remarkably happy one. If Jerome Kingsley was unfaithful to Serena, he was discreet, and there were those of his friends who doubted if he ever did more than indulge in a little light flirtation. He was forty-two now, a tall, powerfully built man with a strong, assertive jawline, his massive shoulders hunched beneath his beaver-trimmed overcoat. He had loved Serena deeply and she was dead at thirty-two.

"Glory be to the Father, and to the Son, and to the Holy Ghost," the priest said in conclusion.

The mourners breathed a sigh of relief and stamped their feet on the snow-covered ground with as much energy as good manners allowed. Jerome Kingsley released his daughter's hand and stepped forward, staring long and silently down at the coffin. All her life Serena had hated the cold and the dark, and now he was leaving her here, alone. Tears blinded his eyes and a muscle ticked convulsively at the corner of his jaw as he gently dropped a long-stemmed, perfectly formed white rose on the casket, and then a handful of the earth that was to cover her. Ashes to ashes, dust to dust. He didn't believe in a resurrection. This was their final parting. And he would not try to replace her.

His daughter squeezed his hand comfortingly as he returned to her side, and then, looking heartbreakingly vulnerable in a black velvet coat with a black velvet tam-o'-shanter perched on top of her pale gold hair, she too stepped forward, a posy of winter violets clutched in her hand. "'Bye, Mummy," she whispered, and with all the grace that had been so characteristic of Serena, she let the delicate blossoms fall lightly on the coffin.

Adam Harland swallowed, chasing away the lump in his throat. His friend's ten-year-old daughter had always held a special place in his heart and now, seeing her dignity at this most traumatic moment, he felt both pride and pity. She would miss Serena terribly. Jerome's financial interests took him to many different parts of the world and his frequent absences from home had forged a deep bond between his Serena and Elizabeth. No doubt school would fill part of the void her mother's death would leave. School and her music.

As the mourners began to walk out of the cemetery toward the gates and the waiting Rolls-Royces, Hispanio-Suzias, and Lanchester Fortys, Adam wondered how

much comfort her music would be to her. It had always
been an important part of her life. He could remember an
evening when he'd stopped at Eaton Place before attending the opera or theater with the Kingsleys. A chiffon-clad
Serena had trotted Elizabeth out of the nursery to sing and
do her party piece for him. She could only have been two
or three years old at the time and already she had had
excellent intonation. It was a talent inherited from Serena
who had a great love and respect for music, certainly not
from Jerome who was tone-deaf and viewed his daughter's
musical talent with indulgent forbearance.

Adam paused at the door of his Austin Swallow,
watching as the chauffeur opened the rear doors of
Jerome's Daimler and Elizabeth stepped inside. He could
see her chin begin to wobble suspiciously and knew that
once the Daimler drew away her tears would fall, fast and
free. Jerome seated himself next to her, his strong-boned
face white and pinched. He was a man unaccustomed to ill
fortune. Adam wondered how he would come to terms
with his loss.

He slid behind the wheel of his Austin, removing his
black homburg with relief, and ran his fingers through his
thick shock of unruly auburn hair. It had been Serena who
had encouraged Elizabeth's talent for music. There had
been piano lessons as well as singing lessons. Adam
followed the chauffeur-driven limousines away from the
cemetery and down the Harrow Road back to West
London, remembering his amusement at lifting Elizabeth
onto a piano stool when she was barely old enough to
walk. By the time she was four she had learned to read
music and had started to compose her own pieces. Serena
had been thrilled. But Adam had always suspected Jerome
was less so, that he would have preferred his daughter's
precociousness to have taken a different form, one he could
have appreciated more easily.

Adam turned left, driving with extreme care down
Edgware Road and into Park Lane. The snow was beginning to settle and driving conditions were hazardous.
Several cars had been abandoned, and only the stout-
hearted were persevering with their journeys. A horse-
drawn cart, undeterred by the weather, rattled in his wake,
delivering ale to public houses. On his right a lone nanny

determinedly pushed a perambulator across the icy vast-
ness of Hyde Park.

He smiled. He liked London. He liked the noise and the
bustle. He liked the flower sellers in Piccadilly Circus, their
giant baskets at their feet, their Cockney cheerfulness
warming the grayest of days. He liked the unchanging
stability of the gentlemen's clubs in Pall Mall, lunching at
Quaglino's, punting on the Thames, driving down to
Goodwood for the races. The Great War and all its
hideousness were over, a slight limp his only legacy from
the years of fighting. Life, for a bachelor of independent
means, was good.

He skirted Palace Gardens, turned left for Eaton Place,
and narrowly avoided a tramp carrying a board emblazoned with the words HELP THE UNEMPLOYED. His
mouth tightened. Life might be good for him, but it was
hell for the million and a half who were out of work. Most
of them were ex-soldiers. Men who had fought at Ypres
and the Somme. Men who had expected a little more from
victory than the misery of the breadline.

He skidded to a halt outside the imposing facade of the
Kingsleys' London home, wondering if the socialists really
did have the answer to the age-old problem of poverty and
if it wasn't about time he became one. He grinned as he
stepped out of his car. Jerome would have ten fits. "Bloody
reds," he called them, shuddering with distaste whenever
they were mentioned. Yet as with most of Jerome's pro-
nouncements, Adam had a shrewd idea his words were
more for effect than a reflection of his true feelings.

As he crossed the snow-covered pavement he saw that
many of the chauffeur-driven vehicles had not yet arrived,
their drivers being more cautious on the icy roads than he
himself had been. The Kingsleys' Daimler was there and he
wondered how Elizabeth would cope with the imminent
funeral party. In his experience, they were never sedate
affairs. It was as if the shadow of death, touching uncomfortably close, had to be banished with loud laughter and
determined gaiety.

The butler opened the door to him, wearing a suitable
expression of somber gravity. Adam suspected that it was
not just a matter of appearance. Serena had been a
considerate mistress and her household staff had been with
her since the early days of her marriage.

"Mr. Kingsley is in the drawing room, sir."

Adam nodded, aware that more mourners were hard on his heels. There was already the sound of muted laughter, nervous tension seeking release in jocularity. He walked into the long, wide, high-ceilinged room that Serena had insisted be decorated in cool tones of ivory and pearl gray. The only color was in the bowls of flowers that graced the Adam mantelpiece, the exquisitely carved occasional tables, the two handsome Louis XV chests, magnificently inlaid and topped with marble. It was impossible to think of Serena in a room without flowers. Adam felt a catch in his throat. It was impossible to think of her as dead.

"Thank God you're here," Jerome said, clasping his hand tightly. "The motions have to be gone through, but I'll be damned glad when this charade is over."

They had been friends for a long time. Jerome was fast-living and selfish, the possessor of deadly charm. Adam was quiet-spoken and reserved, with none of Jerome's flamboyance or charisma, yet the friendship was firm. When Adam had returned from the Western Front with a Military Cross for bravery in action, many of those who did not know him well had been surprised. Jerome had not been. He was well aware of the steely strength that lay beneath Adam's unassuming manner. No matter how famous, how illustrious his other friends, he always turned to Adam in times of need.

"What are you going to do when it is over?" Adam asked, aware that in another second Jerome would be surrounded by people offering sympathy, and private conversation would be impossible.

"Leave," said his friend tightly. "There's no home for me in this house without Serena. Most of my business affairs are conducted from Paris or Geneva. I shall move into the George Cinq in Paris for a few months."

"And Elizabeth?" Adam asked, shocked. "She's just lost her mother, Jerry. If you move to the continent, she's going to feel totally abandoned!"

A slight smile touched Jerome's harrowed mouth. "Don't worry, Adam. Elizabeth will come with me. There's no point in her staying on in London alone."

Adam stared at him. "But her music . . . the academy . . ."

Jerome clearly failed to comprehend Adam's concern for

Elizabeth. "A piano can be played anywhere," he said bleakly. "I need Elizabeth with me. I'm going to be lonely enough without Serena. I don't want to be separated from my daughter as well."

"Hang on a minute, Jerry. I don't think you've thought this through," Adam began urgently, but it was too late. The mourners who had been close behind him when he entered the house now surrounded them.

"Darling Jerome, what a terrible, *terrible* tragedy for you," a pretty young woman with bobbed dark hair said, and kissed him effusively on the cheek. "I was simply *devastated* by the news, darling. Completely *shattered*." She clung to his arm as if for physical support. Adam eyed her ringless left hand cynically. Jerome was once more a prize in the marriage market. Perhaps a retreat to the George Cinq was not such a bad idea after all.

He looked around the now crowded room for a glimpse of Elizabeth, but she was nowhere to be seen. Cloche hats clung to sleekly waved hair, daringly short skirts emerged from beneath minks and sables, cigarette smoke curled upward from long ebony holders.

". . . and so we're going straight from Nice down to Rappallo . . ."

"I dropped a thousand at roulette and another thousand at the baccarat table. Ferdie was *furious* . . ."

"My dear, they were lunching together quite openly and it was *obvious* what their relationship was . . ."

He moved away. Serena had loved gossip, too, but Serena's gossip had always been laced with impish humor and peals of affectionate laughter.

The doors leading into the dining room had been opened and he saw that the long dining table was laden with both cold and hot dishes: kedgerees and sweetbreads, cold salmon and hams, black and red caviar, and oven-hot blinis. The mourners moved toward the refreshments and he knew that, for most of them, Serena was already forgotten, her funeral just another event in a busy social calendar.

The butler approached him and said discreetly, "I believe Miss Elizabeth is in the upstairs sitting room, sir."

Adam thanked him, grateful that at least one other person was anxious about her welfare. The noise of talk and laughter followed him up the sweep of the stairs. How to explain to a ten-year-old that the party taking place was not meant to be disrespectful, but was normal funeral manners? He sighed. Even worse, how was Jerome going to explain to her that he was taking her away from her school and her home? He knew what Jerome's life was like when he traveled. An itinerant round of hotels, restaurants, nightclubs, parties. How could he possibly imagine that Elizabeth would fit in with such a life? He sighed again, feeling suddenly much older than his thirty-four years, and far older than Jerome.

She was sitting hunched up on the window seat, her arms hugging her legs, her eyes huge in her white face. "Hello, Beth," he said, entering the room and closing the door quietly behind him. "Has everything got too much for you?"

She nodded mutely, tears spilling down her cheeks. He was reminded of a stray kitten he had once taken home as a boy. She had the same look of bewildered helplessness, of utter vulnerability. He sat down beside her, wondering what the devil he could say to comfort her. He had no young sisters, no nieces, no previous experience with children at all. He took her hands, saying awkwardly, "Your mother would hate you to cry so, Beth."

It was the diminutive he had always used for her, the name she had called herself when she had been too small to pronounce Elizabeth clearly. Her hand tightened in his and she drew in a deep, shuddering breath.

"But it's all so h-h-horrid, Uncle Adam," she gasped, a fresh flood of tears coursing down her cheeks. "All those people downstairs are l-l-laughing and t-t-talking as if Mummy hasn't died at all!"

A fresh gale of laughter floated up the stairs and Adam's good-natured face tightened. "They know your mother has died, Beth," he said, choosing his words carefully. "And they are all sorry, but they are also frightened. Your mother was young and she was ill for a very short time. They are frightened that if pneumonia could strike her down so suddenly and fatally, something similar could happen to them. And because they are frightened and don't want to think about it, they are laughing and talking and trying to pretend it has never happened."

"Then they're s-s-silly," she said, a sob catching her breath, "and I don't l-l-like them."

"Nor do I," he said, rising to his feet and drawing her to hers. "Let's go for a walk and forget about them, shall we? If we borrow a couple of tea trays from the kitchen, we might even be able to find a hill in the park that we can toboggan down."

"Do you think we ought to?" she asked doubtfully.

He bent down, looking her straight in the eye. "It's the sort of thing your mother would tell us to do," he said firmly, hoping that he was right, then not caring if he was or not when he saw the look of sorrow disappear from her face. "Now come on, find some Wellingtons and a thick coat and some gloves. I haven't tobogganed in years and the snow won't stay forever."

"And so the concerto I played last year at the academy, I'm now going to play with the London Symphony Orchestra at the Central Hall in Westminster," Elizabeth said with shy pride as they plowed for a third time back up the hill, tea trays in hand. "It's a very great honor. Mummy was thrilled. . . ." Her voice faltered. "I don't think Daddy knows yet. Mummy was going to tell him when he came back from Geneva, but by then, she was ill. He'll be pleased though, won't he?" Her expression was anxious, but he was relieved to see that the sting of the cold and the exertion of their climb had put some color back into her cheeks. "The London Symphony Orchestra!" Her voice was awed. "I can hardly believe it!"

They had reached the crown of the hill and were placing their tea trays strategically for the descent.

"And when is this concert to take place?" Adam asked, a frown furrowing his brow.

"Oh, not for ages. I have masses of practicing to do. Miss Rumbatin says I have to learn to think orchestrally, to imagine when I play a piece that Furtwängler or perhaps even Toscanini is conducting a fantastic orchestra. I'm going to every orchestral concert that I can now, not just to piano recitals. All my pocket money goes for tickets."

Adam stared down at her, his frown deepening. "If you were to go away for a while, would it mean you couldn't play with the LSO?"

She settled herself on her tray and turned to look up at him. "No, of course I couldn't. But I'm not going anywhere. You'll come and hear me play, won't you?"

He wondered if he should tell her. If he should gently break the news that Jerome intended to take her away from the academy and disrupt her musical studies. "Beth . . ." he began, then hesitated. Jerome had told him of his plans only minutes after burying Serena. He had been understandably distressed, and without doubt he hadn't been thinking clearly.

"Yes, Uncle Adam?" she asked expectantly, pale blond strands of hair escaping from her woolen beret, her green-gold eyes wide and trusting.

"Nothing," he said with a grin. Jerome was insensitive, but he wasn't so callous as to brutally disrupt Elizabeth's life even further. "Beat you down to the bottom!"

She giggled, pushing herself over the lip of the hill and down, temporarily free from the weight of her grief, finding solace in the company of her father's friend, who was her friend as well.

By the time they returned to Eaton Place it was dusk. The house was quiet, only desultory cliques of mourners remaining.

"Ah, there you are," a weary-looking Jerome said, coming out into the hall to meet them. "I wondered where you had both gone."

"We've been to the park," Elizabeth said, the flush in her cheeks dying, her voice suddenly uncertain. "Tobogganing."

Jerome looked at the tea trays in their hands, the melting snow that had been kicked from their boots. "Of course," he said with a vagueness that irritated Adam. It was obvious that Elizabeth needed reassuring that she had not been disrespectful to her mother's memory, and it was equally obvious that Jerome was unaware of her need and was going to say nothing to set her mind at rest.

"Can I have a word with you, Adam?" he said, taking Adam's arm and steering him toward the now empty drawing room.

"Of course. Beth . . ." Adam turned around to indicate to her that she should follow them, but Jerome's voice cut across his.

"Change back into your black coat and shoes, Elizabeth," he said as they entered the drawing room and she remained standing alone in the hall. "We'll eat out quietly tonight. I've booked a table at the Savoy."

"Yes, Daddy." The exhilaration of the afternoon had deserted her. Her shoulders sagged, her hair hung wispily to her shoulders, and her voice was small and lost.

"I want you to do a favor for me," her father said to Adam, oblivious to her need for comfort, closing the door on her.

Adam checked his rising impatience. Jerome had been his friend for fifteen years. He had many virtues, but sensitivity was not one of them, and it was useless to expect him to begin exercising it now.

"Yes, what is it?" he asked. He poured himself a warming brandy and moved toward the blazing fire.

Jerome seated himself in a leather wing chair, resolutely ignoring the sight of the overfull ashtrays that his guests had left behind and that his household staff had not yet had the opportunity to remove.

"I want you to take roses up to Serena's grave for me while I'm away. I know I can easily pay for the service, but I don't want some faceless minion taking them for me. She'd hate it. Will you do it?"

Adam swirled the brandy around in his glass, glad that his friend's insensitivity was not yet total. "Yes," he said, "but if you're still adamant about leaving London, I think I should tell you that Elizabeth won't wish to accompany you. The academy has arranged for a repeat of the Mozart concerto she played last year, only this time with the London Symphony Orchestra at the Central Hall."

Jerome's shoulders lifted imperceptibly beneath his hand-stitched Savile Row suit. "I'll have to get in touch with the principal. Apologize. They'll easily be able to find a replacement for her."

"For God's sake, Jerry!" Adam said explosively. "Don't you understand? Elizabeth won't *want* them to find a replacement! She's been asked to play with the London Symphony Orchestra, for Christ's sake! Can't you understand what that must mean to her? It's exactly what she needs right now. Months of hard work and total commitment that will ease her over Serena's death."

"I appreciate your concern for Elizabeth," Jerome said tightly, and Adam felt his heart sink. When that particular note of determination entered Jerome's voice, nothing on earth would dissuade him from whatever course of action he had decided upon.

Jerome continued. "But she can study the piano just as easily in Paris as she does here. I think you'll find she will leave the academy without a moment's hesitation when she knows how much I want her to be with me."

Adam groaned. He had no doubt that Jerome loved Elizabeth, but he was showing no understanding of her need for stability. The George Cinq would be no substitute to Elizabeth for Eaton Place and the reassuring routine of the academy.

"You're making a mistake, Jerry," he said tensely. "Elizabeth needs you, but she needs you here, in London. She needs you to be in the audience at the Central Hall when she plays with the London Symphony Orchestra. She needs the day-to-day routine that she has always known."

Jerome rose to his feet impatiently. The house was unbearable without Serena in it. He had no intention of staying a moment longer than was necessary. And he wanted Elizabeth with him. What he wanted he always got.

"We're leaving first thing in the morning, on the boat train," he said abruptly. "Do you want to have dinner with us? I thought the Savoy would be quieter than the West End."

Adam shook his head. "No," he said shortly. "Elizabeth needs you to herself this evening. Say good-bye to her for me."

He was at the door before Jerome said conciliatingly, "Try to understand, Adam. I'm bitterly regretting every business trip I ever took that robbed me of time with Serena. I'm not going to make the same mistake again. From now on, wherever I go Elizabeth goes too."

Adam looked at his friend: rich, successful, powerful, and at that moment almost as vulnerable as his daughter had looked only a little while earlier. His anger disappeared. There were worse sins in life than wanting the companionship of a daughter.

"It's okay, Jerry," he said with an affectionate grin. "Have a good trip across the Channel and send me a postcard from Paris."

Upstairs in her bedroom, Elizabeth heard the distant thud of the front door closing. She pulled a hairbrush through her hair with a pang of disappointment. It would have been nice if Adam had stayed and accompanied them to the Savoy. Almost immediately she felt a rush of guilt. It would be nicer still to be alone with her father. They had hardly had a minute together since her mother's death. There had been arrangements for him to make, his friends had descended in droves, and when he had been alone he had seemed almost dazed. She put the ivory-backed hairbrush back down on the glass tray on her dressing-table and picked up her hat and coat. Black velvet. She hated the touch and sight of it, but her father had insisted it be worn.

She sighed, slipped her arms into the sleeves, and set the tam-o'-shanter on top of her gleaming hair. When she grew up she would never wear black. Not ever. It would always remind her of the loss of her mother. Of standing in the bitterly cold cemetery and knowing that she would never see her again. Never be cuddled by her or kissed by her. Tears sprang to her eyes and she dashed them away fiercely. She mustn't cry. Her father was alone, too, and he needed her to be brave and comfort him, just as she needed him to comfort her. From now on it would be just the two of them together. He would stop spending so much of his time in France and Switzerland. He would be at home when she needed him. He would be able to attend her concerts, perhaps even go with her to the Albert Hall, and the—

There was a light tap on the door and Mrs. MacBride, their middle-aged housekeeper, came into the room. "Are you all right, dear? Your father asked me to tell you that he's ready to leave."

"Yes. Thank you, Mrs. Mac."

Mrs. MacBride regarded her with affection and compassion. Her small pointed face was white and strained. If she had cried over her mother's death, and by the dark rings carved beneath her eyes she had done so long and hard, then it had been in private. There was a strength in her that her ethereal looks belied. A determination of character that was wholly her father's. At the thought of Serena Hughendon's fragile blond beauty being coupled with Jerome Kingsley's reckless zest for life, Mrs. MacBride shuddered. It would make a lethal combination when Elizabeth grew older.

"I'll make sure there's hot chocolate waiting for you when you get back," she said, glad that she couldn't see into the future.

"Thank you, Mrs. Mac."

Mrs. MacBride watched her with pursed lips as she buttoned her coat. The Savoy indeed! There were times when she wondered if her employer was in his right mind. The child was only ten. It wasn't the Savoy she needed, especially not on the day that her mother had been buried. It was scrambled eggs on toast, a milky drink, and an early night.

Her father was waiting for her at the foot of the stairs, and Elizabeth noticed with shock how the grief of the last few days had aged him. The lines running from his nose to his mouth had been gouged deep, and there was a sprinkling of gray at his temples that she had never been aware of before. She slipped her hand into his and squeezed it tight. She loved him and she wasn't going to lose him as she had lost her mother. She was going to look after him and see that he didn't worry, or drink too much, or smoke too much. She was going to make sure that he lived for years and years and years.

"I'm glad we're going to the Savoy," she said, for she had been aware of Mrs. MacBride's silent disapproval. "I like to look out on the river at night."

They walked outside to the Daimler. "I've booked a window table," her father said, grateful for her understanding. "You can look out at the river all you want."

Her hand remained firmly in his as the chauffeur carefully negotiated his way through the icy streets. Trafalgar Square was eerily empty, the biting cold and drifts of snow deterring even tramps.

"I love you, Daddy," she said, nestling close to him as they left the Square and entered the Strand.

Jerome's rich, dark voice was thick as he patted her hand. "I love you too," he said, glad that it was dark in the rear of the Daimler and that she could not see the tears that had sprung to his eyes. "From now on we're going to be together, Elizabeth. We're not going to be apart. Never again."

The car slid to a halt outside the Savoy's palatial entrance, and as Elizabeth stepped out onto the snow-cleared pavement, he felt the first stirrings of comfort, of grief eased. He had lost his wife, but he was luckier than most men for he still had his daughter.

For once, he decided against his customary apéritif in the American Bar and went straight through into the River Restaurant. Many people claimed it to be the most beautiful restaurant in London, and Jerome agreed with them. The long, deep windows, heavily swathed in damask, looked out in the daytime over the embankment gardens and the wide, majestic sweep of the Thames. As they were seated Jerome asked that the drapes beside them be drawn back. There was a slight hesitation on the part of the *maître d'hôtel* and Jerome smiled. "My daughter likes to look out at the river, even though it is dark," he explained, and the *maître d'hôtel* inclined his head.

"Of course, sir." Mr. Kingsley was a valued client. If his daughter wished the balance of the room to be disturbed by having one set of drapes drawn back, then one set of drapes would be drawn back. Besides, hadn't her mother just died? He noted the black velvet dress, the brave set of her mouth, and saw to it that her chair was moved a few inches farther to the left so that her nighttime view of the river was unimpaired.

"Lobster, terrine of duckling, and a bottle of Montrachet 1914," Jerome said, seeing no reason why mourning should spoil his appreciation of a fine wine.

"And for mademoiselle?" the waiter inquired discreetly.

Jerome was vaguely surprised. It was the first time they had dined out together alone and it had not occurred to him that Elizabeth might need help with the menu.

"I'll have lobster too," she said, determined not to let her father down by choosing something childish. "And the duckling, but not the Montrachet."

The waiter suppressed a smile. "Lemonade, perhaps?" he asked helpfully.

Elizabeth hesitated, then shook her head. Lemonade did not sound very sophisticated. "No, thank you," she said with grave dignity. "Could I have a pineapple juice, please?"

The waiter nodded, enchanted by the silk-gold fall of her hair, the medieval severity of her black velvet dress, and her natural gracefulness.

The restaurant was not very full, the bad weather having kept all but the Savoy's residents firmly indoors. With relief, Jerome saw that there was no one he knew at the nearby tables. He was tired of listening to well-meaning friends sympathizing with him on his loss. Their words brought him no comfort at all. They were platitudes, politely uttered but revealing that the speakers had no idea of the depth of his grief. Only Elizabeth had any understanding, and only with Elizabeth did he gain any comfort.

Looking across the table at her, he pondered on what Adam had said to him. Did her music really mean so much to her? She was talented, certainly. Everyone told him that. But then it was to be expected. She was, after all, his daughter. He regarded her with pride. There were music schools in Paris, no doubt better schools than there were in London. He would fix something up for her. Something a little more convenient than the rigid demands of the academy.

The lobster arrived and as he began to eat, he felt the first stirrings of well-being. From now on Elizabeth would be his companion, as Serena had been whenever they had been together. His brows pulled together slightly. Serena had loathed traveling and had seen no necessity for it. Though Jerome always pleaded business commitments, both he and she knew that was not strictly true. If he had wished to remain in London, he could have done so quite easily. As it was, he was a restless man, happier in hotels than in a permanent home, and Serena, loving him, had colluded quite happily in the fabrication that his many absences were necessary for their financial well-being.

"You have never been to Paris, Elizabeth, have you?" he asked as the remains of the lobster were removed and the duckling was placed before them.

"No. Mummy said she would take me as a treat when my French improved."

Jerome stared at her curiously. He hadn't known she was studying French. Nor that Serena had intended a trip to France with her. He wondered how many other things concerning his family's day-to-day life he had been ignorant of.

"Well," he said, slightly disconcerted, "it's a beautiful city, even in winter. I've booked tickets for tomorrow's boat train. We should be there in time for lunch."

Her eyes widened and her mouth rounded on an "oh" of pleasure. He felt himself relax. Adam was a well-meaning idiot to have thought Elizabeth would be dismayed at the prospect. "It's a good place to buy clothes, too," he added, thinking how adult she looked in the black velvet, and what a pleasant change it was from her school uniform.

"That will be lovely, Daddy," she said enthusiastically. "Can we go to the Salle Pleyel and the Théâtre des Champs Elysées?"

"I don't see why not," he said, pleased with her response. Previously it had always been Serena who had taken her to concerts. From now on he would have to undertake the task. He had no ear for music and found it neither pleasurable nor relaxing. However, if Elizabeth wished to attend one or two concerts, he would endure them with good grace.

"We can drive down to Nice if it gets too chilly," he continued affably. "March and April are beautiful months on the Riviera."

"I don't understand." She looked bewildered. "I thought you said we were leaving right away. Tomorrow."

He nodded, helping himself to another glass of Montrachet. "We are."

Slowly, she laid down her knife and fork. "For a holiday? And then later, in the spring, we're going again?"

Her voice had lost its eagerness and was small and unsure. Jerome was unaware of her apprehension. The wine was excellent and he was anticipating the brandy that would follow.

"No," he said easily, signaling for the waiter. "We'll make our base the George Cinq. At the end of the month I have a meeting to attend in Geneva. It's only a three-hour train ride. You can boat on the lake while I attend to my meeting, and then we could stay on in Switzerland and do some skiing if you wish. Later, at the end of March or the beginning of April, we'll move down to the Negresco in Nice. It's just as easy a base to work from, with all the advantages of milder weather and the prospect of some cruising."

Her face was ashen beneath the bright lights of the chandeliers. "But, Daddy, I can't take such a long holiday. There's school. . . ."

"That's no problem," Jerome said confidently. "I'll write to the principal tonight. Explain the circumstances . . ."

The knuckles of her clenched fists were white. "You can't

do that, Daddy," she said. "I've been asked to play at the
Central Hall with the London Symphony Orchestra. I'm
going to have to rehearse very hard and . . ."

He leaned across the table, taking hold of her hands,
imprisoning them in his own. "I'm sorry," he said, and his
voice was sincere, his eyes pleading. "I know it's a
disappointment to you, Elizabeth, but it can't be helped.
There'll be other concerts for you later. Lots of them. At the
moment what's important is that you and I are together."

"Can't we be together in London?" Her hands grasped
his tightly. "Please, Daddy. You can stay in London and I'll
look after you, and—"

"No." Gently, he released her hands, then turned to the
waiter and requested two lemon sorbets and a bottle of
Château Yquem 1921.

Elizabeth's mouth was dry, her heart slamming against
her ribs. She wanted to be with Daddy more than anything
else in the world. The thought of Eaton Square with only
Mrs. Mac for company was horrific. Yet they couldn't leave
London. They couldn't live in France. There was her
music. Miss Rumbatin. The concert.

"You don't understand, Daddy," she said, trying to keep
her voice steady, trying not to let her panic show. "If I leave
the academy now, they won't take me back. I have to stay
on there and I have to work—"

"I'll arrange piano lessons for you in Paris," Jerome said,
a trace of irritation creeping into his own voice.

"I need to go to the academy," she said again, desperate.
"*Please*, Daddy! It's the best school of music in Europe,
and . . ."

The Château Yquem was very good, and Jerome wondered why he had not had the foresight to lay down some
bottles. Elizabeth's eyes were pleading with him across the
table. A smile touched his lips at her naïveté. "There are
other schools," he said reassuringly. "Other teachers.
Don't worry about your music, Elizabeth. Just think how
marvelous it will be for us to be together."

He didn't understand, she thought. He was her father
and he was absolutely wonderful, but he didn't understand about music. He never had. Her throat tightened. He
needed her. He wanted her with him. And it would break
his heart if she refused and remained in Eaton Square with
Mrs. Mac. She shuddered. That was as bad as the prospect

of being torn away from the academy and continuing her studies elsewhere. Her father was talking of being in Geneva at the end of the month. Of being in Nice for March and April. What school could possibly tolerate such absences? As she looked across the table at him, loving him with all her heart, she knew that any future lessons would be not only inferior in quality, but also sporadic. And she also knew that she had no choice. No choice at all.

"Paris will be lovely," she lied bravely.

Jerome did not see the glitter of unshed tears in her eyes or hear the anguish in her voice. He was smiling to himself, thinking how wrong Adam had been and anticipating with relish the fine French brandy that was to follow the Château Yquem.

Chapter Two
❧

*A*ND will mademoiselle require a buffet breakfast for the guests?" the deputy manager of the famed Negresco Hotel asked deferentially. "Kedgeree and scrambled eggs perhaps? Smoked salmon and champagne?"

Mademoiselle hesitated. Her shining, soft shoulder-length blond hair was held back from her face with a ribbon, her cotton dress demurely collared in white piqué, her feet shod in ankle socks and buckled sandals. She knew her father relished his parties, but by five in the morning he was usually happy to sink into a chair with a large brandy and conduct a witty and often malicious postmortem of the proceedings with Adam Harland. An organized breakfast for the hundred guests he had invited to his forty-fifth birthday party would mean no such early morning reprieve.

"It is customary," the deputy manager murmured.

"No, thank you," Elizabeth said with the quiet confidence of one accustomed to making decisions and unawed by the deputy manager's status. "I would like the last drinks to be served at 3 A.M. and the musicians to leave half an hour later."

The deputy manager nodded. He was not in the habit of discussing arrangements with little girls still in the schoolroom, but this one was pretty and charming and certainly knew what she was about.

"And the flowers, mademoiselle?"

"Orchids and franciscea and bird-of-paradise," she said without hesitation. They were not her favorites as they were so lush, but they were her father's favorites and as always she ordered what he would like, and what would bring him pleasure.

The deputy manager nodded. The Kingsleys had a permanent suite at the Negresco, and if Elizabeth had asked for African lilies they would have been flown in without demur.

"Perhaps if you just cast your eye over the menu again, mademoiselle?" he said, proffering the menu that she and the chef had agreed on earlier.

Elizabeth did as she was asked and handed it back to him, satisfied. Everything was in order. It was going to be a lovely party. Adam was coming from London. Friends of her father's were coming from Paris and Geneva and even Rome. There was a gorgeous white chiffon gown hanging in her closet. And in three days' time she would have her father entirely to herself. They were going to Venice, where he had promised her she could indulge in concerts for a whole week. She sighed rapturously. There would be the choir in St. Mark's Cathedral, starlight concerts in the courtyard of the Doge's Palace, opera at the Fenice—

"Will there be anything else, mademoiselle?" the deputy manager asked, aware that he no longer had her attention. A slight flush touched her cheeks at being caught so flagrantly daydreaming.

"No, thank you," she said in her charmingly accented French. "I am sure everything will be perfect."

"*Enchanté, mademoiselle.*" There was a gleam in his dark brown eyes as he inclined his head and took his leave of her. She was like a beautiful flower in perfect bud, just about to blossom. And when she did . . . "*Une belle femme,*" he said beneath his breath as he closed the door of her suite behind him. "*Une très belle femme!*"

Elizabeth poured herself a glass of iced fruit juice from the carafe standing on a glass-topped table and carried it out of the opulently furnished sitting room, onto the balcony that looked out over the Promenade des Anglais and the shimmering blue of the Mediterranean. Despite her father's promises to the contrary, there had not been many concerts in the three years since he had taken her away from Eaton Place. Nor had there been many music lessons. Certainly there had been nothing to compare with the lessons she had been receiving at the Royal Academy of Music in London.

Despite her pleasure at the prospect of the forthcoming party, her heart hurt and she suppressed a sigh. She now knew that it would never be any different. Her father loved her, spent money lavishly on her, adored her company, yet was insensitive to any but his own needs. Music was unimportant to him and so he could not conceive of the importance it played in her own life. She loved him too much to reproach him for his failings. Whenever she could, she sought out lessons in whatever city they happened to be in. It was better than nothing, but she knew that such haphazard coaching would never develop her talent to the full.

The local piano teacher in Nice had been amazed when he had first heard her play. "And you want to take lessons from me, mademoiselle?" he had asked her bewilderedly. "You are not in full-time attendance at a college of music? An academy?"

A shadow had darkened her eyes, then she had smiled and he had wondered if he had imagined it. "No," she had said, and for the first time he had realized that she was not French but English.

"Then I will be delighted to accept you as a pupil. Shall we start now? With a Hanon exercise?"

As her lessons increased in number, he had become more and more puzzled. She had extraordinary talent and a self-discipline rare in a girl so young. Money was not a problem for her. It had taken him less than a week to discover that her father was a wealthy financier and that she was a resident at the Negresco. Why, then, was she not enrolled at one of the major music schools in Paris? It made no sense to him, and neither did her frequently canceled lessons. He could have sworn that they were the most important thing in her life, yet she often canceled them, her voice strained and apologetic when she phoned. With other pupils he would have lost patience, telling them that they must find tuition elsewhere. With Elizabeth he made an exception. She was different from any other pupil he had ever had, striving for perfection with dedicated single-mindedness. There were often times when he suspected that he learned far more from her than she did from him.

"Tell me how you memorize?" he had asked her at her third lesson. "Explain your method to me, please."

She had frowned a little, finding it difficult to analyze the process and to put it into words. She tucked a stray strand behind her ear and said, "First of all, I sight-read, and then I look at the structure of the work, and work on the fingering and write it in."

He had been sitting opposite her and had leaned toward her, his hands clasped loosely between his knees. "And do you *always* write it in?" he'd asked, intrigued.

She had nodded.

"And then what do you do?"

She had shrugged slightly, as though it should be obvious. "Then I memorize the piece from a visual point of view, and then the harmonies." Her voice had grown more confident. "In a sonata, for instance, first you have the exposition, then the development, then the recapitulation, and so you have a union, a connection you can build on."

"And how old are you?" he had asked, wondering if, when she had told him previously, he had misheard.

Her mouth had curved into a dimpled smile. "Thirteen."

He had shaken his head in disbelief, and had asked her to return her attention to a Czerny étude.

Elizabeth looked out across the promenade, again suppressing a sigh. Her lessons had continued, but they were formal and routine, possessing none of the inspirational quality that had been so much a part of her lessons at the Royal Academy.

A white Lamborghini slid to a halt beneath the porte cochere far below her. A smile touched her lips as she saw a stunningly dressed, olive-skinned woman step out of the car, a large circular hat on her head, two chihuahuas skittering around her ankles. She was Princess Luisa Isabel Calmella, her father's latest woman friend. The thirty-year-old princess was a fervent patron of the arts and it was thanks to her urgings that Elizabeth would be going to Venice.

She glanced at the slim gold watch on her wrist. It was nearly one o'clock. The princess was obviously visiting the Negresco for lunch. She put down her glass and hurried back into the sitting room, grabbing a blazer and a schoolbag. It was also time for afternoon classes at the lycée she attended a half-dozen streets away.

The lift came directly and a pageboy, little older than herself, greeted her with a polite inclination of his head. Seconds later she hurried through a reception hall of Versailles splendor, acknowledging the doorman's salute as she stepped out onto the sun-drenched promenade. Within minutes she was in the maze of narrow streets that backed the hotel, no longer "mademoiselle," arranging a deluxe birthday party for a hundred guests with poise and flair, but a schoolgirl sadly lacking knowledge of French history.

The lycée was not the kind of school to which Jerome Kingsley would normally have sent his daughter. It was a little local school neither academically famed nor exclusive. However, other more suitable schools had refused to accept a child whose father insisted that she attend lessons only when it was convenient for him that she do so. The lycée, too, was not overpleased at Jerome's laissez-faire attitude toward his daughter's education.

"C'est une crime!" her despairing French history teacher had exclaimed when Jerome had breezily announced that Elizabeth would not be able to do the extra work assigned to her in order that she reach a satisfactory standard in the subject. He needed her, he had said, to organize his dinner parties and accompany him to social events.

Even Adam had protested. "Beth is still a child," he had said. He was horrified at Jerome's intention of taking her with him on a yachting party with people famed more for their indiscretions than for their good sense.

"Nonsense, Elizabeth hasn't been a child for years," Jerome said airily, with no sign of guilt. "If I don't take her with me, I shall be seduced by my host's wife, and you wouldn't want that to happen to me, would you, *mon brave*?"

They were in the casino at Monte Carlo, relaxing in the Salon Rose after losing badly at baccarat. Jerome leaned back in his wine-red velvet upholstered chair, resplendent in a dinner suit handmade for him in Savile Row. There was more gray in his hair than there had been when Serena had died, but he was still a formidably attractive man. Large, expansive, delighting in the good things of life. Adam regarded him with despair.

"If Elizabeth hasn't been a child for years, then the fault is yours, Jerry. All this spending time with you and your friends is robbing her of her childhood. She needs friends her own age, she needs someone looking after *her* needs, not to be continually looking after yours. She needs to be back at the Royal Academy again, studying music."

"Rubbish," Jerome retorted, one leg crossed nonchalantly over the other. "She would be bored to death in London after the life she has been living these last couple of years *and* she would be bored to death with friends her own age," he added, as Adam began once more to protest. "This mother-hen attitude of yours is becoming tedious. Why don't you marry, for God's sake, and get it out of your system by fussing over a wife and a brood of children?"

Adam grinned, amused at having succeeded in rousing Jerome to irritation. "I just may surprise you and do that one day soon. Meanwhile, when are you going to stop using Beth as protection against predatory females?"

"When females stop being predatory," Jerome said with a return of good humor. "I have no desire to marry again, Adam. And no desire for any relationship that taxes the emotions. A little light diversion now and again is very welcome, but nothing more strenuous."

"Is Princess Luisa Isabel strenuous?" Adam asked, his good-natured face somber for a moment as he considered the prospect of Beth coming to terms with a stepmother. "I understand she's very much in favor at present."

"Ah yes." Jerome almost purred with satisfaction. "Luisa regards music as being a monumental importance to the well-being of mankind and so, naturally, Elizabeth adores her."

"And you?" Adam asked curiously. Jerome's women friends all had three things in common. They were beautiful, they were well-bred, and their reigns were of short duration. The princess was showing signs of surprising durability.

"Luisa is perfect for me," Jerome said with disarming

honesty. "She adores my bank balance, admires my pro-
wess in the boudoir, and, as my antecedents feature
nowhere in the *Almanach de Gotha*, would no more dream of
marrying me than marrying her chauffeur."

Adam didn't know whether to be relieved or sorry. An
indulgent stepmother, sympathetic to her needs, would
transform Beth's life for the better. There would be a stable
home instead of a hotel suite, disciplined schooling instead
of her haphazard attendance at the lycée. He ran his fingers
through his thick shock of sun-bleached hair. It was
obviously an event that was never going to come to pass.
Jerome had discovered he was a bachelor by nature, and he
was enjoying living like one. Adam could only be grateful
that he was, in his way, a responsible parent. He rose to his
feet, mentally calculating his current bank balance.

"Come on, Jerry, I'll have to see if I can win back some of
my losses or I'll be thumbing a lift home."

He had won back enough to be able to enjoy an illicit
week in Paris with the wife of one of Jerome's business
friends. It was an enjoyable diversion but nothing more. At
thirty-seven he had never yet been seriously tempted to
marry, though he regretted the fact that he had no children.

It had been six months since his last visit to the Riviera.
Jerome and Elizabeth had cruised the Adriatic with the
friends he had been so disapproving of, Beth's postcards to
him indicating that the only harm to befall her was a mild
attack of boredom. They had been to Deauville for the
polo, Lausanne for the flower festival, and Oporto for the
wine pageant.

"I'm looking forward to seeing Uncle Adam again,"
Elizabeth said to her father when she whirled in from
school a few hours later. "Has he arrived yet?"

"No." Jerome was amused by the way she clung to the
appellation of uncle to a man who was no blood relation at
all. "He's driving down and I don't expect he'll be here till
nearer seven."

"Then there'll hardly be time to have him to ourselves
before the party starts." She threw her bulging schoolbag
onto a satin upholstered Louis XV chair and shrugged
herself out of her regulation blazer. "Have the buffet tables
been laid yet?"

"They're doing it now," Jerome replied with a slight
gesture of his hand toward the adjoining room.

Elizabeth could hear the clink of silver and the low murmur of the maids' voices as they prepared the room for Jerome's guests. She knew it would never occur to him to go next door to check that everything was to his liking. Such details had become her responsibility, as had his business arrangements. She booked restaurants for him, remembering which merchant banker was a vegetarian, which a fish fanatic. She had a card index file of birthdays and anniversaries, and Jerome's friends remarked with pleasure how much more thoughtful he had become as they received cards and flowers, all with his best wishes, all sent by Elizabeth.

He had already showered and dressed and was sitting on the balcony, sipping a dry sherry, languidly surveying the early evening strollers on the palm-tree-lined promenade below him.

"I'm going to have a bath and change," she said, dropping a kiss on his temple. She wondered if she could also manage to do her homework, and doubted it. She would need to check the food when it was brought up, make sure that the musicians knew which of Jerome's favorite tunes to play, ensure that his surprise birthday cake was brought into the room on cue.

She hurried down the wide, thickly carpeted corridor to her own suite. She had to write an essay on Napoleon's victory at Borodino, the task made no easier by the requirement that it be written in French. Once in her own smaller, but no less opulent suite, she ran a bath, taking her schoolbooks into the bathroom with her. *"On 7th September 1812 Napoleon faced the Russians at Borodino on the outskirts of Moscow,"* she wrote, checking the temperature of the water with one hand. By the time she was describing the heavy losses that the Russians had sustained under General Kutuzov, she was in lace-trimmed lingerie, about to step into the white chiffon creation, hanging tantalizingly on her closet door, that had been designed for her by Elsa Schiaparelli.

"Kutuzov lost nearly half his men," she scribbled hurriedly, hoping that the water splashes decorating the page would dry with no telltale marks. *"Damn* Napoleon," she said under her breath, pushing the book to one side, and slipped the froth of chiffon off its padded hanger with a shiver of delight.

* * *

Two hours later, when Adam belatedly arrived to find the party already under way, he surveyed Elizabeth with pleasure. "You look absolutely fabulous, Beth," he said as she flung her arms around his neck and he hugged her tight. "I can hardly believe it's you! What happened to the little girl in short socks?"

She laughed delightedly, a slight flush touching her cheeks as she drew away from him. "Do you really like my dress? It's a Schiaparelli. Daddy took me to Paris specially to be measured and fitted for it."

Her sun-gold hair fell softly to her shoulders, held back from her face with a pale blue velvet ribbon.

"Mme. Schiaparelli has done you proud," Adam said, aware of a curious tightening of his stomach muscles as he released her. The dress, which fell in a soft swirl to her white satin-clad feet, had not been designed to make her look any older than she was, yet for the first time he realized she was no longer a child. There was a flowering sexuality about her, the more disturbing because it was artless and innocent. The wide, curving neck of the dress and the puffed, full-blown sleeves gathered into a ribboned band a fraction above her elbows emphasized her natural fragility. The bodice was plain, almost medieval, but there was no mistaking the rounding swell of her budding breasts or the minuteness of her waist.

He felt strangely uncomfortable as she guilelessly took his hand and led him into the crowded room to introduce him to the people she knew he had not met before.

By midnight he was happily intoxicated on champagne and was casting his eyes over the single ladies with no apparent escorts. His attention was caught by a petite blonde, a backless dress of shimmering coral silk dancing softly over her honeyed skin, a mischievous light in her eyes. He grinned, confident of his ability to attract, hoping there would be no tiresome husband to evade.

There wasn't, and he found the remainder of the party highly enjoyable. Her name was Francine; she was a Parisian, in her mid-twenties, and had been invited because she was a houseguest of Jerome's close friends, Frank Jay Gould and his wife. In the early hours of the morning he drove her back to the Goulds' luxurious home in Juanles-Pins, kissed her good night with zest, and arranged to see her again that evening.

The top of his Austin Swallow was down as he drove back along the curving coast road to Nice. The sun was rising golden over the Mediterranean, the dew-fresh air fragrant with the tang of the pines, and in a couple of hours' time he would be breakfasting with Jerry and Beth. He swept through Antibes at high speed, whistling cheerfully.

"God knows I don't ask much of you," Jerome grumbled when he returned to the Negresco. "Just a little company when the junketing is over. Where the devil have you been?"

A score of maids was busy removing all signs of the junketing and Jerome was ensconced in his bedroom, clad in an elegant silk dressing gown, a brandy in his hand.

"Escorting a young lady home," Adam said, kicking off his shoes and sinking down into a comfortable chair.

"Selfish bugger," Jerome said, looking pained. "The last guest left an hour ago. I've been sitting on my duff ever since."

Adam tried to look suitably sympathetic and failed. "Where's Beth?" he asked, ignoring the brandy on the glass-topped coffee table and pouring himself a fresh orange juice instead.

"In her room. She insists she has to attend the lycée this morning and that she has an essay to finish before she does so."

"This morning?" Adam repeated incredulously.

Jerome shrugged his massive shoulders. "I've told her she doesn't have to. I fancied a drive up to La Colombe d'Or for lunch, and if she goes to the wretched lycée, she won't be able to come with us. There are times when I suspect that child of selfishness."

Adam ignored the ridiculousness of such a statement and said again, unbelievingly, "She has to finish an essay *this morning*?"

Jerome looked at him with irritation. "Yes. I've said so twice. Quite clearly."

"But she can't have had any sleep! The party didn't finish till five!"

"*I* haven't had any sleep," Jerome said querulously. "I was looking forward to a chat with you when the last reveler had been evicted. A long, leisurely breakfast with you and Elizabeth, a reviving snooze, and then a drive up to Saint-Paul-de-Vence for lunch. You let me down by careering off to God-knows-where, and Elizabeth lets me down by forgoing breakfast in order to write about Napoleon!"

"For heaven's sake, Jerry," Adam said, "you should have squared all this with the lycée days ago."

"The lycée," Jerome said heavily, "is *very* uncooperative. Now, since it doesn't look as if Elizabeth will be breakfasting with us, can we order it now? I'm famished."

Adam was tempted to forgo breakfast himself and instead knock on Beth's door and ask her if she needed any help with Napoleon. He suppressed the urge. A thirty-seven-year-old man knocking on the door of a thirteen-year-old girl at half past six in the morning would definitely look suspect. Especially a thirteen-year-old as tantalizing and desirable as Beth.

He set down his glass so savagely that orange juice spilled onto the table. Desirable! God in heaven, was that really how he had seen her? The answer came thundering back at him and he rose abruptly to his feet, feeling sick and disoriented.

"What the devil's the matter?" Jerome asked in concern. "Are you feeling ill?"

"No, I'm fine. Let's have breakfast," he said tersely, the blood pounding in his temples. "I think I'll sit on the balcony for a while and get some air."

Jerome watched with raised eyebrows as he strode from the room. Adam was the most emotionally stable person he knew, yet something had violently disturbed him. He wondered if it was the pretty French girl he had escorted home, and followed him out onto the balcony. "Women are the very devil," he said sympathetically, "but it's not like you to allow one of them to needle you." He seated himself on one of the wicker chairs and studied his friend with interest.

Adam gave a barely perceptible shrug of his shoulders and said with an air of forced ease, "You're on the wrong track, Jerry. I'm not needled, just a little tired."

"That's okay then," Jerome said, not for one moment convinced. "We'll breakfast out here. The sun is already warm. It's going to be a hot day."

Adam stared out over the Baie de Anges, his back rigid, his fists driven deep in his trouser pockets. God, he thought. Did all men have moments like these? Moments when their sexuality turned traitor on them, taking them by surprise and filling them with horror?

"I'm thinking of doing a little cruising this year," Jerome said as a waiter set scrambled eggs and smoked salmon and apricots down on a cane table. "Do you fancy coming along?"

If he had been asked twenty-four hours ago, Adam would have said yes immediately. Now he firmly shook his head. Beth, clad in a bathing suit or sundress, might face him with more home truths than he could handle.

Jerome shrugged and turned as a shadow fell across the table. "Ah, there you are, Elizabeth," he said with satisfaction. "Has Napoleon received his just desserts?"

"Not yet," Elizabeth said, smiling tiredly. "He's still cock-a-hoop after thrashing the Russians at Borodino."

"Never mind," he said as she sat down. "The retreat from Moscow lies in wait for him."

She turned to Adam. "Did you enjoy the party?" she asked, a smile dimpling her cheeks. "I saw you with Francine. She's very pretty, isn't she?"

"Very," he said, aware of an overwhelming feeling of relief. Elizabeth was wearing a cotton school dress and short socks and sandals, and he felt for her what he had always felt—a love untainted by anything base.

"We're going to La Colombe d'Or for lunch," Jerome said, crumpling his napkin on the table and standing up. "Are you going to come with us?"

Her smile faded and Adam could see the fatigue in her eyes. "No, Daddy, I told you. I have to go to school."

"Then Adam and I will dine without you," he said, not concealing his irritation. "I'm going to lie down now," he continued, addressing himself to Adam. "Let's meet in the bar at twelve-thirty."

Adam nodded, more than ever annoyed by Jerome's cavalier attitude toward Beth. He was going to sleep. She was going to the lycée after no sleep at all, and not even a kind word.

Adam had already decided to leave Nice later in the day. His carnal reaction to Beth, however fleeting, had shaken him too profoundly for him to want to stay. When he saw the tiredness on her face and the unhappiness Jerome's dismissive words had caused her, he was determined that before he left for Cannes or Menton, he would do what he had intended doing for years. He would give Jerry a dressing-down that he would *have* to take note of.

As Elizabeth ignored the covered hot dishes and reached for an apricot, he said concernedly, "You look exhausted, Beth. Have you had any sleep at all?"

Despite her weariness she grinned. "I dozed off once or twice as the Russians were routed."

Although still furiously angry with Jerome, he laughed. "Do you get your French history a little one-sided at the lycée?"

Her dimples deepened. "If you mean, do we concentrate on French victories and ignore French defeats, then the answer is yes."

His own smile faded. She was sitting with the half-eaten apricot in her hand, her hair skimming her shoulders, her green-gold eyes full of laughter despite her exhaustion. He remembered Serena lying in a hammock at the Kingsleys' holiday cottage in the country, wearing an enormous hat, laughing and welcoming and golden. Beth had inherited all her beauty, all her sparkle. His throat tightened. He had loved Serena, but he had never been in love with her. Yet if Beth were older . . .

"Why are you looking so morose?" she asked suddenly, leaning toward him and taking his hand. "Aren't you happy to be back in Nice with us?"

He squeezed her hand tightly, then released it. "I'm leaving for Cannes later this afternoon," he said, hating himself as disappointment flared in her eyes.

"But why?" she asked bewilderedly. "Do you have to?"

He looked down at her and felt something terrible tremble within him.

"Yes," he said, his voice hard and queerly abrupt. "I have to. Good-bye, Beth."

Chapter Three

❧

ADAM didn't see Elizabeth again for two years. By that time his affair with Francine had deepened to the point where he was seriously considering marrying her. She possessed a china-doll prettiness that turned heads wherever they went, and an impish sense of humor. And, despite the diversions of living in Paris, he knew that she was faithful to him during their frequent separations.

They were on holiday in Rome, and had just strolled out of the Hassler after a late breakfast and were walking down the Spanish Steps toward the Via del Corso when Francine said suddenly, "Isn't that Jerome, *chéri*? Standing at the foot of the steps?"

Adam shielded his eyes against the sun. The baroque stone staircase was massed with tourists, smothered in fragrant pink azaleas. At first he could distinguish no one among the clutch of souvenir hawkers and jewelry vendors crowding the bottom dozen steps, then Jerome moved, stepping out of the way of a young priest, and Adam grinned. "It's Jerry all right. Come on."

Taking Francine's hand, he quickened his pace, running lightly down the sun-warmed steps, calling "Jerry! Jerry!"

Jerome turned his head, betraying not the slightest surprise at seeing them. He sported a white carnation in the buttonhole of his double-breasted gray silk suit, carefully tailored to disguise his increasing weight.

"Adam, old chap. Nice to see you," he said warmly as they ran up to him. He caught hold of Francine's hands, gave her a long and appraising look from the top of her sun-gold curls to the tips of her elegantly shod feet, then kissed her with relish on both cheeks.

"Where are you staying?" Adam asked, as Jerome reluctantly released a laughing Francine.

"We're not," Jerome said with no sign of regret. "We're simply passing through on our way to Capri and lingering only because Elizabeth insists it would be sacrilege to be in Rome and not visit the Raphael Rooms at the Vatican."

Adam felt a rush of heat to his groin. Beth. Still loyally and lovingly accompanying Jerome wherever he chose to go. He looked beyond Jerome across the crowded Piazza di Spagna.

She was striding gaily toward them, a scarlet cotton skirt swirling around naked, sun-tanned legs. Her sandals were high-heeled and delicate, her white blouse silk and Parisian. For years Jerome had been trying to hurry her into womanhood and now, at fifteen, effortlessly and without help, she had finally left childhood behind her.

Adam was aware of an overwhelming feeling of relief. She was breathtakingly beautiful, innocently sensual, and pleasure surged through him at the mere sight of her. But it wasn't perverted pleasure. He no longer felt like a pedophile. The emotion he felt now he could come to terms with, even though it would still have to be suppressed.

She saw him and her face lit with joy. "Uncle Adam! Francine!" she cried, breaking into a run. She threw herself into his open arms and he hugged her tight, feeling once more all the love he had always felt for her, ever since she had been a baby. All too soon she drew away from him, her eyes shining. "It's so wonderful to see you again!" She turned to Francine and kissed her affectionately on both cheeks. "He's been hiding away from us ever since Daddy's forty-fifth birthday party, Francine! *We* can't persuade him to join us in Nice, but maybe you can."

"I will do my best," Francine said, her cornflower-blue eyes sparkling. The south of France was always fun, she thought. Nice, for a few weeks at the end of the summer, would be a very good idea.

"Let me take advantage of this *very* fortuitous meeting," Jerome said, placing Francine's hand firmly in the crook of his arm. "We have five hours before we leave for Naples. Five hours in which Elizabeth was intent on dragging me 'round as many museums and art galleries as possible. Now I no longer need to do so." He smiled benignly. "Adam is far better equipped than I to suffer the rigors of the Vatican Museum. He can escort Elizabeth and we . . ." he looked down at Francine and patted her hand ". . . can enjoy a long, cold drink at the Hassler."

Adam gave Francine a quick glance and saw that she was perfectly happy to keep Jerome company for a few hours.

"Okay," he said, tamping down the elation he felt. "We'll meet up at two o'clock at Il Buco on the Via Sant'Ignazio."

"Ah," Jerome said with relish, "Tuscan *campagna* and *crostini* and those delicious little almond biscuits that you dip into the wine. *Benissimo!*"

With Francine prettily decorating his arm, he took his leave of them, sauntering back up the Spanish Steps to the Hassler, his equilibrium restored.

Adam looked at Beth and grinned. "Where to first?" he asked, aware that in her high heels she was nearly as tall as he. "Do you want to go to the Raphael Rooms first, or take a stroll?"

"A stroll, I think," she said, happily linking her arm in his. She was quite unaware that the action added another two or three years to her age, making her look more like a girlfriend than a daughter or niece.

They wandered into the maze of narrow, cobbled streets that led away from the piazza, a not very tall, toughly built man who moved with ease, and a tall, slender girl carrying herself with natural grace and pride, burnished gold hair swinging glossily to her shoulders.

"It's a pity you aren't staying in Rome," Adam said, aware of the number of heads that kept turning in their direction. Italian males flagrantly admired her and envied him.

When she spoke there was a pang of regret in her voice that went far deeper than disappointment that their holiday could not be shared. "Daddy doesn't like sightseeing holidays. He'll be much happier at the Hotel Quisiana in Capri. Lots of his cronies will be there and he'll be able to swim and sunbathe and gossip to his heart's content."

"And you?" Adam asked, his honey-brown eyes darkening. "What will you do?"

"Oh, I will swim and sunbathe as well," she said with a little laugh and a shrug.

Adam's mouth tightened. He knew what she would do. She would sit quietly in the background while Jerome enjoyed himself, flirting and exchanging scandalous stories about mutual friends.

They crossed the Via del Tritone heading in the direction of the Fontana di Trevi. "What about your music?" he asked brusquely. "Do you still play?"

She averted her eyes quickly, but he still saw the unhappiness that flashed through them. "I still play," she said. "I have a Steinway concert grand in my suite at the Negresco."

There was a strange note in her voice that he couldn't define. It was almost one of defiance. He wondered how hard a battle she'd had to fight before Jerome had agreed to her having the Steinway.

"What about your lessons?" he asked relentlessly. "Are your teachers good?"

"I don't have lessons any longer," she said, her eyes still avoiding his, her voice carefully controlled. "We're very rarely in the same place more than two or three weeks at a time and so it isn't possible."

They had reached the fountain. Spray blew softly against their cheeks, the breeze from the water coolly refreshing. Her hair was held away from her face with tortoiseshell combs, her profile, as she kept her face stubbornly turned from his, so lovely and pure that his breath tightened in his chest. There was no bitterness in her voice. He doubted if she even admitted to herself that Jerome had let her down. Yet he could sense and feel the unhappiness that her father's insensitivity was causing her. His jaw hardened.

"Let me speak to him," he said as a group of tourists laughingly tossed coins into the fountain to ensure that they would one day return to Rome. "He has to be made to see what a thoughtless bastard he's being."

She shook her head vehemently, and the sunlight danced in her hair, meshing it to silver. "No, you mustn't do that, Adam. His feelings would be terribly hurt. He sees himself as giving me a marvelous life, and he does. I live like a queen. Sumptuous hotel suites, yacht cruises, dresses from Schiaparelli and Worth. How can you possibly accuse him of being thoughtless or uncaring?"

"Because the hotel suites and the yacht cruises and the clothes mean nothing at all to you and your music does. It isn't too late for you to return to the Royal Academy in London. Jerry has his princess for company now. There is no reason why you should feel guilty or that you're letting him down."

She shook her head again, this time resignedly. "No, Luisa is a darling, but Daddy isn't the most important person in her life, and she isn't in his. He would be dreadfully lonely if I returned to London without him."

"Then he can return with you," Adam said with unconcealed exasperation. "The house in Eaton Place is still fully staffed, though God knows why. Jerry can't have spent more than half a dozen days there in the last five years."

Her eyes clouded. "Neither of us wants to return to Eaton Place. It holds too many memories."

"Then let Jerry do what he always does. Move into a hotel suite. The Dorchester is only five minutes from the academy. It would be ideal."

He could see the longing in her eyes, but then she said with finality, "No, he would hate it. Perhaps if things change between him and Luisa and they decide to marry, then I will. If not . . ." Her shrug was philosophical, and she said with determined gaiety, "Let's toss coins into the fountain and then walk across to the Vatican. The popes were very astute when it came to art, weren't they? Fancy having Raphaels on the walls of your dining room, Botticellis on the walls of your bedroom, and a Michelangelo above your head when you prayed!"

He knew better than to continue talking about music and London. There had been the same note of determination in her voice that he had heard so often in Jerome's. Her mind was made up and no matter how unhappy her decision privately made her, she would not change it. Not until she could do so with a clear conscience.

They strolled in easy intimacy over the Ponte Sant'-Angelo, tourists among a stream of other tourists, all making their way to St. Peter's Square.

It was one of the most perfect mornings Adam could remember. They refused to be sidetracked by the other marvels in the museum, feasting their eyes on Raphael and Raphael alone. When they emerged once more into the sunlight, they bought ice creams and walked along the banks of the Tiber, until Adam realized with a shock that it was nearly two-thirty and that Francine and Jerome had already been waiting for them for thirty minutes. He flagged down a taxi, and they arrived at Il Buco as the waiter was serving Jerome his dessert.

"I thought you'd both disappeared into the bowels of the

Vatican, never to be seen again," he said unperturbedly, helping himself to a lavish spoonful of cream.

"We forgot the time," Elizabeth said, her cheeks flushed and her eyes sparkling. "We've had the most glorious morning, Daddy. I didn't want it ever to end!"

The *maître d'hôtel* handed Adam a leather-bound menu as he eyed Elizabeth admiringly, and Jerome said to Adam, "Try the *pasta con porcini*. It's delicious."

None of them saw the expression on Francine's face. She had been delighted to see Adam and Elizabeth return, had been about to chastise them playfully for their lateness. When Elizabeth innocently said what a glorious morning she and Adam had shared, though, Francine suddenly sat very still, as if she had been slapped, and fettucini slithered from her fork.

Adam had the same glow about him as Elizabeth. He was grinning broadly at something Jerome was saying to him, but his eyes weren't on Jerome. They were on Elizabeth. As were the eyes of the *maître d'hôtel* and the eyes of the businessmen enjoying lunch at a nearby table. For the first time Francine realized that Elizabeth was no longer a child. She was only fifteen, but because of her life-style, because of the sophistication Jerome had thrust upon her, she was a woman. And it was as a woman, a highly desirable woman, that she was now being looked at by the *maître d'hôtel* and the other diners. And by Adam.

Francine's eyes narrowed. Nice no longer seemed such a good idea. She was quite sure that Elizabeth's remarks had been guileless. But how long would that last? With a Frenchwoman's hardheaded common sense, Francine judged it best that Adam and Elizabeth not meet again too often. One could never tell, *n'est-ce pas*? And it was better to be safe than to be sorry.

They did meet again over the next two years, often. Adam now regarded the lust that Beth inflamed in him as normal, if not welcome. He no longer felt like a dirty old man or a sexual pervert. These things happened, he told himself. Sometimes it was a cousin or an aunt that aroused emotions that had to be suppressed and that, eventually, died. It was nothing to be ashamed of. As long as no one but he knew of it.

In the autumn of 1931 he asked Francine to marry him, and both Jerome and Beth attended the lavish engagement party held at the Savoy Hotel in London. Francine, with a Parisian's reluctance to live anywhere but Paris, spent the winter and spring trying to persuade Adam to lease a house in the Sixteenth Arrondissement, telling him that he could easily conduct his business affairs from Paris. Adam showed no sign of being persuaded. His directorships were with London companies, he was London-based, and he had no desire to spend two days out of every seven traveling back and forth between Croydon and Le Bourget.

It was Easter when Francine said that she had found the perfect house and that, once he had seen it, all his objections would be overcome. But Adam had already seen it, and he knew he was not going to take it. If Francine wished to marry an Englishman, he told her, then she would have to accommodate herself to the idea of living in England. Tempers had been high on the drive back from Chantilly to her Montmartre apartment. He knew that Jerome was staying at the George Cinq over Easter and he was tempted to abandon Francine to her ill humor and enjoy dinner with him there.

Something about the set of Adam's jaw and the quality of his silence prompted Francine to think that she had probably gone too far. The wedding was to be in June, and whether they lived in Paris or London, or Timbuktu, she did not want Adam to change his mind about it.

"I am sorry, *cheri*," she said placatingly, slipping her arm through his as they drew up outside her apartment. "It was too big a house anyway. What does it matter? We will forget it."

Adam, who had no desire to prolong the quarrel, gave her an affectionate grin. "Okay," he said, knowing he had won the battle and could afford to be magnanimous. "Pax." With his arm around her shoulders, he led her past the concierge and into her elegantly furnished apartment, and bed.

Jerome was feeling unusually tired. He liked Paris, spending nearly as much time there as he did in Nice, but he was beginning to think that Easter was too early in the year for him to enjoy it to the full. The air was damp, the breezes chilly.

"We'll go back south tomorrow," he said to Elizabeth as she came into his room to see if he was ready to go down for dinner. Her cream silk dress rustled around her knees in a myriad of tiny pleats. As he spoke, the diamond cuff link he had been in the act of inserting into his shirt cuff fell from his grasp, rolling across the pale beige carpet.

Elizabeth bent down and scooped it up. "The Prince of Wales is attending Luisa's party on Friday. I thought you were looking forward to meeting him."

"Not enough to suffer another three days of cold and damp," Jerome said, not moving to take the cuff link from her and to finish dressing. "I feel so cold that I doubt if I'm ever going to be warm again."

Elizabeth looked at him with concern. A light rain had fallen for most of the afternoon, but it wasn't cold. She suddenly realized how overpoweringly warm it was in his suite. He must have turned the central heating up to maximum.

"Are you feeling unwell?" she asked, a slight frown puckering her brow as she fastened his cuff link for him.

"No," Jerome lied. Illnesses were tedious and he had no intention of succumbing to one. "Let's go down for dinner. I shall ask reception to make reservations for us at the Mamounia, Tangier. We'll travel down to Marseilles by train tomorrow and make the crossing tomorrow evening."

"But if you're not feeling well . . ." Elizabeth began, undeceived by his lie. His face was white and pinched, and there were lines of strain around his eyes.

"I am *perfectly* well," Jerome said indignantly. He stood and slipped his arms into the dinner jacket she held out for him. "All I need is a little North African sun."

She knew better than to argue with him. She would telephone his Paris doctor and ask him to make a visit early tomorrow morning. Her father would be furious with her, but at least then she would know if he was fit enough to travel.

"Perhaps Adam and Francine will join us in Tangier," Jerome said as they sat at the window table, overlooking the darkened terrace garden.

"I shouldn't be too hopeful. The wedding is only two months away and they are very busy house-hunting."

"*Francine* is very busy house-hunting," her father corrected her, a twinge of pain darkening his eyes. "Adam has no intention of living anywhere else but where he is living now."

"Daddy! Are you all right?" Elizabeth asked. She forgot all about Adam and Francine, aware only of the effort the last few words had caused Jerome.

He tried to smile, but it was more a grimace. "No," he said, and there was a look almost of fear in his eyes. "I'm sorry, Elizabeth, but I feel most odd—"

She was already halfway around the table to him when he pitched forward, sending cutlery and glasses flying.

"Daddy!"

He was still seated, the top half of his body prone on the disarranged table, his arms hanging limply at his side. She clutched him, her eyes wide with terror. "Daddy! Daddy! Can you hear me?"

The *maître d'hôtel* and an army of waiters were running toward them. His chair was being pulled back. Someone was easing him to the floor, undoing his collar. She could hear the words, "*Un docteur! Un ambulance! Vite!*"

"Oh, God! Don't die, please don't die!" she sobbed, kneeling at his side, her hands still clutching his powerful shoulders, tears pouring down her cheeks. He was inert. His eyes were closed, his face waxen. She stared up at the circle of waiters and diners who had gathered round them. "Oh, where is the doctor? Why doesn't he come?" she cried, distraught.

The *maître d'hôtel* knelt at her side. "He has been sent for, mademoiselle. Please, sit down . . . a brandy . . ."

She ignored him, bending once more over her father. "*Daddy, Daddy!*" she pleaded. "*Can you hear me? Can you open your eyes?*"

Above her head the waiters looked at one another, lifting their shoulders in barely perceptible shrugs. It was obvious that M. Kingsley was dead. That there was nothing anyone could do.

Elizabeth was keening now, cradling him in her arms, knowing he would never hear her again. Never open his eyes and look at her with love and amusement.

"The doctor is here, mademoiselle," the *maître d'hôtel* said, as the crowd parted and a gentleman in a pin-striped suit knelt at Jerome's side.

"Daddy . . . Daddy . . . I love you so . . ." she sobbed, knowing that the doctor had arrived too late.

There was nothing that could be done. In a matter of seconds, in the restaurant of one of the sumptuous hotels he had loved, she had lost him.

For several minutes the doctor attempted to reactivate Jerome's heart. At last he leaned back on his heels. "It is over," he said regretfully. "I am sorry, mademoiselle. There is nothing that I, or anyone else, can do."

There were gentle hands at her elbows, encouraging her to rise. A stretcher was laid at Jerome's side.

"Please, mademoiselle," the *maître d'hôtel* was saying with concern, and she knew that they were waiting for her to release her father so that he could be put on the stretcher and carried from the room. She felt as if she herself were dying. It was impossible to hurt so much and live.

"Mademoiselle," the *maître d'hôtel* said again, and this time the pressure beneath her elbows was more insistent.

She pressed her lips to his still warm cheek. "Good-bye, Daddy," she whispered, and her breathing was ragged. "*Au revoir,* my darling."

She was helped to her feet, her hair spilling in disarray around her shoulders, her eyes bleak. It was all over. There would be no more good times together. He had left her as once, long ago, her mother had left her. She was seventeen, and she was alone.

Chapter Four

❧

THE manager of the George Cinq telephoned Francine's apartment an hour later. There had been no other telephone number that Elizabeth could give him. Jerome's body had been discreetly taken from the hotel to the morgue. The dining room was again functioning perfectly, as if the regrettable incident had never taken place.

The elegantly dressed hotel manager pursed his lips as he waited for an answer to his call. M. Kingsley had been

like many other rich men he had known. Surrounded by an
army of so-called friends and acquaintances in life, strangely lonely in death. If M. Harland could not be contacted at
the telephone number M. Kingsley's charming and distraught daughter had given him, then he could envisage
difficulties ahead. Princess Luisa Isabel Calmella, M. Kingsley's mistress, would certainly not relish undertaking his
funeral arrangements. There were no relatives. No sons or
nephews. No one but the sobbing girl who had given him
the telephone number he was now ringing.

Adam was appalled. At first he thought the telephone
message was a cruel practical joke. It wasn't possible for
Jerry to be dead. He was only forty-nine, for Christ's sake.

"Mlle. Kingsley would very much appreciate it if you
would come at once," the hotel manager finished smoothly. "She is very distressed."

Adam understood. He slammed the telephone receiver
back onto the cradle and grabbed for his clothes as Francine
sat up in bed, her hair tousled, her eyes wide.

"What is it, *cheri*? What has happened?"

His handsome face was bone-white, his lips tight.
"Jerry's dead. He collapsed in the George Cinq restaurant
an hour ago!" He didn't bother to button his shirt,
ramming it down the waistband of his trousers, and
snatched a tie and a jacket.

"*Oh, mon dieu!*" Francine pressed the back of her hand
against her mouth. "Oh, but that is terrible!" Shock flared
in her eyes. "Was Elizabeth with him?"

Adam nodded, stumbling in his haste as he put on his
shoes, blaspheming viciously.

Francine gasped, scrambling from the bed, searching for
her negligee. "*Oh, la pauvre petite! Quelle horreur . . .*"

She was still slipping her arms into the gauzy sleeves
when the apartment door slammed behind Adam.

Adam's heart jackknifed when he saw her. She was
sitting on the edge of her father's bed, her shoulders
hunched, her hands clenched tightly in her lap. The doctor
was still there. He had given her a sedative and had no
intention of leaving her, not until she was more composed
or until someone arrived with whom she could be safely
left. An assistant manager stood uncomfortably at the door,
making sure that no curious undesirables entered the suite.

A maid was removing an untouched tea tray from the bedside table and depositing another in its place. The hotel manager was offering her his condolences, saying what a fine man Jerome had been, and how sadly he would be missed by them all.

She was wearing the cream silk dress she had gone so happily down to dinner in, little more than an hour earlier. Her head was bowed over her hands and her hair hung forward at either side of her face, the light from the chandeliers sparking the gold to silver. She looked terrifyingly fragile. Heartbreakingly alone.

"Beth," he said, his voice catching as he stepped toward her.

Her head whirled in his direction and she sprang to her feet. She ran to him, hurtling into his arms.

"Oh, Adam! Adam! Daddy's dead! He's dead and I can't bear it!"

Tears poured down her face unchecked. The maid slipped unobtrusively from the room. The hotel manager withdrew to a discreet distance, waiting until he could intimate to M. Harland that he would like to speak to him about the various arrangements that would have to be made.

"Oh, Adam! I loved him so, and now he's gone!"

He held her tight, giving her what comfort he could as she clung to him, her body wracked by sobs.

The hotel manager cleared his throat. "M. Kingsley's body has been taken to the morgue," he said quietly. "His lawyers have been informed of his death and—"

"Thank you," Adam said, cutting him short, disconcerted by the man's French practicality. "I'll speak to you later, if I may."

The manager bowed his head. "Of course. I can be found in my office. Good night, M. Harland. Good night, Mlle. Kingsley. Once again, you have my most sincere condolences."

He left the room and the assistant manager followed him. A bellboy would replace him outside the door of the Kingsley suite. It was a mark of respect that the manager favored.

"Sit down, Beth," Adam said gently. "Tell me what happened."

As she leaned against him, no longer sobbing but crying

quietly, the doctor judged that the time had come when he could decently leave. He placed a small bottle containing two tablets on the bedside table, saying to Adam, "I am leaving two sleeping tablets for Mlle. Kingsley. If more are required for tomorrow night and the night after, I will prescribe them, but they will only be dispensed one night at a time. You understand?"

Adam nodded. The doctor checked Elizabeth's pulse. "Are you sure you wouldn't like a nurse to stay with you?" he asked.

She shook her head. "No." She drew in a deep, ragged breath. "Thank you for your kindness, Doctor."

The doctor picked up his bag, grateful that the Englishman he believed to be her uncle was both sensible and sympathetic. "I have left my telephone number on your night table in case it should be needed," he said, walking toward the door. "*Bonsoir, mademoiselle. Bonsoir, monsieur.*"

The door closed behind him and Elizabeth sank down onto one of the chairs, her face deathly white. Adam poured her a cup of tea and stirred in two generous spoonfuls of sugar.

"Here," he said, placing the cup and saucer in her hands and squatting down before her. "Drink this, Beth. It will do you good."

She sipped the tea with childlike obedience, and he said compassionately, "Now tell me what happened, Beth."

Her breathing had steadied, but when she spoke, her voice was full of pain. "He was getting ready for dinner and he said he was cold." Anguish filled her eyes. "I thought perhaps he might be coming down with the flu, but he wasn't feverish and I thought the doctor could wait until morning." Her voice broke and she began to cry again. "If only I'd realized! If only I had rung for the doctor there and then!" Tea slopped over into the saucer and he took the cup from her.

"It would have made no difference, Beth," he said with certainty. "A heart attack or an embolism as severe as the one your father suffered couldn't possibly have been averted. There was nothing you could have done."

"But I cold have *tried*!" she said. "It was so awful, Adam. We were having dinner and making plans. He wanted to leave Paris and travel south, to Morocco. Suddenly he said that he felt most odd and then he—he just keeled over onto the table." Her voice was barely audible, her eyes wide and dark and tragic. "He never spoke again. He never said my name. He just lay there and people came running and someone, the *maître d'hôtel* I think, loosened his collar and tie, but it was no use." She shook her head with disbelief. "He was dead, Adam. Daddy was dead."

He stayed the night with her, sleeping on the sofa while she slept deeply, mercifully sedated. He had left her for only a few minutes when he paid his visit to the hotel manager to discuss the arrangements that had to be made. To the hotel manager's relief, Elizabeth had no desire for any part of the funeral to be held at the hotel. There would be no reception, no wake. Other hotel guests would have no further reminders of the frailty of human existence. The body would remain at a funeral parlor until the funeral service. After that, it would be shipped back to England for burial next to Serena in Kensal Green Cemetery.

A maid had stayed with Elizabeth during his brief absence, and Adam was relieved to see, when he returned, that she had persuaded Elizabeth to eat some scrambled egg and toast.

"I must telephone Luisa Isabel," she said wearily to him. "Other people can wait until morning. I've made a list of everyone who should be informed, and their telephone numbers, and also a list of all those who must be cabled."

He took a list from her, determined to save her the anguish of such a task and to undertake it himself.

"Telephone Princess Luisa Isabel," he said, hoping the princess would not be histrionic in her grief. "I'll send down for a pillow and blankets and make a bed up for myself on the sofa."

"Thank you." Her voice was thick with relief, her eyes telling him how very grateful she was that she was not to be left alone.

If the assistant manager regarded it as odd and unseemly that a single, middle-aged gentleman should ask for bed linen in order that he might share the room of a bereaved seventeen-year-old girl, he gave no indication of it. A death on the premises was anathema to all hotel staff. It disquieted the clients and created a host of minor, and sometimes major, difficulties. If all that had to be endured as a result of M. Kingsley's sudden death was the irregularity of his friend sleeping on the sofa in Mlle. Kingsley's room, then the irregularity could be overlooked just this once.

Jerome had been a nonpracticing Anglican and the funeral service was held at St. George's Church in the Rue Auguste Vacquerie. Princess Luisa Isabel wore black sable with a tiny hat and a wisp of black veil to cover her eyes. She had been Jerome's mistress for four years, and though she had not been so heedlessly in love that she would have forgotten her position and married him, she had been deeply fond of him.

Other friends were there: business friends from London and Geneva; fashionable friends from the Riviera; titled friends that he had met as a consequence of his affair with Princess Luisa Isabel. It was a simple service, short and dignified, and Adam was vastly relieved when it was over. Francine clung to his arm, weeping into a diminutive, lace-edged handkerchief. Elizabeth stood a little apart from them, her face as still and pale as a carved cameo, her silver-blond hair wound into an elegant chignon at the nape of her neck, her narrow-skirted, black wool suit emphasizing her pallor and her willowy slenderness.

He had been terrified that she would break down. That she would find the service and the sight of the coffin, submerged beneath its blanket of flowers, unendurable. She had not done so. Jerome would have wished his funeral service to be conducted with style and good taste, and she was determined to carry out his wishes. Her grief was a private thing and not for public display.

Later that day Adam left Paris with her, as she accompanied Jerome's body back to England. The next morning, in the large, impersonal cemetery in which they had stood seven years previously, when Serena was buried, Jerome was laid to rest. Adam was unashamed of the tears that stung his cheeks. Jerry had been a good friend and he had died, like Serena, too young.

When they left the cemetery the hired Rolls took them, not to Eaton Place, but to the suite that Elizabeth had reserved for herself at the Savoy. Beneath the weight of his grief, Adam was vaguely amused, wondering if she intended to live as Jerry had.

"Will you be moving into Eaton Place or returning to France?" he asked her as they entered her suite.

She flung her coat onto a chair. "Neither." Tea was waiting for them on a silver tray. She crossed the room to it, poured Earl Grey into two wafer-thin cups, and handed him one. "I'm going to sell the house in Eaton Place and buy something smaller and more manageable, something in the country. Kent or Sussex, I think. Somewhere that has no memories."

Her dress was a narrow sheaf of black wool crepe with long sleeves and a high neck, the skirt stopping just short of black suede shoes. Her hair was once again in a glossy chignon. She looked incredibly chic, more French than English.

"Won't you be lonely?" he asked, abruptly walking over to the window and the view of the Thames.

"I shall be lonely wherever I live," she said quietly.

He didn't say anything, but the muscles at the corner of his jaw clenched.

He heard her put down her teacup, then she said, "I shall never be able to thank you enough for all you've done, Uncle Adam. I truly don't think I could have managed without you."

The childhood appellation made him wince. She rarely used it now, and she had chosen to do so just when he had been about to make an almighty fool of himself. When he had been about to say that she needn't be lonely. That she could live with him in London. That he would adopt her, marry her. Anything, as long as he could keep her with him.

"I'll send you the address of wherever I move to," she said, crossing the room to him and slipping her arm through his. "And in June I shall be in Paris for your wedding. I wouldn't miss that for the world." Her voice was warm and loving.

She was not to be a bridesmaid. Francine had apologetically explained to her that she had an army of young nieces all eager for the honor. What she had not said was that Elizabeth, as a bridesmaid, might be more beautiful than the bride, and that was a risk Francine was not prepared to take.

Adam forced a smile. There was no further excuse for him to stay. Jerry had left Elizabeth abundantly provided for, and there was a score of lawyers and business advisers to shield and protect her. Even so, turning to her and saying good-bye was the hardest thing he had ever done.

She walked with him along the thickly carpeted corridor to the elevator. "I shall miss you," she said, squeezing his arm.

"I shall miss you," he said, and his lips brushed her hairline. Then he stepped into the elevator, a handsome man with a thick shock of hair who looked much younger than his forty-two years.

The metal-meshed doors closed between them, and five minutes later he walked out onto the rain-washed Strand, trying not to think of how fragile and vulnerable and achingly beautiful she had looked as they had said good-bye, but of how in eight weeks' time he was to be married. And of how little he was looking forward to it.

Elizabeth walked slowly back into her suite. Now she was really alone. She had to learn to live by herself, and she had to learn to do so bravely.

She stood in the middle of the luxurious room. Silence. No Jerome asking her to book him on a last-minute flight to Zurich; to arrange a luncheon party; to find him his collar stud, his cuff links. No one to care for. No one to fuss over. No one to love.

The chill April day was drawing to a close. The daffodil-colored sky of evening was fading to dusk. She stared out the windows to the broad, gray sweep of the Thames. She was luckier than most people, and she knew it. She had money, financial security, even if she no longer had emotional security. Jerome's lawyers had explained to her the terms of his will, the value of his estate. Until she was eighteen she would be under their guardianship, and there would be restrictions that could not, by law, be lifted until she was twenty-one. However, any of her requests, providing that they were reasonable, would be acceded to, and that included the selling of the Eaton Place house and the purchase of an alternative residence in southern England.

She sat on the sofa, curling her long legs beneath her. She wanted a house of her own. A place where, like an injured animal, she could lick her wounds and adjust herself to a new way of life. A place she could plan her future and come to terms with her loss.

She drew toward her the mass of literature that had been sent by London real estate agents. She knew exactly what she wanted, and only hoped that she would be fortunate enough to find it.

Adam walked down the Strand to Trafalgar Square, and stared glumly at Landseer's enormous bronze lions. Francine would be waiting anxiously for him. Her genuine sympathy for Elizabeth had not been deep enough to override her dismay when he had told her he would be accompanying Elizabeth back to London.

"But, *cheri*, is that necessary?" she had asked, with a Gallic lift of her shoulders. "Surely Jerome's lawyer will be with her, and perhaps Princess Luisa Isabel, and—"

"For God's sake, what comfort will Jerry's lawyer be to her?" he had shouted. "She's going to bury her father! She can't possibly do it alone!"

They had parted on bad terms. Francine was sorry for Elizabeth but had seen no reason why Adam should have stayed with her in her hotel suite the night Jerome had died. It wasn't his place to do such a thing. A nurse could have stayed with her. A woman friend.

"Beth doesn't have any women friends," Adam had said, white-lipped. "She's never been able to make any friends of her own. The only people she ever met socially were Jerry's friends, and they're all twenty years older than she!"

"As you are," Francine had said, her china-blue eyes flashing ferally.

He had sucked in his breath sharply, as if she had slapped him. "Yes," he had agreed, between clenched teeth. "As I am!" Then he had spun on his heel and strode from the room, slamming the door behind him.

Dusk now closed in around him. Red buses and Austins and Fords and taxis vied for supremacy as they roared past the square and down Whitehall. On his massive stone column, Nelson looked out with an indifferent eye over the darkening streets. Adam turned his coat collar up and hailed a taxi. "Victoria," he said without enthusiasm. "The boat train."

Francine greeted him with delight, secure enough, now that he was back with her, to indulge in her pity for Elizabeth. "*La pauvre petite*," she said, as she curled up against him, a mug of hot chocolate in her hands. "Was it very bad for her, *cheri*? Were there no London friends at the cemetery? No one to give her comfort?"

Adam shook his head. It was late the next evening and a log fire was burning in the grate of Francine's apartment. They had made love, eaten a bedroom picnic of hot cheese on toast, and were now sitting half naked in front of the fire.

"No," he said as Francine rested against him and he gazed over her head and into the flames. "Beth did not want another funeral service in London. There were only the two of us there, and the priest."

Francine shivered. *"Alors.* It does not sound very nice." She snuggled closer against his chest. "And now what will Elizabeth do? Live in London and become a debutante?"

Despite his inner turmoil, Adam grinned. "No, she's going to buy a house in the country, and though she didn't say so, I suspect she's going to resume her piano lessons under the very best teacher that she can find."

"Mon dieu!" Francine said, an expression of horror on her face. "She is crazy! She is young and pretty and rich. She could be having a wonderful time in London!"

"Maybe she will," he said, his grin fading. "Later, when she has had time to adjust to life without Jerry."

He needed time himself. He had believed himself to be in love with Francine. He enjoyed being with her more than he enjoyed being with anyone else, except Beth. Francine made him laugh; she made him feel good. Her petite, high-breasted, slightly plump body gave him more pleasure than he had ever before experienced. She was sweet-natured and, for the most part, even-tempered. She adored him and she wanted to marry him and bear his children. And he knew, with pain, that though he was deeply fond of her, he was not in love with her and never would be. The decision he had to make was whether to tell her so and break her heart by calling off the wedding, or to keep the knowledge to himself and settle for the kind of marriage that most practical-minded Frenchmen would envy.

The decision grew harder with each passing day. A wedding dress was bought, a trousseau. The cake was ordered, the invitations sent.

"I have never been so happy, *mon amour*," she whispered

to him one night in the warmth and darkness of her Montmartre bedroom. "Another three weeks and I shall be Mrs. Harland." She giggled, nestling close to him. "Do you think I will begin to look like a Mrs. Harland?"

He did not answer her. She was open and generous with her love, and he knew she was being cheated in return. She was not receiving the single-minded passion that was her due.

When the steady rhythm of her breathing indicated she was asleep, he eased himself away from her and dressed quietly. He knew he had to make up his mind, one way or the other, and whatever decision he made, there would be no going back. He let himself noiselessly out of the apartment, and walked quickly down the curving stone stairs, past the concierge's empty cubicle, and out into the deserted, moonlit street.

It wasn't that he wanted to marry anyone else. There was no other woman in his life, except Beth, and he had long ago rejected that idea as being impossible. If he married Francine, all his creature comforts would be taken care of. He would have a pretty, fun-loving companion. He would have the family life he had always wanted, and he would, no doubt, be happy, because being happy was in his nature. He crossed the cobbled street, passing beneath the chestnut trees, heading for the Rue du Printemps. He would also be living a lie and denying Francine the right to be loved as she deserved to be. He dug his hands deeper into his pockets, walking down the dark, shuttered street toward the milky-pale dome of Sacre Coeur, knowing that when he returned to her, his decision would have to be made.

She looked at him as though he were mad. *"Je ne comprends pas!* Why can't we be married in June? Have you to go away somewhere on business? Is there an emergency?"

She was sitting across from him at the breakfast table in her tiny kitchen, her blond curls tousled, a pale blue chiffon negligee over her lace-trimmed nightdress, her eyes wide and uncomprehending.

"It has nothing to do with business," he said gently, hating himself for the pain he was about to inflict. "I'm sorry, Francine. I should never have asked you to marry me. I'm not the sort of man that should be married."

"That's not true!" She flew from her chair, kneeling down at his side, clutching his hands. "You will make a wonderful husband, *cheri!* You are sweet and kind and understanding . . ."

He looked down into her frantic eyes and knew that there was no way of sparing her the truth. "I don't love you, Francine. I'm sorry. I thought I did. I thought we could have a good life together, but . . ." He lifted his shoulders in an expression of despair.

She gave a little sob, pushing herself to her feet as if she was suddenly old. "You don't love me and you're *sorry!*" she choked. *"Sorry!"* She raised her hand and slapped him across the face with all her strength, tears raining down her cheeks. "It is Elizabeth, *n'est-ce pas?* It is Elizabeth you love! Elizabeth you wish to marry now that Jerome is so conveniently dead!"

He rose to his feet, shocked at how much she knew of feelings he had thought were secret. "No," he said tightly, sick that their affair was ending on such a note. "It has nothing to do with Beth, Francine. I—"

"Liar!" she howled, flying at him, gouging at his face with her nails. "You have always loved her! Always wanted her! Ever since she was a little girl! I've seen it in your eyes!"

"You're wrong." His hands were clenched tight around her arms, holding her back from him.

"I'm not wrong!" Francine spat, her breasts heaving beneath the flimsy covering of her nightdress. "When did the little bitch seduce you? The night Jerome died? Was that why you stayed in her room all night? Was the 'comfort' you gave to her the comfort you never dared give her while Jerome was alive? Is comfort a new, prissy English word for *fuck?*"

His hand caught her across the mouth and she fell against the table, stunned incredulity in her eyes.

"You're wrong and you know it!" he yelled, appalled at the violence she had unleashed in him. "For Christ's sake, her father had just died! I stayed with her because I'm the nearest thing to a relative that she's got!"

"You stayed with her because you're in love with her!" Francine screamed as he stormed into the bedroom. He dragged his suitcase from the top of the closet, then

yanked suits and shirts from their hangers and stuffed them inside. *"You stayed with her because she's a whore! A slut!"*

He slammed the lid of his suitcase shut, not trusting himself to speak.

"I hate you!" she sobbed as he strode past her, out of the bedroom and across the living room to the door. *"I hate you! Hate you! Hate you!"* The door slammed shut behind him and she flung herself on the sofa, battering it with her fists, sobbing as if her heart were breaking.

Elizabeth was stunned when he telephoned her and told her. "But what went wrong, Adam? I thought you were both so happy together."

"We were . . . for a time. She's going around with a friend of Bendor Westminster's now. It will probably end in marriage. He's been crazy about her for years."

"Poor Adam," Elizabeth said sympathetically, and he said nothing to disillusion her. It was easier for Francine if everyone believed that she was the one who had broken off their engagement.

"How is the house coming along?" he asked, changing the subject.

Elizabeth had bought a small manor house near Midhurst in Sussex, only an hour from London by train, but deep in the countryside. Its old English garden looked out over a magnificent view of the South Downs and the distant sea.

"It's fabulous." There was undisguised pleasure in her voice. "Parts of it date from the fourteenth century, and there's even a tiny minstrels' gallery and a solar!"

"And the music lessons?"

"The academy has taken me back." There was so much wholehearted relief in her voice that he laughed.

"Is it very hard going?"

"Excruciating," she said, laughing with him. "My Steinway has finally arrived from Nice and the house had to be nearly taken apart before it could be fitted in. However, it's sitting prettily in the drawing room now and looking perfectly at home."

"And you're happy there?"

There was an infinitesimal pause, then she said, a little too brightly, "Yes, it was the right thing for me to do,

Adam. I couldn't possibly have lived in Eaton Place alone, and I have had enough of living in impersonal hotel suites. I wanted somewhere of my own and Four Seasons *is* mine. You must come down and see it now that you're not traveling to Paris every weekend."

"I'd like that," he said, smiling. " 'Bye, Beth. God bless."

He had purposely restrained himself from visiting her before. He had written to her, had long conversations with her on the telephone, but he had not seen her since the day they had parted at the Savoy. Now that he was no longer spending the best part of every week in Paris, he had no excuse for not visiting her.

He drove down the following Saturday. Once out of London there was very little traffic on the roads. It was a scorching hot May day. The top of his Austin Swallow was down, and the light, sweet scent from the Sussex hedgerows was thick as smoke in the sunlight. Feeling more lighthearted than he had for weeks, he sped south through Guildford and Godalming, enjoying the sight of Georgian houses, their windows sparkling in the sunlight; thatched cottages, their gardens full of lupins and honeysuckle and Michaelmas daisies; and gray stone Norman churches, their lych-gates casting pools of shadow in the sunshine.

She was waiting for him in the driveway when he arrived. Her hair was loose around her shoulders, and she was wearing a red silk shirt and a white linen skirt and summer sandals. Her legs were naked and honey-toned, her toenails varnished a rakish scarlet. She began to run toward him as he stepped out of the car, her arms wide. "Uncle Adam! It's so marvelous to see you again!"

His arms were around her and he breathed in the clean, sweet scent of her, never wanting to let her go. The silky fall of her hair brushed his face and she withdrew, taking his hand, her eyes shining.

"Well," she said with pride, turning toward the house. "This is Four Seasons. What do you think of it?"

It was exquisite. Built of mellowed stone, it stood in its garden as it had stood for centuries, as much a part of the surrounding countryside as the trees that sheltered it. Clematis clung to the walls, spilling clusters of purple blossoms along windowsills and lintels. Roses, in bud but not yet in bloom, edged up the doorway, promising splendor to come.

"It looks perfect," he said truthfully as she led him into the drawing room that had once been the great hall of a Norman knight.

"This is the oldest part of the house," she said as he stared up at the hammer-beamed ceiling in amazement. "The two wings that give it its H-shape were added on much later, sometime in the late sixteenth century."

"Quite modern, in fact," he said, grinning.

She laughed back at him, leading him through the dining room and into the kitchen. "The last owner was an American who spent loads of money on it and restored it with a great deal of love and care."

"I take it he died," Adam said as they walked out from the kitchen into an herb garden. "No one in his right mind would ever leave such a house voluntarily."

"Yes." A small shadow darkened her eyes. "He died about six months before Daddy. The house only went on the market the day I began looking for one."

Adam caught the note of sadness in her voice, and he knew she was thinking of Jerome. He also knew that Jerome would not have thought the house exquisite at all. It would have been too far from London for him. Too quiet. Too secluded.

"Are you happy, Beth?" he asked, no longer smiling, his eyes holding hers steadily. "Have you become used to living on your own?"

Her hair glistened in the sunlight, skimming her shoulders as she turned her face slightly away from him. "I don't think living alone is a thing anyone gets used to, not when one has been happy with someone. I know that you thought Daddy was selfish and that he shouldn't have insisted on my being with him all the time, but it was because he *needed* me. And because he needed me, I didn't mind."

A bee hovered, buzzing, over a clump of sage. In the distance, beyond the rich sweep of the downs, the sky merged into the bright glitter of the sea.

"Why did you break off your engagement with Francine?" she asked suddenly, turning to face him. "She isn't in love with that friend of Bendor Westminster's. Luisa Isabel rang me yesterday to invite me to her summer party and she told me that Francine was heartbroken and still in love with you."

The bee transferred its attentions to a tuft of purple-blue salvia with scented gray leaves. The sun was fierce and he took his blazer off, hooking it with his finger over his shoulder. "Because I discovered I was in love with someone else," he replied, his free hand deep in the pocket of his sporting flannels. "Because it would have been grossly unfair of me to have married her."

She had stopped walking and was staring at him. "But who is it you are in love with?" she asked, bewildered.

He was a yard or so ahead of her. He turned around slowly, facing her in the age-old garden. The bee was still skimming the salvia. The sun was hot on his back.

"You," he said, and knew that his Rubicon was crossed. There could be no going back. Not ever.

Chapter Five
❧

THE bee, replete, winged up and away. Adam sucked in his breath, his nostrils white and pinched, the pain behind his eyes almost unbearable.

"Now that you know, I don't expect you to continue offering me hospitality," he said harshly, wondering how, in the name of all that was holy, he could have been such a fool. "I'm sorry for the offense I've caused."

"Adam—"

"I don't know what possessed me." His voice was stiff, controlled, embarrassed. "I would appreciate it if you would—"

"Adam!"

"—forget what I said. I'm truly sorry, Beth. Good-bye." He turned on his heel and strode quickly from the garden, sick at the numbed incredulity he had seen on her face; sick at his folly that had ruined the happy relationship between them.

"Adam!" She was running after him, her cheeks flushed, her eyes revealing her agitation. "Adam, wait . . ." She caught hold of his arm, but he did not halt in his purposeful stride. He had to get away. He didn't want her sympathy or her pity.

"Adam, please," she panted, trying to keep pace with him. "I don't *want* to forget what you said!" Her voice was urgent. "I never imagined . . . never considered . . ."

He had reached his car. He flung his jacket onto the rear seat as he yanked open the door. "No. I don't suppose you did!" he said as he slid behind the wheel and punched the engine into life. "It isn't what a girl expects from a man she regards as an uncle, is it? A man she's always believed she could trust. I don't blame you for how you feel, Beth." He rammed his foot down hard on the clutch.

"You don't *know* how I feel!" she shouted over the roar of the engine. "I don't *mind*, I tell you! In fact, I'm *pleased!*"

He stared at her, one hand on the wheel, the other on the gear-stick, smoke from the exhaust billowing into the air. Her hands gripped the car door. "I'm glad that you're in love with me! I'm not offended at all, Adam! I'm *glad!*"

Smoke continued to plume into the air. He couldn't move. He stared at her, transfixed, and she began to laugh. "Why are you so surprised? I'm eighteen now. I'm not a little girl any longer. I think your being in love with me is flattering and incredible and quite, quite wonderful!"

He snapped the engine off, his hand trembling slightly, not trusting himself to speak. She stood only inches away from him, a light breeze stirring her hair, her eyes warm and untroubled. She was far more in command of the situation than he was.

"Jesus God," he whispered, then he vaulted from the car, seizing hold of her hands. "I'm forty-two," he said abruptly, "and I'm not just in love with you, Beth. I want to marry you!"

Her eyes flew wide with shock and his hands tightened on hers with bruising intensity. "Is that an idea you could learn to come to terms with?" he asked tautly. "If not, I won't mention it again, but . . ."

She gasped, her eyes still open wide, still incredulous. "I—I think it's an idea I could come to terms with very easily."

He felt as if his chest were encircled with a band of steel. It couldn't be happening. It was too wonderful, too marvelous.

"I love you, Beth," he said again, huskily, and this time his arms slid around her, drawing her close. Her body swayed lightly against his, trembling with uncertainty and expectation. Gently, letting all the love he felt for her show in his eyes, he tilted her face to his. "Dearest Beth," he murmured. His lips brushed her temple, then slid tenderly, slowly, to her cheekbone, the corner of her mouth. "Dearest, beautiful Beth." He felt a moment of doubt flare through her and gently, deliberately, overcame it, bending her in to him, kissing her with tenderness and then, as her doubt faded and she yielded willingly against him, with rising passion.

It was a long, deep kiss and when at last he raised his head from hers, her cheeks were flushed, her eyes sure and certain. "Yes," she whispered, her arms still around his neck. "If you want me to marry you, Adam, then the answer is yes."

He grinned down at her. The gossips would have a field day, he thought. They would say he was marrying her for her money. That he was abusing his position as a family friend. He didn't care. He loved her. He had always loved her. And now he was going to marry her.

Later, sitting in the tiny solarium that she had massed with plants and cushions, Elizabeth said anxiously, "You won't want me to give up Four Seasons when we marry, will you?"

They were sitting on the window seat, sharing a bottle of ice-cold sauternes. Adam put down his glass. For him to move into Four Seasons would do nothing to silence the gossips who would say he was marrying her for her money. He had his own extremely comfortable home in Kensington.

"No," he said, drawing her closer to him. "But we'll keep my house in Kensington for when we're in town, and it will be easier if we are married from there."

"At the Kensington Register Office?" she asked, a smile tugging at the corners of her mouth.

A slight frown furrowed his brow. They had agreed on a quiet wedding, but she was only eighteen. It would be understandable if she wanted a church wedding with all the trimmings.

"Not unless you want to," he said, lifting the bottle of sauternes from its ice bucket and topping up her glass. "We could get married at St. Mary Abbotts, or even St. Margaret's, Westminster."

She giggled, snuggling close to him. "No, thank you. The Kensington Register Office will do very nicely. At least if we get married there, I shan't have to scout around for someone to give me away!"

They were married a month later. Her tutor from the Royal Academy of Music stood as one witness and Princess Luisa Isabel as the other. Elizabeth wore a cream-colored silk dress, high-necked and with short, belled cap sleeves. The midcalf-length skirt swirled lushly around her legs. Her hair was swept high and smoothed into a glistening figure-of-eight knot. Her only jewelry was a single strand of pearls and matching pearl earrings; her bouquet was a delicate cluster of white roses and dew-fresh freesias.

Adam had drawn his breath in on a whistle when she'd walked down the staircase of his Kensington house toward him. "My God, you look lovely," he'd said reverently. "Like a princess in a fairy tale."

She had slipped her hand into his, suddenly shy. The previous night had been the first they had ever spent beneath the same roof, except for the night of her father's death, and she had been suddenly conscious of the night to come. A night that would not be chaperoned by Princess Luisa Isabel, as the previous night had been.

The princess, who was staying as Adam's guest, had been appalled at Elizabeth's decision to marry from Adam's home and not her own. "People will think you have been living together!" she had protested, aghast. "It really isn't done, Elizabeth. You must either leave for the wedding from your home in Sussex, or from a hotel, or a friend's house."

"I have spent enough of my life in hotels and I don't want to leave for my wedding from one," Elizabeth had said gently but firmly. "And I don't have friends of my own in London. All the people I know here were Daddy's friends. I can't very well presume to stay with them when I haven't even asked them to the wedding."

Princess Luisa Isabel had abandoned good sense as an argument and tried superstition. "It is *terribly* bad luck to meet your husband on the day of your wedding, before you meet him at the altar."

"But there's not going to *be* an altar," Elizabeth had said with amusement. "We're being married in a registry office, not a church, Luisa."

The princess had thrown up her hands in despair. A first marriage for both bride and groom and it was to take place in a registry office. It offended her to the very depths of her Catholic soul.

"I, Adam Harland, know not of any lawful impediment why I may not be joined in matrimony to Elizabeth Helena Kingsley," Adam said to the registrar in a strong, sure voice.

Luisa Isabel sighed and dabbed at her eyes with her handkerchief. ". . . I call upon these persons here present," Adam continued, "to witness that I, Adam Harland, do take thee, Elizabeth Helena Kingsley, to be my lawfully wedded wife."

The registrar turned his attention to Elizabeth. "Please repeat after me," he said gently.

There was a slight pause before she spoke, and Luisa Isabel wondered if the girl was suddenly realizing what she was doing: marrying a man who had always been a surrogate father to her. A man twenty-four years her senior. A man who, until four weeks ago, she had never in her wildest dreams visualized as a lover.

"I, Elizabeth Helena Kingsley," she began in a low, husky voice, and Princess Luisa Isabel lifted her shoulders fractionally in a gesture of resignation. It was over now. With God's good grace they would be happy. That Adam loved her and was in love with her was beyond question. Perhaps it would be a long time before Elizabeth discovered that though she, too, loved Adam, she was not in love with him. And perhaps by the time she discovered it, the difference would cease to matter. She hoped so. After the ceremony she kissed them with much affection, laughingly accepted the gift of Elizabeth's bouquet, and showered them with confetti as they all left for a simple wedding breakfast at the Café de Paris.

They had told no one where they were going to spend their honeymoon. The princess assumed it would be on the

continent. Florence, perhaps, or Venice or Rome. Elizabeth's tutor, if asked, would have surmised somewhere
quiet and scenic: Cornwall or the west of Ireland.

They told no one their secret. When the wedding
breakfast was over and their two guests had waved them
off from the front entrance of the Café de Paris, Adam
drove not in the direction of Victoria Station and the boat
train, nor in the direction of the roads leading west to
Cornwall, nor to the ferry for Ireland. Instead he drove
south, out through the London suburbs to Leatherhead
and Guildford, motoring down leafy country lanes to
Haslemere and the rolling countryside beyond. To Four
Seasons and its quietness, its serenity, and its uninter-
rupted peace.

Elizabeth sat close beside him in the open Austin
Swallow, blissfully happy. She had been lonely and bereft
and now her whole world was transformed. She had
someone to love again, someone to care for. Someone who
loved her.

"How does it feel to be an old married lady?" Adam
asked with a grin as the house came into view and they
swooped down through a tunnel of trees toward it.

"It feels very secure," she said, laughing, her arm
hugging his. "Now you can't run away from me. Not
ever."

He pressed his foot down on the brake, sliding the car to
a halt on the gravel that fronted the house. "I can't imagine
there was ever much danger of it," he said with amusement. He slammed his door shut behind him and walked
around the car to open her door.

"It's better to be safe than sorry," she said, her cheeks
dimpling as he swept her up and carried her over the
threshold.

Her arms were around his neck, his thick auburn hair
springy as heather beneath her fingertips. She rested her
head next to his. "I love you, Adam Harland," she
whispered softly as the oak door swung closed behind
them.

His arms tightened around her as he walked with her
across the wood-panelled hall to the staircase. "I love you
too," he said huskily. "And in another few moments I'm
going to show you how much, in every way that I can."

The bedroom was golden, filled with afternoon sun-

shine. He placed her gently on the large brass bed and
walked across the room to close the curtains. They had
never been alone in such intimacy before. Ever since he
had asked her to marry him, he had courted her with the
restraint and propriety of a Victorian suitor, painfully
aware that she had no parent to keep a watchful eye on her,
determined that no one would ever be able to accuse him of
taking advantage of that fact.

She was still wearing the silk dress she had been married
in. She lay where he had placed her, watching him as he
drew the curtains and the room was plunged into muted
light. She had very little idea of what to expect. She had
never had a lover before. Never enjoyed even the most
casual of friendships with a member of the opposite sex.
Her life with Jerome had been a strange one. It had made
her worldly-wise in many ways, assured and sophisticated. She had been at home in the grandest of surround-
ings, unimpressed when confronted by titles or fame. Yet it
had also left her curiously innocent.

She had never had any girlfriends her own age to discuss
boys with, to laugh and giggle with. She had never
enjoyed the easygoing camaraderie that comes from being
a member of a group. Jerome had always been at her side,
shielding her by his presence. She had seen things and
witnessed a way of life that many people twice her age had
never seen or were even aware of, but she had experienced
very little of that life. And nothing at all of love.

Adam took off his jacket and tossed it onto a chair, saying
with obvious tension in his voice, "Would you like some
champagne?"

She pushed herself up against the pillows. "Yes . . .
No . . ." Then, with disarming frankness, she asked, "Is
everyone so scared when they're finally left alone?"

His tension evaporated and a smile tugged at one corner
of his mouth. "Not many would admit to it, but I'm
damned sure they are. I think the champagne is essential. I
told the daily help to leave some to chill in the refrigerator
before she went home. I'll be back with it in a jiffy."

When he had gone Elizabeth rose slowly from the bed
and walked across the room to the dressing table.

"There's nothing to be scared of," she chided herself as
she stared intently at her reflection in the mirror. "It's
Adam I'm going to bed with, not a stranger."

She raised her hands to unclasp the pearls, and laid them down on the glass tray of her dressing table. The drawn curtains were summer curtains and the room was still full of soft light. She took off her earrings and set them beside the necklace. Adam, who loved her. Who made her feel safe and secure. She remembered Francine, chic and sexy and uninhibited. He had very nearly married Francine. And if he had, she knew how different the consummation of his marriage would have been. He was forty-two. He was accustomed to women who were sexually knowledgeable. Was she going to allow him to be disappointed in her?

She lifted her hands to behind her neck and slowly drew down her zipper, letting the cream silk slip from her shoulders to her waist, to her hips, till it slithered into a milky pool about her ankles. Carefully she stepped out of it, then picked it up and draped it on the chair next to his jacket. She couldn't remember a time when she hadn't been happy in his company. When she had been very small he had listened to her sing, tossing her up in the air afterward while she had shrieked with delight and her mother had looked on indulgently. Then, when Jerome had been traveling abroad, he had become a second father to her, taking her to the zoo, the park, the circus. And now she was going to go to bed with him.

Her hand shook slightly as she lifted up her lacy underslip and unfastened her garters. Two months ago she had been disappointed that she was not to be a bridesmaid when he married Francine. She had never been jealous of Francine. It had never occurred to her to wish to be in Francine's place. She slid the sheer silk stockings down her legs. Yet now she was. How had it happened? How had he moved so smoothly from being the Adam of her childhood to the Adam who was now her husband? She stepped out of her cream kid pumps and pushed her stockings off, then again stared at herself in the mirror. Would her father have approved? A slight smile touched her mouth. He would have been too astonished to approve or disapprove. He had always lived his life exactly as he had wanted, taking no thought of other people's desires or wishes. He could hardly be disapproving if she showed the same streak of willfulness herself.

The door opened behind her and Adam stepped into the

bedroom, a bottle of Moët et Chandon in one hand, two champagne glasses in the other. On seeing her dressed only in her slip, her breasts rising creamy and pale from the lush lace that covered them, he halted abruptly, as if he had been punched hard in the chest.

In the mirror, her eyes met his. His hair was rumpled, as if he had run his fingers through it several times on his way down to the kitchen. His handsome, good-natured face was showing signs of strain. She could see tension in the lines around his mouth, uncertainty in the honey-brown depth of his eyes. Her doubts fled. He was Adam. Adam, whose generous, compassionate nature had been her strength and support ever since she was a little girl. Adam, to whom she was now married, and to whom she was going to give her love.

Her eyes continued to hold his and a smile curved her lips. "We don't need the champagne," she said huskily. "I'm not scared anymore."

Her reward was the relief in his eyes. He put the champagne and glasses down on the bedside table and walked toward her. As he slid his arms around her, holding her tight, she leaned against him, looking at their reflection in the glass. He was not much taller than she, a toughly built man who, despite his slight limp, moved with easy strength and confidence. A man whom women admired and other men liked. A man she was going to spend the rest of her life with.

She turned in his arms to face him, her hands slipping around his neck, her body pressing, soft and warm, against his.

With a groan, he lowered his head to hers and kissed her with infinite tenderness, his hands stroking worshipfully over the thin silk of her slip.

"Oh, God, Beth . . . I love you . . . love you . . ." he whispered hoarsely.

She was pliant and willing in his arms, pressing so close to him that he had to exert all his willpower not to lower her to the floor and take her there and then.

"My darling . . . my love . . ." He groaned, then scooped her up in his arms and carried her toward the bed. For years he had restrained his desire for her. Now, at last, it could be expressed. The thought of caressing her small, uptilted breasts, her private places, filled him with awe. She was so young, so pure, so immeasurably precious.

He placed her down gently on the bed. His heart was hammering in his chest as slowly, carefully, he peeled away the delicate straps of her silk-and-lace underslip, revealing the satin smoothness of her flesh, the rose-tipped perfection of her breasts.

Excitement raged through him like a forest fire, but he held it firmly in check. She loved him and trusted him, and he was going to do nothing to alarm or dismay her. He was going to be gentle and patient. Carnality had never had any place in their relationship, and he did not want it to have one now. The thought of seeing shock or disgust in her eyes made him tremble.

"You are so beautiful, Beth. So perfect," he whispered, refusing to give in to his body's demand that he release his engorged penis from the tight constraint of his trousers.

Lightly, barely touching her, he ran his fingertips down the curve of her throat, marveling at the beauty of her milky flesh, her splendor as she lay half naked beneath him.

Her arms slid up around his neck, her lips soft and yielding as his mouth came down on hers. His hands closed caressingly over her breasts, her nipples brushing his palm, erect and taut. He could feel her heart beating under his hand. Her tongue hesitantly met his, then slipped past it, and he knew he could endure no more.

"I want you!" he gasped. "Oh, God, Beth! How I want you!"

He rolled away from her and, standing, pulled off his shirt with shaking hands, kicked off his shoes and socks, and unzipped his trousers.

She watched in shy fascination. She had never seen a grown man naked. The muted sunlight cast golden shadows on the strong muscles of his chest and arms. His belly was flat, a line of crisply curling auburn hair running down from his navel. The blood rose hot in her cheeks.

"Adam, I . . ." she began hesitantly.

The bed rocked beneath his weight as he lay beside her, taking her lovingly in his arms.

"I won't hurt you," he promised fiercely, seeing the sudden apprehension in her eyes. "I promise I will never, ever hurt you."

His mouth closed once more over hers, and as he felt her

relax against him, he very gently slid her slip down to her hips, to her knees, then tossed it free.

"We have all the time in the world," he whispered reassuringly, as only a wisp of lingerie shielded her from his view. "There's nothing to be afraid of, my love. Nothing."

She clung tightly to him, her eyes closed as he lifted her beneath him and reverently removed the last barrier of lace. Her pubic hair, crisp and golden, brushed the palm of his hand like an electric shock. Beth. Toddling to meet him in the drawing room at Eaton Place. Beth. Her face pale, her eyes wide and dark as they tobogganed together on the day of her mother's funeral. Beth. Her arm sliding guilelessly into his as they left Francine and Jerry on the Spanish Steps and set off toward the Vatican Museum. So many memories. So much love. So much longing.

He hardly dared breathe as he straddled her, taking his weight on his elbows, fitting his legs between hers.

"I'm going to be careful, Beth. Careful . . ." he breathed, as slowly, gently, he eased himself into her soft, sweet center.

She stirred against him, her fingers tightening in his hair. His hands on her breasts had stirred something deep and dormant in her. She wanted him to touch them again. To bite and suck them. To kindle her newfound feelings and make them burst into flame.

He scarcely moved after he had entered her, his entire body rigid as if he were terrified of hurting her.

"It's all right," she whispered encouragingly. "It's all right, Adam."

His face was contorted in an expression almost of torment. He could bear no more. She was so small, so tight, so unflinching beneath him. With a single thrust and a deep groan he came, his sperm shooting into her in an agony of relief. As he shuddered and gasped for breath, her arms tightened around him. No spasm rocked her own body, and her breathing was calm and steady. She felt curiously on edge, as if she had been taken to a wonderful party and, having gotten there, had found the doors closed against her.

"Did I hurt you, my love?" he asked, his eyes dark with anxiety.

She raised her face to his, lovingly tracing the line of his brow, the curve of his cheekbone.

"No," she said with a smile. "You didn't hurt me, darling."

It was true. She had felt comfort and gentle pleasure and a hungry, almost frightening feeling when his hands had skimmed her breasts, but she had not felt pain. Nor any other emotion.

"I love you, Beth," he said again drowsily, as his breathing deepened into the slow rhythm of sleep. "Only you. Forever."

She turned her head, kissing his shoulder. She had pleased him. He was happy. Everything was all right.

"Good night, my love," she whispered, curving her body to his. "God bless."

Their lives fell into an agreeable pattern. From Monday to Friday they stayed in Kensington. The Royal Academy was only a few minutes' drive away and no matter what his plans for the day, Adam always drove her there himself. On Friday evening they left London early, motoring down into the heart of Sussex, to Four Seasons. They seldom shared their weekends with any guests. Occasionally, Princess Luisa Isabel would join them with her new lover, a Brazilian millionaire whose only occupation was polo. Other than that they remained alone, content with each other, needing no other diversions.

To Princess Luisa Isabel's dismay, Adam had become a socialist, staunchly supporting Ramsay MacDonald, who led the National Government.

"I don't understand it," she said to Elizabeth. "Adam is a wealthy man. Why is he a socialist? Surely a socialist government will take all his wealth away?"

"They will take some of it away, Luisa, and it is only fair that they should do so," Elizabeth said as they lay in hammocks waiting for Adam and Luisa's lover to return from a polo match at Windsor.

The princess sat upright in her hammock. "My goodness, have you become a socialist too?" she asked, sincerely shocked.

Elizabeth laughed. "I think I'm becoming a pacifist. I like the idea of the League of Nations, and of disputes being settled by international collaboration instead of by armed force."

"It hasn't been very successful in stopping Japan from invading China," the princess said tartly, lying down once again and closing her eyes. "And I don't suppose it will be any more successful in curbing the new German chancellor if he should begin casting his eyes on the Rhineland and complaining that the 1919 peace treaty was unfair to Germany."

"He won't stay in power long enough to complain," Elizabeth said confidently. "He's far too unpleasant to last."

A year later she had to reconsider. The Oxford Union had passed the motion that "this house will in no circumstances fight for its king and country," yet Hitler was growing increasingly obnoxious in Germany, and Mussolini was being equally abhorrent in Italy.

"You can't have patriotism *and* pacifism," Adam had pointed out to her with amusement when she had been indignant at the motion. "Churchill's got it right. The League of Nations needs military power to back it if it is going to act effectively for peace."

By the summer of 1935 Elizabeth had begun to agree with him. Italy had invaded Abyssinia and the league had stood by, powerless. In Germany, Hitler was adopting conscription in defiance of the Treaty of Versailles, and it seemed as if Princess Luisa Isabel's fears had been well-founded. Elizabeth was concerned. However, it wasn't the growth of fascism that was filling her with increasing anxiety, but her failure to become pregnant.

"Do stop worrying, darling," Adam said to her when another month went by and she was disappointed yet again. "There's no hurry for a baby. You're only twenty-one. We've all the time in the world."

She was about to protest that though she was only twenty-one, he had just celebrated his forty-fifth birthday, when she saw the faint lines of strain around his mouth and decided against it. He had been pushing himself very hard lately, painfully aware of the large work force dependent on his company's success; of the long dole queue waiting for them if she should fail them. His curly hair was as thick and as unruly as ever, but it was heavily sprinkled with gray, and the laugh lines at the corner of his eyes and around his mouth had deepened.

"I think I should see a gynecologist," she said, reaching

across the breakfast table for another slice of toast. "I don't *want* to wait any longer, Adam. I'm impatient for motherhood!"

He grinned. "Have you considered how bulky you will look on the concert platform, pregnant and playing Bartok?"

"The Bartok recital is in two months," she said, feeling a quiver of anticipation at the mere thought of it. "I could hardly be bulky by then!" She glanced at her watch, her concentration moving from motherhood to music as he had intended. "Goodness, is that the time? I have a rehearsal class in thirty minutes! Please hurry, darling."

The Bartok recital at the Albert Hall was an overwhelming success. Frank Howes, the music critic of *The Times*, wrote that it was "an outstanding performance, glowing with vitality." At the end of the year she was chosen to represent Great Britain in the first International Chopin Piano Competition in Warsaw. The competition was held in the concert hall of the National Philharmonic Society in Warsaw and to her disbelief she was first after the preliminary stages, only losing her position in the finals. It was a tremendous achievement and from then on she knew, with dizzying certainty, that she was on the verge of becoming what she had always dreamed of becoming: a concert pianist of international repute.

Adam's pride was touched with alarm. He knew how important her music was to her and he had gained pleasure from allowing her to indulge it, but he had never foreseen the extent to which it would affect their lives. The Chopin competition in Warsaw was followed by other competitions in Brussels and in Vienna. It wasn't always possible for him to travel with her and he hated the separations her music brought, and resented the long hours she spent alone practicing.

In May of the following year, she was invited to tour the United States for eight weeks.

"*Eight weeks?*" Adam stared at her in horror. "But it's impossible, Beth. I can't possibly leave London for eight weeks!"

"I know," she said, slipping her arm through his. "I shall miss you terribly, darling."

He couldn't believe what she had said. "You can't mean you intend to go?"

It was her turn to look astonished. "But of course I must go! It's a wonderful opportunity! Two recitals at Carnegie Hall! One in Chicago and goodness knows how many more in other cities."

He felt cold. He knew if she went that she would not miss him. Not as much as he would miss her. There would be other tours. Longer times apart. He closed his eyes, remembering how he had charged Jerome with selfishness for wanting her with him at the cost of her studies. If he refused to sanction the American tour, he would be doing exactly the same thing. And if he didn't, he knew that she would begin to be lost to him. Their lives would grow increasingly further and further apart.

They were in the drawing room at Four Seasons. It was a Saturday morning and Princess Luisa Isabel and her latest boyfriend were coming for lunch. They were flying in from Paris and he was due to meet them at the airport in an hour.

For the first time in his life, Adam was fiercely, burningly jealous. If Elizabeth had been having an affair with another man, she could not be spending more time away from him. His hands clenched. God damn it. If it had been another man, at least he could have socked him on the jaw. But a piano couldn't be socked on the jaw. He moved abruptly away from her, walking across to the windows. He stood with his fists thrust deep into his pockets, so jealous of the time and passion she lavished on her music that he thought he would choke with it.

Elizabeth bit her lip, acutely aware of Adam's distress and suspecting the reasons for it. He didn't want her to go, and he didn't want to have to ask her not to go. Disappointment so acute that she almost cried aloud with it surged through her. To concerts at Carnegie Hall! They would have been the most wonderful, most momentous concerts of her professional life! And she knew, as she gazed at Adam's rigid back, that she would not go. The cost would be too high. She walked across the room to him, wondering how much of her sacrifice was due to her growing guilt at her lack of passionate response to him in bed. For the first few months of her marriage, she had been undisturbed, certain that it would come in time. Now she knew that, though she loved Adam with all her heart, it never would come.

"You're quite right, darling," she said softly, slipping her arm once more through his. "Eight weeks is far too long. I'll decline the offer. Maybe we could go away on holiday for a week or two instead? France perhaps, or Spain?"

Relief swept through him and for a moment he couldn't speak, then he said gruffly, "Not Spain," ashamed of not being able to overrule her decision. At not being able to tell her that eight weeks was not too long and that, of course, she must go. "The whole country is about to be plunged into the most hideous civil war. Luisa Isabel must be distraught at the thought of what is happening there."

"France then," Elizabeth said, glad that his gaze was still avoiding hers and that he couldn't see the misery she felt. She forced enthusiasm into her voice. "Perhaps we'll be able to make a baby there. The gynecologist said that there was nothing physically wrong with me, so it could be that I need to relax more. We'll go down to Antibes and stay at the Eden Roc. It's the easiest place in the world to relax in!"

They swam and sunbathed and laughed and talked, but both of them were aware that a shadow had been cast across the happy surface of their marriage and neither of them was able to dispel it. Adam made love to her with tender frequency, but no baby resulted.

"Does it really matter so much, Elizabeth?" Princess Luisa Isabel asked when they visited her in Paris on their way back to London. "It would interrupt your musical career and make life very difficult for a while. What if you received an invitation to tour America? You couldn't possibly undertake it if you were pregnant. It would be far too grueling.

"Yes," Elizabeth said, her voice oddly flat. "Of course it would be. Do you think it's true what the French magazines are saying about Prince Edward and Mrs. Simpson? There's nothing in our newspapers at home. Only the occasional discreet mention that 'among the Prince of Wales's guests was Mrs. Wallis Simpson!' That sort of thing. Nothing any stronger."

Princess Luisa Isabel was glad for the change of subject. The lack of a baby was obviously beginning to distress Elizabeth.

"The French say that the prince is in love with her and that he wants to marry her. Perhaps he is. If so, I feel sorry for him. He will not be able to marry her." Princess Luisa Isabel spoke with all the authority of her title. "Not if he wishes to keep his crown."

A month later the prince had become king and Elizabeth watched with avid interest as he struggled to make Wallis Simpson his queen. She had thought that the government would make a compromise, enabling him to marry her and remain king, though without bestowing on Wallis the title of queen. She had been wrong. The government and the king did not compromise, and on the eleventh of December he abdicated.

"At least it's a relief from reading about the fascists," Adam said wearily, tossing a log on the drawing room fire. "How our government and the French government can opt for nonintervention in the war in Spain is beyond me. Especially now that Hitler and Mussolini have officially formed an alliance. God help the rest of Europe if those two start hunting as a pair!"

"Will it lead to war?" Elizabeth asked, putting down the music score she had been studying.

Adam's expression was grim. He had fought in one war and had believed, for a time, that it had been the war to end all wars. Now another was looming, one in which most likely he would be too old to participate.

"It will if no one puts a curb on Hitler," he said as the wood took hold and the pungent smell of pine filled the room. "His marching into the Rhineland is only a beginning. That's obvious from his speeches."

They were silent, each thinking of those speeches, which were bringing terror to thousands of European Jews. Hitler had decreed that Jews born in Germany were no longer entitled to German citizenship, and that marriage between Jews and non-Jews was illegal.

"Horrid little man," Elizabeth said, shivering despite the heat from the fire. "How I wish someone would put a stop to him."

No one did. All through 1937 the swastika rampaged triumphantly. By 1938 war was becoming not just a possibility but a certainty. In September the British government mobilized its navy. Hitler shouted that Czechoslovakia was the last territorial demand he would make and Prime Minister Neville Chamberlain flew to Munich to try ineffectually to make peace.

Adam watched events with growing rage. "Can't Chamberlain *see* that he's being taken for a fool? Dictators like Hitler don't honor their word or respect peace agreements! The only thing they respect is force!"

By February of the following year Hitler, not content with Czechoslovakia, was casting lustful eyes on Poland.

"That's it," Adam said decisively. "Another few months, weeks even, and we're going to be at war with Germany. I went to the War Office today. I'm too old for active service. The most I will be able to expect is a desk job." He looked more distressed than she had ever seen him. "I'm damned if I'm going to reconcile myself to sitting behind a goddamned desk!"

Elizabeth had spent all day at the keyboard. She had a Mozart recital in a month and a Bach recital in April, and she had mentally been going over one of the scores she was to play, her left hand moving to the notes and phrases and harmonies that she could hear in her head. With a suppressed sigh of regret she relinquished them.

"Then what are you going to do?" she asked, sensing his inner tension and certain that whatever it was, he had already made up his mind.

"I don't know." He had been pacing the room, but now he stood still and looked at her, and she knew he was lying. "Beth . . ." He took her hands. "Beth, would you mind if we were to leave England before we become trapped here by the war, and before I become billeted behind some bloody useless desk?"

"Leave?" The last strains of Mozart and Bach abruptly fled. She stared at him, the blood draining from her face. "You mean go to America? Run away?"

His eyebrows flew together. "Good God, no! I don't want to run away! I want to be involved!"

"But where can you be involved?" she asked bewilderedly. "I don't understand."

His hands tightened on hers. "The threat of war isn't only coming from Germany, Beth. Japan has been at war with China for five years now, and it's my belief that if we declare war on Germany, the Japanese will take advantage of the fact and move toward Hong Kong and Singapore."

The breath was tight in her chest, the blood drumming in her ears. He couldn't mean what she thought he meant. There was the Mozart recital; the Bach recital; the Brussels Competition in four months.

"I'm sorry, Adam," she said, praying that her fears were groundless. "I don't understand."

His thumbs pressed hard on her wrists. "I want to go to Hong Kong," he said fiercely. "I want to be in a position to fight when the fighting comes!"

Chapter Six

SHE stared at him, her disbelief total. "Hong Kong?" she repeated. Her voice cracked, not sounding as if it were her voice at all.

He nodded, running his hands through his hair. "One of our subsidiary companies is based there. Leigh Stafford, the chap in charge, says that though the vast majority of people out there ridicule the thought of an attack by the Japanese, he thinks it's a distinct possibility. He wants us to wind down our business interests and hold over our investments until the situation is more settled."

She continued to stare at him. In all of the seven years that they had been married, they had never had a serious row. The nearest they had come was when she had been offered the eight-week concert tour of America. She had known then that if she had gone, the very foundations of their marriage would have been shaken. And she had not gone. She had fought her disappointment, determined that there would be other opportunities, opportunities that would not drive a wedge between them. But now Adam was suggesting the impossible. He was suggesting that she leave the academy, that she leave London, that she abandon her musical career as she had been forced to abandon it once before, many years ago.

"No . . ." she whispered, her nails digging deep into her palms. "Oh, no . . . no . . . no!"

He continued as if she had not spoken. "Japan is on good terms with both Germany and Italy. She'll be able to count on support from both of them if she should need it. And she's an aggressor. Look at the way she's been pounding China. Stafford says that Japanese troops are pushing south now. A large contingent have landed at Amoy, three hundred miles northeast of Hong Kong. If they have, it puts them in a very favorable position to attack Hong Kong if they should choose to." His eyes held hers. "It's Stafford's belief, and mine too, that if war breaks out in Europe, that is exactly what they will do."

She had been sitting in one of the deep-cushioned chairs by the fire. Now she rose unsteadily to her feet, the lamplight gleaming on her hair. "And you want to be there if they do?" she asked, her voice low and barely audible, with a strange note in it that he had never heard before.

He thought her strained reaction was because of his age, and a tide of color stung his cheeks. "Yes," he said abruptly, delving in his jacket pocket for his pipe and his tobacco pouch. He furiously stuffed tobacco into the bowl, his eyes avoiding hers. "It isn't half as crazy as it seems, Beth. I'm an army man by nature. I should have realized it years ago and made the army my career, but in the days when it would have been feasible there was no need for me to think of a career. Besides, I believed I'd had enough after the 1914–18 shindig." He lit his pipe and drew on it deeply.

She leaned against the mantelpiece, her face pale, knowing with sick horror that her music, and her future professional life, were the farthest things from his mind. Even now, it had not occurred to him that her incredulity was anything other than that he was, perhaps, too old to once more contemplate active service. She moistened her lips, understanding instinctively that if she cited her musical studies as a reason for their not going to Hong Kong, the battle would be lost before it began. He would see it as proof that her music meant more to her than he did. They would be at an impasse and her earlier sacrifice of not touring the States would have been in vain. She said carefully, trying to make him see how impractical his proposal was, "You're forty-nine, Adam. Surely you can't want to see active service again?"

She knew, even as she said it, that it was the wrong thing to say. The uncomfortable color in his cheeks darkened.

"God damn it, Beth! You're talking like the Army Board! Of course I'm not too old! I'm as fit as any of the runny-nosed youngsters they're so busy recruiting! And I'm experienced! It's men like me the army should be rounding up! Men who have proved themselves on the battlefield and know what they're doing!"

She had never seen him so furious. Her heart began to slam in thick, heavy strokes. His proposal that they go to Hong Kong wasn't a whim. It was something he had thought about long and hard. Something about which he had already made up his mind. A wave of panic surged through her, and she controlled it with difficulty. "But if you are right," she said with what she hoped was sweet reasonableness, "and the Japanese do attack Hong Kong and Singapore, what will happen to the civilian population? Won't it be terribly dangerous for them?"

He frowned, as if he didn't understand what she was saying, and her panic gave way to impatience. She dug her nails deeper into her palms. "You want me to go with you, don't you, Adam." It was a statement, not a question.

He nodded.

She drew in a deep, steadying breath, certain that she had found his Achilles' heel. He would not expose her to unnecessary danger. "But if I go with you," she said quietly, "and the Japanese *do* attack, won't I be in a very vulnerable position?"

His frown cleared. "Good heavens, no!" he said, amused. "Darling Beth, you didn't think I would take you anywhere where I thought you would be in the slightest danger, did you? The Japanese may *attack* Hong Kong and Singapore in order to further their ambitions against the Malay Peninsula and the Philippines, but they will never, not in a hundred years, succeed! Any fighting that occurs will be on the mainland, in the New Territories. You'll be far safer in Hong Kong, my darling, than you will be here if Hitler attacks England."

She slumped back against the mantelpiece, her last hope of avoiding a confrontation gone.

"Cheer up, sweetheart," Adam said, his voice thickening as he walked toward her. He lovingly rested his hand on her shoulder. "It will be an adventure. Stafford says the climate out there is magnificent, the social life unrivaled. We'll have a whale of a time."

"No," she said, and though her voice was low and husky, as it always was, there was no trace of apology or weakness in it. "No, Adam. I'm not going to Hong Kong. How can I? I have the Mozart recital in a few weeks, the Bach recital in April. I have been working for months preparing for the Brussels competition in June. I'm on the threshold of achieving everything I have always dreamed of. I can't turn my back on it now. It isn't possible."

If she had struck him he couldn't have looked more stunned. His hand dropped abruptly from her shoulder and he stepped away from her. "I've explained my reasons for wanting to go," he said tightly. "Surely you can understand them."

The impasse she had always feared was opening wide at their feet. She did understand, but he did not understand her, and she knew with despair that except on a superficial level, he never would. Her music, and her craving for recognition and success, was a closed world to him. Despite his many protestations to the contrary, he had no more understanding of it than her father had had. For him, as for Jerome, her music was an indulgence, something he could take pride in when it suited him to do so, but something that was all too expendable when it came into conflict with his own desires.

"I do understand," she said quietly, moving away from the fireplace toward him. "But it isn't practical, Adam. Even if there is a war in the East, civilians won't play any greater roles than they would if there is a war in Europe."

His jaw clenched and he said with a savagery that was totally alien to him, "Whether civilians will play a major part in the war or not isn't really what is at issue, is it?"

In the silence that fell between them she could hear a clock ticking and the hiss and spurt of flame as burning logs settled in the grate behind her.

"No," she said.

The firelight danced on her glossy hair, and Adam was struck again, as he had been when she was a child, by the strength in her delicately boned face. Beneath the loving gentleness that he found so attractive was a will as resolute as Jerome's had been, a toughness that enabled her to impose on herself long grueling hours of daily practice and study. He turned away from her, frustrated at what he saw as his lack of power over her, knowing, though he would never have admitted it, that one of the reasons Hong Kong had so appealed to him was that it would take her away from the academy and her studies. In Hong Kong she would have more time for him. His growing resentment at the long hours she spent alone at the piano would cease. He knew, defeatedly, that he couldn't browbeat her. He could only plead.

"I have never before asked anything of you, Beth," he said, his voice full of sudden weariness. "Please don't let me down, my darling. I couldn't bear it. Without turning to look at her he walked from the room, his shoulders hunched, every line of his body dejectedly middle-aged.

She knew that he hoped she would run after him, and she did not do so. She turned slowly and faced herself in the large, gilt-framed mirror that hung above the fireplace. She had been confronted once before with the same sort of selfishness in someone she had dearly loved. Then she had been a child and she had had no option but to fall in with the plans that had been made for her.

She stared into the mirror, and smoke-green eyes, thickly lashed, stared back at her. She was a child no longer. The decision was hers and it was a simple one. She could refuse to abandon her career, and go to Hong Kong. Or she could put Adam first in her life and regard their weeks or months in Hong Kong as nothing more than a short sabbatical.

The fire had begun to die down, hissing and spitting desultorily. She bent down to the basket beside the hearth, lifted a log from it, and tossed the log onto the glowing embers. If she did not go to Hong Kong, Adam would go there alone. And their marriage would be over.

"Oh, God!" she said, with a venom that would have startled Adam. "Oh, shit! Oh, hell!" Leaning one hand on the mantelpiece, she stared down into the flames. All through her life Adam had been there when she had needed him. Now he needed her. Her decision was made, but she did not follow him upstairs to their bedroom. She loved him too much to want to hurt him with her bitterness and resentment. She did what she always did when seeking peace of mind. She turned to her piano. When Adam woke, hours later, it was to the taut, savage notes of a Prokofiev concerto.

* * *

"My God, is he serious?" Princess Luisa Isabel asked Elizabeth as they had tea and cakes in Fortnum and Mason's elegant tearoom.

Elizabeth nodded. She didn't want to discuss Adam's decision to travel east, or hers to accompany him, only to apprise Luisa of it. They had been shopping, and lavishly wrapped parcels bearing the labels of Harrods, Hatchards, Swayne Adney & Briggs, Fortnum and Mason were piled high around their feet. "He says that as he is forty-nine, if war does break out, the army will take no notice of him at all. That the most he will be able to hope for is a desk job."

Beneath the lavish veiling of her saucily tilted hat, Princess Luisa Isabel's eyes rose expressively heavenward. "But goodness gracious, if there *is* a war—and your Mr. Chamberlain is quite adamant that there *isn't* going to be one—why should Adam *wish* to be involved? He fought in 1914, did he not? Wasn't he awarded the Military Cross for outstanding bravery? Why on earth should he wish to be physically involved again?"

Elizabeth sighed, knowing that she had been overly optimistic in thinking that Luisa would be satisfied by a cursory explanation. "I'm sure I don't know," she said truthfully. "But he does. And he thinks his chances of involvement are much higher in the East than they are in Europe."

Princess Luisa Isabel regarded Elizabeth with concern as she stroked the lush pelt of double red fox draped around her shoulders. The heads dipped forward over the bodice of her Worth suit while the tails swung flamboyantly down her back. "But what about your music?" she asked bluntly. "What about your career? Surely, he doesn't expect you to go with him?"

Elizabeth flinched and remained silent. The princess rarely lapsed into her mother tongue and even more rarely swore. Now she did both. "*Mae de Deus!*" she said explosively. "How can he be so crazy? So blind? Naturally, you will not go?"

Elizabeth poured herself a second cup of tea, her face white. "Adam has always been very kind to me, Luisa. I can't refuse him this, not as it is so important to him. Please try to understand.

The princess opened her mouth to say that she under-

stood perfectly, then closed it again. What she understood
was something that Elizabeth would not want to hear.

For seven years she had observed the Harland marriage
closely. There had never been one hint of unhappiness or
discord. She had even begun to wonder if she had been
wrong in believing that Elizabeth had married Adam
because he so ably replaced her father, and not because she
was as deeply in love with him as he was with her. Now,
trusting her sixth sense, she wondered no longer. If
Elizabeth was prepared to accompany him to Hong Kong,
just when she was beginning to make a name for herself on
the London concert stage, then it was not because of love.
It was because of guilt.

She wondered when Elizabeth had realized the truth. Or
even if she realized it at all. Looking across at her, Luisa
knew she could not ask. Despite the twenty-year age gap
between them, Elizabeth had never treated her as a mother
figure. It was too late now for her to try to behave as one.
She said abruptly, feeling grossly incompetent, "My God,
but I miss Jerome!"

Elizabeth ground out her cigarette in a glass ashtray.
"Yes," she said tightly. "Me too, Luisa. Me too."

"There's a sailing on the seventeenth of next month,"
Adam said to her. They were in the bedroom of their
Kensington house. She was wearing a negligee and brushing her hair at the dressing table; he was in bed, a notebook
and pencil and a half dozen sailing schedules scattered
around him. She put down her hairbrush slowly. "The
seventeenth is three days before the Mozart concert," she
said, her eyes meeting his in the mirror.

"I know." There was a defiance in his voice she had
never confronted before.

She turned around on the stool to face him, overcome by
a feeling of *déjà vu*. She was once more in the River Room
Restaurant at the Savoy, hearing her father say, "There'll be
other concerts for you later, Elizabeth. Lots of them. At the
moment what's important is that you and I are
together . . ."

There hadn't been other concerts. Not for a long time.
Adam had told her that he'd called her father a selfish
bastard for disrupting her studies, yet now he was doing
the exact same thing himself. She wondered if he was

aware of it, and as her gaze continued to hold his, knew that he was. And that he was ashamed of it.

His hair was rumpled, his pajama jacket open at the neck. "I need you, Beth," he said with boyish simplicity, as if reading her thoughts.

She felt a surge of compassion for him. He needed her and loved her and had always treated her with infinite kindness and patience. Now, just once, he needed something for himself. He needed to feel younger than his forty-nine years. He needed to feel that he was contributing to the defense of England and its outposts. He needed to escape the humiliation of being assigned a desk job while younger, fitter men donned uniforms.

She walked slowly across the thickly carpeted room to him, and he slid his hand around her waist, pressing his face against the smooth flatness of her stomach. She cradled his head against her, feeling as if she were older.

"We'll sail on the seventeenth," she said huskily.

Relief jarred through his shoulders and he drew her down on the bed beside him. "I love you . . . love you . . . love you, Beth," he whispered, his voice choked with gratitude. His hands slid up beneath the delicate silk of her negligee and he rolled her beneath him. "I'll make it up to you, my darling. I promise. Now let me show you how very much I love you . . ."

When he was asleep, she edged carefully away from him, slipping from the bed and wrapping her discarded negligee around her shoulders. It was only a little after midnight and the moon was bright, filling the room with silver light. She went downstairs and made herself a cup of tea, then sat with it in the kitchen, hoping fiercely that at last she was pregnant. For if she was, it would mean an early return to England. A return to normality.

Professor Hurok had been her tutor for the last six years. Russian-born, he was a fierce disciplinarian with an explosive and volatile nature that had terrified her at first. Now, as she came to the end of the piece she was playing for him, he nodded with approval.

"That is very good," he said. "The octaves were faster and louder and much more satisfying." He gave her one of his rare smiles. "And now for the Brahms. I absolutely forbid you to evade him any longer."

Elizabeth groaned in mock despair. The Brahms piano concertos had become something of a joke between them. When Professor Hurok had first suggested that she play the B-flat Concerto, she had been aghast, protesting that her hands were much too small even to attempt it.

"Nonsense!" he had said, dismissing her protestations with a wave of his hand. "The notion that Beethoven's Fourth Concerto and the Schumann Concerto are ladies' concertos, and that the Brahms B-flat is a concerto that can only be played successfully by a man, is ridiculous. Myra Hess has hands that are no bigger than yours. If she can play the Brahms B-flat, and she does so magnificently, then so can you."

Elizabeth had gone away, fired with determination, and for two weeks she had wrestled with a score that was the most difficult she had ever attempted. "Look creatively at the text. Distribute things to make it more comfortable," Professor Hurok had advised her, and she had done so. When she had not been playing it she had been listening to it, convinced that it was the most beautiful piece of music she had ever heard.

"Are you ready?" the professor asked her now, sensing her nervousness. "Then please begin."

She knew he would not correct her, would not even speak to her, until she had played the concerto through, without guidance. Summoning up all her fortitude and all her stamina, she lifted her hands and brought her fingers down on the keys. The music was titanic in scale. She became lost in it, obsessed by it. A small trickle of perspiration ran down her temple. She had thought she had played difficult music before, but the architecture of this score was something outside all her previous experience. It was like a cathedral with no top to it. It reached up forever, demanding more from her than she had ever thought it possible to give. When at last she finished, she was wet with sweat, shaking with exhaustion.

"You see," Professor Hurok said with calm satisfaction, "it *can* be played. You have just done so." As their eyes met across the piano, elation surged through her, intoxicating in its intensity. He sat down, taking a cigarette case and a lighter from his pocket. "Tomorrow we will approach it again, from the first three uprising notes of the *allegro non troppo*."

Her elation died. At the thought of the news she had to break to him, she felt physically sick.

"What is it?" he asked, seeing the expression in her eyes and frowning in concern. "Is it the Brahms? Was it too much for you?"

She shook her head, turning around on the piano stool so that she was facing him. "No," she said stiffly, her hands clasped tightly in her lap. "I have something to tell you . . ."

He stared at her in disbelief, immobile, as she told him that she would be unable to fulfill her coming concert engagements. That she would not be in Europe when the Brussels Competition took place. That she did not know when she would be in Europe again.

"It is not possible," he kept saying. "I do not understand! It is incredible! Unbelievable!"

"I am sorry, Professor," she said at last, her voice tight with pain.

"Sorry?" He pushed his chair away violently, jumping to his feet. "*Sorry*? Don't you understand what you are doing? The chances you are forsaking? Good God, girl! You are one of the most gifted pupils I have ever taught! You are almost certain to win the Brussels Competition. Even before the International Pianists' Competition promoters will be hammering on your door!"

She rose unsteadily to her feet, her face so white that he thought she was going to faint.

"I know," she said bleakly, unable to bear any more. "Good-bye, Professor Hurok."

"*Elizabeth, wait!*" Concern replaced his rage. "Are you ill? Is there something terrible that you are not telling me?"

She shook her head, finding his concern far more distressing than his rage. "No. Good-bye, Professor." And before he could restrain her, she hurried from the room and ran down the corridor, half blinded by her tears.

Two weeks later they left Four Seasons under the care of a housekeeper and closed the Kensington house. They left the keys with Adam's London solicitor, and without any farewell party, any good-byes to anyone at all, they left London for Southampton and the docks.

"You don't mind about not having a crowd coming down to the docks to see us off, do you, Beth?" Adam asked as they sat in the rear of their chauffeur-driven car, driving across Waterloo Bridge toward Waterloo Station.

"No, of course not."

He took her hand in his. "Luisa wanted to come, but she's at a christening in Derbyshire and there was no way she could cry off. It would have caused too many hurt feelings."

Luisa was the only person Elizabeth would have liked to say good-bye to, but Luisa had already explained to her about the family christening.

It was late afternoon when they reached Southampton, and in the mellow sunshine the *Orient Princess* looked magnificent. For the first time in weeks Elizabeth felt her spirits stir. She had never been on a long sea voyage before and a shiver of expectation ran down her spine as they walked up the gangplank and were greeted by the purser.

"She's a magnificent ship, isn't she?" Adam said enthusiastically as a steward led them toward their cabin. "We're going to have a wonderful time on board her."

Elizabeth, her figure slim and svelte in a biscuit-beige suit with wide, fashionable shoulders and a chocolate-brown mink wrap over one arm, smiled in agreement. The steward had just turned round in order to tell them that all the bars on the ship were already open, when he caught sight of her smile and his voice faltered. My God, but she was lovely! he thought. He glanced hurriedly down at his passenger list. She was surely much too young to be Mr. Harland's wife. Perhaps she was his daughter . . . his niece. He found their names and his hopes of a romantic diversion fell.

"Here is your cabin, sir," he said to Adam, throwing open the door for them and envying him for a lucky devil. "I hope you have a good voyage, sir. Madam."

The cabin was large and spacious, with beds instead of bunks, a small bathroom, and ample cupboard space for their luggage.

"Three and a half weeks at sea," Adam said to her exultantly. "It's going to be a second honeymoon!"

Elizabeth laid her mink wrap on one of the beds and he slid his arms around her. "I love you, Beth," he said, and his mouth closed over hers, warm and demanding. She knew that he was about to make love to her, and she knew that she did not want him to. Not now. If he made love to her now she might not be able to pretend. He might realize that though his caresses were agreeable, even stimulating, she did not crave them the way he did hers. He would be dreadfully distressed and their three-and-a-half-week cruise would be ruined.

"Let's go up on deck until she sails," she said coaxingly. "I want to feast my eyes on England while I can!"

He grinned. "The only bit of England you'll see at the moment are the grubby docks of Southampton!"

"The docks will be quite satisfactory," she said, slipping her hand into his. "Come on, we're missing all the fun."

They walked back along the mahogany-lined corridors and up the wide central staircase to the ship's lounge. A huge, fanciful mural of Father Neptune decorated one wall, and the room was full of passengers and their visitors, all saying noisy, exuberant, and sometimes tearful good-byes. Up on deck the breeze was chilly and Elizabeth shivered, wishing she had remembered to bring her wrap.

"The last of the luggage has been swung aboard," Adam said, pointing out the crane that stood on the dockside, its big, empty net hanging limp.

"All visitors ashore, please!" a loudspeaker blared, and they leaned against the rail, watching as the visitors disembarked and the gangplank was lashed into place.

"Only another few minutes now before we up anchor," Adam said with boyish enthusiasm. As he spoke a taxi hurtled onto the cobbles, squealing to a halt. The door flew open and an elegant figure stepped out, her long legs clad in sheer silk stockings, her shocking pink wool suit unmistakably Parisian, her fox furs swinging, her little hat of feathers perched at a preposterous angle over one eye.

"*It's Princess Luisa Isabel!*" Elizabeth cried, waving furiously. "*Luisa! Luisa!*"

The princess ran toward the ship, saw that the gangplank was up, and laughed with an expressive gesture of her hands and a shrug of her shoulders. "*It is too late for me to come aboard*," she called. "*But good luck, Elizabeth! Good luck, Adam! Bon voyage!*"

The siren hooted, drowning their answering shouts, the thick hawsers were cast, and slowly the ship eased itself away from the dock.

"*Good-bye, Luisa!*" Elizabeth cried. "*Good-bye!*"

She waved until her arm ached, until they were so far

away that the princess was no longer discernible. Tears
stung the backs of her eyes as she finally turned away from
the rail and accompanied Adam below. She would miss
Luisa. Apart from Adam, Luisa was all that remained to
her of the past.

The only piano on board was in the first-class lounge.
The ship's resident pianist was delighted to allow her to
use it, and every morning, early, before too many people
were about, she played Chopin and Mozart and Bach on an
instrument that had previously only pounded out Irving
Berlin and Duke Ellington.

The majority of their fellow passengers were expatriates,
returning to Hong Kong after leave in England. She soon
discovered that Leigh Stafford had been correct when he
had said that no one in Hong Kong regarded Japan as a
potential threat.

"*Japan!*" an elderly colonel said to her when she tentatively suggested an attack was a possibility. "*Japan!* Who on
earth has been filling your head with that idea? It's one
thing for the Japanese to fight the Chinese, my dear, but
they would never dare to presume to come into contact
with British steel!" He had laughed heartily at the very
idea.

Even Adam seemed to have given up all thought of
pending warfare. He relaxed visibly as the *Orient Princess*
steamed her way through the Mediterranean toward the
Suez Canal, sunbathing on deck, playing tennis and deck
quoits, dancing with her in the ballroom till late every
night.

It was a casual remark from one of their fellow passengers that made her wonder if she had discovered, at last,
the real reason for Adam's obsession with being part of any
action, if war broke out.

Mrs. Smythe was elderly and partially disabled, and
Elizabeth often accompanied her on deck, sitting in an
adjoining deckchair and keeping her company. One day, as
they approached Port Said, Adam joined them in his tennis
whites. "So pleased to meet you, Mr. Harland," Mrs.
Smythe said. "Your daughter is such a pleasant companion. I shall miss her immensely once we reach Hong
Kong."

Elizabeth smiled, took Mrs. Smythe's arthritic hand, and

said unperturbedly, "Adam is my husband, Mrs. Smythe, not my father." As Mrs. Smythe began to make hasty apologies, Elizabeth looked up at Adam, laughing, expecting him to be as amused as she.

He was not amused at all. The lines around his mouth were white, and his jaw was clenched as he said tightly that he was on his way to a tennis match and would see her later.

"Oh, my dear, I do hope I haven't caused any offense," Mrs. Smythe said agitatedly as he strode away from them. "Whatever could have possessed me to think that you were father and daughter? Of *course* you are married, anyone can see that. What a silly, *stupid* mistake."

"You didn't cause any offense," Elizabeth said soothingly, but as she gazed after Adam there was a small furrow between her brows and her eyes were thoughtful. It had never occurred to her that he might be sensitive about the difference in their ages. It was an intriguing thought. And it might explain why he was so eager not to be classified as too old to fight for his king and his country.

That evening, as they dined, she caught sight of their reflections in one of the wall mirrors. Over the last few months Adam had gained weight and his rugged body had begun to take on middle-aged contours. His hair, though still thick, was now heavily sprinkled with gray, and the lines around his nose and mouth had deepened appreciably. She was wearing an eau de Nil silk dress. The skirt draped into a river of tiny, impeccably executed pleats; the neckline was softly cowled. Her hair was held back from her face with two tortoiseshell combs, falling softly and smoothly to her shoulders. She was twenty-four and didn't look a day over eighteen.

The next morning she didn't leave her hair loose. She swept it all off her neck, piercing the neat twist she created with long ivory pins, determined that Mrs. Smythe's mistake would not be repeated.

Despite all her feelings at leaving London and not fulfilling the prestigious concert schedule that had been arranged for her, she enjoyed the passage to Hong Kong. Once they were beyond the Bay of Biscay the sun shone steadily, and aboard the *Orient Princess* there were no rumors of war or depressing daily newspaper bulletins about Hitler and his bullyboys, or Mussolini and his

Blackshirts. British expatriates returning to Singapore and Hong Kong were reassuringly adamant that nothing would happen to disturb their way of life out there.

"Your husband is quite wrong about the Japanese, my dear," Mrs. Smythe said to her. "Whatever happens in Europe, it won't have any repercussions in the East." She smiled serenely. "Life will go on in Singapore just as it has done ever since Raffles snatched the island from under the noses of the Dutch in 1819, and in Hong Kong, just as it has since Captain Elliot annexed it from the Chinese in 1841. You will have a lovely time there, my dear. Hong Kong is a magical island. There is nowhere else quite like it anywhere in the world."

At the end of March they steamed into the Indian Ocean and a week later Elizabeth woke to the knowledge that within hours they would be in sight of the island that Mrs. Smythe regarded as so magical.

She sat on deck, binoculars in her lap, as the *Orient Princess* threaded its way through hundreds of deserted islands, the offshore breeze heavy with the fragrance of flowers. Adam joined her, watching with her as hills and mountains began to take on distinctive shapes.

"This is the way to approach Hong Kong!" he said with relish, standing by the rail. "In another hour or so we're going to hit her slap on the nose!"

"Can you smell the flowers in the air?" Elizabeth asked him with pleasure. "Isn't it the most marvelous smell? Mrs. Smythe says that the words 'hong kong' mean fragrant."

Adam grinned. "From what Stafford tells me, there'll be lots of other smells when we draw nearer shore. Not all of them quite so pleasant!"

Elizabeth laughed. The strain that had existed between them for their last few weeks in England and their first days aboard ship had now dissipated. She was quite sure that their stay in Hong Kong would be short, and that within a few months they would be on their way back to England. Adam's restlessness would be satisfied and she would once more be able to concentrate wholeheartedly on her music. In the meantime she was determined to be patient and to enjoy the experience as much as possible. "I have it on very good authority that the more unpleasant smells are nothing more than the tang of burnt sugar," she said mischievously.

Adam's grin deepened. "I will allow you to keep your illusions. Just look at those mountains! I'd never imagined them to be so magnificent. That one over there must be five thousand feet at least!"

A tall, well-built man strolled across the deck and joined Adam at the rail. "That is Victoria Peak," he said, "the highest mountain on the island, though there are some others that come very near to it. That's Mount Butler over there to the west, and that one over there, on the right, is Mount Nicholson. I always like to believe it was named after an ancestor of mine. My name is Tom Nicholson." He held out his hand, and his handshake was firm.

"Adam Harland," Adam said, then turned and introduced him to Elizabeth. "And my wife, Elizabeth."

"I'm very pleased to meet you, Mrs. Harland," Tom Nicholson said sincerely. He had been aware of her ever since the *Orient Princess* had slid out of Southampton Water and into the Channel. It would have been impossible not to have been aware of her. She had the kind of beauty that was luminous, that turned heads in the most crowded of rooms. He wondered where Harland had met her. She didn't look much older than twenty or twenty-one. Harland was easily in his late forties, and lacked the sophisticated glamour that was usually the attraction in such marriages.

"Since you know these mountains so well, I assume you're an expat," Adam said, and reluctantly Tom Nicholson turned his gaze from Elizabeth to her husband.

"Yes. An expat," he said with an easy grin. "I've been out here since thirty-two. I'm a minor government official, for my sins. My major worry in life is how to avoid being posted anywhere else!"

Adam's interest quickened. "This is our first trip out here. What's the government's line toward the Japanese? I've heard they're casting their eyes toward the Philippines and Malaya."

"They've been doing that for centuries," Tom said dismissively. "It won't get them anywhere. If they want to enlarge their empire, they'll have to be content with appropriating what they can from the Chinese."

Adam would have liked to discuss the matter further, but they were nearing land now and the deck was becoming crowded. "Isn't it fabulous?" Elizabeth said, leaning her bare arms on the rail. "Can you see all those boats? What are they? Sampans? Junks?"

"The small ones are sampans, the three-masted ones are junks," Tom said, smiling at her. "A vast majority of the population lives, eats, sleeps, and dies aboard them. I've never understood where the Chinese get their reputation for being impassive. They live as noisily and gregariously as Italians!"

Elizabeth laughed and he felt his interest in her deepen. She had a low, husky laugh that was as entrancing as her looks.

"Where are you staying?" he asked Adam, wondering how long they were visiting and what the purpose of their visit was.

"The Peninsula Hotel," Adam said, "though as we intend to be here for an indefinite length of time, I shall be looking about for a suitable property to rent."

"The Peak is the most popular residential district," Tom said, sensing that money was not a problem for the Harlands. "My own house is up there." He took a gilt-embossed card from his breast pocket and handed it to Adam. "Perhaps you would join me for dinner when you have settled in? Next Thursday, or Friday perhaps?"

"Friday will be fine," Adam said agreeably, pleased that the social ball was rolling even before they had stepped on dry land. "We would like that, wouldn't we, Beth?"

But Elizabeth wasn't listening to them. She was gazing rapturously at Hong Kong, its thickly foliaged, steep slopes rising almost sheer from the sea, its glittering harbor massed with junks and sampans and a hundred different colored sails.

Adam felt a surge of satisfaction as he looked at her. Here, in Hong Kong, they would be together in a way that hadn't been possible in London. There would be no concert schedules to detract her from spending time with him. No long hours of arduous practice. His decision had been the right one. Hong Kong was going to be good for them. He breathed in deeply. He was looking forward, with zest, to the next few months.

Chapter Seven

❧

ELIZABETH awoke the next morning to the sharp, white light of a Hong Kong dawn. She stretched luxuriously in her twin bed and then, being careful not to make a noise that would wake Adam, swung her feet to the thickly carpeted floor and slipped her arms into the sleeves of her chiffon negligee. It was barely five-thirty and, as she opened the French windows leading out onto the balcony, the air was cool and fresh and thick with fragrance.

The Peninsula Hotel was situated in Kowloon, on the Hong Kong mainland, overlooking the harbor. Across the shimmering wedge of water lay Hong Kong Island and the bustling, teeming city of Victoria, and over and above it, the great granite rock that Tom Nicholson had referred to as "the Peak." She could see the houses clinging to its slopes, spacious white mansions surrounded by carefully tended, lush gardens. Tom Nicholson had suggested that was where they should look for a house to rent, and she felt a ripple of pleasure run down her spine. She was exiled from London and London's rich musical life, but it seemed there were going to be compensations. She couldn't think of a more wonderful place to live than the dizzy, exotic heights of Victoria Peak.

"Are you all right, darling?" Adam asked an hour later, padding out toward her in his pajamas.

She turned around and smiled, the slow, unknowingly sensuous smile that always made him catch his breath as if he had just been punched. "Yes. I couldn't sleep any longer. I feel like a child at Christmas. I've never seen anyplace so beautiful."

He slid his arm around her waist, looking with her out over the harbor at the flurry of sampans and junk masts and patched sails, and beyond them to the towering mountains of Hong Kong Island and the tortuous valleys and ravines that gashed and scarred their slopes.

"Impressive, isn't it?" he said with satisfaction. "Let's have breakfast and get out there and see it properly."

"I thought you had a meeting with Leigh Stafford this morning?"

"Not till lunchtime." He picked up the telephone and dialed room service. "We can have the morning together and then later, after I've talked to Leigh, we can perhaps do a bit of house-hunting."

They ate breakfast on their balcony: scrambled eggs and bacon, and papaya with limes and mango juice, as well as coffee. By the time they walked out through the Peninsula's glass doors and onto the street, the delicious coolness of the early morning had given way to scorching heat, and Elizabeth was grateful for the light breeze that blew in off the water.

"You'll soon get used to it," Adam said with a grin. "And the houses are air-conditioned. Haven't you seen all the fans?"

She had. Their soft whirr had lulled her to sleep the previous night and she understood now why Tom Nicholson had suggested they look for a house on the Peak. It would be much cooler up there.

"Let's go across to Victoria on the ferry," Adam said as they wove their way between scores of Chinese women in black trousers and jackets, flat straw hats covering their heads, dark plaited hair arrowing down their backs. "There will be a strong breeze off the water and it will help you to acclimate yourself."

The ferry was packed with laughing, talking, jostling Chinese, and Elizabeth remembered Tom Nicholson's observations about them and grinned. He was quite right. They were more like boisterous Italians than the impassive Orientals she had been led to expect.

They landed at the Star Ferry Pier on Hong Kong Island only a few minutes later.

"That has to be the shortest, most spectacular channel crossing in the world," Adam said as he extricated her from a throng of surging Chinese, all eager to be the first to set foot on dry land. "Let's find somewhere to take it easy and have a drink."

For half an hour they sat in the coolness of a traditional teahouse, sipping jasmine-scented tea, adamant that they would not lose face by asking for milk or sugar, or even lemon.

"When in Rome . . ." Adam had said with a grin when the traditional Chinese teacups, without handles and with small lids, had been set down before them. The tea tasted nicer than they had expected, and they each drank two cups before they left in search of a rickshaw and a leisurely tour of the city.

As their rickshaw trundled them away from the harbor, the noise and clamor nearly took their breath away. It seemed as if the whole world were trying to squeeze into the narrow, bustling streets. There were bicycles and trams and taxis, street hawkers and sailors, delicately-built Chinese women carrying their babies on their backs, old people pushing handcarts, shop vendors touting their wares, their goods spilling out of tiny, dark shops onto the street. The air was pungent with the smell of spices and dried fish and the sweetness of flowers; it was deafening with the cries of hawkers.

"A bit different from Bond Street, isn't it?" Adam asked with relish.

"Much more fun," she agreed, affectionately squeezing his hand. "Oh, goodness, look at that jade, Adam! Is it real? It looks too good to be true!"

They bought a jade necklace, an exquisitely carved ivory horse, and a rose-quartz paperweight, then returned with their treasures to the Peninsula Hotel and lunch with Leigh Stafford.

He was a broadly built, stocky man in his early fifties, with an affable smile and an easy manner.

"I must say, I was surprised to hear you were coming to Hong Kong to judge for yourself whether we should pull our horns in or not," he said when initial introductions were over and the soup had been served.

"I had other reasons for coming out here," Adam said easily. "Personal reasons." He didn't expand on what they were. "My fellow directors don't agree with you that there is any danger to the company at present. The general consensus is that there is to be no immediate pulling in of assets."

Leigh Stafford shrugged. It was no more than he had

expected. What he hadn't expected was someone coming out from London to judge the situation for himself. And bringing his wife with him. Leigh tried to stop himself from staring at Elizabeth. If Harland was to stay for any length of time she would certainly cause a flurry in the dovecotes. The expatriate British clung together in a small, exclusive social circle. Entry would be easily and eagerly given to a man of Adam Harland's standing, but it would be his wife who would attract attention. Her ivory-blond beauty would turn heads in any country, but in Hong Kong it was sensational.

"I have to tell you that I am not in agreement with them," Adam was saying to him.

"Er, what? Sorry . . ." Leigh dragged his attention away from Elizabeth and once more toward Adam.

"I'm not in agreement with them," Adam repeated. "I personally think that your assessment of the situation out here is correct. The Japanese *are* casting covetous eyes on the Philippines and Malaya, and if war breaks out in Europe, then I think you're right. The Japs will try to take advantage of it."

Leigh's interest quickened. It was a welcome change to meet someone whose ideas accorded with his own. "Damn right they will!" he said forcefully. "But tell that to the civil servants and they'll laugh at you! No one is taking Japanese aggression seriously. It's the usual story of complacency and facile optimism, and it's grossly misplaced. The Japanese aren't a joke. They're ruthless and fanatical. Anyone in doubt of that should have a word with the Chinese. The Japs are biting deeper into China every day, and they won't be content with China. Not when there are rich pickings of rubber and tin to be had in Burma and Malaya. Take my word for it, when the time is right, they'll make their move, and when they do, we're not going to like it!"

The impassioned authority in his voice sent a shiver down Elizabeth's spine. She had begun to believe that Adam's prediction of war in the East was groundless. That Mrs. Smythe and the colonel were right. The thought of Japanese aggression directed toward Great Britain was ridiculous and not to be taken seriously. Now, after listening to Leigh Stafford, she was no longer so sure.

"What signs have there been of their intentions?" she

asked, tilting her head a little to one side, her green-gold eyes grave.

Leigh was grateful for the excuse to once more turn his attention to her. Her voice as as lovely as her face. Low and warm, with a faint trace of huskiness that he found entrancing.

Watch it, old boy, he told himself chidingly. You're too old for this caper now. But as he answered her query, he knew it was too late. He already adored her. She had a serene, almost untouched quality about her that appealed to his old-fashioned notion of what a woman should be.

"They are widening their grip on south China," he said, "moving uncomfortably close to us, and they are flauntingly gleeful of the fact that Hitler's Germany has recognized them as the rulers of Manchuria. Other than that, they're playing a waiting game. They won't make any moves until our attention is centered elsewhere."

"On Hitler?"

He nodded, then grinned. "And I bet there are still plenty of people back home who are complacent and optimistic about *him*!"

They all laughed and the tension ebbed. As they were lingering over their coffee, Adam said, "Where is the best place to start house-hunting, Leigh?"

"Hobson's in Chater Road. They generally have a good list of what's available. Who is it that's on the lookout?"

"We are," Adam said, amused at his assumption that it was someone else.

Leigh stared at him. It had never occurred to him that Adam Harland intended staying in Hong Kong permanently. Damn it all. Only minutes ago he had been agreeing with him that it would very shortly come under attack by the Japanese! And the man had his wife with him!

He said carefully, "Wouldn't it be wisest to forgo that sort of commitment? Considering what we have just been talking about?"

The smile lines around Adam's mouth deepened. "We're here for the duration, Leigh. When, and if, those little yellow devils attack, I shall be in the forefront, driving them back where they came from! It's a confrontation I wouldn't miss for the world!"

Leigh drew in his breath sharply. Harland was a board director, and Leigh couldn't very well tell him he was a fool. Nevertheless, he was staggered by his naïveté. For over an hour they had discussed Japanese aggression and he had assumed Harland understood the seriousness of the threat. He hadn't. He thought it was a game. A game that, like a little boy, he wanted to take part in. "You must excuse me," he said abruptly, rising to his feet. "I have to be going now. I understand you are chairing our supplies meeting tomorrow? I'll see you then." He nodded courteously and turned to Elizabeth, his fury that her safety should be valued so lightly by her husband white hot. "Good-bye, Mrs. Harland. It's been a pleasure meeting you. I hope we meet again."

"Good-bye," she said, but though her smile was warm, her eyes revealed her curiosity. Leigh Stafford was ragingly angry, and she wondered why. Was it because Adam had stated his intention of remaining in Hong Kong for some time? Was he afraid that his position as company manager would be usurped by Adam's seniority?

"Nice chap," Adam said, oblivious to the undercurrents as Leigh strode quickly from the dining room.

"He's not afraid that you've come out here to check up on how he's running things, is he?" Elizabeth asked, frowning slightly.

Adam laughed. "Good God, no! I've told him I'm here on a sabbatical, not a business trip. After tomorrow I doubt that I'll go near the office. Whatever put an idea like that in your head?"

"Nothing," she said, carelessly dismissive, not wanting to spoil the day by reflecting too deeply on the alternative reason for Leigh Stafford's sudden flare of rage. It was far too disturbing and thought-provoking. She would think about it later, when she was alone.

They found a suitable house to rent on their very first trip to Victoria Peak. Hobson's had supplied them with details of three houses, but they only needed to see the first. It was a long, low, stately white mansion that had been built in the early 1900's by a prosperous merchant. The garden surrounding it was vast and lush, the views stupendous. A swimming pool had been installed by a later owner, and from the terrace surrounding it could be seen the distant harbor, Green Island and Peng Chau Island to the north, Lantau Island and Macau to the west. The furnishings were a pleasing mixture of modern comfort and Chinese elegance: deep, creamy-white sofas and chairs, silk Chinese carpets, jade cabinets, and ivory-framed mirrors. The houses of their affluent neighbors were hidden by forests of bamboo and fern, stunted Chinese pines, hibiscus, and vines, so it seemed as if they were alone in a tropical paradise.

"Tom Nicholson lives only fifteen minutes away," Adam said as they walked in from the garden, both knowing that they were going to take the house. "He seems to be about the only civil servant here that Stafford has any time for."

"Does Leigh Stafford live on the Peak as well?" Elizabeth asked, planning her first dinner party.

"No." Adam was about to say that no company manager could afford the sky-high prices of Peak property when Elizabeth seized his arm.

"Look! Over there, in the trees! It's a monkey, Adam! I'm sure of it!"

"Then I would prefer it to keep its distance," Adam said with equanimity. "Let's drive back to Chater Road and tell Hobson's that we'll take the house as soon as possible, with or without wildlife!"

On Friday evening they drove up to the Peak once more, this time for dinner with Tom Nicholson.

"Whatever sort of civil servant he is, he certainly isn't a minor one," Adam said dryly as they drove along exclusive Plantation Road, catching glimpses of colonial-style mansions hidden behind thick screens of bamboo and pine.

"Perhaps he's the governor," Elizabeth said impishly. She was wearing an ice-blue dress that hung silkily from her shoulders and danced softly over her skin. It had a halter neck and a low V in the back, and her silver-blond hair was swept high into an elegant knot, revealing aquamarines at her ears and throat. She looked sensational and Adam grinned, knowing full well the effect she would have at the Nicholson dinner table. He began to whistle beneath his breath. He was feeling more relaxed and fit than he had for a long time. The change of climate and scenery was doing him good. He no longer felt as if he were hurtling toward a wheelchair and decrepitude. The life of a wealthy expatriate suited him. There was plenty of sport. Tennis and swimming were a part of daily life, as were the cocktail parties and dinner parties. The thought came from out of nowhere that it was a way of life Jerry would have loved. Adam felt a pang of loss as he drove up the wide drive of Tom Nicholson's home. It had been eight years since Jerry had died and he still missed him like hell. His hand closed over Elizabeth's and tightened. "I love you," he said thickly as the car slid to a halt. He had lost Jerry but he would never lose Beth. She was the central point of his life and always had been, always would be.

She leaned across to him, kissing him gently on the cheek, the aquamarines sparkling against her neck. He resisted the urge to draw her into his arms. There would be time, later, for that. For the moment he would be content in showing her off, enjoying the looks of envy in the men of his own age group, the vain hope in the eyes of those who were younger. He knew very well that Nicholson was attracted to Elizabeth, and he also knew that he had nothing to fear. His only rival for her affections was her music and, for a little while at least, he had put that firmly in the background.

A Chinese maid opened the door to them, then Tom strode toward them, his arms welcoming. "Good to see you!" he said expansively, greeting them as if they were old friends and not relatively new acquaintances. "Let me introduce you to everyone."

He led them into a vast, white-carpeted drawing room. Long, high windows looked out over the dark hillside and the distant, glittering lights of Victoria.

"Helena, Elizabeth and Adam Harland. We met aboard the *Orient Princess*. Elizabeth and Adam, Helena Nicholson, my sister-in-law."

Helena shook hands with them warmly. She was a tall, well-built woman with a beautiful square-jawed, high-cheek-boned face and a mass of auburn hair falling untidily to her shoulders. "It's lovely to meet you," she said, and then with disarming directness added to Elizabeth, "Tom tells me that you play the piano."

Tom made an exasperated sound in the back of his throat and she laughed. "Sorry, he said that on *no* account was I to ask you to play. That you were a Bach and Beethoven performer, not an Irving Berlin party-player."

"If Irving Berlin is what you want, I'll happily play it," Elizabeth said, liking Helena Nicholson instantly, and wondering just when her brother-in-law had eavesdropped on her early morning practice sessions.

There were five other guests. Major Alastair Munroe, a soft-spoken Scot in his early thirties, who had been stationed in Hong Kong for over three years; Sir Denholm and Lady Gresby, who had also been residents since 1936; and a tall, languid American, Ronnie Ledsham, and his redheaded French wife, Julienne.

"We could do with a bit of decent piano playing," Ronnie said as they all moved out of the drawing room and onto the cool veranda where cocktails were being served. " 'Land of Hope and Glory' is all Tom can play, and he can't play that very well!"

"I understand you've moved into the Sumnor house?" Sir Denholm said to Adam as Tom's Chinese houseboy served them wickedly dry martinis. "Splendid views from there, if I remember rightly. A marvelous house for parties."

The small talk continued. By the time they went in for dinner Elizabeth had gleaned that Helena Nicholson was a widow and that her escort for the evening was Major Munroe; that Ronnie Ledsham was a flirtatious rogue; and that Sir Denholm was a respected member of the Colonial Government. He talked knowledgeably of the East, discounting all suggestions that the Japanese were a force to watch.

"Certainly they are behaving belligerently," he said to Adam as deep-fried prawns were served. "But their saber-rattling isn't to be taken seriously. It's just so much hot air. Nothing more."

The conversation turned to more important matters. To last Saturday's race meeting, polo, the Royal Scots' chances in a forthcoming army boxing championship.

"I shall certainly not be there to cheer you on," Julienne said to Alastair Munroe in prettily accented English. "It is an ugly sport, the boxing. I do not understand your enthusiasm for it at all."

"And I don't understand your enthusiasm for mammoth shopping sprees," her husband said to her amid much laughter.

Julienne looked up at him from beneath her luxuriant eyelashes and said with obvious mischief, "It is a pity that Raefe Elliot is not eligible to box for the Royal Scots. The result would be a foregone conclusion, would it not?"

Her husband's face tightened and a tide of angry color

stained Sir Denholm's thin cheeks. "My God!" he said explosively, oblivious to the mixed company. "I couldn't believe the verdict when I heard it! Accidental death! Accidental, my foot!"

Elizabeth looked inquiringly at Tom for enlightenment. There was a moment's uncomfortable silence in which Julienne continued to smile as she toyed with her prawns, well satisfied with the furor she had caused.

"We had an unfortunate incident here some months ago," Tom explained to Elizabeth at last, trying to sound dismissive about it and failing. "There was an ugly fistfight and one of the men suffered a severe brain hemorrhage and died. The case came to court last week. Medical evidence showed that he had an abnormally thin skull and the verdict was accidental death."

"It was murder!" Sir Denholm said harshly. "Elliot should be hung! He defamed the character of his wife in order to save his neck! It was a disgraceful, unforgivable exhibition!"

"But what if it were true?" Julienne murmured provocatively, ignoring the silencing glare her husband shot her. "If Melissa *was* taking drugs, and if the gentleman that Raefe found in her bed *was* a drug pusher—"

"Stuff and nonsense!" Sir Denholm barked, pushing his plate to one side, all interest in his food gone. "I've known the Langdon family for over twenty years! Melissa Langdon is a dear, sweet girl who should never have married a rogue like Elliot! The man's a blackguard! He's ruined her life! Done his best to ruin her reputation! And he has the effrontery to pose as the injured party!"

"Some injured party," Ronnie Ledsham said dryly. "He walked into the Hong Kong Club the night he was acquitted with a Malay girl on his arm."

"I hope he was shown the door!" Sir Denholm said savagely. "Insolent young pup!"

"I imagine it's a little hard to show the door to a man of Elliot's wealth and background," Alastair Munroe said quietly. "No doubt he will be asked to resign his membership and honor will be satisfied."

Elizabeth shot him a quick look, wondering if she was correct in detecting a faint note of contempt in his voice. If there were, she was certain it was directed toward the elitist policies of the club, and not toward the scandalous Raefe Elliot.

"And no doubt he will refuse," Helena said, glancing at her brother-in-law. "Personally, I don't blame him. There are surely worse sins in life than escorting a Chinese or Malay girl into the hallowed halls of the all-white Hong Kong Club!"

To Elizabeth's surprise she saw that Tom Nicholson's face had hardened and that a nerve had begun to throb at the corner of his jaw. He cleared his throat to speak, but before he could do so, Lady Gresby said coldly, "You are, of course, entitled to your own point of view, Helena. But I must tell you that it is a singularly naive one. If Mr. Elliot wishes to parade his native mistress in public, then he may do so. But he will not do so in the Hong Kong Club. Not now, nor at any time in the future."

"He shouldn't be in the damn club himself!" Sir Denholm expostulated. "There's more than a touch of the tar-brush about Elliot and no one can tell me any differently!"

"A touch of a tar-brush?" Julienne asked, her cheeks dimpling. "I am sorry, I do not understand."

"The fellow's got wog blood," Sir Denholm said bluntly. "Must have. Hair as black as his isn't natural."

"But I thought Raefe Elliot's pedigree was impeccable!" Julienne said, her eyes widening.

"Elliot's grandfather lived up-country for forty years. You can bet your life that his grandmother was a native," Sir Denholm said.

Before Julienne could bait him any further, Tom asked smoothly, "Is your horse going to run at Happy Valley on Saturday, Ronnie? Julienne tells me that you have a new jockey. Is he any good?"

Later, when they were sitting drinking coffee in the spacious drawing room, Ronnie leaned over to his wife and whispered chastisingly, "You were *very* naughty, darling. I thought old Denholm was going to have an apoplectic fit!"

Sir Denholm was sitting at the far side of the room talking to Helena and didn't hear him, but Elizabeth did. Julienne, aware that Elizabeth had overheard, turned toward her. "We are not really so ill-behaved as we seem. It is just that Sir Denholm loses his temper so quickly and so magnificently, and there are times when I cannot resist provoking him."

"And mention of Elliot *always* provokes him," her husband murmured, taking care that Sir Denholm did not overhear him.

"Who on earth *is* this Raefe Elliot that he arouses such passion?" Elizabeth asked as Adam moved away from her to look at some ancient Chinese scrolls that Tom was eager he should admire.

Julienne's eyes danced. "He is *very* handsome, *very* exciting. An American who lives by no rules but his own. He is also a part of Hong Kong in a way that Sir Denholm and his friends can never be. It is this, I think, that so enrages them."

"He's dangerous," Ronnie said, gazing at his wife with a curious expression in his eyes. "Especially to women." The conversation on the far side of the room between Helena and Sir Denholm and his wife continued; Alastair and Adam were engrossed in examining Tom's antique scrolls. Ronnie settled himself comfortably on the arm of Julienne's chair and with a proprietorial arm around her shoulders said, "The Elliots are an old New Orleans family, though the rumor is that they are descended from the Captain Elliot who first hoisted a Union Jack aloft and claimed Hong Kong for the British. Old man Elliot, Raefe's grandfather, made a fortune by trading. Raefe's father consolidated it with rubber estates in Malaya and a tin mine in Sumatra. Whatever else they've been accused of, they can't be accused of being bad businessmen. Both Raefe and his father were educated in the States and the whole lot of them were, and are, as sharp as needles."

"And just what *have* the Elliots been accused of?" Elizabeth asked, intrigued.

Ronnie grinned. "Whoring seems to have been their main vice. It's said that old man Elliot kept two concubines, aged fifteen and eighteen, when he was well into his eighties. Hence the rumors about Raefe Elliot's ancestry. Raefe's father was no better. He snatched a high-ranking government official's daughter from her home only hours before she was due to be married to another man. By the time her father and his friends retrieved her, she was pregnant with Raefe and compromised beyond all hope. It is said that her father wept all through the wedding ceremony."

"The bride's father may have wept, but if the groom was

as handsome as Raefe, then the bride would not have done so," Julienne said with a wicked chuckle. "She would have been a *very* happy lady!"

Ronnie gave her a playful cuff on the side of her chin. "Don't cast your eyes in that direction," he warned laconically. "Raefe Elliot is far too dangerous a man for your little games. You would get very badly burned, my love."

Julienne's chuckle deepened, but she took his hand, twisting her fingers lovingly through his.

"Can we have some music now, Elizabeth?" Helena asked. "Just for a little while."

The piano was an old Bechstein, its surface crowded with family photographs in silver frames.

"I'm afraid it isn't played very often," Tom said apologetically as she sat on the piano stool and opened the lid. "It's probably grossly out of tune."

She ran her fingers experimentally over the keys. It wasn't what she was used to, but it was still a very lovely piano.

"It's fine," she said. "What would you like me to play?"

He smiled down at her, the expression in his eyes changing from one of easy camaraderie to one that told her how very lovely he thought she was. "Play anything," he said, his voice deepening. "But don't play for a little while. Play for a long while."

His admiration didn't ruffle her. She was accustomed to seeing heat in men's eyes when they spoke to her. And she was accustomed to not being disturbed by it.

Sensing the tastes of her audience, she didn't play any classical music. To Tom's surprise and pleasure, she played delicate blues and then straight jazz, finishing off with a medly of tunes by Jerome Kern, Cole Porter, and Irving Berlin.

"Heavens!" Helena said rapturously, when Elizabeth refused to be pressed into playing any longer. "I would never have believed that old piano could possibly sound like that!"

"A magnificent performance!" Lady Gresby said. "I'm afraid that from now on, there won't be a party in Hong Kong at which you won't be asked to play, my dear!"

As they were all about to leave, Helena took Elizabeth discreetly to one side.

"Just a quick little word, Elizabeth. I would hate Sir Denholm to have left you with the impression that Raefe Elliot is an unconscionable blackguard. He does have *some* redeeming features." Her mouth quirked in a naughty smile. "He's the most damnably attractive man on the island, and that's saying something! What drives Miriam Gresby and her friends wild is that he pays not the slightest attention to them. It's an insult they can't forgive. Julienne has been madly in love with him ever since she first saw him and for once, I don't blame her. Where Raefe is concerned, I could nearly forget my quiet life-style and live very dangerously myself!"

"It's hard to believe it's only our first week here," Adam said to Elizabeth as he lay in bed later that night, watching her as she undressed. "We're having lunch with Sir Denholm and his wife tomorrow, on Sunday we're lunching with Alastair Munroe and Helena Nicholson, and going to a party at the Ledshams in the evening. We're playing a doubles of tennis on Monday with Tom and Helena, going on to a polo match with them, and dining with Leigh Stafford in the evening."

Dressed in her negligee, Elizabeth sat down at the dressing table and began to brush her hair. She was going swimming with Julienne in the morning, shopping with Helena in the afternoon. The social life in Hong Kong was proving as full and relaxed as Adam had promised it would be. And she wasn't remotely interested in it. She didn't want an endless round of parties and dinners. She didn't want to fill her days with swimming and shopping. She wanted to be working. To be practicing hard for the international pianists' competitions, to be extending her range, coming to terms with the new composers whose work Professor Hurok had introduced her to, Vaughan Williams and Busoni and Pfitzner.

She put down her hairbrush, then walked over to the large double bed and slipped in between the cool sheets beside Adam. His arm automatically slid around her shoulders, pulling her close, and she said tentatively, "Sir Denholm is a member of the government out here, and *he* doesn't think there's the slightest possibility of an attack by the Japanese. Wouldn't it be wisest to go back to England? Julienne says that foreign newspapers are full of reports of how war between Great Britain and Germany is only weeks away. I know you don't want to be relegated to a desk job, darling, but desk jobs *are* vital and—"

"No!" His voice was adamant as with his free hand he switched off the bedside lamp, plunging the room into semidarkness. "If the reports in the foreign press are true, then it would be far too dangerous for you in London. You are much safer staying here where, if there is a confrontation, it will be miles away up-country."

His lips touched the side of her mouth as his fingers gently pulled the straps of her nightdress down, revealing the creamy white smoothness of her breasts, the rose-pink perfection of her nipples.

"Forget what Sir Denholm said," he whispered hoarsely. He rolled on top of her, sliding her nightdress up to her waist, revelling in the delicious feel of her flesh against his, savoring her softness and fragrance. "Stafford says the government is blind, that they haven't a true grasp of the situation." Tenderly, his hand parted her thighs and he gently eased himself into her. "God, that's good, Beth!" he panted. "Hold me! Hold me tight!"

She held him tight and thought about Sir Denholm and wondered how on earth she could get Adam to agree to return to London. With a groan he reached a climax, his hands tightening on her shoulders, his mouth closing lovingly over hers. She hugged him tight, telling him how much she loved him, remaining in his arms until he fell asleep. Then, as she always did, she gently disentangled herself. Perhaps Tom Nicholson could persuade him that he was wasting his time remaining in Hong Kong. Perhaps soon the novelty would wear off. She lay on the far side of the bed, gazing up at the moonlit ceiling, hoping fervently that it would be so, that they would soon be back in London.

She went swimming at the prestigious Hong Kong Sports Club with Julienne the next morning.

"Isn't Tom Nicholson a sweetie?" Julienne asked as she came up from a dive, her dark hair sleeked close to her head, her long eyelashes sparkling with water.

"He's very nice," Elizabeth agreed. She struck out for the far side of the pool, and Julienne swam along beside her.

"Don't be so English and reticent, Elizabeth! It's obvious

that he is crazy about you. Tom doesn't fall in love easily, or often, so it's quite a compliment." She glanced naughtily at Elizabeth. "Do you think you could fall in love with him?"

"I'm married," Elizabeth said, laughing at Julienne's ridiculousness as they reached the far side of the pool and hung on to the edge, recovering their breath.

Julienne laughed with her. "Marriage!" she said expressively. "What difference does marriage make?" With a kick of her heels she executed a professional racing turn, not breaking the surface of the water until she was nearly thirty yards away.

Later, as they sat over cold drinks in the bar, Julienne asked her incredulously, "Do you mean that you have *never* had an affair?"

"Never," Elizabeth said, amused by the expression of horror on Julienne's pretty, kittenish face.

"But that is terrible!" Julienne said, then collapsed into giggles. "Oh dear, what must you think of me? But really, Elizabeth, I cannot imagine it. I adore Ronnie, but not to have any little adventures now and again? *Non, je ne peux pas l'imaginer!* You must be very much in love with your Adam!"

Elizabeth's answering laugh indicated that she was, but as she continued to sip her gin and tonic, she knew that her love for Adam was not the kind of love Julienne meant.

As they continued to talk, and as Julienne continued to be indiscreet, telling her about her present lover, who was a major in the Royal Scots, Elizabeth remained unenvious. The love that she and Adam shared was worth far more than the love Julienne enjoyed with her major, or with her other boyfriends. It wasn't a very exciting love, but it was deep and enduring and was surely of far greater value.

"Excuse me a moment," Julienne said, breaking off her laughter-filled account of her latest affair. "I promised Ronnie I would ring him and let him know where to meet me for lunch."

She slipped down from her bar stool, blowing a kiss to a gentleman in the far corner of the room who obviously knew her, then hurried toward the telephone booths.

Elizabeth remained at the bar, reflecting how different social customs were in Hong Kong and London. In London she would *never*, not even for an instant, have remained at a bar alone.

"Another gin and tonic, madame?" the Chinese barman asked courteously.

"No, thank you. I'll have a lemonade this time, please."

As the barman turned to fulfill her request, two casually dressed men entered the room and approached the bar. "I've never heard such a tirade of rubbish!" one of them said darkly as they sat down next to her. "Straight off the boat from England and he believes he knows all there is to know about fighting off the Japs if they should attack! Christ! He believes they'll be fought up-country and that life here will go on as normal! One thing is for sure, he's the kind of middle-aged fool we can well do without! What did you say his name was?"

The barman handed Elizabeth her frosted glass of lemonade.

"Harland," replied his companion.

Elizabeth gasped with shock and indignation, her fingers slipping on the ice-cold glass. It crashed to the floor, its contents gushing down the trouser leg of the man who had called Adam a fool. He spun around savagely. "What the hell . . . ?" he began, his eyes blazing.

His hair was black, straight and sleek, tumbling low over winged eyebrows. His skin was bronzed, his face harsh with high, lean cheekbones and a strong nose and jutting jaw. He looked like a man to be reckoned with; a man who could be a very nasty customer indeed.

"I'm sorry," she said furiously, as his masculinity flooded over her in waves. "It was an accident!"

His eyes were brown. Not the soft, honey-brown of Adam's eyes, but a brown so dark it was almost black. "Allow me to buy you another one," he said, and she could see flecks of gold near his pupils and a small, white scar curving down through one eyebrow. "What was it? A gin and tonic?"

"A lemonade," she said between clenched teeth. "And I would *not* like another one! It may interest you to know that the man you were talking about with such a gross lack of respect is my husband!"

Shock flared in his eyes and was quickly suppressed. "Then I must *insist* on buying you a drink," he said, and to her increased fury she could hear amusement in his voice. "Li, a lemonade for Mrs. Harland, please."

Elizabeth rose to her feet, shaking with anger. She had

no need to wait for him to introduce himself. She knew who he was. Sir Denholm's description of him had been searingly accurate.

"No, thank you!" she said, spitting the words. "Good-bye, Mr. Elliot!" She spun on her heel and marched from the room, her head high, her back rigid.

Chapter Eight

*T*HE doors slammed behind her and she walked full tilt into Julienne.

"Steady on," Julienne said, laughing. "There's no need for us to leave yet. I'm not meeting Ronnie for another hour."

Elizabeth drew in a deep, steadying breath. "Sorry, Julienne. I have to be going. I'll see you later."

"Oh, come on. Just one more gin and tonic," Julienne coaxed, looking genuinely disappointed.

Elizabeth shook her head. There wasn't money enough in the world to tempt her back into the bar and Raefe Elliot's obnoxious presence. "Sorry, Julienne, I really must be going. We're lunching with the Gresbys and I'm going to be late." As she spoke, she continued to walk briskly, hurrying across the lobby and out into the sunshine.

Julienne gave the doors to the bar a last, regretful look and then followed her. There would be other opportunities to waylay Raefe, she thought, surmounting her disappointment with her usual bouncy optimism. And next time he might not have a friend with him. "Well, as you're in a hurry," she said, catching up with Elizabeth, "and I've got time to spare, let me give you a lift. I wouldn't mind a lunchtime drink at the Pen. The barman there mixes the most wonderful manhattans."

As they stepped into Julienne's little Morris, Elizabeth felt her anger begin to subside. Raefe Elliot was an ill-mannered boor, but the friendliness of Julienne and her husband, and Helena and Tom Nicholson and Alastair Munroe, more than made up for it. They didn't think Adam a fool. They liked him and it was *their* opinion that mattered, not the opinion of an arrogant, ne'er-do-well like Raefe Elliot.

As if reading her thoughts, Julienne said suddenly, "Did you see the two men who walked into the bar just before you came out? One of them, the tall dark one, was Raefe Elliot. I saw them when I was on the telephone to Ronnie. I must say he doesn't look very ruffled by his court appearance—or by the new rumors that are beginning to fly around."

Elizabeth knew she shouldn't ask, but curiosity overcame common sense. "What rumors?" she asked as Julienne swung the Morris recklessly onto the busy road.

Julienne's eyes sparkled. "That he's banished Melissa to one of his farms in the New Territories. That he's refusing her a divorce and is keeping her a prisoner, not even allowing her father to know where she is."

"But my goodness, can't the police interfere?" Elizabeth asked, shocked.

Julienne giggled. "He *is* her husband, and the judiciary won't want to interfere with Raefe again in a hurry, not after he made them look such fools over the murder charge that was brought against him. You can bet your life that Colonel Langdon, Melissa's father, would have been far less eager for charges to have gone ahead if he had known in advance that Raefe's defense would depend on revealing that Melissa was a heroin addict! *Mon dieu!* You should have heard the intake of breath when Raefe was forced to part with *that* little piece of information!"

"And was it true?" Elizabeth asked, remembering Sir Denholm's impassioned avowal that it was a monstrous slander, that Raefe Elliot had grossly defamed his wife's reputation in order to save his own neck.

Julienne sped down Chatham Road with scant regard for other traffic and none at all for the pedestrians who leaped hurriedly out of her way.

"Who is to say?" she answered with a Gallic shrug. "Raefe says that she is, her father and everyone else who know her say she is not. But the jury *did* believe that Raefe was speaking the truth when he said that he returned from a business trip to Singapore and found Jacko Latimer in her bed, and Jacko *was* a well-known pusher of drugs among the European community in Hong Kong. For myself, I believe Raefe. What other reason would Melissa have for being in bed with an unpleasant, unprepossessing little man like Jacko? He was the kind of man that has to grovel for sex, not the kind that has it showered on him by a woman as beautiful as Melissa. No, if Melissa allowed Jacko Latimer into her bed, then it was not because she wanted him there. It was because she was paying him for something, and that something could only have been heroin."

They drew up outside the splendid Palladian-style Peninsula Hotel. "But as to why he is refusing her a divorce and is keeping her a prisoner in the New Territories, *je ne comprends pas*. That I cannot understand. I would have thought he would be glad to be rid of her. Certainly I do not believe he is still in love with her."

She giggled naughtily as they walked into the coolness of the Peninsula's lobby. "If he had still been in love with her, the blow that killed Jacko would not have been an accidental one, and would never have been mistaken for an accidental one! He would have torn Jacko limb from limb, and been magnificently unrepentant!" She gave a delicious shiver. "Can you imagine how superb a man like that must be in the bedroom, Elizabeth? If only he didn't prefer his Chinese and Malay girls." She ran the tip of her tongue suggestively over her full lower lip and said, her voice full of laughter, "If only he would give *la belle France* a chance to show what she can do instead!"

After lunch with the Gresbys, Elizabeth excused herself and went to her room to lie down. She still found the hot, humid weather enervating, and the scene with Raefe Elliot had disturbed her far more than she had been willing to admit.

She slipped out of her blouse and skirt and closed the rattan blinds, leaving the room in cool shade. "Damnable man," she muttered as she lay down on her bed and closed her eyes. How *dare* he speak of Adam like that? And how *dare* he suggest that she share a drink with him? Her cheeks flushed as she remembered the way he had looked at her, the naked appraisal in his dark eyes. The lazy amusement

in his voice; the sensual, confident, *arrogant* demeanor that
had so unnerved her.

"Damnable man!" she said again savagely, turning her
pillow over and thumping it with her fist. Julienne was
welcome to her daydreams of him. In Elizabeth's eyes she
was displaying a gross lack of judgment and taste. Raefe
Elliot was *not* an admirable, sexy man coping with an
unfaithful and drug-addicted wife. He was an insolent,
ignorant, loud-mouthed braggart who was not only a
flagrant womanizer and brawler, but possibly even a
murderer as well.

She thumped the pillow again for good measure and
tried to sleep. It was impossible. It wasn't only her
unfortunate confrontation with Raefe Elliot that was disturbing her. It was her own increased knowledge of the
geography of Hong Kong and the conclusions she was
drawing from it.

When she had sailed from Southampton aboard the
Orient Princess, the only thing she had known about Hong
Kong was that it was an island off the coast of China, under
the jurisdiction of Great Britain. Whatever Adam had told
her about it she had believed. That Japan was aggressive
toward it and would eventually attack it; that there would
be fighting in which he would be able to take part and
which would take place "up-country"; that when it was
over he could return to England and though not able to
don a uniform and fight, his pride would be intact; that he
would be able to say he had helped give the Japs a bloody
nose in the East. He would have nothing to feel ashamed of
and, more importantly, he would not feel as if he were an
old crock, too ancient to fight for his country. All this she
had understood. But now, after only a few days in Hong
Kong, she understood far more.

It wasn't the divergent views as to whether the Japanese
would or would not attack that disturbed her. It was the
overwhelming consensus that if they *did* attack, they
would soon be sent packing.

She had been shocked when she had first seen a map of
Hong Kong. She had thought it was a large island, several
miles off the coast of China, with an impressive harbor and
a fleet to match. It wasn't an island in the way she had
thought at all. It was only eight miles wide and eleven
miles long—a mere stone's throw from the mainland.

Across the narrow channel of water lay the Kowloon peninsula and an area of over three hundred and sixty square miles known as the New Territories. This was the area that Adam was presumably referring to when he spoke of fighting taking place "up-country." The only defense that the island and the mainland had against the Japanese warring across the border in China were two Regular Army battalions: the 2nd Battalion Royal Scots, in which Alastair Munroe served, and the 1st Battalion, the Middlesex Regiment. There was no air force to speak of, and only a handful of ships in the harbor.

"Is that it?" she had asked Alastair Munroe in amazement when he had answered her questions regarding the island's defenses.

"It's more than enough to see off the Japs," Alastair had said with amusement. "No point in having a surfeit of men and ships out here when it looks as if they're going to be needed elsewhere against Hitler."

Elizabeth had said, "No, possibly not." But she hadn't been convinced. It seemed to her that it would be exceptionally easy for the Japanese to pour over the border into the New Territories whenever they wanted to. And that once they did, the narrow channel of water between the mainland and Hong Kong island would not deter them for long.

Later that afternoon she and Adam picked up the keys to the house, and the next morning they moved out of the Peninsula Hotel and into their new home on the Peak.

"Household staff is no problem," Helena Nicholson said when she came round to help Elizabeth measure for new curtains and blinds, bringing her two children, aged two and five, with her. "Hobson's will supply them for you, but tell them you only need houseboys and a cook boy and a wash-amah. Tom's houseboy has a sister who is looking for a position. She is only seventeen, but Lee says she is very efficient and it would be nice for them if they were in neighboring households."

She wrote down the measurement of the last window and pushed her untidy mane of auburn hair away from her face. "You didn't mind my bringing Jeremy and Jennifer with me, did you? Since Alan's death they hate me to be out of their sight, poor lambs."

"Of course not," Elizabeth replied. "It's lovely to have

them playing out in the garden." Her eyes had lit up at the mention of the children. "It makes the house seem already a home."

Helena gazed at her curiously. "I would have thought you and Adam would have adored parenthood," she said in her shocking forthright manner. "Do you just not want any, or is there a problem?"

"There's no problem," Elizabeth said, rolling the tape measure into a very tight ball. "They just haven't arrived as yet. There's plenty of time."

"Oh yes, of course," Helena said easily, but her eyes remained curious. There was something odd about the Harlands' marriage, but she couldn't for the life of her think what it could be. They seemed happy enough and she couldn't, for one moment, imagine Ronnie Ledsham or anyone else luring Elizabeth into an extramarital affair.

The children's voices could be heard, laughing and shrieking as they played hide-and-seek in the garden. She looked out the window at them, her blue eyes clouding. It seemed such a little time since they had been playing in front of their house in Singapore. Since Alan had been striding up the path and they had toddled out to meet him.

"Is it still so very bad, Helena?" Elizabeth asked quietly.

She nodded. "Yes, even after a year it still seems . . . impossible. There's a part of me that can't truly believe it. Sometimes, in the morning, before I'm fully conscious, I think he's there beside me, or that he's away on a trip and will be coming home, and then I wake properly and I remember, and it seems too monstrous to be true. How *can* he be dead when I loved him so much?" She quickly wiped the tears from her eyes and gave a self-conscious laugh. "Sorry, I didn't mean to play the poor little widow. I don't usually talk about it at all. It was just seeing the children in the garden, and remembering . . ."

They were silent for a little while, then Elizabeth said tentatively, "Alastair Munroe is a very attractive man."

Helena grinned, her grief once more under control. "He is, and what you mean is that he seems to be in love with me and why don't I marry him?"

Elizabeth laughed. There was no way of coping with Helena's forthrightness except by being equally forthright. "Something like that, yes."

Helena sighed. "He *is* an attractive man, Elizabeth, and

I'm terribly fond of him, but I don't love him in the way I loved Alan. I don't feel ill with worry if he's late, or faint with excitement at the thought of seeing him. I don't want to die with pleasure when he touches me; I don't feel sick with fear at the thought of losing him. I don't want to marry him and him to know he's only second best. I want to be in love with him as I was in love with Alan. As you are in love with Adam. And I don't think I ever will be. Not with anyone, ever again."

That night, lying beside Adam in the darkness, Elizabeth felt curiously restless. It was foolish to allow Helena's innocent words to perturb her. There were more ways than one of being in love. Helena's way certainly wasn't Julienne's way. Helena had loved one man faithfully and wholeheartedly in a way that Elizabeth doubted Julienne ever had. So why did it matter if her way of being in love with Adam was different from their way of being in love?

Adam's rhythmic, heavy breathing deepened into a slight snore and she eased herself away from him to the far side of the bed. She knew the answer to her question. It was because though Julienne and Helena loved differently, they both loved with a physical passion that she was incapable of. She knew the word that described her sexual responses and it was an unpleasant one. For the thousandth time she wondered if Adam was aware of her frigidity, and if he ignored it and accepted it out of his very deep love for her. There was no way of knowing. In many ways he treated her as if she were still a child. A frank discussion between them about sex would be as unthinkable to him as it would be difficult for her.

She sighed and slipped out of bed, then walked barefoot onto the balcony, looking out over the silk-black mountainside to the distant lights of Victoria. She was suffering increasingly from insomnia. Night after night while Adam slept, she found herself making cups of tea, reading the latest Agatha Christie novel, or browsing through her sheet music. She picked up the score of Busoni's *Turandot Suite* that she had been reading earlier in the day. He was an exciting composer and Professor Hurok had been eager that she familiarize herself with his work. She felt a surge of determination. Lack of work was surely the main reason for her restlessness and dissatisfaction, and lack of work was something she could rectify. She would buy a piano tomorrow. Helena would tell her where she could obtain a suitable one. And she would set aside six hours a day for practice. If Adam wanted to swim and sunbathe and play interminable tennis, then he could do so with the new friends they had made. She would accompany him to parties and dinners as she had always done, but through the day she would have her music. And her restlessness and dissatisfaction would surely disappear.

"It's going to take them at least six weeks to ship in the kind of piano you require," Helena said to her as they came out of Lane Crawford, Victoria's largest department store. "In the meantime, why don't you appropriate Tom's piano? It isn't exactly concert quality, but it's better than nothing."

"That would be super," Elizabeth said gratefully, "but wouldn't Tom miss it?"

Helena laughed. "Until you arrived in Hong Kong, that piano was only played at Christmas and birthdays—and then always appallingly." She opened the door of her little open Morgan. "And if time is hanging heavy on your hands, there's another favor you could do for me."

Elizabeth slipped into the passenger seat next to her. "What's that? Arrange for a cooling breeze? An English shower?"

Helena shook her head, her mane of untidy hair bouncing around her shoulders. "No, nothing so easy. The dog I bought Simon for his birthday isn't a dog at all. It's a bitch and she's just had puppies. I've found homes for two of them, but I'm left with the runt. Will you take it? If I don't find a suitable home for it soon I'll have to have it put to sleep." She pulled out into the main stream of traffic, heading toward the Parisian Grill where they were meeting Tom for lunch. "It's a sweet little dog, but a little . . . indeterminate. The mother is a golden Cocker Spaniel and the pups seem to have inherited mainly Spaniel characteristics. Will you take it?"

"Of course I will," Elizabeth said, smiling at her. "Does it have a name?"

"No. The christening can be your privilege, but try and be a little more imaginative than my son. He calls ours Boy and every time Tom calls the dog, the houseboy scurries into the room to ask him what he wants!"

* * *

Tom was already sitting at a table, sipping a Scotch and soda, when they arrived. He looked up at them appreciatively as they entered. They were both tall women. Elizabeth, slender and graceful in a white linen suit and open-necked scarlet silk blouse, her wheat-gold hair swept into a glossy knot. Helena, magnificently Junoesque and brimming with health and good humor.

He was excessively fond of his sister-in-law. He knew Alastair Munroe wanted to marry her and he wished that she would encourage him. Alan was dead and she had to build a new life for herself and the children. She didn't possess Elizabeth's head-turning beauty or Julienne Ledsham's flirtatious femininity, and it wasn't every man who would want to take on the responsibility of two small children. If she didn't encourage Munroe there might be a long wait before another suitor appeared on the scene, and that would be a pity. His nephew and niece needed a father, and Alastair Munroe would fit the bill admirably.

"Were you successful in your hunt for a piano?" he asked as they sat down.

"No. Lane Crawford says it will take at least six weeks to ship one in, and so I've arranged for Elizabeth to borrow yours," Helena said with her usual directness. "I've also arranged that she will take the last pup off our hands." She turned to the waiter hovering at her side. "A large ice-cold gin and tonic, please," she said, satisfied with her morning's work. "I've also got some more news. I've decided that I've presumed on your hospitality long enough, Tom. There's no sense in returning to England with the children until we know what that nasty man Hitler is going to do. And we can't possibly stay with you *ad infinitum*. So I've been to Hobson's and arranged to take a three-bedroom garden flat in Kowloon. I'm moving there tomorrow."

"But there's absolutely no need!" Tom said explosively. "Good God! You can stay with me for as long as I'm posted here and that could be years!"

"No, I can't," Helena said with unusual gentleness. "I'm on my own now, Tom, and I have to learn to live on my own."

Beneath the gentleness her voice was firm, and Tom knew that it was useless to argue. Also, he had a sneaking suspicion that she was right. Her own flat in Kowloon would be far better for her than continuing to live with him. It would give her greater freedom in her personal life. If she wished Alastair Munroe to stay the night with her, then it would be easy for him to do so with no embarrassment to anyone.

"Okay," he said with a broad grin. "I give in. When's the housewarming party?"

All through lunch Tom was aware of male heads turning in their direction and knew it was Elizabeth who was attracting them. He now also knew why Adam Harland always looked so pleased with himself. It was a highly pleasant sensation being the envy of every man in the room. "When are you going to take a trip into the New Territories?" he asked Elizabeth as they were served *filet mignons lili*. "That's where you'll see the real China. The unspoilt China."

"Soon, I hope." The husky note in her voice sent a flare of heat through his groin. On board the *Orient Princess* he had intended, if she were willing, to have an affair with her. It had taken him very little time to realize that extramarital affairs were not part of her life, and now he didn't regret it. His personal life was complicated enough as it was, his true feelings elsewhere, and he had begun to value Elizabeth's friendship.

"Adam *had* planned that we would drive up there this weekend," she continued, a smile touching the full, generous curves of her mouth, "but Ronnie is adamant that we attend the race meeting at Happy Valley. His horse is running and he has a new jockey, and he is convinced he is going to win. He has the celebration party all arranged!"

"He's an eternal optimist," Tom said with a grin, wondering if Ronnie had propositioned her yet. A refusal would be unlikely to offend in that quarter, although it was something he suspected Ronnie didn't experience very often. Not for the first time he wondered how a marriage that seemed founded on mutual, lighthearted adultery could thrive as happily as the Ledsham marriage apparently did. "But if you're not going to the New Territories this weekend, perhaps I could join you when you do go? The country is pretty wild up there and for anyone who isn't familiar with it, it's best to have a guide."

"My goodness, yes," Helena said feelingly. "There are still leopards on the prowl up there, and anteaters and cobras, and a score of other hideous things. The children think it's wonderful, but it scares me half to death. Take my word for it: Happy Valley, and even Ronnie, are much safer!"

Elizabeth laughed, deciding that if the New Territories were as full of dangers as Helena said, then she would be only too glad to postpone the trip until Tom could accompany them. But when she mentioned this to Adam that night, he didn't agree. "There are two well-made roads running from Kowloon to the border," he said. "Whichever one we take, we'll be safe enough as long as we don't leave it."

"What about Ronnie's party?"

"There'll be another party next week, and another one the week after that. A trip north will be far more interesting than seeing Ronnie's horse trail in third or fourth or last. We can accept Tom's offer to act as a guide another time. When we want to explore off the beaten track."

They set off early Saturday morning, driving out through Kowloon and taking the Taipo road toward Fanling and the Chinese border. As soon as they left the crowded, garish streets of Kowloon behind them, Elizabeth was aware of being in a remote and distant country in a way she had never been while on Hong Kong island. There was no trace of westernization. The countryside was bleak and barren, rising on either side into inhospitable mountains clothed with forests of fir. There was little cultivation. The villages they passed through were poor and sparsely populated with a few rice fields surrounding them and very little else. As they drove by, villagers clad in black pajamas paused in their tasks to watch them, large circular coolie hats shielding their heads from the sun, their feet bare and caked with dirt.

"It doesn't look very prosperous, does it?" Adam said, shocked at the difference in living standards between the Chinese working the fields and those living in Kowloon and Victoria.

"There must be *some* prosperous farms," Elizabeth said, remembering Julienne's reference to Raefe Elliot having banished his wife to a farm in the New Territories.

"If there are, I haven't seen any." A frown furrowed his brow. "Did you see that old woman bent double working that rice field? She must be a hundred if she's a day!"

They crossed the Shin Mun River, the water eddying in muddy swirls toward the sea. "Is that a sparrowhawk?" Elizabeth asked, pointing to a bird of prey hovering over the far bank in the still, hot air.

Adam squinted his eyes against the sun. "Could be. Leigh Stafford told me that this place is a heaven on earth for bird-watchers. There are cockatoos, mynah birds, pelicans, the lot."

At the small town of Sha Tin they stopped to pay their respects at the Buddhist monastery. Hand in hand, they walked up the hundreds of stone steps that led to the Man Fat Temple, reaching with relief the temple's veranda and shaded courtyard. Hundreds of small gilt statues of Buddha lined the wall, standing in niches and crevices, a handful of Chinese meditating solemnly before them. On the far side of the courtyard rose a nine-story pagoda, its walls a delicate shell-pink, its Oriental upturned roofs a rich coral red.

An ancient Chinese woman beamed toothlessly at them as she pointed at the steps.

Adam groaned. "Not more steps!"

"I'm afraid so," Elizabeth said relentlessly. "Come on, the view will be worth it."

Breathing heavily, they climbed the cool, circular stone steps that led to the top of the pagoda and emerged, gasping, into the sunlight.

It was like looking out over a painted landscape. Far to the north were the rolling, forest-covered hills of China. To the west was the sea and Tolo Harbor and a flurry of junks, their square sails looking like a cloud of great brown and golden butterflies as they skimmed the silky blue water. And to the south lay the Kowloon Peninsula and Hong Kong island and the soaring peaks of Mount Victoria and Mount Butler and Mount Nicholson.

"Oh, wonderful!" Elizabeth breathed rapturously, leaning on the edge of the parapet and gazing down at the panorama spread before her. At the foot of the hill she could see their Riley, looking like a small black beetle. A hundred yards or so away, half hidden by a clump of pine trees, another European car indicated that they were not the only tourists exploring the pagoda and temple. As she looked down at the squares and courtyards and the black-clad Chinese that had come to worship, she saw a tall, familiar figure stride out of the temple. She seized Adam's arm. "It's Tom! Look! Down there!" She was just about to wave and call his name when Adam asked suddenly, "Who is that with him?"

Her waving hand faltered.

A small, delicate figure was walking with tiny, hurried steps at his side. Her hair was black and sleek, coiled heavily at the nape of her neck. Her cheongsam was richly embroidered, the slits at the side only modestly high. And her hand was very firmly in Tom's.

"Is it a girl from one of the nightclubs, do you think?" Elizabeth asked bewilderedly.

Adam shook his head. "I don't think so. She doesn't look like a bar girl. Even from this distance she looks very respectable and demure."

The two figures were beginning to walk down the hundreds of stone steps that led to their car. As they did so, Tom's arm slid around the girl's waist. They could hear the distant sound of her laughter as Tom stood still, turning her around to face him, drawing her close.

"That's no casual date," Adam said decisively as they kissed. "They're in love. Who the devil can she be?"

"I've no idea," Elizabeth said wonderingly, watching as the two embracing figures finally drew apart and continued to walk, hand in hand, down the remaining steps. "He's never mentioned her to me, but then he wouldn't, would he?"

"Why the devil not?" Adam asked as they turned away from the parapet and began to make their own way back down the stairs.

"Remember our first dinner at Tom's? Remember the remarks Sir Denholm made about Raefe Elliot and his Chinese girlfriend? Chinese girls are regarded as perfectly all right in the bars and nightclubs of Wanchai, but they are most definitely *not* regarded as all right in European clubs and at European dinner tables. Poor Tom. I wonder how long it has been going on."

Adam shrugged. The girl had looked beautiful and well-bred. It seemed nonsense that Nicholson had to keep his liaison with her a secret. "Goodness knows, but I shall have a word with him when I see him again. I don't want him to think that we would disapprove. Life's too short for prejudices of that kind."

She squeezed his hand tightly. "I do love you, Adam. You're the *kindest* man I've ever met in my life."

He grinned. "I hope I'm a lot more than just kind!" he said, pulling her close against him as they ran down the remaining steps.

They continued their journey up as far as Fanling, returning to Kowloon on the Castle Peak Road, past ancient Chinese fish ponds and duck ponds and the medieval walled village of Kat Hing Wai. It was early evening by the time they crossed to Victoria on the ferry.

"Do you still want to catch up with Ronnie's party at the Jockey Club?" Adam asked as they docked.

She shook her head. "No, I don't think so. We're seeing Ronnie and Julienne and Helena and Alastair for lunch tomorrow at the Repulse Bay Hotel. Let's have an early night tonight. I'm tired."

That night in bed she tried to overcome her tiredness and imagine that she was Julienne or Helena. It was no use. Adam's hands on her body were warm and familiar and even pleasant, but they did not inflame her or fill her with passion. She responded to him as always, lovingly and patiently, holding him tight in her arms, wondering what was wrong with her and how she could possibly put it right.

As they lay together afterward, she rested her head against his chest and said tentatively, "I'm sorry if I'm not very sexy in bed, darling. Do you mind very much?"

His arms tightened around her. "What a silly thing to say. I don't want you to be any different. I love you just as you are. I always have."

She twisted onto her elbow, her pale blond hair tumbling around her shoulders as she said with sudden vehemence, "But I don't *want* to be as I am! I feel such a failure!"

He laughed indulgently, pulling her down once again beside him. "You're not a failure, darling. Sex isn't a competition. You make me very happy. Now, go to sleep and stop worrying about something that isn't important."

Sunday lunch at the Repulse Bay Hotel was becoming a regular fixture for them. The hotel lay on the south side of the island, long and white and low, overlooking the most beautiful of Hong Kong's bays. The sand stretched in a perfect crescent of silver, lapped by gently creaming waves and backed by lush, green mountains.

The Ledshams were already sitting on the veranda when Elizabeth and Adam arrived. Ronnie resplendent in white ducks and an open-necked white shirt, his blond hair slicked and gleaming, his grin triumphant. "You missed a sensational day yesterday," he said gleefully as they sat down. "My horse romped home. Julienne lost a fortune because she didn't believe me when I told her it would win and the silly girl put all her money on an old wreck that barely tottered from the starting gate!"

Julienne said something extremely rude beneath her breath and he leaned over to her, kissing her beneath her ear. "I *told* you it would win, darling. Why, oh why, do you never trust me?"

Julienne began to giggle. "Because you are utterly untrustworthy, *cheri*, and utterly adorable." She kissed his nose as Helena and Tom and Alastair strolled out to join them.

"What's this?" Tom asked teasingly as he sat down. "I thought you two wouldn't be on speaking terms after yesterday."

"I have a forgiving nature," Julienne said impishly as he leaned over and kissed her on the cheek. "Besides, I want to make quite sure Ronnie tells me when his horse is going to run again. I lost a *fortune* yesterday!"

"Old Denholm's got a new jockey," Alastair said as the waiter served them ice-cold martinis. "Swears he can outstrip yours any day of the week. He's entering him for the race next week."

A friendly quarrel developed as to whether Ronnie's win had been because of his new jockey or was nothing more than a freak stroke of good fortune.

"It was the jockey, blast you!" Ronnie was saying indignantly for the umpteenth time when they became aware that the tables around them had suddenly fallen quiet.

Elizabeth looked up and saw that Raefe Elliot was walking through the lounge toward the veranda, a diminutive Malay girl at his side.

"*Tiens!*" Julienne said admiringly. "How *dare* he when he knows his father-in-law lunches here?"

Several other people were obviously thinking the same thing, their heads turning around to see if Colonel Langdon was present and if so, what his reaction to his son-in-law and his companion would be. They were disappointed. The corner table normally patronized by Colonel Langdon was empty. Elizabeth, unable to help herself, watched in mesmerized fascination as Raefe neared their table. She was certain that it was a matter of supreme indifference to him whether his father-in-law was there or not.

"Hello, Tom," he said, and his dark, rich voice sent a tingle down her spine. His lean, hard muscled body was taller and broader than she had remembered, and she forced her eyes away from him and down to her glass, furious at the response he aroused in her.

"Hello, Mrs. Harland." The amusement in his voice was blatant. "Be careful with your drink. Martini stains far more lethally than lemonade!"

She was aware of Julienne looking at her with raised eyebrows and Adam looking at her in surprise.

She lifted her head, her eyes meeting his. "Then be careful what you say, Mr. Elliot," she said coolly, and was aware of Adam's surprise deepening into incomprehension.

Raefe Elliot grinned down at her, his eyes bold and black and frankly appraising. "Allow me to introduce my companion. Alute, Mrs. Adam Harland."

Elizabeth rose and shook the Malay girl's hand, seeing with relief that she had no need to feel sorry for her. The almond-slanted eyes were full of confidence. If Raefe Elliot was behaving badly, his companion was happily uncaring.

He introduced her to Julienne and Helena and Ronnie and Tom. Tom, assuming that Adam and Raefe hadn't met, performed the introductions while Ronnie eyed Alute with open lasciviousness and Julienne tried desperately to catch Elizabeth's eye.

"Did you watch my horse run yesterday?" Ronnie asked him. Elliot was an expert on horseflesh and it was nice to be able to let him know that he, too, knew a thing or two about it. "Won by a mile."

"Congratulations," Raefe said, his eyes no longer on him but on Elizabeth again.

"I owe you a fuller apology than the one I made earlier," he said, and she was aware of the blue sheen on his hair and the disturbing sensuality of his finely chiseled, well-shaped mouth. "Perhaps we could have lunch together so that I can make amends?"

She heard Alastair Munroe's quick intake of breath and knew the others at the table were staring at her and Raefe with shock.

"I don't think so," she said with an indifference she was far from feeling. "Good-bye, Mr. Elliot."

The snub was obvious. A smile tugged at the corner of Raefe's mouth, and his broad shoulders shrugged philosophically beneath the linen of his well-cut jacket. "Good-bye, Mrs. Harland," he said, and nodding in Tom and Ronnie's direction, he slid his arm around his girlfriend's waist and strolled off with her toward a corner table.

"My God! The bloody nerve!" Alastair said incredulously. "What the hell will happen if Langdon walks in here?"

No one answered him. Adam said, an odd note in his voice, "I didn't know you'd met him before, Beth. What on earth was he talking about? Why the devil does he owe you an apology?"

A faint flush touched Elizabeth's cheeks. "It's nothing. There was an accident at the club. My glass fell and sprayed him with lemonade, that's all."

Julienne's eyes sparkled. So, the day she had wanted to stay on at the club and speak to Raefe, Elizabeth had already been speaking to him. So effectively that Raefe Elliot had suggested they lunch together, *and* he had asked in front of Adam. It was all *most* intriguing.

"Even Elliot can't expect to get away with squiring a colored around so openly," Ronnie Ledsham said, unwilling admiration in his voice. "Not in locales that Melissa frequents as well."

Tom's face had hardened at Ronnie's words, and his sister-in-law said hurriedly, "Melissa hasn't been seen anywhere since the end of the trial."

"That's because Raefe is keeping her a prisoner," Julienne said with relish. "Ronnie overhead Colonel Langdon fuming about it to Sir Denholm. Apparently Melissa is on one of the Elliot farms in the New Territories, but Colonel Langdon doesn't know where and has had no contact with her since the trial ended."

"He'll need to be keeping her a prisoner if he's going to continue parading his Malay girlfriend around so openly," Ronnie said dryly. "Melissa Langdon's temper is nearly as vicious as Raefe's. We could all be witnessing another murder trial before too long."

"I'm going for a walk," Tom said, rising abruptly.

Elizabeth hesitated for a moment, then said, "Would you mind if I came with you, Tom? I've never been out into the gardens at the rear of the hotel. Helena tells me they're gorgeous."

She stood, uncomfortably aware that Raefe Elliot's eyes were still disturbingly on her.

"You didn't mind my asking to come with you, did you?" she asked Tom as they walked from the veranda.

He grinned down at her. "Heavens, no. Were you suddenly feeling as claustrophobic as I was?"

She gave him an answering smile. "Yes, the atmosphere was pretty tense, wasn't it? You would think Mr. Elliot would have more sense than to dine with his girlfriend in a hotel frequented by his father-in-law." As soon as she had uttered his name she was furious with herself. Why speak of Raefe Elliot? He wasn't of the remotest interest to her.

They walked out of the lobby and into the gardens. "You'd think he'd know better than to bring her here, father-in-law or no father-in-law," Tom agreed.

"Because she's Malay?"

He nodded, the lines around his mouth tightening. "Yes, it's not the done thing. There are plenty of places in Hong Kong where you can take Malay or Chinese girls, but there are some places where you can't. Not without causing talk. And the Repulse Bay Hotel on a Sunday at lunchtime is one of them."

She said carefully, "Adam and I didn't go to the race yesterday. We drove up to the New Territories instead."

"Did you enjoy it?" he asked, making an effort at civility. Only his eyes revealed that his thoughts were elsewhere.

"We went to Kam Tin."

He stopped walking. "Oh," he said, understanding immediately. "You saw?"

"Yes. She looked awfully pretty, and you looked to be very much in love."

He grinned ruefully. "We are. Her name is Lamoon

Sheng. Her father is a real estate baron. If he knew she was in love with a European he'd have her married to a suitable Chinese within twenty-four hours."

"Is that why no one knows about the two of you?"

"Helena knows. There are times when I feel she is a little disappointed in me. You know how direct Helena is. She doesn't see why I don't squire Lamoon around openly, as Elliot does his girlfriend."

"And why don't you?" Elizabeth asked curiously. He wasn't a man she would ever have accused of cowardice, or of caring overmuch what other people thought.

"Because the minute I did, the minute it became known that it was a serious liaison and not just a romp in the hay, my career would be at stake. I would find myself conveniently posted to India or Africa or even Outer Mongolia. And Lamoon would suffer even more. She would be forced into a marriage of her father's choice. At least this way we still see each other. And we can still hope."

They walked back into the hotel and Elizabeth was relieved to see that the corner table on the veranda was empty. Raefe Elliot and his Malay girlfriend were presumably disturbing the Sabbath elsewhere.

"What did you think of Raefe Elliot?" Elizabeth asked Adam as they drove back home up the mountain road toward Wong Nie Chung Gap.

Adam shrugged dismissively. "Not much. An arrogant devil I should imagine. I thought it was consummate nerve, his asking you to have lunch with him."

Elizabeth stared reflectively out at a bank of wild blue irises. "Would you mind very much if I accepted?" she asked at last.

The car swerved slightly. Adam righted it and gazed at her in stunned amazement.

"Of course I would mind! He's a married man and a notorious womanizer! Your reputation would be in shreds if you were seen out alone with him!"

She took his arm, immediately repentant. "I'm sorry, darling. Of course I don't want to have lunch with Raefe Elliot. I can't think why I even contemplated it."

They sped down the curving road that led toward Happy Valley and the racecourse, and into Victoria. A small smile touched Adam's mouth. "Perhaps you suggested it because you want me to be jealous?"

Her eyes darkened and she tightened her hold on his arm. "No, Adam," she said fiercely. "I never want you to be jealous. I shall never do anything that will make you unhappy. Not ever!"

Chapter Nine

❧

ALASTAIR Munroe pressed his foot down sharply on the brake of his battered old Austin, swearing volubly. There were times when negotiating through Kowloon's crowded streets was next to impossible. Taxi horns blared as a bevy of rickshaws blocked the street. A squawking hen, chased by a small Chinese boy, darted between the temporarily halted cars, a flurry of feathers in its wake. A hawker, his wares dangling from both ends of the bamboo pole that arched across his bony shoulders, took advantage of the lull in the traffic and accosted Alastair through the open window of his car.

"Fresh prawns, fresh mussels. You like?"

Alastair shook his head. "No, thank you," he said, averting his eyes from the grimy pails of shellfish.

The hawker persisted and Alastair again shook his head, pressing his palm down on the Austin's horn. Why the devil Helena had moved from the privileged peace and quiet of Victoria Peak to the mayhem of Kowloon was beyond him. The protesting hen was caught. The rickshaws dispersed. Traffic began to move again, and the hawker philosophically trotted off to tout his wares elsewhere.

Alastair took a left turn onto Nathan Road. At least the flat was near a park. It would be easy to take Jeremy there for a game of football. Beneath his trim moustache Alastair's mouth tightened. He wanted to do far more for Jeremy than act as if he were merely a benevolent uncle.

He wanted to become a father to him, and to Jennifer, and he knew he would make a damned good father.

He swerved to a halt outside a block of recently constructed flats. There had been rumors that the Royal Scots were to be stationed elsewhere. It if were true, he wanted an official understanding between himself and Helena before they were separated for months, or even years. Not for the first time he wished she had been widowed for longer than fourteen months. If she had been, he would have felt able to be far more forceful in his demands that she marry him. As it was, it was only reasonable that she wanted to wait a little longer. She was still grieving for Alan, still in love with him. And he knew she felt that to marry again so soon after his death would be an act of disloyalty.

She had only been in the flat a week, but already it looked like a home. He walked into the large, sunlit sitting room, noting the silver-framed photograph of Alan that held pride of place on a lacquered cabinet. The children ran up to him gleefully.

"Can we go to the park, Uncle Alastair? Can we play football?" Jeremy asked, barreling into him.

Alastair swung him high on his shoulders, took Jennifer's podgy little hand, and walked with them out into the garden where Helena was busy transferring geraniums from pots into a freshly dug flower bed. "Trying to create an English garden?" he asked with a grin.

She smiled up at him. She was wearing a halter top that had seen better days, and a pair of shorts that looked as if they had once been Alan's. There was a smudge of dirt on her cheek and her hair hung in its usual untidy mess, cascading thickly over her shoulders.

"And why not?" she asked, rising to her feet to greet him, a trowel still in her hand. Her full, heavy breasts strained against the cotton of her halter top. "I find the sight of familiar, flame-red geraniums distinctly comforting. I only wish primroses and violets would flourish here as well."

He didn't kiss her, although he wanted to. She had, very early in their relationship, insisted that no sign of physical intimacy be demonstrated between them in front of the children, in case it disturbed them. He had respected her fears but was becoming increasingly frustrated by them.

His mouth twisted ironically. He knew the conclusion Tom had drawn when Helena had announced she was moving into a flat of her own. He had assumed it was because they wanted more privacy in which to conduct their affair. He had been wrong. Although Helena had become his lover with a hunger and abandon he had found unnerving, nothing on earth would have induced her to do so beneath her own roof, where the children would be in earshot and where, by some freak chance, they might be not only overheard, but seen.

"I want to talk to you," he said, swinging Jeremy to the ground.

"Oh, can't we go to the park?" Jeremy wailed disappointedly.

Alastair ruffled his blond curls. "Later, Jeremy. I want to talk to Mummy for a little while."

At the expression on his face and the determination in his voice, Helena felt her heart sink. Why, oh why, couldn't he be content with things as they were? He was the one who would be hurt by forcing matters to a head; the one who would feel rejected. And there was no need for it. She was happy in his company, and he slaked her awful desperate sexual loneliness, but he wasn't a replacement for Alan, and never could be. Now he was going to force her to say so.

"Let's find Jung-lu, children," she said wearily, "and ask her to look after you for a little while."

"Don't want to stay with Jung-lu," Jennifer pouted, toddling at Helena's side. "Want to stay with you and Uncle Alastair."

"Later, poppet." Helena gave her a kiss on her chubby cheek and handed her over to the amah. "Look after them for half an hour, Jung-lu. I shall be in the sitting room with Major Munroe and I don't want to be disturbed."

She led the way into the sitting room and lit a du Maurier, inhaling deeply. "I know what you're going to say to me, Alastair, and I don't want to hear it. Why can't we continue as we are?"

"Because the battalion may be moved soon and if it is, I want there to be a formal understanding between us before I have to leave."

She looked at him with affection and despair. He was so punctiliously correct, even now, when he was about to

propose marriage. She knew that his reserved demeanor
was caused by shyness, and it was one of the things she
found endearing about him. He was so competent and in
command in his professional life, and so vulnerable when
it came to his personal life. She said, trying to steer the
conversation away from themselves to a more general
topic, "Why do you suppose the Royal Scots are to be
moved? There won't be many troops left for defense if they
do go."

"The general opinion is that we've been here too long
and that it's a waste of our time. If war breaks out it's going
to be in Europe and that's where the action will be. Not
here. We've been warned to stand by for a return to
England." He took the cigarette out of her hand and
crushed it out in a nearby ashtray. "I want you to marry
me," he said, a faint touch of color on his cheeks betraying
his inner agitation. "I know that you think it's too soon for
you to make such a decision, but circumstances aren't
normal, Helena. I don't want to find myself whisked back
to England with no idea when I will see you again. I want
to *know* that I will see you again." He took her hands.
"Please, Helena," he said gruffly. "I'm not very good with
words, but I love you and I want to look after you."

A lump rose in her throat and she felt her eyes begin to
sting with tears. He was so good and so honorable and she
hated knowing she was going to hurt him. "I'm sorry,
Alastair," she said, and her eyes weren't on him but on the
silver-framed photograph that stood on the lacquered
cabinet. "It's too soon for me. Please try to understand."

He swallowed hard. He had been speaking the truth
when he had said that words did not come easily to him.
He wasn't a man who felt at ease in female company.
Although he was thirty-two, there had been very few
women before Helena, and none that he had considered
marrying. It was Helena's lack of striven-for glamour that
had first attracted him. She was so fresh and open, so
totally without guile. "I'm not asking for an early marriage,
Helena," he said stubbornly. "I know that it would be too
soon for you, but I want a commitment from you that we
will marry some day." He took a ring box from his pocket
and added awkwardly, "I don't know whether the size is
right, but . . ."

It was a solitaire diamond. The tears fell down her face. It was so typical of him to have bought it, hoping to please her, and typical that it was the very worst thing he could have done, for to be able to wear it she would have to remove Alan's ring. She shook her head. "No," she said, her voice strangled. "I couldn't . . ."

He took her right hand, and said, "On this hand, my love, just for a little while . . ."

His understanding shattered her and she crumpled against him, crying unrestrainedly. He knew she was crying for Alan. He rocked her against him, and when her tears subsided he lifted her right hand. He slipped the ring on her fourth finger, and she allowed him to do so.

"We'll move it to the left hand later," he said. "Whenever you're ready to do so."

She gulped and nodded, and wondered for the first time whether she really was a fool for refusing him. "Let's have a cup of tea," she said thickly, and went into the kitchen to make it. Strong and sweet, and with milk, just the way he liked it.

Julienne arched her spine, her spicy red hair curling damply around her face, her eyes closed, her lips parted as she cried out with pleasure.

Derry Langdon lay naked beneath her, his large, strong hands on the pale flesh of her buttocks. She was straddling his face, the glossy mat of her pubic hair skimming his nose and mouth as her hips moved with increasing speed. His mouth was open, hungry for her sweet juices, for that tiny pearl embedded in the velvety soft flesh. She moved faster, her eyes shut tight, her pretty, feline face contorted with pleasure. His fingers gouged into her buttocks, pulling her down, down, down onto his lips, his searching tongue, his nibbling teeth.

"Bon dieu! D'un bon dieu!" Julienne shrieked ecstatically as his rough, hot tongue lapped her clitoris, his lips sucking, his tongue probing. Her hips gyrated wildly as she slipped and slithered over his sweat-soaked face and then, with a scream, she arched backward, her orgasm stabbing victoriously through her.

His hand slid up to her hips, and he twisted her beneath him frenziedly, his hard, pulsating cock ramming deep within her throbbing moistness, his sperm shooting from him as he gave a long, harsh cry of release.

"That was good, *n'est-ce pas?*" she asked, her eyes dancing as she leaned on one elbow, looking down at him.

Derry grunted, unable to speak, his heart slamming within his chest like a sledgehammer, breathing like a man who had just sprinted a mile in under four minutes.

Julienne giggled and wound a lock of his hair around her finger. It was not straight and sleek like Ronnie's hair, but crisp and curling and coarse.

"Perhaps you would like to do it again?" she asked, her voice full of suppressed laughter.

He opened one eye and looked up at her. It was the first time they had made love. He didn't know what sexual athleticism her previous lovers had been capable of, but he was not going to try to compete with them. Death from a coronary in bed with another man's wife was not part of his plans for the future.

"You must be joking," he said expressively, and Julienne gurgled with laughter, sliding down beside him, her head on his chest, her lips against his sweat-damp skin.

After a little while, when his breathing had returned to normal, he asked, "Where does Ronnie think you are?"

Her shoulders lifted against him in an expressive Gallic shrug. "I don't know. The club, shopping . . ."

He slid his arm from beneath her and pushed himself up against the pillows, reaching for the cigarettes and lighter on the bedside table. "It's some hell of a marriage you two have. Does he never question where you've been or how you've spent your time?"

Julienne sighed. It was always the same. Sooner or later her lovers all became obsessed with curiosity about her marriage. Derry was simply displaying his interest much sooner than most. She knelt on the crumpled sheets and faced him, her breasts high and pert, her nipples a rich, ruby red, her hands clasped in pagan demureness on her naked lap. "I do not talk about my marriage with anyone," she said with a seriousness so out of character that he raised his eyebrows. "I am very happily married. I love Ronnie. Ronnie loves me. Whatever you and I do is fun, but it does not affect my marriage. Do you understand?"

"Not in a million years," Derry said truthfully.

A tiny frown puckered her brow and he reached for her, drawing her close against him. "Okay, sweetheart. If that's the way you want it, that's the way it will be. No talk of Ronnie. Who the devil shall we talk about?"

"Melissa," Julienne said promptly. "Do you know yet where she is? Is Raefe really keeping her a prisoner, and if he is, why are you not doing something about it?"

This time it was Derry's turn to frown. Melissa was his sister and he hated the trial and the sordidness that had been publicly revealed, almost as much as his father had.

"Melissa is okay," he said abruptly. "She found the trial an ordeal, and who can blame her? She doesn't feel strong enough to face people yet, not after some of the accusations Raefe's defense counsel threw at her."

Julienne ran the tip of her finger down his sternum and onto the smooth, hard flatness of his belly. "You mean he isn't keeping her in the New Territories against her will?" she asked disappointedly.

"No." Her fingers were feather light in his pubic hair, and he felt his heavy, flaccid sex begin to stir.

"That is a pity," Julienne said regretfully, cupping his testicles in the palm of her hand, enjoying the feel of the weight of them, watching with satisfaction as his splendid cock began once more to swell.

He closed his eyes. It was impossible that she could arouse him again and so soon, but all the same, it was pleasant to lie back and allow her to try. He had no intention of giving her any information about Melissa. Melissa would have to survive her own hell herself. He certainly wasn't going to cross swords with Raefe Elliot and demand that he bring her back to the Elliot home on Victoria Peak.

Julienne twisted onto her knees, not removing her hand from beneath the delicious weight of his scrotum. "Did you know that there were rumors that the Royal Scots are going to leave the island?"

He didn't know and he didn't really care. He was a businessman, not a soldier. She was running the tip of her tongue lightly around the head of his cock, blowing softly on it, her hand firm and warm on the shaft. "How do you know?" he asked, his eyes closed.

Julienne paused in her ministrations, looking down at his cock with satisfaction as it pulsed and hardened. "A friend told me," she said, and wondered whether she should terminate her affair with her Royal Scots major. To continue spending time with both him and Derry might prove difficult, even for her. She sighed. Derry was really a

most promising lover. It seemed as if her connections with
the Royal Scots would have to be severed.

"Adam Harland thinks it will be a great mistake if they
do go. He thinks the Japanese will attack us and that we
should have more regiments stationed here, not fewer."

"Then he's a bloody fool," Derry said thickly. "Don't stop
what you're doing, for God's sake!"

She bent her head again, her tongue running like a river
of fire from the base of his penis to the tip, whorling
around the blood-engorged head, her hand moving with
slow and rhythmic expertise.

"Is Harland the middle-aged Englishman Stafford's been
complaining about?" he asked. "One of the Semco board
directors out here for some kind of sabbatical?"

Julienne nodded, gracefully straddling him, one knee on
either side of his tensed thighs, smiling to herself as she
saw how his penis was straining upward toward the tight
glossy curls of her pubic hair, the honeyed lips of her
waiting vagina.

"His wife is very young and very beautiful and
very . . ." She paused, thinking of Elizabeth's curious,
untouched quality. "Very inexperienced, I think."

Derry was uncaring of Adam Harland's wife. "By God,
you're not!" he panted harshly as with her fingers she
parted the dense mat of her pubic hair and opened the lips
of her throbbing vagina.

"Now, *chéri*," she whispered hoarsely, gently pulling his
penis back from his stomach until it was pointing straight
up in the air, but still not plunging it into her hot, moist
depths. "Let me show you how the second time can be
almost as good as the first!" As he moaned for her to hurry,
she slowly lowered herself onto the swollen tip, shuddering in ecstasy as the soft pillar of her flesh slid down on him
and she was filled to the rim with his hardness and
thrusting strength.

"Oh, that's good, *chéri*!" she whispered as his hands
grasped her hips, and she moved on top of him in
voluptuous pleasure. *"C'est magnifique!"*

Tom Nicholson and Lamoon were lying on cushions on
the floor of the Harlands' summerhouse. Elizabeth had
been prompt in inviting them to dinner, and many more
dinners and suppers had followed. She had also kept her

word about not gossiping about their affair. No one else knew of it, apart from Helena. Not even Alastair or Julienne.

"We can't go on like this, Lamoon," Tom said fiercely. "I have to speak to your father."

"No!" Her dark eyes were enormous in the pale gold of her face. "That would be the end of everything, Tom. He would send me away or marry me to a suitable Chinese. He mustn't know! Not ever!"

"He can't marry you off without your consent!" Tom said savagely, springing to his feet and pacing the wooden floor. "It's 1939, for Christ's sake! Not the Middle Ages!"

"It is still the Middle Ages for Chinese girls of good family," Lamoon said sadly.

He swore, knowing she was right. Knowing that nothing on earth would persuade her father to allow her to marry an Englishman.

She rose to her feet and walked toward him with infinite grace, her long, black hair hanging sleekly down her back. "Don't feel so violently about it, Tom," she said gently, slipping her arm through his. "It is the way things are and we must learn to accept it."

He pulled her into his arms with a groan. He loved her, but there were times when her Chinese placidity nearly drove him mad. "How can you be so accepting of prejudices that are so crass?" he asked despairingly.

He was a foot taller than she was and she stood on tiptoe, kissing the corner of his mouth. "Because there is nothing we can do, Tom. We both know the rules and whether we agree with them or not, we have to abide by them."

"Damn the rules!" he said vehemently. "Not everyone respects them! Raefe Elliot doesn't and the world hasn't caved in around his shoulders!"

"Of course it hasn't," Lamoon said with amusement. "Raefe Elliot is a man. And the Chinese girls who are his friends are not upper-class, respectable Chinese girls. He is not intent on marrying one of them."

"If he wanted to he would," Tom said darkly.

Lamoon giggled. She thought perhaps Tom was right. But Raefe Elliot wasn't Tom, and she wasn't a Wanchai bar girl. For girls like her, mixed marriages were out. There were no exceptions, no alibis, no discussions. As a businessman, her father conducted himself in a manner that his European customers regarded as enlighteningly Westernized. But in his home, Western mores had no place. He was a rigid disciplinarian, as all Chinese husbands and fathers of his class were. If he once knew or suspected that his daughter was consorting with an Englishman, Lamoon knew she would never see Hong Kong or Tom again.

"We must be grateful for what we have," she said practically, her slender body pressed close to the long, hard strength of him. "If it weren't for the nursing classes, we wouldn't be able to meet at all."

"I am grateful," he said huskily, bending his lips to the soft sheen of her hair. "But one afternoon and one evening a week aren't enough."

The war being waged on China by Japan had worked to their advantage. When Lamoon had asked her father if she could attend nursing classes at one of the local hospitals, he had reluctantly agreed. It was an activity that did not lower the family status and it would be as well for her to be useful if international affairs deteriorated.

Lamoon had enjoyed the classes immensely, but she no longer went to them. Instead she met Tom. At first, the difficulties had seemed insurmountable. They couldn't go for drinks at one of the many clubs that Tom's friends went to with their girls. They couldn't dance at the Peninsula, or hold hands across a candlelit table at the Parisian Grill. If they did so, they would be seen. The Chinese grapevine would hum into life and her father would know of her activities within hours, possibly even minutes.

Instead of going to any of the normal venues, they had driven out into the New Territories, avoiding the more frequented roads, walking hand in hand along little-used tracks. It was on one such excursion that Adam and Elizabeth had seen them, and now they had somewhere else to meet.

The summerhouse was tucked away at the bottom of the sprawling garden, out of sight of the main house. Gradually, as their visits to the Harlands had become more frequent, it was accepted that the summerhouse was their meeting place, and inviolate. On Thursday afternoons, her nursing class day, and if Elizabeth and Adam were out, the houseboy would open the door to them and they would walk through the house and out into the garden and down to the summerhouse.

"I don't understand why you will come here, but refuse to come anywhere near *my* house," Tom had said in the beginning, bemused. "It's only fifteen minutes away."

"Because if anything terrible happened, and it was discovered we were meeting, my father would not lose as much face if it was discovered we were meeting in the home of a respectable married couple as he would if it became known that I had visited you in your home, alone."

Tom was too well aware of how important face was to the Chinese to argue the point with her. Their afternoon meetings had continued, and the little summerhouse had become the center of their world.

He lifted her up in his arms and turned back toward the cushions. They had met at Government House, at a party for influential Chinese businessmen and their European counterparts. Her mother had been ill and Lamoon had taken her place at her father's side. He had never in his life seen a woman so beautiful. Her hair had shone like burnished jet, her dark, almond-tilted eyes had flickered once in his direction, then had been demurely cast downward, but he had seen the suspicion of a smile at the corner of her mouth, and he had known that she was as attracted to him as he to her.

He had known, right from the beginning, that to try to date her was crude and impossible. Chinese girls of her social background did not date *anyone* without their father's permission and certainly not Europeans. But he had persisted. He had driven out to her family's mansion at Shan Teng and waited until he had seen her being driven from the grounds in a chauffeured Rolls. The Rolls had taken her to an exclusive hairdressing salon in Victoria. When she came out of the salon an hour later, he was waiting for her on the pavement, and to his indescribable relief, she agreed to meet him. That had been the first of her skipped nursing classes.

The following months had been the most torturous he had ever known. She had come to meet him willingly, her mouth parting shyly beneath his when they had kissed, but he had known that he couldn't make love to her with the same selfish lack of thought as he might have done with a European girl. If she became pregnant, there could be no hasty marriage to make matters right. She was running risks enough in merely meeting him. He couldn't ask her to run even greater ones, ones that would destroy her life.

He wasn't accustomed to celibacy, especially when it was coupled with such raging physical longing. At first, he had been unable to sustain it. He had had a brief and not altogether unsatisfactory affair with Julienne, and there had been occasional forays into the bars and nightclubs of Wanchai. He had soon stopped such expeditions. The bar girls with their long black hair and pale gold skin had been cruel reminders of Lamoon, so like her, and yet so many light-years different from her.

At the beginning of the year, when he had left Hong Kong for a business trip to England, he had been relieved at their separation. It would enable him to think clearly, perhaps to find the strength of mind to end their affair once and for all. When he had seen Elizabeth Harland aboard the *Orient Princess*, he had been filled with hope. If any woman could banish Lamoon from his thoughts, surely the ethereally beautiful Elizabeth could do so. But she had not been another Julienne, sexually indiscriminate and looking for fun outside her marriage. In the end, he had never even propositioned her. He had known that such a venture would end in failure and, by then, he had known that it was too late. No woman, not even Elizabeth, could replace Lamoon in his heart.

"We *have* to be able to marry!" he said fiercely as he lowered her onto the cushions. Christ! He had been in love with her for eight months, and for the last four months he had been totally celibate. It wasn't a situation that could possibly continue. She lay very still, her hair spreading around her shoulders like a pool of black ink. "We cannot marry," she said softly, her eyes holding his, the expression in them one he had never seen before. "But we can be husband and wife to each other. . . ."

His breathing became short and quick; his heart hammered against his breastbone. "No," he rasped. "There are too many risks for you."

She slid her arms around his neck. There were too many risks for her if he did not make love to her. He was a handsome, healthy, thirty-five-year-old man, unaccustomed to celibacy. If he did not make love to her, the risks were that he would turn elsewhere for lovemaking. To the pretty, sexy Mrs. Ledsham, or to the bar girls of Wanchai. And she wanted him to make love to her. She wanted to feel his strong, hard body naked against hers. She wanted to take what happiness she could before their affair was discovered, and before her father sent her far away.

"I love you," she whispered, and as she spoke she was unbuttoning her cheongsam, her fingers trembling. But her eyes were utterly sure as she stepped gracefully free of it.

Tom was a man of iron self-control, but that control had been exercised to the full for the best part of a year. He hesitated for one brief, agonizing second and then, with a groan, he too began to scramble out of his clothes. Restraint was gone, and in its place was a burning, savage hunger, demanding to be satisfied.

"I love you . . . love you . . ." he gasped hoarsely as he flung his trousers and shirt on top of her discarded cheongsam.

He had always imagined that when they finally made love it would be with the utmost tenderness. She was a virgin; she would need time, gentleness. Never in his wildest dreams had he imagined it would be like this. A voracious scramble to free themselves of their clothes, an animallike eagerness to transcend the bounds he had previously placed on them. She knelt in front of him, her breasts pale and beautiful, the dark centers erect and taut. He cupped them in his hands, glorying in her beauty, then bent his head to them, kissing, sucking, nibbling.

"Quickly!" she panted urgently. *"Quickly!"*

He pressed her backward, his hand dropping to the small panties she still wore. His palm closed over her mound of Venus and she moaned, digging her nails into the flesh of his back. She was smooth and hairless, soft as silk. He wrenched her panties down to her knees, to her ankles, knowing as she kicked herself free of them that he was going to be all the things he shouldn't be. Quick. Urgent. Brutal.

"Oh, God!" he prayed, but it was no use. He had waited too long for her to exercise restraint or tender loving care.

His fingers touched her and she gave a willing cry, the cry of a small, wild animal on the verge of copulation. She was hot and moist, as ready for him as he was for her. With a groan that seemed to come from the soles of his feet, he guided his penis to the entrance of her vagina, his mouth bruising and grinding against hers, his tongue plunging deep as he thrust into her dark, sweet center, experiencing a cataclysm of relief that almost robbed him of his senses.

Afterward, when he could breathe again, when his body had stopped shuddering with pleasure, he became conscious of the wetness of tears on his shoulder. He pushed himself up onto his elbows, looking down at her with horror. "Lamoon . . . sweetheart . . . don't! It won't always be like that, I promise!"

Through her tears she began to laugh. "Oh dear, won't it? And I thought it was so wonderful!"

Relief swamped him. Her tears were not because he had hurt or disappointed her. They were a release of her emotions, and he felt tears sting the back of his own eyes. "Oh, God, I love you," he said passionately, folding her once more in his arms, lying with her on the scattered cushions, delighting in the feel of her small, delicate, exquisite body next to his.

She turned her head slightly, kissing his shoulder. "I have to be going," she said regretfully. "The class will be at an end in twenty minutes."

He stifled his disappointment. Chu, her father's chauffeur, would be waiting for her at the front entrance of the hospital. He had to get her down to Victoria and to the rear entrance five minutes before the nursing class ended. Then she would walk through the hospital, emerging from the front entrance as if she had been to class and no questions would be asked.

He sighed, reaching for his trousers. He knew that Lamoon thought that their becoming lovers was as far as they could take their relationship, but for him, today had been only the beginning. Snatched hours one afternoon and one evening a week were not enough. He had been speaking the truth when he had said that a way would have to be found to enable them to marry. He zipped up his trousers and fastened his belt buckle. Perhaps Raefe Elliot could help him. He knew how the Chinese thought. He would know the best way to approach Lamoon's father. He held out his hand to help her stand. He would see Elliot at the earliest opportunity. Lamoon may have accepted that they could never marry, but he would never do so. Not while he had breath in his body.

*   *   *

Ronnie Ledsham sat in the Peninsula Hotel's Playpen Restaurant and watched the doors, a small smile crooking the corner of his mouth. Elizabeth Harland would get the surprise of her life when she asked for Julienne's table and found only him waiting for her. Julienne would be furious when she found out how he had enticed Elizabeth, but he was accustomed to Julie's fury and it never lasted. Within minutes she would be giggling and he would, of course, tell her that his ploy had been in vain and that Elizabeth had rejected his advances. In reality, he was determined that he would do no such thing.

He had already had one double whiskey and soda and he raised his index finger slightly to summon the waiter and order another. The Playpen wasn't one of his usual haunts. He found the long, narrow room, with its lush red carpeting and potted palms and red-shaded table lamps, far too colonial and prim and proper, but it was a rendezvous that would arouse no suspicions in Elizabeth's mind, and it had one mitigating factor in its favor: its windows afforded splendid views, looking out over the harbor and the cloud-wreathed majesty of Victoria Peak.

He glanced at his watch. She was five minutes late. He had thought women only kept men waiting, not their women friends. He wondered if he had been too confident in thinking that his ruse would work. It would have been normal for Julie to have rung Elizabeth and have asked her to lunch, not to send a note. His smile deepened. He had been proud of that note. He had long ago perfected an imitation of Julie's hasty scrawl and he thought that he was now beginning to also capture the flavor of her breathless messages. *"Darling Elizabeth,"* he had written, *"I saw this dog collar in Lane Crawford and thought it perfect for your little dog and please, please, please do me a favor and meet me for lunch at the Playpen tomorrow at one o'clock as I'm in the most awful trouble and Ronnie is going to kill me! Please, please, please! Love and kisses, Julienne."*

Elizabeth would be furious, of course, when she was led to his table, but he was confident that she wouldn't walk away. That she would, at least, stay and have lunch with him. It would be the first time he had been able to arrange matters so that they were on their own. His drink was finished and he ordered another. It had been a long time since he had been in such determined pursuit. Women were to be enjoyed and not taken too seriously. The last thing he wanted was a heavy-weather love affair. He usually knew, instantly, whether a woman would be troublesome or not, and if his sixth sense gave out alarm bells, then he left her well alone. He wanted fun, not a divorce or a rift with Julie.

He sipped his whiskey and soda thoughtfully. It was hard to tell whether Elizabeth Harland would be trouble or not. There was something about her that teased and tantalized him, something he couldn't quite define. There was a self-contained, untouched quality about her that he found very disturbing sexually. A woman so sensually beautiful had no right to carry with her such an air of unconscious innocence. Not for the first time he found himself wondering what her sex life with Adam Harland was like, and his penis swelled hot and hard against his tight trousers. My God, but there were one or two things he'd like to do to her that would take that untouched look from her eyes! He wondered if her pubic hair was as silver-blond as the hair she always wore so sleekly coiled. Why the devil did she never wear it down, loose around her shoulders? He imagined it sliding through his fingers, brushing across his stomach, his thighs.

The doors at the far end of the room swung open and she stepped into the room. The *maître d'hôtel* was at her side instantly. He saw her ask for Julienne's table, her eyes flicking around the room in an effort to locate her. He saw the *maître d'hôtel* mouth the words, "This way, madame," and begin to lead her between the white naperied tables and carved chairs, to where he waited for her. As they approached, the *maître d'hôtel's* eyes were expressionless. Ronnie's generous tip had ensured his wholehearted complicity.

Elizabeth's eyes met his, and he saw a pucker of puzzlement crease her forehead. A brilliant turquoise skirt swirled around her long, sun-kissed legs; a silk shirt of palest mauve tantalizingly skimmed her breasts; her sandals were high and delicate, tiny gold straps so insubstantial he wondered how on earth she could possibly walk in them.

He rose to meet her, his smile wide. "I'm glad you could make it, Elizabeth. You look fantastic."

Her green-gilt eyes were uncertain. "I'm sorry, I don't understand. Where is Julienne?"

The *maître d'hôtel* was pulling out her chair. Ronnie waited until she was seated, and then, sitting opposite her, said, "Julienne was called away. She asked me to take her place. Are you familiar with the menu here? The seafood is out of this world."

Elizabeth wasn't interested in the seafood. She said coldly, "I don't believe you, Ronnie. You're lying."

His grin widened. "Of course I am," he said with what he hoped was endearing charm. "I always do."

She pushed her chair back, about to rise to her feet, and he shot his hand out, circling her wrist restrainingly. "Don't go, Elizabeth. I want to talk to you. Please stay."

For once Ronnie looked and sounded sincere, Elizabeth thought. She sank back in her chair. Perhaps he really did want to talk to her. Perhaps Julienne really *was* in trouble.

"All right," she said reluctantly. "Could I have a martini, please? With lemon."

He ordered her drink, asking for another whiskey and soda for himself. He was beginning to feel pleasantly inebriated and his words were slightly slurred as he said, "You really are the most difficult girl to speak to alone, Elizabeth. I had no choice but to resort to subterfuge."

The waiter was waiting to take their order. "I'll have the melon and plain omelette," Elizabeth said, without looking at the leather-bound menu. She was wrong in thinking that Ronnie wanted to talk to her about Julienne. He was making yet another pass, and the sooner she could decently take her leave of him, the better.

"I'll have the mixed hors d'oeuvres, the beef Wellington, and a bottle of burgundy," Ronnie said, feeling eminently pleased with himself. As the waiter departed, he took her hands across the table. "Elizabeth, Elizabeth, *beautiful* Elizabeth, don't look so cross. I only want to spend a little time with you."

She tried to pull her hands free, but his grasp tightened. She wondered how much he had had to drink.

"We've been through this scene before, Ronnie," she said with as much patience as she could muster. "I like you a lot. I think you're amusing and good fun, and I definitely do not want to have an affair with you. Now can we let the subject drop? Otherwise we'll no longer even be friends."

The wine waiter poured the wine. Ronnie tasted it and

signaled him to fill their glasses. "You have entirely the wrong idea about me," he said, ignoring his hors d'oeuvres and drinking the wine appreciatively. "I'm not at all the womanizer I'm made out to be. The fact is . . ." He imprisoned her hands once more, and the slur in his words was more pronounced than ever. "I'm *terrified* of women. What I need is a woman to be a friend to me, to understand me, to . . ."

She didn't hear the rest of his sentence. Over his shoulder at a nearby table she saw a familiar figure. She felt her cheeks flush scarlet as Ronnie continued to grasp her hands tightly and as Raefe Elliot's eyebrow quirked upward inquiringly.

"Ronnie! For God's sake let go of my hands!" she hissed, aware that it wasn't only Raefe who was casting a curious look in their direction.

Ronnie was reluctant to do so, but the impossibility of both holding her hands and drinking his wine prompted him to acquiesce. He reached for his glass and accidentally sent it flying. A crimson stain flooded the virgin white tablecloth, sprinkling her turquoise skirt with ugly dark spots.

Ronnie looked at the damage in bemusement. He was drunker than he had thought, which was foolish of him when there was so much at stake. Elizabeth was pushing her chair away from the dripping table, a waiter was rushing over to them with a clean cloth, and Raefe Elliot was standing over them both, saying to Elizabeth in lazy amusement, "Glasses are very unstable things in your vicinity, aren't they, Mrs. Harland? Allow me," and he took a napkin from the table and unceremoniously blotted the stains on her skirt while the waiter stood by superfluously.

"I think this lunch has come to its natural end, don't you?" he said in a matter-of-fact tone and, without waiting for her reply, took her hand, drawing her to her feet.

"Give my good wishes to Julienne," he said to Ronnie, who was gazing at him in open-mouthed bewilderment. "Tell her I've escorted her friend home and that no damage has been done."

"Just a minute . . ." Ronnie protested. "What the hell . . . ?"

The expression on his face was so comic that Elizabeth found herself laughing.

" 'Bye, Ronnie," she said, and feeling as if she were drunk herself, she allowed Raefe Elliot to lead her from the room and out through the Peninsula's marbled lobby and into the street.

Chapter Ten

R AEFE made no attempt to release his hold on her as they stepped out beneath the porte cochere. She was aware of the doorman bidding him a respectful good-bye; of a long, low, and sleek, ice-blue Lagonda sliding to a halt in front of them; of the parking attendant stepping out of the car and opening the door for her.

She tried to regain control of the situation, to behave with her usual cool dignity.

"Thank you for escorting me from the restaurant," she began, her voice so still and cracked she barely recognized it as her own. "I'm very grateful, but I have my own car and—"

"I'm sure you have." There was a quirk of laughter at the corner of his mouth and utter assurance in his eyes. "But as I couldn't help but notice that you had left your lunch untouched, I thought we would rectify matters."

"I'm sorry, I couldn't . . ." Her throat was so dry she could hardly speak. Dear God in heaven! If she couldn't sustain a rational five-minute conversation with him, how could she ever hope to survive lunch?

"I insist," he said, and though his amusement at her resistance was naked, his dark, rich voice brooked no argument.

"I have engagements . . ."

His hand was beneath her arm. He had replaced the attendant at the door of the car and was standing so close to her that she could smell the faint tang of his lemon-scented cologne, feel the warmth of his breath on her cheek. She was excruciatingly aware of his lean, hard strength. Of his whipcord muscles beneath the lightweight jacket; of his fingers burning like a brand on the bare flesh of her arm.

"Break them," he said, and, staring into his gold-flecked eyes, she wondered again at the tiny white scar knifing down through his left eyebrow.

Her chest was so tight that she could hardly breathe. No one, ever before, had held her in quite such a way. There was ownership in his fingers. Complete confidence. She knew she couldn't possibly go with him. Adam would be furious. They would be bound to be seen and she had told Adam that she was lunching with Julienne. The complications, when she tried to explain to him, would be endless. Raefe's fingers tightened fractionally on her arm, and she felt a sudden, giddy surge of elation. She didn't care. It was only a lunch. She was doing nothing wrong. Nothing to be ashamed of.

"All right," she said, sitting in the passenger seat, her legs trembling violently. "I will."

He grinned down at her, white teeth flashing in his sun-bronzed face. He had never had the slightest intention of allowing her to refuse. He strode around to the other side of the car, opened the driver's door, and slammed it behind him.

"Now," he said, as he gunned the engine into life, "tell me what the hell you were doing having lunch with a womanizer like Ronnie Ledsham!"

Never had she believed it possible for anyone to drive down Nathan Road at such speed. Rickshaws, taxis, bicycles, hawkers, all were circumnavigated with a skill and dexterity that left her breathless.

"It was unintentional," she said as they rocketed past Kowloon Park and the road that led to Helena's little flat. "I thought I was going to meet Julienne."

He shot her a swift glance and she looked away from him quickly, disconcerted by the immediate understanding she saw in his eyes. It was as if there were already a bond between them, as if they were already speaking in the oral shorthand of long-married couples. But not all couples. Adam would not have understood her so completely. He would have been puzzled. He would have asked her what she meant. Why she hadn't met Julienne as she had intended. Why Ronnie had been there in her place.

She said, trying not to think of Adam, hating her feeling of disloyalty, "Where are we going?"

"To a small restaurant I know near Sham Tseng."

His hands on the Lagonda's wheel were sure and strong. She wondered what such hands would be like on her naked flesh and was appalled at her lasciviousness. Panic swamped her. She shouldn't have come. She should have thanked him for extricating her from Ronnie's company, then she should have declined his invitation to lunch and driven straight home by herself. She wasn't Julienne, she wasn't accustomed to dealing with a man as fast and sophisticated as Raefe Elliot. A man who kept his own wife a prisoner. A shiver ran down her spine. Who was to say what he would do to her, if she were to disappoint him?

"We're nearly there," he said, and as he shot her a down-slanting smile, her panic ebbed. She was behaving like a sixteen-year-old on a first date. Nothing was going to happen to her. She wasn't going to disappoint him because he wasn't going to ask anything of her. They were going to have lunch together. They were going to exchange the kind of conversation they would have exchanged if they had met at one of Tom Nicholson's or the Ledshams' parties. And afterward, she would tell Adam and they would laugh about Ronnie's idiocy and its unexpected consequences and she would probably never see Raefe Elliot again, not on his own.

The Lagonda slid to a halt outside a small building with a plain front, its windows covered by blinds. "It's all right," he said as he saw the expression on her face. "It's not a Triad-run gambling den. It's a very respectable restaurant."

When they stepped inside she wondered if she was dreaming. Small tables were covered with white damask tablecloths; glasses sparkled; silver gleamed. It was like being in a small bistro on the Left Bank in Paris, not a Chinese restaurant fifteen miles from the center of Kowloon.

He ordered dim sum and an ice-cold bottle of Mou Tai. It was obvious that he was as well known to this headwaiter as he was to the headwaiters at the Peninsula and at the Repulse Bay.

"It's little known, but patronized heavily by those who

do know it," he said as the waiter hurried away with their order.

"And who is it that knows of it?" she asked curiously.

"Government officials, high-ranking civil servants, people who want to get away from the tumult of Victoria and Kowloon for an hour or two."

She nodded. She could see at a glance that it was both exclusive and expensive. She had asked for a Cinzano and as she sipped her drink he said, "Until now, you've never given me a chance to say how sorry I am for hurting your feelings, but I am. However . . ." his eyes held hers steadily ". . . I'm not sorry for what I said. It still stands. If your husband thinks he can come out here and enjoy a skirmish with the Japs that will enable him to return to England a hero, he's badly mistaken."

She wondered why she felt no anger. She said, returning his gaze unflinchingly, "My husband was awarded the Military Cross in the Great War. He is already a hero."

"I never said he wasn't a brave man," Raefe said placatingly. "Only that he was ignorant of the situation out here, and that his view is a foolish one."

The dim sum were wheeled to their table on a trolley. As the steaming bamboo baskets were set in front of them, she said stubbornly, "Maybe so, but it's a view that is held by a lot of people who have far more experience of the Orient than Adam. Sir Denholm Gresby is in agreement with him, and Alastair Munroe, and no one could accuse Alastair of being a fool."

"I could," Raefe said with annoying equanimity. "Alastair is a military man, and like most military men he isn't overblessed with imagination. He's been told by his company commander that the Japanese pose no real threat, and he accepts what he is told. But he's wrong."

"And Sir Denholm?" she asked, knowing very well what he would think of Sir Denholm.

He snorted in derision. "Denholm Gresby is a classic example of British obduracy. He actually believes that the Japanese can't see in the dark and that we need never fear any night attacks from them! He's an old duffer who should be pondering the mistakes his kind made in the last war, not seeking to perpetuate them if there's another!"

She suppressed a smile. He was almost as vehement about Sir Denholm as Sir Denholm was about him. "Have you lived in Hong Kong all your life?" she asked with genuine curiosity.

"I was born here, but I was educated in the States."

"And you've never considered returning to America to live and work?"

The grin was back. "No, Hong Kong is in my blood and in my bones. It's where I'm happy and it's where I belong."

She suppressed a smile. Ronnie had said that the Elliots were an old New Orleans family. Although Raefe was adamant that Hong Kong was where he belonged, she could quite easily imagine him strolling through the French Quarter, his hair curling low at the nape of his neck, as swashbuckling and as handsome as a legendary riverboat gambler. There was a fearlessness about him, a daring, an insolence toward life that both excited and intrigued her. She couldn't imagine him ever compromising, ever settling for less than what he wanted. Raefe Elliot wouldn't have abandoned his studies at the Royal Academy to please anyone. Nor would he have left London for Hong Kong if it was in London that his future career was being forged.

His hands reached out across the table and took hers, and at his touch, an impulse of sensuality went up inside her like a flare.

"What are you thinking about?" he asked disconcertingly. "Your eyes are unhappy. I want to know why."

She said, with an ease that stunned her, "I was thinking about my music. About how much I long to be back on a concert platform again. How desperately I resent the opportunities I am missing!"

"You're a musician?" There was surprise in his voice, then he looked down at her hands. At the long, slender, supple fingers, the short oval nails, and he said, "Tell me about it. Tell me all about yourself. Your dreams, your wishes. Your fears."

She made no attempt to free her hands from his. "For as long as I can remember, I have played the piano. It is so much a part of my life that I cannot imagine existing without it. It is what I am. A pianist. And when I am deprived of the opportunity to develop my talent and to progress, as I am now, then I feel . . ." She shrugged expressively. "Then I feel as if I'm being bodily starved."

He nodded, and she knew that he did not think she was being histrionic. He understood. "I think," she said, "I was

born with the ability to play the piano. My mother was
very musical and she taught me from when I was very
small. When I was six, I was professionally taught, and
once it was explained to me how the lines and dots
worked, I was able to read music very quickly. By the time I
was seven, I could sight-read. I learned so fast once I had
started, it was as though it was something I already carried
inside me, as though I knew how to play without needing
to be taught."

"What happened?" The dim sum was forgotten. The
waiters were watching them with resignation, sensing that
it was going to be a long time before they took their leave.

"I won a scholarship to the Royal Academy of Music in
London and then, when I was ten, my mother died."

"And?" he prompted gently.

"And my father needed me to be with him." There was
no resentment in her voice, and he noticed how her eyes
softened as she spoke of her father.

"He was a gypsy at heart." An impish smile touched the
corners of her mouth. "Though a luxury-loving gypsy! We
spent our time traveling between Paris and Nice, Geneva
and Rome. There wasn't much time for piano lessons,
although I had a Steinway in our permanent suite at the
Negresco."

"What happened then," he asked, intrigued, wondering
how the hell she had come to be married to Adam Harland.

"Daddy died when I was seventeen. I moved back to
London, began to study once more at the Royal Academy,
and six months later I married Adam."

"Where did you meet him? Was he at the academy too?"
He couldn't imagine it in a million years.

"Oh, no." Her eyes widened in surprise, as if she were
amazed that he hadn't realized she had always known
Adam. "Adam was Daddy's closest friend. I've always
known him, ever since I was a little girl."

So that was it, he thought, intrigued. No parties. No
boyfriends. Just a bereavement that had left her entirely
alone in the world, and a man she had always known as
her father's friend and whom it had seemed quite natural
for her to marry.

"When I was at school in the States," Raefe said, "my
closest friend was Roman Rakowski, the Polish conductor.
He was there because his parents admired the American

way of education. He was a brilliant musician, even then. Nothing else mattered to him. Not food; not girls; nothing. I learned quite a lot about musicians through my friendship with Roman. I learned that their duty is first and foremost to their music. Not to parents, lovers, or friends."

"But most parents, lovers, and friends cannot understand that," she said, and the pain in her voice sliced through him. "Daddy didn't. Adam doesn't."

"Then as much as you love them, you must hurt them," he said, his lean face hard and uncompromising. "Talent, to survive, has to be exercised."

A shiver ran down her spine. She knew that what he said was true, and that there was only so much time she could allow Adam. Already she had allowed him too much.

"Tell me about Roman Rakowski," she said. "He's in Australia now, isn't he?"

Her hands were trapped by his once again. They were strong hands, olive-toned and well shaped. Hands that gave a feeling of security and safety.

"Yes. As a Jew he found the doors of many of the great European orchestras closed to him. For a time he had been with the Berlin Philharmonic, but Hitler's racist policies made his position there impossible. He was not allowed to play or to conduct, or even to teach. He's in Sydney now and he's composing and conducting and doing everything in his power to persuade the Australian government to give more assistance to Jews desperate to leave Germany and eastern Europe."

Elizabeth looked down at her wristwatch and saw with disbelief that it was nearly four o'clock.

"It's late," she said, knowing that she had to go and that she did not want to. "I must get home."

He didn't argue with her. He would see her again, and when he did she would not have to hurry away from him.

They sat side by side in his car and it was as if something unspoken had been understood between them, making words unnecessary. "My car is parked at the Peninsula," she said as they entered the crowded, noisy streets of Kowloon.

He drew to a halt outside the hotel and she was appalled at the prospect of leaving him. He made no attempt to touch her, to arrange another meeting.

She stepped from the car, hardly able to believe that four hours previously she had driven to her luncheon appointment with no sixth sense of the events that were to follow.

"Good-bye," she said. "Thank you for the lunch."

"You didn't eat a mouthful," he said with amusement, and then Lady Gresby's voice could be heard exclaiming, "Elizabeth! What a lovely surprise. Is Adam with you?"

"This is where I leave you to your fate," Raefe said as Lady Gresby bore down on them. Grinning devilishly, he pressed his foot down hard on the accelerator and swept out into the maelstrom of late afternoon traffic.

"Who was that?" Lady Gresby asked curiously, squinting her eyes against the sun, and then, not waiting for Elizabeth to reply, said, "For one moment I thought it was that terrible Mr. Elliot!"

Elizabeth did not enlighten her. She was suddenly tired and wanted desperately to find somewhere cool and quiet where she could think. She excused herself from Lady Gresby as quickly as she could and then, instead of returning straight home, she drove right to the top of Victoria Peak and parked her car. Folding her hands on the wheel, she leaned forward, staring out over the vista of sea and sky and distant mountain peaks.

It really had been the most extraordinary afternoon. She had been out with the most notorious man in Hong Kong and he had not so much as laid a finger on her. And she had wanted him to. Oh yes, if she was honest, she had wanted him to. Despite the heat, she shivered. She was twenty-five, and for the first time in her life she had met a man with whom she wanted to go to bed. And she couldn't do so for she was happily married to Adam.

She hugged her arms. Raefe would ask her to meet him again and she would have to refuse. She wasn't capable of the kind of affairs that Julienne indulged in, affairs that seemed to have very little effect on her marriage. If she were unfaithful to Adam, the very foundations of her life would crumble. She would never be able to look into his dear, kind face again. And if he ever came to know of it, he would not be able to shrug the knowledge off as Ronnie Ledsham would. He would be devastated, utterly destroyed.

Slowly she leaned back and turned the key in the ignition. Raefe Elliot had revealed to her a side of her nature she had never previously believed existed. As she began to drive back down the Peak toward her home and her husband, she knew that she wasn't grateful to him. She would far rather have remained in ignorance.

"Did you have a nice day, darling?" Adam was sitting out in the garden, reading the *Hong Kong Times* and drinking a cold beer.

"Yes."

He raised his hand to her and she gave it a loving squeeze before sitting down on one of the cane chairs next to him.

"How was Julienne? Still miffed at Ronnie?"

"Yes. No. I don't know."

He put down his paper and looked at her inquiringly. She felt her stomach muscles contract sickeningly. She had never lied to Adam, and there was no need for her to lie now. Her disloyalty to him had not been physical. It had merely been mental. She said, with a quick, bright smile, "I didn't have lunch with Julienne. There was a mix-up over the dates. I'm lunching with her next week."

"You should have come down to the tennis club. I beat Stafford six-two, six-one in straight sets."

She smiled and she waited expectantly. "I ran into Raefe Elliot at the Peninsula," she said, "and he insisted on taking me to lunch so that he could apologize over the drinks incident."

Adam had been looking at her with unfettered pleasure in his eyes. Now the pleasure died, replaced by incomprehension. "But I thought *you* spilt the drink on *him?* It isn't his position to apologize, surely?"

"Oh, he was quite cross at the time," she said, trying to sound carelessly indifferent and failing miserably. "I think it was that he really wanted to apologize for."

"I see." Adam's brow was furrowed and he plainly did not see at all. "So what did you do? Have lunch with him at the Pen?"

"No." She didn't turn her head to meet his eyes. Instead, she studiously watched a blue magpie as it darted down through the trees. "We went to a restaurant out near Sham Tseng. It was very nice, darling. We must go there ourselves sometime. . . ."

"Sham Tseng!" he asked incredulously. "That's miles away!"

"Only about fifteen miles," she said, her gaze still on the magpie's glossy plumage. "He dropped me off at the Pen. I saw Miriam and she invited us for drinks on Sunday—"

"Good God! She didn't see you with Elliot, did she?" Adam exclaimed, jumping to his feet. "I *told* you not even to contemplate having lunch with him!" He ran his fingers through his still thick hair, seriously perturbed. "It will be all over the club by tomorrow!"

"No, it won't," she said soothingly, rising to her feet and taking his hand. "The sun was in her eyes and she didn't recognize Raefe. There won't be any talk, and if there is, why should it matter? I was having a perfectly respectable lunch, just as I often have with Tom—"

"Raefe Elliot isn't Tom Nicholson!" Adam said savagely, disliking the easy familiarity with which she uttered Elliot's Christian name. "Any woman seen out alone with Elliot automatically risks her reputation!"

"I can't imagine why," she said crisply, letting go of his hand and picking up the newspaper and his empty glass. "He was perfectly charming and he didn't make a pass at me, unlike Ronnie Ledsham who *always* makes a pass! And whom you count as your friend!"

"You never told me Ronnie had made a nuisance of himself to you," he said, his voice dangerously harsh. "What happened? When? Where?"

They were on the verge of a furious row and she was desperate to avert it. "Oh, goodness, it doesn't matter, darling. Ronnie makes a pass at *everyone*. All I'm trying to say is that we should make up our own minds about people. Not simply believe everything that we hear. I had lunch with Raefe Elliot; he made his apology. He didn't make a pass at me, and I certainly shan't be having lunch with him again. Now let's go indoors and have a drink and forget all about it." She tucked her hand into his arm. "Miriam says the rumors about the Royal Scots being transferred to Europe are untrue. They are going to be here for another year at least. Perhaps by the time they do go, Helena and Alastair will be married."

She had expected that Raefe would telephone her the next morning. He telephoned her that night. She was in her bedroom putting the finishing touches to her hair and makeup. They were going to a Russian-style nightclub in Wanchai with a group of friends from the tennis club.

There was a light knock at her bedroom door and Mei Lin entered, saying in her bird-soft voice, "Mr. Elliot is on the telephone, missy."

Elizabeth's hand faltered as she put down her hairbrush. "Thank you, Mei Lin." She walked quickly out into the wide, cool hall, grateful that Adam had not been in the room, and had not overheard Mei Lin's message.

Raefe's dark, rich voice sent a ripple of pleasure down her spine. "I'll meet you at one o'clock tomorrow at the ferry."

"No!" She had meant to sound cool and detached and was furious with herself at the panic she could hear in her voice. Her hand tightened on the receiver. "No," she said again, this time with more control. "I can't see you for lunch again."

"How do you know it was lunch I had in mind?" he asked, amused. She could imagine the smile tugging at the corner of his mouth, the dark sheen of his blue-black hair as it tumbled low over his brows.

"Whatever it is, I can't come," she said stiffly.

There was an infinitesimal pause, then he asked softly, "Why? Because you didn't enjoy yourself this afternoon? Or because you enjoyed yourself too much?"

"Because I enjoyed myself too much," she whispered, and unsteadily put the receiver down on its rest, not wanting to hear his voice for a moment longer. She was terrified that she would weaken, that she would tell him she would meet him anyplace, anywhere, anytime.

When he rang back again in five minutes, she instructed Mei Lin to tell him that she was no longer at home. And all through the next few days she adamantly refused to take his calls.

Two weeks later Elizabeth and Adam joined the Ledshams, Helena, and Alastair at a beach party at Tsuen Wan in the New Territories. "This is the beginning of the Gin Drinkers' Line," Alastair said to Adam, pointing up into the hills to a distant line of recently constructed pillboxes. "Work began on those in thirty-seven when there was talk of a division from Singapore reinforcing the garrison. They never came and so work was halted. Not much use having a defense line this far forward if there aren't enough troops to man it."

"How far does it stretch?" Adam asked curiously.

"Eleven miles. It zigzags all the way from here 'round to Ma Lau Tong on the east side of Kowloon. In some places they did quite a lot of work. For example, near the Shingmun Redoubt, a mile or so east of here, they dug trenches, added cement overhead protection, and studied fields of fire."

"Why did they call it the Gin Drinkers' Line?" Elizabeth asked.

"Look at the glass in your hand," Alastair said, laughing. "It's because this spot, where it starts, is so popular for parties."

"Do you think they'll reactivate work on the line if plans go ahead for a civilian volunteer force?" Ronnie asked. He was lying flat on his back on the sand, Julienne's sun hat over his face.

"I shouldn't think so. Even if every civilian in Hong Kong were trained and armed, there still wouldn't be enough men to hold a line so far up-country. The best line of defense is the strait between Kowloon and the island."

"Gee, thanks," Helena said dryly. "And what happens to people like me, living in Kowloon, if yellow hordes come thundering across the border and the British Army is tucked safely away across the straits?"

"They catch the ferry, my love," Alastair said easily. "And the chances of such an event ever happening are extremely remote. Japan is in no position to attack us, or, apart from China, anyone else."

Julienne removed a bottle of gin and a bottle of tonic from a capacious picnic hamper and poured a generous amount of each into a glass. "I have heard you have lots of sick men at the moment," she said to Alastair. She had terminated her affair with her major, but it had been done in a satisfactory manner. In bed, with a lot of laughter and gossip.

"You mean malaria?"

She nodded. "I don't understand why anyone should be sick with it. Not when the army gives out quinine tablets and mosquito repellent cream."

"The Royal Scots think they are under divine protection," Ronnie said, grinning. "No creams and tablets for our brave Lowlanders, eh, Alastair?"

"If men do scorn the medication they're given, then they're fools," Alastair said, refusing to be riled. "Mosquitoes are not respecters of persons. They'll bite a Royal Scot just as soon as they'll bite an Englishman."

"I won't let them bite you, *chéri*," Julienne said to Ronnie, rubbing sun oil into his shoulders. "Mosquitoes, ugh. Nasty, vicious little creatures!"

She began to hum happily beneath her breath. Her affair with Derry was going very well. She smiled to herself, remembering their lovemaking of the previous afternoon. Derry possessed what her major had lacked: a sexual imagination nearly as inventive as her own.

Helena, helped by Alastair, began to spread out picnic food on a crisp white cloth. Yogurt-cheese balls in a jar of golden olive oil, smoked eel pâté with crackers, a crunchy apple salad, fennel and salami and black olives, a raised pork-and-apple pie that she had made herself the previous night, sesame bread sticks, grape tartlets, a melon crammed with raspberries, rum and raisin fudge squares, and, for Alastair, an almond-encrusted Dundee cake.

"Good girl," Alastair said with relish, and seeing the swift deep smile that Helena gave him, Elizabeth wondered if perhaps Helena had changed her mind about not loving him enough. They certainly seemed to be very happy together, and there was a contentment about Helena that had been conspicuously lacking when she had first met her.

"I think I might take a stroll and have a look at those pillboxes," Adam said, rising to his feet and brushing the sand from his trousers.

"It would be much more sensible to have a swim," Julienne said suggestively, her eyes telling him that if he accepted, it would also be a lot more fun.

"Later, perhaps," he said. "When I come back."

Julienne sighed, then giggled at his preferring a climb in the hills to a swim alone with her. She had been flirting shamelessly with him for the last two months and there were times when she wondered if he was even aware of it. Whatever else Adam was, he was not a romantic. She looked across at Elizabeth and wondered if she minded. She was wearing white shorts and a pink cotton halter top, her long legs seeming to stretch forever, her skin honey-gold, her hair coiled high in a loose knot, so blond that it looked like spun silver.

"Why do you never wear your hair down, Elizabeth?" she asked as she wriggled provocatively out of her dress, revealing a daringly cut French bathing costume.

"It's cooler like this," Elizabeth said, plunging two bottles of champagne into a bucket of cool sea water.

"If I had hair that color, I would wear it down all the time," Julienne said, sweeping her own vibrant red curls up beneath her bathing cap. "It would be like a sheet of gold hanging to your shoulders and would make you look even younger than you do already." Her eyes widened, comprehension dawning suddenly. *"Tiens!"* she said as she fastened her bathing cap. "So *that* is why you wear it always so sleek and so prim and proper." She laughed delightedly. "I promise I will not tell!" she said mischievously as Ronnie raised himself up on one elbow, demanding to know what all the hilarity was about. "I shall be as quiet as the little mouse." Still laughing, she ran down across the beach and plunged into the foam-flecked waves.

Ronnie gazed at Elizabeth. Adam was a good hundred yards away, climbing a rocky gully that led to the first of the pillboxes. Helena and Alastair were sitting with their heads close together, deep in conversation. It was the first time, since the debacle of their lunch at the Peninsula, that he had had the opportunity to speak to her alone.

"I rather ruined things the other week, didn't I?" he said regretfully. "Too much to drink too soon, that was the problem."

"There wasn't a problem at all," Elizabeth said easily. "You simply made an error of judgment."

"Meaning that you're not remotely interested in helping me to while away the long, hot days of a Hong Kong summer?" he asked, and though his voice was teasing, there was unmistakable heat in the electric blue depths of his eyes.

"None at all," she said lightly.

He heaved an exaggerated sigh of disappointment, then asked, "You didn't tell Adam about my . . . er, error of judgment, did you?"

"I didn't tell him how you lured me to the Peninsula, but I did tell him that you had made a pass at me. It came out in the course of a conversation about someone else entirely."

"I see." He rolled over onto his stomach, squinting at the small figure that had nearly reached the top of the gully. "I thought he'd been a bit cool toward me lately. That's a pity, I like old Adam." He turned back to look at her. "I don't suppose you will tell me who the person was you were discussing when my name was mentioned?"

She grinned. "No." She drew the champagne out of its makeshift ice bucket and felt it speculatively.

"Is that cold enough?"

"Nearly." She plunged the bottle back into the water and he said, "I hadn't realized till our lunch at the Pen just how very friendly you were with Raefe Elliot."

"I'm no more friendly with him than I am with you or Tom or Alastair. In fact, not nearly so much."

He grinned. "You're a damned sight more friendly with him than anyone realizes. I imagine Julienne would be *very* intrigued if I told her that the last time I saw you, Raefe Elliot was leading you with an iron-strong grasp from the Playpen Restaurant!"

"But you can't tell her any such thing," Elizabeth said, laughing. "Not without revealing what you were doing there and *why* Raefe was escorting me away."

He thumped the sand in mock anger. "Damn me, if you're not right again. However, take a word of warning from one who knows." His eyes were suddenly grave, his voice no longer bantering. "Raefe Elliot isn't a man to tangle with lightly, Elizabeth. I'd steer far clear of him if I were you. Even for a woman like Julienne, Raefe Elliot would mean trouble, and for you and Adam . . ." He shrugged expressively.

"Don't worry about me and Adam," Elizabeth said with sudden fierceness, hugging her knees close to her chest. "I would never let anything hurt Adam, not ever!"

"I'm glad to hear it," Ronnie said with sincerity. "Now, pass me one of those bottles and let's have a decent drink."

It was eight in the evening before they left the beach for home, Ronnie and Julienne in Julienne's little Morris, the rest of them squeezed tight in Alastair's larger car. By the time they reached Kowloon the shadows were lengthening beneath the banyan trees that lined Nathan Road and Elizabeth was on the verge of sleep.

Suddenly her eyes flew open. There was no mistaking

the pale blue Lagonda in front of them, or the virile, broad-shouldered figure at the wheel. She glanced quickly at Adam, but he was talking to Alastair, and no one else seemed to have realized that the car in front of them was being driven by Raefe Elliot.

She looked again, and this time she sucked in her breath sharply. He wasn't alone. A small, sleek, dark head was resting lovingly against his shoulder. She could see the gleam of earrings, the rich brocade of cheongsam. As she watched, he turned his head, laughing down at the delicately featured, pale gold face at his side. Then Alastair turned right toward Helena's flat and the Lagonda continued on down Nathan Road.

There was a pain in her chest as if a dagger had been driven between her shoulder blades. She wondered where they were going. To the Peninsula perhaps, to a dinner dance? To the Parisian Grill? Wherever it was, it was none of her business. She hadn't, surely, expected him to sever all romantic ties merely because he had once taken her out for lunch? Her nails dug deep into her palms. Dear heaven! He hadn't even made a pass at her! On the telephone she hadn't allowed him to say why he wanted to see her again. It was probably only to give one of his girlfriends cut-price piano lessons!

"Here we are, home again," Helena said to her as they slid to a halt. "Hasn't it been a glorious day?"

But Elizabeth didn't answer her. She was sick and tired, appalled at the ferocity of her jealousy, confounded by the depth of her physical longing.

"Let's go straight home," she said to Adam as Julienne's little Morris swerved to a halt behind them.

He looked down into her face, shocked at how tired and drawn she suddenly looked. "Okay, sweetheart," he said, his arm tightening around her shoulders. "We'll go home and have an early night. It's been a long day."

Chapter Eleven

❧

RAEFE rolled over in bed, feeling for his wristwatch on the bedside table. He looked at it and groaned. Five-thirty. He had thirty minutes to reach Kai Tak and the Northrop waiting to fly him to his meeting with Colonel Sandor in Singapore.

By his side Alute began to stir, moving toward him, her hands lightly caressing his chest, moving enticingly lower. Regretfully he swung his legs from the bed and strode into the bathroom.

"Oh!" At his abrupt departure Alute's eyes shot open in disappointment. "You are going so soon?"

Steaming hot water from the shower gushed down over his head and shoulders. "It's five-thirty," he shouted. "Go back to sleep."

"Sleeping alone is no fun," she protested sulkily. She hated his business trips to Singapore. There were so many girls there and she lived in fear that he would find one he preferred to her and bring her back with him. Perhaps, horror of horrors, he would even install her in his house on Victoria Park.

Alute had never been inside the house that Raefe had shared with his wife. He no longer lived there, preferring his luxury apartment in Central, and although Alute often stayed the night in this apartment, she had still not managed to fill the closets and drawers with her dresses and lingerie. To her chagrin, she was still not his number one girl and there were times when she wondered if she ever would be.

He walked back into the bedroom, magnificently naked, and rifled through a drawer for underpants and socks. Water glistened in his hair and gleamed on his strong shoulders.

She wound the sheet seductively tight around her slim body and knelt on the bed. "Can't you spare just ten minutes?" she wheedled, letting the sheet slip down to expose a small, tip-tilted breast and dark-gold nipple.

He grinned, dressing with practiced speed. "No," he said, and there was no regret in his voice. He had more important things to think about than sex.

For the past two years, unknown to anyone, even Melissa, whenever he visited Singapore on a necessary business trip, he also visited military headquarters at Fort Canning, reporting to British Army Intelligence on any suspicious Japanese activity.

After dressing Raefe strode into the sitting room, unlocked his wall safe, and removed two thin files. There were times when he wished the British had never approached him. They asked for information, they received information, and, in Raefe's eyes, they did nothing with it. He slammed the wall safe shut, grabbed a small overnight bag from a chair, and was out of the apartment before his sleepy houseboy could even ask if he wanted coffee.

Colonel Sandor finished reading Raefe's report, then laid the file back on his desk, his mouth tight-lipped. "Do you really believe in the accuracy of this report, Mr. Elliot?"

Raefe met his eyes unflinchingly, his face grim. "Yes, I do."

Sandor drummed his fingers on the file and then pushed it away abruptly. "Even if you are right, and these men *are* Japanese intelligence officers, we can't expect the Foreign Office to expell them, as you suggest. *We're* not at war with Japan. It's the Chinese who are at war with them. Such an action on our part would cause no end of a diplomatic row!"

Raefe's nostrils flared. "Sooner or later Japan is going to attack Hong Kong and Singapore," he said, keeping control of his fury with difficulty. "When she does, we don't want her having access to every detail of our defensive strength! At the moment, there are five Japanese army officers in Hong Kong who are supposed to be learning English, but in fact their sole reason for being here is to build up a finely detailed picture of our present and proposed defenses. They must be expelled immediately! To allow them to remain, knowing what we do, is insanity!"

Two angry spots of color touched Colonel Sandor's cheeks. "Your task is to ferret out facts and report on them, Mr. Elliot. It doesn't extend to commenting on action that is or isn't taken!"

Raefe was enraged. He could only hope he would have the pleasure of seeing Sandor's face when the Japanese poured south, battle maps of the island's defenses in each and every pocket.

"The other Japanese you've named," Sandor continued. "Are you convinced of your facts?"

"Positive," Raefe said through clenched teeth. "The Japanese barber at the Hong Kong Hotel holds the rank of lieutenant commander in the Japanese Navy. At the moment he cuts the hair of the governor, the commissioner of police, the officer in charge of the Special Branch, and the chairman of the Hong Kong and Shanghai Bank!"

Colonel Sandor's face was pale. It was one thing to be told that the barmen and masseurs of Wanchai were listening assiduously to the gossip of British troops and reporting anything of interest back to Tokyo. It was quite another thing to think of men like the governor and the commissioner of police being lured into unsuspecting gossip by their barber. A shiver ran down his spine as he remembered his own trim and shave earlier in the day. He had been bowed from the chair by his Japanese barber, feeling as if he were a million dollars. Under those relaxing conditions it was very easy, for even the most careful of men, to talk carelessly.

"What about the Italian waiter at the Peninsula Hotel? Are you sure of him as well?" he asked tersely.

"As sure as I can be. And the jeweler in the Queen's Arcade."

Sandor grunted. The prospect of Japanese spies in the hotels and bars and shops of Hong Kong was not a cheering one. Even less cheering was Elliot's second report.

"How long do you think this Chinese fifth column, as you style them, has been infiltrating into Hong Kong?"

"Probably ever since the Japanese installed a Chinese as puppet leader over the parts of China they have conquered. It's Wong Chang Wai's followers who will be helping the Japs, if and when they attack. They are being recruited by the Japanese in Formosa and then brought over to the Chinese-Hong Kong border. Entry is easy. All they have to do is mingle with the refugees entering the island every day."

"And you think that the Japanese have armed them?"

"I'm sure they will have partially armed them," Raefe said grimly. "And I'm also sure that they will be well primed as to what acts of sabotage would most damage us."

Colonel Sandor passed his hand over his eyes. He could imagine the damage they could do all too well. Sniping at isolated and vulnerable posts, acting as dispatch riders, spreading false rumors, and signaling to their Japanese masters the positions of guns and pillboxes. Dear God, it would be mayhem. It was hard enough for British troops to differentiate Japanese from Chinese; it was absurd to expect them to be able to differentiate between Chinese sympathetic to them and Chinese prepared to stab them in the back.

He hoped devoutly that Elliot's assessment of the situation was wrong and had the sickening feeling that it wasn't. When it came to the Chinese and Japanese, Raefe Elliot's instinct was unerring. Sandor picked up the files. It was up to the Foreign Office to deal with the Japanese seconded from their army on the pretext of learning English. They, at least, should be easy to get rid of. As for weeding out Wong Chang Wai's followers . . . He doubted if even Elliot himself could accomplish that task.

Raefe slammed out of military headquarters, small white lines etching his mouth. Both the reports he had submitted were damning and he doubted if action would be taken on either of them. There would be those among the High Command who would regard Japanese spies in Hong Kong as a joke. "What harm can they cause?" he could imagine them saying. "The Japs will never have the nerve to attack. Another gin and tonic, old boy?"

He stormed into the blistering heat of early afternoon. The British didn't want the bald truth. They wanted innocuous reports they could write memos about, shuffling them from department to department, theorizing and temporizing over them. His car was waiting at the gates and he yanked open the rear door.

"Raffles," he said curtly to his Malay driver, sinking back

against the cracked leather upholstery. He had other business to conduct while in Singapore, but first he needed a long, cold drink.

As the car sped down wide avenues flanked by trim grass verges and frangipani trees, he wondered why he and his father and his grandfather had preferred Hong Kong. Their business interests had always had firm roots in Singapore. It was Singapore godowns, as well as Hong Kong godowns, that bore the name ELLIOT & SONS in large black lettering. A mirthless smile touched the corner of his mouth. The "& Sons" no longer had any meaning. He had no son and, as long as he remained married to Melissa, there wouldn't be one. Not one he could acknowledge.

The car sped past the spire of St. Andrew's Cathedral and down to the waterfront. Perhaps he had never settled here because such large parts of the city were so English. There was something gentlemanly about Singapore that was lacking in the hurly-burly of Hong Kong. The Malay driver slowed down reluctantly for a policeman directing traffic. Basketwork wings here strapped to the policeman's back so that he did not need to wave his arms in the heat, but merely had to turn his feet in order to direct the cars. The heat was stifling and a trickle of sweat ran down Raefe's neck before they picked up speed to cruise past the green lawn of the Cricket Club, with its football and cricket pitches, tennis courts and bowling greens. He had no time for a game of tennis on this trip.

Two years ago the International Rubber Regulation Committee had raised the output quota to ninety percent of what Elliot & Sons was capable of producing. The reason had been the increased demand by America for rubber, and it had meant vast profits. Extra labor had been employed and very few people, apart from Raefe, had stopped to wonder *why* the Americans were suddenly stockpiling rubber. He had seen it as an indication that the American government was increasingly apprehensive about a war in the East that would cut off their supplies. When he had suggested this in an official report to goad the British, it had been politely discounted.

A year ago the boom had come to an abrupt end. Rubber stocks were so high that the price had slid to rock bottom and now Elliot & Sons was handling more rubber than ever, and losing money at the same time. New markets had

to be found and Raefe was on the verge of closing a deal
with an Australian company. But first he needed to know if
he had the rubber available to deliver. And that meant a
detailed discussion with his general manager at his head
office on Robinson Road.

The car sped up the palm-flanked drive to the rambling,
ornate, Victorian splendor of Raffles Hotel, and he felt his
fury at Colonel Sandor's negative attitude begin to dissi-
pate. With luck his report would reach Whitehall and with
even greater luck, someone, somewhere, would take note
of it.

The tables beneath the vast, roofed veranda were full,
but as he entered, a waiter scurried over to him and a table
was cleared. As he crossed to it, acknowledging people he
knew, he stopped short, his heart hammering violently.

She was sitting near a tall, fanlike fern, her head averted,
her blond hair knotted high at the back of her head. He felt
his mouth go dry, then he moved toward her. She turned to
her companion, laughing at a remark he had made, and
Raefe saw that it wasn't Elizabeth at all. Just an exceptionally pretty woman who had none of Elizabeth's grace, or
sensuousness, or sexually arousing fragility.

He continued to his table, ordering a double Scotch and
soda, thunderstruck at the depth of his disappointment. At
this moment the last thing he needed was an emotional
involvement with a married woman. Despite his very
strong physical attraction to Elizabeth, he had felt an
element of relief when she had adamantly refused to have
any further contact with him. But he hadn't, for one
moment, forgotten her. She was impossible to forget.

The waiter was at his elbow and he ordered a curry tiffin.
Had she really believed he was going to accept her refusal
to speak to him on the telephone, to meet him again? The
woman who was a pale caricature of her rose to her feet
and left the room. He knew that if it had been Elizabeth, it
would have been as if a light had gone out, or the sun had
disappeared behind clouds. There was a luminous
radiance about her, a gentleness that he had never encountered in any woman before. And yet she was tough. He
remembered the way she had spoken to him about her
music, the passion that had entered her soft, smoky voice.
A smile crooked one corner of his mouth. He doubted that
her passion had ever been unleashed on her dull and
steady husband.

* * *

When Raefe's plane touched down at Kai Tak two days later, Derry Langdon was waiting for him, sitting at the wheel of a Jeep, a battered sun hat on the back of his head, a cigarette between his fingers.

Raefe ignored his own car and walked over to his brother-in-law. He liked the easygoing and affable Derry and found it hard to believe that he had been spawned from the same gene pool that had produced Melissa.

"How was Singapore?" Derry asked as Raefe swung himself into the Jeep.

"Hot and colonial," Raefe said briefly. "What's the matter, Derry? New trouble?"

Derry took a last puff at his cigarette, then dropped it to the floor of the Jeep, crushing it out beneath his sandaled foot. "Pa insists that Melissa return to Victoria. He's going to take out a court order claiming you're holding her against her will."

"Your father's a fool!" Raefe said savagely. "Damn it all, can't he get it into his thick skull that I'm trying to save Melissa's life?"

Derry shrugged helplessly. "He doesn't believe things are that bad. He thinks it was unhappiness that drove her to drugs and Jacko, and that you're the cause of her unhappiness. His reasoning is, if he takes her away from you, then she's bound to start recovering."

"If he believes that, he'll believe anything!" Raefe said explosively, running his fingers through the thick tumble of his hair. "Christ! If she comes back to Victoria now, no one is going to believe she was an innocent victim!"

"Pa doesn't see it that way. He says if she returns to Victoria everyone will be able to see that she is fine and it will confirm the belief that she was only labeled a drugtaker in order to provide you with a defense."

"Well, we both know that's not true, don't we?" Raefe said wearily.

They were silent for a minute or two, then Derry asked, "How is she?"

"A mess." His voice was curt but Derry could hear the underlying pain and despair.

He stared moodily out over the airfield. His sister had always been headstrong and willful—and heartbreakingly pretty. Their parents divorced when he was twelve and

Melissa ten. Their mother's new lover had not relished being encumbered with her children, so custody had been awarded to their father. He had compensated for the disruption of their lives by spoiling them both excessively. Derry had enjoyed the spoiling and, as far as he was aware, it had left no long-lasting ill effects on him. But Melissa . . . He sighed.

As a child she had demanded and received instant gratification of all her needs. And she had continued to do so as an adult. Her feline, seductive prettiness ensured that she was rarely crossed. Her father had said it was a pleasure to indulge her, and her many boyfriends had seemed to think likewise.

And then she had married Raefe. The match had alarmed his father who, despite Raefe's wealth, regarded him as socially dubious. If the fellow had a touch of the tar-brush about him, he didn't want it showing in *his* grandchildren. Derry had laughed at his father's fears and thought that at last Melissa was showing good sense. Raefe Elliot was a distinct improvement on the chinless wonders she had previously dated.

Even now he didn't know what had gone wrong. He suspected that Raefe had tried to curb Melissa's childish selfishness and that Melissa, unaccustomed to restraint, had rebelled by indulging in flagrant flirtations with Raefe's friends. If she had hoped that the fear of losing her would make him heel like a pet dog, she had been very wrong. His friends had been embarrassed and Raefe had been indifferent, outwardly at least.

Furious, Melissa had cast her net wider, and from the minute Derry learned of her affair with an officer serving with the Middlesex, he had known that her marriage to Raefe was doomed. He didn't know when the drug-taking had started. Heroin was easily available in Hong Kong and it was her lover in the Middlesex who had introduced her to the habit. She began by using it with what she thought was sophisticated carelessness, plunging with hideous speed into desperate addiction. It was then that his liking for his brother-in-law had turned into respect.

When Melissa confronted Raefe with the truth of her affair, she also maliciously told him she was pregnant, and that though he was the father of her child, he would never know for sure whether she was telling·the truth. Raefe took one look at the blond, blue-eyed, pale-skinned specimen she had broken her marriage vows for and knew immediately that there would be no doubt as to the parentage of the child once it was born. Until it was, there would be no divorce. And no scandal. Melissa discovered that her lover, who had promised to love her for eternity, was not quite so constant when faced with an ultimatum that he either stop seeing her or receive the thrashing of his life. It was then that the family had become aware of her growing heroin addiction.

Raefe had taken her to Perth, to a doctor who specialized in conquering drug addiction, but Melissa had no desire to be freed of her craving and he had been unable to help her.

Raefe had brought her back to Victoria and a week later she miscarried. The baby was dark-haired and brown-eyed and it had died of heroin poisoning before it had even been born.

A month later Raefe returned home from a trip to Singapore and found Jacko Latimer in her bed. Derry didn't know if Raefe had meant to kill Latimer. He wouldn't have blamed him if he had. But, with or without intent, Jacko Latimer had died and they had all had to endure the long-drawn-out agonies of the trial. Melissa had been the least concerned. She was supremely indifferent to Latimer's death, and seemed almost as indifferent to the sentence Raefe would receive if he was convicted of murder. It was while they were in court, Raefe tense and strained, his father hunched and suddenly old, that Derry had come close to hating his sister. He said now, "Is she still on it?"

Raefe nodded. "In decreasing amounts. And the stuff she is getting is clean, unlike the dirt that Latimer was feeding her."

"But how long can you keep it up? She won't stay in the New Territories against her will forever."

A mirthless grin touched Raefe's mouth. "She isn't there against her will, Derry. She's there because she wants to be. She doesn't want to be in Victoria with your father fussing around her, watching her every move. She wants to be where she has access to heroin, even if it is in decreasing amounts."

"And will it work?"

"It's got as good a chance of working as anything else.

Every member of the household staff is one hundred percent loyal to me. She's receiving her heroin under almost medical conditions and she's being weaned, very gradually."

"And when she is?" Derry asked curiously. "Will you both move back to your home on the Peak?"

"Good God no! I'll never live with her again!"

"Then why not divorce her now? Why keep on trying to cure her when all you get for your pains is the accusation that you're keeping her a prisoner and mistreating her?"

"Because she's my wife," Raefe said tightly, "and my responsibility. Because when I divorce her, I want her to be fit and physically able to start a new life on her own."

"And if she isn't?"

The lines around Raefe's mouth deepened. "She will be," he said, swinging himself down from the Jeep. "Just tell your father she's better off where she is than in Victoria, where every petty drug pusher in town can find her and proposition her."

He strode across to his Lagonda, grateful that Derry hadn't asked to visit Melissa. Derry shoved his Jeep into gear, gave him a wave, and then disappeared in a cloud of dust down the road leading toward Kowloon. Raefe wondered if he was still enjoying his affair with Julienne Ledsham and grinned. If the affair was still in progress, he would be enjoying it. Julienne would see to that.

Raefe was at the intersection of Chatham and Salisbury roads when Tom Nicholson, driving his sleek Packard, slammed his hand on the car's horn, waving for him to pull over.

Raefe sighed. He was hot and tired and wanted nothing more than to get home and shower and sleep. He pulled over and Tom screeched to a halt in front of him, then vaulted from the Packard and strode toward him. "You're just the person I want to see. I've been ringing you for the past two days, but your houseboy said he didn't know when you would be returning. How was Singapore?"

Raefe knew Tom wasn't interested in Singapore, so he ignored the question and said, "I only touched down an hour ago. Whatever it was you wanted to see me about, can't it wait?"

"It can," he said reluctantly. "But I'd appreciate it if you could spare me ten minutes, Raefe. I've got problems and I don't know who else can advise me."

They were only a hundred yards or so away from the Peninsula. "Okay," Raefe said wearily. "Let's go down to the Long Bar and talk over a couple of drinks."

"Thanks," Tom said, his eyes showing his gratitude. "I'll follow you."

He walked back to his Packard. Raefe once more put his Lagonda into gear and cruised down the remaining stretch of Salisbury Road and into the Peninsula's luxurious forecourt.

"What's the problem?" he asked Tom when they were sitting with their drinks, fans whirring coolingly above their heads.

"Prejudice!" Tom said succinctly.

A glimmer of a smile touched Raefe's mouth. "Who is she?" he asked, as a waiter removed their glasses and replaced them with two more.

"Lamoon Sheng."

Raefe's brows rose expressively. No wonder Tom had problems. "How the hell have you been managing to meet?"

"Deception," Tom said distastefully. "She goes to nursing classes every Monday and Thursday. The family chauffeur drops her off at the front entrance of the hospital and picks her up."

"Only she never goes to classes?"

"She used to. Before we met. Now she simply walks straight through the hospital to the rear entrance, and those few hours are the only time we have together." His voice was bitter and Raefe, knowing the impossibility of Tom taking Lamoon Sheng anywhere publicly without knowledge of it reaching her father, asked curiously, "Where do you go?"

"To the Harlands'. They are the only people who know about us and Adam Harland has been very supportive."

"He would be," Raefe said dryly, a nerve beginning to tic at the corner of his jaw. "He knows damn all about the Chinese or what would happen if Lamoon's deception were discovered."

"At least he's free of the stinking racial prejudice that seems to afflict everyone else!" Tom said explosively. "It isn't as if it's only the whites! The Chinese are just as bad. Smiling at us and deferring to us, and scorning us behind our backs! The hypocrisy of it drives me wild!"

Raefe's smile was cynical. He knew damn well that Tom had never previously given a thought to the racial undercurrents that divided Hong Kong. Before he had fallen in love with Lamoon Sheng, he would have been as horrified as anyone else if a Chinese had stormed the gates of his favorite club. "It's changing," he said mildly. "If there's a war in Europe, it will come over here and then everything—even Hong Kong—will change."

"Christ! I can't wait for a bloody war to change things! I want things to change now!" He leaned toward Raefe, his hands clasped between his knees, his eyes urgent. "I want to marry her, and I want you to tell me the best way of approaching old Sheng in order to ask for his consent."

Raefe shook his head. "There isn't *any* way you can approach Sheng and ask for his daughter's hand in marriage. Lamoon isn't a Wanchai bar girl with no family to protect her. She's the only daughter of a very rich man. A very rich *Chinese.* He'd have your balls if you even suggested that you wanted to marry her."

"It's 1939, not 1839," Tom said persistently. "He's a businessman. He deals with Westerners every day. There must be *some* way of approaching him!"

"He's a leader of the Chinese community, Tom. He's a respected man, and in his eyes his honor would be shamed if it was known that his daughter was in love with a European. If you persist in seeing her, sooner or later you'll both be found out and then you'll never see her again."

Tom groaned and ran his fingers through his hair. "She isn't a minor. She's twenty-one, for God's sake."

"It would make no difference if she were forty-one," Raefe said, looking at him pityingly. "She's subject to the rigid discipline of a Chinese family bound by autocratic rules impossible to violate, subject to the will of a father whose authority, by Chinese custom, is absolute. It's a system that can't be bucked, Tom. Not yet. Not till European and Chinese ideas about color and culture change dramatically."

"Fuck the system!" Tom said savagely, the skin tight across his cheekbones, his well-shaped mouth thin and straight with pain. "If the only way I can live with Lamoon is by kidnapping her and taking her away from this caste-ridden place, then by God, that's exactly what I'll do! At least in America we could live together openly and not be socially ostracized!"

"Would Lamoon be happy living like that?" Raefe asked quietly. "She's been brought up as a dutiful daughter, deferring to her father in all things. The fact that she risks so much to meet you as she does is remarkable, but would she be able to face the thought of never seeing her family again? Of being the cause of their loss of face? Family honor, to a Chinese, is more important than life itself. I don't see how she could make the adjustment. No matter how much she loves you."

Tom drained his glass. The set of his jaw was determined. "When I need your help with Sheng, can I depend on having it?"

"Yes," Raefe said, rising to his feet. They left the bar together, and he added with grim humor, "When you do face him, you're going to need all the help you can get!"

Raefe left Tom outside the Peninsula and drove with unaccustomed tiredness the short distance to the vehicular ferry. The crossing took only eight minutes, and a quarter of an hour later he was in his flat in Central, standing, his face upward, beneath a gushing shower. One of his houseboys was busily preparing a meal, while the other was pouring him a large Scotch on the rocks.

There was still a lot of work to do for intelligence. He stepped from the shower, shaking water from his hair, and swaddled a towel around his hips. He was in a unique position to ferret out information from British intelligence. He spoke Cantonese and commanded Chinese respect on a far deeper level than the day-to-day, smiling obsequiousness habitually accorded Westerners. His grandmother had been Eurasian, and though he could quite easily have denied it, he never had. He was in the rare position of being acceptable, with only slight reservations, in both Chinese and European society.

He lit a cigarette and strolled across to the huge window that looked out over the streets and squares of Central, and the piers and densely packed harbor.

His wealth cocooned him from the worst aspects of prejudice. Englishmen wishing to do business with Elliot & Sons conveniently forgot that old man Elliot had married a woman whose skin was pale gold and not white. Besides, apart from the dark hair, there was nothing very Eurasian about the Elliots. Both Raefe and his father had been educated at prestigious American universities. They were rich, and old man Elliot's peccadillo was conveniently forgotten. At least it was forgotten unless there was a question of an Elliot marrying one of their daughters. Then prejudice reasserted itself with a vengeance. No one wanted a dark-skinned throwback as a grandchild. It was a risk best not taken. When Melissa Langdon had married Raefe, there had been sighs of relief from anxious fathers, and Colonel Langdon had been, and still was, a man much sympathized with.

Raefe smiled grimly. He was well aware of their fears, and of how groundless they were. His grandmother had been Polynesian, not Chinese. Her skin, and the skin of her forebears, had held only the merest hint of color. The chances of a child of his being born dark were infinitesimal. Not that he cared. His grandmother had been a princess whose line of breeding went back much further than any of the Englishmen who murmured askance about his being allowed into their bars and clubs. She had been beautiful and courageous, working alongside his grandfather in up-country Malaya and in Sumatra, as responsible for the founding of Elliot wealth as his grandfather had been. If she had been as black as coal, he would have been equally uncaring and just as proud of her.

Across the Kowloon peninsula the sky was flushed, the swift pink twilight of the tropics falling swiftly. Whisper-ings about his racial background had long since ceased to perturb him even faintly. But they had made for inner loneliness when he was a child, and that loneliness still remained. He crushed his cigarette out in a jade ashtray. He had thought that his sense of separateness was over when he married Melissa. He had thought he was gaining a beautiful wife who would also be his lover and his friend. The bitterness of his disappointment still seared.

Melissa was incapable of offering loyalty, or the kind of companionship on which a marriage could be built. She had only her body and her face, and they had both been so enticing that, God help him, he paid no attention to her other qualities until he had gotten his ring safely on her finger and enjoyed her tantalizing sexuality at his leisure.

Realization had been torture. She had wanted him to treat her as her father had. To indulge and flatter and pamper, and to seek nothing back in the form of companionship at all. He indulged her financially to the best of his not inconsiderable ability, but he refused to allow her to shout at and be physically abusive to the amahs and houseboys who had served him since he was a child. There were tantrums, sulks. And then the flirting had begun. He exercised a patience he had never known he possessed. Realizing that he no longer loved her, he tried sweetly to make her see how foolish she was being. Because he had not flown into the jealous rages she craved, her flirtations became wilder and more socially embarrassing. His friends made excuses and no longer visited them, and then Melissa, unable to arouse the attention she sought on home ground, sought it elsewhere. At the Cricket Club and the Swimming Club. And men like her major in the Middlesex were only too happy to oblige her.

Raefe stared broodingly out over the harbor. His own behavior had not been blameless. After she had lost his son he had had as many women as he chose to reach out for. Sophisticated, clever, decorative women. Women whose husbands and fathers were the backbone of Hong Kong society. And there had been other women too. Women like Alute. Practiced women of great grace and beauty. And not one of them had touched his heart or his emotions. Until he had met Elizabeth Harland.

He swung away from the window, his frown deepening. What the devil was it about her that so intrigued him? He was accustomed to beauty in the women who graced his arm. It wasn't only her pale, blond beauty that intrigued him, though. It was something else. Some quality he had felt instantly in accord with. Beneath her smiles and her husky laughter she was as desperately lonely as he was, as out of touch with those around her, as untouchable, as unreachable. But not with him. She had felt the same instant recognition as he had. He had seen it in her eyes, heard it in her voice. And she thought that by refusing to speak to him or to meet with him, she could escape the consequences of that recognition.

A smile quirked the corners of his mouth. She was wrong. There were some things in life that were inescapable, as she would very soon discover.

Chapter Twelve

M RS. Harland is not at home," Mei Lin said nervously. Elizabeth stood three feet away from her, every line of her body taut with tension.

Raefe gave a disbelieving chuckle. "You make a bad liar, Mei Lin. Tell Mrs. Harland that if she won't speak to me, I'm coming around. I'll be there within ten minutes."

Elizabeth's hand shot out for the telephone. "No!" she gasped, appalled at her physical reaction to his voice. She knew that the last thing on earth she wanted was to confront him beneath her own roof.

The tone of his voice changed. "I'll meet you at the foot of Peak Road," he said gently.

She opened her mouth to protest, but no sound came. Then she heard him replace his telephone receiver and she knew that she didn't want to protest. She wanted to see him more than she had ever wanted to see anyone in her life.

"I'm going out," she said unsteadily to Mei Lin. "When Mr. Harland returns from his game of golf, please tell him that I've gone for a drive and that I'll be back in time for dinner."

"Yes, missy," Mei Lin said, but her eyes were worried, her voice unhappy. She liked Mr. Elliot, but he had a bad reputation where women were concerned. And she knew that Mr. Harland would not like it if he learned that his wife was surreptitiously meeting him.

Elizabeth ran upstairs to her bedroom. She took a white linen jacket from her closet and picked up her leather, ivory-fastening clutch bag from her dressing table, then paused for a moment to look at her reflection in the mirror. Her hair was glossy and sleek, coiled low at the back of her neck. Her face was pale, almost ashen, her eyes enormous, the pupils dilated. It was the face of a woman on the edge of some dreadful abyss. And all she was doing was meeting Raefe Elliot at the bottom of Peak Road.

She took a deep, steadying breath. She was being a fool. He wasn't interested in her. He was more happy with his petite, fragile-boned Malay girlfriend. And if he were interested in her, it would make no difference. She was happily married to Adam. She was doing what women and men do in Hong Kong every day of the week. She was meeting an acquaintance of the opposite sex for a chat and possible lunch. It was all perfectly harmless and she was revealing a pathetic lack of sophistication by behaving as if it were an event of earth-shattering importance.

Having suitably scolded herself, she left the house. Her hands were steady as she backed her Buick out of the large double garage. She would talk to him about Simon Hausner. She had read in a London newspaper some time ago that Hausner had been instrumental in helping Polish violinist Bronislaw Huberman establish a first-class orchestra in Palestine, composed entirely of Jewish musicians who had fled the Nazis. It would be interesting to find out more about it. Toscanini had conducted the inaugural concert, and she remembered Professor Hurok saying that the program had been a long and demanding one, including works by Brahms, Rossini, Schubert, Mendelssohn, and Weber.

Her hands tightened on the wheel. She couldn't remember the last time she had been able to talk intelligently about music with anyone. Adam listened to her politely when the London papers arrived and she was able to read the latest concert reviews. But he only listened to her. He didn't enter into any discussion, and she knew he was always relieved when the conversation turned to other subjects.

The road twisted down between forests of bamboo and fern and stunted Chinese pines. Raefe Elliot wasn't a musician. Why did she feel she could talk to him about music? Why did she feel she could talk to him about any subject under the sun? She sped past a traditional four-story Chinese house that had been built by a rich merchant in age-old Chinese male chauvinistic style, with one story apportioned to each of his wives. Why did she feel so alive when she was with Raefe? So aware of all her senses? She had looked at his hands on the wheel of his car when he had driven her to Sham Tseng and she had physically ached with the need to have them on her naked flesh. A wave of guilt surged up toward her throat. Why had she never felt like that with Adam? Why, oh why, could she not yearn for Adam in the shameless way that she did for this man she barely knew? This man she was not in love with, never would be in love with, but who by the mere tone of his voice awakened a sensuality in her that had previously lain dormant.

She sped around the last bend and saw his Lagonda parked beneath the trees. For a split second that she was to remember all her life she was tempted to speed past him. Her foot hovered over the accelerator. Then he opened his car door and stepped out onto the side of the road, tall and broad-shouldered in an open-necked silk shirt and white flannels, and her foot came down hard on the brake.

She squealed to a halt in a cloud of dust and he walked over to her, grinning. "That was quite an entrance. I could hear you coming for the last two miles."

She stepped out of the Buick feeling foolish, wondering if he thought she had driven at high speed out of burning impatience to be with him again. Then she saw the dark tilt of his brows and the line of his jaw and the curve of his mouth, and she didn't care what he thought.

"It's the car," she said with an answering grin. "It was made for America and wide, open spaces. It doesn't like cautious driving."

He took her arm lightly, proprietorily, and every sexual nerve ending in her body screamed into life. "We'll drive the rest of the way in the Lagonda," he said lightly. "It's British and much better behaved."

"Where are we going?" she asked as he opened the Lagonda's door for her.

"Somewhere quiet. Shek O or Big Wave Bay."

"I haven't brought a bathing suit with me."

He walked around the car and slid into the seat next to her. "It doesn't matter," he said, and there was a wicked gleam in his eyes. "Neither have I."

He drove with swift expertise to Wong Nai Chung Gap and then, instead of plunging down the steep road toward the south side of the island and the golden sands of Repulse Bay, he turned left onto a narrow road she had never traveled before. It curved through densely wooded country, past a magnificent reservoir, then skirted the foot of Mount Collinson and wound down through giant banks of purple daphne and oleander to the tiny village of Shek O.

The sea was azure, and beyond the headland two small islands lay, bathed in a heat haze, insubstantial as mist. He drove on another mile or so, until the rough and unmade road petered out into the hills. They were at Big Wave Bay. The mountains soared up behind them. The bay was tiny and secluded, and there wasn't another human being within sight.

As she stepped out of the car, happiness pierced her like an arrow. It was a shock of joy so physical, so precisely marked, that she was to know, ever afterward, the exact moment at which her world changed.

"Let's swim." He was already pulling off his shirt, kicking off his shoes.

She hesitated only for a second, then she shrugged herself free of her jacket, unzipped her skirt, and let it fall to the sand.

Naked he was even more hard-muscled and magnificent than she had imagined. His broad chest was covered with a light mat of crisply curling dark hair. His hips were narrow, and he was as assured, as unselfconscious naked as he was when dressed in a tuxedo, summoning the waiter at the Peninsula or the Hong Kong Club.

She unbuttoned her blouse and dropped it at her feet, then he reached out his hand for hers. Dressed only in her bra and panties and lace-edged slip, she ran with him over the silver sand and plunged into the azure waves.

The first shock of the water made her gasp aloud. A wave broke over her head, and she began to swim strongly, shaking the salt from her eyes, laughing with pleasure. He trod water for a second, white teeth flashing in his sun-bronzed face as he grinned at her, making sure that she was at home in the water before he struck out in a smooth crawl.

After the heat of the sand the water was blissfully cool and silky, the waves lifting her buoyantly, filling her with exhilaration. There was a faint breeze blowing off the land, its heady mixture of oleander and pine, sweet and sharp, coming in warm puffs through the salt smell of the sea.

"Happy?" he shouted across to her as they breasted the curve of the bay.

An avalanche of foam crashed down on her, then the next wave lifted her high and clear. "I feel as if I've died and gone to heaven!" she shouted back exuberantly. She twisted over to float and let the waves lift and carry her, closing her eyes against the brilliance of the sky.

He trod water, watching her, knowing that the whole course of his life had changed. He had thought himself in love once before and he had been grievously mistaken. He was not mistaken this time. At thirty-two, when he had thought himself too hardened ever to feel love for a woman again, he was experiencing the *coup de foudre*, the thunderclap of unreasoning, instant love. A love he knew would endure. He swam across to her and his strong hands gently circled her waist.

Her eyes shot open, a moment's panic flared through them, and then she was treading water, facing him, her body pressed close against his as the heavy swell of the sea continued to lift them and let them fall. "I want you!" he said harshly. "I've wanted you from the first moment I saw you."

Spray fell over them in a glittering sheet.

"You're crazy!" she gasped, shaking her face free of water, her hands hard against his chest, excitement spiraling through her.

"I know!" White teeth flashed in a sudden grin. "But it's true. And this is one place where you can't run away from me!"

She could feel his heart hammering beneath her hand. Their legs were intertwined as they trod the green-blue water. Spray cascaded from his hair, running in rivulets down his suntanned neck and onto his powerful shoulders. She heard herself groan, a deep, agonized groan almost of pain, and then her arms slid up and around his neck. As his mouth came down on hers in swift, unfumbled contact, her lips parted, her tongue slipping feverishly past his.

A wave broke over them, forcing them apart. Water drummed in her ears, spray streamed down her face. Then she was above the surface once more and in the circle of his arms, and his hands were on her breasts and her thighs as they swam and twisted and turned and touched like two sea creatures, without restraint or inhibition.

When they made for the shore she swam on her back, her arms rising and falling with supple grace, her nipples dark and erect and taut against the saturated silk of her lingerie. He swam easily and strongly at her side, his dark eyes afire with what had previously only smoldered. He constantly reached out to her, sliding his hand along the satin smoothness of her leg, skimming her breasts, twisting onto his back and enjoying the touch of her body next to his as they effortlessly neared the shore.

She felt the soft sand beneath her feet and stood, the waves foaming around her waist. She no longer felt sober or sane or remotely the person she had always believed herself to be. He stood naked at her side, like a magnificent animal, water pouring from his blue-black hair, the lean, tanned contours of his body rippling with strength and virility.

As their eyes met and he seized hold of her hand, running with her up the sand, she felt a moment's blind panic. What if her body betrayed her, denying her as it always had the pleasure she had merely glimpsed?

"What's the matter?" he asked, his brows flying together in concern as he pulled her down beside him, stripping away her soaked silken lingerie.

"Nothing . . ." She gasped as he rolled his weight on top of her, imprisoning her beneath him. She couldn't continue. She couldn't tell him that she was terrified. That lovemaking had never been more than warmth and comfort and gentleness. That the fury and splendor of it had always been beyond her grasp.

"You taste of salt," he said. Then, as his hands circled her wrists, holding her fast, he lowered his head to her breasts, taking a nipple into his mouth.

There was no hesitancy about his movements, none of the near apologetic reverence with which Adam approached her. Raefe was utterly sure, dominantly masterful, and her response to him was instant.

"Quickly, Quickly! Please!" she moaned, spreading her legs wide, consumed by sexual passion, strung on exquisite chords that reached deep within her, demanding satisfaction.

He released her wrists, and his hands were like fire on

her flesh as they ran down her flat belly, across the curve of her inner thighs, skimming the sea-wet, golden curls of her pubis, the engorged lips, pink and moist and craving for his touch.

"Not yet, Lizzie," he whispered hoarsely as her hands tightened in his hair and her hips thrust upward toward him. "Not yet, my darling . . ."

His mouth ground on hers, his tongue plunging deep as his hands ran down to her knees, back up the smoothness of her thighs, until at last when she thought she could bear no more, his fingers slipped inside her. A low, animal cry choked her throat. She could feel herself slippery and wet as the heel of his hand moved with devilish expertise over her clitoris and then, as her nails gouged his back, as she pleaded with him to take her, his hands were once more on her breasts and he thrust deep inside her, filling her until she thought she would die with the pleasure of it.

It was like nothing she had ever known. They moved together in a frenzy of passion, ascending together toward an unbearable summit. A summit she had never reached before, never even imagined existed. Her hands tightened convulsively around him, her voice cried his name again and again and again as the ecstatic point of physical and emotional explosion was reached.

Afterward she lay gasping beneath him, wondering if, in the last few seconds, she had lost consciousness. The reverberations were still beating through her body, singing along her blood as though they would never end.

He was panting harshly, looking down at her with almost ferocious triumph. He had known she had been scared. He had sensed, too, that despite being married, she was inexperienced, almost virginal. There had been a moment, right at the beginning, when he had felt her panic, her resistance, and he had overcome it as he would have with a filly that needed breaking. He smiled, and then, with utmost tenderness, he lowered his head and kissed her gently on the mouth.

"You're very special, Lizzie," he said huskily, tracing the line of her cheekbone and jaw with the tip of his finger. "So special that I'm never going to let you go."

She gazed up into his dark, gold-flecked eyes, so languorous from his lovemaking that she could hardly move. Slowly she shook her head against the sand.

"No," she said, and there was the regret of a lifetime in her voice. "I'm not yours to keep or to let go, Raefe. I'm Adam's and what happened today . . ." Her voice thickened, as if it were full of smoke. "What happened today can never happen again."

She saw disbelief flash through his eyes, then he rolled away from her. Sitting up, he grasped hold of her upper arms and pulled her toward him. "Don't start being consumed by guilt!" he said savagely. "I'm not wanting a couple of one-night stands. A shallow little affair conducted at the Hong Kong Club and the Peninsula and interminable lunchtime cocktail parties! When I say you're going to be my lady, that's exactly what I mean! Mine! For good. For keeps. Christ!" His fingers tightened on her arms so that she cried out in pain. "I'm old enough to know that this sort of thing doesn't happen twice in a lifetime! At my age there's no such thing as infatuation. It's love, and I'm damned well not going to squander it on a furtive, cheap affair!"

Through the depth of her pain she was aware of a deep, all-pervading joy. He wasn't a man who used words lightly. The cataclysm of passion that had overwhelmed her had overwhelmed him also. He believed himself to be in love with her, and she knew, with a shock that left her almost senseless, that against all reason she was deeply, irrevocably in love with him. But she would not see him again. Her loyalty lay elsewhere. Adam had given her his love for as long as she could remember. Together, slowly and with care, they had built something of value. She wasn't going to jettison it because at last she had discovered the depths of her own sensuality.

"I don't want a furtive, cheap affair either, Raefe," she said gently, "and there is no alternative."

"There is!" His eyes blazed as he sprang to his feet, pulling her up against him. "I want you to come and live with me! I want you to be divorced and I want to marry you!"

She shook her head again and the last remaining pin fell free. Her hair tumbled wetly to her shoulders.

"No," she said again, and though her voice was low, there was no equivocation in it. "My marriage is not like yours, Raefe. I'm not tied to a person I no longer love or respect. Adam has never done anything to harm me. All he has ever done is give me his love, and I would never, ever hurt him."

Raefe took her chin between his fingers, tilting her face to his with almost brutal strength. "But you're not in love with him, are you?" he asked. "What we just experienced isn't what you experience with him, is it?"

She twisted away from him, refusing to reveal to him the barrenness of her marriage bed, knowing that Adam deserved that, at least, from her.

Her clothes lay scattered on the sand. She began to dress hastily, her hands trembling as she zipped up her skirt and fastened the buttons on her blouse. Raefe watched her silently for a few minutes, then strode across to where his trousers and shirt lay in a discarded heap. She pushed her blouse into the band of her skirt, appalled at the rift that was yawning between them. A rift that was of her own making. He dressed with the speed and panther-wary grace that characterized all his movements. It had never occurred to her before that a man could be beautiful. She could have watched him for hours, riveted by his slim suppleness, his athletic muscular coordination, the blue-black tumble of his hair as it curled thickly at the nape of his neck.

"I'm not going to take no for an answer," he said, fastening his belt buckle and picking up his shoes. He walked back to her and slid his free hand around her waist. She tried to pull away but he held her easily. "I want you, Lizzie," he said, and there was such burning desire in his voice and in his eyes that she felt her throat dry and the blood begin to roar along her veins. "And to prove to you how much, I'm going to start divorce proceedings immediately against Melissa."

She leaned against him as they walked back to the car. Only the knowledge of how her action would devastate Adam prevented her from flinging her arms around his neck and telling him that she would live with him anywhere, uncaring of the scandal. Uncaring of anything if only they could be together.

"Tell me about Melissa," she said, her voice oddly flat as she stepped into the car. "All I have heard are the rumors. That you treat her appallingly. That she turned to Jacko Latimer for comfort."

"She turned to Jacko Latimer for heroin," Raefe said

bluntly, gunning the Lagonda's engine into life. "Comfort she gained elsewhere. Mostly with a major in the Middlesex. Sometimes with a junior diplomat at Government House. Sometimes, before she saw fit to tell me about her major, with me."

There was such bitterness in his voice, Elizabeth hesitated before saying, "Did you love her very much?"

"I thought I did." He clenched his teeth. "She soon disabused me of the idea."

The sky above Mount Collinson was flushed a deep rose as they sped out of Shek O village and back along the road leading to the gap.

"Will a divorce distress her?" she asked curiously.

He shrugged imperceptibly. "I doubt it. The only thing that distresses her these days is the thought of having her heroin supply cut off."

Elizabeth was silent. She knew nothing at all about drugs. After a little while she asked, "How does she manage . . . now that Jacko Latimer is dead?"

Raefe turnd his head, his eyes meeting hers unflinchingly. "I supply her," he said with a harshness that made her wince. "If I didn't, she would get adulterated muck from Chinese dealers and be dead within six months. As it is, I can regulate the amount she receives. It's impossible to bring her off it overnight. I tried once, in Australia, before I knew about Jacko, and failed. This way takes time, but at least there's a chance it will succeed eventually. And at least she's still alive."

There were tight white lines around his mouth. Elizabeth remembered Sir Denholm Gresby saying that Raefe Elliot was a blackguard who had ruined his wife's life and done his best to ruin her reputation. He had done neither. He had tried to save her life once before and even now, after her behavior had led to his standing trial for his life, he was still trying to save her and to help her.

The daffodil sky of evening engulfed them as they crowned Wong Nei Chung Gap and began to descend toward Victoria.

"I haven't the slightest intention of taking any notice of what you've said," he said forcefully as he pulled up at the isolated spot at the foot of the Peak Road where she had parked her Buick. "I don't give a damn about your husband or your feelings of loyalty. Your life with him is in the past. It's your life with me now that matters."

She turned away from him, opening the car door, barely trusting herself to speak. He strode around to her, trying to take her in his arms, but she resisted with such passion that he released his hold.

"I can't do as you ask!" she cried vehemently. "I've behaved disgracefully enough already and I can't behave like that again."

"Then why did you let me make love to you?" he demanded, his eyes burning, his brows flying together satanically.

She looked up at him one last time. "Because I needed to prove something to myself," she said quietly, and then, her voice choked, "Because I wanted to." Quickly, before he could reach out for her again, she spun on her heel and ran to her car. She didn't look behind her as she wrenched the door open, turned the key in the ignition with trembling hands, then pressed her feet down hard on the clutch and accelerator.

Raefe made no attempt to stop her. She was on the verge of an emotional collapse, and he knew he could achieve nothing by putting more pressure on her. She had to have time to come to terms with what had happened between them. Time to see that her heart, and future, lay with him and not with Adam Harland.

Elizabeth sped up the darkened twists of Peak Road, the lights of Victoria glittering exotically to her right, the dark bulk of the mountain towering up on her left. It was nearly seven o'clock. She had been away from the house for nearly five hours. She tried to remember if they were going out to dinner that evening, if guests were coming to them, and couldn't. She could still feel the heat of Raefe's hands on her inner thighs, taste his mouth, feel the hard strength of his body. She had never imagined that lovemaking could be so ferocious, so exquisitely joyous. She slewed off the road onto the secondary one that led to her home. And then there had been that moment afterward, that moment when he had traced her face with his finger and kissed her with all the tenderness of absolute love. She began to shake. It would be so easy to turn her back on everything and live with him as his mistress. So easy and, for her, so very, very wrong.

She slammed the car into the garage. Adam's Riley was

already parked, his golf bags still on the rear seat. She caught sight of herself in the driving mirror. Her hair hung dishevelled to her shoulders, her face was bereft of makeup, her clothes looked as though they had been flung on. She stepped out of the car and closed the door behind her. She couldn't allow Adam to see her like this. He would think she was ill, that she had been in an accident. She hurried around to the rear of the house and entered by the kitchen door as quietly as she could.

"Mr. Harland is waiting dinner for you, Mrs. Harland," Chan, her number one houseboy, said, staring at her in surprise as she walked quickly through the kitchen toward the back stairs.

"There's no need to tell him that I'm home. I'll tell him myself," she said, bewildering him even more.

"Is there anything I can get you, missy?" Mei Lin asked breathlessly, running after her as she hurried into her bedroom.

"Run me a hot bath, Mei Lin, and lay out fresh underclothes and a dress for me," she said, her heart pounding in case Adam should have heard her enter the house; should see her before she had time to compose herself, to bathe and change.

"Mr. Harland has been very worried," Mei Lin said, pouring cologne into the bathwater as Elizabeth scrambled out of her clothes. "There has been some bad news I think."

Elizabeth stepped into the bathwater, reaching for her bottle of Elizabeth Arden shampoo. The news was probably about Semco. Adam had been spending an increasing amount of time down at the office, and she knew that he had intended lunching with Leigh Stafford before going on to the golf club. She lathered her hair furiously. Whatever his news, it could scarcely be as bad as the news she had so very nearly brought home to him. The news that she had fallen in love with Raefe Elliot and intended spending the rest of her life with him.

She rinsed her hair and stepped out of the bath, wrapped a towel around her head and another around her body. There were bruises on her arms where Raefe had seized her when she had told him she was not leaving Adam.

"Not the short-sleeved dress," she said to Mei Lin as she

hastily put on fresh underclothes. "The turquoise silk with the long sleeves."

She toweled her hair dry, then swept it up into a smooth chignon and secured it with ivory pins. The turquoise silk dress was cool and elegant. She put on delicately strapped high-heeled sandals, sprayed herself with perfume, and took one last look at herself in the mirror. She didn't look like an adulteress. Nothing showed outwardly. Her hair, her eyes, her skin, were just the same. But she had changed inwardly. She was no longer the same woman who had left the house only hours earlier. That woman had been an emotional virgin, and she was a virgin no longer.

Adam was sitting on the veranda, reading the *Hong Kong Times*, a sundowner on the table by his side. At her approach he turned, his usual smile absent, his face grave.

"Hello, darling. I'm sorry I'm late," she said, slipping her arm around his neck and dropping a kiss on his forehead. "I went for a drive and forgot the time."

He rose to his feet slowly and took both her hands in his. "It's happened," he said, the lines around his mouth grim. "The news was broadcast today."

"What's happened?" She was momentarily disoriented, so sickened at the necessity of her cheap lie that her usual perceptiveness deserted her.

"The inevitable," he said somberly, drawing her close into the circle of his arms. "Great Britain is at war with Germany."

Chapter Thirteen

❧

IN Tom Nicholson's driveway, Chinese chauffeurs leaned against sleek and gleaming Buicks and Packards and Chrysler limousines. It was Jeremy Nicholson's sixth birthday and Helena, realizing the limitations of her small Kowloon flat, was holding his birthday party in Tom's large house on the Peak.

"Oh, goodness," she said to Elizabeth, pushing a thick fall of hair away from her face. "I'd forgotten that children's parties were such hard work. Are there really only twenty children here? It sounds like a hundred and twenty!"

"The magician wants to know if you want him to perform now or after the cake has been cut," Elizabeth said, picking up a small boy who had fallen over part of a train set, a present temporarily discarded.

"Now," Helena said unhesitatingly. "It may keep the sound level down. He's going to perform in the garden, so we had better usher them all outside." She turned to the amahs who were endeavoring to maintain some kind of control over the proceedings. "Jung-lu, could you lead the children out into the garden and ask them to sit quietly for the magic show? Mei Lin, that little girl is trying to put six chocolate cakes into her mouth all at the same time. Please take them away from her. She's going to make herself sick."

Her warning came too late. Mei Lin, accustomed to the childless order of the Harland household, gave Elizabeth a look of pained reproach at having been brought along to assist, then led the offending child toward the nearest bathroom.

"Oh, God, oh, hell!" Helena said as the word "magician" went from mouth to mouth and there was a stampede toward the garden that nearly knocked her from her feet. "What I need is a stiff gin and tonic, but it's such bad form to be clutching a drink in the middle of a children's party!"

Elizabeth giggled and removed a paper streamer from her hair. "There's respectability in numbers. I'll have one with you."

"Two *very large* gin and tonics, Lee," Helena said to her houseboy. They walked outside to the veranda and collapsed on the cane chairs that overlooked the garden and the magician and the exuberant children.

"Oh, gosh, that child who was sick is still eating!" Helena said. "Who on earth is she? She must have a tummy made of steel!"

Elizabeth accepted her drink from the houseboy and sipped it gratefully. "She's Lady Gresby's grandchild," she said with a grin. "Don't you remember? She's out here until Christmas."

"So that's the 'dear, sweet little thing' Miriam Gresby described to me," Helena said, marveling as a fistful of crushed macaroons followed an eclair and two raspberry-jam tarts. "Tom says the Gresbys may have her for longer than they had anticipated. Travel to and from Britain is no longer safe now that the cards are on the table. If things get sticky here as well, I imagine the Gresbys will have to send her on to Canada. That's where most of the children are being evacuated to."

The magician had hit his stride and the noise level had fallen as the children sat cross-legged before him in rapt fascination.

"It seems hard to think of a war as reality," Elizabeth said, gazing out over the smoothly manicured lawn and the painted Chinese lanterns bobbing gaily between the trees. "Nothing has changed here at all."

"It's only been a week," Helena said, swirling the ice cubes meditatively around in her glass. "Give it time. Have you heard of the suggestions that a volunteer force be formed? It's to be something on the lines of the Territorials. Regular drill and training and open to any man who wants to join. Alastair thinks it's a good idea. He's beginning to alter his opinions, I think."

"In what way?"

"He doesn't seem to think the Japanese quite the joke that he used to." Her expressive, animated face was suddenly somber. "And I don't think them a joke at all. Jung-lu has family who have just arrived in Hong Kong from mainland China. The stories they have brought with them, of Japanese rapes and murders, are horrific. If the Japanese *do* invade, it will be the Chinese who will suffer the worst, people like Jung-lu and Mei-Lin."

"*Bonjour!*" Julienne called gaily, swinging toward them with an enormous teddy bear in one hand and a glass of white wine in the other. "*Alors!* What is the matter? Has someone died?"

"We were talking about the Japs," Helena said with a grin. "Not a very jolly conversation, unfortunately."

"Oh, the Japs." Julienne shrugged dismissively. She sank into a luxuriously padded cane-backed chaise longue and held the teddy bear up for inspection. "Isn't he adorable? I couldn't resist him. Ronnie said I was crazy. That no little boy six years of age would thank me for giving him a teddy, *mais, je ne le crois pas*." She gave a gurgle of impish laughter. "He has a very naughty look that reminds me of someone I know very well! If Jeremy doesn't fall in love with him *immédiatement*, then I will keep him for myself!"

"Jeremy will adore him," Helena said, trying to see any similarity between the cheeky-looking teddy bear and Julienne's friend in the Royal Scots. There was none. Alastair had told her that he thought the affair was over and that Julienne had a new boyfriend. Helena wondered who it could be. There had been a time when Julienne had flirted outrageously with Adam Harland, but she was quite sure that Adam had never responded. Even if he had, Helena was sure that the affair would have been short-lived. Adam was too steady and staid for a woman of Julienne's exotic tastes. Which left plenty of other people and one in particular.

Raefe Elliot had been having a drink with her and Alastair the previous Tuesday. She had mentioned Jeremy's forthcoming party, and that Julienne and Elizabeth would be helping her survive it. She had been surprised when, as they parted, he had said laconically that he would drop in for five minutes or so to wish Jeremy a happy birthday. She had wondered then if he had an ulterior motive. Now she was sure of it.

"Is Tom not here?" Julienne asked, shielding her eyes from the sun as she looked out over the lawn and the throng of children.

"Good heavens, no!" Helena said, amused. "He allowed me the use of the house on the strict understanding that he wasn't to have a thing to do with it."

Julienne sighed. Her affair with Tom was long over and she had no desire to rekindle it. Nevertheless, he would have been welcome company. To Julienne, a social gathering without a male was like a gin and tonic without the gin. A slight frown furrowed her brow. "He isn't going to return to England, is he? To, how do you say it in English, join up?"

Helena shook her head. Julienne had an uncanny knack of knowing what people were going to do even before they knew it themselves. "No, why do you ask?"

Julienne shrugged. "There's been quite a rush for the boats since the broadcast. Three of Ronnie's friends have booked passages home. They want to enlist and give Hitler a bloody nose." A smile hovered at the corners of her pink-painted mouth. "And I know of one or two bored husbands who are using patriotism and M. Hitler as an excuse to escape from their *very* dull marriages!"

"Tom couldn't go, even if he wanted to," Helena said practically. "As a junior diplomat he's in Hong Kong until he's posted elsewhere."

"Is there any further talk of the Royal Scots being moved?" Julienne asked, confirming Helena's belief that her affair with her Royal Scots major was over and finished.

Helena shook her head. "No. Alastair says most of the men are impatient for a posting where they will see some action, but it doesn't look as if they're going to get one. There's even talk of the garrison here being strengthened."

"That could be fun!" Julienne's eyes sparkled wickedly at the thought of a fresh input of handsome young officers.

The magician came to the end of his performance, producing two doves amid a cloud of smoke. The children clapped and shouted noisily and then, when it became apparent that nothing else was to follow, began to charge back toward the house and the tea table.

"Tiens!" Julienne cried, seizing her drink as the table beside her was rocked beneath the stampede. "I think I must go now!"

"You will do no such thing," Helena said unmercilessly. "You can help hold the dear little things at bay while Jeremy cuts his cake."

With a horrified expression on her face, Julienne followed Elizabeth into the large, airy, balloon-filled dining room. *"Merde!"* she said expressively as she was surrounded by sticky faces and sticky fingers. "What on earth possessed Helena to invite so many children? There must be hundreds here!"

"Twenty," Elizabeth said, grinning as she removed a brightly painted *papier-mâché* figure from a child who was trying to eat it.

Julienne trod on a cream cake that had been inadvertently dropped to the floor. "I don't believe it!" she moaned, looking down in horror at her ruined suede shoes. "They are like an invading army! Who on earth is that child trying to eat an almond slice and a fairy cake and a brandysnap curl all at the same time?"

Elizabeth giggled. "Lady Gresby's granddaughter. She's quite talented at getting several things into her mouth at the same time."

Julienne shuddered and, following Elizabeth's example, reluctantly joined hands with the children at either side of her as the candles were lit on the cake and everyone began to sing "Happy Birthday" to Jeremy.

It was Mei Lin who saw him enter the room. Her gaze flew to Elizabeth, but she was lifting a child up to see the cake and the candles as Jeremy began to huff and puff, ready to blow them out. He strolled toward the laden buffet table, a lavishly wrapped present tucked beneath one arm, his white silk shirt open at the throat, white flannels hugging his hips. Julienne, immediately sensing the presence of a member of the opposite sex, looked away from the cake. Her eyes met his and her eyebrows lifted in surprise and pleasure.

"Happy birthday to youuuu, happy birthday to youuuu," the children chorused gustily. "Happy birthday, dear Jeremy, happy birthday to youuu."

To Julienne's chagrin Raefe did not accept the invitation in her eyes to come stand beside her. Instead he wove his way imperturbably between the rioting children toward his hostess.

With a great exhalation of breath, Jeremy succeeded in blowing out the last candle. Amidst frenzied cheering Helena hugged him tight, then looked up and saw Raefe. Her mouth widened into a welcoming smile. "My goodness! You actually came! How brave of you! There isn't money enough in the world to tempt Tom to a children's party!"

"It is a bit fearsome," he said with a grin, handing Jeremy his present, not looking as if he found it at all fearsome.

Jeremy tore the paper off his present, revealing a magnificent clockwork sports car. He whooped in delight and Helena prompted, "Say thank you to Mr. Elliot, Jeremy." As she did so, she turned toward Jung-lu. "I think it's time for the children to be given their kites now, Jung-lu. They can take them outside to fly them. And Lee . . ." Her houseboy moved forward. "Drinks, please. A whiskey and soda for Mr. Elliot, two gin and tonics, and a glass of white wine, please."

Relieved that the end of the party was in sight without any accidents, material or physical, Helena pushed her hair once more away from her face and said to Elizabeth, "Gosh, and to think there'll have to be another one next year, and another one the year after that, until he's at least twenty-one!" She was laughing, but as she looked at Elizabeth her eyes widened and her laughter faded.

Elizabeth hadn't moved from her position near the table, only now there were no children crowding around her. Her eyes were wide and dark, her finely etched face so pale that Helena thought she was about to faint.

"Elizabeth, are you all right?" she asked in concern, then she became aware of Raefe, his eyes holding Elizabeth's, with an expression of such burning, blazing desire that she fell back in stunned shock.

The children had surged into the garden, Jung-lu and Mei Lin in their wake. Lee had handed both her and Julienne their drinks and was standing beside Raefe and Elizabeth, his silver drinks tray proffered deferentially. Neither of them made the slightest move toward removing their glasses. Helena doubted if they were even aware of his presence.

"Why won't you speak to me on the telephone?" he asked her harshly. "Why won't you at least talk to me?"

Her hands opened and closed at her sides, as if seeking a support that was absent. She was wearing an amethyst silk shirt and a white linen skirt, little gold sandals and not much else. With a fresh wave of shock, Helena realized how sexy and effortlessly chic her friend was, how unknowingly provocative.

"I told you that I wouldn't see you again . . ." Her voice was barely audible, her eyes bruised with pain.

"*Mon dieu,*" Julienne whispered beneath her breath, staring from one to the other in disbelieving comprehension.

Helena raised her eyebrows sharply in Lee's direction, indicating that he remove himself with all speed. The less he heard the better. As it was, Jung-lu and Mei Lin would be treated to a highly descriptive account of what had happened, and before the end of the day, the Chinese love of gossip being what it was, the staff of every household on the Peak would be cognizant of the facts. Including Adam's.

"This is ridiculous." Raefe's voice was brusque, full of such deep need that Julienne felt a shiver run down her spine and a flush of heat surge through her groin. "I must see you, must speak to you!"

Elizabeth shook her head stiffly, as if she could barely force herself to move. "No," she repeated, through parched lips. "We have nothing to talk about, Raefe. Nothing to discuss."

"Like hell we don't!" His hand shot out, encircling her wrist, and as Elizabeth cried out like an animal in pain, Helena stepped forward. "For God's sake stop it!" she said urgently. "The children will be back at any minute."

Elizabeth sucked in a deep, shuddering breath and with sudden strength wrenched free of his grasp. "You shouldn't have come here!" she told him angrily, her eyes brilliant with anguish. "You shouldn't have come!" She pushed past Helena and ran from the room, tears pouring down her face.

"Lizzie!" He sprang after her, catching up with her in the mosaic tiled hall, seizing her wrists in a grasp she couldn't escape. "Listen to me, for God's sake! I telephoned Roman last night. He's given me—"

"Did you tell *him* we were lovers, as well? Just as you've so publicly told Helena and Julienne? Just as you might as well have told Adam?"

"I told him you were a brilliant pianist," Raefe said, his voice a painful rasp, his expression as agonized as hers. "I told him you needed a teacher! A great teacher."

"Did you tell him that you've never heard me play?" she cried in fury, tears of rage and grief mixing inextricably. "Did you tell him I was a married woman who was bored with her husband and wanted a little diversion?"

"I told him I loved you!" he shouted at her, his fury demonic. *"I told him you were dying inside by inches because your fool of a husband had cut you off from your musical life-blood! I told him—"*

"Adam's not a fool!" If she could have clawed his face, she would have. She hated him; hated herself; hated the spectacle they were making in front of Helena and Julienne. "He's good and he's kind and he's twice the man that you are!"

"There's a man in Kowloon," Raefe continued, not deigning even to respond to her last furiously flung words.

"His name is Li Pi and Roman says he's one of the greatest piano teachers alive today. He's in retirement now, but Roman has spoken to him and he's willing to see you—"

She at last twisted one hand free and slapped him across the face with all the force she was capable of. *"Never! I shall never take anything from you, Raefe Elliot! Not ever again!"*

As she broke loose, running from the house and him, the children surged out into the hall, kites and carefully wrapped slices of birthday cake in their hands. Raefe took a step after her and Helena rushed forward, grabbing hold of his arm. "For God's sake, no!" she whispered urgently. "It will be all over the island!"

He stopped short, his hands clenched, a nerve twitching furiously at his jawline, watching as Elizabeth hurled herself into her Buick, rammed it into gear, and disappeared in a cloud of dust.

Other cars began to drive slowly toward the open door. "Timothy, your car is here," Helena said in a cracked voice, forcing a smile and dispatching one of her guests with relief. "Jonathan, your chauffeur is waiting. Lydia . . . Rosalind . . ."

"I'm sorry," Raefe said to her tautly, the lines of his face harsh as the children tumbled out into the drive. "I didn't intend there to be such a scene."

"I don't know what has happened between the two of you, Raefe," she said bewilderedly. "But whatever it was, there can be no future in it. Her marriage is a good one. She won't throw it away. Not for you or for anyone."

His smile was mirthless. "She will, Helena," he said with utter certainty. "Just give her time and she'll leave him and come to me, and she won't ever regret it!"

"Ce n'est pas possible! I could hardly believe it!" Julienne said, rolling away from Ronnie and lying on her back in their big double bed. "I thought he was going to forcibly pick her up and carry her away!"

Ronnie pushed himself up against the pillows and reached toward the bedside table for his cigarettes and a lighter. "What the hell does Elliot think he's playing at? The news will be all over the Peak by sundown."

"Mais oui," Julienne said admiringly, turning toward him, leaning her weight on her elbow. "But he obviously does not care." She took Ronnie's cigarette from between

his fingers and drew on it meditatively. "What *I* want to know, *chéri*, is when did this all start? I had no idea, and I could see from Helena's face that she didn't either." She handed him back his cigarette and leaned her chin on her hand. "Raefe Elliot and Elizabeth! It is incredible, is it not? I always thought her so calm, so sensible, so—so very English."

Ronnie grinned. There were times when Julie was not half as perceptive as she believed herself to be. "Still waters run deep," he said, pulling her close against his chest. Above her tousled red curls his eyes were speculative. Had Raefe and Elizabeth already been embroiled in an affair the day he had lured her to lunch at the Pen? Or had that been the beginning? Had he, Ronnie Ledsham, inadvertently been responsible for this most intriguing turn of events?

Julienne's fingers ran lightly and arousingly over the smooth, hard contours of his chest and down to the heavy weight of his sex. "I always thought that you were more than a little interested in *la belle* Elizabeth yourself," she said coaxingly. "Perhaps you were, *chéri*, and perhaps *she* was not interested?"

"Rubbish," Ronnie lied good-naturedly, his penis throbbing and hardening in the warm grip of her hand. "*La belle* Elizabeth is too cool and contained for my taste."

Julienne giggled as he rolled on top of her, taking a small, erect nipple into his mouth. "I think you are wrong, *mon amour*," she said, sliding her legs around his waist and arching herself toward him with pleasure. "Yes, where Elizabeth is concerned, I think you are very wrong!"

"I've never been so devastated in my whole life," Helena said to Alastair, her eyes dark with worry. "It wouldn't have mattered where they were. They could have been at a reception at Government House and it wouldn't have made an iota of difference! He would still have thundered at her that he loved her, that he had to see her, had to speak to her."

"And Elizabeth?" Alastair asked with interest. "What did she say in return?"

"I thought she was going to faint. She was so white, so still. She said that they had nothing to talk about. Nothing to discuss."

"Then whatever there has been between them is all

over," Alastair said dismissively, regarding Helena's wide-hipped, ripe, lush body with satisfaction.

They were in bed at her Kowloon flat. Tom was taking Jeremy and Jennifer to the zoological gardens the next day for a birthday treat, so Helena had left them with him for the night and he had returned home alone.

She shook her head. "No," she said, pleasantly comfortable in the circle of his arms. "If you had heard the passion in their voices, seen the expression in their eyes, then you would know that despite all her protests to the contrary, it is far from over."

Alastair's forefinger traced the line of her neck down to her shoulder, to her breast, to the full, dark aureola of her nipple. "The man's a bastard," he said succinctly. "I don't know why you bother with him."

"I like him." She shifted her position so that he could reach both her breasts, loving the slow, unhurried deliberation of his hands. "I like his go-to-hell attitude that takes no account of what people say or think. I like the way he takes his Malay girlfriend with him to all the places he would take a white girl. There's something very feral and primitive about him, something barely veneered by the politeness civilization demands."

"Good grief," Alastair said, sitting bolt upright and staring at her in shock. "You wouldn't like it if *I* behaved in the same manner! Squiring other women around when he has a perfectly sweet wife at home, thrashing Jacko Latimer so that the man dies of his injuries! Gambling tens of thousands at Happy Valley! Racing around in that damned Lagonda of his as if the island were his personal racetrack!"

Helena slid her hands up and around his neck, affectionately pulling him back down against her. "Of course I wouldn't, silly," she said agreeably. "I like you just the way you are."

His light blue eyes darkened fractionally. It was still "like" and not "love." He said, with a trace of harshness, "The fellow is a rogue. He doesn't give a damn about anyone but himself."

"I think you're wrong there," Helena said as he rolled her gently over onto her stomach. She raised herself up on her hands and knees, her heavy mane of hair swinging down onto the bed, her breasts hanging like full, rich fruit, her legs apart as he knelt behind her. "I think he cares very much about Elizabeth. He mentioned a teacher he had found for her. A piano teacher . . ."

Alastair was no longer listening to her. The firm head of his penis pushed hard into the entrance of her vagina, his hands tightening convulsively on her buttocks. "Oh, God!" he groaned, thrusting deep inside her in an agony of relief. *"Oh, God, but I love you, Helena! Jesus, I love you."*

For the second time, Elizabeth slammed the Buick into the double garage beside Adam's Riley. Her hands were trembling when she took them from the wheel. Damn him! Damn him! Damn him! How *dare* he compromise her in such a way in front of Julienne and Helena and God alone knows how many servants and children?

There was a piece of paper tucked securely beneath one of her windshield wipers, but she did not bother to remove it. Several of the cars parked in the Nicholson drive had been littered with party streamers. Her houseboy could remove it when he cleaned the car.

She entered the house, knowing very well what it was she had to do. She should never have come to Hong Kong, never have abandoned her musical studies in London. She was twenty-five, for God's sake. In musical terms that was old. If she wanted to make an international name for herself as a pianist, then she had no time to lose. She had already won two major prizes, and for a short time they had placed her where she wanted to be, on the concert platform. But they had not been enough to establish her. There had been no frantic letters from promoters, demanding that she return to England and undertake engagements for them. She was out of sight and out of mind. To save her sanity—and her marriage—she had to win another major prize and so make a triumphal return.

"Hello, my love. Was it a good party?" Adam asked, stuffing tobacco down in his pipe as he walked toward her.

"Yes . . . No . . ." she replied, appalled at how distressed she still felt.

He laughed, putting his arm around her shoulders. "Make up your mind, love. Either it was, or it wasn't."

She forced a laugh. "Oh, you know what children's parties are like. The noise was indescribable."

"It was far too quiet here," he said, smiling down at her. "I hate it when I come home and you're not in."

"That's what I'd like to talk to you about," she said, knowing that this time she couldn't be a coward. This time she had to tell him exactly how she felt. "I want to go back to London, Adam."

They had walked through the downstairs rooms to the long veranda that ran the length of the house at the back. It was Adam's favorite retreat at dusk. He liked to sit with a sundowner at his side, looking out over the garden and the hillside beyond, and the magnificent views of Victoria and the harbor and the distant hills of the Kowloon Peninsula.

He sat down in his cane chaise longue, saying good-temperedly, "We've been through all this before, Beth. There can be no question of your returning to London now that war has broken out. Good heavens, children are being evacuated *away* from London in the thousands."

"I'm not a child, Adam," she said, sitting down beside him, struggling for calm and control. "And it isn't because of the war that I want to return. It's a far more selfish reason."

A closed, shuttered look came down over his face. It was a look she had grown familiar with. These days, whenever she spoke of her music, he would be conscientiously polite, but the same, shuttered expression came into his eyes. He no longer wanted to hear about it. As far as he was concerned, her music had begun to be an intrusion. He had encouraged her in the early days of their marriage, taking pleasure in indulging her, but when it had come to a choice between moving to Hong Kong, which he wanted to do, or remaining in London so that she could pursue her career, then there had been no choice at all. Just as there had been no choice when her father had wished to live in Nice.

"I'm twenty-five, Adam," she said forcefully. "If I want to continue my career, and I *do* want to continue it, then I have to win a major international prize. You know as well as I that it's the quickest and most effective route to a concert career, not only because of the publicity and prize money involved, but because important orchestral engagements are guaranteed to the winners."

"You can practice here," he said obstinately. "You already spend six hours a day at the piano. I can't see how you can expect to spend any more, no matter where you are."

"Practicing alone isn't enough. I need a critic, a teacher.

Someone like Professor Hurok who will help me to interpret, to look for new insight."

"No." The lines around his mouth hardened. "It's impossible, Beth. There's a war on, for God's sake! There won't *be* any international piano competitions this year, or next year either, if the war continues. The world has got more important things to think about!"

"*I* haven't," she cried passionately. "There *isn't* anything more important to me than my music!"

She had risen to her feet and he looked up at her steadily. "Not even me, Beth?" he asked quietly.

She felt a sob rise up in her throat, remembering the time he had come to her and comforted her when her mother had died, remembering how he had always been there when she needed him, remembering how very much he had always loved her. "Oh, God, Adam! Why can't you see how much it means to me? Why can't you see how forcing me to choose is driving a wedge between us?"

He stood, too, taking her hands in his. "It is you who are driving the wedge, Beth. Not me. You can continue your musical studies here, just as well as you can in London. And later, when we've put paid to Hitler and the world is sane again, then will be the time for you to think about pursuing a career on the concert platform. Until then, there is no point in returning to London. Yours will not be the only promising career to be put in cold storage till the war is over. Musicians will be entering the forces, just as men from every other walk of life are doing. It is the war that is robbing you of London and an international prize, Beth, not me."

She looked despairingly into his eyes. Everything he said was common sense. The war would affect international competitions; there would be other aspiring concert pianists, besides herself, whose careers had been brought to an abrupt halt. And yet . . . And yet . . . She closed her eyes, sick with longing, knowing that Raefe would not have taken such an attitude. Raefe would have understood the depth of her need. Raefe would not have allowed Hitler to interfere with any of his plans for the future.

"I love you very much, Beth," Adam was saying, folding her into his arms and holding her close. "Please be patient. Wait until the war is over and then I'll give you all the support that I can."

Defeated, she felt tears of frustration prick the back of her eyelids. Till the war was over. How many years would that be? And how many other reasons would he then find for a further postponement, and a further one?

"If it isn't possible for me to return to my studies with Professor Hurok," she said tenaciously, "I want to return to London anyway, Adam."

He pulled away from her, looking at her white, set face in bewilderment. "But why? There's nothing I could do there. Here, if the Japs attack, I will at least be able to fight!"

"We've been here for six months," she said, knowing that this was one battle she could not concede. "I'm tired of it, and—"

"Tired of it?" He began to laugh indulgently. "Good heavens, Beth. How can you tire of it? Sun, magnificent beaches, superb swimming, tennis, riding, the best lot of friends we've ever had. Don't be ridiculous, darling. You're suffering from a wave of guilt at not being home and suffering all the agonies of the blackout and evacuation."

"No, I do feel guilty, but it isn't just that. I need to get away, Adam. Have a complete change." He wouldn't return to London, she knew, but there were other places in the world. Places where she would not run the risk of meeting Raefe, of having her defenses stormed; of leaving Adam and never returning to him. "Couldn't we go to Singapore for a while? Helena says it's even more fascinating than Hong Kong."

"I suppose we could go for a week or two if you really want to," he said reluctantly.

She squeezed his hand. A week or two would be a start. She could always encourage him to prolong their stay once they were there. "Then let's go, Adam! Please. Quickly."

He laughed, too relieved that an awful scene had been averted to read anything odd into her sudden enthusiasm for a visit to Singapore.

"Okay," he said. "I'd quite like to see Singapore myself. We'll go at the end of next month, when the dry season starts."

"No!" she said fiercely, and this time he was surprised by her vehemence. "I want to go now, Adam. This week if possible."

"And miss Tom Nicholson's party?"

Her nails dug deep into her palms. Raefe would be at the

party. If he looked at her as he had looked at her at Helena's, then Adam would guess. The whole room would know. "Yes, darling," she said stiffly. "And miss Tom's party."

"All right, Beth, if that's what you want," Adam said with the air of a man who was being more than reasonably patient. "We'll sail there. It will be more pleasant than flying. I'll call the agency and book a couple of berths tomorrow."

Chapter Fourteen
❧

BY six o'clock the next morning she was at her piano, wrestling with the Schubert B-flat Sonata. She had had a sleepless night, lying beside Adam, tortured by how easily she had been unfaithful to him. A week ago her life had seemed so ordered and secure, so predictable. Now nothing was predictable any longer. She had slipped out of bed quietly, so as not to disturb him, then poured herself a lime juice and carried it out onto the veranda. There was nothing she could do to wipe out what had happened. It was something she would have to learn to live with. And to forget.

She had turned away from the view of the distant harbor and the hills of Kowloon, her head hurting and her heart aching, knowing that she did not want to forget. Her betrayal of Adam had not only been physical. It had been, and continued to be, a mental betrayal that she could find no release from. She sat down at the piano, grateful for the salvation it offered her, and launched into the first movement, playing it far more quickly than she usually did. It changed the entire character of her performance and she forgot about Adam, forgot even Raefe, as she began to play the second movement, intrigued at the way that, too, was affected and changed.

It was ten-thirty by the time she had played the third and fourth movements to her satisfaction. She rose reluctantly to her feet. She couldn't remember what Adam's plans were for the day, but he hated having to leave the house without saying good-bye to her. She stretched her fingers, pleased with her new insights into a score she was deeply familiar with. She would return to it after a late breakfast. She would play all four movements through again, then perhaps she would turn her attention to Bartok's Second Piano Concerto. It was a piece of music that had, so far, defeated her. The score looked as if a printer had just thrown a million black notes on the page, and she had always thought it utterly impossible.

As she walked toward the drawing room, Chan hurried to meet her, his expression anxious. "I found this on the windshield of your car, missy. Perhaps it is important?"

It was the piece of paper she had ignored when driving away from the party. She could see now that it wasn't a bit of streamer, and she took it from him. "Thank you, Chan. Is Mr. Harland still in the house?"

"Yes, missy. He's down at the tennis courts checking the nets."

She thanked him again and looked down at the piece of paper in her hand. "Li Pi, 27 Stonewall Mansions, Kimberley Road, Kowloon." The handwriting was firm and strong. He must have slipped it under the windshield wiper before he had even entered Tom's to see her. Which meant he had anticipated her reaction and had not been surprised by it.

From beyond the open windows, the only sound was the chip-chop of the gardener trimming the lawn around the flower beds. The air was heavy, as if a storm was due, the scent from the frangipani trees heady and sweet. She stood for a long time, staring down at the note in her hand. Li Pi. She had heard of him when she had been at the Royal Academy. He was one of the great teachers, and he was now in Kowloon and Raefe had said that, if she went to him, he would see her.

The gardener continued to trim the lawn. Through the window she could see Adam down at the tennis courts, his hands deep in the pockets of his white flannels as he surveyed the nets.

Li Pi. He had taught at the Moscow Central Music

School. His recordings of the Chopin Barcarolle and B-minor Sonata and the Schumann Concerto were incandescent interpretations that had become classics. She stared once more at the piece of paper in her hand and then at Adam, and back again. Would it be a further betrayal to him if she were to accept Raefe's introduction? And if she didn't? Wouldn't that be an even greater betrayal? A betrayal of her talent and all her years of work?

Mei Lin approached her and said in her singsong voice, "I have made fresh coffee for you, missy."

"Thank you, Mei Lin." She looked down once again at the piece of paper, then said decisively, "I'm going out for a little while, Mei Lin. Tell Mr. Harland that I'll be back for lunch."

"Yes, missy," Mei Lin said unhappily. Mr. Harland did not like to be brought such messages. He did not like it when Mrs. Harland left the house and he did not know where she was. He did not even like it when she was in the house and playing her piano. Mei Lin had seen his frown of annoyance only hours ago when he had emerged from their bedroom and heard the music filling the downstairs rooms. And now she would have to tell him that Mrs. Harland had finished playing and had left the house without even waiting to speak to him. Reluctantly she stepped out into the garden and began to walk down past the flower beds and the gardener, toward the tennis courts.

Elizabeth backed the Buick out of the garage, filled with the comforting certainty that she was doing the right thing. Adam had no need to know it was Raefe who had introduced her to Li Pi, and even if he did know, there was no reason why he should be hurt or offended. Perhaps, if her professional life once more had direction and purpose, their personal life would regain the harmony it seemed to have lost.

She spend down the curving road toward Victoria, her stomach muscles tightening at the thought of the interview ahead of her. What if he did not consider her playing good enough? She had brought no music with her. Not even the Schubert score she had worked on all morning. She entered the crowded, colorful streets of Wanchai. Lacquered ducks as flat as pancakes, birds' nests, and sharks' fins hung from shops that were little more than holes in the walls. Colored washing on poles jutted out like flags from the windows of the tall, flimsy buildings. In the harbor sampans were packed so close together that she could see an agile Chinese boatman using them as stepping stones, hopping across the water without wetting a foot. She drove the Buick aboard the car ferry, then got out to stand at the deck rail for the short eight-minute crossing.

Professor Hurok had believed in her talent. She already had a remarkable list of achievements behind her. The Chopin Competition. The Brussels and Vienna competitions. The Bartok recital at the Albert Hall.

The ferry docked in Kowloon and she drove through the gaudy streets, wondering why a man who had spent so much of his life in the gray grandeur of Moscow should choose such an unlikely place for his retirement.

Stonewall Mansions was an old, distinguished block of flats with a doorman on duty at the entrance. She asked for Li Pi, gave her name, and waited while he telephoned and received confirmation that she was expected.

The lift was small, and as it carried her upward, her stomach was cramped with nerves. She had been six months without a teacher. Roman Rakowski, who had recommended her to Li Pi, had never heard her play. Li Pi was seeing her out of politeness and had probably not the slightest intention of accepting her as a pupil. He was merely being kind, doing a favor for Roman Rakowski, who was in turn doing a favor for Raefe.

The lift stopped and she walked along the corridor, stopping before number twenty-seven, her heart racing, her stomach tight. She raised her hand to knock, but before she could do so, a small, black-clad Chinese opened the door.

"My name is Elizabeth Harland. I have come to see Li Pi . . ." she began, thinking that she was speaking to an elderly houseboy. Then she saw the fierce intelligence and the flicker of amusement in his eyes and flushed crimson.

"Please come in, Mrs. Harland," Li Pi said graciously, opening the door wide. "I have been expecting you to call."

The room was huge. The walls were white, the floor covered with sharply colored rugs. The sparse furniture was dark and heavily carved, and dominated by a magnificent Steinway concert grand.

"It's very kind of you to see me. I didn't bring any music with me . . ."

"Please don't be so anxious," Li Pi said, smiling. "Would you like iced tea or coffee, or perhaps a lime juice?"

"Lime juice, please." She could feel her stomach muscles beginning to relax. It was going to be all right. She could sense it, feel it in her blood and in her bones.

He made the drinks himself, pouring the ice-cold lime juice from a vacuum flask. "So, you are a pianist, Mrs. Harland?" he said as he handed hers to her.

Her eyes met his and she was no longer nervous or unsure of herself. "Yes," she said fiercely. "And I want to be a great pianist."

"Ah, yes," he said understandingly. "The dream of so many thousands . . ."

She put down her glass and said, her voice throbbing, "Let me play for you." She had to show him that she was not one of the thousands who merely dreamed. That she had the talent and the determination; the stamina to make her dream come true.

He nodded, giving her no suggestions, no guidance. She crossed to the beautiful piano and sat down before it, her throat dry, her heart slamming hard within her chest. The next few minutes were going to be far more important than her concert debuts at the Central Hall and the Wigmore Hall. More important even than her Liszt and Chopin competition performances. She sat quite still for a few minutes, collecting herself, before she lifted her hands. She brought them down on the keys with deft surety, and the somber, rich notes of Schubert's B-flat Sonata filled the sun-drenched room.

When she had finished, he handed her the score of Brahms's F-minor Sonata and then, when the last notes had died away, the score of Debussy's *Des pas sur la neige*. It was a piece she had never played before and at first she was unsure of herself. Then, instinctively, she captured the melancholy atmosphere, the sadness, the intolerable dilemma that was present in it.

When she was through, she waited tensely for his opinion, the adrenaline produced by her intense concentration singing along her veins. He was silent for what seemed like an age, then he said, with a nod of his head,

"You have talent. Indisputably, you have talent. But for the concert platform mere talent is not enough." He crossed the room to her and took her hands, examining her fingers, her wrists as he went on. "The concert pianist must have many other qualities, Mrs. Harland. He must possess unusual intelligence and culture, feeling, temperament, imagination, poetry, and finally, a personal magnetism that enables him to inspire audiences of thousands of strangers whom chance has brought together, with one and the same feeling. If any of these qualities are missing, the deficiency will be apparent in every phrase he plays."

"And if he has them?" she asked urgently.

"Then he must work, work, work. Practicing must be a relentless occupation with countless monastic hours each day devoted to its perfection. Nothing and no one must be of greater importance!"

Her eyes held his, their sea-green depths no longer cool but burning with passion. "Will you accept me as a pupil?"

He paused for so long, she thought she would faint. "Yes," he said at last. "You have the necessary demons within. They are buried deep, and are not immediately noticeable, but they are there. However, understand this. The energy I shall demand you to expend upon that piano in any one lesson will be equal to the energy a boxer expends upon his antagonist at a prizefight. It will be equal to a matador killing three large bulls. Never ask for mercy for none will be given. At the end of every lesson, you will be ready to drop with exhaustion and you will weep with exhaustion. Then, and only then, will I be satisfied."

Her smile was incandescent. "I'm ready for my first bull, maestro," she said zestfully.

Li Pi smiled. "The Schubert B-flat Sonata," he said. "It was terrible. There were no shadings. The modulations from major to minor were too sudden. The tension must be kept alive in those long melodies and within those long movements. Schubert can present an idea, a subject, from so many different angles. For that you need a particular kind of sensitivity. Now, once again, from the beginning."

"Did Mrs. Harland say where she was going?" Adam asked Mei Lin, the lines running from his nose to mouth seeming deeper than usual.

"No, sir. She said she would be back for lunch."

Adam glanced at his wristwatch. It was already ten-fifty. "All right. Thank you, Mei Lin."

He gave the courts a last, critical check, wondering if Beth had forgotten that they had invited the Ledshams for a game of doubles on Thursday evening. Perhaps she expected that by Thursday they would be aboard a boat bound for Singapore. He still hadn't been down to the shipping line to book a passage. He began to walk desultorily back toward the house.

The truth of it was that he had no real desire to jaunt off to Singapore. Not just at the present moment. Ever since war against Germany had been declared, there had been talk in Hong Kong of forming a volunteer force, just in case the war in Europe triggered off one in the East. If a volunteer force were formed, he wanted to be in at its inception, not lounging on a boat in the South Pacific.

The house seemed empty and bare without Beth in it. He stood at the music room door, staring moodily at the piano that had been specially shipped from Perth. He had always been tolerant about her need to play. He had taken her to concerts night after night in London. Even here in Hong Kong, he lived like a bachelor for most of the day, apologizing for her absense at bridge parties, at tennis matches, at the racecourse, in order that she could indulge in long hours of self-imposed practice. He felt a prick of irritability. She hadn't been as tolerant in return. Wanting to return to London was sheer idiocy. He wondered if she had any idea of the realities of war and he was aware, as he had been lately with increasing frequency, of the twenty-four years that divided them.

He looked at his watch again. It was eleven o'clock. He doubted very much that she would be back for lunch and had no intention of wasting the rest of the day waiting around for her. He crossed the cool, marble-tiled entrance hall, picked up his golf bag, and strode out of the house. He would go to the golf club and have lunch there. And, because he loved her more than he loved anyone or anything, he would call in at the shipping office and book a double berth on the earliest possible sailing to Singapore.

"I didn't expect to see you here today," Alastair said pleasantly when Adam walked into the club bar. "I thought Fridays and Mondays were your days for a round."

Adam slid onto a bar stool alongside him. "I didn't expect to find you here during the week either. What's the matter? Has the army dispensed with your services?"

Alastair laughed. "Not yet they haven't. I'm back on duty at six. What do you want? A stengah or a G and T?"

"A stengah, please," Adam said as the Japanese barman approached. "I don't suppose there's any chance now of your being posted to pastures new?" he asked as Alastair ordered their drinks. "Not now that the government is exercising caution and putting the island on a war footing."

The barman filled two long, iced glasses to the brim with a thirst-quenching mixture of whiskey and soda water and pushed them across the bar toward the two men.

Alastair took a sip of his drink and said reflectively, "I shouldn't read too much into the government's action, Adam. It's a formality, that's all."

Adam looked at him sharply. "You don't still hold to the view that the Japs are harmless, do you?"

The barman had turned his back on them, but was still within earshot as he began to polish glasses meticulously.

"No . . ." Alastair said slowly, his eyes on the barman. "I don't think I do. Not when they are so flagrantly in sympathy with Hitler and Mussolini."

"Makes no difference who the Japs are in sympathy with," Denholm Gresby said knowledgeably, walking up to the bar behind them. "Japan's best interests can be served only by her remaining neutral." He snapped his fingers in the direction of the Japanese barman. "She'd be a fool to be anything else," he said with a snort as the barman waited for his order. "The short-arsed yellow bastards might fight well against a third-rate Chinese force, but they'd get a bloody nose if they ever met with the British Army!"

Adam slid off his bar stool and carried his drink over to the far corner of the room where he had a good view of the golf course. Alastair joined him.

"He's a bit overpowering, isn't he?" he said to Adam. "I can't understand why Tom is so friendly with him."

"It's probably professional necessity," Adam replied absently, wondering if it mightn't have been wiser to have booked the later sailing to Singapore rather than the earlier one. He frowned. He would have to telephone Tom and say they wouldn't be at his party, and he would have to telephone the Ledshams and say the tennis was off, and he would have to cancel a hundred and one other things that he had no wish to cancel.

"Don't let him get to you," Alastair said comfortably, seeing the fierce frown on Adam's brow.

"I wasn't thinking of Gresby. I was thinking of Beth," Adam said in a moment of rare candor.

Alastair raised his eyebrows and remained silent. He had no particular wish to be made a confidant to Adam's marital difficulties, but if it helped Adam to talk about them, he would willingly listen. "What's the matter?" he asked delicately. "Is she . . . er, having problems?"

"Yes." Adam's voice was unusually tight. He had had no intention of talking to anyone about Beth, but he knew that whatever he said to Alastair would go no further, and he badly needed to give vent to his feelings. "I'm having to take her away. God knows, I don't want to. There's the volunteer force to consider and a score of other things."

"Where are you taking her?" Alastair asked awkwardly. He wondered if this particular problem had ever hit the Harlands' marriage before. In the strong cruel light of the sun, Adam looked every one of his forty-nine years. And Elizabeth was only twenty-five. It was an age difference that many marriages bridged quite happily. Obviously the Harlands' was not one of them.

"Singapore," Adam said with more bitterness than he had intended. "We'll be there for a few weeks, I suppose. Until she gets it out of her system."

Alastair cleared his throat and wondered what was the right thing to say. He couldn't imagine how he would feel if, after several years of marriage, Helena were unfaithful to him. He doubted he would be quite as rational about it as Adam was being.

"Best thing to do," he said at last. "She'll soon forget him. It isn't as if Elliot's intentions toward her are honorable. I doubt if the bastard knows what the word honor means."

Adam had turned toward him and Alastair carefully avoided his eyes. "If it's any comfort to you, Elizabeth isn't the first and she won't be the last. Women fall for him like flies. It was the little Chesham girl a few weeks ago, and Mark Hurley's wife a few weeks before that."

Adam was still silent and Alastair drained his glass,

wishing to hell that the conversation had never been started.

"You're crazy," Adam said at last, his voice scarcely recognizable. "Beth isn't involved with Elliot! She hardly knows him!"

Alastair felt the blood leave his face. Slowly and stiffly he turned toward Adam and knew that he had made the most God-awful error. Whatever Harland had been talking to him about, it hadn't been about his wife and Raefe Elliot.

"God, no!" he said, forcing a laugh, trying to remember what the hell he had said. "You've misunderstood me, Adam. What I was saying is that Elizabeth isn't the first woman to make excuses for Elliot's behavior. The Chesham girl and Mark Hurley's wife both did the same thing when he was awaiting trial for Jacko Latimer's murder." He ran a finger along his trim moustache.

"And Beth?" Adam asked, the lines around his nose and mouth pinched and white. "What has he done that she needs to make an excuse for him? What the devil did you mean when you said that she'd soon forget him, that his intentions toward her weren't honorable?"

• "I thought you realized he was making a play for her that day we were all at the Repulse Bay Hotel," Alastair said smoothly, cursing himself for being the biggest fool in Christendom. "Instead of being offended, Elizabeth excused him by saying we were all reading more into it than there was. Give a dog a bad name and all that sort of nonsense. And his intentions certainly *weren't* honorable. They never are. You're lucky that Elizabeth paid him so little attention. Now what do you want? Another stengah?"

Adam was aware that he was on the verge of making himself look a fool. The trouble was he hadn't been listening to Alastair very carefully. He had been thinking of the booking he had made for the *Blantyre Castle* and the numerous arrangements he would have to make before they left. It wasn't possible for Alastair to have meant what he had thought he meant, and to pursue the conversation would only be to arouse preposterous suspicions in Alastair's mind.

"No, thanks," he said shortly. "I must be getting on. Give my love to Helena. 'Bye, Alastair."

He walked away from him and Alastair wiped his

forehead with the back of his hand, letting out a huge sigh of relief. God, but he'd stepped into that one with both feet! He walked across to the bar and ordered another stengah. With a bit of luck he had successfully talked himself out of it, but it hadn't been easy. Gresby came up to him and asked if he'd heard if Ronnie Ledsham's horse was running again on Saturday. Alastair said he thought so, but his thoughts weren't on Saturday's race. Because of his clumsiness, he still didn't know why Adam was so concerned about Elizabeth, or why he was having to take her away.

"Might have a little flutter then," Sir Denholm was saying.

Alastair ignored him. He was still thinking about Elizabeth Harland. If Adam was unaware of her relationship with Raefe Elliot, what the devil else was she up to that was concerning him so much?

Adam walked swiftly out of the club, throwing his golf bag into the rear of his Riley. He no longer had any desire to play. Damn Alastair and his rambling remarks about Beth and Raefe Elliot. What the hell had he meant about her soon forgetting him? He wrenched the Riley into first gear and eased down the drive toward the road. He'd *said* he was only referring to the way Beth had excused Elliot when he made that unpardonable pass at her at the Repulse Bay. He pushed the Riley's nose out into the stream of traffic heading toward Victoria. The damn trouble was that he hadn't really been listening, and Alastair had certainly looked uncomfortable enough when he rounded on him.

It was lunchtime and the traffic was heavier than normal. He overtook a bus and a clutch of Chinese schoolgirls on bicycles. Beth and Raefe Elliot indeed! The whole idea was so patently ridiculous that his anxiety began to ebb. He had misheard. Alastair always was a waffler, never getting to the point of his conversations. He had been talking about Elliot's notorious popularity with women, and citing Beth as a case in point of a sensible woman who, even so, made excuses for Elliot's disgraceful behavior. He certainly hadn't been suggesting anything more compromising than that.

He slewed into Peak Road, traveling far faster than he normally did. He'd been a bloody fool to react in the way

he had. Alastair must have thought he had taken leave of
his senses. He parked the car in the garage and stared at
the empty space where Beth's Buick normally stood. She
had said that she would be home by lunchtime. It was now
one-thirty and she was still out. He frowned as he stepped
out of his car, slamming the door behind him. The idea of
Beth indulging in a wild affair with Raefe Elliot might be
ridiculous, but she was certainly spending far too much
time away from him and away from home. His shoulders
were hunched as he walked into the house. He didn't
relish the thought of having lunch alone. And he didn't
relish the thought of spending long hours wondering
where the devil Beth was, and what she was doing.

When Adam heard the sound of the car engine chugging
to a halt in front of the house, he threw down his
newspaper and hurried to the porch to greet Beth. It wasn't
she. It was Helena, her little open Morgan parked where
Beth's larger Buick should have been.

"Hello," she said cheerily, walking toward him, her mass
of dark auburn hair bouncing glossily on her shoulders. "Is
Elizabeth in? I wanted to know if she fancied an afternoon's
shopping. There's a sale on at Lane Crawford and lots of
goodies to be had."

In actual fact Helena had absolutely no intention of
spending the afternoon jammed amid a crush of shoppers.
She had driven over expecting to find Elizabeth in by
herself, practicing the piano, and Adam at the golf or
cricket club. Elizabeth had not contacted her since the
dreadful scene between her and Raefe at the children's
party, but Helena was sure she must want desperately to
talk to someone. Since the only people she could possibly
talk to were herself and Julienne, Helena had decided to
make herself speedily available. Julienne as an adviser, in
the kind of situation that obviously existed between
Elizabeth and Raefe, would be a disaster.

"She's out, I'm afraid," Adam said, not succeeding in
disguising his gloominess. "Probably already down at the
sale."

Helena did not think so, and by the tone of Adam's
voice, was sure he didn't either.

"That's a pity," she said, wondering whether to take her
leave or not. Seeing the droop of Adam's shoulders, she

said impulsively, "Perhaps I could stay and keep you company until she returns. Alastair has begun dropping hints about civilians being encouraged to return to Great Britain in case there's a flare-up of trouble with the Japs. I haven't the slightest desire to go. You don't think it will come to that, do you?"

Adam led the way into the large, white-carpeted drawing room. "Not a chance," he said with a return of good humor. "Alastair never does get his facts right. What will you have, Helena? A gin and tonic, or a martini?"

"Gin and tonic, please," Helena said, sitting herself comfortably on the deep-cushioned sofa, amused to see that her ploy had been successful. Once the conversation turned to the Japanese and the threat, or the lack of a threat, of war, Adam would happily talk *ad infinitum*.

". . . so the Japs will try to attack," Adam said as they continued the discussion over a light lunch of scrambled eggs and prawns and a chilled bottle of Graves. "But we'll soon shove them off."

"I'm pleased to hear it," Helena said with a laugh as he refilled her glass. "Have you any hope of being placed in the tennis championships next month? I strained my shoulder a week or so ago and it's letting me down. Otherwise Julienne and I were safe favorites for the doubles."

They talked of the tennis championships, the horse Ronnie was running at Happy Valley on Saturday, the staggering way anything planted in a Hong Kong garden flourished and spread. To her surprise, Helena found herself not only pleased that she had taken Adam's mind off Elizabeth's absence, but also effortlessly enjoying herself.

He was an easy companion. He never seemed to think it necessary to bolster his masculinity by flirting, or making the kind of double-edged remarks that Ronnie would have found obligatory in the same circumstances. There was something sweetly old-fashioned about him, a gallantry and dependability that was oddly attractive.

They took their coffees out onto the veranda and to her amazement, Helena found herself talking to him about Alan. She had never done so before to anyone. Not with the same ease. It had been something in the way they had

sat down together after their lunch. Something in the way
he had handed her her coffee cup, after stirring the sugar in
for her. Memory had stirred. Alan passing her the toast
rack, the marmalade . . .

"And so you don't feel that you can ever marry again?"
Adam was asking her.

She shook her head, her expression pensive. "No. What
was between Alan and me was a real thing that we built
very carefully for ourselves, and when we built it, it was
perfect and satisfying. Just because it was blasted to bits by
a drunken driver doesn't mean I'm never going to try to
build anything else among the ruins. Alan isn't a ghost,
tagging along at my elbow. He would have encouraged me
in my affair with Alastair, and if I wanted to marry Alastair,
why, Alan would have encouraged me in that, too."

"But you don't want to marry Alastair?" Adam
prompted gently.

Her usual grin was back on her face. "I don't know,
Adam. I truly don't know."

From behind them they could hear Mei Lin greeting
Elizabeth in the drawing room. The French windows
opened and she stepped out onto the veranda, her eyes
shining, her whole demeanor exultant.

Helena felt shock stab through her. If this was the way
Elizabeth returned from an assignation with Raefe, then it
was beyond belief that Adam had still not guessed about it.
As Elizabeth walked swiftly over to them, taking hold of
Adam's hands and giving him a loving kiss on his cheek,
Helena felt a spurt of anger as well as shock. Up until now
her sympathy had been with Elizabeth. She had never, for
one moment, imagined that the affair was causing her
anything but agony and mental torture. Now she was not
so sure, and the thought of Adam being betrayed so
brazenly enraged her.

"Hello, darlings," Elizabeth said. "I'm sorry I'm so late.
I've had the most *fantastic* morning."

"And afternoon," Adam said dryly, glancing at his
watch.

She hugged his arm. "Please don't be cross. I really did
think I would be back for lunch. I don't know where the
time flew to. It simply vanished."

Helena's eyebrows rose. No doubt it had. It hardly
seemed sensible to admit to it, though.

Elizabeth went on exuberantly. "I discovered that Li Pi, *the* Li Pi, who used to teach at the Moscow Central School, is living in Kowloon." Her whole face was lit with an inner radiance. "I went to see him this morning and he's agreed to take me on as a pupil! Isn't that the most marvelous news, Adam?"

Helena felt the tension leave her body. Elizabeth wasn't as insensitive as she had begun to believe. She hadn't been out with Raefe after all. Helena doubted if even he could have put such elation into Elizabeth's voice and eyes.

"That's wonderful news, my love," Adam said guardedly. "But was there any point in going to see him now, when you are just about to leave for a holiday in Singapore?"

Helena looked at him in surprise. He hadn't mentioned one word to her about leaving for Singapore.

Elizabeth sat down on one of the cane chairs, pouring herself a cup of coffee from the percolator standing on an adjacent table. "I thought about that," she said, her eyes carefully avoiding his as she added cream to her cup. "The important thing is that I've made the contact and that he has agreed to teach me. I told him I would be away for three or four weeks, perhaps longer. It isn't a problem. And he will still be here when I return, and I now have someone to work *for*! There's a purpose to everything again!"

When she had finished stirring her coffee and raised her eyes, she looked not at Adam but at Helena. Everything that she wanted to say and could not say was explicit in her look. They were going away. She was going to get Raefe Elliot out of her system in the only way she knew. When she returned, Li Pi and her piano would be waiting for her, but Raefe Elliot would not be. Helena nodded her head slightly, to indicate that she understood.

"You'll enjoy Singapore," she said, rising to her feet and judging that a *tête-à-tête* was no longer necessary. "When do you leave?"

Elizabeth looked questioningly at Adam. He turned to her, giving her his slow smile, and all the love he felt for her was vividly apparent.

"On Wednesday," he said, and was rewarded by a tight hug.

Looking at them both, Helena felt a lump in her throat. They *were* happy together, and they deserved to continue to be happy together. She prayed to God that Raefe would have the sense to leave Elizabeth alone when she returned from Singapore.

"I'll be going now," she said, knowing that if *she* were Elizabeth, she certainly wouldn't risk losing a man of Adam's worth for a brief, sexual frolic with a roustabout like Raefe.

With her arms still tight around Adam's waist, Elizabeth looked toward her. " 'Bye," she called, knowing full well why Helena had come to see her and deeply touched by her concern. "Everything's going to be fine, Helena. Really it is."

Helena grinned, blew her a kiss, and walked with Junoesque grace through the house and out to her little Morgan. She hoped Elizabeth was right, but she couldn't help remembering that it was Raefe who had given her Li Pi's name and address. Raefe who had gone to the trouble to find a teacher worthy of her. And he had said he loved her. She doubted if he had said that very often in the past. And she doubted, very much, that he would let her go easily.

Chapter Fifteen

❧

B̲UT why the hell have they gone? And for how long?" Ronnie asked mystified as he perched himself on the end of their double bed and watched Julienne as she scooped her spicy red curls up and away from her face. She secured them in a neat twist on the top of her head before she began applying her makeup. "We were supposed to be playing tennis with them tomorrow!"

"I have no idea," Julienne said with a little shrug that sent her bathrobe slipping off one creamy smooth shoulder. "Elizabeth telephoned me yesterday and said that they were leaving for Singapore this morning. She said they didn't know when they would be coming back. In three weeks, perhaps. In a month. They really had no idea."

"Damned odd, if you ask me," Ronnie said, eyeing Julienne's bathrobe as it slipped provocatively lower. "I've never heard old Adam express any wish to go jaunting off to Singapore." He grinned suddenly. "He's not going to inspect its fortifications against the Japs, is he?"

Julienne giggled and applied tiny dabs of foundation cream to her forehead and nose and cheeks. Adam's preoccupation with Hong Kong's defense was a well-known joke between them.

"*Peut-être*," she said, smoothing the foundation cream into her skin with practiced fingers. "Maybe."

The bathrobe had slipped farther and a pleasingly pert breast with a dark, almost russet-colored nipple was now magnificently displayed.

Ronnie rose to his feet and stood behind her, his hand sliding down and caressing the exposed part of her anatomy appreciatively.

"*Arrête-toi!*" she said, with no ill humor. "Stop it, *chéri*. I am in a hurry." She had just showered and in half an hour she was meeting Derry for drinks at the Peninsula. She added a slight touch of color to her cheeks and sucked them in, regarding her heart-shaped face in despair. "*Quelle horreur*! Why can I not have cheekbones like the beautiful Elizabeth? All high and classical and wonderfully, wonderfully photogenic?"

"Because you have a face like a little kitten," Ronnie said lovingly, his hand moving reluctantly away from her breast and resting chastely on her shoulder. He lowered his head and kissed her on the temple, hesitating for a moment and then saying, "Don't go out this evening, Julie. Stay in and keep me company."

Her violet-dark eyes shot open wide. "*Alors, chéri!* What is it? Are you not feeling well? Are you not going to the club to meet Alastair?"

It was Thursday night, and it was a fond fabrication on both their parts that on Thursdays Julie had a meal out with her girlfriends, and Ronnie met up with Alastair or Tom at the club. Both of them were well aware that in fact neither of them spent the evening in quite such a decorous manner and, until now, neither of them had very much minded. It was a mutual deception containing very little real deceit.

Ronnie looked at her pretty, concerned face in the dressing-table mirror. He was supposed to be going to Wanchai to meet a Chinese girl he had been seeing for over two months now. Stray tendrils were escaping from the knot on top of Julie's head and curling forward onto her face. "No, I'm not ill," he said, wondering where she was going and if she was still seeing her major in the Royal Scots. "To tell you the truth, I just felt like a Thursday night at home for a change." He cleared his throat, almost embarrassed by the confession. "Together."

She had been in the process of applying mascara and her hand stayed for a moment in midair. She hadn't seen Derry for five days and the mere thought of him sent an anticipatory tingle down her spine, and a flush of heat to her vulva. "Oh, *chéri* . . . If I had known sooner . . ." she began, not wanting to hurt him.

He gave her a quick—too quick—smile. "It's all right, Julie," he lied. "Perhaps next Thursday . . ."

She put down her mascara brush and twisted around on the stool to face him. His smile hadn't reached his eyes and his voice had sounded distinctly wistful. "*Non.* Not next week," she said decisively, taking hold of his hands and twisting her fingers through his. "We will both stay home tonight." Derry could wait. He was, after all, only her lover. Ronnie was her husband and her friend. Ronnie came first and always would.

She flashed him her wide, brilliant smile. "It will make a nice change, *non?*" she said, hoping that he wasn't suddenly approaching middle age and respectability. If he was, there would be no more Derrys and that would be a pity. Also, she could not imagine Ronnie being respectable. He *enjoyed* philandering. It came almost as easily to him as it did to her.

She giggled and wound her arms about his neck. "Perhaps we should give the houseboys the night off?" she said, her eyes sparkling wickedly. "And then we can enjoy some really *noisy* sex, *chéri!*"

". . . and so I thought that Elizabeth had talked Adam into leaving for Singapore because she wanted to put an end to her affair with Raefe," Julienne said to Helena the next day as they were having lunch in Gripps at the Hong Kong Hotel. "But now, after what Derry has just told me, I don't know what to think!"

"And just what *did* Derry tell you?" Helena asked, keeping her opinions about Elizabeth's motivations to herself.

Julienne picked up her wineglass, and half a dozen gold bracelets cascaded glitteringly down her arm. "He said that Melissa was spending a few days in Victoria and that on Saturday Raefe was taking her to the Gold and Green Ball."

"You mean there has been a reconciliation?" Helena asked, not believing it in a hundred years.

"No-o," Julienne said cautiously. "He didn't exactly say that. He just said that Melissa was bored and wanted to go to the Gold and Green, and that since she didn't have a suitable escort, Raefe had agreed to take her."

Helena's dark brows rose slightly. "Well!" she said at last. "He is her husband. He perhaps thinks that it's far safer for him to take her than it is for her to go with someone who may indulge her in her heroin habit."

Julienne put down her wineglass and began to toy with her asparagus. "But if Raefe had told Elizabeth that his wife was back in Victoria and that he was taking her to the Gold and Green, might that not be why she left for Singapore? Because she thought there had been a reconciliation between them?"

"No," Helena said, with no doubt at all. "Believe me, Julienne. Where Raefe Elliot and Elizabeth are concerned, there are *no* misunderstandings. The only trouble between those two is that they understand each other too well!"

"*On verra*," Julienne said, not totally convinced. "We'll see."

Helena looked at her in amusement. Julienne was always meticulously groomed. This lunchtime the mascara beneath one eye was ever so slightly smudged, and her gold-red curls looked suspiciously mussed. "*When* did you say you'd seen Derry?" she asked curiously.

Julienne had the decency to look slightly discomfited. "This morning," she said, avoiding Helena's eyes. "Isn't that Kaibong Sheng, the Chinese industrialist, over there, by the door?"

"Never mind Kaibong Sheng," Helen said, her suspicions confirmed. "Do you mean to say that you came straight here from Derry Langdon's bed?"

Julienne tried to look as if such a thing was unthinkable, and failed.

Helena shook her head in disbelief. "My God, Julienne! It's barely one o'clock. Couldn't you have waited a bit longer? You only saw him last night!"

Julienne's Thursday nights were as well known to her friends as they were to her husband.

Julienne shook her head. *"Non,"* she said with commendable dignity. "I did *not* see Derry last night. I hadn't seen him for *five* days!"

"So that is why he was pacing the Long Bar at the Pen. Alastair said he looked as frustrated as a caged lion."

Julienne giggled. *"Pauvre petit,"* she said indulgently. "I wasn't able to get a message to him and so, this morning, I drove over to his flat before he left for work."

"And?" Helena prompted, wondering how on earth the Ledsham marriage survived.

"And he did not leave for work," Julienne replied, her eyes sparkling. "Not for quite a while!"

They were still laughing when the waiter came with their bill. "And just who were you with last night that drove that delectable Derry from your mind?" Helena asked as an afterthought as they rose to leave.

Julienne looked at her in surprise. "Ronnie, of course," she said as if it should have been obvious. "Who else?"

Melissa Elliot cast her eyes disinterestedly around the opulent drawing room of her Victoria Peak home. It looked just the same as it had when she had left it. Glossy and immaculate and with as much warmth as a luxury hotel room. A slight frown puckered her brows. All the right ingredients were there and always had been: ankle-deep carpets, lush settees, acres of flowers, and piles of shiny new magazines on the long, low coffee table. Yet she was always aware that it was not quite right and the knowledge irked her. She had an unfailing eye for color and style where clothes were concerned, yet somehow the same flair did not extend to her home.

She walked moodily across the vast room to the windows that looked out over the mountainside and the distant city and the bay. At the moment she didn't give a damn whether the room looked like a hotel room or not. She wouldn't be doing any entertaining here. Raefe's tolerance didn't extend *that* far. He would take her to the Gold and Green, and probably as many other functions as she wished to attend, but he had been adamant that he was not going to play Happy Families with her at Victoria Peak.

She drew deeply on a cigarette, her hand trembling slightly. God, but she needed something stronger than a cigarette and there were over two hours to go before Huang would bring her her scheduled fix of heroin.

She hated Huang with implacable, unadulterated hatred. Nothing on earth would make him unlock his blasted medicine cabinet and give her even a grain of heroin before the appointed time. Or a grain extra. She had tried everything: violence, sex, money. He had been, and still was, impervious to anything she could offer or threaten. "Mr. Elliot says . . ." he would repeat endlessly, and as far as Huang was concerned, Mr. Elliot's word was God-given law.

She ground her cigarette out in an onyx ashtray and continued to stare sulkily toward the distant hills of Kowloon. A sea mist was rolling rapidly landward. The Peak, never slow at succumbing to cloud, was already wreathed in smoky-gray tendrils. Soon cloud and mist would meet and thicken into fog, and visibility would be reduced to a mere few yards. Raefe had said he would drive up to see her that night. To discuss further their joint plans for her return to England.

The telephone on a low, lacquered table some three feet away from her began to ring shrilly. She eyed it distastefully, making no move toward it, waiting till Kwan, one of the houseboys, ran into the room to silence it.

"Good morning, sir. Yes, sir. I will see, sir," he said hurriedly and uncomfortably.

Melissa waited with a sudden feeling of expectancy. Perhaps it was Raefe. Perhaps he was telephoning to say the fog would be too heavy for him to drive up to the Peak later in the day. That she should ask the chauffeur to drive her down to Victoria now, before it grew any worse, and they would meet at his apartment.

"It is Colonel Langdon, Mrs. Elliot," Kwan whispered, his hand firmly over the mouthpiece. "He wishes to speak with you most urgently."

Melissa's small-featured, feline face tightened, the nostrils showing white. "Damn and blast!" she said savagely. "Tell the old fool I'm not here. That I'm still in the New Territories."

"Yes, Mrs. Elliot," her number one houseboy said unhappily. Colonel Langdon was not a man who relished being lied to and his temper was choleric when aroused. Kwan began to lie to the colonel with a smoothness born of years of practice and Melissa threw herself petulantly down onto the nearest armchair.

Her father adored her. He indulged her every whim and thought she could do no wrong. It was all very gratifying but it was not what she wanted at the moment. She wanted the relief of being with someone who knew her for what she was, and accepted her for it without unnecessary pontificating. Her father had naturally expected that she would return to live with him after Raefe's trial. The very thought of it had filled her with horror. There would be the difficulty of obtaining heroin, the endless scenes and recriminations when he was at last forced to realize that the things Raefe had said about her in court were true. She didn't want that. She wanted one person, at least, to continue thinking of her as perfect. And she wanted heroin. And so she had agreed to Raefe's conditions and gone to the farm Raefe's grandfather had bought fifty years ago, way out beyond Golden Hill.

At that time she had hated Raefe even more than she now hated Huang. But even hating him, she grudgingly had to admit to herself that he was treating her with surprising fairness. Their marriage was over, and had been over for nearly a year. After the revelations of the trial it was doubtful that any judge would award her decent alimony. And if she was to live in the style to which she had become accustomed as Mrs. Raefe Elliot, then she would need an exceptionally decent amount. Raefe's conditions had been blindingly simple. If she accepted his help in conquering her addiction, he would see to it that she returned to England with the kind of maintenance agreement that would keep her in luxurious comfort. If she didn't kick her addiction, then there would be no money, no future, nothing.

Her nails dug deep into her palms as she remembered. God in heaven, how she had hated him! He had made it all sound so simple, so easy. And for her, with her craving, it was all so bloody, bloody impossible.

The houseboy put down the telephone receiver and said apologetically, "I don't think the colonel believed me, Mrs.

Elliot. I think perhaps he will come to the house to see if you are here."

Melissa merely glowered at him as if he were personally responsible for her father's actions and he scuttled away, wondering how long she would remain in residence. How soon it would be before the house was once again empty, or occupied by Mr. Elliot and, if the spirits were favorable, a new and more amicable mistress.

Melissa chewed her lower lip fretfully. Her houseboy was right. Her father would undoubtedly be on his way, and would probably still be there when it was time for Huang to give her the heroin she was waiting for so torturedly. She swore and closed her eyes. She knew that she wasn't very bright, but there were times when even she could not believe the mess she had got herself into.

She had never really wanted to go to bed with Paul Williams of the Middlesex. She had merely wanted to arouse Raefe's jealousy. Her eyes, cornflower-blue and still capable of looking surprisingly innocent, opened and narrowed. Even then, two years ago, their marriage had been in difficulties and she had not understood why. She still didn't.

She rose to her feet and again prowled restlessly to the vast window that looked out over the mountainside. There was very little to see now. The cloud and mist had fused and Victoria and the bay were lost to view. She lit herself another cigarette and inhaled deeply.

Derry said that it was her own fault that Raefe had told her their marriage was over. That it would not have happened if she had not been so flagrantly unfaithful to him. Melissa knew he was wrong. Somehow, for some reason that still eluded her, Raefe had fallen out of love with her long before she had embarked on her affair with Paul.

He had never given any indication of it by word or by action, but she had enough experience of her power over men to know when a man was no longer enslaved by her. And Raefe had not been. Not for a long while.

She removed a fleck of tobacco from her tongue, and continued to stare sightlessly out into the swirling mist. She knew now, in retrospect, that she should have settled for what he had given her and would have continued to have given her. His name, his protection, and the remains of his affection. But it had not been enough for her. She hadn't wanted his affection, God damn it! She had wanted his passion. She had wanted him to be as crazy about her as she was about him. And he had not been and nothing she had done had altered the situation for the better. It had only made things indescribably worse.

She shuddered when she thought about Paul Williams. He had been fun for a time, and gratifyingly good-looking, and she had thought herself marvelously in control of the situation. She wasn't in love with him, and so he couldn't possibly hurt her. She was only using him in order to arouse Raefe's jealousy. In order to make Raefe want her again. Only he hadn't, and Paul had hurt her catastrophically. He had introduced her to heroin, and almost instantly she had become agonizingly dependent upon it.

She wrapped her arms tightly around her body as if she were suddenly cold. It was strange how supportive Raefe had been over her addiction. There were times when she could almost believe that if it hadn't been for her unfaithfulness, her addiction alone would not have wrecked their marriage. He had no love left for her, but he had loyalty, and she knew now that as long as she had deserved that, there would have been no other women, no talk of divorce. He would have been scrupulously fair to her, and even now, even after Jacko, he was still more understanding than anyone else she knew.

The throb of a car engine cut through the fog and she glanced quickly at her wristwatch. There was another hour and forty minutes before Huang put her out of her misery. The prospect of enduring her father's anxious company for that length of time, and perhaps longer if she couldn't get rid of him, filled her with horror. She could hear one of the houseboys opening the door to him and low voices in the entrance hall. She took a deep, steadying breath, wiped a trickle of perspiration from her forehead, and turned with a false smile to greet him.

It wasn't her father. It was Raefe. "Kwan thinks your father is on his way here," he said, striding into the room and immediately filling it with his presence. "Which means we won't be able to talk."

He slung his jacket onto a chair, his linen shirt open at the throat, his glossy black hair curling indecently low over the collar. She felt her throat constrict. God damn it, but he could still arouse feelings in her that no other man aroused. Only the knowledge that those feelings were no longer reciprocated prevented her from attempting charm on him. She had been a lot of things, a whore and a fool, but she still had a remnant of pride and would be damned before she showed a man who no longer desired her that she was still enthralled by him.

"He telephoned ten minutes ago," she said curtly. "Derry must have told him I was here."

Raefe poured himself a Scotch and soda and gave his wife a long, assessing look. For three months she had survived on a carefully regulated dosage of heroin, and she had coped with the situation far better than he had thought she would. Drug addiction was no picnic and his rage at her stupidity in first falling prey to it was compounded by his pity for the suffering it was causing her. He said abruptly, "You'd better go and see Huang. If your father arrives in the next half hour, I'll tell him you're resting with a headache."

Her eyes filled with tears of gratitude. "Thank you," she said thickly, and then, in despair, "Bloody, bloody hell! Is it always going to be so bad, Raefe? Is it never going to get better?"

She looked very small, and very defenseless. For the hundredth time he wished Paul Williams into the darkest depths of a tormented hell. "No," he said gruffly. Then to his surprise, and hers, he took her gently into his arms and held her trembling body close to his. "It won't always be so bad, Melissa. You aren't aware of it, but it's getting better every week. You're not on half the amount you used to be. Another three months and you'll be free of it."

"But I won't!" she cried desperately. "I still *want* more, Raefe. God in heaven, I *need* more."

"No, you don't." His voice was firm, his jaw hard as he looked down into her frightened face. "Three months ago you didn't even *want* to be cured. You do now, and it's more than half the battle."

She began to cry and his arms tightened around her, his voice deepening. "I never said it would be easy, Melly. But it is possible. Trust me."

At the diminutive use of her name, which she had not heard on his lips for over a year, she looked up into his strong face and wondered how she could ever have been such a fool as to have lost his love. "I do trust you," she said with childish simplicity.

He released her and she walked unsteadily to the door. She no longer had any bad reactions to the heroin that Raefe obtained for her, but she still felt obscenely disoriented. "Have you thought anymore about when I can return to London?" she asked hesitantly, pausing at the door.

"Not yet, Melly. Not until there is no more need of Huang. Besides," he added when he saw the disappointment in her eyes, "London isn't the best place in the world to be at the moment. Blackouts, gas masks, the nightly waiting for Hitler's bombs. You're better off in Hong Kong."

"And the divorce?" she asked in a small voice. "Won't our appearing together in public prejudice it?"

If she hoped that he would say that the divorce was no longer important, she was again disappointed. "No," he said unequivocally, "we're not sharing the same roof and I damn well won't let anything prejudice it. There's no need to worry on that score."

She looked at him curiously. She had never been able to understand him, never known what he was thinking. She asked with a puzzled frown, "What will you do when we are divorced?"

He grinned at her. The last few moments were the closest they had been in years. "Marry again," he said succinctly.

Her eyes widened in disbelief. "Who?" she asked incredulously. "Surely not the little Chinese girl?"

The amusement in his eyes faded and another expression took its place. An expression of such fierce intentness that Melissa felt the jealousy she thought she had tamed surge through her once again. "No," he said, his voice clipped. "Not Alute."

"A European? Someone we know?"

The moment of closeness was coming to an end. He didn't want to talk to Melissa about Elizabeth. Not yet. Not until Elizabeth had left her husband. He had the irrational superstition that if he talked of it to Melissa, fate would intervene and it would never come to pass. He said only, "Yes, a European."

She saw the tight lines around his mouth, the harsh set of his jaw, and said with sudden insight, "She's married, isn't she?"

A nerve jumped at the corner of his jaw. "You'd better go to Huang," he said, his thoughts no longer on her and her proposed return to England, but on Elizabeth. "Your father will be here any minute."

She knew there was no use in remaining. He had told her all he was prepared to tell her. She hurried off in search of Huang, her mind working furiously. Who the devil could it be? She knew he had had a brief affair with Mark Hurley's wife some months ago. Had the affair been resumed? And if it hadn't? If it wasn't the vivacious Mrs. Hurley?

"Huang!" she called feverishly. *"Huang!"*

There was Julienne Ledsham. She had always had an eye on Raefe and the men Julienne Ledsham eyed nearly always succumbed. A wave of bitterness shot through her at the thought of another woman enjoying the wealth and comfort that was, by marital right, hers. Her nails dug deep into her palms. She damned well wouldn't sink into drug-addicted poverty while Julienne Ledsham, or someone like her, lived royally as Mrs. Raefe Elliot. She would hold Raefe to his promise to provide generously for her. She would damn well free herself of her need for heroin. She would show them all just how strong the weak could be, when they put their minds to it.

The Gold and Green Ball was held in the Rose Room at the Peninsula Hotel and was attended by the elite of Hong Kong society. Julienne looked magnificent, her red-gold curls framing her face like a halo, her gown of starkly simple white velvet chic and very, very French. The top was cut halter-fashion, and the skirt fell in total perfection from her tiny waist to her white satin shoes.

"I can't wait to see Melissa again," she whispered to Ronnie as they greeted a crowd of friends and walked into the chandeliered grandeur of the Pen's ballroom.

"Why? You were never bosom friends," Ronnie said. "Do you think she's going to have a sign around her neck? Whore and drug addict?"

"Of course not, silly," Julienne chided him, squeezing his arm. "It's just that I would like to see if her looks have been affected. It is a reasonable curiosity."

"It's ghoulish," Ronnie said as the band began to play

"It's Only a Paper Moon." He swung her out onto the floor in a pacy fox-trot. "As for me, I hope to God her looks *haven't* been affected and that she's kicked the habit. I always thought Melissa Elliot a remarkably pretty woman."

A tiny frown touched Julienne's brow. "I do not think Melissa Elliot would be at all a good idea for you, *chéri*. I think, in fact, that it would make me quite unhappy."

He looked down into her heart-shaped face and her pansy-dark eyes and grinned. He liked it when he aroused her jealousy. It was such a hard feat to achieve. "Don't worry about Melissa Elliot," he said, and for once he meant it. A woman with the kind of problems that beset Melissa was the last thing he wanted in his life. In fact, there were times lately when he wondered if he needed *any* women in his life. Apart from Julie. It was a thought that had made him wonder if he was ill at first, but to which over the last few weeks he had become accustomed. His only problem was how Julie would receive such an admission. If he began to happily practice monogamy, he would want Julie to do likewise. And Julie, he knew, was in the middle of a hectic affair.

He looked around the crowded room. Who her present lover was he still wasn't sure. If he asked her, she would tell him, but discovering the identities of their respective lovers was part of the game they played and to ask outright would be cheating. His gaze flicked from group to group. Whoever he was, he would be here tonight. And when he saw him with Julie, he would know him.

"It's a pity Elizabeth and Adam aren't here," Alastair said to Helena as he guided her with stiff and correct expertise around the top end of the room. "Adam enjoys full-blown affairs like this."

Helena, seeing Raefe Elliot's distinctive dark head of hair, said dryly, "I don't think Elizabeth would have enjoyed this affair, darling. Have you seen who's over there? And who he's with?"

Alastair looked obediently in the direction she was indicating and his brows shot high. "Good God! He's brought Melissa with him!"

Helena, splendid in a gown of shot-green taffeta with huge puffed sleeves and a skirt that crackled as she moved, said with some amusement, "She *is* still his wife. And I imagine that whatever her reasons for hiding away in the New Territories, it must be pretty boring after a while. She always did enjoy the bright lights."

"Yes, but . . ." Alastair struggled for words. "I mean, they *are* divorcing, aren't they? There hasn't been a reconciliation?"

"Not that I know of," Helena said as they waltzed past the Elliots, who were in conversation with Major General Edward Grasett, the General Officer commanding British troops in China.

As she spoke, Raefe's eyes caught hers and his brows rose in a query. She knew what he was intimating. Where the devil was Elizabeth? She lifted her shoulders in a barely perceptible shrug, indicating that she had no idea. He would find out eventually, no doubt, but not from her.

"Raefe Elliot is quite capable of finding happiness with a woman other than Elizabeth," she said to Alastair as they danced out of his sight. "But Adam Harland isn't."

"And is that where your sympathy lies?" Alastair asked, aware that for the first time in his life, with Helena in his arms, he was actually enjoying dancing.

"Oh, yes," Helena said with a warmth that took him by surprise. "My sympathy is most definitely with Adam. He's one of the nicest men I've ever met."

"Melissa Elliot looks no different now than she did a year ago," Ronnie said to Julienne as the music came to an end and they walked from the floor. "The only thing that's wrong with her is that she's too thin."

"Silly," Julienne said. "A woman *can't* be too thin!" She eyed Melissa appraisingly. Melissa had always dressed well, with a flair more French than English. Her dress of shimmering blue silk emphasized the startling color of her eyes. The neckline was softly cowled, the sleeves were discreetly long, and the back plunged spectacularly to her waist and a nestling gardenia.

"She is still very, very pretty, isn't she?" Julienne whispered to Ronnie as they approached her. Her hair, golden blond and sleek, was waved close to her head, skimming her ears, revealing tiny pearl drop earrings.

She was, but Ronnie still felt no desire to deepen his acquaintance with her. Women like Melissa Elliot were nothing but trouble and best given a wide berth. He tried to steer Julienne in another direction, but it was too late. She was already kissing Melissa effusively on the cheek.

"It's lovely to see you again," she said, and there was no note of falseness in her voice. She *was* pleased to see Melissa again. The thought of any woman being cooped up in the New Territories with no opportunity for fun or gossip or dancing was anathema to her.

Melissa was momentarily disconcerted, looking quickly from Julienne to Raefe. There was nothing on either of their faces to indicate that they were playing out a charade and were, in fact, lovers who wished to marry as soon as possible.

"It's nice to be back," she said cautiously. "Nothing much changes, though, does it? I can't see any new faces. Just the same old crowd."

Julienne wondered if Melissa knew about Elizabeth and hoped Ronnie wouldn't be so unfeeling as to mention the newly arrived Harlands.

"One thing that hasn't changed is Miriam Gresby's dress sense," she said naughtily. "Have you seen her? She looks as though she is wearing a converted barrage balloon!"

Melissa began to laugh. Ronnie glanced at Raefe and saw that his attention was focused fiercely on Julienne. It was obvious that he wanted to speak to her away from Melissa and Ronnie could well imagine what he wanted to speak to her about. It was three days since Elizabeth and Adam had left Hong Kong and Raefe obviously wanted to know where the devil she was.

The band launched into a quickstep and he turned toward Melissa. "Would you like to dance?" he asked gallantly.

"Very much," Melissa said, stepping away from Raefe and toward Ronnie. There had been no dancing at all in the New Territories, and she had noticed the instant they had entered the ballroom that most men were steering clear of her, disconcerted by Raefe's presence at her side, the scandal of the trial still fresh in their minds.

The second they had gone, Raefe said fiercely to Julienne, "Where the hell is she?"

His white dinner jacket flattered his dark good looks magnificently. There was a raw edge to his voice that sent a shiver of pleasure down her spine. Not for the first time she wished it was she who obsessed his thoughts and not Elizabeth.

She hesitated, feeling a surge of erotic pleasure at the temporary power she wielded over him. His voice took on a hint of menace, his eyes narrowing threateningly. "For God's sake, Julienne," he muttered through clenched teeth, *"where is she?"*

Her pleasure could be prolonged no longer. If she didn't tell him he was quite capable of laying violent hands on her. "Singapore," she said, noting how tense his powerful shoulders were beneath the exquisite cut of his dinner jacket. "They left on Wednesday morning aboard the *Blantyre Castle.*"

Chapter Sixteen
❦

THE *Blantyre Castle* steamed languorously through the South China Sea toward Singapore, and Elizabeth tried to retrieve the peace of mind that Raefe Elliot had so disastrously destroyed.

She had hoped the voyage would give her a chance to reaffirm her love for Adam, to show him physically how very much she loved him. Her hopes had been dashed. On their first night at sea, Adam had complained of a severe head cold. He had taken himself to bed alone with a hot brandy and lemon. She had been ashamed of the relief she had felt, but she'd learned something important: no matter how sincere her intentions, it wasn't possible to recreate with Adam the passion she had known with Raefe.

Whatever explosive ingredient existed between her and Raefe Elliot did not exist between her and Adam . . . and never had. They were friends, gentle lovers with a wealth of shared and treasured memories behind them. As Adam began to feel better and they strolled the decks hand in hand, she realized with thankfulness that her passion for

Raefe had not altered her feelings for Adam in any way. They played deck quoits and tennis, they danced together in the evenings and, incredibly, it was as if nothing had changed between them. With utter certainty she knew that nothing would. Not if she were strong. Adam had a right to her companionship and the quiet love she felt for him, and he would have both for as long as he wanted. Her life with him was the same and had no connection with the sexual madness that had erupted with Raefe.

Memories of their fevered lovemaking on the beach rose up to torment her constantly, and she ruthlessly subdued them. It was over. Her true nature had been revealed to her, but for Adam's sake she would never succumb to that animallike hunger again. She had turned her back on Raefe, both metaphorically and physically, and she would not give in to him again. The memory of how she had capitulated, her frenzied, lascivious eagerness, mortified her. But Raefe was a thousand miles away, and no matter how Adam urged her to return to Hong Kong, she would not do so. Not until she had rooted out and killed her carnal desire for Raefe, until she could meet him and be as indifferent to him as she was to Tom Nicholson or Ronnie Ledsham.

"Penny for them, darling," Adam said, smiling at her as they leaned on the deck rail, watching a school of flying fish.

A flush of color touched her cheeks. "I was wondering if Singapore will be much different from Hong Kong," she lied, her gaze remaining resolutely on the fish.

"I imagine not. It's all southeast Asia, isn't it? There'll be the same polyglot mix, the same heat, and the same sort of smells. Sweet spices, dried fish, frangipani. The smell of the tropics. It's never far away, even on board ship."

"I'm looking forward to it," she said with a fierceness that made him raise his eyebrows. "Perhaps we can go up-country. To Johore and to Kuala Lumpur?"

"You really have got the travel bit between your teeth, haven't you?" he asked, amused. "What about Li Pi and the study you were looking forward to?"

The flying fish dived from view, but she continued to gaze across the water. "Li Pi will still be there when we return to Hong Kong," she said with a lightness she was far from feeling. Li Pi was the sacrifice she had to make in

order to free herself from Raefe. Even now, the cost of it
filled her with so much pain she could scarcely breathe.
"Let's go down to the bar and have a drink," she said,
turning quickly so that Adam would not see the anguish in
her eyes.

The talk in the bar was all of war, and as Adam and the
friends they had made on board discussed the news that
Warsaw had surrendered to the Germans, she struggled to
recover her composure and her equilibrium. By the time
the conversation had turned to America and its determination not to be involved in the conflict ripping into Europe,
she was once again cool and in control. She would not
think of Li Pi. She would not think of Raefe. She would
think of nothing but Adam, and his dear, honest face. Of
nothing but how he loved her and needed her. Of how
fortunate she was to be his wife.

"It's a bit flat and drab after Hong Kong, isn't it?" Adam
said, puffing on his pipe as the *Blantyre Castle* approached
the sea lanes outside Singapore's harbor.

"It's not as pretty," Elizabeth agreed, standing beside
him on the deck, the sea breeze cool and refreshing against
her face.

There were no magnificent mountains rising sheer from
the sea. No soaring rocks, silver-gray, silver-tawny. Instead, in the dancing, almost liquid heat, Singapore lay
spread out before them, an unromantic line of godowns
and shining petrol tanks on the left, and on the right a
fringe of coconut palms and a flurry of sampans and junk
masts.

"The terrain is the only thing that *is* different," Adam
said with a grin an hour later, as he guided her down the
gangplank and a blast of hot hair hit them in the face. "Just
listen to that racket! It's even worse that Victoria!"

The dockside teemed with coolies, their clamoring cries
and chants as they loaded and unloaded cargo rising
deafeningly, yet not quite drowning the strident shouts of
their Chinese overseers. Street hawkers added to the din,
plying their wares to disembarking passengers. The boats
around them were unloading spices from Bali and Java and
the Celebes, and the fragrance rose into the air, mingling
with the smell of the Singapore River and the swamp that
stretched out on either side of it.

"God, but it's hot," Adam said, wiping the back of his neck with his handkerchief as they stepped onto the dock. "I thought I'd got used to the heat in Hong Kong, but it's like a blanket here!"

Elizabeth laughed, looking exquisitely cool in a white linen dress that emphasized her slender curves, a broad-brimmed straw hat shielding her face from the sun. She felt headily free. Hong Kong was behind her and she was determined, with all her might, mind, and strength, that she would not return to it until she knew that her marriage was no longer in danger. Leaving Li Pi, leaving Raefe, had been the hardest things she had ever done, but somehow she had found the strength and now, standing on the crowded dock, she was proud at having emerged victorious from her long, hard, private battle.

"Where to now?" she asked, taking Adam's hand as their luggage was trundled ahead of them by a clutch of black-clad coolies.

"Raffles," he said, beginning to think that the trip had not been such a bad idea after all. There *was* something exciting about a new city, and his instinct told him that Singapore was going to be as interesting and perhaps even more exotic that Hong Kong had been.

She walked quickly at his side, her hand held firmly in his, ignoring the appreciative glances she drew from certain sections of the crowd—husbands waiting to greet their wives, businessmen waiting to meet colleagues.

"I'm looking forward to it," she said, her eyes sparkling in a way they had not done for weeks. Then she looked away from Adam to the gate leading from the docks to the road, and her face whitened, her hand convulsively clutched his arm.

"Welcome to Singapore," Raefe said, stepping toward them. His rich deep-timbred voice ripped wide all her hard-won intentions and sent them scattering. "Did you have a good voyage?"

He was speaking to Adam, but his eyes, dark and determined and full of heat, were on Elizabeth. She couldn't look away from him. She was held by his gaze, riveted by it, drowning in it.

"Yes," Adam said with unaccustomed curtness. "I didn't know you were in Singapore." His eyes flicked past Raefe, looking for a taxi. "Are you here for long?"

"I don't know," Raefe replied easily, his gaze still on Elizabeth. "It depends."

His eyes were burning her, scorching through her. She tried to speak and couldn't. She had tried so hard, run so far, and all to no avail. She had merely run from the frying pan into the fire. In Hong Kong, there were friends who simply by their presence could offer her a measure of protection against her crippling desire for him. In Singapore there was no one. And he would pursue her until she capitulated, not just for a few stolen hours, but forever. His eyes and the tight, harsh lines around his mouth told her that. Her fingers dug deeply in the soft linen of Adam's tropical jacket. She felt as if she were going to faint.

"Where are you going? Raffles?" Raefe asked Adam, reluctantly dragging his gaze from her.

"Yes." Adam's voice was chill. He didn't like Elliot. He didn't like his reputation or his negligent, insolent attitude. And he didn't like his being in Singapore, or the coincidence of his being at the docks at the precise moment they had disembarked.

Raefe turned around and raised his hand, and immediately a yellow Ford taxicab purred to a halt at their side.

"Thank you," Adam said stiffly as the coolies began to load their luggage into the trunk.

"Singapore is my city, almost as much as Hong Kong," Raefe said, his eyes once more on Elizabeth's pale, strained face. "I look forward to showing you around."

Adam made a polite, noncommittal reply. He had no intention of spending time with Elliot, in Singapore or anywhere else. He helped Elizabeth into the rear of the taxi and climbed in after her. Then he leaned forward and said to the Chinese driver, "Raffles, please." He did not even look in Raefe Elliot's direction as the taxi pulled away from the curb and into the traffic.

Raefe didn't care. It was about time Adam Harland realized he was losing his wife. And he *was* losing her. Had already lost her. A slight, tight smile touched his mouth. He knew how much she had wanted to throw herself into his arms, how desperately she had wanted to turn her head as the cab drew away and look at him as he was looking at her until she was no longer in sight.

"You tried hard, my love," he said softly as the dockside

crowds and rickshaws and taxicabs surged around him.
"But even you cannot escape the inevitable." Then he
turned to the chauffeur-driven Lagonda waiting a mere few
feet away. "Robinson Road," he said as he settled himself
into its luxurious interior, wondering how he would
endure the hours until he saw her again.

Elizabeth leaned her head weakly against cracked, hot
leather. Dear God, what a fool she had been to think that
she could escape him so easily! As the taxi hurtled away
from the docks she could see a godown, the name "Elliot"
emblazoned in large, scarlet letters across its front. Elliot. A
name synonymous with rubber and tin. A name as well
known in Singapore as it was in Hong Kong. She remembered her first dinner party at Tom Nicholson's, and
Julienne's saying that it was when Raefe had returned from
a business trip to Singapore that he had found Jacko
Latimer in his wife's bed. She closed her eyes as the cab
sped past neatly laid out flower beds and the white, elegant
facades of government buildings. She should have known.
She should have remembered. Ever since she had left
Hong Kong she had been living in a fool's paradise. A man
of Raefe's wealth didn't waste time in traveling to Singapore by ship. He flew down. And he had done so the
minute he had been told where she was.

"Did you know Elliot was in Singapore?" Adam asked,
his voice unusually brusque as the taxi veered onto a tree-
lined road.

"No." She opened her eyes. She felt so drained, so
shattered by the shock of seeing Raefe, of knowing she
could summon up no resistance to him, that if Adam had
asked her then and there whether she was having an affair
with him, she would have admitted it.

"I can't stand the man," he said irritably. "There's
something insufferably arrogant and insultingly self-
assured about him. It wouldn't surprise me at all if he had
murdered Jack or Jimmy Latimer, or whatever his name
was, in cold blood."

It was so unlike Adam to speak harshly of anyone that
Elizabeth felt as if cold hands were on her heart. "He
didn't," she said, hating herself for the position Raefe had
put her in—a woman defending her lover to her husband.
"The members of the jury agreed that his action was

unpremeditated and that he merely meant to give Jacko a thrashing."

"It's a pretty vicious thrashing that leaves a man with a smashed skull," Adam said tightly as they turned left into Beach Road toward the travelers' palms that signaled the approach to Raffles.

She remained silent. She didn't want to discuss Raefe. Her feelings were in tumult as it was, and to hear Raefe's name being spoken so derogatorily by someone she loved and whose opinion she had always respected was almost more than she could bear. She wondered if he knew. The tension emanating between her and Raefe had been almost palpable, and she knew that another, more worldly man would have guessed the truth instantly. But Adam was not worldly, not when it came to sexual indiscretions, and he had never had any reason to suspect her of unfaithfulness.

The cab drew to a halt. Bellboys ran to assist with their luggage. An Indian doorman, tall and turbanned, saluted them into the marble-flagged reception area. Thanks to her childhood, she was a connoisseur where great hotels were concerned, and she had looked forward to staying at the legendary Raffles. Now her pleasure had evaporated, and she scarcely looked about her as a bellboy led them to their rooms.

"I suppose he's down here on business," Adam said pugnaciously, refusing to let the subject drop. He tipped the bellboy and closed the door on him. "The name Elliot was plastered all over the godowns near the docks. He must own half the damned city."

"I don't think so," she said, sitting down on one of the beds and easing off her shoes. God, the last thing she wanted was a discussion with Adam about Raefe's wealth. "I feel suddenly ridiculously tired, Adam. Would you mind very much if I had a nap? We can go for a look around later on, after lunch."

He gazed at her with a concerned frown. Her beautiful face was ivory pale and there were dark shadows beneath her eyes that he had not seen there earlier.

"Of course I don't mind," he said, immediately solicitous. "Would you like me to ring for a cup of tea?"

"No, thank you," she said, forcing a smile. "I just need to sleep, Adam, that's all."

He walked across to her. "I shouldn't have gone on so

about Raefe Elliot," he said apologetically. "It isn't as if the man is of the slightest interest to us." He leaned over and kissed her on the forehead. "Have a good rest, darling. I'll wake you in an hour or so."

The door clicked quietly behind him. The fan, hanging trembling from the ceiling, turned lazily and sunlight fell in slatted shafts through the rattan blinds. She stared up at the glistening white ceiling. All she had to do was not to see him. With a little persuasion, she could surely coerce Adam into leaving immediately for Kuala Lumpur or Johore. Her good intentions didn't have to lay shattered in smithereens around her. She could still salvage a remnant of self-respect from the wreckage.

She thought of the way he had looked when their eyes had met over the heads of the hurrying coolies and disembarking passengers, tall and broad-shouldered, his silk shirt open at the throat, his white flannels snug about his narrow hips, his glossy black hair sheened blue by the sun, and desire shot through her, convulsing her with a physical longing raging to be assuaged. Dear God, but she wanted his hands on her body, his mouth on her flesh. The mere thought of it made her hot and damp, made her quiver in hungry anticipation.

With a sob she rolled over onto her stomach, her fists clenched as she slammed them into the pillows. She would *not* give in to him! She would not sacrifice her life with Adam because of her ravenous craving to lay spread-eagled on her back beneath Raefe Elliot's hard, thrusting body. *She would not! She would not! She would not!*

When Adam returned she had showered and was wearing an apricot cotton dress with a narrow waist and full skirt, and matching peep-toe sandals with a high wedge heel.

"Feeling better, darling?" he asked, sliding his arms around her.

"Yes," she lied, She leaned against him, wishing with all her heart that her body would react to his in the same wild, impassioned way that it reacted to Raefe's. "Adam?" Her arms tightened around him as he looked down at her questioningly. "Could we leave tomorrow for Kuala Lumpur? I've heard that the scenery up-country is superb and—"

"Good heavens, Beth! We've only just got here!" he said,

laughing indulgently. "Let's leave Kuala Lumpur till next week or the week after. It won't run away."

Her heart began to beat in short, thick strokes. She could scarcely remember him refusing her anything, and this was so important! If they didn't leave Singapore, if she had to face Raefe again, then the whole structure of their lives would fall apart.

"Please, Adam," she said, slipping her hands up and around his neck. "Please, darling. It would mean so much to me."

His smile faded. "That's what you said about coming to Singapore, Beth. I gave in to you and we came, but I don't particularly want to find myself in transit again for at least two weeks. It simply isn't reasonable." He squeezed her, then released her. "Come on, darling. I got to talking to a couple of planters and an up-country tin-miner in the Long Bar. I'd like to introduce you to them."

"Please, Adam," she said again, her voice taut. "I know it seems ridiculous, but it *is* important to me!"

"But why?" he asked. "Why this urge to be constantly on the move? Is there something wrong? Something you're not telling me?"

She looked up into his dear, kind, puzzled face, and knew with despair that she couldn't tell him. It would hurt him too much and the dreadful inadequacy at the heart of their marriage would lay exposed. He would know that his gentle, reverent lovemaking had never aroused her. That though she loved him dearly, she was not in love with him in the way a woman ought to be with her husband. And nothing would ever be the same between them again.

"No," she said wearily. "No, there's nothing wrong, Adam."

He took her once more into his arms, holding her close. "I can't bear it if you're unhappy, Beth," he said, his voice muffled against her hair. "I love you so much, sweetheart. You mean everything in the world to me."

"I know." Her voice was choked. "And I love you too, Adam." Her arms tightened around him. At that moment it seemed inconceivable that she could ever hurt him. All she had to do was remember how very dear he was to her. And refuse to see Raefe Elliot ever again.

They had a couple of drinks in the Long Bar and Adam introduced her to the planters and the miner that he had met earlier. Later, as they ate lunch, the sound of music filtered through into the dining room. "That's the band," Adam said with a grin. "There's dancing here every afternoon. Rather decorous, I suspect, but still fun."

When they had finished their coffee they strolled along the arcade that led to the dance floor. "How about a slow foxtrot before we launch ourselves on the town?" Adam asked her, putting his pipe away in his pocket. "It's years since I did this sort of thing at two o'clock in the afternoon. It makes life feel quite *risqué!*"

For the rest of the day, as they explored Singapore by rickshaw and taxi, she wondered when Raefe would next attempt to get in touch with her. And where.

The city was more open, more laid out, than Hong Kong, the contrasts between the different parts of the city sharper and more obviously defined. The Chinese part of the city, the crowded and dark little shops, was familiar enough to them after Hong Kong, but only a few streets away the noise and bustle vanished and Chinese faces were replaced by Indian faces, black pajamas by vivid silk saris, hectic frenzy by Asian languor.

They paid off their taxicab and strolled through a street market, its stalls piled high with mounds of mangoes and papayas and pomelos and chilies, the ground daubed with the scarlet stains of betel nuts. Later, when they were tired, they took a rickshaw back to Raffles, the narrow, crowded streets replaced by broad avenues with trim grass verges and luxuriant and carefully tended flower beds.

"That's the Tanglin Club," Adam said, pointing out a low, white building amid spacious grounds. "If we're going to be here for any length of time, we must become members. Alastair says it has the best swimming pool in the city."

As they neared the government and business section, she saw the name "Elliot" emblazoned high over an office block and her stomach muscles tightened. She didn't want to be in Singapore long enough for it to become necessary for them to join prestigious, all-white sports clubs like the Tanglin. She wanted to leave Singapore, and Raefe Elliot, far behind her.

"It's a far more attractive city than it first looked, isn't it?" Adam mused as their rickshaw bowled down the broad tree-lined expanse of Battery Road. "Every street leads to either the sea or the river. There's water and ships everywhere."

She agreed with him. Singapore *was* a beautiful city, with its parks and gardens and its straight streets bordered by exotic flame trees, but she couldn't enjoy it as Adam did. Nearing Raffles Place, she could think only of Raefe. Of whether he would be at Raffles when they returned. Of how he would take her adamant refusal to see him again. Of how she would summon the strength to remain steadfast against her crippling need for him.

Dusk was falling rapidly as their rickshaw drew up with a flourish in front of the travelers' palms. "You go ahead for a shower, Beth," Adam said as they walked into the hotel. "I'm going to slip into the bar for five minutes and have a cooling stengah. My throat is parched."

She was only too happy to go straight up to their room. A brief glance into the barnlike lounge had shown no sign of Raefe, but he would be nearby somewhere, she was sure of it. Her hand trembled slightly on the banister as she walked quickly up the wide stairs. She was filled with such a mixture of dread and longing that she felt as though she was being inwardly torn apart. Once in the comparative safety of her room she closed the door and leaned against it, her eyes closed.

Would he have the temerity to join them for dinner? Was he even now sharing a drink with Adam? His determined pursuit sent waves of aching pleasure licking through her. He could have any woman he wanted for the asking. And he wanted her. She opened her eyes and moved across the room, switching on lamps, closing the blinds against the moths and the nighttime sounds of crickets and bullfrogs. When she listened to people talking about him, even people who liked him, such as Julienne and Helena, she felt as if they were talking about a stranger. They weren't talking about the Raefe *she* knew. The Raefe who was as oddly vulnerable and as inwardly lonely as she herself was. The Raefe with whom she identified so completely.

She unbuckled the narrow belt of her dress and stepped out of her shoes. There had been an almost instant fusion between them, not only physically but also mentally. She felt as if she had known him all her life. She laid her dress on the end of the bed and walked into the bathroom, turning on the shower.

The water gushed hot and strong and she stepped beneath it, turning her face upward. She wanted to be with him more than she had ever wanted anything, ever, in her life. Even more than she wanted success as a pianist. She wanted his face to be the last thing she saw at night, when she closed her eyes. She wanted him to be the first thing she saw when she woke. She wanted to eat with him, sleep with him, laugh with him, cry with him. She wanted to sit across the breakfast table from him, she wanted to watch him shave, she wanted to share his dreams and hopes. She wanted to be part of his life. Tears mingled with the hot rush of water. If only they had met years ago. If only she hadn't married Adam. If only . . . If only . . .

"There's quite a good bunch down in the bar," Adam called out to her as he entered the bedroom. "Tin-miners out on the town. What they don't know about the Japs isn't worth knowing. You don't mind if I have another chat with them later, after dinner, do you, Beth?"

"No, of course not." Beneath the roar of the shower her voice was unsteady. She wiped the futile tears away, deeply ashamed. How could she ever wish that the last few years with Adam had never taken place? It wasn't possible. Adam had always been a part of her life. His strong, compassionate nature had been her support and her sustenance ever since she was a child, and she could not wish herself free of it now, simply because the deeply sexual side of her nature had been unleashed at last.

She stepped out of the shower and wrapped a towel around herself. "Was there anyone else in the bar?" she asked, forcing herself to sound uninterested. "Anyone we know!"

"No," he said, his brows pulling together in a slight frown. "It would hardly be likely, would it? The only person we know who's in Singapore is Elliot."

She crossed to the dressing table, sat down before it, and reached for her makeup. He had told her all she wanted to know. Raefe wasn't in the bar. And he hadn't approached Adam suggesting that they all dine together. She felt a surge of relief that was immediately followed by fierce, excruciating disappointment.

Adam gave her a long, puzzled look, then walked into the bathroom to shower. Had she been referring to Elliot?

he wondered. Was she expecting him to be in the Long Bar this evening? Had she perhaps known all along that he would be in Singapore? He unbuttoned his sweat-soaked shirt and tossed in onto the floor. The Singapore heat was getting to him and he was being ridiculous. Elliot's appearance at the docks when they had disembarked had been nothing but coincidence. And there was nothing remotely odd about him being in Singapore. His business interests must demand that he visit the city often.

The hot water flowed over his head and as he reached for the soap he began to whistle. The idea of Beth indulging in an adulterous affair with Raefe Elliot was as ridiculous now as it had been when Alastair had first hinted at it. He grinned to himself, thinking how outraged she would be if she knew he had even considered such a thing a possibility.

"Put your silver dance shoes on," he called to her as he soaped his chest and shoulders. "We'll have another spin on the floor and a bottle of champagne to celebrate our first night here!"

All through dinner Elizabeth tried to relax and failed miserably. While Adam talked about the differences between Singapore and Hong Kong, her eyes flicked nervously away from his animated face and around the crowded dining room. There was no sign of Raefe. Her throat was tight, and she was torn by conflicting emotions.

"One of the chaps I was drinking with earlier used to be a stockbroker," Adam said, "traveling up to town from Brighton every day on the eight-fifteen. He threw it all in five years ago and came out here. He says he hasn't regretted a day of it."

Elizabeth smiled and toyed with her *satay,* wondering if, concealed by one of the many giant potted ferns, Raefe was watching them as they ate and talked.

Later, in the Long Bar, she did her best to listen attentively as Adam and his new-found friends discussed the Japanese and their empire-building intentions.

"I'm sorry . . . I didn't quite hear," she said apologetically as one of the planters waited, his eyes appreciative, for her to respond to the last remark he had made to her.

"I said that the war in Europe has been no bad thing for Malaya," he repeated obligingly, wishing to God that her husband wasn't there and that he could let his eyes rove below the enticing neckline of her dress. "America is panicking like mad and demanding more rubber than she has been doing for an age. We have over three million acres of it under cultivation, you know, and half the world's tin." His Australian-accented voice was full of pride, as if he were personally responsible for the country's natural richness.

She managed a smile. "Then it's no wonder the Japanese have an unhealthy interest in Malaya."

The Australian laughed. She was intelligent as well as stunning to look at. "Have another drink," he said expansively, turning around and banging his fist on the bar to attract the barman's attention.

Elizabeth suppressed a shudder and touched Adam's arm lightly. "I really don't want any more to drink, darling. Or any more of this conversation. Do you mind if I slip away? It's been a long day and I'm tired."

"No, of course not," he said, his eyes darkening with concern as they always did at the least indication that she was uncomfortable or unhappy. "Do you want me to come with you?"

She shook her head, knowing he was enjoying his conversation about Japanese intentions and Britain's ability to deal with them. "No, of course not. I'm going to go for a short walk in the grounds and then have a long bath before I go to bed." She gave his arm a loving squeeze, said good night to the disappointed Australian, and walked quickly through the lounge and along the arcade that skirted the ballroom and led to the gardens.

Raefe hadn't been in the dining room, and he hadn't been in the bar. She had been wrong in her assumption that he would be. As she stepped out into the hot, sultry darkness she knew that if only she could persuade Adam to change his mind and leave Singapore in the morning for Kuala Lumpur or Johore, then the confrontation she so dreaded would be avoided.

The narrow gravel path she had taken wound down between soaring travelers' palms and high banks of ghostly blossomed hibiscus and sweet-smelling juniper. Thousands of stars spangled the night sky, burning with breathtaking brightness, and she paused, looking up at them, recognizing the Pleiades and Orion and the familiar curve of the Hyades.

From somewhere behind her, in the scented darkness,

there came a soft footfall and the sound of a match spurting into flame. She spun around, her heart leaping into her throat, knowing who it was even before he rounded the curve of the path. A second later the hibiscus blossoms trembled, milk-white petals fluttering to the ground.

"I thought you were never going to have the sense to come out here," he said, and the match and the cigarette he had just lit both went fizzing down among the dry juniper needles as he covered the distance between them in an easy stride and took her into his arms.

Chapter Seventeen
☙

SHE tried to push herself free of him, tried to cry out in protest, but the touch of his hand on her flesh, the hard, muscular strength of his body, the feel of his heart pounding close against hers, were too much for her. With a groan she swayed against him, brought almost to insensibility by the pleasure of his touch.

"No . . ." she whispered desperately as he raised her face to his. "Oh, please, Raefe, no . . ."

In the moonlight his lean, high-cheekboned face was merciless. "Yes," he breathed harshly and lowered his head to hers, holding her with brutal strength.

Vainly she tried to wrest her mouth from his, but her need for him, her raging, urgent desire confounded her and left her helpless. For one brief, brave moment she struggled, then his hair was coarse beneath her fingers, his hands hard upon her body, and his mouth was dry as her tongue slipped past his lips.

Her surrender was total, irrevocable. When his hands slid up beneath the soft silk of her dress, she made no protest, pressing herself closer to him with shameless hunger.

"I want you, Lizzie . . . Want you . . ." he said hoarsely.

Though beyond his shoulder she could see the lights of the ballroom gleaming between the trees and the painted Chinese lanterns that decked the terrace, she said only in a wanton, raw voice that she no longer recognized, "Yes! Here! Now! Oh, please! Quickly. *Quickly!*"

There were no preliminaries. He didn't even lower her to the ground. Like a stag in heat that cannot wait another moment, he slammed her against a tree and took her where she stood.

Afterward, as they clung together in the hot, moist darkness, reverberations of their shattering climax still shuddering through them, he said, "You will, of course, tell Adam what has happened. And return to Hong Kong with me."

She moved away from him, and her hair, which had fallen free of its pins, shimmered in wild disarray about her shoulders. "No," she said quietly, her voice brooking no argument. "I shall not tell Adam. It would break his heart. And I shall not return to Hong Kong with you."

His brows flew together. "This isn't a repeat of what you said to me at Shek O, is it?" he asked fiercely. "You can't possibly imagine that you can walk away from me again! That I would even *allow* you to."

She shook her head and her hair gleamed in the moonlight, pale as ivory. "No," she said softly, her arms tightly around his waist, her head against his chest. "I shall never walk away from you again, but if you want me, Raefe, it must be on my terms."

"And those are?" he demanded harshly, tilting her face to his.

"That I remain with Adam." He made a savage sound of protest and she continued, her voice almost as fierce as his had been. "I owe Adam my loyalty, Raefe. He has loved me and cared for me all my life, and I care for him. Very much." His frown deepened and she said more gently, "Don't confuse my loyalty with my love, Raefe. I can only give one to Adam. You have both. Surely it is enough?"

He said, his voice still tight, "It isn't what I want."

"It's all I can give."

Around them crickets rattled their legs in continuous whirring. From the terrace there came the sound of subdued laughter, and the clink of glasses. There was a long silence, then a small grin crooked the corners of his mouth. "Then it's what I shall take," he said, and this time when he kissed her, it was with the knowledge that she would never be lost to him again.

She was sitting at the chintz-flounced dressing table in her nightdress and negligee, brushing her hair, when Adam returned to their room.

"I thought you'd have been in bed and asleep long ago," he said cheerily, happily inebriated from having drunk many more stengahs than he was accustomed to.

He shrugged himself free of his white evening jacket and draped it over a convenient chair, then undid his bow tie and tossed it on his bed. As he walked across the room to her, he unfastened the top button of his dress shirt, then gave her a kiss on her cheek.

"Mmmm, you smell nice, sweetheart," he said appreciatively, and instead of walking away and continuing to undress, he slid his hands up her arms, cupping her shoulders. "I miss you when you're not with me, Beth. I didn't see another woman all evening who was half as beautiful."

She forced a smile, putting down her hairbrush with an unsteady hand. Her passionate, physical, total love for Raefe had not diminished the deep affection she felt for Adam. But she couldn't make love with him tonight, not while the heat of Raefe's hands still lingered on her body. "I'm glad," she said, rising to her feet. She walked over to the chair and picked up his discarded jacket. "Did the ex-stockbroker from Brighton join you after I had left?"

"No." His voice was deflated. He had never, ever made love to her when he thought she was tired or unwilling. Her moving away from him signaled that tonight she was perhaps both, and he felt acute disappointment. He sat down on the edge of his bed and slipped off his shoes. "I have some news for you that you will like, though," he said, pulling his shirt over his head, his spirits rising as he anticipated her pleasure. "There's a train leaving for Kuala Lumpur at ten tomorrow morning, and we can be on it if you still want to be." He turned his head so that he could see the delight on her face.

She was in the act of hanging his jacket in the closet. He saw her hand falter, but she didn't turn her head in his direction and when she spoke, her voice sounded oddly high and brittle. "That's very kind of you, Adam, but I've changed my mind. I'm quite happy not to do any further traveling."

She began to pick imaginary specks of dust from the lapels of his jacket and, puzzled, he said, "But I thought you were quite desperate to go. You said it was important to you."

His kindness, and the knowledge of how she was repaying it, made her cheeks burn with shame and mortification. She kept her back firmly to him, beginning to examine a lightweight suit for nonexistent dust as well. "Not any longer," she said, trying to inject a note of lightness into her voice, as if her contrariness was an example of female perversity and should be laughed away.

Adam shook his head in mock despair. "I can't keep up with you, sweetheart. You haven't set your heart on any other far-flung destination, have you?"

She emerged from the closet at last. She had set her heart elsewhere. Not on a destination, but on Raefe. "No," she said. She gave Adam a quick squeeze, then moved away toward her own bed before he could interpret her gesture as sexual willingness. "And from now on, we'll go where *you* want to go, Adam. I promise."

He grinned. "Okay," he said, settling himself into bed. "That means that tomorrow we hire a car and drive across to the north of the island. I want to see for myself how easily Singapore can be defended against the Japs. And I want to see what defenses have been built, and if there's anything Hong Kong can learn from them."

She smiled at him, her affection for him so deep that she felt tears sting the backs of her eyes. "You should have stayed in the army and become a general. Good night, darling. God bless."

He blew her a kiss across the narrow divide of their beds and turned off the bedside light, happy that he wasn't traveling to Kuala Lumpur the next morning, and happy that Beth was no longer consumed by the restlessness that had begun to seriously worry him.

She didn't see Raefe for three days. Unspoken but understood between them was their mutual desire that Adam should be treated with as much respect as possible.

There would be no apparently innocent meetings when Adam was present.

She was no longer torn apart by inner turmoil. She had reached her Rubicon and crossed it, and there could be no going back. The knowledge brought with it a peace of mind that she had thought she would never regain. The next morning she and Adam hired a car and explored the island at their leisure. It was rich and verdant, the city sprawling out till it merged into an exotic jungle of casuarina trees and flame trees and bushes with thick, juicy leaves, infested by screeching monkeys and vividly colored birds. They drove to the north coast, looking out over the narrow strait that separated the island from the Malay Peninsula.

"The Japanese couldn't possibly attack Singapore in the same way that they could Hong Kong," Elizabeth said, standing on the palm-fringed beach and shielding her eyes against the sun as she looked toward Johore. "They would have to fight their way down the entire peninsula. It simply couldn't be done. The ground is too mountainous and the vegetation too thick, even for tanks."

She was wearing a pair of white slacks and a cornflower-blue blouse, open at the throat. Adam looked at her and grinned. "You sound even more knowledgeable than Denholm Gresby."

She laughed, then said, a small frown puckering her brow, "I don't think Sir Denholm is knowledgeable at all. At least, not where Hong Kong is concerned."

Adam raised his binoculars, sweeping them around in an attempt to locate strategically placed pillboxes. There were none to be seen. He was not unduly surprised. There was no urgent necessity for them. Singapore, unlike Hong Kong, was an impregnable fortress, and he had been wrong in thinking there would be anything to learn in the way of coastal defense.

"Well, where Singapore is concerned, there's not too much to worry about," he said, lowering his binoculars. "Though with the Japs, anything could happen. They're just crazy enough to believe an attack could succeed." He wiped a trickle of perspiration from the back of his neck with his handkerchief. "Where to now? What about the Sea View Hotel for a nice curry tiffin? The fellows in the bar highly recommended it."

"Fine," she said agreeably, and they turned away from

the sea and walked back toward their car. "Where is it? Back in the city?"

"No, it's on the east coast road. Apparently the Britishers here treat it as a kind of English village pub. You know, drinks before lunch on a Sunday and a good old singsong into the bargain."

She slipped her arm through his. "You're making me feel homesick. I haven't thought of Four Seasons for ages. Do you think Sundays at home are still the same, or do you think the war will have altered everything?"

"For the moment, I suspect they will still be the same," Adam said as he opened the door of their hired Mercedes tourer. "The newspapers are calling it the phony war. Nothing seems to be happening at the moment. Let's hope nothing does."

On Wednesday Adam asked her if she would like to spend an afternoon, free of his company, shopping. She knew immediately that he had plans of his own that he wanted to follow.

"Where is it that you want to go?" she asked teasingly. "On a binge with your drinking chums of the other night?"

"Not exactly," he said good-humoredly, filling the bowl of his pipe with tobacco. "There's a card game on and I wouldn't mind chancing my luck. That is, if you don't mind."

"Of course I don't mind. Just make sure you don't lose your shirt, that's all. I imagine that those rubber planters are pretty sharp card players!"

She telephoned Raefe at the number he had given her, and told him she was free for the whole afternoon. "But I'm supposed to be shopping. Could you pick me up at Robinsons? I'll call in there first and buy a dress."

"You have ten minutes," he threatened, his voice husky with desire. "If you're not at Robinsons' front entrance by ten past one, I shall come into the dress department and carry you bodily out of it!"

"I'll be there," she said. Her eyes were shining, her cheeks were flushed as she put the receiver back on its rest, grabbed her handbag, and ran from the room.

Robinsons was a huge store on Raffles Place, only a stone's throw from the hotel. She hurried up to the dress department, bought the first dress she saw, and waltzed it over to be wrapped and boxed without even trying it on.

"But, madam, surely it would be wisest to see if it fits," the shop assistant protested in dazed bewilderment.

"It will fit perfectly," Elizabeth said, feeling as euphoric as if she were drunk. "Please wrap it for me quickly. I'm in a terrible hurry!"

He was waiting for her as she emerged five minutes later. "You only just made it," he said, laughing at her as she raced into his arms. "I was on my way in to get you."

His black hair gleamed in the strong sunlight and the lean, sun-bronzed planes of his face looked almost Arabic. Heedless of the shoppers thronging around them, she slid her arms around his neck and parted her lips eagerly as he lowered his head to hers.

A few shoppers gave them bemused glances and made detours around them, but one particular shopper stood rooted to the spot, staring at them in stunned disbelief.

Miriam Gresby had been about to enter Robinsons to meet a woman friend for coffee in the new air-conditioned restaurant. Her husband was in Singapore on official business and was, that morning, meeting Sir Shenton Thomas, the island's governor. She far preferred shopping in Singapore to Hong Kong, and so she had accompanied him. Now she stood, hardly able to believe her eyes, as the cool, beautiful, exquisitely mannered Elizabeth Harland threw herself publicly into Raefe Elliot's open arms.

It was disgraceful behavior for anyone, but *Elizabeth Harland!* She watched as the fervent embrace came to an end and he took her hand, leading her across the pavement to an open-topped Chrysler. Her mouth, that had at first dropped open in amazement, closed like a trap. There would be no more dinner invitations issued to the Harlands, and she would certainly see to it that none would be accepted from them.

As the Chrysler pulled away, she remembered the other occasion when she thought she saw Elizabeth Harland with Raefe Elliot. It had been outside the Peninsula Hotel, but the idea was so ridiculous that she assumed she had been mistaken. Her eyes narrowed as the Chrysler was lost to view. She knew now that she hadn't been. The flagrant affair was one of long-standing duration. She marched into Robinsons, her rocking-horse nostrils flaring, eager to share her outrage with the friend who was waiting for her.

* * *

Raefe had never taken any of his Singapore girlfriends to his house at Holland Park on the outskirts of the city, and Melissa had never visited it. It was a large, sprawling white bungalow and it had been his childhood home. Perhaps, subconsciously, that was the reason he had never used it as a love nest. Whatever the reason, as he lay beside Elizabeth's creamy pale body on the large brass bed, he was supremely glad that no woman had lain there before her.

They hadn't drawn the blinds and there were no curtains, but outside the window there was a vine sifting the sunlight so that the walls of the bedroom were delicately patterned with the moving shadow of leaf and tendril.

"Slowly," he said, his rich, dark voice full of love as she turned toward him, pressing the length of her body against his, her breasts soft against his chest. "This time, my love, there's no need to hurry."

Teasingly his lips played with hers as his hands caressed, aroused, explored. She had a tiny mole beneath her left breast, a small scar on her hip, and her pubic hair was golden-blond, crisply curled.

"You're so beautiful," he said as he held himself in firm control, his hands running over her silky flesh, marveling, fascinated, enchanted.

"Ahhh, Raefe . . ." She sighed deeply as she lay beneath him, her fingers curled in the ram's fleece of his hair, filled once again with that fierce, chaotic tumble of urges to unite with him, to be part of him, to complete herself by joining with him.

"I love you, Lizzie. I'll love you always," he said passionately, his mouth open on hers.

She arched herself toward him, aching for him to take her. "I love you," she whispered against the heat of his flesh.

He looked down at her, his dark face brilliant with an expression of fierce love. "Always?"

"Forever."

They pressed themselves close to each other, savoring each moment of their leisured lovemaking and then, at last, he entered her and she gasped and then purred with pleasure, her body melting bonelessly into his. He took her to the very brink of sexual convulsion, holding her there with infinite skill, teasing, tantalizing, until she begged and pleaded for release.

He refused to acquiesce, withdrawing until she thought she would die, and then plunging deeply into her, his eyes tightly closed, a look of agony contorting his features. "Now!" he said harshly. *"Now!"* And she cried out beneath him, brought to an orgasm so stabbing, so victorious that it filled her with joyous terror. Their bodies were slippery with sweat, the sheets tangled around them as they lay intertwined, the sunlight streaming golden across the floor.

Colonel Sandor put down Raefe's latest report and said, with a note of weariness in his voice, "It would seem that every photographer and barber in southeast Asia is a Jap spy!"

"Mr. Mamatsu, the photographer who plies his trade behind Raffles Hotel, certainly is," Raefe said grimly. "He makes a feature of giving cut rates on soldiers' souvenir photographs to send back to wives and sweethearts, that sort of thing. His shop is crammed with military personnel at all hours of the day and night."

Colonel Sandor rose from behind the desk and walked over to the window to stare thoughtfully out across a green-lawned square. It irked him that his best intelligence officer was American and not British. He disliked Americans. All Americans. They were too cocky, too self-assured. And with Elliot he could never rid himself of the feeling that he was being held in contempt. "As long as we know who these beggars are," he said coldly, "and as long as we can intercept and decode their messages, I don't think too much damage is being done."

Raefe's mouth tightened. He hadn't expected the colonel's view to be any different. It had been a while since his last visit to Fort Canning and the five Japanese seconded from the Japanese army for the supposed purpose of learning English were still happily ensconced in Hong Kong, as was the barber at the Hong Kong Hotel. "I beg to disagree," he said tightly.

Coloney Sandor turned reluctantly away from the window. The sun was shining and the grass was green. It was a perfect day for cricket.

"It isn't your position to agree or disagree, Mr. Elliot," he said, holding on to his patience with difficulty.

Raefe's eyes smoldered furiously. Sandor was a White-hall wallah. Following the official line laid down by men in pin-striped suits, thousands of miles away. Men who had no real understanding of the East or the Eastern mind.

"With respect, Colonel," he persisted, "we're being too complacent. I've traveled the length and breadth of Malaya, I know the country like the back of my hand. Whitehall's boast that it is unassailable is misplaced."

Colonel Sandor picked up his swagger stick and slammed it against the four-foot-high map pinned to the wall. "A backbone of granite mountains rising to seven thousand feet, zigzagging the length of the country! Four fifths of the land covered with dense, tropical jungle, with rain forests. How can it be?"

"Despite what army intelligence would like us to believe, the Japanese Army is highly trained, and it is highly trained in bush warfare. They'll land on the coast and they won't be deterred by jungles or by rain forest. They are accustomed to those conditions in a way British troops aren't. They'll use enveloping tactics rather than a head-on assault, and they'll be at the Johore Straits before we've had time to blink!"

Colonel Sandor's nostrils were pinched and white. "I find that kind of talk defeatist, Mr. Elliot. The Japs have to be so sure of our military superiority that they will never dare to attack! Our belief in ourselves and in our ability is crucial!" He strode back to his desk. "Your report about Mr. Mamatsu will be dealt with. Good day, Mr. Elliot!"

Elizabeth sat in a wicker chaise on the glass-covered veranda of the hotel, a notepad on her knee. She was writing her regular monthly letter to Princess Luisa Isabel, but was not filling the pages up as rapidly as she usually did. She looked down at what she had written. "Singapore island isn't mountainous or as magnificently beautiful as Hong Kong, but the city is far lovelier and Adam is enjoying himself hugely, making friends with rubber planters and tin-miners, and brushing up on his poker-playing."

The words were innocuous, accurate, and very misleading. She was conjuring up a picture of an idyllic vacation, and she was giving no hint at all of the cataclysmic turn that her life had taken. She put down her pencil and stared out across the gardens. At the frangipani trees. At the hibiscus.

Voluptuous pleasure licked through her. Hibiscus, and Raefe rounding the path in the darkness, and their shameless, fevered lovemaking. She picked up her pen again. "There is so much I would like to talk to you about, Luisa. So much has happened that is hard to put down on paper." She paused, knowing she could not be more explicit, that it would not be fair to Adam.

A small bird with jewelled colored wings darted down from a nearby tree, and as she watched its flight she knew with sudden certainty that if, and when, she told Luisa about Raefe, Luisa would not be surprised. That she would have been expecting such an event for a long time. "The East has brought me to maturity," she wrote, her pen beginning to flow more easily across the paper. "I have been a little girl in a woman's body for too long. I am so no longer . . ."

She saw Raefe only once more before he flew back to Hong Kong. Adam had fixed up a game of singles with the ex-stockbroker from Brighton, and she had left him on the tennis courts and taken a yellow taxicab to the padang on the waterfront where Raefe was waiting for her.

"I haven't got long," she warned as she slid into his car. "Only an hour or two."

"Then don't waste time talking," he said practically, and pulled her to him and kissed her.

They drove to Holland Park and made love, and then they went down to the river, walking along its banks, their arms around each other's waist, painfully conscious of the sun sliding away to the west and the precious minutes ticking rapidly by.

"How long will it be before you return to Hong Kong?" he asked, hating the thought of leaving her, acquiescing only because he understood her feelings for Adam and respected them.

"I don't know. A week, perhaps two weeks."

"And you will be sailing back?"

"Yes."

"So it could be over a month before I see you again."

She was silent, knowing how much he wanted her to leave Singapore with him, knowing how impossible it was for her to do so. The river wound through the heart of the city, narrow and alive with sampans.

"What will you do when you return to Hong Kong?" she asked, her head resting against his shoulder as they walked.

He flashed her a sudden, down-slanting smile. "I won't be seeing Alute, if that's what you're thinking."

"I wasn't," she said gently, utterly sure of him, as she knew he was of her.

His smile faded. "I shall probably be spending most of the next few weeks with Melissa," he said, a slight edge to his voice. "She needs all the support I can give her at the moment."

"Is it very bad for her?" she asked curiously. "I don't know anything at all about heroin."

"It's a killer," he said briefly, "a by-product of opium. In liquor-drinking terms, if opium is regarded as a light hock, heroin is a mixture of brandy, methylated spirits, and cyanide."

A light breeze from the sea blew coolly against their faces, heralding a tropical shower.

His profile was grim. "It's been hellish for her. She isn't a person who has ever had to fight for anything. Whatever she has wanted, some man has supplied. Her father always indulged her, her boyfriends indulged her, and, God help me, I indulged her. Instant gratification was what she always demanded and to hell with the consequences. If you'd asked me six months ago if she could have fought a nightmare like heroin addiction, I would have laughed in your face. But she is doing it, and she's doing it with more guts than I ever gave her credit for." He stared out at the sampans, so closely packed together that children were jumping across from one to another. "I've come to respect her in a way I never did when I lived with her. She's . . ." He sought for the word, then said with a crooked smile, "She's gallant. And she'll come through, in the end."

The next morning, just after dawn, Raefe flew away from Singapore, piloting his Northrop himself. Elizabeth had slept restlessly, and as morning sunlight seeped through the shutters she slipped out of bed and dressed, careful not to disturb Adam. She wanted to breakfast by herself. She wanted just a little private time in which to come to terms with the knowledge that Raefe was once again thousands of miles away from her.

The dining room was deserted except for a few planters up early to catch a flight north. She could never in her life remember missing anyone so badly. Not her father; not Adam. She ordered papaya with fresh limes, the porridge that was Raffles' specialty, toast with Cooper's Oxford Marmalade, and coffee. Even as she ordered, she knew that the only thing she wanted was coffee. The rest was just something to toy with, an excuse to remain in the dining room, to delay returning to Adam.

The fruit and the porridge were returned to the kitchen untouched, but she ate a slice of toast and sipped her coffee. Then she became aware that she was not only feeling heartsick, she was feeling physically sick. She took another sip of coffee and put down her cup. It tasted foul.

A middle-aged American couple, looking as if they were tourists, sat down at a nearby table.

". . . and so I thought we could take a rickshaw this morning and buy some silks," the wife was saying.

Elizabeth took a deep breath and swallowed. It was no use. She had only eaten a slice of toast and drunk half a cup of coffee, but incredibly she was going to be sick. She rose abruptly to her feet and ran from the room.

The Americans stared after her with raised eyebrows. "I wonder what's wrong with her?" the husband said. "She looked white as a sheet. Where did you say we could buy the silks?"

Elizabeth knelt on the cool tiled floor of the lavatory, retching. The toast and coffee came back easily. After that she continued to retch, bringing up dark green bile. At last it stopped and she staggered to her feet, crossed to the sink, and poured herself a glass of water. Gingerly she sipped it, wondering what on earth could be wrong with her.

The middle-aged American woman came in and took her makeup purse out of her handbag.

"Heavens, what we suffer to become mothers," she said, beginning to repair her makeup.

"I'm sorry, I don't understand," Elizabeth said, still leaning weakly against the sink.

The woman laughed. "Morning sickness," she said understandingly. "If men suffered from it, the birth rate would soon fall!" She pressed her lips together to set her lipstick, popped her makeup purse back into her handbag,

and said as she walked to the door, "Never mind, honey.
It's worth it in the end. I have three and I wouldn't be
without one of them!" The door swung to behind her and
Elizabeth was left hanging on to the sink for support,
ashen-faced and trembling.

Chapter Eighteen

*S*HE told herself that the American woman had jumped to
a ridiculous conclusion. People were often taken suddenly
ill in a climate like Singapore's. She had eaten something,
or drunk something, that had disagreed with her.

The next morning it happened again. And the next.

"Oh, God!" she whispered as she knelt on the floor,
heaving up the scrambled egg she had manfully forced
down in an attempt to prove that there was nothing wrong
with her. "Oh, God! What now? What on *earth* do I do
now?"

She crawled out of the bathroom and sat at her dressing
table, opening a drawer and lifting out a small diary. She
had kept it meticulously for over three years. It was the
diary her gynecologist had advised her to keep when she
had first become anxious about her fertility. The dates of
her menstruation were carefully marked. As were the dates
when she was most likely to conceive, and the dates when
she and Adam had made love. She turned the pages with a
shaking hand, knowing what she would find.

Her last period had come to an end shortly before she
had gone to Shek O with Raefe. Guilt had ensured that she
had not made love with Adam in the immediate ensuing
days, and then they had left Hong Kong aboard the
Blantyre Castle for Singapore.

She had been lovingly affectionate with him on the
voyage, wanting to make up to him for her betrayal of him,
wanting to reestablish the firm foundation of their mar-

riage. But there had been no lovemaking. Adam had been tired, suffering from a severe head cold and a general feeling of malaise. They had held hands, danced together, stood at the deck rail with their arms around each other's waist, but they had not made love.

She put the diary down. She had no need to check the days since their arrival in Singapore. Although Adam had approached her lovingly several times, she had always made a gentle excuse, wanting to give herself more time before she committed what she saw as the final act of treachery—entering his bed with the feel of Raefe's hands still on her flesh, his kisses still hot on her lips.

She stared at her reflection in the dressing table mirror. She looked like a ghost, her eyes darkly ringed, her face deathly pale. It had been obvious that she was unwell and she had told Adam that she thought she was coming down with the virus he had been suffering on the voyage out. His concern had only made her feel more wretched.

"Oh, Adam," she breathed despairingly "Oh, darling, *darling* Adam! I didn't want it to come to this! I didn't want to hurt you!"

Tears slid down her face. She had thought she could continue to give him all the deep affection she had always given him. That their life together would continue as it always had, unscathed by her passionate love for Raefe. Now she knew that it was not possible. There could be no balancing of the two separate halves into which her life had fallen. She could not have both her calm, steady, sheltered life with Adam, and the turbulence and tumult of her love for Raefe. One of them must be lost to her. And she was bearing Raefe's child. She pressed her hands against her face and the tears rolled mercilessly down between her fingers, and onto her negligee.

"*Damn, damn, damn!*" she sobbed. She had longed for a child for years. She had counted dates. She had waited in a fever of hope and longing month after month. And at last, what she had most longed for had been given her. She was expecting a baby. And the father was the man she loved. But it was not her husband. It was not the baby she had dreamed about, the baby that would make Adam so happy. The baby that would be the crowning happiness of their life together. "Oh, God, Adam!" she whispered brokenly, lowering her head to her arms. "I'm so sorry, darling. So desperately sorry!"

* * *

"So you've changed your mind completely about this jaunt to Kuala Lumpur?" Adam asked her as they ate lunch at the Sea View.

She had been toying listlessly with the sweet-and-sour prawns on her plate, and now she put down her chopsticks. "If you would like to go, Adam," she said carefully, "then I'm quite happy to go with you. But there's no need to visit Kuala Lumpur for my sake."

He had been smiling, happy with the game of tennis he had played earlier before leaving Raffles, happy with life in general. Now he frowned with concern. "Are you sure you're all right, Beth? I mean, are you not wanting to travel north because you feel so unwell?"

She shook her head and pushed her plate away. "No, there's no need to worry, Adam."

She knew that she had to talk to him, but she couldn't bring herself to do so yet. She didn't know the words to use. She didn't know how it was possible to break such devastating news to someone she cared about so much, someone who loved her so much.

His frown deepened. "I really think you should see a doctor. It's ridiculous saying that you'll be all right in a day or two. You're hardly eating anything and you look ghastly."

She forced a smile. "That's not a very complimentary thing to say to a lady!"

He grinned. "You know what I mean. It isn't safe to let things run their course in a climate like this."

He was wearing an open-necked cotton shirt and a pair of shorts, but the sweat still gleamed on his forehead and glistened on his neck. He turned around, looking for a waiter, then raised his hand to indicate that he wanted another stengah.

"If you don't want to travel farther north," he suggested, turning back to her, "then perhaps it's about time we returned to Hong Kong."

"Yes," she said, avoiding his eyes and looking seaward to where a small group of Malay fishermen were collecting their catch from their fishing traps. The sooner they returned to Hong Kong, the sooner she could tell Raefe about the baby. And the sooner Adam would have to be told.

A Chinese waiter, balancing a tray of gimlets and stengahs and Tiger beer, weaved his way dexterously between the crowded tables toward them. Adam signed for his drink, then said, "So we'll sail for home on the first available ship."

The fishermen were walking away across the beach with their catch. In the brilliant sunlight, the small green islands in the distance were as insubstantial as mist. She drew her gaze away from them and back at Adam. "You really do think of Hong Kong as home now, don't you?"

He shrugged. "Why not? It feels like home."

"And Four Seasons?" she asked, wondering if she would ever return there. If it would ever be a home to her again.

"I've never thought of Four Seasons as home," he said with his usual honesty. "I always think of it as being exclusively yours. Which it is."

"But you enjoyed living there?" she persisted, suddenly wondering if she had always assumed his contentment and his happiness. Wondering if, perhaps, there was far more to him than she had previously suspected.

"I would enjoy living anywhere with you," he said, reaching across the table and taking her hands. "A palace or a shack, it would make no difference. As long as you were there, Beth, I would be happy."

She couldn't have spoken, even if she had wanted to.

He squeezed her hands and said decisively, "That's it, then. We'll call in at the shipping office on the way back to the hotel and book two berths. I wonder if much has changed while we've been away? I imagine Alastair is still trying to persuade Helena to marry him and that she is still refusing."

As they rose to leave, Elizabeth felt dizzy at the thought of how much had changed. Their whole lives. And he didn't know. Not yet. And she hadn't the courage to tell him.

They walked along the Sea View's pillared terrace and beneath an incongruous dome of Grecian splendor, toward their waiting Mercedes. Adam had discovered that driving in the Singapore heat was not much fun and after their first few days there he had hired a *syce*, a Malay chauffeur. The *syce*, who had been squatting down, sheltering in the shade of the car, jumped to his feet at their approach and opened the doors for them with an efficient flourish.

"Julienne's probably notched up at least three new lovers," Adam said dryly, wincing against the heat of the leather seat. "God knows how that marriage survives. I don't."

Again Elizabeth said nothing. There was nothing she could possibly say. They called in at the shipping office on Robinson Road and booked a double berth on a ship leaving the following Monday. She was both longing to leave and loath to, her feelings as agonized and contradictory as they had been when she had left Hong Kong.

"I'm tired, Adam," she said truthfully, as they stepped out of the air-conditioned coolness of the office and into the blistering heat of the street. "I don't know what you have planned for this afternoon, but I'd like to rest for an hour or two."

He looked down into her wan face, distressed at the deep circles beneath her eyes. "You should have said so sooner," he said, concerned, his hand beneath her arm as they walked to the car. "I'll tuck you up and then go for a swim at the club." Their *syce* drew out into the traffic, refusing to be intimidated by aggressive rickshaw drivers who regarded crowding a foreign car off the street a duty. "And if you're feeling no better by the time I return," Adam continued sternly, "then I'm calling for a doctor, no matter what you say."

She rested and drank some milk of magnesia and by the time Adam returned, she was able to say, with an element of truth, that she felt much better and that there was no need for him to carry out his threat.

On the following Monday, they sailed out of the great harbor and turned northward, toward Hong Kong. If Adam thought her unduly quiet, it was only because he believed her to be still suffering from the enervating virus he, himself, had suffered from for a while. He had enjoyed their trip to Singapore far more than he had anticipated, but he wasn't sorry to be leaving. He wanted to be in at the inception of the proposed Hong Kong Volunteer Force. He wanted to have a good old chin-wag with Leigh Stafford about the apparent invincibility of Singapore. He wanted to sit on his veranda, a sundowner in his hand, and look out across his garden and the lush, tropical greenery of the Peak down to the glittering harbor and the distant, cloud-capped hills of Kowloon.

"We're home," he said with satisfaction, as their ship nosed its way up the Lei Yue Mun Channel between a scattering of small, stony, uninhabited islands.

Elizabeth stood beside him, her hands on the rail, her knuckles white. She no longer knew where home was, or who it was with. It was late afternoon and the Peak was half hidden in clouds, scudding shadows of high cirrus smoking down the ravines and ridges, the scent of hibiscus and frangipani drifting fragrantly across the water.

She had not told Raefe that she was on her way back to him. Unless he had tried to contact her at Raffles, he would think her still in Singapore. He would not be waiting for her when they docked and she did not want him to be. When they did meet, she wanted to be the one who was in control of the situation. Whatever decision was taken about the future, it would be *her* decision. Not Adam's. Not Raefe's. Hers.

There was the usual pile of mail. Business letters for Adam. Cards and invitations. A half dozen envelopes bearing Princess Luisa Isabel's embossed coat of arms. Chan and the other houseboys carried the luggage upstairs and while Mei Lin supervised the unpacking, Adam retreated to a comfortable chair, a gin and tonic in his hand as he settled down to read the backlog of letters.

Elizabeth pushed her pile neatly to one side. There was no way she could cope with party invitations and frivolous gossip at the moment. She didn't even want to open Luisa's always cheery letters. Feeling restless she went upstairs. Mei Lin was deftly sorting the unpacked clothes into piles for the laundry, piles to be pressed, piles to be put neatly away. "Have there been any messages for me, Mei Lin?" she asked.

"All the messages are on the telephone pad, missy," Mei Lin said, her gold cheeks rosy with pleasure at having her mistress back in residence again.

"But have there been any other messages?" Elizabeth persisted. "Any personal messages?" She had already flicked an eye over the names written with meticulous care by Mei Lin on the telephone pad. Raefe's had not been there.

"I very careful," Mei Lin said, a trifle defensively. "I put every name down, missy. I leave none out."

So he hadn't telephoned. But then he had had no reason to. She had told him that she would get in touch with him when she returned. From downstairs she could hear Adam calling her name and she hurried out to the head of the stairs.

"There's a letter here from Leigh," he called up to her. "Sounds as if I should see him straight away. I'll be back in an hour."

A second later the door slammed behind him. She walked slowly down the wide open staircase, her heart beginning to hammer in her chest. She was on her own and she had to take advantage of that. She had to ring Raefe now, before Adam returned.

"I have sent a message to the wash amah to tell her that you are back and that she is needed," Mei Lin said, panting as she carried the laundry through into the kitchen. "She will be here in an hour."

"Thank you, Mei Lin."

Elizabeth stood looking at the telephone on the hall table for a long moment, then walked quickly into the drawing room where she would have more privacy. She wouldn't tell him about the baby over the telephone. She would only tell him that she was back. And that she had missed him every single second she had been away from him.

His houseboy answered the telephone.

"Could I speak to Mr. Elliot, please?"

"Verry sorry," his houseboy said in broad pidgin. "Mr. Elliot not in. Can I take message?"

Her disappointment was so intense, she actually slumped against the wall. "Tell him Mrs. Harland rang," she said, feeling ridiculously as if she were going to cry. "Tell him that I am home again. That I am in Hong Kong."

"Yes, missy. Verry good, missy."

She was filled with the sudden humiliating thought that he had probably taken hundreds of such messages in the past. From Mrs. Mark Hurley; from Alute. From women whose names she didn't know and had no desire to know. The feeling of humiliation was fleeting. He had never before taken one from a woman with whom Raefe was in love, of that she was sure. She walked over to the large window that looked out on the Peak and the bay, and despite all her misery at the hurt she was about to inflict on Adam, happiness bubbled up inside her. He would ring her back within minutes, within hours. They would be together soon. "Oh, but I love you," she whispered, hugging her arms around her waist as she looked down toward Victoria. "Raefe Elliot, *I love you!*"

Raefe took the message from one of his Chinese informers. This time the tidbit was not about Yamishita, the Japanese barber at the Hong Kong Hotel, or any of the other known Japanese spies masquerading as photographers and waiters.

"Your friend Mr. Nicholson is in great trouble," the familiar singsong voice said urgently. "Mr. Kaibong Sheng knows of his involvement with his daughter. The tongs are on the streets looking for him."

Raefe blanched. The tongs were the hired killers of the Chinese underworld, and if Sheng had discovered that his daughter had been deflowered, then there was nothing more certain than that he would have hired the tongs to exact his revenge.

"Do you know where Tom Nicholson is now?" he demanded urgently. "Do you know where Lamoon Sheng is?"

"No." The singsong voice expressed neither regret nor curiosity. "I only know that Sheng was told an hour ago that the Englishman has soiled his daughter's honor. And that the tongs have been given their orders."

Raefe blasphemed, looking at his watch. It was four-twenty and it was Thursday. The day that Lamoon Sheng ostensibly attended nursing lessons at the hospital. By four-thirty, Tom would have taken her back to the hospital so that she could slip in through a side door and emerge seconds later through the main door where the chauffeured Rolls would be waiting for her. Only today, the chauffeur would not be the only person waiting outside the hospital. The tongs would be there as well.

Raefe yanked open his desk drawer and took out a revolver and a shoulder holster. He strapped the holster on as he strode from the room, grabbing his jacket from the hall coat stand. Tom would be unarmed and unprepared and the tongs were not likely to have had instructions to give him merely a beating. For the sin Tom had committed, Raefe doubted if old man Sheng would be satisfied with anything less than his death.

He vaulted into his Lagonda and gunned the engine into life. The tires squealed as he shot out of the parking bay and into the heavy late afternoon traffic. Thank God he had been at the apartment when he had received the message, and not at the Peak. If he had been, there would have been no chance at all of him reaching Tom in time. He swerved past a taxi, pressing the heel of his hand on the horn, making no concessions for rickshaws or cyclists or even pedestrians.

What car did Tom drive? Was it a Mercedes or an Opel? A Packard. It was a Packard. He sped across a busy intersection, aware of the squealing of brakes in his wake. It was four twenty-nine. Tom was probably there now. He was never late in delivering Lamoon back to the hospital, doing nothing, as he thought, to arouse her father's suspicions. Raefe screamed around a traffic island, sending rickshaw boys scurrying for their lives. Tom had been a naive fool to imagine the affair could continue without someone, somewhere, seeing them and informing on them.

The hospital loomed up on his right, and he saw the unmistakable powder-blue Sheng Rolls-Royce parked outside the front entrance. He took the next corner on two wheels. The tongs would be waiting for Tom at the side entrance. They would wait until Lamoon Sheng had entered the hospital before they pounced. Their orders would be not to involve her in the violence. And if Lamoon had still not walked out of the front entrance . . .

It was four-thirty. The side street was crowded with office workers leaving as early as they could for home. There were black-clad Chinese on bicycles and half a dozen Chinese stall-holders and a peddler selling jade, all a mere yard or two away from the side entrance door. Raefe was just about to breathe a sigh of relief, believing he had got there before Tom, when he saw the Packard parked at the other side of the street and Tom's tall, broad-shouldered figure walking through the crowds toward the entrance, Lamoon's diminutive figure at his side.

Raefe was still fifty yards away from them and the street was jammed with traffic. He squealed to a halt, slamming his hand hard upon the horn as he did so. The crowd of office workers turned their heads, staring at him as if he had lost his senses, but Tom was too deep in conversation with Lamoon to take any notice of a maniac letting loose on a car horn. Raefe jumped from the car, shouting Tom's name, forcing his way at a run through the office workers and shoppers and tourists who crowded the pavement.

"Tom! *Tom!*" he yelled. The Chinese cyclists were no longer with their bicycles. They were all moving in behind Tom as he approached the side entrance of the hospital. One of the stall-holders, too, was no longer intent on selling his wares to passing pedestrians.

Tom and Lamoon were at the side entrance. A Chinese was standing over the open bonnet of Tom's Packard, busily disabling it to ensure there would be no escape in that direction.

"*Tom!*" Raefe yelled at the top of his lungs. This time Tom heard him. His head swung around, his eyes widening as he saw Raefe hurtling toward him. Lamoon was still in the doorway, a bewildered expression on her face. The crowds who a second earlier had thronged the street had now, sensing danger, hurriedly scattered, leaving the side entrance of the hospital an open space apart from Tom, and the Chinese, and Raefe.

"*It's the tongs!*" Raefe shouted as the jade peddler, judging that there was no longer time to wait for Lamoon Sheng to disappear before launching his attack, hurled his tray at Raefe and dived toward Tom.

The tray caught Raefe full on the chest and he fell to his knees. Instantly he scrambled to his feet again, gasping for breath, seeing through a blood-red haze the gleam of a blade and then Tom's fist as it shot out, sending the jade peddler sprawling.

Desperately he tried to reach Tom, but there were hands around his throat, choking him, pulling him backward, fingers gouging at his eyes. He kicked back, knocking his assailants off balance, and snatched his gun from his holster.

Tom was on the ground, barely visible as he thrashed beneath a welter of kicks and punches. Then the stall-holder grabbed hold of the peddler's knife and as Tom was held, pinned to the ground, he sprang forward, the knife lunging down toward Tom's heart.

The blow from the gun's butt knocked the assassin senseless, just as the blade pierced Tom's flesh. Raefe was aware of Lamoon screaming, of a police siren wailing, of feet running. Tom gasped, dazedly imprisoned beneath the weight of his attacker, blood oozing from the shallow wound in his chest. Raefe tried to tell him to lie still, but when he spoke the words were fuzzily incoherent and to his surprise and indignation his legs buckled beneath him and he dropped forward onto the pavement. He pressed his hand to his side to ease his breathing, and when he withdrew it his fingers were dark and sticky with blood. Tom wasn't the only one who had been stabbed.

The whine of the police siren came nearer and nearer. Lamoon was running toward them, her eyes wide with terror, then Raefe saw the Sheng chauffeur sprint from around the front of the building. He tried to warn her, to tell her to run toward the approaching police car, but his desperate warning was barely audible. He was going to faint. "Christ!" he whispered disgustedly, and slumped forward into a deepening pool of blood as the chauffeur seized Lamoon and dragged her, kicking and screaming, away.

When the telephone rang Elizabeth leaped toward it, her heart racing. Adam was down at the tennis courts, inspecting the nets in the last flush of light before darkness fell.

"Yes," she said eagerly. "Elizabeth Harland speaking." It wasn't the rich, dark voice she so longed to hear.

"It's Helena," Helena said briefly. "I knew you were back. I saw Adam with Leigh Stafford in the Long Bar at the Pen a couple of hours ago."

"Oh, Helena, it's lovely to hear from you," Elizabeth began, trying to tear her thoughts away from Raefe. "I was going to call you, but—"

"There's been an accident."

Elizabeth's hand tightened on the telephone receiver. She knew now what the strange curtness was in Helena's voice. It wasn't pique because she hadn't called the instant she had returned from Singapore. It was the sound of sobs being barely suppressed.

"Oh, God," she whispered, her stomach muscles tightening, thinking immediately of Jeremy and Jennifer. "What is it, Helena? What has happened?"

"Someone told Kaibong Sheng of Tom's affair with Lamoon." She paused, trying to steady her voice. "He ordered the tongs to kill him . . ." She began to cry and

Elizabeth sat down very slowly, keeping the telephone pressed tightly to her ear.

"Yes, Helena?" she prompted, terrified of what Helena was about to tell her.

"They were waiting for him when he brought Lamoon back to the hospital . . . They tried to stab him . . ."

Elizabeth clung tightly to the word "tried." "But they didn't?" she asked urgently. "Tom isn't hurt? He's still alive?"

"Yes." There was another pause while Helena blew her nose. "I can't stop crying. It's the shock. The thought of that evil old man giving orders for Tom to be killed."

"What happened?" Elizabeth asked again. "Tom brought Lamoon back to the hospital and the tongs were waiting for him. What happened then?"

"Someone, I don't know who, rang Raefe and told him what was planned. He reached the hospital just in time to shout a warning to Tom and to help him . . ."

Elizabeth felt the blood drain from her face.

"There was a dreadful fight on the pavement. Tom's nose is broken and two of his ribs are cracked and he has a shallow knife wound in his chest." Her voice trembled. "It would have been much worse. It was Raefe who saved his life . . ."

"He's hurt, isn't he?" Elizabeth said tightly. "Raefe's hurt?"

Helena began to cry again. "He was stabbed. The knife punctured the pancreas. They operated on him an hour ago . . ."

"Jesus God!" The room rocked sickeningly around her. "I must go to him. What ward is he in? Where is he?"

"He's in a private room just off Ward Three, but you can't go to him, Elizabeth! There's Adam to think of! I'm going down there now. I'll see him. I'll tell you how he is!"

"No!" Elizabeth shook her head frantically. "I'm going there myself!" She slammed the receiver down and ran for the door.

"What on earth is the matter, Beth?" Adam asked as he entered the room and she crashed into him. "Where's the fire?"

He had put his hands steadyingly on her arms and she wrenched herself free. "I'm sorry, Adam," she gasped. "I have to go down to Victoria."

She raced out into the hall, scooped up her handbag from the hall table, seized her jacket from the bamboo coat stand.

"But why?" he asked perplexedly as he followed her. "What on earth has happened?"

She was scrambling in her handbag for her car keys. "Lamoon's father has discovered she is having an affair with Tom." Her fingers curled around the keys. "He sent the tongs to kill him!"

"Dear Lord . . ." Adam's face paled.

She ran to the door, opened it, and looked back at him, her eyes anguished. "He's all right, Adam. He has a broken nose and a couple of cracked ribs, but he's all right."

"Then I don't understand why there is all the urgency." He took a step toward her. "We can visit him tomorrow, together."

She shook her head. "No!" she whispered, knowing that she could not stay to explain to him, that every minute was precious. "Raefe's been hurt, too. He's been stabbed. They operated on him an hour ago!" She ran out of the house and across the gravel toward the garage, never looking back toward him.

For a long moment Adam couldn't move. He felt as if he had been kicked savagely in the chest. By the time he managed to stumble to the door, her car was already screeching down the drive toward the road.

"Beth!" he shouted vainly. "Beth!" He ran down the shallow steps of the portico but it was no use. With a scream of tires she slewed out onto Peak Road, and he could hear the engine tone change as she slammed through the gears and into fourth.

He leaned against one of the portico's flower-wreathed pillars, sick and disoriented. *What* had Beth said? Surely she couldn't have meant it? Surely he had misheard, as he had misheard Alastair in the golf club bar. A flock of blue magpies, disturbed by the raucous noise of her departure, wheeled over his head. *Elliot?* She had gone racing down to Victoria like a woman demented, all because Raefe Elliot had again involved himself in an act of violence? It didn't make sense. It *couldn't* make sense.

He could no longer hear the sound of her car engine. The magpies had settled down again in the branches of the flame trees. And it did make sense. It made the most awful, most diabolical sense. Like an old man he pressed his hand against the pillar in order to launch himself into a tottering walk. He hadn't misheard Alastair. He had told Alastair they were leaving Hong Kong because Beth was having problems. And Alastair had immediately assumed that her problem was Raefe Elliot.

He walked slowly into the house, his shoulders hunched, his hands pushed deep into the pockets of his cardigan. Alastair was a man who hated gossip and never indulged in it, yet he had known about Beth's passion for Elliot. And if Alastair knew, then Helena must know, and Julienne and Ronnie. He poured himself a large measure of whiskey. Probably everyone on the whole island knew. His hand shook as he raised his glass to his lips. He had never felt such pain. He couldn't even begin to imagine how he would live with it. A world without Beth. It was inconceivable. The glass fell to the floor, whiskey seeping and staining the pale beige carpet as he lowered his head to his hands and wept.

Helena was in the hospital foyer, waiting for her when she arrived.

"How is he?" Elizabeth asked, running across to her, her eyes fierce with anxiety.

"I haven't been allowed to see him. I don't think he's fully recovered consciousness yet. The sister says there's no need to worry, that he's going to be all right. The knife missed the lungs, and though it pierced the pancreas, she says that no lasting harm has been done."

Elizabeth's relief was so intense, she swayed slightly. "I must see him, Helena."

"They won't let you. It's a strictly next-of-kin situation so soon after surgery."

A new look flashed into Elizabeth's eyes. "Does Melissa know yet? Has anyone told her?"

Helena pushed an untidy mass of dark hair away from her face. "I don't know. Perhaps the hospital has. I never gave Melissa a thought."

"She should be told!" Elizabeth said vehemently. "I'm going up to the ward now. The sister will know if she's been told or not."

"And if she hasn't?" Helena asked, her beautiful, square-jawed face troubled.

"Then I will tell her," Elizabeth said, and left Helena with slightly raised brows as she walked swiftly off into the direction of Ward Three.

"No, Mrs. Elliot hasn't been informed," the ward sister said apologetically. "I understand that Mr. and Mrs. Elliot were separated and that Mrs. Elliot was living in the New Territories."

"They are separated, but she isn't living in the New Territories," Elizabeth said, her gaze going to the door of the private room opposite the sister's office. "She's at the family home and she should be told what has happened."

"Of course." The ward sister paused. "Perhaps, if you are a family friend, it might be less of a shock if you were to contact her?"

"Yes," Elizabeth said, her gaze still on the door of the private room. "I will telephone her when I leave. After I have seen Mr. Elliot."

"I'm afraid Mr. Elliot only returned from surgery two hours ago. There will be visiting tomorrow evening," the sister said pleasantly.

Elizabeth turned and looked at her. "Please let me see him. I don't want to be here tomorrow when perhaps Mrs. Elliot may be visiting."

The sister drew in a deep, understanding breath. It hadn't occurred to her that the lovely Mrs. Harland was here in any other capacity but that of family friend.

"Please!" Elizabeth repeated, her expression urgent.

The sister hesitated, then said compassionately, "All right, but only for five minutes. And don't expect him to make much sense, because he won't. He'll still be fuzzy from the anesthetic."

With her legs almost buckling with relief, Elizabeth followed her out of the office and across the corridor to the private room.

"Five minutes only," the sister said again as she opened the door.

Raefe made beautiful sense. "Hello," he said as she reached the bed, his voice heavily slurred as if he had been drinking. "I love you, Lizzie."

Tears stung her eyes. "I love you too," she said softly, shocked at how pale he looked.

He gave her a crooked smile. "Goddamn tongs," he whispered expressively. "They can't do anything right. It was me they damn near killed, not Tom."

She took hold of his hand. "It would take more than tongs," she said with a wobbly smile.

His hand tightened faintly on hers. "I'm glad you're back. Another week and I would have come for you, Adam or no Adam!"

She thought of the way Adam had looked as she left him. White-faced and shocked, knowing at last of her passion for Raefe. "Don't worry about Adam," she said somberly. "I shall never leave you again, my love."

The sister stood at the door. "Your five minutes are up, Mrs. Harland. Any further visiting will have to be at the appointed times."

She squeezed his hand. "Melissa doesn't know yet. I'll telephone her tonight."

"Good," he said wearily. "She'll be grateful. Good night, sweet Lizzie."

She reluctantly withdrew her hand from his. "Good night, my love," she said, blowing him a kiss, knowing that from now on her life would be shared with him. There were no more decisions to make, no more choices to agonize over.

The door closed behind them. "So you will telephone Mrs. Elliot?" the sister asked, disguising the prurient curiosity she felt.

"Yes. Could I do it from your office, please?"

The sister nodded. It would be as well to know that the news was broken in the proper manner. "Of course," she said, leading the way across the corridor. "You will need to ask the switchboard for an outside line."

Helena was waiting for her when she walked back into the foyer. "How is he?" she asked, rising to her feet. "Did they let you see him?"

Elizabeth nodded. "For five minutes. It was strange to see him so weak and so pale."

"But he's going to be all right?" she asked anxiously, not able to imagine Raefe either weak or pale.

"Yes," Elizabeth said as they stepped out into the darkened street. "He'll probably be discharged by the end of the week." Her voice was tired, drained of energy.

"Let's go for a drink somewhere," Helena suggested, knowing exactly how she felt. "The Pen, perhaps, or Grips?"

Elizabeth shook her head. "No, Helena. I have to get back home. I need to talk to Adam."

They had stopped near her car. Helena looked at her in alarm. In the garish light of the street lamps Elizabeth looked almost ill. "You're not going to tell him about Raefe, are you?"

"There's no need," Elizabeth said wearily. "He already knows."

Helena's face was horrified. Elizabeth bent down and unlocked the car door. She didn't want to talk to Helena about Adam. Not yet. Perhaps not ever. "You didn't tell me what happened to Lamoon," she said as she opened the door and slid behind the steering wheel. "Was she hurt as well?"

"No. At least, I don't think so." Helena was still thinking of Adam. How on earth would he have taken such news? Of all the men she knew, he least deserved such a blow.

"Where is she now?" Elizabeth asked.

"Lamoon? I don't know." Helena dragged her thoughts away from Adam. "I don't think anyone knows. I don't think we will ever see or hear of Lamoon again."

Elizabeth turned the key in the ignition. "Poor Tom," she said bleakly. "Good night, Helena. I'll give you a ring tomorrow."

Helena stood on the pavement, watching as Elizabeth drove away. "Poor Tom," she repeated, heartsick. "And poor Adam. I wonder what he will do now?"

Elizabeth sped away from the hospital, driving through Victoria's neon-lit streets and squares and toward Garden Road and the slow climb up to the Peak. Magazine Gap Road was deserted, and as she climbed higher she could see the silky blackness of the bay and the distant twinkling lights of Kowloon. The feeble orange glow of the street-lights lit her onto Peak Road. She drove carefully, mindful of the precipice on the left, catching occasional glimpses of white stuccoed mansions hiding palely between the trees, thinking of her telephone call to Melissa.

Melissa had sounded disoriented when she had first spoken to her, and then, when she understood what the message was and what had happened to Raefe, she had been genuinely distressed.

"Can I see him now? Tonight?" she had asked uncertainly, wondering if the chauffeur was in his quarters and if he would drive her to Victoria.

"I think it is probably too late now," Elizabeth had said awkwardly. "There is visiting tomorrow."

There had been a long pause, then Melissa had said, "You've already seen him, haven't you?"

"Yes," Elizabeth had said unhappily. "Yes, I've already seen him."

Another long pause. "I'm sorry," Melissa had said at last, "but I don't know your name."

"Elizabeth. Elizabeth Harland."

There had been a slow intake of breath on the other end of the telephone, then Melissa had said in a flat, defeated voice, "Thank you for telephoning me, Elizabeth. It's more than I would have done if our positions had been reversed."

She had hung up the phone and the conversation had come to an end. What the listening sister had made of it Elizabeth neither knew nor cared.

The road wound tortuously between high banks of thick foliage and tall, dense pines. It had been a disconcerting conversation, but one that had done nothing but increase her sympathy for Melissa. There was a far more terrible conversation lying in wait for her. She eased the Buick off Peak Road and onto the narrow track that led to the drive of her home. The lights were on as she had known they would be. She slid the car into the double garage and, hating herself to the bottom of her soul, walked reluctantly toward the house, and Adam.

Chapter Nineteen
❧

JULIENNE and Derry were in a small sailboat, drifting pleasantly in a dead calm off Cape d'Aguilar.

"I can't understand why the devil he wasn't arrested," Derry said, a note of admiration in his voice as he sprawled at the helm, wearing nothing but a small gold crucifix on a

chain and a pair of white shorts that had seen better days.
"It's only been a few months since he was cleared of Jacko's
murder. How he can rampage the streets with a loaded
revolver and get away with it is beyond me."

Julienne leaned against the side of the boat, her hand
trailing languorously in the jade green water. "But he knew
the tongs were lying in wait for Tom. And he didn't burn
the gun. He only pistol-whipped the Chinese who was
attacking Tom."

"Fire," Derry corrected her in amusement. Julienne's
rare lapses of idiom always entertained him. "You fire a
gun, sweet love. You don't burn it."

Julienne shrugged a naked shoulder unconcernedly. Her
shorts were cerise, very brief, very French, and her halter
top was a sizzling shade of apple green. "Fire, burn, what
does it matter? All that matters is that he did not shoot the
man. He simply prevented him from murdering Tom. And
for that, *mon amour*, I am very grateful."

Derry gazed at her speculatively. He wasn't sure, but he
thought she had once been Tom's mistress. If she had been,
he didn't want the affair to be rekindled now that Tom's
rash liaison with Lamoon Sheng had been brought to an
abrupt conclusion. If he didn't know himself better, he
would have said that he was headlong in love with
Julienne. As it was, he merely considered himself delight-
fully infatuated. But infatuation or not, he was seriously
disturbed at the thought of losing her. He could come to
terms with Ronnie. He had no choice. But the thought of
Julienne romping in bed with anyone else made cold sweat
break out on the back of his neck.

"Come over here," he said, his voice little more than a
growl. He felt a rising in his groin as Julienne withdrew her
hand from the water, her nipples straining full and taut
against the thin cotton of her top.

She smiled lazily at him. "A sailboat is not a very good
place for what you have in mind, *chéri*. You will get
yourself very wet and very bruised!"

"I'll get myself very fucked and I won't care about the
bruises," he said, his electric-blue eyes dark with heat.
"Now, for God's sake, get yourself over here, Julienne!"

She giggled and rose to her feet, moving carefully as the
sailboat rocked gently. "I think, *chéri*," she said mischievously, "that you are going to have to be very, very careful!"

She slid down next to him and he slipped his arm around her shoulders. "How long will Raefe be in the hospital?" she asked. "Does anyone know?"

"No." A light breeze had sprung up and Derry eyed the sails doubtfully, wondering if he should put a couple of reefs in them. He didn't want to capsize off Cape d'Aguilar with his shorts around his ankles. The breeze petered away, the sails flapping desultorily. He relaxed, saying, "Melissa went to visit him. They seem to be on extraordinarily good terms at the moment. You would think, now that the divorce is going ahead, that they'd hardly be speaking to each other."

"Divorce?" Julienne asked curiously. Her cheek had been resting against his shoulder. Now she turned her head and looked up at him. "I didn't know that they were getting a divorce. I thought she had moved back in with him?"

Derry shook his head. The sun had bleached his hair and the spray from the sea had tightened his curls so that he reminded her of a statue she had once seen of a Greek god. "She's back in the house they used to share, up on the Peak. But Raefe isn't living there. He's moved permanently into his apartment in Victoria. I can't imagine him staying there once he has remarried. It's so small."

"Remarried?" She sat bolt upright, her eyes wide. "*Tiens!* He can't be going to marry again! It isn't possible!"

"It's very possible," Derry said, frowning slightly. "You haven't had any hopes in that direction yourself, have you, Julienne?"

She looked genuinely shocked. "*Non!* How can you think such a thing?" She kissed him, open-mouthed, pressing herself against him. Derry enjoyed the embrace, but did not allow himself to be distracted.

"Then why does the news shock you so much?" he asked when he finally drew his mouth away from hers.

"Because I know who it is he is in love with. And never, in a million years, would I have believed it possible that she would leave her husband for him. It is amazing! Incredible!"

The breeze was beginning to lift again, filling out the sails. Derry ignored them. "Who is she?" he asked, fascinated. "I know it isn't Mark Hurley's wife because she's been looking as miserable as sin lately. And I haven't seen him with his Chinese girlfriend for weeks."

"I don't think I should tell you, *chéri*," she said teasingly. "It would not be very discreet of me."

"To hell with discretion," Derry said thickly, his hand sliding down inside the low neckline of her halter top. "Now who is it? Tell me or I'll throw you overboard!"

He had begun to caress her nipple, prompting her to feel familiar sweet urgings. "I don't think you would do such a thing," she said, her eyes beginning to cloud over with her desire. "But just in case—" She broke off to laugh throatily as he lowered his head to her breast. "It is Elizabeth Harland, *chéri*. And never did I think she would be so reckless. So very un-English!"

"We English," Derry said hoarsely as he slid her down beneath him and the boat rocked wildly, "can be *very* reckless . . ."

His hands were on the waistband of her shorts. She undid the button and zip, and wriggled obligingly as he eased them down over her hips.

"Why is it your pussy hair is an even spicier red than the hair on your head?" he asked as the tight tousle of curls sprang erotically against the heel of his hand and his fingers slipped inside her.

"*Ils sont joli, non?*" she whispered, pushing herself up against him, her eyes closed, her lips parted. "Oh, but that is good, *mon amour*. Very, very good."

The breeze was blowing landward, filling the sails. Derry felt the boat begin to scud, and an edge of water creamed over the side, splashing down on them. He ignored it. The tide was on the turn. The worst that could happen was that they capsized or were blown ashore. He kicked his shorts from around his ankles. Julienne's silky-dark nipples were erect against his chest, her legs were wide. Neither of them cared about the sea water that now slopped around them. He took his prick in his hands. He wasn't going to stop now. Not even for old Father Neptune. He grinned as he thought of the sight they would make as they neared the shore. He hoped no one would be so daft as to think they were in trouble and send out help. He didn't need any help. None at all. He was going in hard and strong and with all flags flying.

Late the next afternoon Helena visited Tom for the second time that day. She felt incredibly tired. Tom had not wanted to stay another night in the hospital and it had taken all her persistence to ensure that he did so. He wasn't badly hurt. His nose had been broken and would probably set a trifle crooked, but his good looks had always been of the rugged kind and she did not think they would suffer. His broken ribs had been strapped. The wound on his chest had required only half a dozen stitches. His mental suffering far exceeded his physical suffering.

"I must see Lamoon!" he said to her fiercely when she entered his room. "I must know that she is all right!"

"She wasn't hurt," Helena repeated for the twentieth time. "You told me yourself that the chauffeur merely dragged her away."

Tom slammed his fist down on the tightly tucked-in sheets, his eyes blazing. "She was fighting him for all she was worth! Anything could have happened to her! A man crazy enough to try to have me killed isn't exactly going to be lenient with a daughter who is completely in his power, is he? Christ!" He ran his hand through his hair. "And I just lay there! I didn't lift a finger to help her!"

"You can only have been semiconscious," Helena said practically. "When the police arrived seconds later, you were flat out and that horrid Chinese was lying senseless on top of you. How could you have helped her?"

He swung his legs from the bed, wincing with pain from his ribs as he did so. Helena put her hands restrainingly on his shoulders. "Oh, no, you don't," she said firmly. "You're not leaving here till tomorrow morning at the earliest. Even if you did, it wouldn't do any good. You can hardly call in person at the Sheng mansion and ask for her, can you? Not unless you want more thugs to complete yesterday's unfinished task!"

"But I have to know what has happened to her," he repeated despairingly. "I'm responsible! I knew the risks she was running and I encouraged her!"

"Lamoon knew the risks as well," Helena said quietly.

Tom groaned, not wanting to put into words what he most feared. That she was no longer even in Hong Kong. That he would never see her again.

"I'm going across to see Raefe," she said, satisfied that Tom had accepted the futility of storming out of the hospital. "He has Chinese friends who will be able to tell us what has happened."

"How is he?" Tom's eyes darkened. "I tried to go over and see him this morning, but that dragon of a ward sister said the doctor was with him and that I couldn't see him until tomorrow."

"She probably had her instructions from the police," Helena said dryly. "I imagine they want to keep the two of you apart until they have finished taking statements from you both."

"They can take statements till they're blue in the face!" he said savagely. "Any injuries we inflicted were in self-defense. If Raefe hadn't shouted out to me when he did, that bloody chink would have knifed me with no one on the street even being aware of it!"

"And if he hadn't slugged the supposed stall-holder, after your first attacker failed, the second would have succeeded," Helena said, her face going pale at the thought of how near he had come to losing his life. "I hope the powers that be decide it wisest to take no action against Raefe. He's suffered enough as it is. I don't believe he was half so indifferent to the murder charge that was brought against him as he would have had us believe."

"I don't believe he's half so indifferent about a lot of things as he would have us believe," Tom said wryly. "Underneath that devil-may-care swagger of his hides a damned nice bloke."

"Yes," Helena agreed wearily as she turned to leave. Raefe Elliot *was* a damned nice bloke. And he had saved Tom's life, which made it all the more difficult for her to blame him and to dislike him for the unhappiness he was causing Adam.

"So there's no news at all of Lamoon?" Raefe asked Helena. He was propped up against some pillows, his hard-boned face oddly pale, his eyes burning blackly.

"No. You're the only person I know who has access to the Chinese grapevine. I wondered if you could find out what has happened to her?"

"Yes," he said unenthusiastically. "I can do that, Helena. But I can already make a pretty good guess. She won't be in Hong Kong, that's for sure. She will have been sent to relatives as far away as possible. And she will stay with them until a suitable marriage can be arranged for her."

"Poor Tom." Helena's deep blue eyes were bleak. "He

loves her so much." She crossed the small room to the window and stood for a moment, looking out, seeing nothing.

"There was never even the faintest hope of their being able to marry," Raefe said, his voice oddly flat. "For families like the Shengs, mixed marriages are out. There are no exceptions."

Helena continued to stare out of the window. "What a stupid world we live in," she said bitterly. "There is so much unhappiness that can't be avoided. You would think that by now the human race would have stopped inflicting misery that *can* be avoided, simply because one person's skin is a different shade from another's. Surely all that matters is that they love each other? Surely loving each other is the *only* thing that matters?"

"It may be, one day, but that day hasn't dawned yet, Helena."

"Do you think it will ever come?" she asked, turning toward him once again. "Not an ideal world with everyone loving one another, but a *decent* world. A multiracial world, where people are judged by their worth, and not by their color or social status?"

"If enough people want it, and work for it, and are prepared to die for it, then it will come," Raefe said somberly. "But it won't come in a world dominated by Hitler or the Japanese."

Helena managed a tired smile. "Oh, dear, what a subject to bring into a sick room! I meant to cheer you up, not cast you into a pit of depression."

"Then cheer me up," he said, watching her closely. "Where the hell is Lizzie? I haven't seen her since yesterday evening, and I was too groggy then from anesthetic to appreciate her visit properly. I expected her to be here this afternoon."

"Perhaps she thought Melissa would be visiting," Helena said awkwardly. "I know that she telephoned her from here late last night."

Raefe's eyes narrowed slightly. "Melissa has been and gone. A telephone call to the ward would have told Lizzie that. Where is she, Helena? What do you know that you're not telling me?"

Helena wished that she had remained standing at the window where she could avoid Raefe's all too perceptive eyes. "I don't know," she said uncomfortably. "We parted outside the hospital at about nine last night. I had suggested we go for a drink together, but she . . ." Helena faltered, cursing herself for a fool.

"But she what?" Raefe asked, his nostrils pinched and white, his mouth tight.

"She said she was tired," Helena finished lamely.

Raefe's near-black eyes held hers mercilessly. "Don't lie to me, Helena. Why wouldn't she go for a drink with you? What did she say?"

Raefe had saved Tom's life. Helena couldn't lie to him, no matter how much she wanted to. "That she had to go home to talk to Adam," she said at last, defeatedly.

"Talk to him about what?" Raefe demanded, every muscle in his body tightening with tension.

"She said that Adam knew about her affair with you. I imagine that was what she needed to talk to him about. He loves her very much and—"

"Christ!" He swung his legs over the bed, pulling free the IV needle that was inserted in his arm.

"Now see what you've done!" Helena cried, horrified. "Stay where you are! Don't move until I can get a nurse!"

"I don't need a damned nurse!" he snapped, but to his fury the sudden movement had made him sick and giddy. As Helena rushed to the door to get assistance she was relieved to see that he was swaying unsteadily and was not hard on her heels.

The ward sister came in answer to Helena's call for help. She took one look at Raefe, his face bone-white, and said crisply, "Thank you, Mrs. Nicholson. Perhaps you would leave now. Mr. Elliot is far weaker than he believes himself to be."

"Telephone Lizzie," Raefe said to Helena, knowing defeat when he met it, and accepting it with appalling grace. "Tell her I want to see her. Tell her if she doesn't come to me, then I'm coming to her!"

"Not without my permission you're not," the sister said tartly.

Helena grinned. She doubted if Raefe had ever been spoken to in such a way before. Then, sensing that a full-scale battle was about to commence, she made a hasty and diplomatic exit. At the public telephone booth in the hospital's foyer she dialed Elizabeth's number.

"Mr. Harland, Missy Harland not home," Chan said before she could even state with whom she wished to speak. "Please to telephone back another time."

"Could I leave a message—" Helena began, but Chan had already severed the connection. The line was dead.

Helena replaced the receiver, perturbed. It was unlike any of the Harlands' houseboys to be rude or curt. As she walked through the busy foyer and out into the street she was convinced that Chan had been rude because he had been lying. Adam and Elizabeth *were* at home. But they weren't answering the telephone, not even to her. She unlocked the door of her car and slid behind the wheel, wondering what on earth was happening in the Harland home, and whether she should drive up there.

Julienne walked with hip-swinging pertness down the hospital corridor toward Tom's private room. Her red hair was glinting, and her eyes were bright with health and love of life. She was wearing a suit of sizzling lemon linen, the waist nipped in tightly, a peplum emphasizing the curve of her hips. She wore no blouse beneath the jacket and the collar was open deeply, revealing honeyed skin and a small diamond on a chain nestling at the cleavage of her breasts.

"Mr. Tom Nicholson, please," she said to the ward sister.

The sister put down the sheaf of notes she had been perusing. The private lives of her two most recent patients were growing increasingly interesting. She knew very well who Julienne was—and of her reputation. "Certainly," she said, her face revealing none of her thoughts. "This way, please."

Julienne's treacherously high-heeled shoes tip-tapped in the sister's wake, along the corridor toward Tom's room. "How is Mr. Elliot?" she asked the sister, her gaze flicking over the names on the doors of the few private rooms. "Is he going to be all right?"

The sister turned her head, her eyes meeting Julienne's. "Yes," she said, wondering which man Julienne was most interested in, and what her relationship with both of them was. "But he needs rest."

If there was any irony in the sister's voice, Julienne was blithely unaware of it. *"Vous avez été très gentille,"* she said as the sister opened the door of Tom's room. And, indeed, the sister had been very kind. Then, on seeing Tom, his chest heavily bandaged, Julienne's smile faded. "Oh, *mon pauvre petit!*" she exclaimed, the heady fragrance of her French perfume filling the room as she hurried to his side.

Tom was genuinely glad to see her. They hadn't been lovers for over two years, but unlike most of the women he knew, Julienne had a capacity for friendship as well as love, and his affection for her ran deep.

"*Ça va?*" she asked urgently, taking his hand. "Are you all right?"

"I'm fine, Julienne," he said, not looking fine at all. "A couple of cracked ribs and a broken nose. That's all."

She ignored the stiff-looking chair beside his locker and perched on the bed. "You do not look fine, *chéri*," she said, her kittenish face unusually somber. "You look very, very unhappy."

"I am." Worry and anxiety had carved deep lines on his handsome face, and his long, mobile mouth was tight with strain. "You know about Lamoon?"

Julienne nodded. Helena had told her, and she had not been surprised. She had known that a man as virile as Tom must have been conducting a love affair with someone, and the fact that he had never brought that someone with him to picnics and parties indicated that she was, perhaps, Chinese.

"I am very sorry for you both," she said sincerely, "but you must have known it was hopeless, Tom. A girl like Lamoon Sheng . . . I don't even understand how you managed to meet undiscovered for so long."

"Elizabeth and Adam Harland gave us hospitality and the use of their summerhouse," he said bleakly.

"*Tiens!*" Julienne's pansy-dark eyes were wide with shock. "I would never have believed it in a million years! I always thought the Harlands so prim and so very proper, and now I discover that Adam is really a romantic at heart and as for Elizabeth . . ." Words failed her.

Tom looked at her curiously, unused to such an occurrence. "What about Elizabeth?" he asked, sensing that something was wrong.

"She's in love with Raefe," Julienne said simply. "Derry tells me that Raefe intends to marry her."

Tom stared at her. "I don't believe it," he said at last.

Julienne's shoulders lifted in a tiny shrug. "I do not blame you, *chéri*, but I think it is the truth. I think that very soon the nice, steady Adam is going to be a very unhappy man."

"Christ!" Tom continued to stare at her in disbelief. "Raefe and Elizabeth. It never occurred to me."

"It has been going on for quite a while," Julienne said knowledgeably. "Since before Jeremy's birthday party."

"Christ!" Tom said again. He had been so immersed in his affair with Lamoon that he hadn't given a thought to his friends' private lives for months. "Poor old Adam . . ."

Julienne took his hand. "And poor Tom," she said gently. "There will be no more Lamoon, *chéri*. You are going to be very lonely."

His face tightened. "I can't accept that yet, Julienne. I *have* to see her again! God damn it! I *will* see her again!"

Julienne shook her head slowly. "No, *chéri*," she said regretfully. "I think not. I think your Lamoon is already very far from you." She rose to her feet looking down at him compassionately. "Perhaps in a few days, if you *are* lonely, perhaps it might be a good idea to telephone me? Old lovers should be able to give comfort when it is needed. *C'est compris?*"

Despite his grief, he grinned. He understood very well. "You never know," he said, his heart breaking inside him. "I might just do that, Julienne."

She smiled and blew him a kiss. "*Au revoir*," she said, hoping very much that he would do so. "God bless."

Dusk had fallen and the lights were on in the corridor as she walked toward the sister's office. She hesitated a moment outside the door that bore Raefe's name. She wanted very much to go in and see him, if only for a minute. A few yards away from her, in her glass-fronted office, the sister put down her pen and watched her with interest.

A small frown puckered Julienne's brow. Surely Raefe would not mind if she went in and asked how he was? But she wasn't sure. Nothing about Raefe was predictable. It was one of the reasons she found him so devastatingly attractive. She knew very well the kind of reaction she could arouse in Ronnie or Derry, or even Tom. But Raefe Elliot was different. And she didn't want the humiliation of forcing her company on him if he preferred to be alone.

"Another time, *chéri*," she whispered, and smiled to herself as she continued to walk down the corridor toward the stairs. Elizabeth was a very lucky lady, and Julienne didn't blame her in the least if she was about to burn all her boats behind her. If she were in Elizabeth's position, she would be very tempted to do the same thing. But tempted only. After all, she was married to Ronnie, not Adam. And Ronnie was fun and made her laugh. She ran down the last few steps and into the foyer. She felt very sexy and Ronnie was meeting Alastair at the Pen at seven o'clock. She would have to hurry if she wanted to detain him before he left the house.

Adam stared at Elizabeth as she entered the drawing room. He looked hunched and gaunt and suddenly very old.

"You're in love with him, aren't you?" he asked without preamble.

"Yes."

The word fell between them like a bomb. She saw him stagger slightly and then regain his balance. He was standing in front of the flower-filled fireplace, his pipe clutched tightly in his hand, the tobacco long since burnt out.

"Oh, Adam, I'm so sorry," she said heartbrokenly, moving toward him. "So very, very sorry."

He fended her off with his arm. "No!" he said, his voice hoarse with grief. "Don't come near me, Beth! Don't touch me! I can't bear it! Truly, I can't!"

The tears were pouring down her face. "Sit down, Adam. Let me fetch you a drink."

"I don't want a bloody drink!" he shouted. "I want what I've always wanted! I want you, Beth!" He pressed his hand against his eyes. "I want you," he said again, brokenly. "God help me, Beth. I don't know how to begin to live without you. You're all I've ever wanted . . . ever since you were a little child."

She moved toward him once more, and took his arm and led him to a chair. "Sit down," she said gently. He did and she crossed to the table that held decanters and glasses, and poured a large brandy. "Drink this," she said, pressing it into his hand. "Oh, Adam, oh, my dear, if only you knew how hard I've tried not to let this happen!"

He drained the brandy in one swallow and set the glass down unsteadily. "So you've *tried* to stay with me, have you?" he said with sudden bitterness. "You've *tried* to love me and not him?" His face was ashen with anger and grief.

"I don't understand, Beth! I thought we were so happy together!"

"We were . . . we are . . ."

She was crouching at his feet and he leaned forward, seizing her wrists with surprising strength. "Then *why*?" he howled. "In the name of God, Beth! *Why*?"

He was hurting her but she couldn't pull away. "I don't know why," she cried truthfully. "But when I'm with him, I feel whole. Complete. I feel as if he is the other side of my personality. I want to be with him all the time." She saw the agony on Adam's face, but she couldn't stop. "I want to share his life . . ."

He released his hold of her, springing to his feet with such suddenness that she fell to her knees. "You've taken leave of your senses! Men like Elliot don't marry the women they sleep with! You don't mean anything to him, Beth! He doesn't love you! *I* love you!"

She pulled herself up against the chair, tears dripping down onto her hands, her dress. She hated what was happening to them, hated herself for allowing it to happen. "No. It isn't like that, Adam. He does love me. He wants me to share his life with him."

He flinched as if he had been struck. "You can't mean that. . . . You can't intend *leaving* me for him? For a man who doesn't know the meaning of the word faithful? A man who is a *killer*?"

The room was suddenly very still. Elizabeth felt as if she were on a stage. As if nothing that was happening was real. She said, unutterably wearily, all passion spent, "I have to leave you, Adam." As he stared at her, refusing to believe her, she added with brutal simplicity, "I'm carrying his child."

Adam's groan was deep and terrible. He put his hands out, like a blind man, seeking for somewhere to sit. "Oh, no . . ." he said as he lowered himself into a wing chair. "Oh, no . . . no . . . I don't believe it. I won't believe it!"

She walked across to the mantelpiece and leaned against it for support. "I don't know what I'm going to do," she said bleakly. It wasn't a cry for help, it was simply a statement of fact. "Raefe doesn't know yet. Whatever I do, though, I can't stay here, Adam. I'm going to move into the Pen."

He shook his head, struggling for words. When they came, he said desperately, "No! There's no need, Beth! Stay here. Stay with me!"

"I can't," she said, her heart breaking. She walked over to him and knelt down in front of him, taking his hands in hers. "There is no way I can expect you to understand, Adam. But I love you. I've always loved you."

His expression was tired in defeat, aged by pain. "But not the way you love him?"

Her hands tightened on his. "No," she said, her voice cracking. "Not the way I love him."

For a long time neither of them spoke. Then, at last, Adam said, a new note of desperation in his voice, "There's no need for you to leave, Beth."

She raised her face to his.

He was struggling inwardly, coming to terms with the most dreadful crisis he had ever faced. "You say Raefe doesn't know about the baby? Don't tell him. Don't tell anyone."

"I'm sorry, Adam, I don't understand. . . ."

His thumbs pressed so hard on the backs of her hands, she winced with pain. "*We'll* have the baby, Beth! *I'll* be the father! We can live together as we've always lived! We've been happy, Beth. You said so yourself! We can be happy again! *Please*, my darling. Please stay! Please let me take care of you both!"

She began to cry, great wracking sobs that could not be controlled. She had always known that he loved her, but that he loved her so deeply he would forgive her infidelity, accept another man's child as his own, tore her apart. He was offering her all he could possibly offer and it wasn't enough. Nothing ever could be. Their life together had come to an end, buried beneath a carpet of hibiscus blossoms.

"No," she whispered sadly, rising unsteadily to her feet, wondering if her life would be long enough for her ever to forgive herself. "I think you are the kindest, most loving man in the world, Adam, but I can't do as you ask. I can't live with you anymore. I'm going back down to the Pen tonight."

He made no move toward her. He didn't even try to rise from his chair. His world had collapsed around him. She was going and there was nothing he could do to make her stay.

"I love you," he said tonelessly as she walked to the door. "God help me, but I still love you, Beth."

She swayed, one hand on the knob of the door, then walked blindly out of the room. She packed only one suitcase, carrying it down the stairs herself, not calling for Chan or for Mei Lin. She paused in the mosaic tiled hallway. The drawing room door remained closed. She didn't move toward it. There was nothing more she could say to him. The most horrible thing of all, the most horrible part of the whole, dreadful scene that they had endured, was that, deeply as she cared for him, not once had she had any doubts about the decision she had made. She had none now as she walked tiredly out of the house and across the dark gravel to the garage and her car.

"My God, I don't believe it!" Helena said, thunderstruck. It was nine in the morning. She had driven over from Kowloon, determined to see either Elizabeth or Adam, worried sick by the repeated refusal of Chan to put through any of her calls.

Adam smelt of stale brandy. His cardigan looked as though it had been slept in. "It's true," he said bleakly. "She's at the Pen."

"But she'll come back!" Helena cried with desperate reassurance. "When she has had time to think, she will come back!"

Adam shook his head. "No," he said flatly. "She won't come back, Helena." He paused for a moment, then said, "She's pregnant by him."

"Holy God!" She stared at him, so shocked that she felt physically ill. "Oh, Adam, my dear. I'm so sorry . . ."

"It isn't pity I want," he said tautly. "I just want Beth back again." His eyes met hers urgently. "Talk to her for me, Helena. Try to make her see sense. I've told her I don't care about the baby. I don't care about anything as long as she comes back to me."

"I'll talk to her," Helena said, but her voice, even to her own ears, sounded defeated. Elizabeth's decision would not have been made lightly, and if she was pregnant with Raefe Elliot's child, then Helena could not imagine her returning home. "Come along," she said to Adam. "You look ghastly. Have a shower and change your clothes and we'll have breakfast together. I'll ask Chan to put on some eggs and to set the table."

"Thank you, Helena," he said gratefully, knowing through his pain that her maternal bossiness was exactly what he needed.

He left the room slowly, his limp more pronounced than she had ever seen it before. "Damn you, Raefe Elliot," she whispered beneath her breath. "Why the hell couldn't you have fallen in love with Julienne? Then no hearts would have been broken."

Chapter Twenty

*E*LIZABETH booked into the Peninsula, tired and drawn, asking for a single room and saying that she would want it indefinitely. She knew that Raefe, when he found out, would immediately want her to move in with him, but she had no intention of doing so. Not yet. She had not left Adam in order to live with another man. She had left him because she was carrying another man's child. Because she could no longer give him the love and loyalty that was his due.

She moved wearily around her room, putting her toilet things on a small glass shelf in the bathroom, and laying her nightdress on the bed. There was a carafe of iced water on the dressing table and she poured herself a glass and drank deeply. She didn't want room service. She didn't want a meal, a hot drink. She didn't want to do anything but sleep.

She undressed with slow, tired movements. Her face was swollen from the tears she had shed, her head ached. She hung her clothes on the back of a chair, took a long, cooling shower, and lay down on the bed.

She had left Adam. Her agonized mind sought oblivion in sleep. The day mercifully began to recede, grow confused, grow dim. The sound of traffic on nearby Salisbury Road blurred and faded. . . . She had done the only

thing she possibly could do. She had told Adam of her love
for Raefe. She had told him about the baby. And she was
going to have the baby. The merest touch of a smile
softened her lips as she closed her eyes and slept.

The next morning she didn't drive first to the hospital.
She drove instead down Nathan road to Li Pi's Kowloon
apartment. If she was embarking on a new chapter of her
life, then her music was going to have first priority. It had
taken a backseat for far too long.

She looked ill and pale when he opened the door to her,
but her eyes were burning with an expression he was all
too familiar with. He wasted no time in upbraiding her for
her absence. Neither of them had time to spare.

He took her straight to the keyboard, but not in order
that she could play for him as she had played previously.
This time they were starting from the beginning. "I would
like you to play for me a C-major scale in double octaves,"
he said to her without preamble. "As legato as possible and
in one continuous gesture."

He stopped her after only the first note. "You must sit
differently. You must sit on the *thighs* so that the pelvic and
knee joints are mobile. Now, once again."

It was exactly what she needed. For three hours she did
not think of Adam once. Or of Raefe. Or even of the baby.

At lunchtime, as they shared a light meal of fish and rice,
she told Li Pi how difficult she always found Bartok's
second piano concerto. He smiled, his aged face creasing
into a hundred lines.

"There is no such thing as a difficult piece, Elizabeth. A
piece is either impossible, or it is easy. The process
whereby it migrates from one category to the other is
known as practicing."

She laughed, knowing he was right, loving the feel of
once again working, of having achieved something of
worth.

"You will be here tomorrow?" he asked, when at last he
escorted her to the door.

"I shall be here every day," she said, and her beautiful
face was no longer etched with strain. She felt clearheaded
and confident.

"Remember," he said. "Remember when you practice,
that in performing the scale, the tempo must not be too
slow, otherwise it will break down into a series of isolated

impulses, nor must it be too fast, or staccato emerges." He
gave her his gnomelike grin. "Till tomorrow. Good-bye."

It was late afternoon and the streets were crowded as she
drove back toward the ferry and Victoria. She felt almost
light-headed. Her life was not lying in pieces all around
her. It was beginning to take shape. She no longer felt as if
she were being manipulated by emotions outside her
control. She felt in command of what was happening and
the feeling brought with it a heady sense of freedom. When
she walked into the hospital it was with the swing of new-
found confidence. Her full-skirted dress of pale eau-de-Nil
silk rustled against her legs.

"Is Mr. Elliot feeling stronger?" she asked the ward sister
as she passed her in the corridor.

The sister raised an eyebrow slightly. It was because Mrs.
Harland hadn't visited earlier in the day that Mr. Elliot had
been demanding he be discharged.

"If his temper is anything to go by, he is," she said dryly.

Elizabeth grinned. Raefe wouldn't make an easy patient.
"Can I see him now?"

"The sooner the better," the sister said, "but if he tells
you he's discharging himself, dissuade him. He won't be fit
to go anywhere for at least another week."

Elizabeth nodded and walked on to Raefe's room.

His head spun toward the door the instant she opened it.
"What the hell time do you call this?" he asked, but his
eyes told her his anger was only feigned. They blazed with
pleasure at seeing her. "It's nearly six, God damn it!"

"I had things to do," she said casually, walking across
the room and sitting demurely on the stiff little chair beside
his locker.

"Come here, woman!" he growled. "Where I can get my
hands on you!"

She did as he demanded and despite the IV drip and his
heavily bandaged chest, it was a long time before either of
them spoke again. When she finally pulled herself away
from him, she said hesitantly, "I have something to tell
you."

"I know." She was sitting on the bed, her hands
imprisoned in his. "Adam knows about us. Helena told
me."

There was unconcealed satisfaction in his voice. She

withdrew her hands from his and walked over to the window.

Raefe's brows flew together. "What is it, Lizzie? He had to know sometime. What's the matter?"

"I didn't want him to know so suddenly, so dreadfully." She paused for a moment, then said, "I've left him. I had no choice. I've taken a room at the Pen."

Raefe's elation was tempered instantly by the realization that there was still something she hadn't told him. He waited, every muscle in his body tense.

At last she turned to face him. The sunlight streaming through the window behind her burnished her hair to silver. "I'm going to have a baby," she said simply.

He didn't even ask her if it was his. He didn't need to. "The devil you are!" he said exultantly. "Come over here where I can kiss you!"

A smile curved her lips. "Are you pleased?"

"Let me show you," he said, reaching his hand out to her and pulling her down against him. "Why on earth did you move into the Pen? You should have gone straight to the apartment."

"No." She pulled away from him a little. "I'm not moving into the apartment, Raefe. Not yet."

He stared at her, as if she were out of her mind. "Whyever not? It's large enough."

She shook her head. "It has nothing to do with size. It's just that I don't want to walk out of Adam's life and immediately into another domestic arrangement. Does that make sense?"

"None at all," he said, his brows once more flying satanically together. "I want you with me every minute of the day. You want to be with me. We're having a child. You living at the Pen and me living alone in the apartment just doesn't make sense!"

She had known he wouldn't understand. "It makes sense to me," she said quietly. "It's what I need."

"What you need is a good hiding," he said grimly, "but I'm in no condition to administer it."

She smiled. "Then you'll have to accept what I'm saying."

There was a new-found assurance about her, and a determination that he knew he could not argue with. Not yet. "How will you manage?" he asked, thinking that he had found her Achilles' heel. "The Pen is ruinously expensive. I can't imagine Adam footing the bill, and I'm not going to."

Her smile deepened. "There's no need for either of you to foot any of my bills," she said, enjoying her independence. "My father left me very adequately provided for."

"Blast him," Raefe said, his eyes gleaming once more. He didn't imagine that little fact had pleased Adam Harland. A financially independent lady was one who could call her own shots, and it was obvious that that was exactly what Lizzie intended on doing. "Who was your father?" he asked curiously. She had talked about him but she had never told him his name.

"Jerome Kingsley."

Raefe frowned, trying to remember. "Kingsley, Kingsley," he muttered, then his face cleared. He'd got it. Jerome Kingsley, financial wizard of the thirties. No wonder the Peninsula's bills left her unperturbed. "At least," he said wryly, drawing her gingerly back into his arms, "you're not marrying me for my money."

"I'm not marrying you at all," she said, a shake of laughter in her voice.

He grinned complacently. "Oh, yes, you are. Just as soon as Adam can be persuaded to divorce you. Do you think you could rearrange yourself a little? I have a knife wound there that's giving me hell. What I need is a glimpse of your breasts to take my mind off it!"

"Je ne comprends pas," Julienne said bewilderedly. "Raefe is now out of the hospital and living in Victoria. And you are in a single room at the Pen. It doesn't make sense."

"So I've been told," Elizabeth said, amused.

"Doesn't Raefe *want* you to move in with him?" Julienne asked, wondering if she had been unnecessarily tactless.

They were at the swimming club, relaxing at the poolside with tall, iced drinks.

"Yes," Elizabeth replied. "Don't look so concerned, Julienne. I'm at the Pen because I want to be there."

"*I* wouldn't want to be there. Especially in a single room!" Julienne said emphatically. She gazed at Elizabeth lying on her sun-lounger, her bathing suit still wet from their swim. "You know, Elizabeth," she said thoughtfully, "I do not think that staying at the Pen is very good for you. I think perhaps you are beginning to eat a little too much."

Elizabeth grinned. Julienne did not yet know about the baby. "Yes," she said contentedly, eyeing her slightly thickening waistline. "I think you could quite possibly be right, Julienne!"

The last few weeks had not been easy for her. Although adultery was rife in Hong Kong, the desertion of a husband or wife was not. Her action in moving out of her marital home had shocked and dismayed many. Lady Gresby had crossed her firmly off her list, and so had a lot of other people. Leigh Stafford had been excruciatingly embarrassed when they had met accidentally at the Hong Kong Club. People she had regarded as friends now no longer spoke to her and openly avoided her. She didn't care. She was living her life as she wished to live it, and the friends who mattered to her had all stayed loyal.

"Adam tells me that you've asked him for a divorce," Alastair said to her when they met one day for lunch at the Parisian Grill. "Is that wise, Elizabeth? So soon? It's a very final step."

"So is having a baby that isn't his," she said quietly.

Alastair blanched. "I'm sorry. . . . I didn't realize." He toyed with his smoked duck, then asked, "Wouldn't it be easier if you moved in with Elliot? People wouldn't find the situation quite so puzzling."

"I can't help it if people find my personal life puzzling, Alastair," she said with unusual crispness. "And it doesn't bother me. It isn't any of their concern."

"No," Alastair agreed, with little conviction. He was a man who liked things to be neat and tidy. He didn't like loose ends or messiness in personal situations, and he was growing increasingly miserable over his failure to persuade Helena to marry him.

"How are things with you and Helena?" Elizabeth asked, sensing the direction of his thoughts.

He shrugged dismally. "The same as they have always been. I love her. I'm damned sure that she loves me. But she won't marry me."

"Perhaps it's still too soon for her. She's only been a widow for two years."

"Just over two years," Alastair corrected her. "It's nearly three now. She used to talk to me about it, but she won't anymore. I think she talks to Adam more than she talks to me."

"Adam can be a very sympathetic listener."

"Yes." He gazed at her curiously. "You still see him, don't you? I mean, not just casually and by accident. You see him by arrangement?"

She nodded. They had needed to meet and talk, and she had not wanted to keep returning to the home they had shared. Adam had suggested they lunch at the Pen, and they had continued to do so at least once a week.

"Is he happy about a divorce?" Alastair asked.

"No." A shadow crossed her eyes. She didn't like talking about Adam with anyone, but Alastair had been a good friend to her and he deserved to know something of what was going on. "He won't instigate proceedings yet. He's still hoping that I will return to him."

"And you won't?"

Her green-gold eyes met his unflinchingly. "No, Alastair. I'm in love with Raefe. Even though, for my own reasons, I'm not living with him, my future is with him."

Alastair sighed. "I wish to God Helena felt that her future was with me," he said wearily. "If the Japs continue being belligerent, I can see women and children being ordered to leave the colony. And if Helena goes, then I may never see her again. She may just slip away from me, and I couldn't bear that, Elizabeth. Truly I couldn't."

"Are things really getting worse with the Japanese?" Elizabeth asked, unable to give him any words of comfort where Helena was concerned.

"Oh, yes. They're playing a waiting game, but I don't think they will wait much longer. An expeditionary force landed at Bias Bay last month. That's only thirty-five miles northeast of Hong Kong. Canton has been captured. In practical terms our isolation is almost complete."

"And as if it weren't enough, the Germans are rampaging all over Europe, the Russians have invaded Finland . . ." she said bleakly. She looked around the luxurious restaurant. It was very hard to believe that half the world was at war. Silver gleamed on white linen, a trio of musicians played discreetly. There were Sydney rock oysters for hors d'oeuvres, smoked salmon, strawberries, champagne, and fifteen-year-old brandy.

"I know," he said, reading her mind. "It doesn't seem possible, does it? But it will come here as well, Elizabeth. It's just a matter of time."

* * *

"Would it help this period of adjustment you're giving yourself if we took a trip to Australia?" Raefe asked her as they lay in bed in his Victoria flat.

"Australia?" She turned her head toward him, her hair brushing his shoulder. "Why Australia? Do you have to go on business, or does Fort Canning want you to go?"

"Neither, sweet love," he said, his hand resting comfortably on the growing rise of her belly. They had no secrets from each other. She knew far more about his intelligence work than he should ever have told her. "Roman is on tour there. The orchestra is giving concerts in Sydney, Melbourne, Adelaide, and Perth. I thought we could meet up with him on the last leg in Perth."

She sat up in bed, looking down at him, her eyes shining. "Oh, that would be wonderful, Raefe. It seems forever since I heard a great orchestra!"

He leaned back against the pillows, loving her so much his heart hurt. "He wants to hear you play."

Her eyes widened in horror. "You're joking! He's one of the greatest conductors in the world! What could I possibly play for him?"

"Bach, Schubert, Beethoven, anything that you like," he said, grinning. "Don't tell me you're not capable of it. Not after the months of work with Li Pi."

She laughed down at him. Her horror had only been because he had taken her by surprise. She knew her capabilities very well and she was more than ready to play for a conductor of Roman Rakowski's stature. The prospect sent adrenaline singing along her veins. "Roman Rakowski," she said again in awe. "I can hardly believe it."

Raefe pulled her down beside him. "Don't say his name with quite such adoration or I might change my mind and keep you as far apart from him as possible!" His hands reached out for the full lusciousness of her breasts. "They're getting bigger, Lizzie. How many months is it yet?"

"Ages and ages," she said languorously, sliding her legs between his, luxuriating in the pleasure of his touch. "Another six months at least."

He lowered his head and his tongue circled her silk-dark nipple, his lips pulling gently. She gave a soft moan, pushing her pelvis against him, hot and damp with reawakened desire.

"Twice before breakfast can't be very good for my health," he murmured teasingly as her hands moved caressingly downward. "I'm thirty-two, sweet love, not twenty-two."

"You're wonderful," she murmured, her lips on the bronzed flesh of his shoulders, her legs spreading wide. Her breath exhaled on a low, deep sigh of fulfillment as he entered her. "Wonderful . . . wonderful . . . unbelievably wonderful . . ."

They arrived in Perth on Christmas Eve. Neither of them had wanted to spend Christmas in Hong Kong. It was too emotional a time. Raefe was sure that Adam would ask her to spend the day with him, and if he did, knew that she would feel bound to do so. As it was, she had been able to tell him that she would be in Australia and she had been deeply relieved when Helena invited Adam to spend Christmas with her and Alastair and the children.

Melissa had gone, for her own choice, back to the farm in the New Territories. She didn't want to be surrounded by the curious eyes of family and friends. Every day was still a battle for her, and she wanted to fight her battle alone and in private.

"It seems funny to see Christmas trees and imitation snow and snowmen when the sun is blazing down," Elizabeth said as they window-shopped in Perth, looking for a Christmas present for Roman. Raefe tucked her hand more tightly in the crook of his arm. "I keep forgetting that you've never spent a Christmas in the southern hemisphere before. We'll spend tomorrow on the beach. That will really disorient you."

They passed a newsstand, the headline on the month-old papers from England a defiant "COME ON, HITLER! WE'RE READY FOR YOU!"

"I wonder what next year will bring," she said, suddenly somber.

He patted her hand. It was Christmas. He didn't want to think of Hitler, or the Japanese, or the darkness the world was plunging into. "It will bring a baby," he said, deliberately misunderstanding her. "*Our* baby!"

Her seriousness lifted as he had intended it should. She

hugged his arm. "The nurse at the clinic says that it should start to move within the next few weeks. I wonder what it will feel like?"

"Uncomfortable, I should imagine," he said with a grin.

They were passing a shop window. Backed against a neutral screen of shot-gray silk stood an exquisite bronze head.

Raefe turned and glimpsed it. He stopped. "Our window shopping is over," he said, drawing her near to the window. "Look."

She looked and saw the name, edged in gold: Wolfgang Amadeus Mozart.

"Oh," she said, letting her breath out slowly. "It's beautiful, Raefe."

"And perfect for Roman. Come on. Our shopping expedition is over."

"It's wonderful!" Roman Rakowski said, his eyes shining as he carefully lifted the bronze from its tissued wrappings. They were in the empty auditorium of Perth's concert hall. Elizabeth and Raefe had sat, spellbound, as Roman took the great orchestra through its rehearsal for the evening's performance. Now the three of them were alone, with Elizabeth excruciatingly aware of the Steinway grand standing off-center on the platform above them. Roman's present to them was a small painting of the boy David, his sling in his hand, his eyes fearless, as he faced Goliath and the Philistines.

"I thought it apt," Roman said, his deep voice filling the empty hall. "A small force facing a larger one. It reminded me of your situation in Hong Kong."

"It's lovely," Elizabeth said truthfully. The colors glowed with vibrancy and there was something so pure, so brave about the boy's stance that her throat tightened.

Roman Rakowski was not at all what she had expected. He was a big bear of a man with a shock of unruly dark blond hair, and an engaging habit of running his fingers through it whenever he explained a point to the musicians. He was ridiculously young for a conductor of such stature, but she could see why he had achieved such eminence. There was a presence, a vigor, an authority about him. Enthusiasm emanated from him in waves.

"What do you think, my friend?" he had demanded,

bounding down from the rostrum after the musicians had been dismissed. He hugged Raefe as if he were a long-lost brother. "The sound has changed, eh?" He had turned toward Elizabeth, his smile wide, his eyes welcoming. "The sound of the orchestra now comes from the string section. Did you hear it? We are softer in the brass section, not so dominating as other orchestras, and in the strings we do not have this very spiccato off-the-string way of playing. I think, especially for classical music, it is wrong. This is better, don't you agree?"

He put his arms around them both, leading them to the far right of the platform where he had a flask of coffee tucked away.

"It's not much to greet you with," he said, shrugging his huge shoulders apologetically. "But the champagne will have to wait until after tonight's performance."

There was a permanent undertone of suppressed laughter in his deep bass voice and Elizabeth felt herself instantly drawn to him, liking him unreservedly.

When they had drunk the coffee he had looked down at her, lines crinkling around his eyes as he said, "The concert platform is yours, Elizabeth. Make yourself comfortable. Play whatever you want."

A moment of pure, undiluted terror coursed through her, then, as he touched her arm encouragingly, she remembered who she was, and what she was, and she stepped up onto the concert platform with the confident knowledge that it was where she belonged.

The first, flawless notes of Grieg's Piano Concerto filled the hall, and Raefe let out a sigh of relief. She hadn't been overcome by nerves. She was playing to the best of her ability. God damn it! She was playing like an angel!

Afterward, as they sat in a tiny Polish restaurant that served the icy borscht soup that Roman loved, Raefe asked him, "Where do you go next?"

Roman broke a roll of rye bread in half. "Palestine," he said with deep satisfaction, "as guest conductor."

Raefe whistled. "That must mean a lot to you," he said, pouring more wine into Elizabeth's and Roman's half-empty glasses.

"It does." Roman's voice was suddenly somber, and all three of them fell silent, thinking of the musicians who formed Palestine's national orchestra. Musicians who had fled the horror of Hitler's Germany.

When Roman spoke again it was to say tersely, "Did you know that the British are restricting the entry of refugees into Palestine?"

Raefe nodded and Elizabeth said uncertainly, "I'm sorry, I don't quite understand . . ."

"There are hundreds of thousands of Jewish refugees seeking to enter Palestine," Raefe said to her quietly, "and because Palestine is a British-mandated area, the British have control of the numbers being accepted."

Elizabeth's face was pale. "What happens to the refugees that Britain refuses entry to? Where do they go?"

"They are shipped back to whatever country they fled from," Roman said, his gray eyes bright with fury. "And the persecution they tried to flee continues. They will be herded into ghettoes, sent to concentration camps."

Raefe took Elizabeth's hand. "It isn't only the British who are being deaf and blind," he said gently, sensing her shame. "The Americans are being just as bad."

Roman ran his fingers through his hair. "Why the hell can't they realize the gravity of the situation?" he asked despairingly. "Why can't they forget about numbers and quotas? The bureaucracy of it all is beyond belief!"

"Bureaucracy always is," Raefe said tightly, and his rage and frustration weren't directed only at the faceless governments who were closing the doors against those needing sanctuary. They were directed at the bureaucrats of Fort Canning as well, at the high-ranking military personnel still obstinately adamant that there would be no war in the East.

That evening Elizabeth and Raefe sat in the concert hall in the seats Roman had reserved for them. The atmosphere was electric. Many of the music-lovers in the audience had never been to a Rakowski concert before, but they knew of his reputation and were waiting in tense anticipation to see if it was justified.

"I can't believe he is as brilliant as the critics say he is," a cynical male voice said to his companion in the row behind them. "He's too young."

There was a suppressed feminine giggle. "You are silly, darling," the woman said indulgently. "A conductor doesn't have to have white hair and be ages old in order to be great. Look at Leopold Stokowski and Arthur Rubinstein. They're only in their late forties and they've both been conducting for over twenty years!"

There was a noncommittal grunt and then, as the orchestra members filed in and took their places to enthusiastic applause, he said dryly, "I wonder why talent on the podium is so peculiarly Polish? Rubinstein and Stokowski are both Poles, and so is Rakowski."

"Sssh, darling," she said as the auditorium fell silent, awaiting Roman's entrance. "And Stokowski may have a Polish name but he's English by birth."

"Good Lord, is he really? I thought—"

What he thought was drowned by a storm of applause as Roman strode out onto the concert platform.

Elizabeth felt the familiar surge of almost unbearable excitement that she always experienced in the few moments before the baton was raised. Only this time it was different, even more heart-stopping. This time the superbly elegant figure in white tie and tails was not a stranger. It was Roman. Raefe's friend, and now her friend.

She withdrew her hand from Raefe's, clapping wildly as Roman took his place on the podium and turned to the audience, acknowledging their applause. His unruly dark gold hair had been brushed into submission and gleamed sleekly. His exquisitely cut evening jacket emphasized his powerful physique. As he bowed and the applause intensified, Elizabeth felt a sense of shock run through her. It was obvious, even before he raised his baton, why he aroused such fevered enthusiasm in his audiences. There was a virility about him, a personal magnetism that was overwhelming.

"I'll say one thing for him," the cynical voice behind them said as the applause finally died down and Roman turned to face the orchestra. "For sheer nerve, Poles take some beating!"

Elizabeth slipped her hand once more into Raefe's, squeezing it tight. The concert hall fell silent. There was a long, pregnant moment of waiting, then Roman raised his baton. Elizabeth could hear her heart beating. He was opening with Mahler's Fourth. It was one of her favorite symphonies and one she had heard conducted magnificently by Wilhelm Furtwängler at the Albert Hall in

London. That the performance she was about to hear could even begin to compare with Furtwängler's seemed an impossibility.

In the utter silence Roman brought his baton down, and almost from the first instant she knew that she had no need to worry. Roman was in complete and utter command of the orchestra, his rhythm flawless. The music flowed and surged, sank and rose again with glorious unforced urgency.

She sighed rapturously, succumbing to Mahler's sensuous richness and lush lyricism. Roman was a bold conductor, his use of rubato so adventurous he nearly took her breath away. At times he would pause for an instant of delicious expectation before launching into a heart-easing melody; at others he would press forward within a phrase toward its climax. Whatever he did he did with utter confidence, revealing a deep, almost mystical understanding of the score. "Oh, wonderful! Wonderful!" she breathed when the last exquisite notes had died away and the auditorium erupted in applause.

"Do you need any more convincing, darling?" the woman behind shouted to her companion.

"No," he said, clapping vigorously. "The man is a born conductor! Truly magnificent! I've never heard Mahler performed better!"

The applause died down, only to break out again when the young man who was to play the solo in Tchaikovsky's Violin Concerto in D walked onto the platform.

"It can't be as good as the Mahler," the man behind them whispered. "It would be an impossibility."

It was as good as the Mahler. Roman's conducting was big and bold and soaring. He possessed a charisma that not only excited the audience, but magnetized the orchestra as well. They played like angels for him. As the last, unbearably beautiful notes died away, Elizabeth could feel tears pricking the backs of her eyes, then she was on her feet with the rest of the audience, shouting out *"Bravo! Bravo!"* and clapping until her hands hurt.

"I told you he was incredible!" Raefe shouted to her as Roman strode from the concert platform and the applause rose frenetically, demanding his return.

"I know. But I'd never imagined he would be quite so *demonic!*"

Raefe laughed and the applause reached fever pitch.
Once again Roman strode across the concert platform to
the base of the podium, sharing the applause generously
with the orchestra. Perspiration gleamed on his forehead,
and his dark blond hair was no longer smooth and sleek
but gloriously unruly.

"*Bravo! Bravo!*" the shouts continued, the orchestra
clapping as unstintingly as the audience.

As he took his fifth and final bow Roman looked
laughingly down to where Elizabeth and Raefe were
cheering, his eyes shining with elation and satisfaction.

"Do you always achieve such an effect when you
conduct Mahler?" Raefe asked later as they sat at a candlelit
table in the same little Polish restaurant.

Roman grinned. His hair was still damp with perspiration, his eyes as brilliant as live coals. "What effect is that,
my friend?" he asked, attacking mushroom-stuffed beefsteak rolls with relish.

"For the entire audience, it was as if they had died and
gone to heaven!"

Roman laughed. "Was that how it felt? Then that is
good. That is how Mahler *should* make you feel."

Elizabeth and Raefe sat opposite him, their plates empty.
They had eaten before the concert and were not hungry,
but Roman signaled for the waiter and asked for a fruit
compote to follow the beefsteak. "I'm not usually a big
eater," he said apologetically to Elizabeth, "but after a
performance it takes hours for my nervous energy to
subside and while it is doing so, I eat like a horse!"

She smiled at him and at that moment, as their eyes met,
she knew they were truly friends, that they would have
been friends even without Raefe's influence. She knew
exactly how Roman felt after such a performance, and he
knew that she knew. She sipped the Polish wine that
Roman had insisted they drink, wondering if she could
ever acquire a taste for it, and asked, "Is Mahler very
difficult to interpret?"

The plate of mushrooms and beefsteak was cleared away
and replaced with the compote. Roman ate a spoonful
appreciatively, then said, "No, for me he is one of the
easiest of composers."

Elizabeth rested her arms on the table, leaning forward

slightly. Her hair fell softly to her shoulders. "Why is that?" she asked with professional interest.

Raefe grinned. The rapport between Roman and Elizabeth delighted him. He loved watching Elizabeth's face, laughing and animated, as she and Roman enthusiastically discussed musical personalities and orchestras, and the vital question of whether there should be breaks after the fermatas in Beethoven's Fifth. That he was able to take very little part in these discussions bothered him not in the least. Music was the world in which Elizabeth belonged and one in which he was determined she should take her place. The day would come when Roman, with his connections and his influence, would be a great help to her.

"Mahler was a conductor himself," Roman was saying exuberantly, "and it shows in his scores. He puts in so many marks and verbal instructions that it is impossible to go wrong. For instance, in the second symphony—"

Raefe gave a mock groan. "It's nearly three in the morning, Roman. Have some pity, please."

Roman chuckled. "You are a Philistine, my friend," he said indulgently. "But, for your sake, no more Mahler for the moment. Instead, let us drink *Bruderschaft* together."

"*Bruderschaft*?" Elizabeth asked, hoping fervently it wasn't another Polish wine.

"It is a ceremony we have in Poland. A declaration of lifelong brotherhood. You fill your glasses so . . ." He generously replenished their half-full wineglasses. "And then, still holding your glasses, you link your elbows around each other, so . . ." He linked his elbow with Raefe so that their arms were intertwined. "And then we drink from our own glass at the same time. It is a pledge. A promise that our friendship is forever."

Entranced, Elizabeth watched as, their eyes holding each other's fast, the two men drank. Despite the difference in their coloring, there was something uncannily similar about them, as if they really were brothers. They were both tall and broad-shouldered, and though Roman was more heavily built than Raefe, he possessed Raefe's pantherlike grace, moving with the easy strength and agility of a rigorously trained athlete. They shared other qualities too. With both of them there was a sense of power under restraint, an impression of controlled vigor and sexuality,

and a self-confidence so total it was almost insolent. She
suppressed a smile, wondering how their prestigious
American university had survived them.

"And now *we* will drink *Bruderschaft* together," Roman
was saying to her.

Feeling slightly drunk she lifted her glass and linked her
elbow around his. As she drank, she felt overcome by her
good fortune. She had Raefe, whom she loved with all her
heart; she had all her friends in Hong Kong; and now she
had Roman's friendship too. Looking into his brilliant gray
eyes, she knew it was a friendship that would last
throughout her life.

Four days later, when the time came for the three of them
to part, their regret was almost unbearable. Roman was
returning with the orchestra to London, and then flying
out immediately to Tel Aviv. Elizabeth and Raefe were
returning to Hong Kong. None of them knew when they
would meet again.

"The next time we share a concert platform," Roman
said to her, hugging her so tightly she thought her ribs
were going to crack, "it will not just be at a rehearsal, it will
be before an audience." He turned to Raefe, his eyes
suspiciously bright. "Take care, my friend. Good-bye."

It was early dawn when they arrived back in Hong Kong.
Their airplane squealed to a halt on the tarmac of Kai Tak
Airport, and through the windows she could see the sun
rising golden over the Peak.

"We'll soon be home," Raefe said to her, a curious gleam
in his eyes as they stepped down onto the tarmac. She was
carrying the painting that Roman had given them, holding
it close to her chest. It had stood on the dressing table of
their hotel room all the time they had been in Perth. Now
she would have to part with it. It had been given to them
both, but it belonged in Raefe's flat, not in her impersonal
hotel room.

"You had better take this now," she said regretfully,
handing it to him as they walked to his car.

He opened the door for her, making no move to take the
painting. "Oh, I don't think so," he said airily.

She stared at him. "But surely you want to hang it in
your apartment?"

"Of course," he said after he had slid behind the wheel. "Most definitely."

The engine snarled into life and as they drew away from the airport she said suspiciously, "You're playing games with me, aren't you? What is it that is so amusing you?"

He flashed her a smile. "*You* amuse me, sweet Lizzie." He pulled out into Argyle Street. "You don't really think, after the week he have spent together, that I'm going to docilely return you to the Pen, do you?"

"The majority of my clothes are still there," she said without much vehemence.

His smile deepened. "No, they're not, dear love. They were removed the day we flew to Perth. They are now cosily nestling against my clothes in the extraordinarily large wardrobe that had to be bought to accommodate them. You are a very *greedy* girl where clothes are concerned. I've never seen so much stuff. Armfuls and armfuls of—"

"Your bedroom at the apartment has fitted wardrobes," she interrupted. "A large wardrobe would look preposterous in it. I don't believe a word you're saying!"

He turned left onto Waterloo Road. "You're quite right. A wardrobe *would* look preposterous in the apartment. However, it does not do so in our new bedroom."

She gurgled with laughter, still holding the painting against her chest. "And where is that?" she asked. She had no intention of arguing with him. She had known ever since Christmas that the period of adjustment was at an end. She no more wanted to return to the Pen than he wanted her to.

"Sit still, keep quiet, and you'll soon find out," he said, shooting down Nathan Road toward the ferry.

Once on Hong Kong island, he drove east through the still quiet streets of Victoria and the gaudier streets of Wanchai. "Where on eart are we going?" she asked, her arm through his, her head resting on his shoulder.

"Patience," he said in loving chastisement, taking the road out toward Sai Wan Ho.

He drove on past Lei Yue Mun Bay and Chaiwan and then, as the morning sun bathed Mount Collinson and Pottinger Peak in liquid light, he took a small road up into the foothills. The track wound around, and the car bumped and swayed over the ruts that marked the course of winter floods of mountain rain. They churned their way up around a steep bend and ground to a halt, the dust of their wake hanging thickly in the air behind them.

"Oh," she breathed rapturously. "Oh, Raefe, it's beautiful."

The house was small and secluded, nestling against a backdrop of fern and mountain pine. Away in front of it the hills rolled down to the bright blue glitter of the sea.

"I warn you now, it isn't furnished," he said as they stepped out of the car and began to walk toward the house. "Apart from two or three essential items, that is."

It was unlike any other house she had seen on the island. There were no pillars, no porticos. It bore no resemblance at all to the luxury houses of the Peak. It was built of stone, with an outside staircase leading to the floors above. Every step was whitened at the edge, and on each were terracotta pots and tubs of flowers: deep drowned purple pansies, scarlet geraniums, milk-white anemones with lamp-black centers, a tangle of honeysuckle tumbling riotously. The doors and shutters had been painted cornflower blue and were thrown open welcomingly.

"We can have something much grander if you like," he said, seized by sudden doubt about its suitability as they stepped over the threshold.

She shook her head vehemently. "Oh, no, Raefe. This is what I want. This is perfect."

The sun streamed in through the windows onto white-washed walls and gleaming pine floors. She walked through the rooms, the scent of the flowers drifting in fragrantly through the open windows. The two or three essential items of furniture were a large brass bed, the linen snowy white and lavishly trimmed with lace, an enormous wardrobe holding all their clothes, and a Steinway concert grand. "I thought you would want to choose the rest of the furniture yourself," he said, standing close behind her, his arms around her waist. "I want your personality in every room, Lizzie."

She turned in the circle of his arms, touching his face tenderly and with absolute love. "We can start furnishing it now," she said softly. "This very minute." She gently freed herself from his embrace and walked out to the car, returning with Roman's painting of the boy David.

They hung it in the sun-filled room that looked out over the sea. Raefe held her close. "And we can start living in it now," he said huskily, lifting her up in his arms, then carrying her to the bedroom and the snowy-white bed.

Chapter Twenty-one
❧

THE master bedroom of Tom Nicholson's house was in deep shade, the blinds drawn against the fierce brightness of the afternoon sun. A slight smile touched Julienne's lips as she lay on her back, her hands moving caressingly over Tom's shoulders and up into the dark thickness of his hair. Tom had never been a very imaginative lover. He, unlike Derry, would never have considered making love in a rocking sailing boat off Cape d'Aguilar. But his very prosaicness made a change, and her appetite for change was inexhaustible.

"That is good, *n'est-ce pas?*" she whispered, her hips moving with increasing speed as she sensed he was coming to a conclusion.

She closed her eyes, the sexual images she conjured up amply compensating for Tom's deficiencies. His mouth ground deeply on hers, his hands tightened convulsively on her breasts, and as he groaned in the agony of climax, she knew without offense that he wasn't making love to her at all. It was Lamoon who was filling his head. Lamoon he was mentally expending his passion on. She was merely giving him sexual relief, easing his pain. Her arms cradled him close, the knowledge giving her a satisfaction that was far deeper than the transient satisfaction of successful copulation.

When at last he rolled away from her, lying exhausted on his back, she raised herself up on one elbow and looked down at him compassionately. "Do you feel better now?" she asked, her fingers playing slowly across his chest.

He grinned. "You sound like a nurse."

She giggled. "I *feel* like a nurse. A very *personal* nurse."

His grin faded and his eyes darkened with affection. "You're worth your weight in gold," he said huskily, pulling her down beside him, grateful for her sexual generosity and her blessedly uncomplicated nature.

She nestled against him, her vibrant red hair tousled, her breath soft against his flesh. "I am having lunch with Elizabeth tomorrow," she said as he reached over to the bedside table for cigarettes and lighter. "Having a baby suits her. She looks more beautiful than ever."

Tom blew a wreath of cigarette smoke into the air. "I still can't believe she's left Adam." A smile tugged at one corner of his mouth. "I had ideas myself once where Elizabeth was concerned."

"*Quand?*" Julienne demanded, sitting upright, her eyes widening with interest. "When? Tell me!"

"It was when I first met her, aboard the *Orient Princess*. I thought maybe an affair with her would help me to say good-bye to Lamoon." He was silent for a minute or so. He never talked about Lamoon. The pain was too deep, too raw. Julienne waited and at last, when he had regained control of his voice, he said, "I never approached her, of course. She seemed to be so happy with Adam, and I couldn't imagine her being unfaithful to him in a million years."

Julienne gurgled with laughter, swinging her legs to the floor and reaching for her scattered clothes. "That is where you made your first mistake, *chéri*. You should never assume. Especially where women are concerned!"

The next day, at the Floating Palace Restaurant in Causeway Bay, she said to Elizabeth, "Lamoon Sheng might just as well have vanished off the face of the earth. No one knows where she is, or what has happened to her. Tom won't speak of it. If he did, I think he would simply go to pieces."

Elizabeth put down her menu, unable to decide whether to have lobster or oysters or fresh crab. Raefe had done everything he could to discover Lamoon's whereabouts, but even he had failed. The Chinese grapevine was ominously silent. It was almost as if Lamoon had never existed.

"Raefe thinks she was bundled out of Hong Kong and married to a man of her father's choosing, while he and Tom were still in the hospital," she said, her voice vibrant with the rage she still felt. "It's unbelievable that in this day and age a woman of twenty-one can still be treated as if she's nothing but chattel!"

Julienne lifted her shoulders in mutual disbelief. "I agree with you, *chérie*. It is medieval. Thank your lucky stars that you are a European."

A waiter weaved his way between the crowded tables toward them. The restaurant had been decorated to resemble a Mississippi steamboat and he looked curiously out of place with his Oriental face and high-collared, white-buttoned jacket.

"I'll have oysters, please," Elizabeth said, her choice dictated by the knowledge that the lobster and crab were at present swimming below the restaurant in large cages.

"I will have the lobster," Julienne said, suffering from no such qualms. "And a bottle of Chablis, please."

She looked around at the neighboring tables, but there was no one she recognized. She felt unbelievably tired. Keeping Ronnie and Derry happy, as well as Tom, was proving to be quite a feat, even for her.

"You're looking unusually pensive," Elizabeth said, resting her hand on her tummy as the baby gave a definite kick. "Is anything worrying you?"

"No," Julienne said with a little sigh. "I was just thinking that maybe it is time I settled down a little. I shall be twenty-seven in June. Perhaps I should be thinking of having a baby, like you."

"Have you told Ronnie about this burgeoning maternal instinct?" Elizabeth asked, amused.

Julienne's pansy-dark eyes finished their reconnoiter of the restaurant. She had seen no one of interest. "I do not think Ronnie would mind," she said, a note of surprise in her voice. "I think he might even be quite pleased."

The waiter was at their side again, piling the table with appetizers of spring rolls and spare ribs and dumplings. Elizabeth ignored them. She was six months pregnant now and the baby was playing havoc with her appetite. Some days she was ravenously hungry; others she had to force herself to eat even the lightest of meals.

"Doesn't it give you a guilty conscience, Julienne?" she asked musingly as Julienne lifted a dumpling from its basket with her chopsticks.

"Comment?" Julienne asked, startled, wondering if Elizabeth was referring to Derry or to Tom.

"All this food," Elizabeth said, indicating the laden table. "I don't know what things are like in France, but ever since the beginning of January, bacon and butter and sugar have been rationed in Britain, and now the government has announced that every Friday will be a meatless day, and that no beef or veal or mutton will be sold on Mondays or Tuesdays."

"It is those pigs of U-boats in the Atlantic," Julienne said graphically. "Ronnie says that once the navy has gotten rid of them and supplies are able to reach Britain from America, without hindrance, then there will be no further restrictions on how much food people can buy."

"I'm sure Ronnie is right," Elizabeth said without much conviction. "But it's March now. How much longer can it go on?"

It went on all through April. On the ninth, two German divisions invaded Denmark and Copenhagen was taken within twelve hours. On the same day German troops landed near Oslo and the fierce and bloody battle for Norway began.

"At least we're fully prepared against an enemy attack in Hong Kong," Adam said at the beginning of May. He and Elizabeth were seated at a corner table in the Peninsula's flower-filled restaurant. Their weekly meetings had continued, but the reconciliation that Adam had hoped for was as far away as ever. Elizabeth was happy. She was in love with Raefe. And with great reluctance, prompted by the existence of the child she was carrying, Adam had agreed to institute divorce proceedings against her on the grounds of her desertion and adultery.

He was trying hard not to think that about now. For the next hour he had her entirely to himself. It was what he had looked forward to and lived for all through the week. With dogged determination he refused to allow thoughts of their pending divorce to blight his fleeting happiness.

"The Hong Kong Volunteer Defense Corps will soon be a force to be reckoned with," he said with pride. "We're carrying out training now on a regular basis. Leigh Stafford has joined, and even Denholm Gresby is giving us his support."

The formation of the Volunteer Defense Corps was Adam's major interest. It ensured that when the time came, men like himself would be able to fight in an officially recognized unit. "We have all types of men offering their services," he continued enthusiastically. "Businessmen and bankers, customs officers and clerks. My God, but we'll give the Japanese a run for their money when the time comes!"

Elizabeth smiled. No matter what his age, there was something eternally boyish about Adam.

"A lot of people still think that the volunteers are unnecessary and that there will be no call for them," she said. She had been toying with her sweet and sour pork, and now finally pushed the plate away.

She didn't feel very well. The baby was lying uncomfortably and she had been awake through most of the previous night with a severe attack of heartburn.

"I hope you're not one of them," Adam said, shocked.

She managed a smile. "No, of course not. I've been aware that the Japanese threat is real for a long time now."

"Then who is it who thinks the volunteers are unnecessary?" Adam persisted.

"Late-night drinkers at the Jockey Club," she said vaguely, knowing that if she gave any names he would immediately single the offenders out the next time he met them, demanding that they explain themselves.

"Then they're misinformed idiots," he said contemptuously.

Elizabeth's smile deepened. One gentleman in the Jockey Club bar who had loudly stated that the volunteers were full of hot air and there wasn't the remotest possibility of an attack by the Japanese was a high-ranking executive of the Hong Kong and Shanghai Bank. She shifted uncomfortably on her chair, wishing the baby would rearrange itself.

"Are you all right, Beth?" Adam asked quickly, immediately concerned for her.

"I'm fine," she said reassuringly. "It's just that I'm so big now, it's difficult to be comfortable."

"How much longer have you to go?" To her bemusement he had never found any difficulty in talking about the baby. It was Raefe whom he would never mention.

"Six weeks or thereabouts."

An all-too-rare smile touched his mouth. "I'm surprised that you can still sit at your piano."

"It isn't easy!" she said with feeling. "I must be the only

pupil Li Pi has ever had who has to have her back rubbed at half-hourly intervals!"

They laughed and for a few brief seconds it was almost possible for Adam to believe that she had never left him. That they were sitting as they used to at Four Seasons, or on the terrace of their home at the Peak, sharing a drink and chatting about each other's day. His laughter died. They weren't in their own home. They were in an impersonal hotel restaurant and the baby they were referring to was not his. He asked tersely, "Are you happy, Beth? Truly happy?"

The old pain coursed through her. She was, but the agony of telling him so almost crippled her.

He had stretched his hand out toward her across the table and she took it. "Yes, I'm happy, Adam," she said quietly, her throat tight. "Please don't keep asking me. My answer hurts you so much and I can't bear it."

"Then come home!" he said fiercely, his fingers tightening on hers. "It isn't too late, Beth! The baby can have my name. We'll leave Hong Kong. We can go to America or to Canada. No one there will ever know. We can be a family again."

She shook her head, tears of futility stinging the backs of her eyes. "No, Adam. I've made my decision and it has been the right decision. For me."

His shoulders slumped and he looked suddenly ill and tired. "Then that's it," he said defeatedly. "I won't ask you again, Beth. But the offer will always be there. Even after the baby is born. Even after the divorce."

She squeezed his hand, unable to speak. The musical trio in the far corner of the room began to play "Night and Day" and she stood. "I must go," she said thickly. Raefe was leaving that afternoon for a flight to Singapore and a meeting with Colonel Sandor, and she wanted to drive him to the airport. "Good-bye, Adam. Take care of yourself."

"'Bye, Beth." He rose heavily to his feet. "Take care of yourself, sweetheart."

She nodded, aware that Miriam Gresby was lunching with a friend a half dozen tables away, and that she was staring at them with outraged curiosity. Elizabeth walked quickly from the room, her back was straight, her head high, graceful despite her advanced pregnancy.

Miriam Gresby had seen to it that no one in Hong Kong

had been left uninformed of Elizabeth's desertion of her husband. The most surprising people no longer even spoke to her. And the most surprising people had continued to be unfailingly kind and courteous. Major General Grasett's wife, for example. And Lady Northcote, wife of Sir Geoffrey Northcote, the Colony's governor.

She slid with difficulty behind the wheel of the car. Raefe had tried to persuade her to allow a chauffeur to drive her, but she enjoyed the mechanics of driving and she wanted as few household staff as possible intruding on their privacy. Their only resident servants were Mei Lin, who had timidly asked Adam if she could follow Elizabeth to her new residence, and Raefe's long-term houseboy.

The vehicular ferry was nearly empty, and she stepped out of the car and leaned her arms on the rail as the ferry made the short crossing between Kowloon and the island. She still didn't feel very well. Her stomach muscles were uncomfortably tight and there was a pain low in her back that she couldn't ease.

They docked in Victoria and she drove off the ferry, wondering if perhaps Raefe was right, and it wouldn't be more sensible to have a chauffeur, at least for the next five or six weeks. The temperature was in the eighties and the heat, unalloyed by any breeze, glared down from the sky as from a burning glass. "Next time I venture into pregnancy," she said to herself as she turned toward Mount Collinson, "I'll make sure that the last few months are in the winter!"

The sea was glorious as she skirted the coast, rippling out through jade green to aquamarine to deepest indigo. She turned right, twisting up into the flank of the mountain, wishing that Raefe wasn't leaving for Singapore. He would only be away for three or four days, five at the most, but she knew how intensely she would miss him. The Chrysler's tires rolled over a bed of dried verbena as she turned the last corner before the house.

She slowed to a halt, savoring the sight of her home. Blue convolvulus looped down the side of one wall in long, belled strands. Scarlet geraniums flamed against the blue paint, carnations of every shade, from deep flame to mother-of-pearl, crowded the white-edged steps. She slid the car forward again, happiness striking through her like an arrow. This was where she belonged. This was where her heart lay.

Raefe was in the bedroom, putting the last of his things into a small overnight case. "I was beginning to think you were planning sabotage," he said with a grin. "Delaying coming back until it was too late for me to catch my flight."

"It would have been a very sensible idea," she said, stepping into the circle of his arms and laying her head against his chest. "I wish I had thought of it."

His arms tightened around her. "It won't be long," he murmured tenderly against her hair. "Just a few days."

She nodded and he hooked a finger under her chin, raising her face to his. "I shall miss you," he said, and kissed her lingeringly.

The drive back across the island to Kowloon and Kai Tak Airport was one she could have done without, but it never occurred to her to tell him she was not feeling very well. She wanted to be with him right until the last possible moment. And that meant driving with him to the airport, and then driving herself home again.

It was six o'clock by the time she wearily took the coast road eastward for the second time. She was determined to go to bed early when she arrived home. She would ask Mei Lin to make her a cup of hot chocolate and she would have a long, leisurely bath, then she would go to bed and read. A trail of lilacs lay unbruised across the track. She steered the car around them, leaving them as perfect as before, and as she did so, something damp and warm seeped between her legs and her abdomen was seized by a cramping pain, as if it were in a vice.

She sucked in her breath sharply, her hands clenching the wheel. The car wavered slightly, then straightened. The pain eased and began to die. She let out a grateful sigh of relief, the alarm bells in her brain awakened but not yet ringing. By the time she reached the house they were ringing so loudly that she was deafened by them.

The doctor who had been attending her at the antenatal clinic had told her exactly what to expect. And it wasn't what she was now experiencing. He had told her the pains would start gradually and intermittently, that she would have plenty of time to arrange to be driven into Victoria to the maternity hospital.

She stumbled into the house, gasping for breath as

another strong, convulsive pain seized her. "Mei Lin," she
called, an edge of panic in her voice. *"Mei Lin!"*

"Yes, missy," Mei Lin answered, stepping forward to
meet her, a smile of welcome on her face. It vanished in an
instant as Elizabeth leaned against the wall for support,
beads of perspiration on her forehead, her face chalk-
white. *"Missy! What the matter? What happened?"*

"The baby is coming," Elizabeth gasped. "Help me to
bed, Mei Lin. Telephone the doctor! Telephone Mrs.
Nicholson!"

"Yes, missy! At once, missy!" Mei Lin panted as she
helped Elizabeth into the bedroom.

Elizabeth fell onto the bed. The pains were getting
harder, *and they were six weeks too early.* They began to merge
into one another so that there was no respite, no abatement
in which she could gather together her strength and her
stamina. Six weeks too early! The words beat like a tattoo in
her brain. Something had gone terribly, dreadfully wrong.
She should be in the hospital. Raefe should be at her side.
She should be welcoming decently spaced out contractions, feeling in control, not thrashing in agony attended
only by a terrified Mei Lin.

By the time the doctor came she was barely conscious.
"It's all right, Mrs. Harland," he said reassuringly, his voice
reaching her from what seemed like a vast distance. "An
ambulance is on its way. Now do exactly as I tell you."

She clung to consciousness and to the sound of his voice.
She was dimly aware of towels being spread on the bed, of
her underclothing being removed.

"The baby is breech," she could hear him say tautly. "I'm
going to have to try to turn it around . . ."

He tried once, twice, three times. Someone was screaming long and low. Mei Lin placed a wet cloth against her
brow and she realized with horror that the person screaming was herself.

"Have . . . you . . . done . . . it . . . yet?" she
croaked, her voice barely audible.

He shook his head, knowing it was too late to transfer
her by ambulance to the hospital, knowing that unless he
succeeded in turning the baby soon, he would lose both
child and mother.

"Now! Again!" he said fiercely. "When the pain is at its
height!"

Some dim, far removed part of her brain wanted to laugh. When the pain was at its height! It had never been anything else. It ripped through her, stunning her with its savagery. She sucked in her breath, groaning in agony as once again his hands reached deep inside her. This time he gave an exclamation of relief.

"That's done it! I'm sure of it! Now summon up all your strength, Mrs. Harland. Push!"

She could no longer do anything of her own volition. She could only cling desperately to the last shreds of her strength, praying for it to be over. Praying for the baby to be born. Praying for it to be all right.

"That's it! Wonderful! Once again!"

She was drenched in sweat, barely able to hear him, no longer able to see. She was being split apart, rent in two. She heard herself cry out, a long, primeval ululation of victory as her exhausted body finally succeeded in expelling the child from her womb. She wanted to open her eyes, to see, to speak, but she was falling into a vortex of black, rushing winds.

"My baby," she whispered. "My baby . . ." As the winds closed over her head, submerging her, she was aware that something was wrong. Something was not as it should be. She tried to think what it was and at last, as the darkness became total, it came to her. There was no noise in the room around her. No murmur of congratulation. No sound of a baby's cry.

Helena's car bucketed up the rough track toward the house. Mei Lin had sounded panic-stricken on the telephone, and Helena had asked to speak to Elizabeth, in order to ascertain exactly what was happening. Mei Lin had told her that Elizabeth couldn't come to the telephone. She was having the baby.

"You mean her contractions have started?" Helena had asked, puzzled.

"No!" Mei Lin had sobbed. "Baby come now, Missy Nicholson! This minute!"

She rounded the last corner of the track and saw with relief that the doctor's car was already parked outside the house. In Helena's experience first babies always took their time in coming. She had been in desultory labor for eighteen hours with Jennifer. She stepped out of her car and as she did, a long, agonized scream froze her to the spot. "My God!" she breathed, her eyes rounding in horror, then she broke into a run.

"Something verry wrong, Missy Nicholson!" Mei Lin gasped as she entered the house. "Baby coming fast and not the right way round!"

The bedroom door was closed against them, but beyond it they could hear the doctor saying urgently, "That's it! Wonderful! Once again!" And then there was silence.

The ambulance had rolled to a halt beside Helena's car by the time the doctor walked slowly out of the bedroom. He was a burly man with a thatch of still thick hair and a deeply lined face.

"I'm sorry," he said to Helena as he stepped into the corridor. "The baby is dead."

Helena pressed a fist to her mouth. "Oh, no!" she whispered, sinking down onto a chair. "Oh, no!"

"I'm sorry," he said again bleakly. "It was breech and it was six weeks premature." He rolled his shirt sleeves down, fastening his cuffs. "I've given Mrs. Harland a sedative and I don't think she will regain consciousness until she reaches the hospital. She'll have to stay in for several days."

"Can I travel with her?" Helena asked.

The doctor nodded, then turned away from her to the ambulance attendant, giving them low, terse instructions. Half an hour later, the small, doll-like body of the baby, heavily swathed in white linen, was carried out of the house by an ambulance attendant, and into the ambulance. Elizabeth was transferred next, her eyes closed, her hair tangled and damp, her skin bloodless.

Helena turned to Mei Lin. "Please telephone Mr. Harland for me," she said tonelessly. "Tell him I'm accompanying Mrs. Harland to the hospital. And tell him that the baby is dead, Mei Lin."

Mei Lin nodded. She had already left a message at Raffles Hotel in Singapore for Mr. Elliot to telephone home immediately.

"What shall I tell Mr. Elliot, missy?" she asked anxiously.

Helena pushed a dark fall of hair away from her face. Singapore was sixteen hundred miles away. It would be days before he returned. He couldn't be left for all that time thinking he had become a father. "Tell him the truth," she said bleakly. "Tell him that Mrs. Harland is in the maternity hospital in Victoria and that the baby is dead."

"Yes, missy," Mei Lin said unhappily, then, as Helena followed Elizabeth's stretcher to the door, she asked, "Missy Harland will not die, will she, Missy Nicholson?"

"No," Helena said thankfully. "Tell Mr. Elliot that she will be all right, but that she will have to stay in the hospital for several days."

Mei Lin nodded. Helena stepped out into the waning sunshine and crossed the flower-filled terrace to the waiting ambulance. It was the baby that had prompted Elizabeth to leave Adam and go and live with Raefe. Now the baby was dead. As the ambulance attendants closed the doors behind her, she wondered if the baby's death would change anything. If perhaps now Elizabeth would return to Adam.

The ambulance began to jolt over the stony track that led down to the coast road, and in the Moses basket near her, a shock of spiky black hair peeped from the tightly swathed sheeting. Tears stung Helena's eyes. Raefe's child and Elizabeth's child. She didn't even know its sex. She clasped her hands tightly in her lap, hoping fervently that Adam would be at the hospital and waiting for them when they arrived.

Chapter Twenty-two
❧

THERE was an appalling few minutes as they approached the hospital and Elizabeth drowsily recovered consciousness. "My baby . . ." she murmured to Helena. "Where is my baby?"

Helena had squeezed her hand tightly and wished to God that the doctor was with them to answer her, instead of following behind them in his own car.

"The baby died, Elizabeth," she said gently. "I'm so sorry, darling. So very sorry."

Elizabeth gave a long, low cry, memory returning, then she twisted her head sharply away, the tears falling unrestrainedly.

Once at the hospital she was transferred to a private room far away from the maternity ward and the healthy, lusty cries of the newborn. An ambulance attendant had carried the Moses basket into the hospital, but it did not reappear in Elizabeth's room. Helena wondered where it had been taken and if they would ever see its lifeless, dark-haired little occupant again.

"I must ask you to leave now," a nurse said to her. "Mrs. Harland needs medical attention and the doctor is on his way to her."

Reluctantly, Helena let go of Elizabeth's hand. "I have to leave the room, Elizabeth, but I'll only be outside, in the corridor."

Ever since their brief exchange of words in the ambulance, Elizabeth had kept her head averted from Helena. She now turned it slowly. Her face was deathly pale, her eyes bruised black with grief. "I want Raefe," she said simply.

Helena felt her eyes sting with tears. "I'll get him for you," she said thickly. God in heaven, what on earth had possessed him to leave for Singapore at a time like this? Mei Lin had said he could be contactd at Raffles, but that didn't mean he would be resident there for the duration of his trip. If he was in Singapore on business, then he would most likely be visiting his rubber plantations up-country. Which meant that it could be days before he could be contacted, perhaps even a week or longer.

Trying to get a long distance connection to Raffles from the telephone in the hospital foyer would be a near impossible task and she didn't even attempt it. Instead she telephoned Alastair, telling him briefly what had happened and asking him to do his damnedest to get in touch with Raefe. Then, after only a moment's hesitation, she dialed Adam's number.

Adam left for the hospital immediately. He had been pruning roses when Helena telephoned, and the secateurs were still in his cardigan pocket and stray rose clippings clung about his person as he limped hurriedly up the hospital stairs and along the corridor to Elizabeth's room.

"I'm sorry, Mrs. Harland is resting. No visitors are allowed for another twenty-four hours," the staff nurse on duty said primly.

"Rubbish," Adam said, anxiety overcoming his customary good manners. "I'm her husband! I want to see her now. Immediately!"

"Oh, of course. I'm sorry, Mr. Harland," the nurse said, flustered. The ward sister had given her to understand that Mrs. Harland's husband was in Singapore and had still not been contacted. "I'm sorry," she repeated. "I hadn't realized your identity. You may see her for five minutes, but I must ask you not to stay a second longer. Normal visiting hours finished an hour ago. The night staff will be coming on duty in ten minutes. Please come this way."

Adam followed her into a dimly lit room, pity and rage and hope all striving for supremacy. His pity was deep and genuine. He knew how much Beth had longed for a child. He knew what her pregnancy had meant to her. And now it had all come to nothing.

His rage was directed at Elliot. How could the man have left her when she was so near the end of her pregnancy? Helena had said he was in Singapore on business. Adam very much doubted it. He had heard rumors that Alute, the Malay girl Elliot had squired so openly and for so long, had left Hong Kong for Singapore. If she had, Adam could well imagine the purpose of Elliot's visit. And if it wasn't Alute, then it would be another woman. Elliot had never been renowned for faithfulness. Not to his wife; not to his girlfriends. And now, quite obviously, he was being unfaithful to Beth.

A nerve jumped convulsively at the corner of his clenched jaw. Now, at last, Beth would know Elliot for what he was. A no-good roustabout, incapable of deep feelings for her or for anyone else. When she was strong enough to leave the hospital he would take her away, so that she could recuperate. They would go to Australia or New Zealand, or maybe even America. Hope intoxicated him. When Beth had needed Elliot, he had not been at her side. He, Adam, had been at her side. As he always would be.

"Oh, my dear, I'm so sorry," he said huskily as he leaned over her. He kissed her tenderly on her forehead, appalled at how white and exhausted she looked. "I'm so very, very sorry."

Elizabeth closed her eyes for a moment, summoning up what little strength remained to her. It was typical of Adam that, even though she had lost the child that had driven them so irrevocably apart, there was no underlying note of satisfaction in his voice. His sympathy was sincere and deep. His generous, compassionate nature would have been incapable of anything less. Yet she didn't want his commiserations. She wanted Raefe, and Raefe was still hours, perhaps even days away from her.

"Thank you for coming, Adam," she said, forcing a small smile. "It was very sweet of you."

"Sweet of me, be damned," he said huskily, sitting down on the chair beside the bed and taking her hand. "You can't think that I would leave you on your own at a time like this?"

"Helena has been with me," she said tiredly, touched as she always was by his loving concern for her. There were deep shadows beneath her eyes and her voice was so weak, he could barely hear her.

"You need to rest," he said. "You're in no condition to even talk. I'll come back in the morning and we'll discuss where you can go to recuperate. New Zealand, perhaps, or maybe America."

"Yes," she said wearily. "New Zealand would be nice." She closed her eyes. New Zealand and Raefe. Perhaps they could make another baby there. Perhaps, with Raefe, the agonizing hurt would heal.

Adam rose heavily to his feet. She was already asleep. He looked down at her long and tenderly, then he turned and walked slowly from the room. He would be there when she awoke. He had no intention of returning to the Peak, not even for a change of clothes. If there was nowhere he could stay in the hospital, then he would check into one of the nearby hotels. If he was needed, he would be with her within minutes.

Helena was waiting in the hospital corridor. "How is she?" she asked.

"Exhausted," he said, grateful for her presence. "I'm going to ask if I can stay at the hospital tonight. If not, then I'll book into one of the nearby hotels. Either way, I'll be here within minutes if she should need me."

Helena looked at him oddly. "I don't think they will let you sleep here," she said doubtfully. "I don't think they would even let Raefe sleep here."

"My God! I should hope not!" Adam said explosively. "If I had my way the bastard wouldn't even be allowed in to see her!"

Helena took his arm. "Elizabeth isn't the only one who needs a good night's sleep," she said firmly. "You've undergone a long period of stress, Adam. If you won't return home, then at least book into a hotel. Trying to sleep on a couple of chairs in one of the hospital waiting rooms isn't at all a good idea. And it isn't necessary."

"I'm going to take her away," he said as she led him down the corridor toward the stairs. "New Zealand or America. Somewhere where she can forget the last few months and we can start again."

Helena swung her head sharply toward him. "Have you told her that?" she asked incredulously. "Has she agreed?"

He looked at her in surprise. "Why yes, of course. She said New Zealand would be nice."

Helena stared at him helplessly. Despite his graying hair and his now pronounced limp, he still had the deep-chested, chunky build of a useful-looking middleweight, yet there was a naïveté and a vulnerability about him that aroused all her protective instincts. She didn't for one minute believe that the death of her child had altered Elizabeth's feelings for Raefe. Whatever Elizabeth had said to Adam about New Zealand, he had surely misunderstood.

"Don't make any plans, Adam," she said gently. "Not until Elizabeth has seen Raefe. It would be fatal."

Her hand had been resting lightly on his arm and he pulled himself away from her, saying savagely, "For a sensible woman, you can be very obtuse, Helena! She won't want to see Elliot! Why should she? He's let her down in the most awful way that a man *can* let a woman down! Whatever might once have existed between them, it's over now!" He swung away from her, hurrying out of the hospital foyer and into the forecourt, the secateurs still bulging incongruously in his cardigan pocket.

Helena sighed and pushed her hair away from her face. It was no use going after him. Whatever she said, he wouldn't listen. She shoved her hands deep into the

pockets of her skirt and was halfway to the hospital car
park before she remembered that her Morgan was not
there, but miles away, parked beside tubs of geraniums and
carnations and sweet-smelling stocks.

Wearily she altered direction, walking toward the street.
She would have to get a taxi. And even when she arrived
home there would be little comfort awaiting her. Alastair
was on duty and wouldn't be able to see her until the end
of the week. The children would be in bed. She scanned
the street, looking for the familiar light of a taxicab. If
Adam had been sensible, they could have enjoyed a meal
together and a reviving drink. But he hadn't been sensible,
and she was tired and on her own.

"Damn!" she said bad-temperedly to the world at large
as a taxi finally slid to a halt beside her. "Why does a man
who is so nice have to be so pathetically idiotic?" There was
no answer and she climbed dispiritedly into the cab,
unhappily aware that the main cause for her despression
was not the death of Elizabeth's baby, or Alastair's unavoid-
able absence. It was something far more disturbing:
Adam's stubborn belief that he and Elizabeth were on the
point of reconciliation.

The next morning, when Elizabeth awoke, her room was
full of flowers. "Your husband sent them," the nurse who
took her pulse and checked her blood pressure said.
"Aren't they gorgeous?"

They were, but Elizabeth was unclear whether the
sender had been Adam or Raefe. If it had been Raefe, then
it meant that he knew what had happened and was on his
way to her side.

"Is there a card with them?" she asked, pushing herself
slowly into a sitting position.

The nurse beamed and passed it to her. It read simply
"From Adam, with love."

Elizabeth put it down on the sheet. She should have
known that if Helena or Mei Lin had succeeded in
contacting Raefe, he would not have wasted time in
thinking of flowers. He would have slammed the telephone receiver down and left immediately for the airport.
She thought of him hearing the news in a distant,
impersonal hotel bedroom, and her heart twisted in
anguish. "Oh, my sweet love," she whispered. "Hurry
back so that I can comfort you. So that we can comfort each
other . . ."

When the doctor came to see her he stayed with her a long time, making quite sure she understood that there was no reason why she should not, in the future, bear healthy children. She was grateful for his kindness, but she did not want to think of other, as yet unborn children. She wanted only to grieve for the child she had lost. When he had gone, she lay weakly back against the pillows and cried and cried. The doctor, when a member of the nursing staff told him of her reaction, nodded with satisfaction. Tears were far healthier than silent, numbed grief. "She's going to be all right," he said prophetically. "She's a much tougher little lassie than she looks."

Adam came in to see her the minute he was allowed to do so. The ward sister had told him of her tears, and that they were not only perfectly natural, but healthily therapeutic.

"What she really needs is rest," the sister had added. "Please don't overtire her by staying with her for too long."

Elizabeth's hair was down around her shoulders, making her look ridiculously young. She had dried her tears, but her face was still pale and there were dark shadows beneath her eyes.

"Did you sleep, sweetheart?" Adam asked, pulling the chair as near to the bed as he possibly could.

"Yes." She had been given sedatives and pain-killers and her sleep had been deep and unnatural. A faint smile touched her mouth. "You're still wearing your gardening cardigan, Adam. Where on earth did you spend the night?"

He grinned sheepishly. "I didn't want to travel back home in case you needed me. I slept 'round the corner, at the club."

"Oh, Adam," she said, a catch in her voice. "You're the kindest person I know."

She had said the same thing to him scores of times before. When she was a little girl; when he had comforted her after Jerome's death. When they had been happy together at Four Seasons. Hope for the future surged through him. "You'll be out of here within ten days to two weeks," he said, euphoric at once more making plans with her, once more contemplating a future together. "We can leave straight away for New Zealand. The doctor says you'll be perfectly strong enough."

She stared at him uncomprehendingly. "I'm sorry, Adam. I don't understand . . ."

"I'm taking you to New Zealand to recuperate," he reminded her tenderly.

Her eyes widened, a new expression coming into them, but before he could understand it, they heard an angry altercation in the corridor.

"Mrs. Harland's *husband* is with her at present!" the ward sister was protesting indignantly. "Only husbands are allowed to visit so early in the day!"

There came the sound of a deep, dismissive reply, then the door flew open and Elizabeth cried, *"Raefe!"* the sound seeming to come from her very soul. Her arms were outstretched and even as Adam stumbled, disconcerted, to his feet, Raefe strode to her side and crushed her in his arms.

The ward sister ran into the room, saying, "Only *husbands* are allowed—" then stood stock-still, her eyes wide with disbelief at the sight of Adam, standing futilely by, while his wife was kissed with demented passion by the man who had just stormed into the room.

"Oh, my love!" Raefe whispered fiercely against her hair as she clung to him. "Oh, my sweet, sweet love!"

Adam blundered toward the door. He knew now what expression had been in her eyes in the last few seconds before Elliot had burst in on them. It had been horror at the enormity of his assumption. And pity.

"Mr. Harland!" the sister cried. "What is happening? I don't understand?"

Adam pushed uncaringly past her. He understood. He had seen Beth's face as Elliot strode toward her, and it had been transfigured with an expression of such love that he had hardly been able to breathe. Never, in all the years they had lived together, had he seen her look at him like that. He couldn't even conceive of it. He staggered out into the corridor. Finally and at long last he understood. She was never going to come back to him. It was over. Finished.

A Junoesque figure was running down the corridor toward him, dark hair cascading untidily around a beautifully-boned, expressive face. "Adam! Oh, my God! Are you all right? *Adam!*" He allowed her to seize his arm, to take some of his weight. "What's happened?" she asked urgently. "Is it Elizabeth? Is she dead?"

He shook his head. "No," he said, his voice cracked with defeat and weariness. "No, she's not dead, Helena."

Helena glanced swiftly down the corridor. The door to Elizabeth's room was open and the ward sister's voice rose clearly. "Only *husbands* are allowed to visit, Mr. Elliot!"

"Oh, God," she said beneath her breath, understanding. She turned once more to Adam. "Come along, my dear," she said compassionately. "Let's go and have a coffee somewhere."

He nodded. Helena was an inch or two taller than he with her wedge-heeled sandals on, but he didn't mind. There was something very comforting about Helena. Something he had begun to depend upon.

Raefe arranged for the baby to be buried in the Elliot family vault. The quiet, simple service, attended only by themselves and Helena, brought Elizabeth a measure of peace. Raefe had intended that she have a long period of rest and recuperation when she was discharged from the hospital, but she shook her head vehemently at the thought. She didn't want rest. It would give her too much time in which to brood. She wanted to ease her pain with work.

For the first few weeks, to avoid her becoming overtired by the journey into Kowloon, Raefe hired a chauffeured car to bring Li Pi to the house, and her lessons took place in the large, sunlit room that looked out toward the sea.

The war being waged by the Japanese on the Chinese had intensified in recent weeks, and Li Pi had begun to smile less and less. "Fighting is taking place just beyond the border now," he said to Elizabeth at the beginning of June. "Red Cross trucks bring wounded from China into Hong Kong every day. It is growing bad. Very bad."

"It's horrendous," Helena said to her on the telephone. "Several schools in Kowloon have been turned into makeshift hospitals, but I'm sure the wounded that are brought over the border are only the tip of the iceberg. I drove up toward Fanling yesterday and the smell of dead bodies was unmistakable. I doubt if any proper burials have been carried out in weeks.

* * *

"You are going to have to leave," Raefe said to her grimly when he returned from a visit to Government House and a meeting with Sir Mark Young.

"Leave?" She looked up at him startled. "I don't know what you mean." She was sitting on the sofa, her legs curled beneath her, a music score in her hands. She put it down as he sat beside her.

"The government is going to demand that all European women and children leave the colony immediately," he said wearily. "It will be official tomorrow."

She had known for days that something was very wrong. Intelligence meetings now took place in Hong Kong as well as Singapore, and they had begun to last until late into the night. "Are the Japanese going to attack?" she asked quietly.

"The government thinks so. The fighting in China is only miles away now."

"But that's against the Chinese. It doesn't necessarily mean that the Japanese will turn their attention toward us."

"No," Raefe agreed, "but it's a risk the government can't take. It's been arranged that two Canadian ships, the *Empress of Asia* and the *President Coolidge*, take evacuees to Australia."

"How soon?" she asked, her voice fearful.

His hand tightened on hers. " 'By the end of the week," he said bleakly.

She did not argue with him because she knew it would be pointless. He loved her, and he would miss her as agonizingly as she would miss him. Yet rather than have her remain in Hong Kong in danger, he would forcibly carry her aboard the *Empress of Asia* himself. If she was to stay behind when other women left, then she would have to do so by subterfuge.

Very early the next morning, before Raefe was awake, she tiptoed downstairs and telephoned Helena.

"Thanks for the information," Helena said appreciatively. "It might be sensible to leave now, but I don't think I will. Not yet"

"Will you have any option if it's a government demand?" Elizabeth asked.

"I'm a State Registered Nurse," Helena reminded her. "I haven't practiced for years, but that makes very little difference in a situation like this. No one enlisting as an

auxiliary nurse, or an air-raid warden, or stenographer or
cipher clerk will have to leave. They will be too necessary."

"Thanks, Helena," Elizabeth said, now knowing what
she had to do.

"Darling, I really would be happier if you left for
Australia," Ronnie said miserably. Julienne was sitting at
her dressing table. She was wearing an oyster silk, lace-
edged camisole and nothing else, and was carefully var-
nishing her fingernails a searing scarlet.

"I am not going, *chéri*," she said for the twentieth time.
"*C'est compris?*"

"No, I don't understand," he said irritably. "All the other
wives are going. It isn't just the usual scare. This time it
really does seem as if something is going to happen."

Julienne inspected her nails carefully. "What is going to
happen is that I am going to stay here, with you," she said,
waving her hand gently in the air to encourage the polish
to dry. "I am *not* going to be packed like a sardine aboard a
ship crammed with hundreds of crying, fretful children.
Merde alors! How can you ask it of me?"

Ronnie was ashamed of the relief he felt. The thought of
Julienne thousands of miles away was unbearable.
"Perhaps you're right," he said, standing behind her and
sliding his hands down over her shoulders. "It's just
scaremongering. It won't come to anything." His hands
slid lower, cupping her breasts.

"Be careful of my nails, *chéri!*" she protested laughingly.

"To hell with your nails," he growled, lifting her up in
his arms and carrying her toward the bed. "Let's celebrate
the fact that you're staying here, with me, where you
belong."

"But of course," Julienne said, a delicious shiver rippling
down her spine. "After all, I love you very much, *chéri*. It is
something you must never forget!"

Raefe spent the next two days making arrangements for
Elizabeth to leave aboard the *Empress of Asia*. He was tight-
lipped, his face grim. He didn't want her to go, but there
was no alternative. And God knew when he would see her
again.

Her cases were packed and sent down to the docks to be
winched aboard. She had hardly spoken to him since he

had told her what she must do, and he guessed it was because if she spoke, she would also cry.

Adam telephoned her, his voice harsh with anxiety. "Are you leaving aboard one of the evacuee ships, Beth?"

She glanced over to the desk where Raefe was checking her travel documents. "Yes," she lied, hating herself for the deception she was playing on both of them.

"Thank God!" he said thankfully. "Perhaps you would have a word with Helena. She's adamant that she's staying. I can't seem to make her see sense at all!"

"Yes," Elizabeth promised, wondering what on earth would happen when the *Empress of Asia* sailed without her.

She went through all the motions of leaving. She said good-bye to Mei Lin and clung to Raefe in the last few minutes before he led her outside to the car.

"Oh, God, but I love you, Lizzie!" he said hoarsely, his face ravaged by grief at the prospect of parting with her.

She wanted to tell him, her very soul crying out in protest at the deceit she was exercising. But she knew that if she told him she had no intention of leaving, he would force her to do so. The only way she could remain was to carry out this charade.

Both ships were berthed at the Kowloon docks, their funnels spouting black smoke as hundreds of rickshaws and cars descended on the dock, spilling out women and children and mountains of luggage.

For one brief second, as Raefe walked her to the foot of the gangplank, she wondered if, for his sake, she should leave with the others for Australia. She looked up at the high sides of the ship, the rails crammed with waving, departing women, and then back at him and knew that she could not do so. Most of the women who were leaving had children. If the baby had lived, then she would have gone without a second thought. But the baby had not lived, and if war came to the colony, there would be plenty of work for her to do. She wasn't a trained nurse, but she was competent and quick-witted. An overworked hospital would surely be able to put her to use.

"I love you!" Raefe said savagely when the time came for them to part. *"Only you, Lizzie! Forever!"*

Tears spilled down her cheeks. She had never lied to him, never been deceitful, and her guilt was crucifying.

"I love you too," she whispered, touching his strong-boned face with her hands. "Oh, my darling, I love you too!"

There were hordes of people pushing past and around them. Unable to endure any more he kissed her deeply, then swung on his heel, forcing his way through the crowds back to the car, knowing that if he stayed a second longer, good sense would desert him and he would plead with her to stay.

Elizabeth watched him through her tears, wondering what expression she would see in his eyes when next they met. He would be enraged. She was prepared for his anger and knew that she could bear it. But what if there was another expression in his eyes? What if he was disappointed in her? What if her childish deceit diminished her in his opinion?

Dark was beginning to fall and the last clutch of anxious women were boarding. Elizabeth began to make her way back down the gangplank, easing her way past a member of the crew. "We're sailing in a few minutes, ma'am," he said warningly.

"I've forgotten something. I won't be long," she lied.

The dock was crowded with husbands waving final farewells. She pushed a way between them, looking for a rickshaw boy. She would go to Helena's and in an hour's time, when the *Empress of Asia* and the *President Coolidge* were far out at sea, she would telephone Raefe.

"I don't imagine he's going to be very pleased," Helena said dryly as she poured Elizabeth a large gin and tonic. "Why couldn't you have told him to his face that you weren't going?"

"Because he would have made me," Elizabeth said simply.

Helena dropped ice cubes into the glass and did not argue with her. "If you need somewhere to sleep tonight, or for subsequent nights, there's room here." She handed her the gin and tonic, then poured another for herself.

Elizabeth's skin lost a fraction more color. "Oh, God, Helena, do you think it will come to that?"

"I think he's going to be extremely angry," she replied. It was an understatement.

* * *

"You're *what*?" he shouted into the telephone. "You're *where*? My God! Of all the idiotic . . . stupid . . . crazy . . ." The phone was slammed down in her ear, his furiously flung words still vibrating.

"He's angry," Helena said unnecessarily.

Elizabeth clasped her hands together in her lap to prevent them from trembling. "Yes," she said unsteadily. "He's angry."

Less than twenty minutes later they heard his car skid to a halt in the street outside. "I think," Helena said nervously, "that another gin and tonic is called for."

They could hear the pounding of his feet as he took the stairs two at a time. He didn't bother to knock. The door rocked back on its hinges and he stormed into the apartment, his brows pulled together demonically, his lips white. *"Do you realize the danger you've put yourself in?"* he thundered, seizing her by the arms and pushing her down into a chair. *"Do you realize what you've done? There'll be no other sailings, for God's sake! You'll have to stay here now!"*

"I want to stay here," she said quietly, her face white. "I've enlisted as a volunteer nurse."

He ran his hand through his hair, staring down at her in disbelief.

"I *wanted* to tell you, but I knew that if I did, you would have me locked aboard the *Empress of Asia* until she sailed."

"You're damned right I would!"

She bit her bottom lip, steadied her voice, and said, "If you don't want me to return home with you, I can stay here with Helena."

His brows shot high. "What the hell are you talking about? Of course I want you to return home! Jesus God, Lizzie! Don't you realize that I nearly died when I said good-bye to you on that goddamn ship?"

"Then tell me you're not angry with me," she said urgently, rising to her feet.

His arms closed around her. "I'm *furiously* angry with you, but I'm not a certifiable lunatic! I'm not going to banish you from my bed!"

With unspeakable relief she slid her arms around his neck. Raefe lowered his head to hers, a blaze of such fierce love in his eyes that Helena discreetly turned away. She poured herself another gin and tonic. Her spare bed was not going to be needed after all.

* * *

All through the remainder of the month, reports of heavy fighting beyond the border continued, but the Japanese made no attempt to cross into the colony. By the end of the month, when Raefe flew down to Fort Canning, it was generally agreed that the crisis was over.

Elizabeth was pruning back the lush azaleas that crowded down from the hillside toward the house when she heard the throb of an engine. She paused, a slight frown creasing her brow. Raefe wasn't due back for two more days at least, and she wasn't expecting Julienne or Helena to call on her. A Jeep lurched into view, a cloud of dust in its wake. She put down her secateurs and removed her gardening gloves as she walked curiously to meet it. The sun was strong in her eyes and for several seconds she couldn't see who was driving. Then, as the Jeep shuddered to a halt and a huge, bearlike figure emerged, a huge grin splitting his face, she dropped her gloves to the ground and began to run joyously toward him. "Roman! *Roman!*"

He swung her up in his arms easily, swinging her around and off her feet. "*Witaj!*" he said exuberantly, a deep laugh rumbling up from his chest. "Are you trying to tame the azaleas and hibiscus into a neat and tidy English garden?"

She giggled. "No," she said happily as he set her back down on her feet. "I'm just trying to prevent them from smothering the house completely."

His grin deepened, his eyes creasing at the corners. "Where is Raefe?" he asked as they walked toward the house.

"He's in Singapore. But he's only there for another two days. You'll be able to stay until he returns, won't you?"

Regretfully he shook his head. "I'm afraid not," he said as they stepped into the sun-filled room where her concert grand held pride of place. "I just made a brief trip back to Perth, and from here I go on to London. I'm going to apply for a commission in the Royal Air Force. My ship leaves at nine tomorrow morning."

"Oh!" She was devastated with disappointment. "Raefe will be furious when he finds out he missed you! It might be ages before he sees you again." She paused, her voice suddenly desolate. "Years even."

The shadow of the war fell across them. Roman dismissed it with firm optimism. "The fighting may be over by the spring. When it is, I shall want you to play for me. In Palestine perhaps."

She grinned, dizzy at the thought, knowing that he was going to ask her to play for him now and that her fingers itched to do so.

"What is it to be?" he asked, strolling over to the concert grand, his tall, powerful physique filling the room. Musingly he ran his fingers over the keys.

"Would you play for me?" she asked impulsively, no longer overawed by him as she had been in the concert hall in Perth. She was as at ease with him as if she had known him all her life.

"A farewell performance before the rigors of fighter command?" he asked, his blue eyes grim despite the lightness of his voice. "Of course I will. There's nothing I would enjoy more."

He sat himself at the keyboard, adjusted the piano stool, and flexed his strong, large, beautifully sculpted hands. She stood beside him, tense and waiting, forgetting all about the war raging in Europe, forgetting even the disappointment that Raefe was not with them. Roman was a conductor, not a pianist, and she was uncertain of what to expect. His fingers touched the keys, and the opening notes of Beethoven's "Appassionata" filled the room. She sighed rapturously, knowing immediately that if he had wished, Roman could have made the piano, not the rostrum, his life.

The music ebbed and flowed, enveloping and consuming her. She closed her eyes, rocked by a feeling of such unity with him in the passion they shared, that it was almost sexual. The ordered calm of the *Andant* was followed by the great tidal wave of the *Allegro*, the musical menace so relentless and mounting that she opened her eyes, wondering how she could possibly bear the terrifying beauty of it. Li Pi had described the last movement of the "Appassionata" as mounting until, amid the thunder of sudden *sforzandi*, the edifice of the world collapsed. Lucifer, once the bearer of light, plunged down from heaven into eternal darkness. Li Pi had not exaggerated. For several minutes after the final chord reverberated throughout the room, neither Elizabeth nor Roman spoke. Then Roman said, "I once had the privilege of playing Beethoven on an old piano, an 1803 Broadwood. The excitement of playing the 'Appassionata' on the kind of piano it was composed for was indescribable. I was convinced that the piano was going to break at any moment under the stress, but that terror became part of the wonder of it."

A shiver of pleasure ran down her spine. "I know what you mean," she said, feeling so emotionally and mentally close to him that the breath was tight in her chest. "It's as if Beethoven is shaking his fist in the face of heaven."

Roman nodded, his eyes holding hers, the rapport between them electric. "Beethoven thought it his greatest sonata," he said, appalled at the mood that had sprung up between them and trying to bring it back to normal. "I'm in complete agreement with him. What about something entirely different? Something lyrical and joyful. The sonata he wrote immediately following the 'Appassionata.' Sonata Number Twenty-four in F-sharp, Opus Seventy-eight?"

For some unaccountable reason she was trembling. "It's a devil to play," she said, her voice unsteady as he rose from the piano stool and indicated that she was to play it.

"It isn't," he said gently, a smile hovering at the corners of his mouth. "Not for you."

Nervously she took his place at the piano. It was as if all her senses were stretched and heightened. Never before had she been in such close intimate contact with someone whose passion for music was as deep and as integral as her own, and it was a heady experience.

Mei Lin came into the room to ask if Elizabeth wanted refreshments for her guest, but though she said, "Excuse me, missy," several times, neither Elizabeth nor the huge, golden-haired man at the piano paid her the slightest attention.

The long afternoon tapered to dusk. Rachmaninov followed Beethoven; Grieg followed Rachmaninov; Mozart followed Grieg.

The windows were open to the scent of the flowers and the light breeze blowing across the bay. Two gulls skimmed low over the water, their dark shadows identifiable only by their long, grieving cry. At last, when it was too dark to see anymore without leaving the piano and switching on the lamps, Elizabeth leaned back on the piano stool and said apologetically, "I'm exhausted, Roman. Whatever is the time?"

"It's time to eat," he said, closing the piano lid. "Are there any Polish restaurants in Hong Kong?"

She flexed her tired fingers. "If there are, I don't know of them. Would you like to eat here? Mei Lin is a very good cook."

"I'm sure she is," Roman said agreeably, "but I think I would like to take you out on the town. I'm staying at the Peninsula and I thought it would be a good idea if we had dinner there. It's one of Raefe's favorite haunts, isn't it?"

She smiled. "It's the haunt of every expatriate on the island. If we're going there, I need to change my dress. I spent all morning gardening in this and it's full of grass and azalea stains."

"I'll wait for you outside," he said, walking to the open door that led to the terrace. "I want to look at the sea by moonlight. No wonder the two of you love this house. Its setting is pure theater."

"I'll send Mei Lin out with a drink for you," she said, wondering with amusement who would see them dining together at the Pen and what sort of harebrained rumors would result.

She discarded her cotton dress and slipped on a pale mauve voile dress that swirled softly about her legs. Raefe would want her to be a credit to Roman, and she complemented the dress with ivory stockings and ivory kid pumps, then swept her hair high into a smooth chignon and clasped a heavy rope of pearls around her neck. It was almost as if she were going out on a date, and she sat down suddenly on the edge of the bed, overcome with panic. What on earth was happening to her? She loved Raefe. She loved him utterly and completely and it was impossible that she could feel any emotional or sexual attraction for anyone else. But she did.

The closeness that had sprung up between Roman and herself while they had played Beethoven and Mozart and Grieg together had not just been the closeness of two friends with a shared talent. It had been stronger than that. So strong that she had to admit with brutal honesty that if it hadn't been for her commitment to Raefe and her deep love for him, the closeness between her and Roman would have transcended the mental and become physical.

Shocked at her own vulnerability, she went downstairs to join him. He turned toward her, his thick unruly hair gleaming gold in the moonlight and his eyes crinkling at the corners as he smiled down at her. Her panic ebbed and a feeling of safety swept over her. Whatever her own vulnerability, Roman had a moral strength that could be trusted absolutely. He was Raefe's friend and he was her friend, and it was a friendship he would never violate.

They drove to Victoria in the Jeep, the night air warm and scented. Early stars, king stars, burned bright and steadfast, and the moon was pale and luminous as they sped down Chai Wan Road, Pottinger Peak looming dark and magnificent on their left.

In Wanchai the neon lights flashed on and off with dazzling brilliance, a cacophony of noise emanating from the bars and nightclubs.

"Just the place for a quiet night out," Roman said with a broad grin. The laughter that always seemed such a part of being with him welled up inside her.

"The night is only just beginning here. Things don't start to really heat up until the early hours of the morning!"

The Peninsula's dining room was full as usual, but they had no trouble obtaining a table. Roman had already made a reservation for three, and as Raefe's place setting was speedily cleared away, a sharp pang of regret knifed through Elizabeth.

"I think someone is trying to attract your attention," Roman said as a waiter brought them gin and tonics. "The red-haired lady, over there on the left."

Elizabeth looked in the direction he indicated and encountered Julienne's raised eyebrows and astonished expression. Ronnie, who was for once at her side, looked merely startled at the sight of Elizabeth with a man he had never seen before, but Julienne was in a fever of curiosity.

"Who is he?" she mouthed, then collapsed in a fit of giggles as Elizabeth teasingly raised her shoulders as if to say that she didn't know.

By the time their second drink and the menu had arrived, Julienne could contain her curiosity no longer. Promising Ronnie that she would be no longer than five minutes, she rose from their table, and, hips swaying seductively, walked over to Elizabeth and Roman.

Elizabeth's amusement deepened as she introduced Roman and Julienne, and saw the naked approval in Julienne's violet-blue eyes.

"Enchanté," Julienne said, her eyes sparkling as she sat in

the chair that had been reserved for Raefe. "Will you be staying long in Hong Kong, Roman?"

She rolled the first letter of his name in her provocative accent, and Roman's smile deepened.

"Unfortunately not," he said. "My ship sails in the morning." Elizabeth was sure there was genuine regret in his voice. There was certainly genuine regret in Julienne's as she said, her cheeks dimpling prettily, "That is a pity, *n'est-ce pas*? It would have been nice for us to have made friends."

Elizabeth restrained her laughter with difficulty. She knew exactly the kind of friendship Julienne had in mind and wondered, not for the first time, where Julienne found her inexhaustible energy.

As the waiter came to take their orders, Julienne rose reluctantly to her feet. If Roman Rakowski was leaving Hong Kong in twelve hours, it was pointless prolonging their meeting. Nothing delightful could come of it. All the same, she envied Elizabeth her dinner date and her eyes, as they met Elizabeth's, indicated that.

"*Au revoir*," she said to Roman as he stood as well. Then, her laughter-filled eyes meeting Elizabeth's, she added, sotto voce, "Be good, *chérie*!"

Roman, as aware as Elizabeth of the quality of the rapport that had sprung up between them earlier at her house, and aware of what had ignited it, steered clear of music as a subject while they ate dinner. Instead, he talked about the war in Europe and his hopes of a commission in the Royal Air Force.

"I first started flying when I was in America. Raefe used to let off steam on the polo field, but I've been in love with flying ever since an uncle took me up in a Curtiss Jenny when I was eight years old. If it hadn't been that I loved music more, I would have made flying a full-time career. Now, for a time at least, I'm going to have to."

Elizabeth was silent. In previous wars, Britain had had to rely on her navy and her sailors. Now she was relying on men like Roman. Men volunteering to fly Hurricanes and Spitfires against the might of the German Luftwaffe.

After dinner, and after she had introduced him to Mei Kuei, her favorite rose-flavored Chinese liqueur, they left the Peninsula. She suggested that she take a taxi back home so he could have an early night before his departure the next day.

"Nonsense," he said in a voice that brooked no argument. "I shall enjoy the drive. The landscape fascinates me. By moonlight, it's pure Grand Guignol."

They spoke very little on the drive back toward the east coast. The night air was now cold and Roman slipped his jacket around her shoulders, ignoring her protests that he would freeze without it.

"I'm a hardy animal," he said, his white teeth flashing in the darkness as he grinned across at her.

Male tweed tickled the nape of her neck and her cheeks as she snuggled warmly down in it. He would need to be hardy to survice the rigors that lay ahead of him. She was filled with sudden terror for his safety, shuddering at the mental image of his plane spinning down in flames over the English Channel.

"What's the matter?" he asked, looking swiftly across at her. "Still cold?"

"No," she lied, wishing fervently that Raefe was with them. If he had been, he would have sensed her fears and her reason for them.

The whitewashed walls of the house gleamed silver in the moonlight as they approached, the scent of hibiscus and azaleas still heavy in the air.

After stopping, Roman walked around the Jeep to help her as she stepped onto the uneven ground in her perilously high heels. "I won't come in," he said gently, before she had time to ask him. "Give my love to Raefe. And keep safe, both of you, till this damned war is over and we meet again."

He didn't touch her, didn't kiss her good-bye or hug her, as he had done when they had parted in Perth, and she was deeply grateful.

"Good-bye, Roman," she said, her voice breaking slightly. She was uncomfortably aware that the flame that had sprung up between them earlier had erupted once more into life.

"*Do widzenia*," he said, his voice suspiciously gruff. "Good-bye, Elizabeth. God bless."

She turned quickly and walked into the house, not looking back. As she closed the door behind her she could hear the sound of the Jeep's engine revving into life, then its ever-receding throb as it sped away.

Next morning, even before she was dressed, the telephone rang imperiously and she knew, as she hurried to answer it, that the caller would be Julienne.

"I thought you might not be in," Julienne said mischievously. "I thought that perhaps you would be waving good-bye to Roman's ship."

"No," Elizabeth said serenely, refusing to be baited. "And now that you have found me respectably at home, have you any other reason for calling?"

Unabashed, Julienne admitted that she hadn't. "You never told me how *devastatingly* handsome Roman Rakowski was when you met him in Perth," she chastised Elizabeth. "I thought all musicians and conductors were slim and slender and effeminate. I had no idea he was such a big, *gorgeous* hunk of a man!"

Despite herself, Elizabeth laughed, vastly amused at Julienne's misconceptions about the physical attributes of the great majority of the musical profession.

"What I can't get over," Julienne continued, with a note of awe in her voice, "is how *alike* Roman and Raefe are. I know that Raefe is very dark and Roman is startlingly fair, and though they are both tall and broad-shouldered, they are built differently. Roman is a huge *bear* of a man, whereas there is a lean, lithe, whippiness about Raefe. But despite those differences, there is *still* something uncannily similar about them." She giggled. "Perhaps it is because there is something feral and a little primitive about both of them. Raefe doesn't give a damn about accepted standards of social behavior, and I doubt if Roman does either. It makes both of them very exciting." She gave a pleasurable sigh, but whether at the thought of Roman or Raefe, Elizabeth wasn't sure. "Are you playing tennis today?" she continued, abandoning a subject Elizabeth knew she would return to again. "Helena said she would be at the club at lunchtime, and I think Alastair is going to try to be there as well."

"I don't know," Elizabeth said vaguely. "I'll see." She said good-bye and hung up, knowing that the last thing she wanted at the moment was an afternoon of gossip at the club. All she wanted was for Raefe to come home, and to be at home when he did so.

When he did return, late the following afternoon, she rushed out of the house to greet him, hurtling into his outstretched arms. "Darling! I thought you were *never* going to come home! It seems as if you've been away for *ages!*"

He hugged her tight, kissing her deeply. Rapturously content, she twined her arm around his waist as they walked back into the house.

"We had a surprise visitor while you were away. One you will be sorry to have missed."

"I find that hard to believe," he said. As he grinned down at her, the quality of his smile was so much like Roman's, she missed her step and stumbled against him. His arm tightened around her and she said, an odd little note in her voice, "It was Roman."

"Then you're right," he said, looking down at her, sensing that something had disturbed her and wondering what it was. "I am sorry to have missed him. What the devil is he doing in Hong Kong?"

They sat down on the white-upholstered sofa, in the long, large room they used as a sitting room, and she leaned against him. "He isn't here any longer. He'd been to Australia again and was just passing through on his way to London. He's going to apply for a commission in the Royal Air Force."

"I thought he might," Raefe said, his voice suddenly grim.

They sat in silence for a minute, his arm around her shoulders and her head resting against his chest. After a little while he asked curiously, "And what happened while he was here that has so disturbed you?"

Her head flew upward, her eyes, wide with amazement, meeting his. "How on earth do you know that anything has?"

He chuckled and pulled her closer. "I know everything about you, my love. I know when you're happy and when you're unhappy, and I know when you're fretting your head over something. Now what is it? Did he ask you to play for him and did you lose your nerve? Or, even worse, did he not ask you to play for him?"

"It's nothing like that," she said slowly. "I did play for him, and he played for me. He's a marvelous pianist." She hesitated, wondering how she could tell Raefe of the fierce sexual attraction that had sprung up between them as they had played, and which they had both been so painfully aware of. Surely she couldn't tell him such a thing had happened. It didn't mean that her love for him wasn't one hundred percent total, or that she would ever, in a million years, be unfaithful to him.

His dark eyes held hers, and she knew with a rush of thankfulness that he *would* understand. Between her and Raefe there had never been any secrets and there would be none now. She slid her fingers through his, clasping his hand tightly on her lap, and said awkwardly, "We played for hours, all afternoon and until it was quite dark, then he took me for dinner at the Peninsula." She paused, searching for the right words, and he waited patiently, knowing already what she was trying so hard to explain to him.

"It was a wonderful experience, Raefe. The music drew us together, and it was as if . . . as if . . ."

"As if you were lovers?" he asked gently.

She gasped as if she had been struck. "You know! How can you possibly know?"

He fought down the loving laughter that surged up in his throat. "Because I know you, my love. And I know Roman. And I know what kindred spirits you are. I also know how powerful and erotic such a shared experience can be."

"Oh!" Relief overwhelmed her. "I couldn't understand what was happening to me, or why."

"For a beautiful, wonderfully talented woman, there are times when you are touchingly naive, my love. Music *is* sexual. At least, I know it is for Roman and I'm pretty sure it is for you as well. I'm not surprised the sparks flew when the two of you were together." His winged eyebrows pulled together slightly. "It wasn't anything deeper than that, was it? You haven't suddenly discovered that he's the great love of your life?"

"No, silly," she said, touching his face tenderly. "*You* are the great love of my life! I love everything about you. The way your hair looks blue in the sunlight, the tiny motes of gold that fleck your eyes." Her voice became husky. "The touch of your hands on my flesh . . ."

As she spoke he had begun kissing her, his mouth moving from her temples to her cheekbone, to the corner of her mouth.

"I love you completely and utterly," she whispered as he slid her down beneath him on the sofa, "and I always will. Always and forever." And then, for a long time, neither of them spoke again.

* * *

The news from Europe continued to be grim. France fell. The Germans marched into Paris. In darkened cinemas in Victoria and Kowloon, the Pathé News left expatriates in no doubt at all as to what was happening half a world away. By the end of the summer, the Battle of Britain was under way, the skies above the English Channel thick with Spitfires and Messerschmidts. The Blitz followed. Night after night London was bombed, and the flickering news-reels revealed horror and devastation, and the dogged refusal of Londoners to be defeated.

In Hong Kong, signs advertising first-aid classes and air-raid precaution lectures proliferated. Work was renewed on defense positions. Barbed wire sprang up around the golf course at Fanling. More pillboxes were erected. Ammunition dumps were sited in the hills, discreetly camouflaged. In Kowloon and Victoria sandbags protected government buildings. Beaches were closed to the public and covered with wire fences and machine-gun posts.

In November Raefe received a letter from Roman. He had been successful in joining the Royal Air Force, and was fighting alongside Polish and American volunteers. The letter was heavily censored, and subsequent letters were rare and so briefly worded that the only information they gave was that he was still alive.

Raefe and Elizabeth spent Christmas at the house, putting a fir tree up in the large drawing room and decorating it with tinsel and baubles. Melissa had moved back into the home she had once shared with Raefe, on the Peak. It had been over two months since her last injection of heroin and she had emerged from her long ordeal quieter and more reflective.

"I'd thought of inviting her to spend Christmas day with us," Raefe said to Elizabeth as he helped her fix colored streamers across the hall.

"Then why didn't you?" she asked him. She had still not met Melissa, but they had talked several times on the telephone and a hesitant friendship had sprung up between them.

"She's spending the day with Derry. Apparently his affair with Julienne is not going too smoothly at the moment. She's spending less and less time with him and has told him she can't see him at all over the holidays."

Elizabeth secured the last paper streamer and stood back to admire it. "Ronnie will be pleased. I don't think he has a girlfriend at all now."

Raefe grinned. "Julienne has quite some way to go before she's in the same position. Even if she puts an end to her affair with Derry, there's still her little liaison with Tom. That's been going on ever since Lamoon disappeared."

They were silent for a moment. Lamoon's disappearance had affected Tom deeply. He rarely socialized now and, apart from Julienne, there had been no subsequent girl-friends.

"What's he doing for Christmas?" Elizabeth asked, frowning in concern.

"God knows. Helena asked him to spend the day with her and Alastair and Adam, but he refused. I asked him to come to us, but he said he'd prefer not. Since Ronnie and Julienne are coming, I can't say I blame him. I don't suppose Julienne would mind, but Ronnie might."

"Poor Tom," Elizabeth said compassionately as Raefe's arm slid around her shoulders. "I can't bear to think of him being so unhappy. Perhaps if he knew for certain what had happened to Lamoon, he would be able to begin to forget her."

"If he knew what had happened to her," Raefe said somberly, "it might make it even worse."

There was a glimmer of good news in January when Tobruk fell to the Allies, but the rest was bad news. German U-boats continued to sink Allied ships in the Atlantic. German planes continued to bomb London and major cities such as Bristol and Plymouth and Glasgow.

"I feel so guilty," Elizabeth said to Julienne as they knelt on the floor of a church hall at a first-aid meeting, cutting up old sheets for bandages. "Everything is so horrible. Hitler and Mussolini, and London being ravaged by bombs . . ."

"Why feel guilty?" Julienne, who had never felt guilty in her life, asked practically. "You are not responsible for Hitler and Mussolini, are you?"

Elizabeth grinned. "Don't be an ass, Julienne."

"Then why feel guilty?" Julienne persisted.

Elizabeth leaned back on her heels. "Because it is such a

terrible time for so many hundreds of thousands of people, and because I have never been so happy."

"*Alors!* Is that all?" Julienne asked in disbelief. "Never feel guilty about happiness, Elizabeth. It is far too precious an experience. Do you think this bandage will ever be of any use? It started off three inches wide, and now it's nearly a foot wide! It will have to be a very curiously shaped soldier who finds need of it!"

Chapter Twenty-three

*I*N March, Raefe and Melissa's divorce was made absolute. "Now there is only your divorce to wait for," Raefe said to Elizabeth, holding her close. "Why the hell do these things take so long?"

She didn't answer him. After the stillbirth of her baby, Adam had begun to waver about the wisdom of a divorce. He had withdrawn proceedings and had only recently, reluctantly, instituted them once again. She asked instead, "Will Melissa leave Hong Kong now?"

Raefe frowned. His sense of responsibility for Melissa was still strong, but the future he had envisaged for her, and which she had been looking forward to so much, was no longer possible. A return to London was out of the question. And Melissa had no friends or family in Australia or America. "I don't know," he said, his frown deepening. "There was a time when she couldn't wait to shake the dust of Hong Kong off her heels. Now she says she would much rather stay here than go to a place she doesn't know."

"You can't blame her. I wouldn't want to go alone to Australia or America either."

They were silent, both of them knowing that the day might come when she would have to go. Last summer's invasion scare had died down and many of the women who had left aboard the evacuee ships had returned. But though an increasing number of people now believed it would never happen, invasion by the Japanese was still a possibility.

"It might help if her father could be persuaded to leave for Perth or Los Angeles," Raefe said, his voice full of exasperation as it always was when he spoke of his former father-in-law. "She won't live with him here, but she might in a different environment."

"Have you told him that?"

His mouth tightened. "I've tried to, but he won't even speak to me on the telephone, let alone meet me!"

Three hours later Raefe drove up to the Peak to speak to Melissa. She was on the telephone when he arrived, but she brought her conversation to a quick conclusion, saying, "That will be lovely, Julienne. I'll look forward to it."

"Was that Julienne Ledsham?" Raefe asked as he moved toward the drinks trolley. He poured himself a Scotch and soda.

"Yes." Her voice was stilted. She had received the same documentation in the mail that morning as he had, and she had known that he would call to see her. She had had a long time in which to adjust to the idea of no longer being his wife, and she had thought she had done so. The sensation of bitter shock she felt at the reality came as an unpleasant surprise.

Raefe dropped a couple of ice cubes into his drink. There had been a time when he was unable to approve of any of Melissa's friends. Now he said with a grin, "What is Julienne up to these days? Is she still leading Derry a chase?"

Melissa felt her tenseness begin to seep away. "Yes," she said, a slight smile touching her mouth. "The last time I saw him he said he was thinking of asking her to marry him."

At the thought of a confirmed bachelor like Derry even contemplating marriage, Raefe's grin broadened. "He stands no chance. Julienne is quite happy as she is."

The slight smile that had touched Melissa's mouth faded. There was never any dislike in Raefe's voice when he spoke of Julienne, and yet Julienne was quite immoral. When *she* had behaved in a similar fashion, he had not shown an iota of tolerance. He had simply refused ever to sleep with her again. She said, with an edge to her voice, "The Ledsham marriage survives adultery. Why didn't ours?"

He felt a familiar heaviness weigh on his shoulders. "Because you are not Julienne," he wanted to say. "Because there was no generosity in your promiscuity. No regard for my pride. No love for anyone but yourself." He said instead, "Because we are not Julienne and Ronnie. When they married, it was with the understanding that faithfulness was not necessary to them. It was for me. It still is."

"And is Elizabeth faithful to you?"

"Yes." There was no doubt in his voice, no equivocation.

Melissa felt a flare of her old vindictiveness, wishing with all her heart that Raefe would, one day, find his precious Elizabeth in bed with another man. Jealousy surged through her. If he did, would his reaction be the same as it had been with her? Would he discard Elizabeth and never have anything more to do with her? Or had he discarded her, Melissa, so totally because he had been *relieved* by her adultery? Because it had given him the excuse he needed to free himself of her? She said passionately, with sudden insight, "My unfaithfulness didn't end our marriage! Our marriage was over long before I tried to make you jealous by sleeping with someone else! It was over within weeks of the wedding when you realized that you weren't in love with me! That you had never been in love with me!"

He turned away from her, unable to deny it, and set his glass back down on the trolley. "I came here to talk about the future, not the past," he said tersely. "You know that you can have the use of this house for as long as you want, but you need to think of where you're going to go when you leave here."

"London," she said with equal curtness. "When this bloody war is over and life returns to normal."

He sighed, aware that their newfound friendliness was fast slipping away. "God knows when that will be," he said, turning once more to face her. "Hong Kong isn't the safest place in the world, Mel. I'd rest far easier if you were in America or Australia."

She met his eyes unflinchingly. "Elizabeth isn't in America or Australia. Julienne isn't. Nor is Helena Nicholson or Miriam Gresby or a score of other women I could mention.

I don't particularly want to stay here, though things aren't quite so bad now that I seem to be socially acceptable once more. If the Germans weren't intent on bombing London to a pulp, I'd be on the first ship home. As it is, I'll wait. Living alone in a city I don't know holds no appeal for me at all."

"What if I could persuade your father to leave as well?"

She laughed derisively. "My God! The thought of my father in Australia hardly makes Australia more palatable! And he certainly wouldn't go if the suggestion came from you. He still thinks you're hell-bent on ruining me. If you suggested he should accompany me to Australia, he'd be convinced it was because you had inside information and knew that the Japs were about to land there at any moment!"

He knew what she said was true. "Would you leave if Julienne left?" he asked, his eyebrows arching curiously.

"I might, but I can't imagine Julienne leaving without Elizabeth. And I can't imagine the three of us decorously sitting out the war together, can you? The best you can hope for is that Hitler comes to a sticky end. That the Germans say 'sorry, chaps' and beat a hasty retreat to their own borders, and the Japanese don't get ideas above their station. Then no one will have to go anywhere unless they want to, and those that do want to will be able to go where they choose. Which in my case is London."

Raefe chuckled, knowing there was no use in pursuing the subject further, at least for the time being. "'Bye, Mel," he said, relieved that they were at least parting amicably. "Give my regards to Julienne when you see her."

Melissa felt a catch in her throat, not wanting him to go. Not wanting to be left. "'Bye," she said, digging her nails into her palms. Damn it all, she was a grown woman, not a child! And her newfound pride would not allow her to pine any longer after a man who had never loved her. "'Bye," she said more firmly, walking to the door with him. She was going to Julienne's party in an hour. She wondered whether to wear her red chiffon or her sapphire-blue silk, and decided on the red chiffon. It would be her first night out as a newly single woman. And at Julienne's, anything could happen.

Julienne wandered through her flower-filled drawing room, checking that the houseboys had distributed enough ashtrays and enough small dishes of hors d'oeuvres. She enjoyed giving parties and did so with effortless ease. However, this evening's party was going to be one with a difference. It was going to be the last party she would ever give as a happily faithless wife.

The flowers were perfect. She had arranged them herself earlier in the day, great, lavish bouquets of jungle flowers that filled the house with a heady fragrance. On the buffet table in the dining room, silver gleamed and cut glass shone. It was really quite a momentous occasion: the beginning of a life of monogamy, perhaps even mother-hood. A small smile played on her wide, full mouth. The idea had at first appalled her, then intrigued her. But before her plans could be put into practice, there were one or two things that had to be dealt with.

The first little difficulty was Derry. She was excessively fond of him. He possessed a careless gaiety and a zest for life that matched her own. And he was an extremely satisfying lover. She sighed a little. She was going to miss her laughter-filled, crazily athletic, passionate afternoons with Derry. She restraightened an already perfectly straight Georgian silver table knife. It was a pity, but it was a necessity. She could no longer bear to see Ronnie looking so downcast. He tried to hide his dejection from her, still resolutely flirting with all her friends, but she knew that he did so without any real enthusiasm. It was as if he had outgrown his days of philandering and was waiting wistfully for her to follow suit.

She stepped back from the laden table, appraising it for a second time. So . . . she had come to her decision, and there would be no more Derry, and no more Tom, and no one to replace them. It would, no doubt, be strange at first, but Ronnie would be happier and that would be compensa-tion enough. All that remained was to inform Derry and Tom of her decision.

She crossed to the cocktail cabinet and mixed herself a very dry martini. Derry would think she had taken leave of her senses. He might even miss her quite deeply, but he would recover. She wasn't worried about Derry. It was Tom who was causing her concern. She opened the French windows and stepped from the dining room onto the terrace that ran the breadth of the house. Fairy lights had been strung among the trees and Chinese lanterns glowed in the deepening dusk. Tom was not in love with her, but she had become his one source of comfort. Since Lamoon's disappearance, he had withdrawn into himself, no longer socializing. He blamed himself for what had happened, and for the suffering he was sure Lamoon was undergoing.

No, she could not leave Tom with the same ease as she could leave Derry. He would not trouble to find a replacement for her and he would need one, very much. Since it was a task he would not undertake for himself, she knew that she must do it for him, though without his knowledge. She had pondered long and hard over a suitable candidate and had been surprised at the conclusion she had reached: Melissa Langdon Elliot.

She wondered at first if her usually sound judgment was letting her down, but on reflection had decided that it wasn't. Melissa was beautiful, lonely, and emotionally insecure. Tom was a good-looking man who possessed a strong sense of protectiveness. The battle that Melissa had successfully waged against heroin addiction would raise her in his estimation, not diminish her. The more Julienne thought about it, the more sure she became. Tom's old-fashioned gallantry had been appalled at the public disclosure of Melissa's private life at the time of Raefe's trial, but Julienne felt that his dismay had been more for the humiliation that Melissa had endured than for the revelations themselves. From the front of the house there came the distant sound of a doorbell. Her guests were beginning to arrive. She sipped the last of her martini, put down her glass, and stepped back into the house to greet them.

By the time Derry arrived the ground floor rooms were crammed with people, the crush crowding the stairs and spilling out into the garden.

"How are you, old boy? Nice to see you," Leigh Stafford said expansively as Derry eased himself into the drawing room, trying to locate Julienne.

"Hello there, Derry. Are you going to be playing in the rugger match against the Middlesex?" someone else shouted to him.

A white-jacketed houseboy squeezed his way toward him, proffering a tray of drinks.

"I hear that horse of Ronnie's is still performing miracles!"

"And so it looks as if poor old Roger will have to marry the girl now!"

The laughter and raised voices were deafening. Derry ignored the back-slapping from old acquaintances, continuing his search for Julienne. It didn't perturb him in the least that the party was in her marital home. What did disturb him was the presence of Tom Nicholson's Packard in the drive outside. His suspicions about Julienne and Tom had increased over the last few months, but he still wasn't sure. Were they having an affair? Or was the idea ridiculous? He pushed his way toward the far side of the room where he thought he could see the telltale glint of Titian hair. God damn it! She *couldn't* be having an affair with Nicholson! He was too taciturn. Too strait-laced. Sir Denholm Gresby detained Derry, wanting to know if it was true that Ronnie's horse was odds-on favorite for Saturday's race. Derry didn't know and didn't care. A peal of delighted laughter confirmed that it *was* Julienne in the center of the nearby dinner-jacketed group, and as he approached them he saw that one of the dinner jackets belonged to Tom Nicholson.

He pushed his way determinedly to her side.

"*Alors, chéri!* How lovely to see you!" Julienne said uninhibitedly, kissing him on the cheek. "You know Tom, don't you? And Charles Mills, and Graham Storey . . ."

"I want to talk to you!" he whispered harshly in her ear.

"Later, *chéri*. For the moment I have to be the hostess." Her voice was regretful. When Derry approached her in a crowded room with that look in his eye and that tone in his voice, it meant not that he wanted to talk to her, as he said, but that he wanted a quick, reckless coupling in a bathroom, or a convenient bedroom.

The last such exhilarating escapade had been when they had excused themselves from the table at a mutual friend's dinner party. The nearest available room had been a spare guest room, the bed piled high with coats. Julienne had been fascinated to discover, as she rearranged her lingerie, that the topmost coat on which they had just fornicated belonged to Miriam Gresby. Ever since, whenever she had seen it on its owner's back, she had eyed it with affection and a dimpling smile of reminiscence.

"To hell with being a hostess!" Derry said in a savage, low voice. "I need to talk to you, Julienne!"

She shook her head firmly. *"Non!"* she said, turning away from him to greet Melissa who had just entered the room. "Later, *chéri!*"

There was nothing he could do. Tom Nicholson was regarding him coldly. Mills and Storey were eyeing him curiously, and his sister was approaching them, wearing a dazzling red chiffon dress and something of her old sparkle.

"Nice to see you out and about," he said to her after Julienne had kissed her and completed the introductions.

"Nice to *be* out and about," she said dryly. Both of them knew that since her return from the New Territories, she had not been inundated with party and dinner invitations. The truth, not believed at the time of the trial, had since gained credence. Melissa Elliot *was* a heroin addict. The fact that she had apparently beaten her addiction cut no ice with the leaders of European Hong Kong society. They had been extremely reluctant to welcome her back into the fold, and social invitations had been few and far between. It had been Julienne, inviting her to join parties at the racecourse, at the beach, at the tennis club, that had turned the tide.

"I say, you're looking pretty gorgeous," Ronnie said to her, coming up to them and slipping his arm around her shoulders. "How about coming out onto the terrace for a dance?"

He was wearing a sharkskin suit, a silk shirt, and handmade shoes. His blond hair was glossily slicked back, his moustache was meticulously trimmed. There had been a time when Melissa had referred to him disparagingly as an upper-class spiv. She did so no longer. Beneath his heavy-handed flirtatiousness was an easygoing tolerance, and tolerance was a quality she had begun to appreciate.

They wove their way through the crowd toward the terrace, and Derry turned once more to Julienne. She was deep in conversation with Tom Nicholson, and he ground his teeth frustratedly. God damn it! What on earth did she see in the man? And why didn't Ronnie put a stop to it? Was he blind?

The conversation showed no sign of coming to a conclusion and was obviously one that would not welcome interruption. He turned away bad-temperedly, in search of another drink. The present state of affairs couldn't continue. He would have to have a serious talk with Julienne and soon.

"It really would be a favor to me, *chéri*," Julienne was saying, her pansy-dark eyes holding Tom's.

"What? Taking Melissa Elliot to the Government House dinner?"

"I know you've been invited . . ." she continued coaxingly.

"And don't intend to go."

"It is exactly the sort of function that Melissa needs to be seen at again. She has suffered very much, *chéri*, since that terrible trial. Even Raefe has said how very gallant she has been."

"I'm sure she has, but I can't see that it's any reason for me—"

Julienne squeezed his arm lovingly. "It is not nice to be a social outcast, Tom. Nor to be lonely, especially when one is so unaccustomed to it. I think you will find the new Melissa very different from the old Melissa."

"I should hope so," Tom said feelingly. "The old Melissa would have eaten me for breakfast!"

Julienne giggled. "The new Melissa will not do so. I think you will like her very much. She needs someone strong to help her not to care about the gossip and the wagging tongues."

"All right," he said reluctantly. "I'll take her to the Government House dinner, but after that she's on her own again, Julienne. I'm not going to make a habit of squiring her around."

"Of course not," Julienne said demurely. "And now, *chéri*, I think that it is time that we talked about ourselves. There is something that I have to tell you . . ."

It was not quite so easy explaining to Derry that their affair was over and that she was, in the future, going to be a faithful wife. They were in one of the upstairs bathrooms, the door securely locked against all those needing its facilities.

"Use the bathroom downstairs!" Derry roared in answer to an inquiring knock upon the door. There was the sound of aggrieved indignation, then a defeated retreat. "I don't believe you!" he repeated, a perplexed expression on his handsome, rawboned face. "Why is it over? Nothing has gone wrong between us, has it?"

"No, *chéri*. Everything has been most wonderful," Julienne said sincerely.

"Then why, in God's name . . . ?" He ran a hand through his thick sun-bleached hair, struggling for understanding.

"I am twenty-seven," Julienne said with a slight shrug. "It is time I began to think about settling down, of perhaps becoming a mother."

"You can become a mother anytime you want," he said with a sudden grin, refusing to take her seriously. "Right now, this very minute, would be as good a time as any!"

He had her pinned against the sink and he lifted her skirt, pressing close against her.

"No, *chéri*," she murmured regretfully, refusing to capitulate to the delicious tide of sensations he was arousing. "No more. It is over. Finished."

His grin vanished. Concern began to replace perplexity. "You're joking, Julienne. You have to be. This is just another cock-tease, isn't it?"

She shook her head, wishing that it was. "No, Derry," she said, her accent rolling his name in a way that made his scalp tingle. "No, I have made up my mind. It is sad, but it is necessary."

He looked down at her in horror. "You can't do this to me, Julienne! I love you! I want to marry you!"

She giggled, touching his face lovingly. "I do not think it would be a very good marriage, *chéri*. I would be always knocking on the doors of cloakrooms and bathrooms, trying to retrieve you!"

He had the grace to grin slightly. He couldn't quite imagine Julienne in the role of the slighted wife. "I do love you, Julienne," he said thickly. "I've never enjoyed anything as much as I have the time we've spent together."

"It has been very special," she agreed, knowing that the hardest part was over and that all that remained was to say good-bye.

He hesitated, then asked suspiciously, "You're not having an affair with Tom Nicholson, are you, Julienne?"

Her eyes held his steadily. "No," she said emphatically. "How can you think such a thing?"

"Promise?"

"I promise." It was true. She wasn't. Not any longer.

He frowned. At least he wasn't being jilted in favor of someone else. And he might not be jilted for very long.

Julienne would surely get bored with faithfulness and then they could continue their affair as before. He decided to take advantage of the present and not worry about the future. "If we're going to say good-bye, then we'd better make the last time very good indeed," he growled, his arms tightening around her.

She pressed her hands against his chest, pushing him away. "*Non*! Truly, I meant it when I said I was not going to be unfaithful to Ronnie again!"

"You *can't* mean it, Julienne!" His voice was agonized.

From the far side of the door could be heard the sounds of people impatiently lining up for the bathroom. Her mouth quirked at the corners. "I shall keep my word, *chéri*, but I shall also say good-bye in a way you will like very, very much." And she slipped down onto her knees before him, her fingers reaching for the fly of his trousers, her tongue moistening her lips in delicious anticipation.

In June Raefe said to Elizabeth as he drove her to Li Pi's Kowloon flat, "I saw Lamoon Sheng yesterday."

She twisted sharply toward him. "You did? Where? Who was she with? Did you manage to speak to her?"

He shook his head, a lock of dark hair tumbling low across his brow. "No. She was with a prosperously dressed Chinese. They were crossing Des Voeux Road."

He didn't tell her that the Chinese had been holding Lamoon's arm in a viciously tight grip, or that Lamoon had looked like death, her face gaunt, her eyes wretched.

"Does this mean she's living at home again? That even if she isn't allowed to socialize with Europeans, we can at least write to her?"

Raefe bore left on the road curving around Chai Wan. "I doubt it," he said somberly. "I made a few discreet inquiries after I saw her. The man she was with is a distant cousin. He's also her husband."

"Oh!" Elizabeth sank back into her seat, deflated. "Then her father *did* force her into marriage." She was silent as they motored on toward Shau Kei Wan. After a little while she said hopefully, "Perhaps her marriage isn't too unhappy. If he is also a cousin, then presumably she has known him a long time. She may even be happy."

Raefe said nothing. He had seen at a glance that Lamoon was not happy, but he didn't want to distress Elizabeth unnecessarily. It wasn't as if they could do a damned thing about it.

After a little while Elizabeth asked, "Will you tell Tom?"

Raefe changed gear and swept down toward Wanchai. It was a question he had considered long and hard. "No," he said as he overtook a taxicab. "What good can it do? He's going out with Melissa now, and if I told him that Lamoon was back in Hong Kong . . ." He shrugged expressively. "It might spoil things between them and I wouldn't want that."

"But if Lamoon is back in Hong Kong, surely other people will see her and tell him? He might even see her himself."

Raefe shook his head. "I doubt it. For one thing, I don't think this is anything but the briefest of family visits. For another, as a traditional Chinese wife, she isn't going to be seen in public very often."

"But we must let him know that she's alive," Elizabeth persisted.

A trolley bus rattled along beside them, crammed to the doors with strap-hanging Chinese.

"And that she's married?" Raefe asked, looking at her questioningly.

Elizabeth hesitated, then nodded. "Yes. It's best that he knows. He has to realize that it's finally over. That she will never be able to return to him."

In August Elizabeth gave her first concert performance since leaving London. She had been ready to do so for a long time. At the Imperial Concert Hall, in front of the largest audience the Imperial had seen for several months, she played a selection of works by Mozart, Rachmaninov, and Berlioz. The music critic of the *Hong Kong Times* was ecstatic, writing that it was "an outstanding performance played with the utmost skill and grace," and that her piano playing "glowed with rare vitality."

Friends who had thought they knew her quite well were stunned by the enormity of her talent. They had expected to hear a few party pieces nicely executed. They had not expected to hear a Mozart piano concerto and Rachmaninov's Rhapsody on a theme of Paganini played with almost terrifying assurance.

Miriam Gresby decided it would no longer be socially

wise to continue shunning her. At the party afterward, in
the Hong Kong Hotel, she maneuvered herself to the front
of Elizabeth's admirers and said gushingly, "What a *wonderful* performance, my dear! I remember when I first heard
you play, within hours of your arrival in the colony. I said
then to Denholm that you were *outstandingly* gifted. I'm
having a small dinner party next week. I'm hoping that the
governor will be in attendance, and perhaps the French
attaché. I would so much appreciate it if you could join us."

"I'm sorry, Miriam," Elizabeth said with commendable
politeness, "but I have commitments next week. Perhaps
another time?"

"Oh, but I could change the date . . ." Miriam Gresby
began, but Elizabeth was already talking to someone else.
She drew in a sharp, angry breath, knowing that she had
been snubbed. To her dismay, she saw that Major General
Grasett was among those waiting to give Elizabeth his
congratulations. There was no way, if she was to maintain
her position as a leader of Hong Kong society, that
Elizabeth could remain absent from her dinner table. She
would just have to swallow her pride and approach her at a
later date. She turned away, smiling stiffly at those around
her, murmuring, "*Wonderful* piano playing, wasn't it? Of
course, I've heard her play privately *many* times before."

Julienne Ledsham was standing with her husband on the
fringe of the throng. Miriam's smile remained fixed. She
didn't like Julienne Ledsham but Julienne was a very close
friend of Elizabeth's. Perhaps if she invited the Ledshams
to dinner as well . . .

"What a *glorious* evening it has been," she said to
Julienne, wondering how anyone with red hair could
possibly get away with a dress of searing pink. "I've always
known that Elizabeth was *very* talented, of course."

"Oh, but of course," Julienne said, her lips twitching in a
smile. "That is a very lovely coat, Miriam." She touched
the sealskin lightly with her forefinger. "I imagine it is a
coat that can give great pleasure, *n'est-ce pas?*"

Miriam looked at her as if she were mad. Allowances had
to be made for the fact that Julienne was a foreigner and
that often her English left a great deal to be desired, but
really! Sometimes she was incomprehensible.

"It is a very *serviceable* coat," she said, wondering if
Julienne was somehow making fun of it. "I find sealskin
the only possible fur in a climate like this."

"*Mais oui*, I quite agree," Julienne said, her eyes sparkling wickedly. "It is *very* comfortable indeed!"

"What was all that rot about Miriam Gresby's coat?" Ronnie asked as they moved away and toward Elizabeth.

"Nothing for you to worry about, *mon amour*," she said, tucking her arm in his. "Nothing at all."

For many long months the news from Europe continued to be grim. After the surrender of Tobruk to the Allies in January, Rommel had mounted an advance against it. By April the city and port were isolated, the remainder of the Allied force having retreated to the Egyptian border. It was still under siege. In the skies above Germany, RAF bombers continued to make nighttime sorties, their losses heavy. Roman was a member of the 249th Squadron, flying a Hurricane. They received a card from him in September and then, after that, there was nothing.

"Do you think he's still alive?" Elizabeth asked Raefe anxiously. "What are his chances?"

Raefe had just returned from an intelligence meeting at Fort Canning and his face was tired and drawn. "Not good," he said solemnly.

To the best of his knowledge Roman had been on active operations since August, and he knew that the average life span of a pilot was only three months. It was a statistic that didn't bear thinking about.

In November, the aircraft carrier *Ark Royal* was sunk by U-boats, and the Germans were at the gates of Leningrad.

"It's not going to be a very jolly Christmas, is it?" Helena said to Elizabeth as Elizabeth drove her back to her Kowloon flat after one of the auxiliary nursing meetings.

"There's the Chinese Charity Ball at the Pen tomorrow night," Elizabeth said, trying to look on the bright side of things. "Alastair is coming, isn't he?"

"Yes, if he can. There's been something of a fuss this last day or two. Rumors that the Japanese are building up their forces beyond the border."

"We've had those rumors before," Elizabeth said cynically.

"Yes, I know." The Buick's top was down and Helena pushed her windblown hair away from her face. "The trouble is, we've heard the cry 'wolf' so often, we may not take any notice when it's the real thing. And then we may get taken by surprise. It's not a very nice thought, is it?"

"Major General Maltby isn't the kind of man to be taken by surprise," Elizabeth said. "His last command was the Northwest Frontier!"

Helena chuckled. Major General Maltby had replaced Major General Grasett a month ago and had made an immediate good impression among both troops and civilians. "He's rather nice, isn't he? Very English and very correct."

Smiling, Elizabeth agreed as she drew up outside Helena's block of flats. As she stepped from the car, Helena asked, "Are you going to Happy Valley tomorrow to watch Ronnie's horse run?"

Elizabeth shook her head. The nursing classes she now attended had wrought havoc with her disciplined hours of piano practice. The time had to be made up and she was going to do that to an extent the following afternoon. "No. I'll see you at the Peninsula tomorrow night. 'Bye, Helena."

She drew away from the curb and into the mainstream of traffic, humming beneath her breath. The world situation was ghastly, but her own personal situation was blissful. She wasn't sure yet, but she was almost certain that she was pregnant again. "There'll always be an England," she began to sing softly to herself. "And England will be free. As long as England means to you what England means to me." It was the song they sang every Sunday lunchtime when they all met for drinks at the Repulse Bay Hotel.

Her hands tightened on the steering wheel as she thought of Roman and of the men like him, fighting lone battles in the sky, facing enemy flak night after night. "Please be safe, Roman," she whispered as she drove toward the Star Ferry Pier. "Please, *please* be safe!"

Chapter Twenty-four

꧂

*T*HE Chinese Charity Ball at the Peninsula had been named the "Tin Hat Ball." Its purpose was to raise £160,000 toward the purchase of bombers, which Hong Kong then intended to present to Britain. As Elizabeth parked Raefe's Lagonda and walked into the brightly lit lobby, she wondered if the ball would achieve its objective.

She had spent all morning and afternoon at the piano, and her back and wrists ached. If Raefe had been at home she knew she would have been tempted to stay there and miss the ball. As it was, he had been at an intelligence meeting at Government House since early morning and had arranged that, instead of coming home, he would meet up with her at the Pen.

As she walked into the ballroom she saw her reflection in one of the giant gilt-framed mirrors. She had begun to wear her hair down again, and it fell in a long, smooth wave to her shoulders, pushed away from her face on one side with a tortoiseshell comb. Her dress was of cream silk, the skirt falling sensuously over her hips to midcalf in a swirl of soft pleats. Three long strands of enormous pearls hung from her neck at precisely the right depth of the softly draped neckline. They had been her first present from Raefe and she wore them at every possible opportunity. She stepped into the ballroom, the silk of her skirt rustling softly against her legs.

Julienne and Ronnie, and Helena and Alastair were seated at a large round table at the far end of the room. Tom Nicholson was also at the table, and with an involuntary tightening of her stomach muscles she wondered where Melissa was. Julienne had never, as yet, invited Tom and Melissa to any gathering at which she and Raefe would also be present, and she was sure that Tom was equally careful.

As she approached them, Ronnie rose to his feet, pulling back a chair for her, and Julienne said lightly, "*Chérie*, how lovely to see you! You're looking wonderful!" Her gaze flicked curiously from Elizabeth to the door. "But where is Raefe? I understood he was coming too."

"He's at a business meeting. He's coming straight on here when it finishes." Raefe's frequent visits to Government House were a closely guarded secret.

"That is a pity," Julienne said with genuine regret. "But you will be able to keep Tom company. Melissa has at last decided that she is going to leave Hong Kong for America, and she has gone to the New Territories, to the farm, to collect the things she wishes to take with her and to arrange for her other possessions to be put into storage."

Elizabeth breathed a faint sigh of relief. She was not at all apprehensive about meeting Melissa, but she hoped that when she finally did so, the occasion would not be quite so public.

Julienne was wearing a turquoise satin, ankle-length gown lavishly encrusted with crystals and beads. The bodice was very décolleté, revealing the lush ripeness of her breasts, and the back plunged to her waist. Her fox-red hair was a short, riotous mass of curls, tiny tendrils springing forward and lying seductively against her cheeks.

"We are all morose," Julienne continued, not looking in the slightest morose. "Ronnie's horse behaved very badly this afternoon. He was, I think, not very well." She began to giggle. "I saw Sir Denholm placing a bet at the five-hundred-dollar window. I think perhaps he is very angry with Ronnie."

"So are a lot of other people," Tom said dryly. "Old Gresby wasn't the only one putting a packet on that wretched horse."

Both Ronnie and Julienne looked blithely unconcerned and Elizabeth was sure that neither of them had staked any of their money on their own horse, or had lost any.

"What was the Middlesex rugger match like?" she asked Alastair, changing the subject. "You were there this afternoon, weren't you?"

"The Middlesex have a long way to go before they play a

game of rugger equal to the game played by the Royal Scots," Alastair said with a grin. "Still, it wasn't a bad game all in all."

Rivalry between the 1st Middlesex and the 2nd Royal Scots was intense, with the Royal Scots considering themselves vastly superior.

Ronnie hooted with laughter. "My God, Alastair! The Middlesex can thrash the Royal Scots to pulp on a rugger pitch and you know it!"

A waiter, depositing a fresh round of drinks on the table, mercifully subdued Alastair's reply.

The band was playing "It's Only a Paper Moon" and on the crowded dance floor Elizabeth could see Leigh Stafford, dancing very stiffly with Miriam Gresby, and Derry Langdon moving with practiced ease, a diminutive blonde in his arms. Seeing where her gaze was directed, Helena leaned across to her and whispered, "Derry's latest is Anthea Hurley."

"Mark Hurley's wife?"

Helena nodded. Elizabeth looked at the china-doll-pretty Anthea Hurley with interest, well aware that she had once been one of Raefe's girlfriends. She was dancing indecently close to Derry, and Derry, far from looking pleased with the arrangement, was looking distinctly discontented, his gaze roving constantly around the room.

His eyes met hers and shot swiftly from her to Julienne. She saw by the change of expression in their vivid blue depths that he had at last found what he was looking for. The discontent gave place to open misery. Elizabeth looked away from him, feeling sorry for him, but glad that she no longer had to feel sorry for Ronnie.

"What are the two Canadian battalions like, that arrived last month?" Ronnie was asking Alastair, one hand cradling his whiskey and soda, the other resting lightly and proprietarily on Julienne's satin-clad knee. "Are they going to be any good to us if the Japs attack?"

"Any reinforcements are better than none," Alastair said. "And they appeared fit enough when they landed."

"They are extremely confident and well-equipped," Julienne said, deliberately avoiding Derry's pleading gaze. "I saw them just after they disembarked. They were being led through the streets to the Shamshuipo barracks by a magnificent army band. They looked wonderful!"

"Maltby must be grateful for them," Tom said as the band swung into "Blue Moon." "Especially with this current scare."

A cascade of streamers was released, drifting down over the heads of the dancers.

"It still leaves us dangerously under strength," Alastair said, removing a streamer from his shoulders. "And I've a feeling that this situation is the most serious one yet."

Julienne could see Derry making his way determinedly toward their table, Anthea Hurley hurrying in his wake. "Let's dance, *chéri*," she said, her hand closing over Ronnie's. "In a moment there is to be a floor show and then we will not be able to."

Ronnie obligingly rose to his feet and by the time Derry had woven his way through the couples on the dance floor, his quarry had flown.

"Hello, Derry, old boy," Tom said affably. "How's the polo?"

Derry was a renowned player with an incredible nine-goal handicap. "Fine," he said shortly, turning away from them and once more trying to locate Julienne. Since Julienne had terminated their affair his playing on the polo field had suffered. At his last match he had ridden like a barbarian and had been disqualified in the second chukker for "riding at an opponent in such a manner as to intimidate and cause him to pull out." He had been uncaring, his only wish that the player he had unseated had been Ronnie Ledsham.

A breathless Anthea caught up with him and was embarrassingly ignored by him. Tom, aware that she had once been one of Raefe's passing fancies, decided it might be best if she was not still at their table when Raefe joined them. He rose gallantly to his feet. "Would you care to dance, Anthea? I'm wretchedly partnerless at the moment."

Anthea looked at Derry, obviously hoping that he would object, but when no such objection was forthcoming, she had no alternative but to unwillingly acquiesce.

"Why the hell won't Julienne let me speak to her?" Derry said savagely to Elizabeth. "I haven't seen her alone since the night of her party!"

Alastair, who disapproved of all extramarital affairs, was listening to him frozen-faced, and Elizabeth knew that at any moment angry words would be exchanged. "Let's dance," she said to Derry, rising to her feet.

He nodded obligingly, moving with her out onto the dance floor. "I don't understand it," he said gloomily for the thousandth time. "We were happy together. I've never in my life enjoyed myself as much as I did when I was with her. Why has she spoiled everything? Has she suddenly got religion, or fallen sick? What is it?"

As he led her into a smooth quickstep, a smile touched the corners of Elizabeth's mouth. "She certainly hasn't got religion and she isn't sick," she said soothingly. "In fact, I don't think Julienne has changed at all. It is Ronnie who has changed. He still flirts, but he hasn't been seen with another woman for nearly a year now."

"But what has that got to do with Julienne?" Derry demanded, mystified.

"Julienne loves him," Elizabeth said gently as they skimmed past Tom and Anthea Hurley. "She may have fallen in love lightly and often elsewhere, but her love for Ronnie has always been the mainspring of her life. Once she knew that her affairs were beginning to cause him anguish, she ceased having them. It's as simple as that."

"It isn't simple to me," Derry said grimly. "I can't eat, I can't sleep, I can't think. I can't even play a decent game of polo any longer!"

The dance was at an end and it was announced that Miss Hilda Yen was now going to sing for them.

"Let her go, Derry," Elizabeth said to him pleadingly as the couples around them began to return to their tables.

He looked across to where Ronnie was escorting Julienne from the crowded floor. "I can't!" he said fiercely. "God in heaven! I love her, Elizabeth. I *can't* leave her alone!"

The floor was emptying and people were beginning to look in their direction. "You will make her very unhappy if you don't," Elizabeth said soberly, then reluctantly she stepped away from him, leaving him where he stood as she walked back to her table.

Hilda Yen, a beautiful Chinese girl with raven-dark hair streaming silkily to her waist, sang a romantic song in Chinese. While she did so, Elizabeth wondered if her own friends had felt the same despair when she and Raefe had first fallen in love. She empathized totally with Derry. His love for Julienne was dominated by sexual passion and she knew from her own experience that once in the grip of such joyous madness, there was no room for restraint or common sense.

Hilda Yen's song came to an end and was enthusiastically applauded. The dancing continued, and Elizabeth waltzed with Alastair and fox-trotted with Ronnie, waiting hungrily all the while for Raefe to enter the ballroom and stride toward her.

Raefe's expression was grim as he drove through the darkened streets to the Peninsula Hotel. He had trusted his informants, not his own judgment, and it was a mistake he would never forgive himself.

For weeks, all the information he had received from Shanghai and Canton had stated positively that the concentrated Japanese military activity in and around Canton was preparation for an attack on the Chinese city of Kunming, to the northwest. Canton was a mere hundred miles north of Hong Kong and he had not been convinced. He had voiced his doubts to the British at Fort Canning, but the consensus was that any visible Japanese preparations around Canton were more likely to be defensive than aggressive. They were taken note of. Reports were written and reports were filed.

His jaw tightened as he swerved to a halt outside the Peninsula's glitteringly lit Palladian entrance. Defensive be damned. There was now at least a full division of Japs mustering on the border and they were facing south, not north.

He strode into the hotel, cursing himself for not having acted earlier. For not having put Elizabeth on a ship or a plane. For allowing her to remain with him.

"Good evening, Mr. Elliot," a junior manager said respectfully as Raefe crossed the lobby.

"Good evening, sir," a bellboy said with genuine warmth as Raefe continued on his way toward the ballroom. Mr. Elliot was a generous tipper. The bellboy wished there were more like him.

Raefe acknowledged their greetings curtly. He had only minutes in which to speak to Elizabeth before returning to the tense meeting still in progress at Government House. He had excused himself peremptorily, knowing he had to tell her himself that an invasion was imminent. He had to see her. It might be days, even weeks, before he would be able to do so again.

As he entered the crowded ballroom the orchestra was playing "The Best Things in Life Are Free." Ignoring the greetings he received from all sides, he made his way quickly to the far end of the room and the large circular table around which Helena and Alastair, Julienne and Ronnie, and Tom and Elizabeth were sitting.

Elizabeth turned her head at his approach, her face lighting up joyously at the sight of him. "Darling! I thought you were never going to get here!" It was nearly midnight and though she had disguised it beneath smiles and laughter, her anxiety had been growing.

He took her hand, drawing her to her feet, and said low and urgently, "I can't stay, Lizzie. The invasion is imminent. Leave now and return to Victoria. You'll be far safer on the island than you will be this side of the water. Whatever happens, don't be tempted to cross back here. Do you understand me?"

"Yes, but—"

"No 'buts.'" His dark eyes burned hers. "Be safe for me, Lizzie! That's all I ask!"

His arms closed tightly around her, his kiss hard and savage, almost brutal. "I love you!" he said harshly as he drew his head away from hers. Then, before she had the chance to ask where he was going, what he was going to do, he was gone, pushing his way through the laughing couples that thronged the floor.

"Well!" Julienne said, her eyes wide. "What was all *that* about, *chérie*?"

Elizabeth did not answer her. She was still staring after Raefe, fear roaring along her veins. What if anything happened to him? What if he were killed? What if . . . ?

The music came to an abrupt end. The president of the American Steamships Line appeared on the balcony above the dance floor, waving a megaphone for silence. "Your attention, please, ladies and gentlemen! Your attention, please!" he shouted.

Helena and Alastair, Ronnie and Julienne and Tom, who had all been mesmerized by Raefe's sudden appearance and his abrupt, passionate leavetaking of Elizabeth, transferred their attention to him, their smiles and laughter fading.

"Any man connected with any ship in the harbor," the president of the American Steamships Line continued to shout, "report aboard for duty. At once!"

There was a second's unbelieving silence, then scores of chairs were scraped back as men rose hurriedly to their feet, the dance forgotten.

"My God! Is this it?" Ronnie asked, stunned.

"Looks like it," Alastair said grimly. "I'd better be getting back to the barracks." He stood up. "Good-bye, my dear," he said soberly to Helena. "I'll be in touch with you at the earliest opportunity."

She stared at him aghast. All around them men were saying good-bye to wives and sweethearts and making for the doors. As Alastair turned to join them, she pushed her chair away from the table, rising hastily to her feet.

"No! Wait a moment, Alastair!"

He turned and hesitated, and she threw her arms around him, hugging him tightly. "I love you!" she said fiercely. "I know I haven't said it very often lately, but I do, Alastair! Truly I do!"

He didn't speak. He couldn't. He would have wept with relief, for he had begun to believe that she had never loved him and never would. He held her close for a brief, precious moment, and then, his eyes suspiciously bright, he swung on his heel, breaking into a run as he made for the doors.

Julienne and Ronnie, Tom and Elizabeth and Helena stared at one another. The orchestra had begun to play again, but only a few couples had taken to the floor.

"What do we do?" Ronnie asked awkwardly. Both he and Tom were members of the volunteer force. "Do we report for duty, too?"

"I shouldn't think so," Tom said doubtfully. "Not until there's been a more official announcement."

"Raefe said that an invasion was imminent," Elizabeth told them in a low voice. "He also said that when it came, the island would be far safer than Kowloon." She looked at Helena. "You'd better move in with me, Helena. We can go and collect the children now."

Helena shook her head. She was dressed starkly and sophisticatedly in a black cocktail dress, and it did not suit her full-blown beauty. "No," she said stubbornly. "I have to stay in Kowloon. The hospital I have been assigned to is there."

"Whatever happens, the Japs will never fight their way as far south as Kowloon," Tom said, defusing the tension. "All the fighting will be around the border."

Ronnie grinned, his natural buoyancy reasserting itself. "We'll soon shove the little men off," he said confidently. "To tell the truth, if this *is* the real thing, I shall be relieved. The sooner it starts, the sooner it will be over."

Elizabeth rose to her feet. "I'm going home now," she said quietly. "Are you sure you won't come with me, Helena?"

Helena shook her head again. "Positive. By tomorrow everything will have probably blown over. If it has, I'll see you for drinks as usual at the Repulse Bay."

"I hope it blows over," Tom said with a wry smile. "The uniform I've been handed out as a member of the volunteer force isn't exactly Sandhurst standard. The jacket was made for a man half my size and I'm not sure whether the trousers are long shorts or short trousers. Whichever they are, I look ridiculous in them!"

Even Elizabeth found herself laughing as she said her good-byes, but her laughter faded once she was on her journey home. As the ferry made its way across to Victoria she stood in the bow, looking out over the silk-black sea. The Peak was in darkness. She didn't know where Raefe was, or when she would see him again. For the first time since they had moved into it, she did not drive home to their house near Mount Collinson. Instead she drove to the apartment in Victoria. It was more central. Wherever Raefe was, she would be nearer to him there than she would be out near the coast, on the east of the island.

The next morning Victoria seemed, on the surface, much as usual. Elizabeth had a light breakfast and then she telephoned Adam. He hadn't been at the ball the previous evening, and there was still a chance that he knew nothing of the latest rumors.

"Mr. Harland not here," Chan said civilly to her. "Mr. Harland a volunteer. He been called up."

She put down the phone, her earlier optimism diminishing. If the volunteers had indeed been called up and deployed, then it meant things had gone much further than they ever had before.

She made herself a cup of coffee, drank it, and then telephoned Helena. "It looks as if there'll be no prelunch drinks at the Repulse Bay today," Helena said wryly. "The whole garrison has been ordered to battle positions, the volunteers included. The Royal Scots are on the mainland, up near the border. The volunteers are somewhere on the island. It's all beginning to look extremely grim."

"Don't you think you should bring the children over here and all of you stay with me?" Elizabeth said again. "I'm at the apartment in Victoria, not the house. You can travel by ferry to the hospital each day quite easily."

"Not yet," Helena said again, obstinately.

"But why?"

"It looks so cowardly," Helena said briefly. "Can you imagine the panic among the Chinese community of Kowloon if all the Europeans did a quick flit across to the island? There would be pandemonium."

Elizabeth didn't argue with her. She had met that note of obstinacy in Helena's voice before and knew that arguing was useless. And, at the moment, there was no imminent danger. Whatever fighting took place would be as Ronnie had said, far to the north of the New Territories, in and around Fanling.

She suddenly went cold, remembering Melissa. "Oh, my God," she whispered. "Melissa . . ."

"What about Melissa?" Helena had not overheard Julienne and Elizabeth's conversation the previous evening.

"She's out at the farm." Elizabeth had no need to say any more. Everyone knew that Melissa had spent much of the last two years living on the isolated Elliot farm in the New Territories.

"Does Raefe know she's there?" Helena asked sharply.

"I don't know. He might. I have to go, Helena. I have to try to get in touch with him!"

She put down the receiver with a crash. Where could she start? Government House? Flagstaff House? Fortress Headquarters? Where was he likely to be? Hastily she dialed the number for Government House and a harassed male switchboard operator answered the call.

"Could you tell me if Mr. Elliot is at Government House, please?"

"I'm sorry, ma'am, there's an emergency on. No private calls are being taken."

"This is very urgent! I have to know if he is there or not. If he is, then I can leave a message."

"I'm sorry, ma'am, but—"

"Then please could I speak to Sir Mark Young?" Elizabeth said in her best accent. "It is Elizabeth Harland speaking."

The switchboard operator hesitated. He had heard of Elizabeth Harland and remembered seeing a photograph of her in the *Hong Kong Times*. She had been at a dinner and the gentleman sitting next to her had been the governor.

"I'll see what I can do, Mrs. Harland," he said doubtfully. "Please hold the line."

It was nearly ten minutes before the switchboard operator came back to her. "Mr. Elliot is here, Mrs. Harland, but he is in conference and there is no way he can be disturbed."

Elizabeth felt her anxiety begin to ease. "Please give him a message for me. Tell him that Mrs. Elliot is at the farm in the New Territories. Have you got that?"

"Yes, Mrs. Harland." The switchboard operator was beginning to understand her concern. If the rumors flying around Government House were true, the last place on earth any woman should be was on a farm out in the New Territories. "I'll most certainly see to it that he gets the message," he said reassuringly.

"Perhaps if you telephoned me back . . ."

"Yes, Mrs. Harland. I'll do that." The switchboard operator had also remembered that Elizabeth Harland was the stunning, ice-cool blonde who had caused such a sensation at the Imperial a few weeks ago.

It was half an hour before he called back. The message had been passed on to Mr. Elliot. Elizabeth thanked him, then made two more telephone calls. One was to Mei Lin, telling her that she would be staying in the flat in Victoria for the next few days and asking her to join her there. The other was to her nursing station. There was no need for her to report for duty as yet, but they would appreciate it if she would stand by in readiness.

It was the strangest Sunday in Hong Kong she had ever experienced. There were no prelunch drinks at the Repulse Bay Hotel, no parties, no gossip, no water picnics. All the men, including the volunteers, were at battle stations. She wondered where Adam was. Alastair had told Helena that the volunteers were being deployed on the island and not the mainland. Presumably he would be stationed somewhere on the coast.

When she went for a walk in the afternoon she could see Royal Navy motor torpedo boats out at sea, guarding the approaches to the colony. The sight sent a shiver of apprehension down her spine. After so many years of speculation, it seemed that those who had always said the Japanese would eventually attack had been proved right. Certainly the Chinese thought so. They stood in huddled, anxious groups, saying to her as she passed by them, "Is it true the Japanese come soon, missy?" "Who look after us when the Japanese come?"

"The Japanese will never reach Hong Kong island," she said reassuringly, but the Chinese continued to look anxious. For years the Japanese had ravaged China. They knew very well what to expect if the Japanese also overran Hong Kong. The pictures of Japanese soldiers in Manchuria gleefully bayonetting Chinese prisoners had been widely circulated among the Chinese community.

Mei Lin arrived at teatime, not asking where Raefe was or why Elizabeth had decided to spend the next few days in Victoria. She immediately began to prepare a light meal for Elizabeth, grateful that she hadn't been left in isolation on the east coast.

In the evening Elizabeth read through a Moszkowski score and then, unable to concentrate properly, she wandered over to the French windows. She threw them open and stepped out onto the veranda, looking down over the rooftops of Victoria to the bay. The evening was warm and scented with hardly a breath of air, the setting sun a riot of crimson and vermilion and vivid streaks of yellow. The stillness was unpleasantly reminiscent of the threatening calm before a typhoon. She returned to the music score, trying not to wonder where Raefe was, where Adam was. In a few days, if the experts were to be believed, the Japanese would have attacked and been repulsed and life would return to normal. She could only pray that when it did so, Raefe and Adam, and Alastair and Tom and Ronnie, would all be safe.

She slept restlessly, disturbed by the heat and the atmosphere of waiting and watching. At seven o'clock, after lying awake for two hours, she gave up all hope of further sleep and, wrapping a cotton dressing gown over her nightdress, wandered into the sitting room. She drew back the drapes and looked once more out across the bay.

"Would you like coffee and scrambled egg, missy?" Mei Lin asked, hurrying from her own room to be of service.

"No eggs, Mei Lin. Just coffee and toast, please."

At seven-thirty Mei Lin went down into the street to buy the morning paper. This was usually the houseboy's task, but since he was still at the main house and since Mrs. Elliot had not asked him to move to Victoria, it was a task Mei Lin happily imposed on herself. When she arrived back at the flat, she was breathless and terrified.

"We are at war, missy! We are at war with Japan!"

Elizabeth snatched the newspaper, but the only reference to Japan was a small paragraph on the front page reporting that Japanese transport ships had been sighted off Thailand.

"Not the paper, missy!" Mei Lin gasped, trembling violently. "A policeman told me. He say we've been at war with Japan since quarter to five this morning!"

Elizabeth dropped the paper. If it was true, then she had to report immediately to her nursing station. "Make some more coffee, Mei Lin," she said. She hurried into the bedroom and quickly slipped out of her dressing gown and nightdress. "I'm going straight to the Jockey Club. I want you to stay here, do you understand?"

It had been arranged months ago that the Jockey Club would serve as a relief hospital. At least it wasn't far to drive.

"Yes, missy, anything you say, missy," Mei Lin said, bringing the coffee into the bedroom. "Do you think—"

A loud crescendo of noise ripped through the still morning air. The coffee cup crashed to the floor, steaming hot liquid seeping into the carpet.

"They're coming, missy!" Mei Lin screamed, pressing her hands over her ears. *"Oh, what have we to do? We will all be killed!"*

"Don't be silly!" Elizabeth said sharply, bending down and picking up the broken pieces of china. "It's only the air raid warning. You've heard practice alerts before!"

Mei Lin began to cry. Not like this she hadn't. Not at eight o'clock in the morning. "No, missy!" she protested vehemently. "The Japanese are coming! *Look!*"

She was pointing to the window and Elizabeth turned swiftly, just in time to see fighter planes hurtling down on Kai Tak Airport. Her first desperate hope was that they were Royal Air Force planes on maneuvers, but then the bombs began to rain down, sheets of flame shooting skyward.

"Oh, my God!" she gasped, dragging on her skirt and her blouse. "Put your tin hat on, Mei Lin, and stay indoors!"

"Don't leave me, missy! Please don't leave me!" Mei Lin sobbed as Elizabeth grabbed her own tin hat and began to run toward the door.

"You'll be perfectly all right here," Elizabeth shouted back over her shoulder. "They're bombing the airport, not the residential areas! Just stay indoors till it quiets down!"

She slammed the door shut after her and ran out into the street. She had left the Lagonda parked by the curb the previous evening, having been too tired to garage it. Now she jumped in and roared the engine to life. She was wrong when she told Mei Lin that the Japanese were only bombing the airport. Bombs were raining down on Kowloon now, columns of smoke billowing skyward. She thought of the hundreds of Chinese refugees cramming the narrow streets and fought back a sob of rage. The casualties would be appalling, and this was only the beginning. God only knew what was to come in its wake.

Chapter Twenty-five
❦

*F*OR eight hours Raefe could do nothing about the message he had received. When at last the strategy meeting he was attending drew to a close, it was ten o'clock at night. He requisitioned a Jeep and, ignoring the request that he remain at Government House throughout the night, he drove at high speed through the darkened streets toward the ferry.

He knew that the Royal Scots were at battle stations in the north of the New Territories, and he knew that a platoon of Punjabis and the Volunteer Field Engineers had been given instructions to blow up all bridges that would give the Japanese access to the south. If the bridges were blown up before he could return with Melissa, then the two of them would be helplessly trapped in the path of the advancing Japanese.

The eight-minute crossing seemed interminable. The instant the ferry docked he revved the Jeep's engine. His foot pressing down hard on the accelerator, he careened through Kowloon's narrow streets, making for the Tai Po road leading north. He was stopped over half a dozen times by army patrols, but his identity card and rank as an intelligence officer ensured he was detained for only seconds.

Inky darkness pressed in all around him as he hurtled north. God, what a fool he'd been not to warn Melissa not to leave the Peak. He knew she had finally made up her mind to leave, but it had never occurred to him that she would return to the farm to collect any of her possessions. Mountain peaks pierced the skyline in black silhouette. At Pineapple Pass, just north of Tai Po, he was stopped by a large contingent of Royal Scots who warned him that the nearby railway line was soon to be blown and the road impassably blocked.

By the time he reached the farm it was nearly two o'clock. There were no lights on, no signs of life, but the minute his Jeep approached the houseboys tumbled out into the darkness, their hands high in the air, certain they were being overrun by Japanese.

"Is Mrs. Elliot here?" he asked, vaulting from the Jeep and running toward them.

"Oh, yes, *tuan!* Missy Elliot asleep. Take us back with you, *tuan!* Japanese come, but Missy Elliot no believe us!"

He ignored them, slamming his way into the house. Taking the wide stairs two at a time, he shouted, "Melissa! *Melissa!*"

She stumbled from the bedroom as he ran down the broad hall toward her. "What on earth . . ." she began. Her hair was tousled, her eyes glazed by sleep.

"We're at war with the Japs!" he said tersely, seizing her arm and propelling her back into the room. "Get dressed!

The Tai Po road is about to be blocked and the bridges
blown!" As he was speaking he was rifling through her
wardrobe, tossing a skirt and a sweater toward her.

"But my things!" she protested dazedly. "I haven't
finished packing yet."

"There's no time now, not unless you want to ask the
Japs to help you!"

She stared at him as realization of their danger dawned,
then she hurriedly began to slip her arms out of her
negligee.

"I'll be waiting for you in the Jeep," he said curtly,
turning away from her. "Be quick, Mel! Every second is
vital."

The moment he was out of the room she slipped her
nightdress over her head and pulled on her underclothes,
trembling in her haste.

Raefe hurried down the stairs, calling for the houseboy.
"Is anyone else on the premises?" he asked the servants as
they stood shivering in the doorway.

"No, *tuan*, only us. Please, *tuan*, can we—"

"Get in the Jeep," Raefe said tersely.

They obeyed with alacrity. Raefe followed them, revving
the engine into life. Where the hell was Melissa? It was at
least five minutes since he had left her. Just as he was about
to furiously go in search of her, she came running out of the
house, her hair still dishevelled, the buttons of her blouse
undone, her jacket in her arms.

Even before she had slammed the Jeep's door behind her,
Raefe was driving off, bucketing over the dusty track that
led to the road, fearful that at any moment he would hear
the dull blast of the Tai Po road being demolished.

"When did you hear the news?" Melissa asked, gasping
as she pulled her jacket around her shoulders.

"We haven't yet, officially, but it's no false alarm. There
are at least two battalions of Japs only a couple of miles to
the north. They'll be fighting their way south within
hours."

"Oh, God." She held on tight to the door as the Jeep
rocked and careened around potholes and gullies carved
by heavy rain. "Where is Tom? Do you know?"

He shook his head. "No. The volunteers are all on the
island, except for the Field Engineers. They're out here

with the Royal Scots and the Punjabis, demolishing bridges and making movement difficult for the Japs."

The Jeep thudded onto a smoother road surface, and Raefe pressed his foot down hard on the accelerator. No one knew he had left Government House. With luck, if the Japs held off till daylight, he could be back without anyone's being any the wiser about his absence.

"How did you know I was out here?" Melissa asked as they thundered toward Tai Po.

"Lizzie phoned me. I was in a strategy meeting. There wasn't a damn thing I could do about it for hours. Why the hell did you come up here alone? You must have heard the rumors."

"I've been hearing rumors for over two years," she said defensively. "How did Elizabeth know where I was?"

He swerved to avoid a pothole. "She was at the Chinese Charity Ball at the Pen on Saturday night. Everyone was there, Julienne included."

There came the sound of a dull explosion in the distance and she sensed his knuckles tightening on the wheel. She bit her lower lip. He had known the risks he was taking when he'd driven out for her, and yet he had done so unhesitatingly. When Elizabeth Harland had informed him of where she was, she must have known what he would do. Melissa hugged her arms around herself, knowing that if she had been in Elizabeth's place she would never have told him.

"We've about another half mile to go before we reach the pass," he said, and as he spoke his headlights picked out large heavy rolls of barbed wire coiling across the road. He swore vehemently and slammed on his brakes, skidding to a halt. Melissa was thrown violently against the dashboard and one of the Chinese toppled from the rear jump seat and into the road. The vicious wire was all around them and Raefe shouted at the Chinese to stay where he was and not to move.

"Can we get free of it?" Melissa asked fearfully.

Raefe yanked open the glove compartment. There was a wrench and a pair of pliers. A very small pair of pliers. "God knows," he said grimly. "Can you yank the sleeves out of your jacket so that I can wrap them around my hands?"

She did so, her heart in her mouth as he began to work, inch by inch, severing the wire that was jammed up against his driver's door, edging his way out of the Jeep, slowly and bloodily cutting and clipping.

It was an hour before he furiously kicked the last remaining section of wire away. As he did so there came the sound of another explosion, this time behind them, to the north. Neither of them spoke. If it was the bridge over the Sham Chun that had been blown, it would make no difference to their journey to Kowloon. But if the blowing of the Sham Chun was a signal for the other objectives to be demolished, then they would find themselves on the wrong side of a mass of impassable rubble.

It seemed an eternity before Raefe said with relief, "Whatever the hell it was they just detonated, it wasn't the railway or the road." In the light of his headlights the entrance to the pass loomed eerily, the troops still standing by like wraiths. They waved him down and he skidded to a halt, flashing his pass.

"You've only just made it, sir," one of the soldiers said respectfully. "We're all set to blow the line the minute the word comes through."

"Is the rest of the way clear into Kowloon?"

"Yes, sir."

Raefe pressed his foot once more on the accelerator. They were going to make it. A half mile farther on there was an ear-splitting crack and the Jeep veered violently out of control as a front tire burst.

He fought down his rising frustration, bringing the Jeep under control and bumping to a halt. "Will it take long to change the tire?" Melissa asked nervously as he sprang to the ground.

There was a moment's silence, then he said savagely, "It wouldn't, if we *had* a spare tire, but it looks as if we're the victims of a goddamn fifth columnist."

"But we're not in danger now, are we? I mean, the road is clear behind us and the Japs certainly won't be bowling down behind us. Not with the Royal Scots out in strength."

He grunted agreement, his immediate problem not the Japanese but his superiors who would soon be wanting to know where the hell he was.

The remainder of the journey was conducted at a snail's pace and it was nearly eight o'clock by the time they crawled into Kowloon's crowded outskirts.

"I'm going to dump this and put you in the first taxi I

see," he said, then was deafened by the screaming approach of planes, wave after wave of them, hurtling down from the north toward Kai Tak.

There was no time for them to take shelter. Split seconds later bombs rained down on the airfield, then a plane wheeled away from the others, swooping low over Kowloon. Raefe jammed on the brakes, shouting to the Chinese to run for cover. As he grabbed Melissa's hand, dragging her from the Jeep, there was a terrific whistling sound, then the crash of an exploding bomb blasted their eardrums. There were other planes screaming overhead now, and bombs were falling directly in their path. There was a culvert at the side of the road and Raefe threw Melissa down beside it, rolling on top of her as the bombs cracked the street wide open. He was deafened by the crash of impact, by screams; blinded by dust and thick, black, acrid smoke.

An eternity later he raised his head and looked back across the road. The Jeep was a flaming mass of twisted metal. Chinese were running in all directions, some with their clothes on fire, some with blood pouring down their faces.

Melissa was sobbing hysterically beneath him, her hands pressed desperately over her ears. Another plane dive-bombed and he ducked his head, tightening his hold on her and then, as the explosion thundered in his ears, he was wrenched away from her, lifted bodily into the air and slammed down twenty yards away in the middle of the blazing road.

He choked for breath, heat searing the back of his throat, dust filling his mouth. As he stumbled to his knees amid billowing smoke, he half fell against a soft, moist object. He looked down at it, swaying dizzily. It was an arm, bloodily severed from the shoulder. He clapped his right arm to his left, reassuring himself that they were both still intact, then he saw the bleeding body to his right. It was a Chinese, still alive, screaming frenziedly, his arm and shoulder socket a hideous black hole.

He staggered to his feet and ran back between burning cars to the culvert and Melissa. She was lying facedown, part of her skirt and blouse ripped from her body, blood pouring from a gash in her head. He felt her pulse, then ripped another length of material from her torn skirt, made a pad with his handkerchief, and bandaged it clumsily in place. He had to get her to a hospital, and the hospitals would be crammed with the Chinese victims of the attack. Scooping her up in his arms, he ran with her across the road and into a maze of side streets. The Kowloon hospital would be the nearest. It was crazy to wait for an ambulance, even though he could hear their sirens screeching toward him. Glass littered the streets, doors hung crazily askew, sobbing, terrified Chinese ran in all directions. He could taste blood in his mouth and wondered where it was coming from, then he wove around the last corner and into the forecourt of the hospital. A white-coated figure ran toward him.

"What the hell happened?"

"Bombs! A whole stick of them! There must be thirty dead!"

Melissa was swiftly taken from him and placed on a trolley. "Who is she?" the doctor asked as a nursing attendant began to propel the trolley at high speed toward an examination room.

"My wife. My ex-wife."

The sound of sirens pierced the air as the first of the ambulances returned with their bloody cargo.

"It doesn't look good," the doctor said a few seconds later as he examined Melissa. "Nurse, have this patient prepared for surgery at once."

It was only then that Raefe realized that the nurse at the doctor's side was Helena.

"Yes, Doctor." Helena was already doing as he instructed.

As Helena started to peel away what was left of her clothes, Melissa groaned, her eyes flickering open. "Raefe?" she whispered with difficulty. "Raefe?"

He took her hand, bending over her, saying gently, "I'm here, Mel. I'm with you."

For one brief moment her fingers pressed feebly against his and a smile touched the corners of her mouth. "Good . . ." she breathed. "Good. I'm so glad . . ." Then her eyes closed and she was still.

"Dr. Meredith!" Helena called urgently. The doctor was instantly back at her side. He felt for Melissa's pulse, lifted the eyelid of one eye, then did all he could to resuscitate her. His efforts were in vain. "It's no good," he said at last. "She's dead."

He couldn't waste time in commiseration; his casualty ward resembled a battlefield. The curtain whisked closed behind him and it was left to Helena to say, "I'm sorry, Raefe."

He stood looking down at the face of the woman he had married only brief years before. There had been a time, when he was standing trial for Jacko Latimer's murder, when he had thought her death would be a matter of supreme indifference to him. It was so no longer. Over the last two years they had slowly and painfully forged a new relationship. A relationship based on acceptance of the past and one far finer than anything that had gone previously.

"Thank you, Helena," he said thickly. He couldn't stay. His duty was at Fortress Headquarters. "Make sure her body is treated with respect," he said, and before she could suggest that she should tend to the deep gash over his left eye, he was striding away between the wounded and the dying that were being brought in off the streets.

Julienne had reported early to her nursing station and had been told that she was not needed yet. Volunteers were needed, however, at the Peninsula Hotel, and she was asked if she would report for duty there and help the Red Cross nurses turn it into a temporary hospital. She had happily agreed and driven to the Peninsula in her little Morris, enjoying the novelty of being up and about so early in the day. It was still not eight o'clock. She giggled to herself, wondering what Ronnie would say when she told him. It was a standing joke between them that in all the years they had been married, she had never been up and dressed before ten o'clock.

The Peninsula Hotel was a hive of activity when she arrived. Bellboys were busily rolling up the luxurious carpets, guests were cheerfully helping to stack chairs and tables at the far end of the ballroom, and blackout material was being hastily cut to fit the windows.

"Morning, Mrs. Ledsham," a bellboy said, pausing in his work to give her an admiring grin as she walked exuberantly into the lobby, in her high-heeled shoes, her skirt tight and with provocative side slits similar to those the Wanchai bar girls wore in their cheongsams.

"Bonjour," Julienne returned, her smile wide. "Where can I find the Red Cross sister in charge?"

The sister in charge regarded her with despair. "We are no longer playing at war, Mrs. Ledsham," she said coldly. "We *are* at war. Kindly remove your makeup and nail varnish and then assist the other nurses in preparing cots for the wounded."

Julienne was about to make a most unsuitable reply when her future nursing career was saved by a tall, good-looking Dutchman who was standing at one of the far windows.

"My God," he called out to them. "Come over here and look at this!"

They did so and stared in disbelief at the planes bearing down toward Kai Tak Airport.

"They must be ours," Julienne said, aghast. "They can't possibly be Japanese." And then, a moment later, the bombs began to fall.

Within a few hours of leaving the lush splendor of the Peninsula ballroom, Alastair found himself in the far north of the New Territories. His orders were straightforward. He and his men were to maintain observation on the frontier and report any Japanese troop movements. They were also to ensure that all bridges were successfully demolished, then they were to withdraw in an orderly manner to the Gin Drinkers' Line, farther to the south, where a stand would be taken. All through Sunday the Japanese were well within their sights, massing on the far side of the border, but making no move to attack.

"They will, though," Alastair said grimly to his captain. "Just give them enough time and they will."

At ten minutes to five on Monday morning he received a terse message over the field telephone, telling him that Britain and Japan were officially at war. By seven-thirty the Japanese were pouring over the border and Alastair was leading his men into the first bloody engagement of the war.

Elizabeth drove straight to the Jockey Club. The streets that had been so quiet the previous day were now choked with cars and trucks as people hurried to their posts. She drove with one hand nearly permanently on the car horn, refusing to be intimidated by daredevil rickshaw boys or the crowded buses that kept hurtling past her.

"It looks as if this is really it," Miriam Gresby said nervously to her when she arrived.

Elizabeth looked at her in surprise. She had never known Miriam to be anything but aggressively bombastic. To her horror she realized that the older woman was frightened. "Come on, Miriam, it will soon be over," she said with an optimism she was far from feeling. "Let's get to work."

A truck was already discharging equipment and they set to, ferrying camp beds into the Jockey Club, putting them into position, helping to set up the operating room on the first floor. Within an hour their patients had begun to arrive. Most of them were very old and sick, refugees who had been sleeping on the streets of Kowloon for weeks, some of them for months.

"Oh, God, who would have thought one bombing raid could cause so many injuries?" a tired-looking blonde said to Elizabeth at lunchtime as they snatched a sandwich and a cup of coffee. "If this is only the beginning, how are we going to cope with what comes later?"

The morning raid was followed by others. A military post, established in the nearby members' enclosure, let off deafening rounds of antiaircraft fire as the planes swooped low overhead. Though no bombs were dropped in their vicinity, the noise and the sight of the smoke still billowing over Kowloon rendered most of their patients half sense-less with terror.

It was ten o'clock at night before Elizabeth was told to go home and get some rest. She walked wearily out to her car, her legs and back aching, her head splitting. For the moment the skies were silent. Perhaps, she thought as she turned the key in the ignition, the rumors about the Japanese not being able to see in the dark were true. She fervently hoped so. She needed a decent night's sleep if she was to face another equally arduous day in a few hours' time.

Mei Lin ran to greet her, sobbing with relief. "Oh, missy, I think something terrible happen to you! All day I've been here alone and there has been such noise and such smoke!"

"It's over for the moment, Mei Lin," Elizabeth said wearily. "Pour me a gin and tonic, will you?" She eyed the chairs and the sofa longingly, but did not sit down. She had an urgent telephone call to make before she allowed herself such luxury.

She dialed Helena's Kowloon number, praying that the line was still in working order and that Helena was back from the Kowloon Hospital.

When Helena's calm, deep voice answered, she leaned against the wall in relief. "Helena? It's Elizabeth. You can't continue to stay over in Kowloon with the children. It's far too dangerous. Drive over here and stay with me, please."

"No." Helena's voice was as tired as her own. "It's impossible, Elizabeth. The situation in the hospital is beyond belief." She paused for a moment, then said, "There's something I have to tell you—"

"Then you must send the children over here! I'm going to telephone Li Pi in a minute. I want him to come here, too. He could bring the children with him—"

"Melissa is dead. Raefe brought her into the hospital at ten past eight this morning."

Elizabeth slid slowly down the wall until she was sitting on her heels. "Oh, no," she whispered. "Oh, no."

"They were caught in the raid this morning. She was alive when he brought her in, but she died within minutes."

Elizabeth was silent. It was a strange experience to feel grief for a woman she had never met; a woman who had once been the center of Raefe's life. Whatever she said would sound trite and so, since there were no words to describe her feelings, she said nothing.

"I'm grateful for your offer to take the children," Helena said tactfully, when they had both been respectfully silent for a moment. "But they are just as safe here as they would be in Victoria. The bombing is going to be pretty indiscriminate."

"I wasn't thinking only of the bombs," Elizabeth said, wrenching her thoughts away from Melissa. "I was thinking of the Japanese advance."

"They won't advance very far. The Royal Scots will be sending them back across the border with their tails between their legs. They're certainly not going to advance as far south as Kowloon."

"All right," Elizabeth said reluctantly. "But if things change for the worse, promise me you'll send the children to me."

"I promise," Helena said affectionately. "Good night, Elizabeth. I must get some sleep. I'm back on duty in five hours and I've never been so tired in all my life."

Elizabeth grinned. "Me too. Good night, Helena. God bless."

Mei Lin brought her an ice-cold gin and tonic and she sipped it gratefully as she dialed Li Pi's number. He was as adamant as Helena that Kowloon was in no worse danger than Victoria. "I will come to you, if necessary," he promised at last, "but not before."

She was forced to put down the telephone with both her objectives unrealized.

"Will you be out all day again tomorrow, missy?" Mei Lin asked, her eyes wide and frightened.

Elizabeth sank down into one of the chairs. "Yes," she said, wondering how she would find the strength to get undressed and go to bed. "If there are air raids tomorrow, Mei Lin, you must go down to the shelters. You will be safe there."

Mei Lin gave a little sob. The thought of the dark, crowded shelters terrified her almost as much as the Japanese did. "Yes, missy," she said obediently, but she had no intention of doing as Elizabeth suggested. She would hide in the apartment under the table, as she had done all day. The apartment was in an elegant European area. The Japanese would surely not bomb European houses. Such an outrage was inconceivable. If she was going to be safe anywhere, she would be safe beneath Missy Harland's table.

"I run you a bath, missy," she said, eager to please, feeling suddenly braver. "Japanese soon run away from British soldiers. Everything soon all right again."

Chapter Twenty-six

❧

EVERYTHING was not soon all right again. For the next two days the bombing of Kowloon and Victoria continued. The casualties at the Jockey Club increased from a steady flow to a barely containable torrent. The supplies that had seemed so adequate when they were being loaded off the trucks now proved to be barely sufficient. Old sheets were torn into strips for bandages. Chlorine and rock salt were used to eke out the diminishing supplies of disinfectant. The fierce enthusiasm that most volunteers had exhibited on the first day began to be replaced by ever-increasing anxiety.

"I don't understand it," Miriam Gresby said petulantly. "What are our troops doing? Why aren't the planes being shot down?"

"Because land-based antiaircraft guns aren't very effective," Elizabeth said with as much patience as she could muster, "and we haven't planes of our own in which to do battle with theirs. What planes we had were all destroyed in the first raid on Kai Tak."

"Nevertheless, *something* should be done," Miriam said querulously. "It's been three days now and my nerves are in shreds."

Very little outside news filtered through to Adam and his fellow volunteers manning a pillbox on the south side of the island, overlooking Aberdeen harbor. On Wednesday morning a motorcycle messenger gave them the news that there had been fierce fighting in the New Territories since first light on Monday, and that the Japanese had broken through the Gin Drinkers' Line and were now fighting their way toward Kowloon.

"Jesus," one of Adam's companions said, stunned. "I

thought the Gin Drinkers' Line was supposed to be as far south as the Japs would get."

Adam had thought so, too, and now he watched the sea approaches to Aberdeen harbor with even greater vigilance. If any Japanese sailed into the sights of his gun, they would have a very nasty surprise indeed.

"Do you think they'll try to make a surprise landing?" a former clerk in the Hong Kong and Shanghai Bank asked him nervously.

"I wish they would," Adam said grimly, impatient for action. "I just wish to God that they would!"

Up on the heights of Sai Wan Hill, looking out toward Kowloon and the mainland, Ronnie had been under intermittent air attack for two days.

"The bastards really mean business, don't they?" he said to Leigh Stafford, who was his platoon commander.

"They do, and the military made a gross error in underestimating them," Leigh said bitterly. "All that cock about the Japanese Air Force being of a low standard and their bombing poor! Their bombing was accurate enough at Kai Tak. Every bloody plane we had was destroyed before it could even take off! They've got us by the short and curlies, old boy. These next few days are going to be critical. If they once chase us off the mainland, we'll be in a siege situation and they'll be able to lobby us with mortar fire from Kowloon all day and all night."

By dusk on Tuesday, Alastair and his men had made a bloody but planned retreat to the Gin Drinkers' Line. Here, in the underground tunnels and pillboxes and observation posts of the Shingmun Redoubt, they were to make their stand against the Japanese and prevent any further advance to Kowloon.

"It isn't exactly the Ritz, is it?" he heard one of his men say as they hurled themselves down into the dank, claustrophobic depths of tunnels that had been dug and cemented years before, as a precaution against an attack that no one had believed would come.

It wasn't the Maginot Line either. Alastair had long been dubious as to the benefits of fighting from such a fixed position, and his doubts grew by the moment. Some embrasures in the pillboxes were so constructed that it was impossible to depress the machine guns sufficiently to cover the steep slopes below them. The scrub-filled ravines that surrounded them offered treacherously covered approaches to any attacker, and the rugged, jagged terrain made mutual support between positions a near impossibility.

"When an attack comes, we'll use the redoubt mainly for cover," he told his men crisply. "Our main fighting positions will be on the outside."

There was a general murmur of relief, but when darkness fell and the attack came, it came with such suddenness and such ferocity that it was in the dimly lit passageways and foul-smelling pillboxes that most of them died.

Alastair had time only to press one hand against the breast pocket containing Helena's photograph, then the screaming hordes swarmed down on them, heedless of the Royal Scots' machine-gun fire, heedless of the casualties they were suffering.

Grenades were lobbed through pillbox embrasures and hurled down ventilation shafts; steel doors were blown in, exits were sealed off.

"The bastards are coming in!" Alastair yelled, leaping away from the guns and toward the tunnel from which he heard the pounding of running feet and frenzied cries of *"Banzai! Banzai! Kill! Kill!"*

In the smoke-filled, acrid darkness, Alastair let off every round in his pistol and then, as ever more Japanese surged forward over the bodies of their dead comrades, he resorted to a bayonet, knowing now that he would never marry Helena. Never even see her again. Blood was pouring from a bullet wound in his shoulder and from a shrapnel wound in his head.

"They're falling back, sir!" a young corporal, fighting hand-to-hand alongside him, cried out triumphantly.

There was a second's respite as the Japanese no longer tried to storm the passageway, then a grenade came whistling toward them, landing and rolling on the floor between Alastair and the corporal. There was no room to back away from it, nowhere to sweep it to. Alastair saw the youngster's terrified face and then, with a savage cry of *"Helena!"* he hurled himself onto it, taking the full force of the blast, his flesh and blood spattering the cordite-fumed tunnel and raining down on the unconscious but barely injured boy.

The first intimation Helena had that the Gin Drinkers' Line had given way and that the troops were in retreat was when Miss Gean, her hospital matron, took her to one side and informed her that the news was grave and that, because she knew Helena had children still in Kowloon, she was giving her permission to leave her post and remove them to the greater safety of Hong Kong island.

"But what of everyone else?" Helena asked aghast. "Are the other nurses to leave too?"

Miss Gean shook her head. "No. Even if the troops withdraw to the island, we shall not. We are needed here and we shall stay here."

Helena ran from the hospital still in uniform. She drove through the bomb-blasted streets, cursing herself for her blind belief in the Royal Scots' ability to thrash the Japanese. She had foolishly put her children's lives at risk, ignoring Elizabeth's pleas that she take them to Victoria while it was still relatively easy to do so. Once the news Miss Gean had imparted to her became general, it would be impossible to get a place on one of the ferries. And God only knew what would happen to Jeremy and Jennifer if they fell into the hands of the Japanese.

She screeched to a halt outside her block of flats and ran up the stairs. There was still time. She could have the children and their amah at the ferry within fifteen minutes, then Jung-lu would take them directly to Elizabeth's. She mustn't think of Alastair. Alastair would be safe. Alastair would come back to her. She would be able to tell him that she was sorry she had been so hesitant about marriage. That she had changed her mind. That she wanted to marry him more than anything in the world.

"Missy Nicholson! What happen? What wrong?" Jung-lu cried as she raced into the flat.

"The Japanese are approaching Kowloon! Pack one bag and then I'm taking you and the children down to the ferry. You are to go and stay with Mrs. Harland in Victoria. This is the address. Her household staff will be expecting you."

"No, missy," Jung-lu said, shaking her head vehemently. "Me not leave Kowloon. My family here. My mother, my father, my cousins."

Helena was already throwing the children's toilet things and a change of clothes into a large canvas holdall.

"Where are we going, Mummy?" Jeremy was asking curiously. "Can I take my toy soldiers?"

"Want to take teddy," Jennifer said, toddling around the room after Helena. "Please can I take teddy?"

"Of course, darling," Helena said, adding toy soldiers and a teddy bear to her mental list of absolute essentials that had to be taken with them.

"You *must* take the children to Victoria," she said fiercely to Jung-lu. "I have to return to the hospital. I'm desperately needed there!"

Jung-lu shook her head. "No, missy, I not leave my family. Not now, not even for you."

The canvas bag was nearly full. Helena scooped up her silver-framed photograph of Alan and laid it on top of the clothes, and zipped it up. "Please, God," she was thinking, "don't let Alastair be killed, too. Don't let the grieving begin all over again."

"You can return immediately after you have left the children with Mei Lin," Helena said, casting a last, hasty look around the room to make sure that she had not forgotten anything of vital importance.

"No." Jung-lu's mouth had set defiantly. "Sorry, missy. Me no go."

Helena felt sobs of frustration rising in her throat. She had brought all this on herself with her damnable optimism that such a move would be unnecessary. If she took the children herself, Miss Gean would understand. After all, she had given her permission to leave the hospital and not to return. But in Helena's eyes, leaving now would be deserting her duty. The little hospital had been originally built to accommodate one hundred bed patients, and now there were close to a thousand Chinese crammed in the wards and corridors, all of them hideously wounded as a result of the savage air raids, and all of them desperately in need of help. No, she could not remain in Victoria with the children herself, not if there was an alternative way in which she could be sure of their safety. The alternative way occurred to her as she lifted Jennifer high in her arms, and picked up the bulging holdall. Li Pi. Li Pi was still in Kowloon and she knew that he had been as adamant as she in refusing Elizabeth's request to take shelter with her in Victoria.

"'Bye," she shouted to Jung-lu in the last few seconds before she closed the door of the flat behind her. Any anger she had felt now dissipated. She only prayed that wherever Jung-lu went she would be safe. The Japanese were reputed to be utterly merciless where the Chinese were concerned.

She bundled the children into the car and drove through the rubble-filled streets toward Li Pi's luxury apartment.

". . . and so you see, I really would be most grateful if you could take the children to Elizabeth's for me," she said, trying to sound less desperate than she felt.

"Is this the man who teaches Auntie Lizbeth to play the piano?" Jeremy asked curiously, looking around at the unusually bare room and the concert grand piano dominating it.

Li Pi smiled down at him. "Would you like to be able to play the piano?" he asked.

Jeremy nodded, his eyes bright. Helena took a deep, steadying breath. Perhaps she had been wrong in keeping panic from her voice. Perhaps Li Pi had not appreciated the seriousness of the situation. "Our troops are no longer holding the Japanese," she said carefully. "They are in retreat. It is only a matter of days before they reach Kowloon."

Li Pi had been bending down, talking to Jeremy. Now he stood upright, holding Jeremy's hand, and said, "And so you wish me to take the little ones to Victoria?"

Helena nodded. "Please, Li Pi. They will be much safer there. Even if the Japanese do reach Kowloon, they'll never be able to cross to the island."

"No," Li Pi said, smiling. "Of course not."

Helena stared at him, suddenly certain that it was not what he really thought. *Oh, God*, she thought despairingly, *am I being an optimistic idiot again? Could the Japanese invade the island?* "The *Prince of Wales* and the *Repulse* are on their way to us," she said confidently. "Once they arrive, the Japanese will give us no more trouble."

Li Pi nodded and smiled and said, "I will be more than happy to take the little ones to Victoria for you. But I would not put my faith in battleships that have still not arrived, Mrs. Nicholson. The Japanese have probably already taken them into account."

* * *

Tom found himself with the Volunteer Field Engineers, helping the Royal Scots blow up the bridges over the Sham Chun. When the Japanese poured over the border at seven-thirty in the morning, he was on his way to give a message to a nearby platoon, and from then on remained with them, cut off from the engineers, fighting with the Royal Scots as they withdrew to battle positions on the Gin Drinkers' Line, a few miles to the left of the Shingmun Redoubt. By early Wednesday morning, they were falling back even farther, this time to Golden Hill, where he had often walked with Lamoon.

There was no pleasant walk in store for him on the night of the tenth of December. Exhausted by the retreat from the Gin Drinkers' Line, weighed down with equipment and ammunition, he followed his orders, climbing and crawling up the steep slopes in almost total darkness.

"At least we'll be able to see the bastards coming from here," one of his companions said as they finally hauled themselves onto the bare summit.

Tom wasn't so sure. At the Gin Drinkers' Line, the Japanese, their uniforms heavily camouflaged by twigs and grass inserted in the cross-stitching, had attacked in rubber-soled shoes, approaching so silently that no one was aware of their presence until they were nearly on top of them.

He slapped his arms around himself, trying to keep warm, trying to forget that he was tired to the point of exhaustion and desperately hungry.

"Have a tot of rum," his companion said dourly. "It's the only breakfast you'll get today."

The attack came as dawn was breaking. Mortar shells rained down on them, the impact area igniting in sheets of flame, a thick pall of smoke enveloping them as they fired relentlessly back, only to be savagely mortared yet again. Tom hurled himself forward, firing his Bren gun, hurling hand grenades, shouting barrack-room obscenities that he didn't even know he knew. All around him men were falling, screaming out in pain, the ground beneath their feet slippery with blood. He heard a voice to his left yelling for him to get under cover but he ignored it. *"Bastards!"* he yelled as he ran forward like a dervish, his gun firing. *"Motherfucking bastards!"*

He heard a voice at his side saying, "I've bought it, mate!" and he turned his head fleetingly just in time to see his breakfast companion, a look of disbelief on his face, slide to the ground. Tom plowed on in a man-made fog of smoke and dust and cordite fumes. The earth seemed to be blowing up all around him. The noise was deafening. And then, inch by inch, he knew he was being pushed back. They were losing the fight for Golden Hill, just as they had lost the fight for the Gin Drinkers' Line.

When the order finally came for them to pull back to less exposed ground closer to Kowloon, Tom sobbed in bitter rage and frustration. They were being defeated. Defeated by bloody, motherfucking *Japanese*.

They had scarcely reached their new positions when a further order came. The mainland was to be evacuated, and anything of any use to the enemy was to be denied them. Cement works, power stations, dockyards; all were to be destroyed. From now on, all further fighting would take place on Hong Kong island.

Helena had safely deposited Li Pi and the children aboard the ferry the previous day and was sincerely glad that she had done so. Gunfire could be heard on the Kowloon streets, the air raids had increased, and the Chinese dead lay in the streets, their bodies rotting alongside the living. The medical staff of the Kowloon Hospital, doctors and nurses, were gathered together and somberly told that despite the evacuation of the troops, it was the governor's wish that they all remain at their posts.

Even in the hospital, the sound of the disorder in the streets could be heard. Windows were being smashed in Nathan Road; riots had broken out and looting was rife. Helena returned to her terrified patients, wondering where Julienne was, where Elizabeth was, and if Alastair and her children were safe.

Tom fumed and swore all the time he was being driven down toward Kowloon Point. After all they had gone through, he and his companions were being ferried down to the embarkation point in a bus! To Tom it was the final indignity.

"Looks a bit nasty 'round 'ere, don't it?" one of the men

with him said as they saw evidence of looting and a rotting pile of Chinese dead.

Tom was just about to turn his head away from the chaotic street scene when he went rigid, the blood draining from his face. "Lamoon!" he uttered with a strangled cry. *"Lamoon!"*

She was pushing and battling her way in the midst of the crowds streaming toward the docks.

He couldn't believe his eyes. For a long, near fatal moment, he couldn't even move. "Lamoon!" he shouted again as the bus continued to speed away from her. "My good *Christ! Lamoon!"*

He leaped to his feet, ignoring the shouts and cries around him. "Let me off this bloody bus!" he yelled, and then, not waiting to see if it would stop, not caring if he was court-martialed and shot, he launched himself from the bus platform and into the road.

He fell heavily, rolling over and over, then scrambled to his feet and ran back up the street shouting *"Lamoon! Lamoon!"* like a man demented.

She stood still as the crowds milled around her, turning her head to see where the shouts were coming from, her almond eyes wide and fearful.

"Lamoon!" he shouted at the top of his lungs, barreling his way through the hurrying Chinese. "Oh, good God! *Lamoon!"*

When she saw him she swayed on her feet, kept upright only by the pressure of people jostling and pushing her.

He cleaved his way through the throng, his eyes blazing with joy. "Lamoon!" he breathed as he swept the last human barrier easily aside. "Oh, my love! My darling! *Lamoon!"*

She fell into his arms, her head against the broad safety of his chest, tears streaming down her face. He crushed her against him, sobs of thankfulness and joy rising in his throat. "Oh, my little love," he said chokingly. "Where have you been? What did they do to you?"

Air raid sirens screamed into life.

"I thought I would never see you again!" she said rapturously, raising her face to his.

All around them Chinese and Europeans were running for cover.

"My love, my life," he whispered hoarsely, then kissed her with all the pent-up passion of months of longing.

There was a sudden blinding roar as the planes swooped down on the narrow streets. *"Quick!"* he yelled, seizing her wrist. *"I'm sure as hell not going to be killed now!"* He sprinted with her across the road and thrust her into a doorway, shielding her with his body. The sky darkened as the planes roared overhead, then there came the terrible whistling sound of falling bombs.

"Don't let me die! Dear God, don't let me die!" he prayed silently for the first and only time since the war had begun. He couldn't die, not now, when he once more had Lamoon. He had to be alive to protect her, to love her, to keep her safe.

The bombs tore into streets some distance away. The ground rocked beneath their feet, a shower of white concrete dust falling over their heads and shoulders.

"Is it over?" Lamoon shouted above the roar of falling buildings and the continuing scream of sirens.

"I think so." Cautiously Tom lifted his head, peering upward. The sky was as blue and as clear as it had been minutes earlier before the attack. "Come on, I've got to get you out of here. Where were you going when I saw you?"

They were back out in the street. To the left of them, about half a mile away, tongues of flame were shooting skyward, great billowing clouds of smoke beginning to choke the air.

"The ferry," she gasped as they wove and dodged through the crowds erupting from the street shelters. "I thought it would be safer on the island."

"Damn right it would!" Tom said grimly. My God! The mere thought of what might happen to her if she fell into Japanese hands made him go cold with terror.

"The trouble is I haven't got a permit!" she said as he lunged across the street toward a taxicab abandoned by its driver.

"To hell with bloody permits!" Tom exclaimed, half throwing her into the front seat of the taxi and running around to the driver's seat. "Let's hope this old jalopy has some petrol in it!"

It had, and seconds later they were speeding through the congested streets toward the docks.

"You haven't told me what happened to you yet," he said, swerving to avoid the fire engines and ambulances screaming their way to the fires and the injured.

"I was married," she said simply.

He jerked his head toward her, the taxi veering dangerously. She gave a small smile. "It is over now." Her smile faded. "He was killed in a raid. We were visiting my father." She looked away from him, out to the ravaged streets. "They were all killed. My father. My brothers. There is no one left."

"Yes, there is," he said gently, removing one hand from the wheel and placing it over hers.

Her eyes were bright with tears as she turned her head once more toward him. "I love you," she said softly. "For all of my life, I love only you, Tom."

Kowloon City Pier was a shambles. European women, amahs and small children in their wake, were thronging the area streets. Extra launches were waiting to ferry them across to Victoria, taking on board so many passengers that by the time they put out into the channel it seemed a miracle they didn't sink beneath the weight.

Tom shouldered his way through the crush toward a Royal Naval Volunteer seemingly directing operations. "This lady has lost her permit," he said urgently. "She needs to be able to cross immediately."

"Sorry, mate," the harassed naval officer said. "No one crosses without a permit."

All around them children were crying, frightened by the noise and the crush and the unmistakable smell of fear.

"To hell with that!" Tom said furiously. "This lady is Lamoon Sheng and my fiance! I want her aboard one of these boats, Lieutenant!"

"I don't care if she's the Queen of Siam," the lieutenant said, rapidly checking permits and waving thankful women through toward the launches. "She's a chink and she hasn't a permit and she'll have to wait, is that understood?"

Tom's eyes blazed and his fist clenched. Lamoon pulled desperately on his arm, begging him to come away, then a deep voice shouted out, *"Over here, sir! The Chinese are storming the boats!"*

Just as Tom was about to hit him, the lieutenant turned and forced his way toward his junior officer, and Lamoon almost sobbed with relief. "Please, let's go away, Tom. I'll cross later, when there is no longer a panic." Very faintly, above the noise and shouts around them, both of them could hear the distant sound of gunfire.

"There isn't going to be a later," Tom said harshly. "The Japs can't be more than a couple of miles away."

"There's room in this boat," the nervous underling who had been left in charge said to Tom. "And would you go as well and try to keep order? These women will have the boat six feet under the way they're carrying on."

Tom didn't need to be asked twice. He hurled Lamoon forward onto the pier, running with her toward the launch. He would take her to the Hong Kong Hotel. He was known there, and the name Sheng was known there. At the Hong Kong Hotel, even in war, she wouldn't be just another "chink." And then he would rejoin his unit, though how the hell he would ever find it again he couldn't imagine.

In the Kowloon Hospital the stench drifting in from the streets was almost insufferable. Bodies were beginning to decompose where they had fallen, sewage was seeping from bombed and broken mains, hundreds of tons of fruit and vegetables were rotting as the refrigeration system in the godowns broke down.

Helena's patients lay squeezed into any inch of space they could find. The lucky few lay in beds; others lay under the beds, on the floor, in the corridors. Operations in the two small operating theaters were continuous. By Friday evening, Helena couldn't remember when she had last slept, or eaten, or even taken a drink. Her uniform was stiff with blood, her fingernails caked with it. There was no more disinfectant, no linen for bandages, and their precious water supply was dwindling fast.

All through Friday night she tended the maimed and the dying and the dead, not thinking of Adam or Alastair, not even thinking of her children, knowing that if she did so she would not be able to continue. Instead she stanched hideous wounds, stitched gaping holes in arms and thighs, and tried to give comfort to young men who had lost their legs and would never walk again.

At nine o'clock the following morning, the pitch of the noise drifting in from the surrounding streets altered ominously. There was no sound of bombs falling or air raid sirens screaming into life. Seconds later there came the heavy tramp of marching feet and the doors were kicked open by Japanese soldiers, rifles at the ready, bayonets fixed.

The Chinese began to scream, struggling to leave their blood-strained beds, to drag their injured bodies to a place of safety.

The leading Japanese officer ignored them. He was grinning at Helena, his eyes behind his gold-rimmed spectacles lustful as they feasted on her Junoesque proportions and her magnificent bosom.

"You come," he said leeringly, jabbing his bayonet only inches away from her face. "You come with Japanese officer. You find out what defeat for European women means."

Chapter Twenty-seven
❦

RAEFE had spent the last week at Fortress HQ, helping the British interrogate Japanese informers, trying to elicit enough information from them to enable Major General Maltby to assess where his preciously few troops could best be deployed.

The main question was whether to keep troops back in a central position, moving them forward in strength to meet an attack when an attack came, or to spread them out, trying to cover as much of the coastline as possible.

The information that Raefe was able to pass on was not decisively helpful. He was told that the Japanese would land by parachute, at night, in the central area around Wong Nei Chung Gap. This information was disregarded since the Japanese had not yet, at any time, operated a bombing raid at night, and the feasibility of landing an army of men by air over the treacherous ground of the gap was practically nil.

A second informant said that the Japanese would cross to the island from the Devil's Peak Peninsula, west of Kowloon, landing at Sau Ki Wan. The Devil's Peak crossing was the shortest of all possible crossings, and foreseeing that it was one the Japanese would want to use, withdrawing forces had been ordered to scuttle ships in it, making the channel impassable.

"They won't be able to cross at that point," a senior officer said confidently. "They're going to land on the south coast where we least expect it."

Major General Maltby did the best he could in an impossible situation. Keeping the vast majority of troops in a central position until an attack came was not a feasible option. He did not have enough trucks to facilitate the speedy movement of large numbers of troops to any one spot. Instead, he deployed the Canadian troops to the south of the island, the Indian regiments to the north coast, the Punjabis to the west of Victoria, and the Rajputs to the east, overlooking the Lei Yue Mun Strait. The Royal Scots and the Middlesex remained centrally stationed, as many units as possible being supported by the volunteers.

By Friday evening Raefe knew that there was little left for him to achieve at Fortress HQ and he was thirsting for action. His orders were clear. As an undercover agent for the British, if and when Hong Kong fell, he was on no account to allow himself to be captured. He was to escape, making his way to the Japanese-held mainland and then traveling through enemy territory to Chungking in free China, where he would help the Chinese form British-led guerrilla units. They would be an Asian counterpart of the French maquis, doing everything possible to undermine and dislocate the authority of the enemy.

Meanwhile, with the Japanese still making no move to land, Raefe's sense of impotence was acute. "At least let me join a volunteer unit," he begged Sandor. "I can't remain buried away here any longer. It will only create suspicion about what I am really doing. And if word gets to the Japanese, I'll have even less chance of making a successful getaway should the need arise."

Permission wasn't given until the following Thursday. By then the Japanese were swarming all over the island and Raefe found himself holding the honorary rank of captain and commanding a unit whose officer had been killed. And fighting by his side was Adam Harland.

Elizabeth remained on duty at the Jockey Club. On the evening of Friday, December 12, it was announced on the

radio that HM ships *Prince of Wales* and *Repulse* had been
sunk off Singapore. She heard the news with stunned
disbelief, knowing that there was now no real hope for
Hong Kong's survival. The next morning she was greeted
with the news of the mass evacuation from the mainland.
By midday the Japanese could be clearly seen on the
Kowloon waterfront, sandbagging buildings and setting
up gun emplacements.

When her long hours of duty came to an end, she did not
grab what sleep she could. Instead, ignoring an air raid
and almost constant mortar fire, she drove through the
wrecked streets to the apartment and Mei Lin.

"No, Missy Harland," Mei Lin said tearfully. "Missy
Nicholson not come. Children not come. Oh, when will it
end, Missy Harland? When will it be safe again?"

There was nothing that Elizabeth could do. There had
been no telephone link to Kowloon for days. If Helena was
trapped there, Elizabeth could only pray that she and the
children were alive and well. If she wasn't trapped there, if
she had managed to join the other civilians in the previous
day's mass evacuation, then there was the hope that they
would eventually turn up at the apartment. That when she
was next able to drive home, she would find Helena
waiting for her.

As the week progressed the streets of Victoria became a
nightmare. The bombing and mortar fire was incessant, the
thousands of Chinese refugees pathetically easy targets.
The makeshift hospital was hit and hit again, even though
a large red cross had been painted on the roof. One of the
operating theaters was wrecked and one shell went right
through the top floor, causing many casualties. On
Wednesday, December 17, fourteen bombers attacked the
crowded streets of the Central District and Wanchai.

"They're softening us up," one of the medical orderlies
said darkly. "You mark my words, this will be the last day
they content themselves with bombs and shells. This time
tomorrow the bastards will have landed!"

Elizabeth wiped the back of her hand wearily across her
forehead. Once the Japanese landed she would probably
never see Mei Lin again. An hour later, when there was a
lull in the terrible bombing, she made a dash for her car,
determined to make one last trip to the apartment. She
would collect as much tinned food and bed linen as she

could transport to eke out the rapidly dwindling hospital supplies, and give anything remaining to Mei Lin.

The roads were so cratered and bomb-blasted, so littered with fallen tram wires and lamp standards, that they were nearly impossible to negotiate. It took her nearly an hour to make the five-minute journey. As she neared the apartment apprehension began to cramp her stomach muscles. The area had received several direct hits. Fires were still raging out of control. Doors and window frames hung lopsidedly from buildings whose fronts had been ripped away. An ambulance clanged vociferously in her wake. Air raid wardens were climbing cautiously over a mound of rubble that had once been a human habitation.

Her hands slid sweatily on the wheel; she felt sick and disoriented. It couldn't be her apartment block. It couldn't. She stumbled from the car, running across to the men still searching the smoking wreckage.

"This your 'ouse, lady?" one of them asked solicitously.

"Yes," she gasped, hardly able to breathe. "My apartment was here . . ."

"Ain't 'ere no longer," the man said unnecessarily. "Anyone in 'ere when it caught it?"

She shook her head, weak with relief. "No, I told my amah to always go down to the shelter."

"We've found someone!" a man shouted from a few yards away. "A Chinese! A girl! Poor kid, must have been hiding under the table. Didn't even have her tin hat on."

Elizabeth began to struggle toward him, slipping and sliding over blasted concrete and shattered wood and the incongruous remains of her kitchen.

The air raid warden heaved a heavy tabletop away and bent down, beginning to lift Mei Lin from the rubble. "You take 'er 'ead, I'll take 'er feet," the first man said, hurrying to assist. "Cor blimey, what a nasty mess and no mistake."

Mei Lin's golden skin was covered with a white film of concrete ash. Dark red blood oozed through the bodice of her blouse. Her head lolled back at a grotesque angle as they lifted her free.

"She your amah, luv?" one of the men asked Elizabeth. She nodded, the tears streaming down her face.

"She was a silly girl," the air raid warden said as they transferred Mei Lin's body to a stretcher. "Tabletops are no protection against Jap bombs. When will they ever learn?"

The two men lifted the stretcher and began to carry it with difficulty back down over the constantly shifting wreckage.

"Pretty though," the first man said, looking down at Mei Lin's still, white face. "Very pretty little thing she was."

Elizabeth slipped and slid in their wake. Mei Lin had been pretty. She had been pretty and sweet-natured and touchingly loyal. And she had died alone, hiding in terror from the thundering volley of falling bombs.

"You all right, miss?" the air raid warden asked as they pushed the stretcher into the rear of an ambulance.

Elizabeth nodded, her tears falling unrestrainedly. She had been tending the dying and laying out the dead for over a week, but Mei Lin's death was the first to touch her personally.

She watched as the ambulance doors slammed shut, crippled by fear. Where were Helena and the children? Where was Li Pi? Where were Julienne and Alastair and Ronnie? Where were Adam and Raefe? Were they safe? Were they alive and well, or were they, too, lying dead or maimed, the victims of a Japanese bomb or a mortar shell?

She walked slowly back to her car. She had no way of knowing what was happening to any of them. She could only continue her work at the Jockey Club and pray fervently that the war would soon end. There had been rumors that the Chinese were sending troops to their aid. If it were true, and if they arrived within the next few days, then it was just possible that the Japanese would capitulate and there would be peace by Christmas.

The drive back to the Jockey Club was grim. Now that the raid was over, the Chinese had swarmed from the shelters and re-formed in long, disorderly queues for food. Nearly all of them looked as if they were in need of medical treatment. With sores openly exposed, their clothes often little more than tattered rags, they waited with rusty tins and battered bowls for the daily distribution of rice and beans.

"We have been requested to send someone to help with the sick at the Repulse Bay Hotel," her nursing officer said to her when she returned. "Will you go? I'm afraid the military are unable to provide an escort, but it shouldn't be too bad a drive if you go at dusk. There's not much chance of a raid then."

The Repulse Bay. Elizabeth thought of the laughter-filled, happy afternoons she had spent there. "Yes," she said wearily. "I'll go."

The nursing officer managed a small smile. "At least Repulse Bay won't be under intensive air attack like Victoria is. It should be quite a picnic out there. I almost wish I were going with you!"

Thursday had been an unusually cold and damp day, and Ronnie's discomfort was acute. He hadn't had a hot meal for twenty-four hours and he couldn't remember the last time he had slept. Ever since ten in the morning, bombers had been flying over Victoria and even now, late at night, black smoke from the Anglo-Persian Company's petroleum and oil storage tanks at North Point billowed into the air. The Japanese batteries in Kowloon had his position under almost constant mortar fire. Of the seven men in his platoon, one was seriously wounded by shrapnel and another was out of commission with violent stomach pains and diarrhea.

"Nerves," Leigh Stafford had muttered disparagingly. "There's nothing physically wrong with the fellow. He's just scared to death."

Ronnie didn't blame him. He was pretty scared himself. At teatime they had seen about two hundred Japs approaching the Devil's Peak Pier. They were obviously unconcerned about the scuttled ships in the channel. The landing was imminent and it was going to take place exactly opposite his gun position.

"I'm ready for the little yellow bastards," Stafford said fiercely, conscious of the need to give a good impression to the younger man. "I've waited for this moment for a long time."

The night was so dark they could barely see a yard in front of them. Heavy clouds obscured the moon, and thick black smoke from the still burning oil tanks hung chokingly low. The rubber boats and rowboats and sampans sliding out into the channel did so unobserved, shielded from sight by the high sides of the grounded merchant ships.

"There's something out there," Ronnie muttered edgily, his eyes straining to see through the darkness. "I can feel it in my bones."

"Blast those scuttled ships," Stafford said viciously. "I can't see a bloody thing for them."

A huge flare of burning oil suddenly shot skyward, fleetingly illuminating the channel, the scuttled ships, and the scores of small craft edging their way around them.

"I can see them!" Ronnie rasped, adrenaline shooting along his veins. *"There's a battalion out there! And it's coming this way!"*

"Positions, men!" Stafford commanded, forgetting his weariness, forgetting his hunger. "Get ready to fire!"

Out of the darkness the black shapes of boats and men began to take on substance.

"Targets!" Stafford yelled, his voice throbbing and then, as shadowy figures began to leap onto the shore, *"Fire!"*

"My God, there's an entire Jap army down there!" the *hors de combat* corporal howled. "There's bloody hundreds of them!"

"Keep firing!" Stafford bellowed. *"We mustn't let them gain a foothold! For Christ's sake, keep firing!"*

They kept firing and, for a few miraculous minutes, held the disembarking Japs at the water's edge. In the distance, at either side of them, they could hear the guns of the antiaircraft batteries roaring into action.

"We'll soon send them on their way!" Stafford crowed, but even as he spoke, more boats were sliding ashore, more men sprinting and leaping over the bodies of the dead and wounded.

"They're going to overrun us!" Ronnie shouted as, despite the withering fire, heedless of their casualties, the Japanese swarmed toward them. *"There's no way we can hold them!"*

A hand grenade was lobbed through a loophole and just as speedily lobbed back again.

"We *have* to hold them!" Stafford shouted back, then another grenade entered the pillbox, exploding and blasting them off their feet. Cement and plaster rained down on them. Ronnie could hear someone screaming and prayed to God it wasn't himself.

"Out!" he heard Stafford shout through the dust and fumes and blinding smoke. *"We have to get out!"*

Ronnie was in full agreement with him. He staggered to his knees, his uniform ripped, blood trickling down into his eyes, and half fell over the corporal who had been suffering so violently with a stomachache. He was suffering no longer. He had taken the full force of the blast and had been cut almost in two, sliced open from the neck to the navel, his entrails spilling bloodily to the floor. Ronnie gagged, falling over two more prone bodies as he struggled in the older man's wake.

The Japanese were all over the pillbox now, exhorting them to give themselves up. To surrender.

"It's no good, old boy. We have to do as they say," Leigh panted, throwing down his revolver and stepping out of the pillbox toward the Japs, his hands raised.

"No!" Ronnie screamed at the top of his voice, but it was too late. The gentlemen's war that Leigh Stafford imagined he was fighting was no gentlemen's war at all. The Japanese jeered at him in derision as he did as they demanded, then fell on him, bayonets raised, plunging them time and time again into his defenseless body.

Ronnie raised his revolver and fired and kept on firing. A piercing pain in his shoulder sent him stumbling to his knees, then, as they closed around him, a blow to the back of his neck sent him sprawling to the ground. He couldn't see, couldn't hear, couldn't breathe. There was blood in his nose and his eyes and his mouth. *Julienne!* he thought desperately. *Julienne!* Then he was dimly aware of the Japanese surging away from him, away from the pillbox. He lay motionless, fighting back cries of pain as scores of rubber-soled feet pounded past him on their way inland.

"Bastards," he whispered as the last reverberation died away and he crawled in crucifying agony on his hands and knees. "Bastards! Bastards! *Bastards!"*

Adam heard the news of the landings in the early hours of Friday morning. "The Japs have landed on the southeast coast," he was told tersely. "Get yourself and your men over to Brigade Headquarters. That's where they're heading."

Adam slammed down the phone and immediately gave the order to abandon their position. Brigade Headquarters was at the Wong Nie Chung Gap, and the gap stood on high ground in the virtual center of the island. If it fell into the hands of the Japanese, then they would have achieved a terrible tactical advantage.

"Who are we linking up with, sir?" one of his men asked as they rocketed across country in an army truck.

"I don't know," Adam retorted grimly. "And I don't care. Just as long as we throw the bloody Japs back into the sea!"

Julienne had been posted, much to her disgust, with Miriam Gresby, who had been with Elizabeth at the Jockey Club. She would have preferred a more congenial companion, especially in a dressing station as isolated as the one they had been detailed to. They were to the east of Wong Nei Chung Gap, their patients mainly men from the Rajputs who had come under intense shelling from the Japanese batteries in Kowloon. It was a small station with only three medical officers, a British nursing sister, four other British Voluntary Aid Detachment nurses, three Chinese Voluntary Aid Detachment nurses, and three medical orderlies. By the time the Japanese swarmed inland early Friday morning, they had over a hundred patients in their care.

"The Japanese have landed," the senior medical officer said to them grimly. "I've just been warned they're coming this way."

Julienne, her gray cotton nursing dress creased and spattered with blood, did not pause in her ministrations to a young Canadian boy whose leg had been blown off by a shell. If the Japanese came, they came. There was nothing she could do to stop them. But she was damned if she was going to cringe with fear at the mere mention of their name.

"My God! You know what they'll do to us if they capture us, don't you?" Miriam Gresby hissed to her, twisting her hands convulsively and ignoring the boy whose wounds she had been in the process of dressing.

"No." Julienne was applying sulphur to a pus-ridden stump. "But whatever it is, talking about it will make no difference." She looked over at the young boy Miriam was neglecting. His face was shiny with sweat, his knuckles clenched against the pain. "Your patient needs you to finish changing his dressing, Miriam."

Miriam's lips tightened, querulously thin without their usual careful application of lipstick. "Don't take it upon yourself to tell *me* what to do, Julienne Ledsham! I'm not surprised you're unconcerned at the prospect of rape! It's exactly the kind of activity you enjoy, isn't it?"

Julienne was startled at how little anger she felt. Miriam

had always been a fool, and now she was a frightened fool. "No," she said, readjusting a draining tube. "I have never had any experience of rape, Miriam, and I doubt if I would enjoy it at all. Would you like me to help you with that bandage?"

They worked together in silence, Miriam's hands trembling as she lifted her patient's leg while Julienne deftly bound the cumbersome dressing pad into place.

At the slightest sound all heads swiveled toward the doors. The patients lay still, tense and apprehensive.

"We are a hospital," one of the Chinese nurses said nervously to Julienne. "The Japanese will not harm sick men, surely?"

"No," Julienne said reassuringly. "Of course not." But she remembered the stories she had heard of Japanese behavior in China and she was not at all sure.

"They're coming," one of the orderlies said suddenly. "I can hear them."

Julienne wiped away a trickle of blood from the corner of the mouth of a Rajput whose right lung had been pierced with shrapnel. He was dying, but he was still lucid. "What is happening, nurse?" he whispered. "Why has it gone so silent? What is wrong?"

She took his hand and gave it a comforting squeeze, saying gently, and praying that she was speaking the truth, "There's no need to worry about it, Sergeant."

The outer doors of the dressing station were slammed open and a barrage of running feet thundered toward them. Julienne's hand tightened on that of the dying Rajput, then the doors to the ward were flung open and a squad of Japanese, rifles at the ready and bayonets fixed, burst in on them.

"*Out of beds!*" they screamed. "*Out of beds!*"

"This is a hospital," the senior medical officer said forcefully, stepping forward and addressing himself to the officer in charge. "These men are all seriously injured. They cannot leave their beds. I must ask you to with—"

The officer raised his rifle butt and hit him full across the side of the head, sending him sprawling across the floor. "When Japanese officer gives order, English pigs obey! Now out of beds! Everyone out of beds!"

Those that could tried to do as they were ordered; those that couldn't remained helplessly where they were.

"Out! Out!" a Japanese screamed, jabbing his bayonet toward the young Canadian boy Julienne had been so recently tending.

Julienne withdrew her hand from the dying Rajput's and flew across to the injured Canadian, throwing herself in front of him.

"*Non!*" she spat, knocking the bayonet aside as contemptuously as if it were a toy. "*Ça n'est pas possible!*" Her riot of Titian curls tumbled from beneath her crisp white nurse's cap, and her violet-dark eyes blazed. "This patient has only one leg! He cannot stand! Do you understand? He cannot stand!" She spread her arms wide so that the Japanese could approach no farther.

The Japanese goggled at her and stepped backward, and as he did so, his commanding officer barked an order. It was the signal for a bloodbath.

The retreating Japanese retreated no farther. He lunged forward and with a cry of horror Julienne flung herself protectively over the body of the helpless Canadian. The bayonet went through the flesh of her arm and into the Canadian's stomach, skewering them bloodily together. Through her screams of pain, Julienne was aware of the other soldiers, pausing for a moment half crouched over their bayonets, and then storming forward, dragging patients from their beds and bayonetting them with murderous glee.

A booted foot was stamped down on her pinioned arm as the soldier sought leverage to wrench his bayonet free. As she slithered to the floor she caught a glimpse of Miriam Gresby cowering in a corner and of one of the Chinese nurses being hurled away from the patient she was trying to protect. A bayonet went into the senseless body of the senior medical officer, another through the throat of the dying Rajput.

Julienne crawled to her hands and knees, slipping and sliding on the blood-soaked floor, trying to reach a scalpel, a surgical knife, anything that would end the life of one of the beasts rampaging around her. There were no instrument trays within her reach and she staggered to her feet, sobbing in frustration, deafened by the screams of the dying men and the shrill, gleeful laughter of the Japanese.

"*Murderers!*" she howled as she lunged toward the nearest Japanese. "*Murderers!*" She hurled herself at him, clawing at his face with the hand of her uninjured arm, her nails raking his flesh.

His rifle butt came down hard on the side of her head, sending her sprawling in blinding agony to the floor. All around her, as she lay unable to move, barely conscious, she could hear the screams of the dying Rajputs. Then there were no more screams, only gasping, agonized groans, then silence.

"What are you going to do with us?" Miriam asked in a quavering voice. "Dear Lord, what are you going to do with us?"

Julienne tried to move. Her vision was dislocated, objects dancing and merging together, but she was sure she could see the glint of metal just inches away from her.

"You soon see," a Japanese said to Miriam as the nurses were dragged from wherever they had tried to hide. Stumbling and falling, they were hauled over the bodies of the dead medical staff and the few patients who had managed to die on their feet.

Julienne stretched her hand a fraction of an inch farther. It was a knife. A surgical knife. Her fingers closed around the haft.

"How old are you, Englishwoman?" the Japanese snapped at Miriam.

Julienne lifted her head, the knife safe in her grasp, and dizzily tried to focus. Miriam looked as if she were about to faint. Her steel-gray hair, usually so elegantly styled, hung damply against her cheeks. Her hands, naked without their lavish decoration of rings, looked pathetically old.

"Forty-seven," she said waveringly.

The Jap hooted with laughter. "Too old," he said derisively. "Too old, old woman. No good." And as the four British women and the three Chinese women were herded forward, she was pushed contemptuously aside.

One of the Chinese girls was whimpering in fear; another was praying rapidly and urgently, a rosary sliding with desperate haste through her fingers. The men pressed around them, bloody and sweaty, jostling for position, and then the screams began.

Julienne held the knife concealed in the palm of her hand. She would only be able to kill once, but she would kill with merciless relish. Brutal hands seized her, throwing her onto her back, and she could see nothing but lustful

yellow faces closing in on her, and rampant cocks held in
blood-soaked hands.

She had only one hand in which to hold the knife, but
she held it firm, and as the first of her ravagers fell on top of
her the knife slid unerringly in and up beneath his ribs. She
saw an expression of dumb amazement on his face, heard
his choking intake of breath, and knew it would be the last
he would ever take. As his companions realized what she
had done, they fell on her with howls of rage, but Julienne
was triumphant.

The soldier whose dead body was being dragged off
from her to make way for the others was the one who had
so brutally bayonetted the young Canadian.

"Vous avez été vengé, chéri," she whispered as her victim's
comrades fell on her like ravening wolves. *You have been
avenged.*

Chapter Twenty-eight

❧

THE night sky lightened imperceptibly, presaging dawn,
as Adam and his companions hurtled in their army truck
toward Wong Nei Chung Gap.

"How the hell did the bastards manage to get so far
inland, so quickly?" their driver asked as he took a perilous
corner at the foot of Shouson Hill with a screech of tires.

"God knows," Adam said tautly. "They must have
overrun the Rajputs on the north coast *and* the volunteer
batteries at Sai Wan Hill and Jardine's Lookout."

"Ronnie Ledsham was at Sai Wan Hill," one of the men
behind him said as the truck bumped and rocked over the
uneven ground. "I wonder if he copped it or not?"

"That bloody horse of his ought to cop it," another voice
said darkly. "I lost a bloody packet on it last Saturday."

There was a burst of nervous laughter, then the driver
said brusquely, "Pack it in, chaps. I can hear gunfire."

Adam leaned forward, straining to see into the darkness. To the left was the dense black mass of Mount Nicholson. With a painful stab he recalled Beth leaning against the rails of the *Orient Princess* as they steamed into the harbor. Tom Nicholson had pointed out to her Victoria Peak and Mount Butler and Mount Nicholson, then laughingly said that he liked to think Mount Nicholson had been named after an ancestor of his. He wondered where Tom was now.

There was a rattle of gunfire and the flank of the mountain was suddenly thrown into lurid relief as flames from exploding mortar shells soared skyward.

"Jesus, but they're bloody close!" the man who had lost a packet on Ronnie's horse said apprehensively.

"The Japs aren't heading toward the gap, they're *on* the gap!" the driver exclaimed as volley after volley of machine-gun fire ripped out over the sound of the rifles and the crump of exploding shells.

Adam's hand tightened on his rifle. They had only the ammunition in their belts and a small supply of hand grenades. His driver flashed him a quick glance. "It looks as if we're not going to be meeting up with anyone, sir," he said grimly. "It looks as if we're going to be on our own."

"Keep your eyes on the road," Adam ordered, and as he did so a machine gun opened fire on them. Bullets raked the windshield, spattering across the chest of the driver, burrowing into the door. From behind him Adam heard screams as men were hit, and he yelled at them to get down. The truck was veering wildly out of control and he seized the wheel, trying to hold it on the road, to drive through the crucifying hail of fire.

"*I'm hit, sir! I'm hit!*" the youngest member of his platoon shrieked, stumbling toward the front of the truck, blood pouring down his face and over his hands.

"Get down!" Adam shouted at him as he fought to hold onto the wheel, to keep the truck on the road.

There was another withering blast of fire and the young corporal screamed in agony, lifted off his feet by the momentum of the shots plummeting into him. When he fell, it was forward, over the rear of Adam's seat. Vainly Adam tried to free himself of the boy's weight, but it was too late. He last control of the wheel and before he could regain it, the truck toppled off the edge of the road, crashing and rolling and splintering down the side of a ravine.

Adam was sandwiched between the driver and the dead corporal, and when the disintegrating truck finally rocked and slithered to a halt on the dark, scrub-filled hillside, he knew he owed them his life. Without the protection their bodies had afforded, he would have been smashed to a bloody pulp.

Pain screamed through his shoulders and legs as he tried to move, tried to free himself from them. He had to get out of the truck before the gas tank exploded or a hand grenade went off, and he had to get his men out with him.

"I've got you, sir," someone said, and Adam recognized the voice of Freddie Hollis, the middle-aged punter who had lost money on Ronnie's horse. "Just hang on tight, sir, and I'll have you free in a jiffy."

"Get back!" Adam shouted to him. *"The gas tank is about to go!"*

"Not yet it isn't," Hollis panted with the confidence of a man accustomed to long shots. "Not till I've got you free, it isn't."

With a massive heave, he pulled Adam from beneath the dead driver and out of the truck's shattered cab.

Adam crawled painfully on his hands and knees, looking about him with horror. "What about the others?" he asked, stumbling to his feet, sick and stunned. There was no movement from the wreckage. No sound.

"I didn't see what happened to the two who were behind me," Hollis said, fighting for breath. "But the three in front of me are all goners."

With a choked cry, Adam staggered forward toward the wreckage.

"There's nothing you can do for them!" Hollis protested urgently. "We need to get the hell away from here!"

Adam agreed with him completely, but before he left he had to satisfy himself that he wasn't leaving wounded men behind him. His hands, moving feverishly and bloodily over the mangled bodies still trapped in the rear of the truck, assured him that he was not.

"Come *on*, sir!" Hollis hissed. "That tank is going to go any minute."

Adam sucked his breath between his teeth. Apart from one man, his entire platoon had been wiped out without even having had the chance to fire on the enemy.

"Let's go," he said harshly, hardly able to speak for grief, and they began to run and stumble over shale and between stunted Chinese pines. As they did so, there was another long, chattering burst of machine-gun fire. The gas tank was hit, and it exploded with hideous force, flames leaping into the air, the heat blasting their retreating backs.

"That was a near one," Hollis gasped, throwing himself facedown on the scree.

They lay still for a few moments, trying not to think of the bodies being incinerated only yards away from them.

"Come on," Adam said, when the machine gunner had been given time to direct his attention elsewhere. "We have to try to skirt this ambush and regain the road. Somehow or other, we still have to make it to the gap."

"I can't see a bloody hand in front of my face," Hollis whispered back to him. "Can't we just sit it out until it gets light?"

"And find a score of Japs having breakfast fifty yards above our heads?" Adam asked savagely. "No, we can't. Our orders were to make it to the gap and give what assistance we could. And that is what I intend to do."

Hollis sighed. Adam had always been a stickler for discipline. He knew he could always refuse and say his legs wouldn't carry him, but he didn't fancy the idea of spending hours alone on a treacherous hillside with the Japanese breathing down his neck. "I'm with you, sir," he said resignedly. "Lead the way."

Adam led the way. Slowly and carefully they traversed the scree, the predawn darkness intensified by a thick fog rolling in from the sea. Finally, bruised and bleeding, they crawled back onto the road a good hundred yards farther on from the point where they had been ambushed.

"We can't just stroll along it as though it's Pall Mall on a Sunday morning," Hollis whispered apprehensively. "What do you intend to do?"

"What I don't intend is getting shot," Adam retorted crisply. "We'll cross to the higher ground, taking what cover we can, but keeping the road in view to give us our bearings."

Crouching low, rifles in their hands, they ran across the narrow road and into the scrub beyond.

"I can hear an engine," Hollis said suddenly. "Coming toward us, from the gap. Is it one of ours, or one of theirs, do you think?"

Adam listened. "It's one of ours," he said with sudden certainty. "It's a Bedford. I'm sure of it."

As the truck lumbered into view and he saw the familiar shape of the bonnet, he sprang forward, waving it down.

The truck skidded to a halt and the driver leaned out, yelling, "Don't go any farther that way! The gap's alive with Japs!"

"There's a party of them this way as well," Adam warned. "They've got a machine gun positioned above the road."

"Jesus Christ! Which way should I go then?" the driver asked desperately.

"Back the way you came," Adam snapped, disgusted by the man's determination to retreat. "And you can take my corporal and myself with you."

The driver rammed his truck once more into gear. "No bloody fear," he said forcefully. "I'm not driving back into that hellhole! Everyone is falling back. There's only one other platoon still trying to fight their way through to headquarters, and that's led by a madman. He's about five hundred yards ahead of you." With that, he pressed his foot down hard on the accelerator and sped away.

"Did you tell him about the Jap ambush?" Hollis asked as Adam sprinted back across the road.

"Yes. He seems to prefer that to whatever is happening at the gap."

"And what *is* happening at the gap?" Hollis asked, knowing damn well he would soon be finding out. If Adam had been going to retreat he would have hitched a lift with the departing truck driver.

"Hand-to-hand fighting by the sound of it," Adam said, dropping down into the scrub and beginning to run at a steady pace. "There's one platoon still trying to fight their way through, though."

"And we're going to join it?" Hollis asked, running at his side.

"Yes," Adam panted, wondering how long he could keep up his speed over rough ground. "We damn well are!"

The sound of fighting was all around them. Dawn was beginning to break, and as the pale gold light seeped over the horizon, it was easier for them to locate the sources of fierce enemy rifle fire.

"Jesus, Mary, and Joseph!" Hollis said as they threw themselves to the ground for the twentieth time. "The bastards are forming a ring around the gap. No one is going to get out of there!"

There was the sound of a truck accelerating wildly, speeding in their direction down the nearby road. They raised their heads cautiously, and as the British army truck veered into view, a barrage of shell shots were let loose on it. There was a scream of brakes and it keeled over, the cab a mass of flames. Spurts of fire flicked along the ground and splashes of dust pitted the road. No running figures fled from the truck's rear. It lay where it had fallen, burning brightly, and the shellfire died.

"Poor devils," Hollis said heavily. "They were making a run for it. There's no sense in trying to go any farther. The Japs have the gap. The best thing we can do is to try to retreat."

Adam's mouth tightened obstinately. He hadn't waited years for a military confrontation in order to make a retreat before he had even engaged the enemy. "No," he said stubbornly. "We're not retreating while there's still a platoon fighting ahead of us. We're going to join up with them and fight with them."

A shell exploded in a dip of ground to their left, showering them with debris.

"But there's no point!" Hollis protested when he had satisfied himself he was still all in one piece. "Even if we manage to fight our way through to Brigade Headquarters, we'd never be able to fight our way out! It's surrounded!"

The pale gold of early dawn was deepening to rosy red. Adam crouched on his haunches, looking around him. They were above the gap, and the gullies and ravines running down to it from the surrounding mountains were full of Japanese. Brigade Headquarters was a hundred yards or so on the west side of the Wong Nei Chung Gap Road, and he could see the bunkered roofs and the nearby company shelters half buried in the hillside, and the ammunition dumps. The Japanese had closed in a tight ring around them, but they had still not broken through. From all around the headquarters there were pockets of fierce fighting, and the one nearest to them was now clearly visible.

Adam's fingers tightened purposefully around his rifle.

There were six men, probably seven, all in volunteer uniform, except for the officer leading them, and all were running low through the dense undergrowth toward a Japanese machine-gun post. He didn't wait to see what would happen when they came within firing distance of it.

"Come on!" he snapped to Hollis. "There's a party going on and we've been invited! Get moving!"

Braving sniper fire and falling shells, they raced over the potholed ground. "Christ! I don't know who those chaps are in front of us, but they've been busy!" Hollis said as they swerved to avoid the bodies of butchered Japanese. "What are they fighting with? Carving knives?"

Adam didn't answer. His heart was pounding against his ribs, the blood drumming in his ears. Please don't let my leg let me down, he was praying as he ran and leaped and surged down the hill toward the volunteers in front of him. Then, as the volunteers opened fire on the machine-gun post and he hurled himself into battle alongside them, he found himself uttering the prayer of a man who had entered into battle over three hundred years earlier. "'O Lord! Thou knowest how busy I must be this day,'" Sir Jacob Astley had prayed before the battle of Edgehill. "'If I forget Thee, do not Thou forget me.'"

Bullets, heavy and hissing, flew past his head like swarms of angry bees. Mortar shells began to plop down into the ground around him, exploding in sharp blasts and sending shrapnel flying. One of the men in front of him caught a piece in his throat and fell to his knees, choking on blood.

"We have to put that gunner out of action!" the officer leading the volunteers yelled.

Adam was aware that Hollis had fallen, but whether through injury or to take shelter from the withering blast of machine-gun fire he didn't know.

"I've got a grenade!" he shouted, aware that the men he was fighting with had long since exhausted such supplies.

"Then give it to me, man!" the officer said, whipping around to face him. His steel helmet was gone, his dark hair falling damp with sweat across his forehead. His bayonet dripped blood from his earlier hand-to-hand engagement, he had an ugly gash in his left forearm, and his eyes blazed with fanatic determination.

Adam felt himself falter and half fall as he thrust the

grenade into the officer's blood-soaked hand. "Thanks!" Raefe said with an exultant grin. "This will put the bastard out of action! Give me all the cover that you can!"

There was no place to hide, no place to take cover. If Elliot was going to lob the grenade with any hope of accuracy, then he was going to have to suicidally expose himself to enemy fire.

As Raefe sprang forward, heedless of the gunfire ricocheting around him, Adam opened fire at the machine gunner. Bullets beat down on him like hail, and other pellets bounced off the ground, casting gigantic firefly sparks into the air. Through the smoke and fumes he saw Raefe raise his right arm and lob the grenade with deadly accuracy. Crazily, as the machine-gun post erupted in screams and smoke and flames, all he could think was what a magnificent spin-bowler Elliot would have made.

"Thank God," Hollis croaked, crawling up beside him. "That bloody gun has been silenced."

"Not for long!" Adam whooped gleefully. "Now we can turn it on the bastards and give them a taste of their own medicine!"

There was still heavy sniper fire as he crouched low and sprinted forward to Elliot's side. "That was bloody marvelous!" he exclaimed, seizing Elliot's uninjured arm and slapping him on the back. "I've never seen anything like it! Why the hell you're not gutted with bullets I'll never know!"

"I've got my fair share," Raefe said wryly as the blood continued to run down his left arm. "Now, let's put this machine gun to good use."

Adam didn't move. He suddenly realized what it was he had done. This man he was congratulating on his foolhardy bravery was the man he hated most in the world. The man who had taken Beth away from him. The man he had yearned to put a bullet through.

Raefe grinned and for the first time Adam was aware of the force of the man's personality, of the reckless zest for life that had so attracted Beth. "I know what you're thinking, Harland," he said as a shell whistled close over their heads. "But forget it for the moment. All that matters now is that we get through to Lawson."

"Brigadier Lawson?" Adam asked, wondering what the hell Elliot was doing holding the rank of a British Army captain.

Raefe nodded grimly. "He's in there with only a handful of men. The Winnipeg Grenadiers who were with him were detailed to Jardine's Lookout shortly after midnight. His only reserve company left two hours ago to try to capture Mount Butler."

"Then who has he got in there with him?" Hollis asked, reaching them in time to hear the tail end of the conversation.

"Clerks, cooks, signalers, store men," Raefe said tersely. "They're putting up a hell of a fight, but you can see for yourself what the odds are."

Another shell plummeted heart-stoppingly near them.

"Yes," Hollis said fervently. "I can, but I don't see what we can do about it. We can't take on the entire Jap army single-handed. There must be two divisions at least swarming over these hills."

Adam and Raefe ignored him. The other volunteers who had been pinned down by fire were now running toward them. Of the six, there were only four left.

"We leave two men here to man this gun," Raefe said decisively. "The rest of us keep going forward, is that understood?"

Hollis squirmed slightly. He wasn't a coward and he didn't like being made to feel like one. If the madman giving the orders had an ounce of sense, he would realize that continuing forward was nothing short of suicide. As it was, he didn't have sense and of the two options open to him, Hollis much preferred the thought of remaining with Adam, whom he had begun to regard as a lucky mascot.

"If Captain Harland is staying with the gun, I'll stay with him."

"I'm not," Adam said unhesitatingly. "I'm going forward with Captain Elliot."

Hollis wondered what the odds were on their ever coming back. "All right," he said fatalistically. "I'll go forward too."

They had gone only fifty yards when a party of Japanese surged over the lip of the hill, bearing down on them with frenzied shouts of *"Banzai! Banzai!"*

In the long, hideous days afterward, when Adam had plenty of time to remember and reflect, it was Raefe's sheer physical strength that remained his clearest memory. As hand grenades fell among them like fine rain, Raefe shouted blasphemous encouragement to the men he was leading, and hurled unspeakable oaths at the enemy. When his rifle would no longer fire, he clubbed the Japanese to death with the butt. When his bayonet remained pinioned in the body of a soldier who had been bearing down on Hollis, he wrested a sword from an officer and decapitated him with it. He picked up grenades and threw them back at the attacking hordes. He fought with his boots and with his bare fists. He wasn't one man, he was ten men, and by the time the Japanese lay dead around them, Adam knew he would never again be able to speak of Elliot with contempt.

They lay on the ground among the fallen Japanese, gasping for breath. Hollis was badly wounded, blood pouring from a shrapnel wound in his leg. One of the original volunteers had died at the end of a Japanese bayonet thrust, his last, anguished cry being for his mother. Adam had been wounded in the shoulder and the thigh, but he could still lift his arm, still limp at a creditable rate on his good leg.

The gunfire in and around the headquarters was fiercer than ever.

"They're still holding out," Adam panted. "Surely to God there should be reinforcements breaking through soon?"

Raefe was just about to answer him when he saw a score of Japanese emerge from the scree on the east side of the Wong Nei Chung Gap Road and take up sniper positions perilously close to the beleaguered headquarters. Dragging himself to his feet, he waved Hollis and Adam on behind him. Before they had gone a dozen yards, they could see more Japanese, this time on the roof of the medical aid shelter, only thirty feet or so from Brigadier Lawson's command post.

"We can't get there in time to be of any use," Hollis gasped, then he heard Raefe Elliot's savage intake of breath and Adam's choked cry. Down below then, where the gap road wound through the converging hills, toward Repulse Bay and the sea, the Brigade Headquarters was completely surrounded and under a barrage of gunfire. Half a dozen men, one of them in the distinctive uniform of a brigadier, burst out of the shelter, firing from the hip. There were almost instantly cut down.

"Oh, God," Hollis said, sinking to his knees. "Oh, God! Oh, shit! Oh, hell!"

Adam and Raefe looked down on the now silent headquarters, the skin stretched tight across their cheekbones, their mouths grim. There was no more gunfire, only exultant Japanese swarming down into the bunkered recesses of what had been Brigadier Lawson's command headquarters.

"What now?" Adam asked bleakly, turning away, unable to bear seeing any more.

Raefe was silent for a minute. The Japanese had closed in a tight ring all around them and he knew they would have to fight just as fiercely to break out of the ring as they had to break into it.

"We head toward Repulse Bay," he said at last. "The Japanese will have their work cut out for them consolidating their positions on the ground they've taken. Any counterattack will have to come from East Brigade, and they're down around the bay and the peninsula."

Hollis groaned. "But that's nearly two miles over rough ground. There's no way I'll be able to make it."

"There's an advanced dressing station between here and the bay," Raefe said, helping Adam haul Hollis to his feet. "We'll leave you there. They'll soon patch you up."

They were so exhausted by the time the dressing station came into view, none of them noticed how suspiciously quiet it was.

"I'll get them to put a pad on this wound in my thigh," Adam said as they limped up to the door. "It isn't deep, but it's bleeding like the devil."

The door swung open and he didn't speak again. Not for a long time. It was a charnel house. The senior medical officer lay directly across their path, hideously bayonetted. Men with only stumps for legs lay half dragged from their beds, killed despite their obvious wounds.

Hollis choked, vomiting over the floor as Adam and Raefe stepped disbelievingly forward. The nurses had been herded together and lay in a pathetic discarded heap, their broken bodies bearing dreadful witness to the way they had been used before death.

"Christ Almighty!" Adam whispered, turning his head away. "It's beyond belief—" It was then that he saw Julienne. She was lying apart from the other nurses, a dead

Japanese a few feet away from her, a surgical knife protruding from his chest.

Adam sobbed, kneeling down at her side. "The bastards," he wept, taking her hand. "The unspeakable, unbelievable, goddamned *bastards!*"

Every muscle and tendon in Raefe's body was rigid. "*Lizzie!*" he was screaming inside his head. "*Lizzie! Lizzie!*" If the Japs had raped and murdered once, they would rape and murder again.

Adam turned his chalk-white face toward him. "What about Beth?" he whispered hoarsely. "What if the Japs overrun the Jockey Club?"

Raefe was taking off his jacket, bending down over Julienne. "There's a huge concentration of troops around Wanchai and the Jockey Club," he said tersely, praying to God they were still there. "Lizzie will be safe."

His voice was odd, so tight that it was almost strangled. With unutterable tenderness he wrapped the jacket around Julienne and closed her pansy-dark eyes.

"At least she took one of the bastards with her," he said, and as he spoke Adam realized it wasn't rage or horror that was transforming his voice, but tears.

"We can't just leave her here," Adam said helplessly. "We can't just leave any of them here. It's indecent. It's—"

A noise from a large cupboard only a yard or two away from them made them both spring to their feet.

"*Bastard!*" Adam sobbed. He leaped forward and yanked open the door, his bayonet ready in his hand.

Miriam Gresby toppled out on top of him, no longer elegant and aggressive, but a barely recognizable, incoherent wreck.

"*They killed them all! Killed them! Take me away, oh, take me away!*" she cried, sinking to the floor at Adam's feet, grasping his hands and then, as he tried to help her to her feet, his legs. "*Oh, God, help me! They killed them! Raped them!*" Her words were lost in a fit of hysterical sobbing.

Raefe looked down at Julienne. She was still beautiful, despite the obscene way she had died. Her spicy red hair clung in damp, curling tendrils around her kittenish face; her full, soft lips were tranquil. He pressed the first two fingers of his hand against his lips then bent down and pressed them against hers. "'Bye, Julienne," he said huskily. "*Au revoir, ma petite.*"

"What are we going to do with Miriam?" Adam asked, as she sobbed and clung to him.

Raefe stood up, took one last look around the ward and the dead men bayonetted in their beds, and said, "We'll take her with us to the Repulse Bay."

The scene he had just imprinted on his memory would stay with him for life. Whatever the outcome of the fighting now taking place, he made a deep, bitter resolve that the world would know of the infamy of the Japanese who had overrun the dressing station. "If I die," he said harshly to Adam, "make sure that what has happened here becomes public knowledge."

Adam nodded, deciding to make sure no harm came to Miriam. She was a witness to what had taken place, and one day, maybe years hence, she would be able to tell her story and the perpetrators would find themselves on the gallows.

It was a long, miserable retreat to the bay. Hollis's leg wound was severe, and though Adam bound it as best he could with pads he found at the dressing station, the blood was still oozing through, dark and thick, as they limped their way across the hills toward the hotel.

"I don't feel too good, old boy," Hollis said with difficulty to Adam as the long, low, gleaming white hotel finally came into view. "I don't think I'm going to make it."

"Of course you're going to, make it," Adam said grimly, grateful that his thigh had stopped bleeding and the wound in his shoulder had proved to be not seriously incapacitating.

"Help Corporal Hollis," Raefe said brusquely to Miriam Gresby. He wondered how soon it would be before he was able to commandeer a car or a truck and storm a way through the Japanese-held center of the island to the Jockey Club.

"Sorry about this, Lady Gresby," Hollis said with a weak grin. "I never thought we'd get to know each other quite so intimately."

Miriam sobbed and allowed him to rest his arm around her shoulders, and they traversed the last few yards of uneven ground and dropped down onto the road. It was blessedly clear.

"Thank God," Adam said with heartfelt relief. "At least the Japs haven't reached the bay."

As they limped toward the sumptuous hotel gardens, they were seen, and over half a dozen guests ran out toward them.

"Jesus Christ! What's happened?"

"Lady Gresby! It *is* Lady Gresby, isn't it?"

"Give that man to me, I can support him."

The voices clamored around them and Raefe said tersely, "The Japs have overrun Brigade Headquarters at the gap. Are there any troops at the hotel? Any telephone communications?"

"We have a platoon of C Company of the Middlesex," a middle-aged man incongruously dressed in a white dinner jacket and evening trousers said, "and some naval ratings and a small party of Royal Navy Volunteer Reserves. About fifty men in all."

"Who's in command?" Raefe asked as he led his depleted party between the luxuriant flower beds that lay at the rear of the hotel.

"Second Lieutenant Peter Grounds," another of the guests, who was helping to carry Hollis, said. "He's very competent. He has everything under control."

"And the telephone?" Raefe asked, desperate to communicate to Fortress HQ the atrocity that had taken place at the dressing station, and to reassure himself that the Jockey Club had not suffered similarly.

"There's a non-military telephone link. Second Lieutenant Grounds is keeping in touch with Fortress HQ on it."

Raefe breathed a sigh of relief and, bloody and dirty, stepped inside the familiar, opulent Repulse Bay Hotel.

Chapter Twenty-nine

W E'VE had reports of other atrocities," he was told when he had made his report. "The fifth antiaircraft battery of the volunteers was bayonetted to death *after* they had made an honorable surrender. The Silesian Mission at Shaukiwan has been overrun and the medical staff butchered." The second lieutenant eyed the ugly gash on Raefe's forearm. "You'd better get that seen to. We have a resident nurse here, a formidable Scotswoman, and also a couple of auxiliary nurses. They'll soon sort you out."

Raefe walked slowly out of the luxurious lounge that was serving as a temporary military headquarters, and toward the rooms being used as a sick bay. For the first time since the fighting had begun, he felt unbelievably tired. There was no immediate danger now to send the adrenaline surging along his veins; no outlet for the bitter, burning hate that had consumed him ever since he had stood amid the carnage of the advanced dressing station. His orders from Fortress HQ had been precise. He was to stay at Repulse Bay, giving whatever assistance he could, and helping in the formation of sorties against the encroaching Japanese. If the island were overrun and there was no further hope of driving the Japanese back across the straits, he was to avoid capture and make his escape to Chungking, where he would continue the war giving help to British intelligence. He ran his hand through his hair. The word surrender had not been used, but it had been implicit. And he had categorically been refused permission to try to cross the island and reach Happy Valley and the Jockey Club.

"Lizzie," he groaned as he stepped inside the crowded sick bay. Ever since he had gazed down at Julienne's mutilated, broken body, he had been consumed by an emotion totally alien to him. He had been consumed by fear. *Lizzie, Lizzie,* he prayed to himself, his knuckles clenching white. *Please be safe! Please survive!*

And there she was. Her gray cotton nursing dress was blood-spattered, her lovely face tired and drawn, but she was there, only yards away from him, her blond hair coiled at the back of her neck, her smile reassuring as she sponged the dried blood from Hollis's leg.

"It's going to need several stitches, Lance Corporal Hollis," she was saying in her low, warm voice. "And we don't have a doctor—"

"*Lizzie!*" He didn't give a damn about Hollis's leg. He didn't give a damn about anything anymore. "*Lizzie!*"

She spun around, dropping the bowl she had been holding, the blood draining from her face.

"Just a minute," Hollis protested plaintively. "I don't mind there being no doctor, but at least let me have a nurse!"

She left his side, she left the upturned bowl on the floor, she took three paces across the room and like an arrow entering the gold, hurled herself into Raefe's outstretched arms.

"Oh, my love, my darling, my sweet, sweet love!" he murmured hungrily against her hair, her skin, as he crushed her to him like a man demented.

"If he gets that sort of treatment for a fleabite to his arm, why didn't I get it for my leg?" Hollis complained to the rest of the fascinated, bedridden onlookers.

"It's because he's a captain," someone said cheekily. "Captains always get special privileges."

"Wish I was a bloody captain then," another voice chimed in. "I wouldn't mind that sort of privilege."

"I can't believe it!" Elizabeth said joyously, her face upturned to his. "I've been so worried about you! There have been such dreadful reports. Every time I heard of a Japanese advance or the massacre of a volunteer unit, I kept thinking that perhaps you were there. That you were lying out on the hillside dreadfully injured or even dead!"

"Not me, Lizzie," he said, and the old grin was back on his mouth. "I'm like a bad penny. I always turn up."

"Kiss me!" she said urgently. "Oh, God, make me believe it's true and that I'm not dreaming! *Kiss me!*"

He lowered his head to hers and as Hollis and the wounded Canadians clapped and cheered, he kissed her long and deeply, overwhelmed by the love he felt for her, knowing that she was his very life.

"Very nice!" Hollis called out to them weakly. "But what about my leg? If it doesn't get stitched up soon, it won't be worth wasting the catgut on it!"

"Oh, goodness," Elizabeth gasped, horrified. "Lance Corporal Hollis's leg!" She fled from Raefe's arms, and made effusive apologies to a vastly entertained Hollis as she ran fresh water and filled a clean bowl.

"When you've finished with that reprobate, I have a slight scratch on my arm that needs loving attention," Raefe said, grinning down at Hollis, who winked up at him. "And you have another patient, too. Adam."

"Adam!"

She spun her head around to him and Hollis groaned in despair. "Never mind Adam Harland," he said with feeling. "If it wasn't for him, I wouldn't be in this pickle. Adam first-to-the-front Harland will just have to wait his turn."

Elizabeth returned her attention to his injured leg. "Is he badly hurt?" she asked tremulously.

"No," Raefe said. "A bullet grazed his shoulder and there's a peppering of light shrapnel in one leg." He paused, then said, "He's quite a fighter. If he hadn't come to our assistance, I doubt if Hollis or I would still be alive."

She put the bowl and the sponge unsteadily down. "Do you mean that you and Adam have been fighting together?"

Raefe nodded, amused at seeing how competent she was in a task so alien to her. "Yes, and if I say so myself, we made rather a good team."

"I'm going to give you an injection before I start suturing," she said to Freddie. "It will help numb some of the pain, but it's not going to be very nice."

"Oh, God," Hollis said, raising his eyes to heaven. "I knew my luck would run out eventually."

Raefe watched as Elizabeth began to put in the sutures. He couldn't tell her about Julienne now. He didn't want to have to tell her at all. He said quietly, "I'll see you later, Lizzie. After you've had a chance to say hello to Adam."

She nodded, grateful for his sensitivity. She wondered

how Adam must feel at having had to fight alongside a man he felt so much contempt for.

It was eighteen hours before she and Raefe had an opportunity to be alone together. She had been on duty all day and she remained on duty all night. Not until six the next morning was she able to leave the sick bay and the wounded Canadians who had been brought in from the gap. As she stepped out into the wide, lushly carpeted corridor, Raefe was waiting for her, his arm in a sling.

"Your senior companion dealt with me herself," he said, sliding his free arm around her waist. "And a very efficient job she did too. How was Adam's leg? Is he going to have any problems with it?"

She leaned wearily against him, rejoicing in the physical and emotional strength he afforded her. "No." She had cleaned and bandaged Adam's leg and shoulder herself. It had been a strange experience, knowing that Raefe was only rooms away from them, that they were all now together in an intimacy from which there was no escape. "He won't be able to fight anymore. He can't move quickly and he should never have had to walk so far over such rough ground. What he needs is rest, but it isn't something easily obtained at the moment, is it?"

"No," Raefe said, his arm tightening around her. "Which is why we must take our opportunities while we can."

In an hour he was to leave with a hastily assembled party of the Middlesex, their destination the Japanese-infested gap. He did not tell her of his imminent departure. He wanted their lovemaking to be as joyous, as uninhibited, as it had been in the sun-filled bedroom of the home he doubted either of them would ever see again.

"Come with me," he said, his voice thick with rising passion. "I have a surprise for you."

If anyone had told Elizabeth that an unoccupied bedroom could be found in the hotel she would have laughed in disbelief. Ever since the Japanese had overrun the New Territories, nervous residents from all parts of the island had made their way to Repulse Bay, regarding it as a possible haven of safety. There were now one hundred and eighty of them, cheek by jowl, with two hundred soldiers and more stragglers arriving every hour. Deluxe suites were being shared by elderly American men and Chinese babies; by aristocratic Englishwomen and the young wives

of French and Portuguese businessmen. At night, every
bed, every sofa, every chair was occupied. The idea of
finding privacy was ludicrous. Until Raefe opened the door
of the huge, walk-in linen cupboard and turned the key in
the lock behind him.

"Now," he said huskily, pulling a blanket from a shelf
and tossing it to the floor. "Let me show you how very
much I've missed you, Lizzie!"

Afterward, whenever she remembered their lovemaking
in the small, lavender-scented linen room, it seemed to her
as if it had taken place in slow motion. She knelt, facing
him on the blanket, and he tenderly touched her face with
his hands, his forefinger softly tracing the pure line of her
cheekbone and jaw. Then, as her excitement had mounted
unbearably, he removed her white nursing cap and the
pins holding her hair so primly at the back of her head, and
her hair slid, heavily and silkily, over his hands, spilling
down onto her shoulders.

"You are so beautiful, Lizzie," he said reverently. "So
incredibly, amazingly beautiful."

He kissed her forehead, her temples. His mouth tantalizingly skimmed the corner of her mouth and trailed down
her neck. Then, with slow deliberation, he began to undo
the buttons of her dress.

"I love you, Lizzie. Love you," he whispered hoarsely as
he slipped it down over her shoulders, exposing them and
her lace-covered breasts. She rose in a smooth, fluid
movement, letting the dress fall to her ankles, stepped free
of it, then knelt down once more before him for his
adoration.

Gently he removed her white lace brassiere, cupping her
breasts in his strong, olive-toned hands, his thumbs
brushing the rosy-red nipples, his eyes darkening in
pleasure as he saw them harden proudly. He lowered his
head to them, his thick shock of blue-black hair soft against
her skin as he pulled gently with his mouth on first one
nipple and then the other, his tongue lapping and circling,
his teeth softly nipping. She heard herself groan in
submission, felt the hot dampening between her thighs as
exquisite chords of longing vibrated deep within her.

"Oh, Raefe, I've missed you so," she whispered as his
hands ran caressingly down over her breasts to her waist,
then over the full, gentle curve of her hips and her thighs.

Not until she was brought to near insensibility with need of him did he swiftly rid himself of his shirt and pants and ease her down on the floor beneath him. Restraining his own passion with iron self-control, he lowered his head to the mound of golden curls between her thighs, his hands stroking her flesh as his tongue found the small pearl of her clitoris.

She lay in an ecstasy of passivity, her arms stretched out languorously above her head, moaning with pleasure as his tongue moved slowly, hot and sweet. At last, when he could bear no more, he covered her body with his own, parting the lips of her damp vagina with strong, sure fingers. "Oh, God, Lizzie!" He groaned as he entered her. "I love you! Only you! Forever!"

They moved slowly at first, two lovers with an intimate knowledge of the other's needs, savoring every step of their climb toward a long, drawn-out, magnificent climax. Her hands slid over his shoulders, up to the nape of his neck, her fingers burrowing in his coarse black curls. Their bodies would no longer allow them to halt along the way. Her hips ground relentlessly against his, her breasts crushed against his chest as he drove deeper and faster into her. She heard his name on her lips, felt her back arch, her nails score his flesh as they reached a mutual peak of earth-shattering, cataclysmic relief, no longer two separate identities, but one.

Afterward she lay in his arms, tears wet upon her cheeks. Before he gently drew away from her she said softly, "I'm having another baby, Raefe. I've thought I was for a week or two. Two days ago I was sure."

He looked down at her, his near-black eyes brilliant with love. "This time it will be all right, Lizzie," he said huskily, his hard-boned face certain.

Her arms tightened around him. The Japanese were advancing indefatigably; the world they had known was falling apart. And yet at that moment, lying in Raefe's arms and sharing with him the joy of her pregnancy, she had never been happier.

It wasn't until they were dressed and the door of the linen room was closed behind them that he gently told her of Julienne's death.

She was too shocked, too grief-stricken for tears. "Oh,

no," she whispered, time and time again. "Oh, no! I can't believe it! I won't believe it! Not Julienne. It isn't possible!"

"I'm sorry, my love," he said, holding her close, hardly able to believe himself that Julienne's dauntless buoyancy was stilled forever. "But it's true. Miriam Gresby was a witness. And one day, the Japanese who overran that dressing station will pay for what they did. On the gallows."

He kissed her and left her, knowing she would have to come to terms with her grief herself. He could not help her. White-faced, she returned to the room she was sharing with ten other women, and knowing that she would have to be back on duty in the sick bay by lunchtime, she desperately tried to sleep. But despite her physical exhaustion, sleep was a long time in coming. She thought of Julienne, laughing and merry and dazzling. It seemed inconceivable that she would never see her again. Never hear her infectious giggle. Never again be dazed by her outrageous, good-humored behavior. And when she thought of Ronnie, living a life unsustained by Julienne's irrepressible zest, she turned her face to the wall and wept.

Six hours later she went back down to the sick bay and reported for duty to the Repulse Bay's resident nursing sister. The sister's face was harrowed as she told Elizabeth that Second Lieutenant Peter Grounds had been killed while leading an attack on the hotel's garage.

"On the garage?" Elizabeth asked, stunned. "You mean the Japanese are on the grounds?"

"I'm afraid so," the nursing sister said grimly. "And they had prisoners with them. Second Lieutenant Grounds led a very brave attack on the garage to free the men the Japanese were blatantly ill-treating, and though the attack succeeded and the Japanese have been flushed out, Second Lieutenant Grounds died in the confrontation."

From then on in the hotel was an atmosphere of siege. Adam helped the staff and guests sandbag the windows, and when one of the guests, a Dutch engineer, suggested that they use a large drain as an air raid shelter, Adam was in keen agreement with him. The drain was plenty big enough, at least eight feet in diameter, and it ran from the rear of the hotel, beneath the road, emptying out onto the beach. All through Saturday and Saturday night, everyone who was able worked under the Dutchman's direction, inserting an entrance and ventilation shafts. By the time Raefe and the men from the Middlesex returned from their bloody and abortive attempt to rid the gap of Japanese, women and children from the hotel were sheltered snugly in the drain, equipped with sandwiches and coffee, and temporarily safe from the shells that were now landing with terrifying frequency.

"This isn't like a usual Sunday at the Repulse Bay, is it?" Adam said dryly to Elizabeth as he helped the Dutchman tap a central heating pipe for water. The hot water system had been turned off due to lack of fuel, but as the hotel's water supplies were dwindling fast, the water in the boilers and pipes could not be allowed to go to waste.

Elizabeth smiled wearily. It certainly wasn't. She remembered the Sunday prelunch drinks they had enjoyed with Ronnie and Julienne, and Helena and Alastair, and Tom, with Ronnie gustily leading them into a rip-roaring rendering of "There'll Always Be an England." Now there was no singing. The stink of unflushed lavatories permeated every room, the cocktail bar and the card room and the dining room were full of weary soldiers, exhausted after their hopeless expedition to the gap.

Raefe ran toward them. "We're coming under sniper fire from the rear of the hotel," he shouted urgently to Adam. "We need your ability as a marksman to try to pick them off."

Adam's face tightened, not because of Raefe's presence, but with resolution. "Just let me have the chance!" he said fiercely, grabbing the rifle that Raefe thrust at him. "Where are the bastards?"

"About fifty yards away, on the west side." Raefe gave Elizabeth's shoulder a quick squeeze, then spun on his heel, breaking into a run after Adam.

That night, Major Robert Templar of the Royal Artillery was sent by Fortress HQ from the Stanley Peninsula to take command of the various units milling beneath the hotel's roof. The situation was clearly desperate. A party of volunteers had fallen back to the hotel earlier in the day, telling of bitter fighting taking place not only in the center of the island, but all along the southern coast as well. They had been part of the East Brigade's last-ditch effort to recapture the gap, and they were all that was left of their party.

"You'll be pleased to see one of them," Raefe said to Elizabeth as he directed the line of fire from a sandbagged window. "It's Derry."

"Derry!" She ran down the candlelit corridors to the main lounge where the newcomers were drinking preciously rationed coffee and taking what rest they could. He looked for all the world as if it were any normal Sunday evening. His tin helmet was crammed on his sun-bleached hair at a rakish angle, giving him the look of a medieval pikeman. His raw-boned, handsome face was smeared with dust and smoke but his grin was wide, his eyes undefeated.

"Derry!" she cried, squeezing past half a dozen soldiers and a squalling Chinese toddler. "Derry! How wonderful!"

He swung her up in his arms, whirling her around, and smacked a large kiss on her cheek. "You look as beautiful as ever," he said appreciatively. "But do you think that gray is really your color?"

She giggled and felt for one brief, delirious moment that the world had returned to sanity. Then she remembered Julienne. Derry saw the expression on her face change, and with dreadful premonition, his own smile faded.

"What is it?" he demanded, the hair on the back of his neck rising. "What's happened?"

"It's Julienne," she said, stepping away from him, her voice thick with pain. "She's been murdered by the Japanese."

He stared at her disbelievingly for a moment, then with an anguished cry he turned and forced his way back through the crowded lounge and out into the darkness.

"I don't understand it," Adam said to her later. "Where did he go? We need every able-bodied man we have to defend the rear of the hotel."

Elizabeth thought of the dark hills outside the hotel, infested with Japanese. "I think," she said slowly, "that he's gone to kill all the Japs he can."

For the next twenty-four hours she hardly saw Adam or Raefe, and Derry did not return. A three-man committee had been formed to try to bring some order to the chaos, but there were some problems that were insurmountable. Food and water were fast running out. By dusk on the twenty-second, there were only enough rations left for two more days. Many of the sick and injured desperately needed the services of a doctor, but despite many agonized requests over the telephone to Fortress HQ there was no doctor that could be spared. The sanitation was abominable, and if it hadn't been for the Dutchman's organizing parties of volunteers with pails, Elizabeth was sure that an epidemic would have broken out.

When the order came through from Fortress HQ on Monday night that all troops were to evacuate the hotel and leave the civilians to the mercy of the Japanese, she was horrified. "But it's an invitation to murder," she said to Raefe, aghast. "How can headquarters even suggest it?"

"Because it's the only hope there is of saving lives," he said, hoping to God he was speaking the truth. "Our position here is untenable. There's no chance we can fight our way out. The Japs are on the grounds and all around us. When they close in for the kill, it will mean the annihilation of everyone within the hotel walls."

"And if the troops leave?"

"Then as civilians, the guests and staff will have a slight chance of survival," he said tautly, knowing the gamble that was being taken. If the Japs about to storm them were the same troops who had stormed the dressing station, the chance of anyone's surviving was slim.

She was silent for a moment, then said, her voice so low he could hardly hear her, "Will you be going with the troops? Is this good-bye for us again?"

He took her hands, holding them tightly in his. "I'm leaving with the troops and I'm taking you with me."

She gasped, staring up at him bewilderedly.

"Not only is the hotel untenable," he said grimly, "the whole island is untenable. There can be no alternative to an eventual surrender. When that happens, my orders are clear: to evade capture and escape. And I'm certainly not leaving you behind to face the Japanese. Not after what happened to Julienne. From now on, where I go you come as well."

The exodus of troops took place at 1 A.M. the following day. All alcohol in the hotel was carefully destroyed so that the Japanese would not be tempted into a drunken orgy of raping and looting. The last telephone message was received from Fortress HQ, then the telephone lines were ripped from the walls. The evacuation was to be made via the drain tunnel leading to the beach, and then south across country to Stanley, where the Japanese had not yet penetrated. As the troops assembled, all in stockinged feet so they would make less noise, Adam took Raefe to one side. "Beth's told me what you plan to do if there's a surrender. I'm coming with you. I want to continue the fight against these murdering bastards, and I won't be able to do that if I'm stuck in a prison camp somewhere. I will be able to do it from Chungking."

Raefe's hesitation was fractional. Adam's leg injury was a nuisance, but not gravely incapacitating. And he was a fearless fighter. Two of them would be able to give far greater protection to Elizabeth than one of them could. "All right," he said. "If it comes to it, we go together."

Slowly and apprehensively, the troops began to file out through the drain.

"Been nice knowing you, nurse," one of the Middlesex said to Elizabeth, never imagining for a moment that she was going to go with them.

"See you in good old London town," another said, giving her an appreciative wink.

One of the volunteers, leaving with the rest of the troops, hesitated at the last moment, then changed into a suit of civilian clothes and disappeared upstairs. "Put his trousers and jacket on," Raefe said to Elizabeth. "You'll be far less conspicuous."

They waited until the end of the line and then, wishing the white-faced, apprehensive civilians luck, they slipped into the drain, aware that the Japanese were only a few feet above their heads.

Emerging in the darkness of the beach, they ran, taking whatever cover the could, to the Lower Beach Road and on past the Lido until they reached the main Island Road. No shots were fired at them. No Japanese were lying in wait.

"We've done it!" Adam whispered exultantly to Raefe. "We've slipped past them!"

In the still darkness a familiar voice could be faintly heard. It was the redoubtable Dutchman and he was shouting out into the darkness from the hotel, "Come in . . . Come in . . . No soldiers here! No soldiers here!"

The paused for a moment, overcome with fear for those they had left behind. Then the long line of figures once more broke into a steady run, off the road, into the hills, and over the rough, treacherous ground to Stanley.

Chapter Thirty

❦

THEY reached Stanley village at six in the morning, and by the time they did so, every one of those who had fled the hotel knew that the battle they were waging was hopeless. The Japanese had control of all the high ground and they had come under heavy sniper fire several times. At one point, as they had skirted South Bay, they had stumbled over the bodies of dead Canadians, their hands tied behind their backs, their bayonet wounds hideous witness to the way they had died.

The brigadier in charge of the troops assembling in Stanley for a last-ditch stand was adamant that he would keep on fighting, even if it meant doing so with his fists.

"And it looks as if he'll have to," Raefe said somberly to Adam. "There are hardly any mortars and no mortar bombs. All the heavy machine guns have been knocked out. There are some spare rifles, a small quantity of hand grenades and bayonets, and that's all."

"Then it will have to do us," Adam said, his jaw set hard. "I just wish to God we could catch some sleep before we go into action again."

"You've no chance," Raefe said with his old grin. "The Japs are on Stanley Mound and that's where we're going now, with the Royal Rifles."

Adam wiped his hand across his forehead. He was exhausted to the point of collapse. His shoulder hurt and his leg throbbed, but he would have died rather than let the younger man know how beaten he felt. The minute they arrived in Stanley, Beth had offered her services to the overworked dressing station. Seeing her hurry off, uncomplaining about her long days and nights without sleep, and the arduous walk they had just endured, he had wondered if he would ever see her again.

A barrage of shells exploded uncomfortably near to them. "Come on," Raefe said, his grin dying. "Let's show the bastards the battle isn't over yet."

Elizabeth swayed with fatigue. There was nowhere for the wounded to be evacuated to. Apart from small, isolated pockets of resistance, the Japanese had control of the entire island. Bombing had cut the water mains and the water tanks had been hit by shellfire. Nearly the only thing that could be done for the hideously maimed men was to pour sulfur into their gaping wounds.

All through the long, bomb-blasted day, she remained at her post, not knowing where Adam and Raefe were, praying they were still alive.

"My arm!" a young boy screamed "Aaaahhh, my arm! Please, please, somebody help me. Oh, my arm!"

Running to him, Elizabeth could see that the trooper's arm had been riddled by shrapnel from an exploding shell and was hanging in shreds, blood pouring out of the terrible wounds.

"Stanch the bleeding, nurse," the medical officer said to her tersely. "Let's see if we can save it."

By nightfall her hands were caked with blood. The shellfire was almost ceaseless and the Japanese on Stanley Mound had not been forced into a retreat. Instead, they were steadily gaining ground.

"There's only one way we can go now," one of the wounded men said to her bitterly as she dressed his leg, "and that's into the bloody sea!"

Up on the smoke-blackened slopes of Stanley Mound, Raefe and Adam fought side by side, exhorting each other forward, firing their rifles until they were too hot to hold.

"Watch your fronts, men!" Raefe yelled suddenly. "There's another wave of them coming!"

He saw Adam drop to one knee, firing at the chest of the Japanese who was leading the charge. The shot went wild, and as Raefe pulled the pin from a grenade, holding it for as long as he dared and then hurling it underhand into their midst, he was aware that the Japanese officer was nearly on top of Adam.

Adam staggered to his feet, the Jap too near for him to

take aim and fire. Desperately he grasped his rifle by the barrel, wielding it club fashion. The Jap knocked it contemptuously aside and as Adam fell, there was the gleam of a sword raised high above his head. With a bloodcurdling cry that put the Japanese shrieks of "Banzai!" to shame, Raefe hurled himself at Adam's attacker, circling his neck with his good arm, wrenching it back until it broke and the soldier fell against him like a rag doll. He had his back to the enemy for a second too long. The bullet hit him in his right shoulder, spinning him around, and then Adam was giving him covering fire as they ran and leaped to the nearest dip of ground they could find.

"It's Christmas Day in the morning, nurse," an injured Cockney who had trekked with them from the hotel said, incredulity in his voice. "It don't seem possible, do it?"

Elizabeth stared down at him. The days and nights had long since merged into one. Christmas. She thought of Christmas two years ago; of walking the sun-drenched streets of Perth with Raefe; of Roman Rakowski giving them the painting of the boy David.

"No," she said, hardly able to speak for weariness. "It doesn't seem possible at all."

Toward dawn she was able to snatch a couple of hours of desperately needed sleep, and when she awoke, it was to the news that Stanley Mound had fallen to the Japanese and that a retreat was going to be made to Stanley Fort at the very tip of the peninsula.

"Did Captain Elliot and Captain Harland return?" she asked fearfully.

The officer she was questioning gave a hopeless shake of his head. "God only knows," he said despairingly. "It's a shambles." Then, as an afterthought, he said, "Merry Christmas. I've spent better, haven't you?"

It was lunchtime before she knew for certain they were both still alive.

"I've just dug a bullet out of Captain Elliot's shoulder," one of the medical orderlies said. "He's lost a lot of blood but he insisted on returning to the front."

"He wouldn't have been hit at all," said one of the volunteers who had been fighting with them. "Not if he hadn't broken the neck of the Jap about to decapitate Captain Harland."

Elizabeth put out a hand to steady herself. "Is Captain Harland safe? Is he hurt?"

"No," the volunteer said cheerfully. "He was going like the bloody clappers the last time I saw him. The British bulldog at its best, that's Captain Harland. He can certainly show some of the youngsters a thing or two!"

Just after lunch she heard rumors that there had been a general surrender, but the fighting around them continued. "The brigadier won't believe it," one of the orderlies said crisply. "Says he's fighting on until he receives orders in writing that he's to stop."

Two hours later a staff car carrying a British staff officer and flying a white flag crossed the enemy line to Brigadier Wallis's headquarters. Minutes later the men were listening, stunned, as they were bitterly told that Hong Kong island had surrendered to the Japanese.

"By order of His Excellency the Governor and General Officer Commanding, His Majesty's forces in Hong Kong have surrendered," a young captain read from the order Wallis had issued to all the units under his command. "On no account will firing or destruction of equipment take place as otherwise the lives of British hostages will be endangered. Units will organize themselves centrally forthwith."

Tears streamed down Elizabeth's cheeks. It was over. All the fighting and all the suffering had been in vain. Hong Kong had fallen. The Japanese were triumphant.

When the advancing Japanese had disappeared into the darkness, Ronnie had begun to drag himself forward, inch by inch, aware that blood was coursing freely from the wound at the back of his neck and that try as he might, he could not raise himself to his knees, let alone his feet. As dawn broke, he heaved and hauled himself onto the dust-blown road and then, his last reserves of energy expended, lay semiconscious, facedown, praying that the vehicle to discover him would be British. It was.

"We thought you were a goner, mate," a voice was saying jovially, and he was aware of excruciating pain in his neck and head as he was bounced and shaken. "Then I recognzied that blond thatch of yours and I said, 'Cor blimey, if it ain't Ronnie Ledsham.' We'd still have left you where you were, but Lance Corporal Davis said he badly wanted a word with you. Something about a horse that he put a week's money on and that limped home last."

Ronnie tried to smile, but his facial muscles wouldn't respond. He was in the back of a truck and if God was good to him, there would be a hospital bed and morphine at the end of his journey.

"From the way those Japs tried to decapitate him, they must have had money on his horse as well," another voice said, and there was a ripple of laughter.

A shell exploded in the road ahead of them and the truck swerved sharply. Pain streamed through Ronnie, robbing him of all coherent thought. When they reached the nearest hospital, he was unconscious again.

The next thing he heard was an incredulous voice saying, "You're a lucky bastard, Ledsham. There can't be many men who survive a sword blow to the back of the neck."

Ronnie struggled to open his eyes. The hideous shaking and bumping had stopped. He was prone and blessedly immobile and there was a large dressing supporting the back of his neck. He focused hazily on a weary-looking doctor and managed a mockery of a grin. "It would take more than a Japanese sword to put me out of the running," he croaked gamely. "Where am I?"

"The hospital," the doctor said, satisfied that his patient would live.

"Thank God," Ronnie whispered, and once more closed his eyes.

Six days later, when a grave-faced chief medical officer informed the men in the crowded ward that Britain had surrendered, Ronnie was one of the few who were elated by the news. As far as Ronnie was concerned, it meant that he had survived the fighting, and it meant that he would soon be reunited with Julienne.

"What do you think the Japs will do with us?" a soldier asked him.

Ronnie, now one of the walking wounded, was helping a hard-pressed nurse to change a dressing on the boy's leg. He shrugged slightly, wincing with pain as he did so. He still felt as if he were recovering from the world's worst hangover. "Intern us, I suppose," he said optimistically. "Life will be uncomfortable for a time, but it won't last forever. Nothing does."

The little nurse at his side remained silent. She had heard hideous rumors of the brutal treatment meted out to patients and staff in some of the more isolated dressing stations, but they were rumors her own patients were still blessedly ignorant of. Only minutes ago a Jeep had screamed up to the hospital and a high-ranking officer had hurried inside for urgent talks with senior members of the staff. Less than a minute later, orders had been given for all stocks of alcohol on the premises to be destroyed, even though such stocks were proving enormously valuable as substitute antiseptics and pain-killers.

"It's being done in the hope it will prevent the Japs' indulging in a drunken orgy of rape," one of her colleagues had said, white-faced with fear. "But there will be plenty of alcohol to be looted from the shops in Wanchai, and if they find out what we've done, it may make them madder than ever."

The staff officer who had been dispatched from Fortress HQ to warn the hospital of the treatment they might expect was striding past the end of the ward on his way back to his car when he caught a glimpse of Ronnie, supporting a patient's leg as a nurse deftly bandaged it. He knew Ronnie well, having often shared a drink with him at the Jockey Club, and he stood stock still, the blood leaving his face.

"What is it, sir?" the medical officer escorting him back to his car asked.

"That man, Ledsham. His wife was one of the nurses raped and murdered in the attack Captain Elliot reported."

"Christ!" The young medical officer looked in Ronnie's direction, horrified.

The staff officer tightened his lips and turned in the direction of the ward. "I have to tell him," he said resolutely. "The man can't be left in ignorance."

"But what if the report is incorrect?" the medical officer asked, hurrying at his side. "So many nurses have been transferred from post to post. She may not even have been there when the attack took place."

"She was there all right," the staff officer said grimly. "Captain Elliot identified her himself."

Ronnie turned around at the officer's approach. As an American, and an American once more in civilian clothes, he knew better than to reveal to a British officer just what good news he personally thought the surrender was. From the hospital window he could see white flags fluttering in the streets, and for the first time in what seemed an eternity, there was no sound of exploding shells or detonating bombs. "Good morning, sir," he said, mindful of his drinking companion's rank and feeling very chipper. His volunteer's uniform had been so saturated in blood that it had had to be destroyed and no replacement had been found. Ronnie had been grateful. He felt much more comfortable in the cotton trousers and white linen shirt and slip-on shoes that had been given to him.

The staff officer felt sickly disoriented. It was impossible to talk to Ronnie and not remember the other occasions they had talked. The crowded, laughter-filled bar at the Jockey Club. The parties at the Ledsham home on the Peak. The palm-filled Long Bar at the Peninsula.

"I need to talk to you, Ronnie," he said, wondering how the man would take the news. There had always been gossip that the Ledsham marriage was on the rocks, gossip fed by Ronnie's blatant army of girlfriends. But the staff officer remembered that there hadn't been quite so many girlfriends of late, and even when there had been, he had always had the uncomfortable feeling that Julienne Ledsham had known all about them and had not thought them worth her notice.

"What is it going to be for us all?" Ronnie asked chattily. "Internment at Shamshuipo Barracks?"

The staff officer didn't know. It probably would be. The Japs would have to put them somewhere. He said, wishing that he had never looked into the ward on his hurried dash toward his car, "I'm awfully sorry, Ronnie, but Julienne is dead."

Ronnie's smile remained fixed on his face. "What was that you said? I don't think I heard you correctly."

"Julienne is dead," he repeated gently. "I'm sorry, old chap, I—"

"I don't believe you!" Ronnie backed away from him, laughing nervously. "I don't believe you. There's been a mistake."

The staff officer shook his head. This was far worse than he had thought it would be. "No, Ronnie. It was Raefe Elliot who telephoned the report into Fortress HQ. The dressing station to which Julienne was posted was overrun in the early hours of the nineteenth. There was only one survivor, and that was Lady Gresby. The rest of the nursing staff were raped and murdered. Elliot identified Julienne himself."

Ronnie was swaying slightly, taking in great gulps of breath, trying to speak and failing.

"As soon as it's possible to do so," the officer continued, "we'll make sure her body, and the bodies of those who died with her, are brought back to Victoria and decently buried."

Ronnie stared at him.

The staff officer clapped him comfortingly on the arm, then turned and marched swiftly out of the ward.

Ronnie continued to stare after him, and then looked toward the windows. The white flags were still fluttering.

"Thank God the fighting is over," a man in a nearby bed said to him, seeing the direction of his gaze. "We're going to have to tolerate the bastards now, aren't we?"

Dead. Raped. Murdered. Julienne. It wasn't possible. They were going to start a family. They were going to have years of happiness together. Years and years of it. He began to walk slowly toward the door, in the staff officer's wake. The ward behind him was so crammed with injured men, the nursing staff so overworked and exhausted, that no one noticed him leave. Julienne dead. He stood on the street in Wanchai, looking dazedly around him. Scores of British and Canadian soldiers were squatting on the pavements, smoking as they dispiritedly awaited the arrival of the Japanese. The streets were riddled with potholes, littered with damaged cars and abandoned trucks. Steel helmets and gas masks and armbands lay discarded in the gutters.

"We're just going to have to tolerate the bastards now, aren't we?" The words rang in his ears and he shook his head fiercely. No, by God! Never. Julienne was dead and the world had gone dark around him. The bulky dressing at the back of his neck made his movements difficult and he raised his hand, feeling for the bandage that secured it, and ripped it free.

At the corner of the street a group of soldiers sat beside an empty Jeep, tommy guns on the ground beside them. "Have you finished with those?" he asked them tersely.

They looked up at him, hungry and weary unto death.

"Everyone is finished with them," one of them said bitterly. "We've surrendered, didn't you know?"

"I haven't," Ronnie said. He bent down, lifted two of the tommy guns, and threw them into the back of the Jeep.

"And where do you think you're going with that lot?" a sergeant major asked, making no move to apprehend him.

"I don't know," Ronnie said, frozen-faced, as he opened the Jeep's door and slipped behind the steering wheel. "Anywhere, just as long as there are Japs."

"Then you've got an easy task!" the sergeant major said with a savage laugh. "Because there's nowhere on this bloody island that there *aren't* any Japs!"

Ronnie turned the key hanging in the ignition. At the third try the Jeep hiccoughed into life.

"Maniac," the sergeant major said as Ronnie pulled away from the curb and drove away down the bomb-blasted street. "My God, what wouldn't I give for a decent meal and a beer!"

Ronnie drove slowly. He wanted to think of Julienne. He wanted to remember her. He knew where there would be Japs. The hills around the gap would be thick with them. He drove away from the built-up streets and the shell-pocked buildings and the piles of dead Chinese. There hadn't been a day when he had been unhappy with her. There had never been a day when he had arrived home and she had not been pleased to see him. The streets petered out behind him. He could see the Japanese now, hundreds and hundreds of them, squatting on their haunches at the side of the road, awaiting the final order for the victory march into Victoria. None were disturbed at his approach. The surrender was hours old. White flags flew. The fighting was over.

Ronnie creaked to a halt at a curve where Stubbs Road merged into Wong Nei Chung Gap Road. The stench of rotting bodies fouled the air. He wondered how many men still lay out on the hillsides. He wondered how many of them were not yet dead, just dying horribly, with no access to food or water, terribly maimed.

He walked around to the rear of the Jeep and lifted the tommy guns out, tucking one under either arm. She had never knowingly hurt him. Not ever. She had loved him more than she had ever loved anyone else. He had been her life as she had been his. The Japs had seen him now and were looking at him curiously. Some of them were beginning to rise to their feet.

"Bastards!" Ronnie howled, flinging himself down on his belly and opening fire on them with the first of the guns. "Bastards! *Bastards! BASTARDS!*"

Tom stood, heartsick, at the gates of Murry Barracks. He and the other men he had been fighting alongside had been ordered to retreat there hours earlier when the surrender had been declared. The fighting was over. The Japanese, with an army Hong Kong society had always regarded as a ludicrous joke, had beaten them to their knees. Tom's shame was so intense that he wanted no one else to see it, and so, instead of remaining with the rest of the men, he stood alone, wondering if Lamoon was still at the Hong Kong Hotel. Wondering if she was still safe.

The next morning, Boxing Day, the Japanese came into the barracks and lined them all up and searched them. The weather was beautiful, the sun blazing down from a brilliant blue sky as they stood before the Japanese on the parade ground. A Japanese private, attracted by the silver badge on the fore-and-aft cap of an adjutant to the Middlesex, pulled the hat from the adjutant's head. Tom felt his stomach muscles tighten. There had already been gross scenes of unnecessary violence and now they waited tensely as the adjutant said in a calm voice to the Japanese warrant officer in charge, "Tell that man to give me my hat back."

Immediately the warrant officer strode over to him, screaming abuse, and gave him a series of hard insulting slaps across his face. Tom looked uneasily at his neighbor. If this was how things were going to be, life as a prisoner of war beneath the Japs was going to be no picnic.

Two days later they were herded together and told they were crossing to Kowloon to be interned at Shamshuipo, the barracks that had once been home to the Middlesex. Degradingly they were marched through the streets, hemmed in by grinning Japanese sentries in ill-fitting, shabby uniforms. The Chinese watched them, cowed and dejected. There was no one to arrange food distribution for them now. No one to protect them from the bullying victors. White flags hung desultorily from windows, interspersed with the Japanese flag of the rising sun. The streets were filthy, littered with the bodies of dead Chinese, and the bombed and shattered sewers gave off a dreadful stench. Tom's eyes narrowed as they passed close to piles of the dead. Some of the bodies did not look as if they had been out beneath the sun for long, certainly not since Christmas Day. Which meant that they had died since the surrender. He thought of Lamoon and was nearly crippled by the fear he felt. The European women at the Hong Kong Hotel would be taken away to internment camps. But what would happen to Lamoon? Would she be taken with them, or would she be left to fend for herself, just one more of the many thousands of Chinese now openly starving?

"Think there'll be a chance to cut and run for it?" the man marching next to him asked in a low voice.

"I don't know," Tom replied. It had been exactly what he had been thinking himself. Breaking free from the column as they were marched past the Hong Kong Hotel, seeking out Lamoon, and fleeing with her. But where to? Chungking, the wartime Chinese capital, was over a thousand miles away. There would be a British embassy there, and safety, but between Hong Kong and Chungking lay hundreds of miles of Japanese-occupied territory.

As they neared the shell-pitted walls of the Hong Kong Hotel, he looked hungrily at the windows. If only he could see her! If only he could reassure himself that she was still safe! He scoured every window for a glimpse of her, but she wasn't there. Sick at heart, he trudged on toward the ferry, wondering when he would see her again. Wondering if he would ever see her again.

Lamoon wearily wiped her forehead with the back of her hand. Ever since her arrival at the Hong Kong Hotel she had taken on the role of nurse, and for the last six days and nights she had hardly slept. She did not know that British and Canadian troops were being marched past the hotel on their way to internment until long after they had been herded down to the pier and the boats waiting to take them across to Kowloon.

Even though there might have been the faint chance of seeing Tom among their numbers, a part of her was glad she had not witnessed their humiliation. She could not bear to think of it. It seemed beyond belief that the soldiers of the greatest empire the world had ever known were being jeered at and laughed at by Japanese troops.

The Europeans around her were stunned with shock, dazed by the finality of the capitulation, pathetically incredulous.

"But where were the Chinese? I thought the Chinese were sending an army to help us?" an elderly British woman asked, time and time again.

"Perhaps they will come now," another said hopefully. "Perhaps we will be relieved."

Lamoon remained silent. She knew that if the Chinese army had been able to reach them, it would have done so, but it was three years since the Japanese had driven the Chinese army back across country in order to capture Canton. There had been no sign since of the Chinese being strong enough to regain the territory lost, territory that would have to be crossed before they could reach Hong Kong.

It was on her second day in the hotel that she overheard one of the auxiliary nurses saying worriedly to a colleague, "But we can't just leave two European children in the care of an elderly Chinese. It isn't right."

"They won't be parted from him," her colleague replied wearily. "The little boy is adamant that his mummy said they had to remain with the old man. Though he's only five or six, he objected like the very devil when it was suggested he and his sister should be cared for by one of the women with children his own age."

"If it comes to internment, then they'll *have* to be separated," the first nurse said darkly. "The Japs have no respect for the Chinese. They certainly won't waste food on them by feeding them in camps."

Lamoon tried not to think of what might happen to her if the Europeans in the hotel were interned. She looked across to the old man and the two children that the nurses had been discussing, and stared at them incredulously. She had never met Tom's nephew and niece, but she had seen photographs of them and had been struck by the little boy's likeness to Tom.

"Why is that lady looking at me like that?" Jeremy asked, turning to Li Pi. As he did so, Lamoon's suspicions deepened into certainty. There was something in his movements that bore a definite Nicholson stamp. She hurried across to them and said shyly to Li Pi, "My name is Lamoon Sheng. I am a friend of Mr. Tom Nicholson and Mrs. Helena Nicholson."

Li Pi's anxious face creased into a smile. "I, too," he said with gentle dignity, "am a friend of Mrs. Nicholson."

"And these are her children?" Lamoon asked as Jeremy and Jennifer stared gravely up at her.

Li Pi nodded. "I was entrusted by her to take them to Mrs. Harland's." His smile faded and he looked again very old and very anxious. "But Mrs. Harland's apartment has been destroyed by bombing and so we came here. The management knows me. My name is Li Pi."

His name meant nothing to Lamoon. She thought, as the Europeans thought, that he was an old family retainer. She stared at him and asked fearfully, "And Mrs. Harland? Is she safe?"

For the first time Li Pi's suffering showed in his eyes. The thought of Elizabeth's brilliant talent being snuffed out by the blast of a Japanese bomb was almost more than he could bear. "I do not know," he said. "The local ARP men told me that one body was found. A girl's body. But they said that she was Chinese."

They looked at each other, both knowing the mistakes that were so easily made when bodies were hastily removed from blasted buildings. "We must pray," Li Pi said, sensing how deep Lamoon's concern for Elizabeth was. "It is all that we can do now."

For the next four days Lamoon prayed. She prayed for Tom, and for Helena and for Elizabeth. And she prayed for herself and Li Pi and the children. On the day after Boxing Day, when the Japanese stormed into the hotel, the children clung to her fearfully.

"We're not going to be taken away from you, are we?" Jeremy whispered. Jennifer began to whimper, holding on to Lamoon's skirt, her eyes big and wide, as bandy-legged Japanese swarmed through the rooms with fervent shouts of "Long live the Emperor!"

"No," Lamoon said to him reassuringly, her heart hammering painfully as she wondered what she would do if such an attempt was made.

"All American, all British, all Dutch together," the Japanese officer in charge ordered.

"What is to happen to us?" a young American woman asked bravely. "Where are our husbands?"

The Jap found her last question beneath contempt and did not deign to reply to it. "You are going to Japanese internment camp," he said magnanimously. "All things there will be good. Food will be plentiful and conditions will be pleasant. I hope that you appreciate this kindness from the Imperial Japanese Army. As you know, the soldiers of Nippon are always kind to women."

No one listening to him believed him. As the Europeans were pushed and jostled together, the Chinese refugees who had taken shelter with them were driven at bayonet point out into the street.

"I must go," Li Pi said to Lamoon unsteadily, releasing his hold of the children's hands. "They may allow you to stay with them, but they will never allow me. I cannot cause an incident. Not in front of the little ones. *Joi Gin*. Good-bye."

"No!" She tried to catch hold of his arm, but he had gone and as she took a step after him, a Japanese bore down on her, a bayonet in his hand.

"All Chinese out!" he shouted, seizing her shoulder.

Jennifer tightened her hold on Lamoon's skirts, beginning to cry. Jeremy stood white-faced. "Let go of her!" he said bravely to the savage-looking Jap. "Don't you dare to hurt her!"

Lamoon, terrified that he would be hurt, tearfully tried to disentangle Jennifer from her skirt. The young American, who had asked what was to happen to them, stepped forward. "That young woman is not Chinese," she said authoritatively, not knowing if Lamoon was or not. "She is Eurasian and those children are hers. She must be allowed to remain with them."

The Jap paused, uncertain.

"That is correct," the nurse who had been anxious about Li Pi's guardianship of them said with equal certainly. "If we go into internment, she must be allowed to come with us. And the children also."

The Jap hesitated for a moment, then nodded. "You go with others," he said to Lamoon. "But you bow to Japanese officer. Everyone must bow to Japanese officer!"

Lamoon bowed, tears stinging her eyes as the children huddled at either side of her. For the moment she and the children would remain together, but what would happen to Li Pi? How would he survive the harsh brutality that the Japanese were meting out to the Chinese?

The American woman crossed the room to her, defying the Japanese order that she remain subserviently stationary. "Come along," she said forcefully. "Stay with me. We don't want you being separated from the rest of us again, do we?"

Lamoon smiled gallantly through her tears. She had found a friend. She was determined that she would also find Helena. And one day, if God was willing, she would find Tom and Li Pi again too. "Thank you," she said, with a hint of her habitual shyness. "I would like that very much." And with the children's hands clasped tightly in her own, she crossed the room to where the European women were awaiting instructions for where they were to go.

Only the thought of the children, the absolute necessity of surviving in order that she might be reunited with them, enabled Helena to endure the days and nights after the Japanese ransacked the hospital. At one point she had been forced to lie on the bodies of the dead while the Japanese abused her again and again and again. When news had come that she was being taken to Hong Kong island to be interned in a civilian camp at Stanley, she had sobbed with relief.

The ferries had been crowded with numbed, dazed civilians, the women's eyes darkly shadowed from the experiences they had undergone. Helena barely recognized the harbor. The water was green and dirty, full of the wreckage of junks and sampans, and thick with floating, distended corpses. She averted her eyes, lifting them upward toward the towering grandeur of the Peak, taking comfort in its enduring beauty.

Trucks ferried them down to Stanley, the scenes of devastation so dreadful that many of the women began to weep. Bodies still lay unrecovered on the hillside. Burned-out remains of Jeeps and trucks bore silent witness to the ferocity of the fighting that had taken place.

At the gates of what had once been a large, rambling jail, they halted. There was a great mass of civilians already there, suitcases by their sides, pathetic bundles of personal belongings tucked beneath their arms.

"Where are they from?" Helena asked urgently, feverishly searching the bewildered, defeated faces for a glimpse of Elizabeth. For a glimpse of Jeremy and Jennifer.

"Heaven only knows," the elderly lady crammed next to her said. "Victoria probably, or Repulse Bay. I heard there were a lot of civilians trapped at Repulse Bay."

She couldn't see the distinctive gleam of Elizabeth's pale gold hair, but suddenly she saw a lone Oriental face. A very beautiful face. "Lamoon!" she shouted, leaning over the side of the truck and waving furiously. "Lamoon!"

Lamoon's head turned swiftly in Helena's direction, then as Helena continued to call her name and wave, and as Lamoon saw who was calling out to her, her face lit up with unalloyed joy and she began pushing and shoving through the milling crowd, toward the stationary truck.

"Lamoon!" Helena shouted again, then she saw the tiny figure in Lamoon's arms and the slightly bigger one running at her side, and tears of joy began to flood down her cheeks. "Oh, God!" she gasped, leaning out over the side of the truck, her arms outstretched. *"Oh, God! Thank you! Thank you!"*

A guard was racing toward them, but by the time he roughly pushed Lamoon and Jeremy away from the truck, Lamoon had thrust Jennifer up into her arms. She could see that Jeremy was undisturbed at the Jap's action, too overcome by relief at seeing her again to care that he would have to wait a little longer before he could throw himself into her arms.

"Let's go in there defiantly," she shouted down to him as the gates opened and the trucks began to move forward. "Let's go in there singing!" And pressing Jennifer's cheek close against hers, she began to sing in a clear, lovely contralto, "'There'll always be an England.'"

The motley assortment of civilians in the accompanying trucks and on foot took up the strain. "'And England will be free!'" they sang out, their heads high, their hearts filled with determination to survive as they entered Stanley Gaol. "'As long as England means to you, what England means to me!'"

Chapter Thirty-one

~

In the hours immediately following the surrender the men on the Stanley Peninsula were dazed and bewildered, exhausted beyond belief. Elizabeth continued to care for the wounded, crippled by guilt at the knowledge that she would soon be leaving them. Raefe made a final report to Brigadier Wallis, informing him of the instructions he had been given. Adam hurriedly collected provisions for their long march.

"The brigadier wants us to take two men with us," Raefe said as they met together at dusk. "Captains Henry Bassett and Lawrence Fisher. Bassett speaks fluent Cantonese and Fisher is a doctor. Bassett, especially, will be useful if we should become split into two groups or if anything should happen to me." Elizabeth drew in her breath sharply, but he ignored it, saying to Adam, "Are you sure you want to come? It's going to be quite a trek."

Adam knew that Raefe was obliquely referring to his lame leg. "I'm coming," he said staunchly. "I've lived with my lameness for years and it's never hindered me. It isn't going to do so now just because it's been peppered with shrapnel."

Raefe didn't argue. If Adam had been anyone else he would have adamantly refused to have him as a member of the party. As it was, a strange bond had been forged between them as they had fought and risked their lives for each other. And he couldn't order Adam to stay behind. Not when he was going to take Elizabeth with him. "All right," he said, knowing at least that Adam would give his life for Elizabeth if it became necessary. "What provisions have we got?"

They had tins of bully beef and sardines and condensed milk and, strangely, Quaker Oats. "It was all I could scrounge," Adam said apologetically.

Knowing how long it was since any of the hundreds of dispirited troops around them had eaten, no one argued with him.

"When do we leave?" Elizabeth asked quietly.

"In an hour. When it's dark. Bassett and Fisher are to meet up with us down on the beach."

"And where do we go first?" Adam asked as Raefe spread a Crown Lands and Surveys Office map out on the ground before them.

"We're requisitioning the motorboat that the Chinese have been trying to ferry provisions across the bay in. It's old and it's leaky and it's too great a risk to try to make for the mainland in it, but if we can reach Lamma Island, there will be a motor torpedo boat waiting for us off the west coast."

Adam had long ago realized that Raefe had connections with military intelligence. If he said there would be a motor torpedo boat waiting for them, then Adam believed him.

"With luck," Raefe continued, "the motor torpedo boat will be able to land us at Mirs Bay, to the northeast of the New Territories. There are Chinese guerrilla forces in action there and we should be able to rely on them for help."

"And then we walk?" Adam asked, tracing the coastline on the map with his forefinger and halting when he reached the broad expanse of Mirs Bay.

Raefe nodded. "Sixty miles to Waichow. That will be the most difficult part of the journey. The ground is mountainous and it will be infested with Japs. From Waichow things should become easier. We'll then be within the territory of the Chinese Regular Forces, and we'll also be able to travel by boat. The East River runs from Waichow to Leung Cheun, about two hundred miles farther north. From there we will be on foot again until we reach Kukong, and from Kukong we should be able to travel to Chungking by rail."

"What will you do then?" Adam asked, squatting on his haunches and looking at Raefe curiously.

"My orders are to stay there and help the Chinese form British-led guerrilla units. There's also going to have to be an organization established to arrange the escape of prisoners of war and internees from Hong Kong. If there is, I'd like to be a part of it."

Adam remained silent. There was a British embassy at

Chungking and no doubt he would also find himself under orders, but he had no intimate knowledge of China and could not speak Cantonese. His orders certainly wouldn't be the same as Raefe's. He would probably be sent to India or Burma, somewhere where he would have to take a back-seat until the war was over. It occurred to him that he would, in all likelihood, have Elizabeth with him. They were still husband and wife. He wondered if the same thought had also occurred to Raefe, but if it had, he gave no sign of it.

His sleek black hair fell low across his brow, and his face was weary. "Let's go," he said, and Adam noticed that he rose to his feet without his usual pantherlike speed. The sling he had discarded so contemptuously shortly after leaving the Repulse Bay Hotel was still discarded, but his bandaged arm and shoulder were obviously giving him pain. Adam felt a wave of apprehension flood through him. It was twelve hundred miles to Chungking, and without Raefe their chances of ever reaching it were virtually nonexistent. As they hoisted their haversacks onto their shoulders and began to walk down toward the beach, he took comfort from the fact that Raefe would not be attempting it if he wasn't confident of success. He would put his own life at risk without so much as a second thought, but he wouldn't put Beth's life at risk also.

From the darkened beach they could see fires raging intermittently all along the coastline. "The Japs are probably putting private houses to the torch," Captain Bassett said, and Elizabeth shivered, thinking of the home she and Raefe had shared and which she was now sure she would never see again.

Captain Bassett was a short, chunkily-built young man with fair straight hair and a ready smile. If he had been stunned at Elizabeth's presence on the beach and the realization that she was to accompany them through China, he had hidden it magnificently. As they walked across the pebbled beach and into the shallows to the waiting motorboat, he told her that he spoke not only Cantonese but French, Italian, Urdu, and Pushtu as well. He asked her if she was Scandinavian, with an eye to learning another language as they trekked, and was disappointed when she said no.

Captain Fisher was far more taciturn and reserved. He

had taken Raefe to one side, objecting strongly to the
presence of a woman on such an arduous undertaking, and
his objections had been curtly overridden. Mrs. Harland,
he was told, was coming with them. As they scrambled
across the beach he looked curiously at Adam Harland. He
didn't look a very influential figure. Fisher wondered what
pull he had that ensured a man like Elliot giving way to
him over the question of his wife.

The Chinese who had been ferrying provisions to the
troops cut off on the peninsula, risking heavy enemy fire
each time they did so, had remained with their boat.

"We go now," they said anxiously as Raefe helped
Elizabeth aboard. "The Japanese coastal batteries quiet
now. We go now, while it's safe."

As they squatted down in the damp, smelly boat,
Elizabeth saw the dark shape of a child huddled in the bow.
She smiled reassuringly, but the pale little face, barely
visible in the darkness, did not smile back.

"Is this your little boy?" she whispered to one of the
boatmen as the boat's engine throbbed into life and they
began to chug steadily out from shore.

The Chinese shook his head, answering her question in
Cantonese.

"It's a girl, not a boy, and he says he doesn't know who
she is," Raefe interpreted for her, his eyes scanning the
shoreline behind them for signs of activity from any of the
Japanese coastal batteries. "He says their village was
bombed and that after the bombing he found her crouched
in the bottom of his boat. She's been here ever since, living
on whatever scraps they can give her. Her parents are
dead."

The child continued to stare at Elizabeth, her eyes wide
and dark. "But she looks as if she's starving!" Elizabeth
protested, horrified.

Raefe glanced at the child. The bewilderment in her eyes
and the dumb acceptance of her fate were expressions he
had seen on too many faces, too often in the last few
weeks.

When Elizabeth began fumbling in her rucksack he
didn't deter her, even though Fisher said coldly, "We
haven't enough rations to hand out willy-nilly."

Elizabeth ignored him, pressing a tin of sardines into the
child's hand. She was so huddled up and so thin and

scrawny that it was impossible to judge how old she might be. She was possibly seven or eight, though her eyes were ages old.

The tin was seized eagerly and the girl pressed it close against her chest, as though defying anyone to remove it from her.

"It's all right," Adam said reassuringly to her. "It's yours."

Suddenly, a brilliant arc light blazed out from the shore and shells slammed into the water around them.

Elizabeth threw herself down on the waterlogged floor of the boat, pulling the child with her. Adam heard Raefe give a low, harsh cry as machine-gun and rifle fire opened up on them, and then, just when Adam thought all hope was lost, the blazing light swung sharply away from them to the east as another target, more worthwhile than a village motorboat, came into their sights.

Adam began to ease his way toward Raefe, asking urgently, "What is it? Have you been hit?"

"No!" Raefe snapped harshly. He was hunched in the stern, peering into the darkness as he tried to see what vessel had attracted the gunners' attention.

Adam sat back, knowing better than to persist with his questioning. He stretched out a hand to Elizabeth, pulling her back into a sitting position. The child crawled upright with her, huddling against her for comfort as every minute took them farther and farther away from the coastal guns.

Eventually all sound of gunfire faded. The night wind was bitterly cold and Elizabeth hugged the thinly clad child, trying to warm her as best she could.

"It seems ironic that when we pick up the motor torpedo boat, we're going to have to backtrack on ourselves, rounding the Stanley Peninsula in order to reach Mirs Bay," Captain Fisher said as Lamma Island appeared in the darkness, a low, black hump.

"It can't be helped," Raefe said brusquely. "No motor torpedo boat could have come ashore to take us off. This one is lying out of sight of the Jap guns on the west side of the island. Once we're aboard her, she can keep well away from land as she rounds the peninsula and travels up the New Territories' coastline."

"If she's there," Fisher said dryly. "What happens if she's not?"

"This motorboat will stay anchored for four hours on the east side of the island. If we don't pick up the motor torpedo boat, then we return to it and tomorrow night we try to cross to the west side of Kowloon and strike out for the Chinese border from there."

"That sounds a dodgy proposition," Captain Bassett said with a shiver. "I shouldn't fancy our chances anywhere within a twenty-mile radius of Kowloon. Mirs Bay sounds much more attractive."

The Chinese at the helm turned off the engine and the boat rode ashore on stones and sand.

"How far to the east coast?" Fisher asked as they waded ashore.

"A mile, perhaps less. It's a very narrow neck of land here," Raefe said abruptly, his jacket pulled close about him.

Elizabeth crossed the sand to him and slipped her hand into his, needing brief physical contact with him to express her relief that so far none of them had been hurt. Raefe gave her hand a tight squeeze, then released it. He strode over to the boatmen and confirmed that they would wait for four hours.

Captain Bassett looked after him, then back to Elizabeth, bewildered. He had been given to understand that she was Harland's wife. If she was, and if she was also Elliot's mistress, then the trek ahead was going to be fraught with more than one kind of danger.

Raefe took the lead and they set out on a wide, earth-covered path winding through the sweet-smelling fir trees. They had only gone twenty yards or so when Fisher halted abruptly. "We're being followed!" he whispered. "Listen."

Everyone froze, listening intently. There was nothing to be heard but the soughing of the wind in the trees.

"You're mistaken, old chap," Captain Bassett said, heaving his rucksack into a more comfortable position on his back. "Come on, that motor torpedo boat won't wait for us forever."

Once more they began to move forward, walking in single file, Elizabeth immediately behind Raefe, Adam behind her, Captain Fisher and Captain Bassett taking turns bringing up the rear.

The track climbed steeply at one point, then began to run down, toward the sea. "I can see it!" Adam whispered to

Raefe, pointing out a single boat low in the sea. "How do we manage to attract its attention without making noise and alerting any Japs that might be lurking around?"

"We can't," Raefe said with unusual sharpness. "We have to take a risk."

Hurriedly they scrambled down to the shore. Captain Bassett stripped off his shirt and began to wave it furiously as they all shouted across the sea at the top of their lungs. Minutes later they could see a skiff being lowered and Elizabeth leaned against Raefe, weak with relief.

"It's going to be all right," she said as his good arm closed around her waist. "Once we're aboard the boat, we'll be relatively safe."

There was a small sound from behind them and this time they all heard it. "What the devil—" Captain Bassett exclaimed, whipping around, his gun in his hand.

A small, weary figure began to walk toward them across the narrow strip of sand.

"It's the child!" Adam said incredulously. "She's followed us."

"Then she'll have to go back," Fisher said brusquely. "It's bad enough that we have to take the responsibility for a woman without having a child tagging along as well."

The child, sensing how unwelcome she was, hung back. Elizabeth looked pleadingly at Raefe. "We can't leave her here! She'll starve! At least let us take her with us as far as Mirs Bay. There'll be a village there. People. We'll be able to find someone to leave her with."

"My God, I've never heard of anything so ridiculous!" Fisher said contemptuously.

"*Please*, darling!" Elizabeth said. "It will only be another few hours and then she will be safe as well!"

Raefe gazed at the pathetic figure of the child. Her dress was ragged, offering her no protection at all against the cold night wind, and her feet were bare. "All right," he said curtly. "But she's your responsibility, Lizzie. No one else's."

The skiff had grounded ashore and a dark-uniformed figure was herding Bassett and Fisher aboard. Elizabeth ran over to the little girl. "Come on," she said, taking her hand. "Stay close to me."

Adam looked at Raefe curiously as they were ferried from the skiff to the boat. The bones of Raefe's face seemed to have taken on sharper lines than usual and beneath his heavy jacket his injured arm hung far more awkwardly than it had previously.

The captain of the boat immediately commandeered Raefe, and Adam was unable to ask him again if he was all right.

Crouching low in cramped but far dryer conditions than they had experienced on the motorboat, they slipped out into the China Sea at a brisk twenty knots. They sailed steadily east through the darkness, giving the gaunt outline of the Stanley Peninsula a wide berth, then continuing northward along the indented coast of the New Territories toward Mirs Bay.

"Where do you want us to put you ashore, sir?" the captain asked Raefe as the first rays of dawn began to streak the sky.

"There's a small bay, just north of Nam-O," Raefe said, glad of the disguising darkness as he stood at the captain's side. "Put us ashore there."

The captain sailed in as near to the coast as he dared. The skiff was lowered into the water and they climbed down into it, shivering with cold as they were paddled ashore.

"What now?" Adam asked as they wearily waded ashore just as the sun was rising. "It's pretty lonely here. How far do you think the village is?"

Raefe looked gray with exhaustion. "Not far," he said tersely. "About half a mile."

"Can't we lay up here?" Bassett asked him and then, seeing the look of veiled contempt that Fisher gave him, added hurriedly, "I was thinking of Mrs. Harland. She must be extremely tired."

Elizabeth was, but she shook her head in denial, sensing that Raefe desperately wanted them to push on. "No," she said, still holding the hand of the little Chinese girl. "Please don't worry about me, Captain Bassett. I'm fine." She smiled at him and Bassett felt a rush of heat to his groin. Even in the darkness of the previous evening he had realized she was a remarkably beautiful woman. Now, in the pale golden light of the rising sun, he saw for the first time just how beautiful. Her silvery blond hair was pulled away from her face, secured at the nape of her neck with coral pins. Her green-gold eyes were thickly lashed and full of staunch endurance. He noted the creased and blood-spattered volunteer's uniform beneath the army jacket she was wearing for warmth, and wondered what her civilian profession was. Probably she didn't have one. Her husband, Adam Harland, was obviously crazy in love with her, if the concern in his eyes whenever he looked across at her was anything to go by. As Captain Elliot was.

Bassett wondered if Adam Harland knew of the liaison between his wife and the captain. There was such a close sense of unity among the three of them that he thought Harland couldn't possibly know. Still pondering on the relationship of his companions, he brought up the rear as they walked away from the beach and inland, between carefully tended paddy fields to the village.

"It's a Hakka village," Raefe said briefly to Adam as they entered it. "The people should be friendly, but I doubt if there will be any Chinese guerrillas here to give us help. If there aren't, we shall just have to press on by ourselves."

Although it was still very early, half a dozen small children ran to meet them, waving their arms in greeting and shouting for others to come see the funny foreigners. The children led them into the heart of the village, past primitive dwellings where pigs nosed for food, and into a small paved courtyard with a fung-shui tree growing in the center.

"This is obviously the village square," Adam murmured to Elizabeth as an elderly headman in a blue cotton jacket and long trousers invited them all to sit down with him around a large stone table. The village women, wrinkled and bent from hard work in the fields, and dressed in traditional black trousers and tunics, grinned toothlessly at them and offered them tea.

They drank it gratefully, and Adam remembered the first time he had drunk Chinese tea, sitting with Beth in the little teahouse near the waterfront on their first morning in Victoria. It seemed so long ago, so much a part of another age, that he couldn't believe it was barely two years.

Raefe had been speaking to the headman in Cantonese, with Captain Fisher watching him closely. At last he turned to them and said, "The headman is going to give us one of his young men as a guide to the nearest guerrilla camp. He has also invited us to eat with them."

"Jolly good show," Bassett said cheerily, beaming at the women as they brought rice bowls and chopsticks and set them on the table in front of them.

"I need to talk to you," Raefe said quietly to Adam. While Elizabeth was busily filling the little Chinese girl's bowl with rice and vegetables and fish from a large central dish, he quietly slipped away from the table.

Adam followed him to the fung-shui tree, full of his old apprehension. He had known something was wrong ever since the coastal battery had opened fire on them when they were crossing to Lamma Island.

"You're going to have to go on without me," Raefe said to him harshly when they were out of earshot of the others.

Adam stared at him, stupefied. Whatever he had expected, it had not been a calamity of this proportion. "But you *have* to come with us," he said. "It's over a thousand miles to Chungking! We don't stand a chance without you!"

"You don't stand a chance with me," Raefe said grimly, and slowly and with difficulty he opened his heavy army jacket.

The makeshift pad was dark with blood. Near black, deoxidized blood.

"Oh, my God," Adam whispered. "I knew it! I knew you'd been hit!"

"And I knew there wasn't any point in letting anyone know," Raefe said. Adam was horrified at how difficult he was finding it to speak. "I just wanted . . . to be sure you had a guide."

He swayed on his feet and Adam seized his arm, supporting him. "What do you want me to do?" he asked urgently, knowing with sickening horror that Raefe could not possibly survive his wound.

"The maps and compass and medical supplies are . . . in my rucksack," he said, beads of sweat trickling down from his forehead. "The Hakka guide will take you to the guerrillas." He paused, drawing in a deep, ragged breath, then said, "Keep on the right side of Fisher. He's an irascible devil, but you need him."

"Elizabeth won't leave you behind," Adam protested. "We'll stay here, in the village . . ."

Raefe shook his head. "No," he said adamantly. "This is Japanese-controlled territory. It isn't safe. If the motor torpedo boat was sighted as we came ashore . . . then there'll be Japs here within the hour. You have to leave now. Immediately."

"Beth will never agree to that! There's no way on God's earth I could persuade her to leave you behind."

Raefe managed a slight grin. "I know, and I'm glad." He drew in another deep breath, and when he could speak again, he said, "Leave Lizzie to me. I'll tell her that I'm bringing up the rear and will meet up with you at nightfall. But for God's sake, don't allow her to talk to me for more than a few seconds or she'll guess the truth."

"Oh, Jesus," Adam said brokenly. "Oh, God!"

Raefe licked his lips. "I want you to do one thing for me, Adam."

"Anything!" Adam was near to tears. This was the man he had hated with every fiber of his being, and it was the man whose death was going to nearly destroy him with grief.

"Lizzie is pregnant." Raefe saw the incredulity in Adam's eyes and the old grin touched the corners of his mouth again. "Look after her for me, Adam. And look after the child."

Their hands were tightly clasped. Adam could feel the tears streaming down his face. Elizabeth was walking toward them, revived by the hot tea and the plentiful food.

"Are you having a private conversation, or can anyone join in?" she called out good-humoredly.

"Don't let her stay with me!" Raefe hissed fiercely to Adam. "Not for a second longer than necessary!"

Adam gave Raefe's hands a last, tight squeeze, then turned away, unable to speak. Elizabeth did not notice his distress. She had eyes only for Raefe, and was shocked at how exhausted and gaunt he looked. "You haven't eaten," she said gently. "You'll feel better if you do."

He gathered up the last reserves of his strength and flashed her a brilliant, down-slanting smile. Her hair was like spun gold and he longed to reach out and touch it, but he knew if he did so, his shaking hand would betray him. He leaned against the tree, feigning his old nonchalance. "I want you to leave with Adam and Bassett and Fisher," he said, making a superhuman effort to keep the pain from his voice. "I'm going to bring up the rear, keeping well behind."

She nodded. She didn't like the idea of marching all day without him at her side, but he was in command and she had no intention of making his task any harder than it already was.

"Jung-shui doesn't want to remain behind in the village. She wants to come with us. Can she? I'll share my rations with her and make sure that she is no trouble."

"Jung-shui, is that her name?" He was playing for time, trying to think. It might be best if the child went with her. Having such a responsibility might help her through her grief when she discovered he would not be rejoining her. "Yes," he said. He knew that Fisher wouldn't like it, but Adam would be able to deal with the situation. "Take her with you if you want, but you'll have to be parted from her eventually."

Elizabeth was not so sure. The child had no family. The idea of keeping her with her permanently had already begun to take root.

Adam was gazing at them anxiously. Raefe knew that in a second he was going to do as he had asked and ensure that Lizzie remained with him no longer. "You must go," he said harshly. "The others are waiting."

"And I'll see you tonight?" She was smiling up at him, all the love she felt for him glowing in her eyes.

"Yes," he said, feeling his heart break within him. "I'll see you tonight, Lizzie."

She stood on tiptoe, not caring what Captain Bassett or Captain Fisher thought, and kissed him tenderly on the mouth. "I love you," she said, thinking joyously of all the years that lay ahead of them. Then she strode swiftly back to the others, picked up her rucksack, and, holding Jung-shui's hand, followed Adam as he walked quickly out of the village in the Hakka boy's wake.

The village children scurried along at their side. At the edge of the village Adam paused, thanking the village headman for his hospitality and his help. As Bassett and Fisher shook hands with other village elders who had come to wave them on their way, Elizabeth turned for a last glimpse of Raefe. He was leaning against the fung-shui tree, looking as relaxed and as insolently nonchalant as he had the first time she had set eyes on him in the bar of the Hong Kong Club. The sun gleamed on his tumbled dark hair, sheening it to blue-black, and an odd, ironic smile touched the corners of his mouth as he lifted his hand in farewell. She pressed her fingers to her mouth and blew him a kiss, then she turned and plunged after Adam as he strode onto the narrow path leading between the paddy fields and toward the hills.

Despite their lack of sleep, they trekked all day. At one point, as they reached a high ridge, they could see the shimmer of the sea, then it was lost to view as they clambered down into a ravine thick with fir and bamboo. Jung-shui kept up a valiant pace at Elizabeth's side, not asking where they were going, not caring, grateful merely to have Elizabeth's protection.

Shortly after midday their young Hakka guide became increasingly nervous, constantly stopping and cupping his ear, as if listening to sounds that the rest of them couldn't hear.

"What is it?" Adam asked nervously. "Are we being followed?"

"Not sure," the Hakka boy said succinctly. Moving with ever-increasing caution he cut away from the track, leading them up a steep slope through shaded groves of bamboo. At the summit he lay flat, signaling for them to follow suit. They did so only just in time. A Japanese patrol was marching down the track, in the direction of the village.

"It would seem a good moment to take a rest," Fisher said dryly, heaving his rucksack wearily from his shoulder.

The Hakka boy nodded in agreement and spoke rapidly in Cantonese to Bassett.

"He says we should stay here until dusk, in case there are more patrols following," Bassett translated. There were no protests; everyone was desperate for rest.

"What about Raefe?" Elizabeth whispered urgently to Adam. "Will he be safe?"

Adam thought of Raefe, his lifeblood seeping away beneath the heavy army jacket. "Yes," he said abruptly, not able to look her in the eyes. "He'll be safe."

At dusk they began to walk again, bypassing many villages that had been bombed and were now charred ruins. It was shortly after midnight when they reached the guerrilla headquarters at Wang Nih Hui.

"Thank God," Bassett said thankfully, sinking down onto a pile of straw. "I couldn't walk another step."

"You'll have to tomorrow," Fisher said tartly.

Bassett didn't care about tomorrow. Fully clothed, he closed his eyes and in seconds was asleep, snoring loudly.

"I don't understand," Elizabeth said worriedly to Adam. "Where is Raefe? Why hasn't he caught up with us?"

"He will," Adam said, wondering how the hell he was going to break the news to her. "Try to sleep, Beth. We're going to have just as long a trek to face in the morning."

She slept restlessly, waking often, aware that Raefe had still not joined them. At dawn the guerrilla camp bustled into life. Sausages were provided for them and also the unexpected luxury of hot cocoa.

"Today we have to cross the Tah Shui-Shao road which is heavily used by Japanese patrols and convoys," the guerrilla leader told Bassett, squatting down at his side. "A party of our men is going ahead now to plan the best way of crossing it."

Bassett relayed the information to the others. Adam and Fisher received the news in silence, knowing very well what fate would be in store for them if their attempt failed and they were captured by the Japanese.

"We can't leave!" Elizabeth said urgently to Adam. "Not until Raefe catches up with us."

Bassett and Fisher were hoisting their rucksacks onto their backs. The young Hakka boy was showing no signs of returning to his village, but was standing with the guerrillas, obviously intending to stay with them.

"We have to go," Adam said as the guerrillas and Bassett and Fisher began to file their way out of the camp.

"We can't go! I won't go!" Her distress tore at his heart.

"You have to, Beth," he said, knowing that the terrible moment could be postponed no longer. "Raefe isn't going to join us. He was injured when we came under fire from the coastal battery. He's staying behind at Mirs Bay so that he won't slow us up."

"I don't believe you!" She took a step backward. "I don't believe you! It isn't true! Oh, please tell me it isn't true!" Her eyes were frantic, her face bloodless.

"My dear, I'm so sorry," he said compassionately, reaching out to take her in his arms. "Raefe knew that if you were told you wouldn't leave him, and he *wanted* you to leave him. He *wants* you to be safe."

"*No!*" she said. "*Oh, no!*" She turned and ran away from the guerrillas and Fisher and Bassett, running in the direction they had come from. Running toward Raefe.

He sprang after her, seizing her wrist, violently swinging

her around. "It's no good!" he said desperately. "You can't go back! There are Japs on the road!"

"*I don't care!*" She was fighting him, struggling to get free. "*I'm not leaving him to face capture alone! I'm going to him! There's nothing you can do to stop me!*"

"He won't *be* there when you return!" he shouted at her. Then, hating himself for his brutality, he said as gently as he could, "He was dying, Beth!"

She sucked in her breath, staring at him disbelievingly, and then she began to scream.

He had never struck a woman in his life and he would have thought himself incapable of striking Beth. His hand caught her savagely at the side of her face, stunning her into silence. "*He's dying and there's not a goddamned thing anyone can do about it!*" he yelled. "*Now for God's sake, don't make his dying alone worthless! Don't bring the Japs hurtling down on men who are risking their lives to help us!*"

She was sobbing hysterically, the tears streaming down her face. He tightened his hold on her, dragging her with him. "Come along," he said brokenly, his rage dying, tears scalding his own eyes. "We have to catch up with them, Beth. We mustn't be left behind."

Chapter Thirty-two

❧

SHE remembered very little of the long, arduous journey to Chungking. They crossed the Ta Shiu-Shao road, narrowly escaping being sighted by a convoy of Japanese trucks. From there on the way became very steep, and Henry Bassett began to suffer acutely from the heat. Adam relieved him of his rucksack, carrying it along with his own as they trudged over rough ground, each day and every day. He also helped the little girl in every way possible. A week later they reached Waichow and then, for a blissful few days, they were able to travel by barge up the East River to Leung Cheun.

Only the conviction that Raefe was still alive sustained her. The people in the village where they had left him had been friendly. They would have taken care of him and they would have hidden him from the Japanese. One day they would be reunited. So sure was she of it that it gave her the strength she needed to cope with the lack of food and the lice-ridden blankets that served as bedding and the constant, never-ending weariness.

At Leung Cheun they were given a lift to Kukong in a truck driven by a captain in the Chinese Nationalist Forces. From Kukong they traveled by rail to Chungking, with money lent to them by the staff of Kukong's Methodist mission.

"I never thought we'd make it," Bassett kept saying. "Truly, I never thought we'd make it."

Adam smiled at him wearily. There had been times when he, too, had doubted that they would ever reach Chungking. The two-month trek had broken his health and he knew it. He would never be robust again. He scarcely recognized himself when he entered the luxury of a bathroom at the British embassy and looked at himself in the mirror. He had become an old man. His still thick hair was no longer a grizzled gray, but pure white, and his luxuriant beard made him look like a grotesque and half-starved Father Christmas. He clipped it, then soaped the stubble to razor it off, marveling at Beth's constitution. She looked so delicate and fragile, and had proved to be so tough. She was still carrying the baby, her thickening waistline visible evidence of its continuing existence.

They had been greeted by embassy officials as husband and wife and treated as such, both of them too weary to face the inevitable confusion that would follow if they stated they were separated.

"This is much easier," Adam had said to her, "especially in view of your condition."

Elizabeth didn't care whether it was easier or not. Her one concern was how soon she would be able to receive confirmation that Raefe was alive.

"There'll be official lists of all prisoners of war captured, won't there?" she asked Adam, her eyes tormented, her face ivory pale.

"Yes," he answered, wondering if the Japanese would be mindful of the Geneva Convention. "But it will be months, possibly longer, before the Red Cross will have access to such information."

"Then I'll wait," she said quietly, her hand passing lightly over her rounding stomach. "But Raefe is alive, Adam. I know he is."

Within hours of his arrival Adam had been asked to make an official report to the military authorities. He did so, giving all the information he could about the situation in Hong Kong. He also told them of the atrocities that had taken place at the dressing station, giving an estimated number of the dead and a description of the way they had died. He also told them of how Raefe had been gravely injured and had stayed behind rather than hamper the others' escape chances.

Colonel Lindsay Ride, who had been commander of the Hong Kong volunteers' field ambulance and who had escaped from Shamshiupo, reaching Chungking only days before them, asked quietly, "In your opinion, could Captain Elliot still be alive?"

Adam hesitated for a moment, thinking of Beth and her fierce insistence that Raefe had survived. Then he said, "No, sir. Captain Elliot knew his wounds were fatal. He knew he was dying."

There was a small silence and then Lindsay Ride said, "Thank you, Captain Harland, that will be all."

Adam knew there would be no further posting for him. He was physically unfit for active service of any kind.

"We can't get you back to England, old boy," a colonial officer said to him regretfully. "The best we can do is fly you and Mrs. Harland to Rangoon. Rangoon is still safe. From there, with luck, you might be able to get a flight out to India."

Elizabeth refused to leave until official permission was given for her to take Jung-shui with her.

"If you want to adopt her, the Methodist Mission will help," Adam said, appalled at the prospect of leaving the little girl behind. "Shall I go and see them for you?"

"Please," she said, squeezing his hand gratefully. He was looking after her as he had always done, with infinite tenderness. But even though they were outwardly living together as man and wife, it was inconceivable to either of them that sexual relations should be resumed between them.

In April they left for Rangoon, taking Jung-shui with them. The international situation had worsened. Singapore had fallen to the Japanese and even Rangoon was no longer secure. A week after their arrival they were hurriedly ferried to Calcutta on an army flight.

"Which is where we'll be staying for the rest of the war, I expect," Adam said resignedly.

Elizabeth watched the earth falling away beneath them, and wondered where Helena was, and Li Pi, and Alastair and Tom and Ronnie. She was sure she knew where Raefe was. He would have recuperated from his wounds now and would be leading Chinese guerrilla units into the New Territories in the ongoing fight to oust the Japanese. And if he wasn't, if he had been captured, then he would be in an internment camp and she had only to wait for the war to end and for him to be released.

British officials in Calcutta made them as comfortable as possible, putting a bungalow at their disposal. Adam found something reminiscent of Hong Kong in the way their European neighbors still clung to the colonial way of life. Elizabeth was vaguely surprised when he mentioned it to her. She noticed very little anymore. She had withdrawn into herself, waiting for the baby to be born, waiting for the war to end. Waiting for Raefe to return to her.

Adam moved heaven and earth to find a piano for her, and on the day it was moved into their large drawing room, he knew his fears about her mental health were groundless. The old discipline soon claimed her. She practiced for seven or eight hours a day, remembering all that Li Pi had taught her, striving for perfection in order to be worthy of him.

In July the baby was born and the hospital staff, taking it for granted that her attentive husband was the father, were astounded when she asked that the name of Raefe Elliot be entered on the birth certificate as the father.

"What are you going to call him?" Adam asked her, standing at the foot of the bed as she held the dark-haired, shawl-wrapped baby close to her breast.

She smiled up at him. Her hair was loose around her shoulders, and she didn't look a day older than the eighteen-year-old girl he had married. "Nicholas Raefe," she said, her cheeks flushed with happiness, her eyes so full of love that his heart twisted within him. He felt no jealousy, no bitterness, that the child she was holding was Raefe's. Those emotions had all died within him when his respect for Raefe was born. But he did feel almost unbearable regret. If only the child she was nursing were *his* child. If only he and Beth and Jung-Shui and the baby could be a family together.

"Why Nicholas?" he asked, knowing it was a dream that would never come to fruition. Beth was living with him now, quite contentedly, as a sister might live with him. But she would not stay with him. Not when the war was over.

"Because I like the sound of it," she said, and her joy was so deep, it reached out and touched him. He found himself smiling, and said tenderly, his heart full of love for her, "So do I, Beth. So do I."

In September, Colonel Ride forwarded them the information that Tom Nicholson was a prisoner of war in Shamshuipo Camp in Kowloon, and that Mrs. Helena Nicholson was a civilian prisoner in Stanley internment camp, and that her two children were with her.

"Thank God," Adam said, time and time again. "Oh, thank God they're safe!"

In October they received the news that Alastair Munroe had died in the fighting at the Shingmun Redoubt. There was still no news about Ronnie, or about Raefe.

"We're damned lucky to know about Helena and Tom and Alastair, and to have Ride as a source of information," Adam said. "There must be thousands of families who don't know if husbands and fathers and sons are alive or dead."

"Raefe is alive," Elizabeth said with quiet confidence. "I know he is. I can feel it in my blood and in my bones. He's alive and he's going to come back to me."

He didn't argue with her. He was sure she was wrong, but to tell her so would be to rob her of the hope that was sustaining her.

In January of the following year came the news that Ronnie Ledsham was dead. The information from Chungking was far more explicit than normal official information would have been. "He died at the gap," Adam said bleakly. "God alone knows what he was doing there. He was supposed to be at Sai Wan Hill." He put down the telegram, his hand trembling slightly. "He was by himself and there were over a dozen dead Japs scattered around him."

Tears slid down Elizabeth's face. "He must have known about Julienne," she whispered, all the old grief surging through her. "He did what Derry did. He went out and fought the bastards by himself."

In early 1944 they returned to England via Portugal, and Elizabeth traveled down to Four Seasons with Jung-shui and Nicholas Raefe. Adam remained in London. He knew she did not want him to accompany her. Four Seasons had once been their marital home. Returning to it together would have meant that she wanted their lives to continue together. And she didn't. Now that they were back in England she wanted him to once more begin divorce proceedings. She wanted to be free in order that she could marry Raefe.

Jung-shui stared out the train window at the neat fields and the woods and the rolling splendor of the downs. "It's very pretty, isn't it?" she said with gentle gravity.

Elizabeth hugged her tight. "Yes, darling, it is *very* pretty, and it's your home now. I do hope that you will like it."

Jung-shui gave her an accepting smile. "Nicholas has never seen it before either, has he? Do you think Nicholas will like it too?"

"Yes," Elizabeth said, tears glittering on her eyelashes. She looked out over the familiar countryside, wondering if Raefe had ever seen Sussex. It was difficult to imagine him in the Sussex countryside, tall and lean and olive-skinned. She wondered what the villagers in Midhurst would make of him, and she wondered how much longer she would have to wait before she could share a drink with him in the village pub, and walk with him on the downs and by the sea.

Princess Luisa Isabel was waiting on the station platform to greet them, as Elizabeth had known she would be. She had written to her from Calcutta and from Portugal. That morning, when she had telephoned from London and told her she was traveling down to Midhurst on the two o'clock train, Luisa had been almost incoherent with delight.

Now she ran along the platform toward them, a slightly plumper Princess Luisa Isabel than Elizabeth remembered, but still with a ridiculous little hat dipping coquettishly over one eye, and still with fox furs swinging.

"Luisa!" she cried, running toward her, Nicholas Raefe

held in one arm, Jung-shui clinging to the hand of her free arm. *"Luisa!"*

Fox furs and an exotic fragrance enveloped Jung-shui and Nicholas Raefe, the tiny pillbox hat and its veil tilting more precariously than ever.

"What *beautiful* children!" Luisa crowed, cupping Jung-shui's golden face in her gloved hand, winning the little girl's heart at once. "And is this your brother? My, isn't he a big boy? I thought he would still be a baby!"

"Not a baby," Nicholas Raefe said as Elizabeth set him down on fat little legs. "Can walk. Babies can't walk."

Laughing and crying, Elizabeth threw her arms around the older woman. "Oh, I'm so glad to see you again, Luisa. I'm so glad to be home!"

Luisa drove them through the high-hedged, winding Sussex lanes in a splendid Rolls-Royce that attracted the attention of everyone they passed.

"However do you manage to get the gas for it, Luisa?" Elizabeth asked incredulously. "I thought everything was rationed to the hilt?"

"It is," Luisa said mischievously, "but I have my contacts. The worst thing about the war has been that I have been without a chauffeur. Every time I got one, the army commandeered him for what they termed 'essential war work.'"

Elizabeth hugged her arm, laughing at her silliness. "Oh, Luisa, if only that *was* the worst thing about this horrid, horrid war!"

Luisa stayed with her for two weeks. An advertisement for a housekeeper was inserted in *The Times* and a pleasant, middle-aged Scotswoman applied for the job. Her husband had died in the fighting when British troops had fallen back on Dunkirk and Elizabeth immediately engaged her, impressed by the woman's quiet courage as she set about, alone, building a new life for herself.

When Luisa had reluctantly departed, the house seemed oddly empty. She wandered through the rooms, looking out of the windows at Jung-shui and Nicholas Raefe romping together on the terrace. They, at least, were safe. She thought about Helena's children, wondering if they had suffered during the long years of internment, and she thought, as she always did, about Raefe. Whether he had been free or a prisoner, he, too, would have suffered. Four

Seasons would be a haven for him when he returned to her. A place where he could rest and recuperate and where their lives together could begin anew.

She busied herself in transforming a sunny, ground floor sitting room into a study for him, decorating and furnishing it herself. She planted roses along the south wall of the house, Zephirine Drouhin and Ophelia and Madame Alfred Carriere, so that the house would be clothed in blossom. She worked hard at her music, knowing how eager he would be that her dreams of the concert platform should be speedily fulfilled.

It was a rain-washed April day when her first visitor, apart from Adam and Luisa Isabel, arrived. She was on the terrace dressed in an old violet-colored tweed skirt and a lavender sweater, with her hair pulled away from her face and tied in a ponytail with a hair ribbon borrowed from Jung-shui. She was lifting and dividing the clumps of Michaelmas daisies that grew along the edge of the terrace by the house wall when she heard the sound of a car approaching.

She put down her trowel and walked along the terrace to the shallow stone steps that led down to the drive. Adam hadn't telephoned to say he would be visiting her, but then their relationship was so close that there was no reason why he should have done so. The car swung around the curve in the drive and she stood still, rocked by surprise. The car wasn't Adam's carefully polished Daimler, but a battered old Morris that reminded her, with a sudden pang, of the little battered old Morris that Julienne had driven in Hong Kong. It stopped twenty yards or so away from her and a big bear of a man in an RAF uniform pulled himself with difficulty from the car's cramped interior.

The April sun shone on his thick dark gold hair. There was the word POLAND on the insignia on his shoulder. For a moment she was overcome by an overpowering sense of déjà vu, remembering Hong Kong and the perfume of azaleas, then she was running down the steps, shouting incredulously, "Roman. *Roman!*"

White teeth flashed in a dazzling grin as, moving with an athletic grace and agility rare in a man of his size, he strode toward her. She took the last few steps two at a time and hurtled into his arms, hugging him tightly. "Oh, Roman!

How wonderful! I can't believe it's really you!" she cried, looking up at him with shining eyes.

"*Nie do wiary!* Whenever I come upon you unexpectedly, you are always knee-deep in flowers," he said, his grin deepening. As she continued to hug him, he added, "If I'd known I was going to get this sort of welcome, I'd have visited earlier."

Laughter bubbled up inside her as she feasted her eyes on him. Even in an RAF uniform he had about him a hubris that was totally mid-European.

"You don't mean to say that you're *stationed* near here?" she asked disbelievingly as he reluctantly released his hold on her and she tucked her arm through his, leading him toward the house.

"I'm afraid so. I'm about ten miles away at Westhampmett."

She began to giggle, joyously light-hearted. Roman was home and soon Raefe would be home.

"Oh, but that's wonderful, Roman!"

She led him across the terrace and through the open French doors into the large drawing room dominated by her Steinway grand.

"I'm glad to see that you are still working," he said affectionately, moving immediately across the room to the piano to see what she had been playing.

She nodded. All of a sudden the world was once again a sane place. She had someone to talk to about music, and she had someone at her side who was a bridge into the past, a living proof that the most unexpected reunions took place every day.

"Chopin," she said a trifle defensively. "I find him so soothing."

He gave a deep chuckle. "You forget that I am a Pole, Elizabeth. There is no need to apologize to me for playing Chopin."

She laughed, as at ease with him again as she had been in Perth. On the podium he was Roman Rakowski, Maestro. Here he was Roman, her friend, the man she had drunk *Bruderschaft* with. Feeling easy and confident, she sat at the piano and he stood by her side, filling the room with his presence.

"Chopin is far more than a rose-colored salonist, surrounded by violets," he said, the old bond of their mutual passion for music enclosing them in a world of their own. "He must be played with verve and daring."

For the first time since her last lesson with Li Pi, she sat down at the piano and played to a critical audience. It was bliss. A totally freeing experience that made her feel as if she were alive again after long months of hibernation.

"*Dziekuje*! That's good," he said when she finished, his voice full of encouraging enthusiasm. "Now play a waltz. The waltzes are marvelous, a little hackneyed perhaps, but who cares? They are unsurpassably beautiful."

The war faded from her consciousness. She played waltzes and then nocturnes. The great Fantasy in F minor, and the Barcarolle.

"Oh, wonderful!" Roman said exuberantly, running his hands through his hair in a gesture she remembered from Perth. "These nocturnes show Chopin's enormous talent for condensation. He is a *much* greater composer than he is often made out to be. You must always play him like that, Elizabeth, dynamically and with inner drama."

When she had played the last note of the Polonaise-Fantasie, he was quiet for a few moments, the question he had not asked hanging in the air between them. As she closed the lid he said softly, "Tell me about Raefe."

She told him, sitting in front of a log fire, serving Earl Grey tea from a Crown Derby teapot into wafer-thin cups. He listened in silence, not interrupting her, making no comments, until she said finally, "And so, there is nothing for me to do now but wait for him."

The log fire spat and crackled.

"And his name has not been listed by the Red Cross as a prisoner of war?" he asked, his expression grave.

She shook her head, and something moved within him, an emotion both shocking and disturbing. "No," she said, not seeing his quick frown, or the way his brilliant onyx eyes had suddenly darkened. "But then there must be hundreds and hundreds of men who are still alive but whose names aren't on any list. I don't imagine the Japanese are being very cooperative with the Red Cross, do you?"

He shook his head and he reluctantly stood, knowing it was time for him to go.

"Oh, must you go so soon?" she asked, disappointment

flaring in her eyes. "I want you to meet the children. Jung-shui is down in the paddock, riding the pony I bought her for her birthday. Nicholas Raefe is with his nanny. She's a local girl from the village and she takes care of him while I practice. She's taken him to feed the ducks at the local pond, but they'll be back at any moment. Please stay."

He was sorely tempted, but he knew that he had to have time to himself to think before he stayed with her any longer, or before he agreed to see her again. She was desperately in love with Raefe, and one day, God willing, Raefe would be returning for her. To fall in love with a woman so unobtainable would be crass foolishness, and he wasn't a man who suffered foolishness easily.

"*Nie,*" he said. His great height and massive shoulders seemed to fill the room. "I'm sorry, Elizabeth, but I must go."

She walked with him out to his car, urging him to visit her again. Her loneliness, when he had driven away, was so acute that it almost robbed her of breath.

It was a week before he telephoned her and said that he had leave the following weekend. He had never been down to Brighton. Would she care to drive there with him and have lunch?

She accepted unhesitatingly. This was what she would one day do with Raefe. That she was doing it now with Roman seemed to her the best possible omen.

They went to Brighton. A few days later they took Jung-shui and Nicholas Raefe to Bodiam Castle and picnicked, chilly but happy, beneath the great Norman battlements. From then on, Roman visited her regularly, swinging Nicholas Raefe up onto his shoulders as they walked the downs or the seashore, Jung-shui hurrying eagerly along at his side, chattering about her pony and her English school while Roman listened to her with genuine interest, displaying a patience rare in a man of his mercurial talent.

The war in Europe was rapidly coming to a close and Elizabeth knew that Roman couldn't wait for the day when he would be discharged and able to return once more to the concert platform.

"Where will you go first?" she asked as they walked along a pebble beach where, a thousand years earlier, Julius Caesar's Romans had first struggled ashore.

"Palestine," he said unhesitatingly. "Nowhere in the

world is there a people so hungry for music. I want to give every ounce of support I can to an orchestra that will one day be the greatest in the world."

She thought of the men who composed that orchestra, the great musicians of Eastern Europe who had escaped Hitler's genocidal machine.

"Perhaps I shall play with them one day," she said with a little smile.

"You will," he said with fierce confidence. "And when you do, I shall conduct you."

Roman's regular visits, interspersed with visits from Adam and from Princess Luisa Isabel, relieved Elizabeth's relative isolation, but her sexual loneliness remained acute. There were times she lay in bed at night, damp with longing, when she almost wished that she had never been awakened to sexual passion. She hungered for sexual relief so fiercely that it shocked and appalled her. "Not sexual relief!" she would say furiously to herself as she swung her legs from the bed and walked over to the window to look out over the moonlit terrace. "Raefe. It's Raefe that I'm hungry for. Raefe that I miss."

But on May the eighth, when Sir Winston Churchill announced over the wireless that German armed forces had surrendered unconditionally, it was sexual need that brought her world tumbling down around her ears.

Roman had been on leave that day and the minute the announcement was made he ran to his car, leaped into it, and raced away from camp in the direction of Four Seasons.

Elizabeth's housekeeper had already told her the news and they stood in the large, slate-floored kitchen, celebrating the event with cooking sherry.

"Find a flag!" Elizabeth said joyously to Nicholas Raefe's nanny. "We must fly a flag from the windows!"

"But no one will see it, ma'am. We're over a mile from the road," the young nanny protested, dazed by the momentous announcement and the generous amounts of cooking sherry that Elizabeth was pouring for her.

"It doesn't matter!" Elizabeth said determinedly. "We must fly a flag!"

They found a flag in one of the garages and hung it from the window above the main door. Jung-shui and Nicholas Raefe begged to be allowed to go into the village, where bells were ringing and people could be distantly heard singing.

"I'll take them, ma'am," the nanny said, eager to take a part in the festivities. Elizabeth waved them off, and her housekeeper began to bake a special cake for the children's tea, listening to the wireless and the commentator's description of the crowds gathering outside Buckingham Palace and Number Ten Downing Street.

Elizabeth walked back into the drawing room, sensing her housekeeper's need to be on her own. After all, her husband would not be one of the men thankfully returning home. Her joy at the announcement of peace was mixed with a fresh surge of personal grief.

Elizabeth stood in the large, sun-filled room, wondering when and if Raefe would receive the news. Then Roman's battered Morris screeched to a halt in the drive, and she ran out the French windows to greet him.

He took the shallow stone steps in two giant bounds and was halfway across the terrace when she catapulted into his arms. "Isn't it the most wonderful news!" she shouted exultantly, flinging her arms around his neck. "It *must* mean that war in the East will be over soon as well!"

When Roman had driven through Midhurst, perfect strangers had been flinging their arms around each other and kissing each other, and it seemed the most natural thing in the world that he should crush Elizabeth against him and kiss her exuberantly.

The exuberant, sexless kiss that he had intended died almost before it was born. Like a spark setting a tinderbox alight, the instant their lips touched, reason and sanity left them. Her mouth parted, her tongue slid past his, and her fingers tightened in his hair. His response was immediate. He swung her up in his arms and strode with her into the drawing room. He lowered her to the rug and tore off his jacket, his tie, his shirt. She didn't even remove her clothes. With her skirt hastily shoved up to her hips, her brief panties pushed to one side to allow him to enter her, she pulled him down on top of her, half senseless with need. He gasped her name and plunged into her hot and hard. As he felt his sperm shoot from him like hot gold, he knew with dreadful certainty not only that he loved her, but that Raefe was dead. He couldn't have made love to her, his body would not have allowed him to, if Raefe were still alive.

She was sobbing beneath him, her cries no longer the savage cries of satisfied love, but of horror and grief and deep, burning shame. "Oh, no!" she sobbed, twisting and turning in an effort to get away from him. "Oh, no! Oh, Raefe! Raefe! What have I done? Oh, God, what have I done?"

He eased his weight off her, saying awkwardly, "Elizabeth, please . . ."

"No!" She pushed her fists against his chest, fighting to be free of him.

"Elizabeth, please . . ." he began again as he rose unsteadily to his feet, but she wouldn't listen to him.

"No! Oh, God, please go away! Please go away and never come back!"

He stood for a moment, his magnificent shoulders glistening with sweat, then slowly put his shirt back on. He picked up his tie and crushed it into his pocket, then hooked his jacket with one finger and swung it defeatedly over his shoulder. Because of a moment's uncontrolled passion, everything that had been forged between them now lay in irreparable ashes. His pain was so intense, he didn't know how he was surviving it.

"You have to listen to me, Elizabeth," he said, his voice raw with urgency.

"No!" She was trembling convulsively, hugging her arms around her as though holding herself together against an inner disintegration. "No, please go! Oh, please go!"

"I love you," he said with fierce simplicity. "I wouldn't have done such a thing if I didn't love you."

"No!" she whispered again, shaking her head, the tears still falling. "I don't want to listen! Please leave me! Please go away!"

There was nothing further that he could do. From outside, he could hear the distant sound of the village bells ringing joyously, and knew he would never be able to listen to them again without reliving the pain he now felt.

"Good-bye," he said hoarsely. "I'm sorry, Elizabeth, more sorry than you'll ever know. With his heart breaking within him, he turned away and walked out of the room.

She covered her face in her hands, sobbing convulsively. Oh, God, how could she have done such a thing? How could she have pulled another man down on top of her in such hungry, urgent need?

"Oh, Raefe, I'm so sorry," she gasped. "So very sorry. Please come back to me, my love! Please come home!"

Chapter Thirty-three

Roman telephoned her early the next morning, but she refused to speak to him. He wrote to her and she destroyed his letters unread. The shame she felt was so mortifying, so total, she couldn't imagine ever facing him again.

In June, Adam drove down to see her and as soon as she saw his face she knew he brought bad news with him. "What is it?" she asked fearfully, rising from the piano stool and walking swiftly to him. "What has happened?"

"I'm sorry," he said, taking her hands. "Truly I am." Ever since they had returned to England he had been ceaseless in his efforts to try to trace Raefe as a prisoner of war. Now, at last, he had official notification, but it was not the kind of notification that Beth had been so steadfastly awaiting. She knew immediately.

"No," she said, pulling her hands away from his. "I don't believe it! He's alive, I know he is!"

Slowly Adam took the piece of paper from his inside jacket pocket. "He's missing, presumed dead, Beth."

She wouldn't look at the paper he held out to her. She turned on her heel and walked away from him, staring out through the French windows at the roses in early bloom. "No," she said, and her voice was quiet and sure. "He's alive, Adam. And he's going to come back to me."

On August 16 the Japanese surrendered and war in the East was finally over.

"Soon Daddy will be home," she said joyously to Nicholas Raefe, cuddling him on her knee. "Soon he will be able to come for walks with us and he'll teach you how to play football, and we'll have such lovely times together, just you wait and see."

Nicholas Raefe looked at her lovingly. He had been waiting so long to see the Daddy who was only a name to him that he didn't really mind waiting a little longer. He couldn't imagine what this strange daddy would be like and he didn't really need him to teach him how to play football and cricket, because his Uncle Adam already did that. He kissed her on her cheek, then wriggled off her knee and ran on sturdy little legs to where Jung-shui was waiting for him down in the paddock.

Now, every day, she waited for news. A Hong Kong Fellowship had been formed in London for the wives and widows and relations of prisoners of war and those interned, and she attended the London-based meetings regularly, hoping to glean some information about Raefe from the newsletters that the fellowship published at regular intervals and that were a great comfort to many. Extracts were published from POWs' letters, though they contained only reassuring news for otherwise the Japanese censors would not have let them through. At the end of September, the fellowship was informed that over a thousand men, former prisoners of war in Hong Kong, had sailed aboard the *Empress of Australia*, her destination Vancouver, via Manila.

"They are beginning to come home," Elizabeth whispered to herself. "It can't be long now. Oh, please, Raefe, please write. Please let me know where you are!"

But he didn't write and she knew it was because he could have no idea where she was. She would have to wait for the army to redirect his letters to her. Helena wrote to her, her letter forwarded by the Red Cross. She was alive and well, though after the years of imprisonment, much slimmer than before. She would be returning to England at the earliest opportunity.

"And Lamoon is with her," Elizabeth said joyously to Adam. "Isn't that incredible? Lamoon is with her and she and Tom are going to be married at the earliest opportunity."

The first ship to arrive in England bearing Hong Kong prisoners of war was the *Ile de France*, sailing from Canada. Members of the Hong Kong Fellowship were advised by the authorities that it was not advisable for them to travel to Southampton to meet the returning men. The men were going to be whisked straightaway to resettlement camps for at least three days and there would be no opportunities for reunions until then. Elizabeth took not the slightest bit of notice. She would be there when the *Ile de France* docked, even though there was still no confirmation that Raefe would be aboard, even though the authorities still adamantly held to the view that he was missing and presumed dead.

Adam drove her down to Southampton, terrified at what her reaction might be if Raefe was not among those disembarking. It was a chill autumn day and they had to wait with a small huddle of other eager relations for the men to begin to file down the gangplanks and to once again touch English soil. She stood, her coat collar up against the cold breeze, her eyes fierce with determination. Raefe would be one of those disembarking. He *had* to be.

Gaunt face after gaunt face hurried down the gangplank. A woman standing next to her gave a joyous cry and ran forward, calling out to one of the hunched, emaciated figures, his kit on his shoulder. Elizabeth saw the look of disbelief on the man's face; saw his disbelief turn to wonder and then to joy as he slung his kit to the ground and opened his arms wide.

In single file the men continued to disembark, but there was no tall, broad-shouldered figure with a pelt of blue-black hair. Only tired men, thankful to be home again, slightly bewildered that there were so few people at the docks to greet them.

When the last men had disembarked, she still stood there, her coat collar turned up against the wind, her eyes overly bright.

Adam touched her gently on the arm and she said fiercely, "There will be other ships, Adam. Lots of other ships." Then she didn't speak to him again and he drove her back through the winding country lanes to Four Seasons in silence.

That night he asked her if she would remarry him. She stared at him, knowing why he was asking her.

"No," she said, her throat dry. "Raefe is still alive, Adam."

"Oh, my dear," Adam said tenderly, taking her hands and holding them tightly in his. "And if he isn't? Will you marry me then, Beth? Will you let us be happy as we used to be?"

Tears sparkled on the thick sweep of her lashes. "No, Adam," she whispered, loving him with all her heart, but loving him as a friend. "No. Those days are over. They will never come again."

There were other ships bringing back POWs and internees as she had said there would be. Helena and Jeremy and Jennifer arrived home on October 28, having sailed via Manila and Singapore and Colombo and Aden. Elizabeth drove up with Adam to Liverpool to meet them, and as Helena walked toward them, her square-jawed, high-cheek-boned face still beautiful despite the gross amount of weight she had lost, Elizabeth gave a low sob.

"Helena. *Oh, Helena!*" she cried, running toward her. She hugged her tight. "Oh, Helena, I'm so glad to see you!"

"The feeling is mutual," Helena said unsteadily, and there were lines around her eyes and mouth that had never been there before.

Adam held her close, too, shocked at the suffering etched on her face, knowing that she, too, was probably shocked at the change in him. He was only fifty-four, but the fighting and the trek to Chungking had taken its toll on him. He had aged prematurely, his limp now severely pronounced, his hair snow white.

"Oh, Adam," she said, kissing him on the cheek, her deep blue eyes bright with tears. "It's so wonderful to see you again!" Suddenly, as he tucked her arm in his and began to lead her toward his car, he no longer felt so old and so decrepit.

"It's wonderful to see you too, Helena," he said, his voice thick with emotion. "Beth has a room ready for you and the children at Four Seasons. You will stay there, won't you? For as long as you want."

"Yes," she said. As the children clambered into the rear of Adam's Daimler, she added bleakly, "You know that Alastair is dead, don't you?"

Adam nodded. They all knew now the way Alastair had died, and he had been posthumously awarded the Victoria Cross.

"I loved him and was a fool and never really realized it,"

she said, her voice unsteady with regret and grief. "I shan't ever make the same mistake again."

"No, my dear," he said, knowing now what the future held for him and full of the kind of happiness that he had thought he would never feel again. "I know that you won't." As they drove away, he knew that although Beth's long years of waiting were still not over, his own had finally come to an end.

"And neither of us ever saw Li Pi again," Helena said quietly.

They were sitting at the dining table at Four Seasons. Jung-shui and Nicholas Raefe had welcomed Jeremy and Jennifer, Jung-shui with shy gravity, Nicholas Raefe with boisterous exuberance. They had gone immediately down to the paddock to view the pony and after a specially indulgent high tea, retreated to Nicholas Raefe's bedroom where they played a spirited game of Monopoly until it was time for bed. Now the house was quiet and Elizabeth and Helena and Adam sat around the candlelit dining table.

"He may still be alive," Helena said tentatively, but all of them knew there was very little hope. He had been old and he had been Chinese. His chances of survival in Japanese-occupied Hong Kong would have been tragically slim.

"Tell us about Tom and Lamoon," Adam said gently, knowing how deep Beth's grief was at the thought of Li Pi's death and wanting good news to leaven the bad.

Helena smiled and her mane of dark hair, now heavily streaked with gray, swung forward against her cheeks. "They were married in Shamshuipo Camp three days after liberation. The troops were still confined there because there wasn't anywhere else for them to go, and Lamoon and I hitched a lift from Stanley to Shamshuipo. Tom said he'd waited so long to marry her that he wasn't going to wait any longer, and he insisted that the padre marry them immediately."

"Let's give them a toast," Adam said. He walked over to the cocktail cabinet where he knew a bottle of champagne lay hidden, saved by Beth for just such an event. He uncorked the wine and poured it into their glasses.

"To Tom and Lamoon," he said, raising his glass high.

"May they know only peace and happiness from this day forward."

"To Tom and Lamoon," Elizabeth and Helena echoed, and for both of them tears were not very far away.

Christmas came and went and still there was no news of Raefe. "There were other camps apart from the ones in Hong Kong," Elizabeth said obstinately when Adam gently asked her if she shouldn't now accept the official report of his death. "There were camps in Singapore and Formosa and Manchuria. Quite a lot of officers from Hong Kong were sent to Shirakawa Camp in Formosa. He may have been there. He may have been sent anywhere."

"But the men in those camps are all accounted for. The authorities have lists of their names and nearly all of them have been returned home," Adam said, his heart hurting at her steadfast refusal to face reality.

"Not all of them," she said, her face pale, deep shadows bruising her eyes. "Not Raefe."

In the New Year Adam told her that he had asked Helena to marry him and that she had accepted.

"I'm so pleased," Elizabeth said, hugging him tightly. "It's the most sensible thing that you've ever done, Adam. She'll make you a marvelous wife."

"We're going to be married in April, on Helena's birthday. You will be there, my dear, won't you?"

"Of course I'll be there," she said lovingly. "Wild horses wouldn't keep me away!"

In February Tom and Lamoon drove down to Four Seasons. They were on a visit to England so that Lamoon could meet Tom's parents and be formally welcomed into the family.

"This is quite like old times, isn't it?" Tom said as they sat around the dinner table with Adam and Helena, happily unaware of the shadow that passed across Elizabeth's face.

Lamoon looked as impossibly lovely as ever, her almond eyes shining with happiness, her cheongsam glitteringly exotic. The years in captivity had sat lightly on her, but there were flecks of gray in Tom's dark hair and his lean face still bore traces of the emaciation he had been suffering from when he was released.

"If only Alastair were here," Helena said quietly. "And Julienne and Ronnie. Then it really would be like old times."

They were silent, all of them thinking of the past and suddenly, as clearly as if it were a vision, Elizabeth could see Alastair, laughing and talking in the Jockey Club Bar, and Ronnie, his blond moustache as trim and sleek as that of a matinee idol, and Julienne, her mop of spicy red curls tumbling around her heart-shaped face, her eyes dancing with mischief. Somewhere in the background, she was sure she could hear the faint, rousing strains of "There'll Always Be an England," and then Alastair and Ronnie and Julienne faded into the background and she could see only Raefe.

He was standing nonchalantly at ease, his hair falling low across his brow, his dark eyes looking at her with love and tenderness. And again she saw the smile on his mouth, the same ironic smile with which he had bade her good-bye at the village on the shores of Mirs Bay. She sat absolutely still, waiting for him to come nearer to her, but the sound of singing faded and Tom was saying, "We shall be returning to Hong Kong on the twentieth. I still have my job with the government, and even if I hadn't, I couldn't imagine living anywhere else. It's my home."

Small drops of ice were dripping down her spine. The ghosts were all receding and Raefe was receding too.

"There'll be a lot of changes there now," Adam said. "I'm surprised the Chinese didn't hold out to have it handed back to them."

Suddenly, and with absolute certainty, she knew he was dead. She rose abruptly to her feet, trembling violently, her face chalk white.

"The day will come," Tom said, pouring more wine into his glass. "The British government will have to surrender Hong Kong to the Chinese eventually."

"Excuse me!" she said in a strangled voice, and walked swiftly from the table.

"And then what will become of it?" Helena asked Tom.

Tom was holding Lamoon's hand and Adam was watching Helena's face, thinking how beautiful she was. None of them realized that Elizabeth had left the table for anything more than to bring in the dessert. None of them realized how deeply distressed she was.

She stood in the hall for a brief second and the sound of their laughter drifted out to her. Tom had been reunited with Lamoon. Adam was reunited with Helena. But she knew now that she would never be reunited with Raefe. The belief had sustained her and given her strength for over three years, but now that belief was gone. Raefe himself had personally come to her and gently removed it.

The kitchen door was open, the desserts standing on a tea tray, waiting to be transferred to the dining room. She ignored them. Without pausing for a coat or a jacket, she ran from the house and across the gravel drive to the garages. Her car was parked alongside Adam's Daimler and Tom's hired Ford. She slipped behind the wheel and turned the key in the ignition. She didn't know where she was going and she didn't care. With a screech of tires she reversed out of the garage, then swung the wheel around and shot down the drive and out into the dark, high-hedged lanes beyond.

He was dead. The realization beat at her in waves. He was dead and he was never, ever going to return to her. She drove south, across the South Downs, toward the sea. He had said good-bye to her in the dusty, Chinese village, and he had meant good-bye, but she had not meant good-bye. Not good-bye forever.

"I can't live with it," she whispered as she raced seaward, out to the loneliness of Selsey Bill. "I can't live with such pain! It isn't possible!"

The sea gleamed, slickly and blackly, and she brought the car to a halt. She tumbled out of it and ran down onto the beach, slipping and sliding over the loose pebbles until she reached the shingle and the gentle creaming waves.

He was dead and he was never coming back to her. "Oh, Raefe!" she cried in agony, raising her face to the heavens. "Oh, Raefe! Why did you leave me? Why did you go?" Then she sank to her knees on the sea-damp sand, and covered her face and wept.

Epilogue

THE sun beat hotly on her back and the azure blue South China Sea glittered. She had survived that night on the English coast, as she had survived the hundreds of agonizing nights that had succeeded it. There had been her music, and Jung-shui and Nicholas Raefe, and somehow because of them, she had found the will to live and the courage to endure.

She rose slowly to her feet. This was the last of her pilgrimages. Yesterday she had visited Julienne's grave and had laid a posy of exotic blossoms on it, then she had driven to the military cemetery at Stanley. She had laid flowers on Alastair's grave and on Ronnie's and Derry's and had walked slowly up to one of the graves on which the inscription on the headstone read only "Known but to God." She had ordered the small bouquet of flowers especially. It was an English bouquet of all the flowers that grew at Four Seasons and that he had never seen there. Creamy white roses and yellow-eyed daisies and pale lilac anemones with indigo hearts. She had stood for a long time, thinking about the past, knowing that finally she had come to terms with it.

The intervening years had brought their own happiness. She had achieved her dreams of concert platform stardom, and she remembered the words she had whispered to herself on the first night that she played to a large audience. "For you, Li Pi," she had whispered. "And for you, Raefe, my love." And she had not let either of them down.

Slowly she walked back down the hill to her car. People were beginning to emerge from the long, white, peaceful serenity of the hotel for early-morning swims. Lamma Island was beginning to take on shape and form as the early morning heat haze lifted and disappeared. She opened her car door and slid behind the wheel. She had no more doubts, no more uncertainties. The man who had loved her for seven years was waiting for her in their hotel suite and in two hours' time she would become his wife.

She drove away from the bay and up Repulse Bay Road toward Wong Nei Chung Gap. New buildings were springing up on the hillsides, luxury homes standing where the Rajputs and the men of the Middlesex had so bravely died. The road topped the gap and began to wind down toward Happy Valley and the outskirts of Victoria.

She had served a long and lonely seven years. There had been no other men in her life, not until three months ago when she had found herself staring with stupefied horror into Roman Rakowski's fierce gray eyes.

They were on the concert platform of the Hollywood Bowl. The Los Angeles Philharmonic was to play Tchaikovsky's Piano Concerto No. 1 and Mahler's Symphony No. 9 in D, under the German conductor Otto Klemperer. She was guest pianist. Rehearsals had gone satisfactorily and though it was the first time she had played in the immense, natural amphitheater of the Bowl, she had her nerves well under control.

The orchestra had taken its place to enthusiastic applause. She herself had walked out to a warm, reassuring welcome from the stunningly large audience. But still Klemperer had not taken his place on the podium. There were impatient coughs and mutterings throughout the open-air auditorium and a sense of growing unease from the members of the orchestra. There had been rumors that the sixty-seven-year old conductor was not in good health. In rehearsal he had looked tired and strained.

The minutes spun out and she half expected the musical director to walk out and apologize for the conductor's absence due to sudden indisposition. Just as it seemed they could wait no longer for him, there was a cheer from the audience and an outburst of applause. Elizabeth breathed a sigh of relief, closing her eyes as Klemperer strode toward the podium. In these last few seconds before she commenced to play, she needed to steady herself, to harness the adrenaline surging along her veins, to be in complete and utter control. Klemperer reached the podium amid continuing applause. She flexed her fingers, drew in a deep, calming breath, and opened her eyes, fixing them on Otto Klemperer.

Only it wasn't Klemperer. It was Roman. The world dropped away beneath her feet, leaving her sick and giddy. Roman saw the shock she had sustained, saw the blood drain from her face, the black satin evening gown she wore emphasizing her pallor. The applause at his entrance finally died down and he lifted his baton, his eyes riveting hers.

"Don't go to pieces!" he silently pleaded with her. "Remember who you are and what you are! Play for me as you played for Klemperer!"

The breath was so tight in her chest, she was in physical pain. She could read the messages his eyes were sending and she tried vainly to comply with them. Just when she thought she couldn't possibly move, when she thought she was frozen forever, she remembered the tiny candlelit restaurant in Perth where they had drunk *Bruderschaft* together. Slowly the pain in her chest eased.

He gave her a sudden grin and she felt the world right itself on its axis. She was going to play for Roman as she had played for Klemperer. A sudden blaze lit her eyes. No, she was going to play far, far better than she had played for Klemperer. She was going to play better than she had ever played in her life.

He sensed her returning confidence and his thick eyebrows, so many shades darker than his deep gold hair, rose questioningly. She gave an imperceptible nod, and relief flooded through him. He brought his baton down in a characteristic firm downbeat and from the moment that her fingers touched the keys, he knew the rapport between them was total.

The excitement in the audience was palpable. Elizabeth felt as if she were riding a magic carpet as she and the orchestra entered into another world. Their collaboration was brilliant, flawless, as the dialogue between them flowed and ebbed and climaxed in a surge of spirit and sound at the end of the long first movement.

There was hardly a breath from the audience in the pause before the second movement. Elizabeth knew that her sleekly coiled chignon was damp with perspiration, that she was playing on a level she had never reached before. Roman leaned forward on the podium, his eyes blazing into hers as softly, almost imperceptibly, he summoned in the strings. The flute entered, delicate as the pipes of Pan, and then Elizabeth, and then Roman merged them all into a Ukrainian dance of rhythmic pungency.

In the rondo finale the battle for ascendancy between piano and orchestra reached a climax so passionate, so earth-shaking, that when Roman's arms whipped them all into the final, desperate chords, Elizabeth thought she was going to die. She sagged over the piano as the last notes died away and the audience exploded into frenzied applause. Dazedly she raised her head, trying to orient herself. Roman's face was sheened with perspiration as he weakly stepped down from the podium and walked toward her. The audience was on its feet as he did so, shouting, stamping, clapping . . .

"Amazing!" Roman shouted over the din of the applause. "You were wonderful! Incredible!"

His hand gripped hers, his eyes blazing triumphantly with love and pride as he raised her to her feet. Unsteadily, her knees so weak she couldn't imagine how they were supporting her, Elizabeth walked offstage with him.

"It's good the Bowl has no roof!" Roman said in her ear. "Otherwise it would have been lifted off!"

They paused for a second offstage, the applause drumming against their eardrums, and then, their hands tightly gripped together, sweating and trembling, they walked back on again. The orchestra was stomping its feet, the audience shouting hoarse "Bravos!" and "Encore! Encore!"

They took bow after bow, and at last Roman shouted across to her, laughing, "It's no good! We'll have to play the last movement again!"

It had been the triumph of her career, and it had been the moment when she had known that her destiny, and Roman's destiny, were irrevocably linked, as her destiny with Raefe had been.

The streets of Victoria were beginning to hum with life. As she drove toward their hotel she could see a giant placard advertising their forthcoming concert, and on a newspaper stand she saw the giant headline, "RAKOWSKI AND HARLAND TO MARRY! Concert platform greats to tie the knot!"

She smiled, wondering what the next day's headline would have been if her pilgrimage had had a different outcome. It was Roman who had suggested they return to Hong Kong. He had realized there could be no future for them until the past lay at peace. She parked the car outside the hotel and Lee Yiu Piu hurried to open the heavy glass doors for her. She smiled at him and walked into the opulent foyer, conscious of the buzz of newsmen as they hurried toward the flower-filled room where, in a little while, she would marry.

She pressed the button for the elevator, unnoticed by them, and wondered why it had taken her so long to understand that this was what Raefe would have wanted for her. He would not have wanted her to live alone and he would not have wanted her to grieve forever. His great gift to her had been in showing her how deeply and passionately she could love. And in loving Roman, she knew that the love she had felt for Raefe was not diminished. That love, and the richness it had bequeathed to her, would be hers forever.

She walked down the deeply carpeted corridor to her hotel suite and quietly opened the door. Princess Luisa Isabel was removing her wedding bouquet from its cellophane cover and laying it carefully on the bed. Jung-shui was surveying herself in the full-length mirror, her sleek black hair decorated with a single white rose, her bridesmaid's dress emphasizing her willowy slenderness and the burgeoning breasts of a fifteen-year-old. Nicholas Raefe was busily trying to pin a carnation to the lapel of his morning suit, his dark hair tumbling untidily in the way it always did, and in a way that never ceased to make her catch her breath. He was ten years old now, and already had the lean, whippy look that had been so characteristic of Raefe.

It was Roman who saw her enter the room first. He swiftly strode across to her and took her in his arms. She leaned against him, hugging him tightly. He gently tilted her face up to his and asked, his handsome, strong-boned face revealing none of the anxiety he was feeling, "Are all your ghosts laid to rest, my darling?"

"Yes," she whispered, loving him with all her heart, grateful for his patience and his understanding and his acceptance of the place Raefe held in her life, and always would.

"Then let's get married," he said huskily, and as Princess

Luisa Isabel handed her her wedding bouquet, and as Jung-shui and Nicholas Raefe announced that they were both ready for the wedding and had been waiting for her for ages, a deep smile of happiness curved her lips. She slipped her arm into Roman's and walked with him out of the room and along the corridor and down the stairs, to where the reporters and photographers were waiting.

Special Offer
Buy a Bantam Book
for only 50¢.

Now you can have Bantam's catalog filled with hundreds of titles plus take advantage of our unique and exciting bonus book offer. A special offer which gives you the opportunity to purchase a Bantam book for only 50¢. Here's how!

By ordering any five books at the regular price per order, you can also choose any other single book listed (up to a $5.95 value) for just 50¢. Some restrictions do apply, but for further details why not send for Bantam's catalog of titles today!

Just send us your name and address and we will send you a catalog!

THE LATEST BOOKS
IN THE BANTAM
BESTSELLING TRADITION